NOTHING BUT!

NOTHING BUT!

BOOK-6

FAREWELL MY LOVE

Brigadier Samir Bhattacharya

PARTRIDGE
A Penguin Random House Company

ISBN: Hardcover 978-1-4828-1788-1
Softcover 978-1-4828-1787-4
Ebook 978-1-4828-1786-7

To order additional copies of this book, contact
Partridge India
000 800 10062 62
www.partridgepublishing.com/india
orders.india@partridgepublishing.com

CONTENTS

DEDICATION

This book is dedicated to all my grandchildren Adi, Aryaman, Abhiveer, Arjun, Neel, Naina, Nachiketa and Rumi and who as the fifth generation of my family inspired me to complete this epic saga.

Family Trees of the Eight Families (Principal Characters Only)

1 Sikandar Khan—Muslim Family from Kashmir
First Generation—Sikandar Khan—Wife Zainab Khan—Brother Sarfaraz Khan
Second Generation—Curzon Sikandar Khan—Wife Nusrat Shezadi
Third Generation—Ismail Sikandar Khan
Fourth Generation—Shiraz Ismail Khan (Adopted Son of Ismail Sikandar Khan)
Fifth Generation—Paramveer Singh Bajwa (Peevee for short) son of Shiraz Ismail Khan and Shupriya Sen—adopted by Monty and Reeta Bajwa

2 Harbhajan Singh Bajwa—Sikh Family from Kashmir
First Generation—Harbhajan Singh
Second Generation—Gurcharan Singh Bajwa—Wife Harbir Kaur
Third Generation—Daler Singh Bajwa—wife Simran Kaur
Fourth Generation—Montek Singh Bajwa—wife Reeta—sister Loveleen
Fifth Generation—Rohini Bajwa (Dimple—nickname—Husband Bharat Padmanaban

3 Sonjoy Sen—Bengali Hindu Family from Calcutta
First Generation—Sonjoy Sen
Second Generation—Naren Sen—Wife Shobha Sen
Third Generation—Samir Sen—Ronen Sen—wife Mona Sen—Purnima Sen
Fourth Generation—Shupriya Sen
Fifth Generation—Paramveer Singh Bajwa (Son of Shiraz Ismail Khan and Shupriya Sen)

4 Apurva Ghosh—Bengali Hindu Family from Chittagong
First Generation—Apurva Ghosh
Second Generation—Debu Ghosh—Wife Hena Ghosh
Third Generation—Arup Ghosh—Swarup Ghosh—Anup Ghosh—Mona Ghosh
Fourth Generation—Lalima Ghosh daughter of Arup and Galina Ghosh and Shupriya Sen (daughter of Ronen Sen and Mona Ghosh)

Fifth Generation—Paramveer Bajwa (son of Shiraz Ismail Khan and Shupriya Sen—adopted by Montek and Reeta Bajwa)

5 Haji Abdul Rehman—Afridi Pathan Muslim Family from Peshawar
First Generation—Haji Abdul Rehman
Second Generation—Attiqur Rehman—Wife Nafisa Rehman
Third Generation—Gul Rehman—Wife Zubeida—Aftab Rehman—Arif Rehman—wife Ruksana—Shenaz Rehman(wife of Nawaz Hussein)
Fourth Generation—Aslam Rehman—Wife Farzana—Fazal Rehman—wife Samina—Mehmooda—Husband Karim Malik—Saira Rehman wife of Riaz Mohammed Khan(Shiraz Ismail Khan)—`Salim Rehman-wife Aasma
Imran Hussein(son of Shenaz and Nawaz Hussein—adopted as Shiraz Ismail Khan by Colonel Ismail Sikandar Khan
Fifth Generation—Samir Rehman(son of Aslam and Mehmuda) Nasreen Rehman(Daughter of Aslam amd Mehmuda—Shezadi Rehman(Sherry—Gammy daughter of Saira and Shiraz(Riaz Mohammed Khan)Tojo(son of Saira and Shiraz) Samira Rehman(daughter of Fazal and Samina)—Shafiq Rehman (son of Fazal and Samina Rehman—)

6 Shaukat Hussein—Muslim Family from Calcutta
First Generation—Shaukat Hussein
Second Generation—Dr Ghulam Hussein—Wife Suraiya Hussein
Third generation—Nawaz Hussein—wife Shenaz Hussein
Fourth Generation—Imran Hussein(Shiraz Ismail Khan) later found and adopted by Colonel Ismail Sikandar Khan
Fifth Generation—Paramveer Singh Bajwa (son of Shiraz Ismail Khan and Supriya Sen adopted by Monty and Reeta Bajwa)

7 Edwin Pugsley—Anglo Indian Family from Calcutta
First Generation—Richard Pugsley
Second Generation—Edwin Pugsley—wife Laila Pugsley
Third Generation—Shaun Pugsley—Debra Pugsley—Sandra Pugsley—Richard Pugsley-Veronica Pugsley

8 Colonel Ronald Edwards—Only son of Roland and Gloria Edwards—British Family from England—First Generation

Chapter-1

Fifty Long Years and Yet No Solution in Sight

While the Foreign Secretary level talks between India and Pakistan kept progressing in a cordial and constructive manner, but the Kashmir issue once again remained as the major stumbling block for both the sides. While Pakistan kept insisting that Jammu and Kashmir was a disputed territory, India's stand was that it was very much a part and parcel of India.

This was also the golden jubilee year of India and Pakistan's independence and while both the countries geared up to celebrate their forthcoming 50th Independence Day in August, the British on 1st July, 1997 handed over the island of Hong Kong to the People's Republic of China. That morning as the Union Jack was lowered for the last and final time, and the flag of the People's Republic of China was hoisted with a lot of fanfare in Hong Kong, Reeta who with Monty was watching the handing and taking over ceremony live on television said to her husband.

"But darling tell me if Britain after their victory in the Opium Wars against an Imperial China that took place during the early years of Queen Victoria's reign, can after so many years of rule give up the strategic island that is also an international financial centre so very gracefully, why can't India and Pakistan once and for all sort out the Kashmir issue in a peaceful and friendly manner too. It is now 50 years since Maharaja Hari Singh's so called kingdom of Heaven on Earth became a damn Hell hole, and even today most of his subjects on either side of the Line of Control do not seem to know as to which country they really belong to.?

'Yes it is indeed rather sad that the political leaders from both sides in all these years have done little or nothing to have the problem resolved amicably, and this has already led to three bloody wars. And that is if one takes 1971 into account also. And with the ongoing proxy war that Pakistan triggered off nearly a decade ago, the rampant militancy and the killings of poor innocent Kashmiris even today shows no signs of receding at all. And I therefore will not be the least surprised if the damn balloon goes up again soon," said Monty when Unni rang up to say that Joginder Singh, the boss of the CBI had quietly not only been shown the door, but he had also been shunted out from the backdoor to some obscure appointment as a special secretary in the Home Ministry.

It was at around four o'clock on that very morning of 1st July, 1997 that Joginder Singh on his return from France came to know about his immediate transfer. He had gone to France in connection with the Interpol notice that was to be served on Quattrocchi, Win Chaddha and a few others in the Bofors case. But even before his aircraft could land at New Delhi's International Airport, his future had been nicely and properly sealed. Besieged by a mob of waiting journalists at the airport who wanted to know his reactions to his hasty removal from that powerful chair, the man with his mystic smile feeling like a hero simply said. "I think your guess is as good as mine,"' and then got into his official staff car and headed home.

That morning, when Monty met Unni at the Press Club to find out what could have been the likely reason for Prime Minister Inder Gujral to so very unceremoniously remove Joginder Singh from that powerful chair overnight, Unni simply smiled and said.

"Well with the speed at which Joginder Singh was pursuing both the Bofors and the Fodder scandals, and the manner in which he was hobnobbing with the politicians and sometime even rubbing some of them on the wrong side, I think it was expected. One must remember that this government also is functioning with the blessings of the Congress, and with Sonia Gandhi now in the party and with Gujral's requirement to also keep her and Lalu in good humour, there was therefore a need for the IB boss to be a little more discreet in his actions and to go a little slow on both these contentious issues. And by serving an Interpol alert notice on Quattrochhi who was once very close to the Gandhi family, he somehow did not realize that he had inadvertently kicked his own damn goose. Moreover it was also a question of Mr Gujral's own survival and that of his ragtag 13 party coalition government, and Gujral must have been indirectly cautioned by the Congress high command to rein in the CBI chief or else lose his job. And that is exactly what has happened. Moreover the appointment of RC Sharma an IPS officer of 1963 vintage who had been given a year's extension in January to replace Joginder Singh has also set tongues wagging. Mind you Joginder Singh had done only 11 months in that chair and is due for retirement in October. But for the Congress and for the Gujral government he it seems had become a real pain in the neck, and poor Mr Gujral therefore had no other option but to shunt him out and get a pliable R.C.

Sharma on that politically sponsored powerful chair. And therefore this only goes to prove my point that the all powerful politicians and the political lobby in the Indian parliament of both honest and crooked parliamentarians are more interested in sticking to their damn chairs, rather than finding out the real truth and punishing the culprits. And mind you this is the same RC Sharma, who headed the Bofors enquiry for five years starting from 1991 and made little or no progress on it because it was the Narasimha Rao Congress government which was in power during that period. And the current rumour is that Joginder Singh was also planning to question Sonia Gandhi on her close friendship with the Quattrochis and that for Gujral would have been suicidal. But for Gujral to give the lame excuse that Joginder Singh was not competent enough to sit on that important chair is nothing short of bending backwards to the Congress high command and that indeed is a real pity,' added Unni with a sly impish grin on his face.

"Well if that be the case, then I am afraid we have only a total sham democracy in this country, This undoubtedly was India's Watergate, but it was with a big bloody difference. Whereas in the Watergate investigation, the system took over from where journalistic endeavour to get to the truth ended, and the democratic institutions responded in a manner that were expected of them. But in the Bofors and the Fodder scam case it is the other way round and the system is being made to buckle in order to serve the interests of the corrupt power hungry politicians and their 'Babus," said an angry Monty.

"That is exactly what I have always been saying that India is God's own country where though the national motto is 'Satyemewa Jayete"(Truth Always Triumphs) but in reality it is always subverted, And many more Bofors will come and many more Bofors will go, but these corrupt politicians will go on forever," concluded Unni as he raised a toast to the late Feroze Gandhi, the son-in-law of Jawaharlal Nehru,the husband of Indira Gandhi and the father of Rajiv and Sanjay. Unni had always held Feroze Gandhi in very high esteem because as an honest parliamentarian in the then ruling Congress government he had the guts to take on the very establishment that he was very much a part off. According to Unni it was Feroze Gandhi, the Congress Member of Parliament and the Prime Minister's son-in-law who had the bloody guts to accuse the Nehru government of corruption and that was way back in 1958. On the floor of the house that day Feroze had openly challenged Nehru's finance minister TT Krishnamachari with rampant corruption in the Haridas Mundra case. And when during that heated debate it was established that the government had secretly and clandestinely helped the industrialist's sinking companies with finances, the finance minister had no other option but to put in his papers and go home.

"Thank God Feroze Gandhi died soon thereafter and he did not have to live long enough to see the names of his own immediate family members bearing his surname being castigated and tarnished for corruption by all and sundry," said Unni who always felt that had Feroze Gandhi lived longer, he would have probably been a better Prime Minister than his wife Indira Gandhi.

Though the Golden Jubilee independence year celebrations for both India and Pakistan had crossed the half way mark, there was nothing much to revel about. While India got into a chaotic political and economic limbo, in Pakistan the arrest of Aimal Kansi and his immediate deportation to the United States not only angered the tribals of Baluchistan, but it also gave the radical Pakistanis an opportunity to vent their growing hatred on the Americans, To add to Pakistan's embarrassment, when the American Ambassador at Islamabad, Thomas Simons in late August informed his own government that Pakistan's involvement with Mulla Omar was more than just providing food and fuel, and that the ISI was also training and supplying young armed Mujahideens to strengthen the Taliban, Salim Rehman too was disillusioned with Pakistan's growing friendship with that radical diehard Muslim organization.Therefore to take it off his chest Salim Rehman in a private letter to his brother-in-law Riaz (Shiraz) in Paris that was sent through the diplomatic mail said very candidly that as per the Pakistan Foreign Ministry's information and one that has come from a very reliable government source, it was the ISI that not only advocated Pakistan's recognition of the Taliban government, but it had also warded off the closing of certain pro-Taliban 'Madrassas' (Seminaries) that are located near the Pak—Afghan border, and which have now become spawning grounds for the future Taliban hardline fighters. Moreover, the presence of the Pakistani Harkat-ul-Ansar militants who are presently being trained in various camps inside Afghanistan by the ISI, and who are primarily meant for carrying out clandestine operations in Indian occupied Kashmir was also a very disturbing factor because the foreign office feared that they too in the long run will also get Talibanised and that could spell real danger for their own country.'

No sooner had Shiraz received that long informative letter from Salim Rehman, in which Salim also hinted obliquely that Pakistan militarily may soon also join the nuclear club, and that Pakistan despite the ongoing foreign secretary level talks with India was well on the road to try and once again internationalize the Kashmir issue, Shiraz quickly in his own code jotted down the salient points in his little red diary. Apprehensive that such kind of jingoism by the Pakistan ISI and the military may well lead to a breakdown to the ongoing talks, he initially thought of indirectly warning his Indian counterpart in the Indian Embassy in Paris, but on second thoughts gave up the idea for fear of being compromised. He was also aware that the long arm and the eyes and ears of the ISI were very much in evidence within the four walls of his own embassy and it was not worth taking any chances

Meanwhile In India, the clout of the 'Bhais'(Dons) in Bollywood was also evident when Gulshan Kumar, the son of a juice seller from Daryaganj, Delhi who had founded the Super Cassettes Industries, and who was also now a well to do film producer was shot dead in broad daylight on the morning of 12th August, 1997 while he was on his way to pray at the Jeeteshwar Mahadev temple in Juhu. Juhu was a seaside suburb for the rich and the famous in Mumbai and the beaches nearby were popular tourist spots. But that morning as Gulshan Kumar approached the temple, he was brutally gunned down by a hail of bullets and died practically instantaneously. The man who had started promoting religious music for the Hindus and who was responsible to introduce talented young singers like Kumar Sanu, Anuradha Podwal and Sonu Nigam to Bollywood and who served free food to all the pilgrims who visited the famous Vaisno Devi temple near Jammu was suddenly no more. The great devotee of Vaisno Mata Devi' the Indian Goddess also popularly known as "Sherawali Maa' (The Tiger Lady) had succumbed to his wounds even before he could say 'Jai Matadi'(Glory to the Goddess) on that windy Monsoon morning.

Though the police called it a vendetta killing and accused Nadeem of the successful music duo Nadeem-Shravan fame in being the man who had hired the assassins to get rid of the multi-millionaire proprietor of that music production company, but the fact remained that the police were not able to lay their hands on the real hired assassins who fired those bullets. The finger of suspicion also pointed to Abu Salem, whose real name was Salem Qayoom Ansari. Salem hailed from Sarai Mir, a small village in the Azamgarh district of Uttar Pradesh, and had started his life in Mumbai as a tailor. He subsequently ran a telephone booth and sold cutlery in the suburbs of Mumbai But he was now in the extortion business racket targeting Bollywood bigwigs and others who had large sums of black money to throw around. Abu Salem was also a prime suspect in the March 1993 serial bomb blasts that shook Mumbai, India and the world, but the police force simply could not lay their hands on him.

The brutal daylight murder of Gulshan Kumar on the streets of Juhu and the assassins having got away scot free while people kept watching the grotesque murder had shocked the stars of Bollywood and Peevee (Deepak Kumar) was no exception either. Late that very evening, when Shupriya learnt about the killing of the Super Cassette magnate through the PTI, (Press Trust of India) news channel, she immediately rang up Peevee and advised him to hire a team of bodyguards from some trusted and reliable private security agency, and of which there were now many in the city.

"Please try and get some ex—policemen who are also good sharp shooters and preferably those who have performed VIP duties with 'Z' category politicians, and if you pay them handsomely, I am sure you will find them in a city like Mumbai. And for heaven's sake do not get on the wrong side of these goons. Deal with them diplomatically and in a friendly manner, but without showing that you are afraid of them," said Shupriya.

"Yes Mom, but you don't have to worry because I already have an ex-serviceman sharp shooter who has recently retired and who is now all the time shadowing and tailing me. He is from the Bravo Company, of the 4th Battalion Jammu and Kashmir Rifles and has also served in the elite Black Commandos earlier. He also holds a valid license for small arms' including the Sten gun and Papa was kind enough to send him to me. Papa had met this Havildar when we were shooting in Kashmir for the film on the late Major Shiraz Ismail Khan that was titled 'Sherdil', and since he had only just retired from service, he was only too happy to be hired by me,'.added Peevee.

On hearing her late husband's name coming from her own son, Shupriya eyes became moist and for a few seconds she was completely carried away."'Oh that is indeed very good news, but please do not leave everything to him. You have to become more security conscious yourself and never ever become complacent and lower your guard," added Shupriya as she slowly recovered her composure

"Oh you just don't worry Mom, the goon who wants to take my life is yet to be born," said Peevee very confidently while wishing her a very good night.

That day Shupriya was really in high spirits because. Peevee for the first time ever had addressed her as only Mom and without suffixing the traditional number 2 tag to it. Late that evening a lonely Shupriya took out the photograph of Shiraz in uniform from her secret hiding place, and switched on the cassette recorder to listen to an old Kishore Kumar number titled 'Ye Sham Mastani'. It was from the hit film "Kati Patang.'and it was this very song that Shiraz had sung to her on the day they were secretly married and that was way back on 15th,September, 1971.

Four days later on 16th August, while Bollywood was mourning the brutal killing of Gulsham Kumar, the whole of Pakistan and all those who loved Sufi music were also mourning the untimely death of Nusrat Fateh Ali Khan. The King, Emperor and Shahenshah of 'Qawali', the traditional music maestro of the Sufis was on his way to Los Angeles to receive his kidney transplant, but he had to be hospitalized on 11th August while transiting through London. He was taken ill with kidney and liver failure and died on 16th August of a sudden cardiac arrest at Cromwell Hospital, London and he was just forty eight years old and only six years senior to Gulshan Kumar. "Born on 13th October, 1948 at Lyallpur in a Shia Muslim family, Nusrat Fateh Ali Khan was initiated into this unique form of traditional Sufi devotional music by his father Ustad Fateh Ali Khan. Tragically his first performance at the age of 14 in 1964 was at the graveside of his own father. It was during the ceremony known as 'Chelum' that is traditionally held after 40 days after the death of an individual that his talent was recognized. His first major hit was the song 'Haq Ali Ali, 'and thereafter there was no looking back for him. 'He was a man who sang to God and made everybody else to sing to the Almighty also," said Shiraz to his daughter while explaining to her the nuances of the popular qawali. Shiraz was an ardent fan of the man who had also contributed to the song 'Gurus of Peace' in the album 'Vande Mataram' that AR Rehman had composed to celebrate the 50th anniversary of India's independence and Shiraz knew that his untimely death was a great loss to both the nations.

Chapter-2

From One Shocking Tragedy to Another

Having completed her 18th birthday on 6th June,1997 Sherry (Shezadi) was allowed for the first time by her father to attend a formal official cocktail and dinner party that was being hosted by him in honour of the outgoing Egyptian Ambassador who was also a dear friend of the family. Dressed in a traditional peacock blue salwar kameez, Sherry on that evening of 30th August looked stunningly gorgeous as she escorted by her parents entered the 'Bar Hemingway' inside the luxurious Hotel Ritz Paris that was now owned by the Egyptian billionaire Mohamed Al Fayed who was also the owner of 'Harrods', the huge departmental store in London.

"Let me tell you that this famous hotel in Paris with its stunning logo had been hosts to many a rich and the famous like Edward VII, King Reza Pahelvi of Iran, Charlie Chaplin, Greta Garbo and even Rudolp Valentino, and of course the famous novelist Ernest Hemingway who always stayed here whenever he visited Paris and therefore the bar has been named after him," said Shiraz very proudly.

"Yes and the famous couturier Coco Chanel too stayed here for 30 long years and she had literally made this her home," added Saira.

"Then I must also tell you that the hotel also has a very sophisticated and important guest tonight and she is none other than Princess Diana. And more importantly she also is guest of a very well to do Egyptian who now owns this hotel. But nonetheless I must also admit that you are equally very pretty and charming too young lady," said the gallant Egyptian Ambassador very proudly on being introduced to Sherry.

"But Your Excellency if the Princess is present in the hotel right now, will it be possible for us to meet her, if not to see her at least from a distance," said Sherry in an excited tone.

"Oh that I am afraid is simply not possible my dear because it is supposed to be a closely guarded secret. And according to inside information she arrived only today with her latest boy friend Dodi Fayed, who incidentally is also the hotel owner's son. They couple had spent the preceding week on 'Jonikal' Dodi senior's luxury yacht on the French Reviera," said the Ambassador as Shiraz raised a toast to Pakistan-Egyptian friendship and got the party going.

"Well I must say that you are very well informed my dear husband,"said the Egyptian Ambassador's wife with a look of surprise on her face.

"Well on a day like this I guess I have to be on the ball and a little more secretive too. After all I am still the Egyptian Ambassador to France and the lovely ex-Princess of Wales is an honoured guest of a fellow very well to do and well connected Egyptian too," said the jovial man while extending an invitation to Shiraz and his family for a cruise on the Nile and a visit to the famous tourist spot of Luxor during the coming winter season.

After the party ended around 11 PM that night, and after Shiraz and Saira had seen off all their guests, the family decided to end the evening with some hot coffee at the exclusive L'Espadon restaurant inside the hotel. After the coffee and while they were waiting near the foyer for the embassy chauffeur to bring the car, Saira on having noticed the large number of people waiting outside the hotel with their cameras and flashguns loaded and on the ready remarked rather casually.

"I think the celebrity status for people like Diana and others like her is not only a handicap for them, but it is also a damn nuisance for those who want to enjoy a little bit of privacy on the quiet. And I won't be the least surprised if the paparazzi with their high resolution cameras and zoom lenses even manage to enter her bedroom. Frankly speaking all this is simply ridiculous and there should some decency shown to the poor Princess, who after all has suffered so much mentally during these last few years."

"Yes I fully agree with you my dear, but for the paparazzi this is their profession and business, and an exclusive intimate photograph of the Princess in the company of Dodi can earn them quite a packet," said Shiraz

"So does that mean that Dr Hasmat Khan is not in the running anymore," asked Sherry somewhat matter of factly.

"Well I must say that you too are also well informed my dear, but it could be that Diana wants to make Hasmat a little jealous. Because the little that I know, I think she is still very much in love with the handsome Pathan doctor, but who unfortunately off late for family reasons I am told has been avoiding her," added Shiraz.

"That is indeed rather sad and I only hope and pray that after so many tragic love affairs and a broken marriage, Dodi Fayed at least should now make her happy," said Saira.

On reaching home a little after midnight, when Shiraz got into his night suit and while in bed was browsing through the book "The Land of the Pharoahs," that the Egyptian Ambassador had presented him with that evening, the telephone rang. Shiraz looked at his watch, It was 0050 hours and a new day had already begun

"Do pardon me Monsieur, but there has been a terrible car accident involving Princess Diana, and it took place inside the Place de l' Alma underpass, which is not very far from the Hotel Ritz, and I hope you and your family are safe," said the man on duty at the Pakistan Embassy.

"But are you sure that it was Princess Diana's car," asked Shiraz as he got out of bed and got into a pair of jeans and a polo shirt.

"Most certainly Sir because a group of paparazzi on motorbikes were following the Mercedes-Benz S280, and one of them who happened to be a friend of mine gave me that information on telephone just now," said the caller.

"I hope she is alright and you go back to sleep and I will return soon," whispered Shiraz softly into Saira's ears after he had conveyed the terrible news to her.

A few minutes later, Shiraz got into his big black Puegeot with the diplomatic number plate and flag and made his way to the accident site. But by the time he reached, the tunnel had already been cordoned off by the police and all the four occupants including the driver had been taken either to the mortuary or to the nearest hospital so he was told. According to the police, Dodi Fayed and the driver Henri Paul both had died at the scene of the accident, while Princess Diana and the bodyguard Trevor-Rees Jones both of whom were badly injured still had a little life in them and were rushed to a hospital. According to one of the paparazzi's, the Princess was bleeding heavily from the nose and ears, while the bodyguard had serious injuries to his face. But the saddest part was that seeing her in that terrible state some of the paparazzi were shamelessly clicking away and taking pictures of her, till the police arrived and arrested all of them.

It was around midnight that Dodi Fayed decided that he with the Princess would go back to their apartment on Rue Arsene Houssaye and they would spend the night there. And in order to give the paparazzi the slip, a decoy vehicle at 12.15 AM on that 31st August took off from the main entrance and quite a few photographers kept following it. Five minutes later the couple escorted by the bodyguard and Henri Paul the driver quickly got into the Mercedes that was parked at the rear entrance of the hotel on the Rue Cambon exit. In order to avoid the papparazi from chasing them,

Henri the driver took off at breakneck speed. But at around 12.25, as the car approached the entrance to the Place de L'Alma tunnel, the driver lost complete control of the vehicle and the car swerved left on the two lane carriageway before colliding headon with a pillar that was supporting the roof. It then spun around backwards and crashed against the solid stonewall of the tunnel with a big bang.

Ironically that was the thirteenth pillar of that tunnel that had caused the tragic accident. While the critically injured Diana kept murmuring the words 'Oh My God' and 'Leave me alone', the paparazzi still kept taking pictures. Once the ambulance arrived, Diana was taken to the Pitie-Salpetriere Hospital. Her injuries both internal and external were extensive and though the team of doctors desperately tried their level best to save her life, but it was not to be. At 4 AM that morning the lovely Princess Diana was no more. It was later revealed that the driver Henri Paul had been drinking quite heavily that night and the accident occurred as he tried to elude the paparazzi by driving at a very high speed.

Next morning at breakfast, when Shiraz conveyed the news to his family, there were tears in Sherry's eyes. It seems that she on that very night had dreamt that she had been introduced to the Princess and Sherry had even presented her with a bunch of roses that she had quietly picked up from the Hemingway Bar, and now she was no more.

That month of August it seems was a month of death and destruction not only for those who were rich and famous, but also for the poor as a spate of brutal massacres of innocent men women and children were reported from Algeria, which was once a thriving French colony.The civil war in Algeria that had erupted after the cancellation of the 1992 election by the military had intensified manifold, and though a state of emergency had been declared, but the killings continued unabated. The trouble started after the FIS, the Islamic Salvation Front was all set to win the elections, but was denied that honour. And it got worse as the years went by.

In the month of August itself there were four deadly massacres, and the one on 29th August at the village of Rais was the bloodiest and the worst of the lot so far. Hooded members from the GIA, the Armed Islamic Group during the night of 29th August armed with guns, bombs, axes and knives having arrived in trucks and cars mercilessly killed nearly 400 innocent men, women and children, and in some cases even their animals were not spared. The firing and looting carried on till the wee hours of the morning and what was even more surprising was the late response by the Algerian security forces whose barracks were only a few kilometers away from that village. Even more worrying to Shiraz was the fact that quite a few in the rival guerrilla groups that were fighting each other now had also fought together in Afghanistan against the Russians, and some of them were also closely linked to the dreaded Al Qaida.

A week later there was still more bad news for the world, when on the 5th of September, 1997 that was known as 'Teacher's Day' in India, the world lost one of its greatest teachers. She was a revered Nun who was an epitome of love, compassion and sacrifice for the poor and the needy, and Shiraz who always kept a photograph of the little lady in a blue bordered white saree inside his leather wallet decided to write a poem on her. Mother Teresa, 'the Saint of the Gutters' had died at the age of 87 in her own little convent in Calcutta.

'You came to us as a gift from God,
To show us the way of truly serving the Lord.
With Jesus in your heart and compassion for the poor,
You served them all, the unwanted, the destitute and the leper.

For caste, creed or religion you made no distinction
And like an angel from heaven you gave all love and comfort with true devotion.
As a mother to this world you were a beacon of light
Always shining in the wilderness, day and night.

You served the Lord among the poorest of the poor,
And gave whatever it takes to do good to one another.
You breathed new life into the missionaries of charity,
And thus presented the true face of God to humanity.

Though you have left us, your spirit shall always remaln,
Guiding us through life while shining from Heaven.'

"By God Papa you are a good poet too,' said Sherry as she read the poem aloud a second time to her mother and brother.

"Oh the little lady from Albania always inspired me and frankly speaking the words of this poem simply came to me as I kept thinking about her life of selfless devotion to the poor," added Shiraz while showing them Mother Teresa's photograph that he had in his wallet.

On 13th September, while Shiraz watched the live broadcast of Mother Teresa's funeral service that was being attended by Queens, Kings, Cardinals,

Prime Ministers and Presidents from all over the world, he wondered whether another saintly and selfless woman like her would ever come to this world again. She had taught the world that it is more blessed to give than to receive. And when the wine for the Eucharist was brought into the hall by a leprosy patient and the bread by a handicapped man, and the water by a woman who had recently been released from prison, the moistness in Shiraz's eyes was quite evident. After the conclusion of the services at the Netaji Subhas Bose Indoor Sadium in Calcutta, when her body draped in the Indian tricolor of her adopted homeland on a military gun carriage escorted by a military honour guard was being taken back to Mother House, which was the headquarters of the Missionaries of Charity for a private burial, it seemed as if the whole of Calcutta with flowers was on the streets to bid a final goodbye to the diminutive lady who was not only God's gift to Calcutta and the world, but perhaps God's greatest gift to all mankind. As the televised news cast that was being shown live came to an end, Sherry who was sitting next to her father cuddled up to him and tenderly kissed away the little tear drop that was slowly dribbling down his cheek.

Chapter-3

What Price Sea food and Pizzas

"Abbajaan' how I wish we were in Charlotte, North Carolina and we could have become millionaires overnight, and there would have been no need for you to work so hard at all," said an excited Tojo to his father as he walked in with the latest copy of the Time magazine that had covered another unprecedented bank robbery, which took place in the United States of America on 4th October, 1997 and resulted in the robbers carrying away 17.3 million dollars in hard cash. But since 11 million dollars of that cash was all in 20 dollar bills, the robbers could not carry the entire amount and they left behind 3.3 million dollars in the back of the armoured cash van that they had used in transporting the money to the lonely spot where the bulk of the money was transferred into the waiting getaway cars. It was an inside job by the very man who was the armoured car driver and the vault supervisor in the regional office vault of Loomis Fargo and Company.

"But Papa, the heist was the second largest cash robbery in the history of the United States and surprisingly it was only a month earlier that 18.9 million dollars in cash was robbed by another insider in the Dunbar Armoured robbery case in Los Angeles, California. And therefore it only goes to show that even in a country like America that always boasts about their so called hi-tech security systems and the FBI and the CIA of being the best in the world, they too cannot stop their own people from perpetrating such kind of daylight robberies," added Tojo

"But as compared to Zardari and Benazir and others who were in power in our own country, or those who are presently right now in power, this is chicken feed. At least in the case of banks, the money is always insured, and what is 17 or 18 million dollars as compared to the billion dollars that Zardari and Benazir quietly swiped away while they were in power, or to the measly 50 odd million dollars that the Gandhis and their friend the Quatrochhis, the Win Chaddhas and the Hindujas are alleged to have made in the never ending Bofors scam," said Sherry.

"'True, but in America these people who were responsible for these heists will definitely be caught and tried, but as far as India and Pakistan are concerned, they will be all hailed as saviors and may will be awarded the 'Bharat Ratna' and the 'Nishan-e-Haider for looting the nation,' said Shiraz in a lighter vein, when his wife Saira reminded him that he must apply for his leave and take them on the cruise on the River Nile and to Luxor as was promised by the outgoing Egyptian Ambassador.

"Of course, the cruise is very much on the cards and it has been planned during the third week of November," said Shiraz while presenting a tourist guide book on the ancient monuments of Egypt to his wife.And while Shiraz and his family were looking forward to the grand cruise on the Nile and the visit to the ancient sites of the Egyptian civilization, Peevee decided to visit his Mom number two in Havana. He was in any case going for the shooting of his new film to Miami and Orlando in Florida that was scheduled for early October and he looked forward to spending at least a quiet week with her in Castro's Cuba.

"My God with this new Shirley Maclaine hairstyle, you simply look gorgeous and who will ever say that you are soon going to be fifty soon," said an excited Peevee as he touched Shupriya's feet and presented her with a bouquet of 50 red roses. And as the big Mercedes Benz with its diplomatic number plate and the Indian tricolor flag fluttering in the autumn breeze made its way to the Ambassador's house, Peevee observed that Cuba was not the kind of Iron Curtain Island that the western press made it out to be. Yes, it was still a communist country and Fidel was still the big boss, but by and large the people on the streets looked fairly happy and contented.

That evening, when Shupriya threw a grand party in honour of Peevee for the entire Embassy staff and their families, and she also invited the handful of Cubans who worked as drivers, cleaners, and as domestic helpers in the mission, Peevee was surprised to learn that 'Deepak Kumar' the actor was also fairly well known on that tiny little island.

"I think he looks better than Cary Grant and more like Gregory Peck,' said Imelda the 60 year old housekeeper who as a young teenage girl regularly saw Hollywood movies till they were banned by Castro in 1959. In 1960, Imelda married her childhood friend Raul Santos who had fought during the revolution under Che Guevara, but died defending his country when the Americans launched their disastrous Bay of Pigs campaign in April 1961. As a young childless widow she first looked after an orphanage for children in Santa Clara and in 1965 after the Indian Embassy in Cuba employed her as a housekeeper, she has remained there ever since and was now more like a family member.That evening, when Imelda learnt that the Madame Ambassador with her young guest would be going to her hometown Santa Clara on 17th October where the remains of Che Guevara would be finally laid to rest with military honours in a specially built mausoleum, she without feeling shy expressed her desire to accompany them and Shupriya immediately gave her the nod. It was at Santa Clara, Imelda's home town where Che Guevera the young revolutionary had won the decisive battle for the Cuban revolution 39 years ago, and where she as a young nurse with a guerrilla outfit had first met her future husband.

Early morning of that 17th October, as they drove from Havana along the 300 mile National Highway to Santa Clara, Imelda vividly and proudly narrated to Peevee as to how Che Guevera and his band of guerrillas had timely derailed and blasted the train that was bringing in strong government military reinforcements from Havana, and which ultimately resulted in a decisive victory for the revolutionaries, Peevee was indeed very impressed by her knowledge of modern Cuban history, and when he further suggested to Imelda that the decisive Battle of Santa Clara would make a good motivational war film for the young Cuban generation and that a talented Cuban film director like Humberto Solas would surely do a great job of it, it was Imelda who was highly impressed by Peevee's knowledge about Cuban cinema. And a little while later, when Peevee in his baritone voice started singing the ever popular number Guantenamera (The Girl from Guantenamo), Imelda was completely floored.

During the solemn ceremony that day when the remains of Che Guevara was finally laid to rest with full military honours, there were tears in Shupriya's eyes. It reminded her of her late husband, a war hero of India who too had sacrificed his life for his country. Next day morning, while Peevee was getting ready to catch his flight back to Mumbai via London, Shupriya presented him with a pair of pure silver cuff links and a matching tie pin that had two concentric circles engraved on them. She after her wedding on 15th September 1971 had ordered it from Cooke and Kelvey at Connaught Place and wanted to gift it to her husband on his return from war, but her loving Dablo (Double O) unfortunately never returned.

Knowing Peevee's appetite for good genuine sea food, Shupriya on the way to the airport took him to the El Floridita restaurant for lunch. Many years ago and even after the Cuban revolution this too was Ernest Hemingway"s favourite eating place. It was at this very restaurant that the Nobel laureate while sipping his favourite Diaquri wrote many of his books and articles.

While Peevee relished the big spread of rich seafood with his chilled beer, Shupriya hinted to him that there was now a possibility of her going as an Ambassador to a bigger and a more important country soon and Moscow was being tipped as the most likely choice.

"By Jove Mom that will be simply great, and with Moscow being much closer to what is now called Mumbai, it will also give me the opportunity to visit you more often,"said Peevee while thanking Shupriya for the delightful lunch. That evening as she lay in bed with her late husband's photograph in her hand, she felt doubly happy because this was the second time that Peevee had addressed her as Mom and not as Mom Number 2.

'While Peevee was on his way back to Mumbai via London, he was pleasantly surprised to learn at the Heathrow airport that a young Indian lady by the name of Arundhati Roy had won the prestigious Booker prize for her novel 'The God of Small Things.' It was a story of two fraternal twins who become victims of circumstances that were beyond their control and how it affected their lives. Born in Shillong on 24th November, 1961 to a Syrian Christain mother and a Bengali father, Arundhati was a product of Lawrence School Lovedale and had initially aspired to become an architect. But now with her very first novel she had become a celebrity overnight. Peevee on seeing the book on display at an airport bookstall immediately bought a copy and by the time he landed in Mumbai he had finished reading through the young lady's 340 page debut novel.

A fortnight later and as promised, Shiraz with his family on 9th November landed at the Cairo International Airport. And after having spent two days as guests of his dear old friend the Ex Egyptian Ambassador who with his wife proudly showed them around the popular tourist spots of the capital city, the family on the 13th departed on a four day cruise on the River Nile to Luxor. They had planned to stay at Luxor for two days and see the ancient temples on both sides of the great river, and on the 18th return by the late evening Egyptian Airways flight back to Cairo. The four day lavish cruise on the Nile and that too on the luxury boat the M/S Liberty was a wonderful experience for the family and specially because they were in one of the six Presidential suites that had a private balcony overlooking the serene river. Very early on the morning of 17th November, when they landed at Luxor that was also known as Thebes in ancient times,they found the place teeming with tourists and most of them were Europeans, Americans and Japanese. Shiraz having studied the guide book very thoroughly had decided to spend the first day visiting the more renowned ancient temples on the west bank of the river and on the second day visit the tourist sites on the east bank because that was where the airport was also located.

"Come on let's all hurry up or else we will miss the next tourist ferry to the west bank,"said Shiraz loudly as all of them with their individual rucksacks on their backs ran down the gangway. The overcrowded tourist ferry boat took only 20 minutes to get to the west bank, and when Shiraz checked the time it was only a minute past eight in the morning. After haggling with the taxi driver for an eight hour comprehensive guided tour, when it was finally decided that they would first visit the 'Mortuary Temple of Hatshepsut' that was the farthest away from the ferry,and later make their way back through the Temples of Remeses and the Valley of Queens in order to catch the 5 PM tourist ferry back to the east bank, the Egyptian taxi driver who by then had realized that his passengers were fellow Muslims from Pakistan simply smiled and said 'Maalish aur Salaam Wale Kaum. Huzoor,' meaning thereby that it was no big deal and that he was delighted to be their driver and guide.

There was no doubt that the spectacular mortuary temple of the only female Pharaoh Hatshepsut with its many columns and layered terraces located deep beneath the high cliffs was the most popular tourist spot on the west bank, and Shiraz with his family was keen to get there as early as possible and before the large groups of other tourists on guided bus tours arrived on the scene. But having had a very late night on board the Liberty the previous evening, and with no time for breakfast in the morning, they were all feeling very hungry. So when they stopped at a restaurant that was also named after the same Queen Pharaoh for a quick bite, the happiest person was young Tojo.

"The pizza is our specialty and the choice of vegetarian and non-vegetarian is entirely yours Sir," said the polite waiter in his broken English as he ushered them to a table for four.

"In that case make it a magnum size mutton pizza with whatever toppings you have ready and please do serve it fast with some good hot coffee," added Shiraz as he took a few photographs of the blue domed restaurant that had the unusual sign "No Galag' meaning 'No Problems' emblazoned in big letters on top of the dome. But soon after breakfast, when they resumed their journey to visit the famous temple they did not realize that they were in serious danger of becoming victims of a deadly terrorist attack. Fortunately they were still a good five hundred yards away from the site, when the sound of rapid gun fire reverberated from inside the temple complex.

"Stop, stop," yelled Shiraz loudly to the driver as he looked through his field glasses that was around his neck and noticed a group of uniformed men inside the temple complex. They were firing at the group of tourists who were already inside the temple and were now trying to escape the mayhem. Realizing the imminent danger, the driver immediately reversed this vehicle and they made their way back to the ferry. Had they arrived there even a few minutes earlier, they too would have become victims of that ghastly massacre. The unscheduled quick pizza breakfast at the restaurant had virtually saved their lives.

It was around 9 AM that morning, when a large group of around 75 foreign tourists mainly from Switzerland and Japan together with a few from England, Germany, France and a few other countries who were on a conducted tour arrived at the popular tourist site. But no sooner they were inside the temple complex; they were attacked and brutally killed by six armed terrorists who were armed with automatic weapons and knives. It was a well planned operation and the killers had come disguised as members of the security forces. The final body count put the death toll at 63, which included 36 Swiss, 10 Japanese, 6 British, 4 Germans and 7 others. The wounded included 12 Swiss, 2 Japanese, 2 Germans, 1 French tourist and 9 Egyptians But the saddest part was that among those killed were four young Japanese couples who were on their honeymoon.

It was indeed a close call for Shiraz and his family as they on that very evening decided to cut short their visit and to fly back to Cairo. And it was only a few days later that they came to know who perpetrated that ghastly crime and why.The brutal killing of innocent tourists was the handiwork of the Al-Gama'a al-Islamiya, Egypt's largest Islamic fundamentalist group and the manner in which the massacre was carried out by the six armed men indicated that they were also well trained. According to one reliable source they had all been trained in Afghanistan by Bin Laden's Al-Qaida and had carried out the killings with the aim of destabilizing the Egyptian economy, which virtually thrived on tourism. There had been similar killings of foreigners in Cairo earlier also, but not on such a massive scale. The Islamic militant group had started targeting foreign tourists ever since they took up arms in 1992, and with the primary aim to topple the government and set up a purist Islamic state in Egypt. It was evident that the group had carried out a thorough reconnaissance of the target area prior to taking up vantage positions in and around the temple compound. And since there was no armed security in that area, they had a free run for nearly 40 minutes, while the tourists were trapped inside the vast complex. The attackers then hijacked a bus, but they ran into a check post that was being manned by armed Egyptian tourist police force. During the brief shootout, one of the terrorist's was critically injured, while the rest fled into the hills. Soon a massive manhunt was launched and a few days later the Egyptian government declared that all the six terrorists had been killed. But there was another unconfirmed report that said that their bodies were found in a cave and that they had apparently committed mass suicide.

"But I wonder what they are trying to achieve by killing innocent civilians. Because by committing such brutal acts not only are they bringing a bad name to Islam, but they are also losing out on their so called aim and desire to set up a purist Islamic Caliphate in the world. In fact I think it is nothing but sheer stupidity and madness, and if the leaders of these so called young Fidayeens and Jehadis think that violence and terror will subjugate the rest of the world and make them follow their diktat, then I am afraid they are all living in a fool's paradise," said Saira after she learnt that a five year old child was also gunned down by the terrorists inside the temple of Haptepshut.

"But unfortunately terror has no religion and it is these damn half illiterate Mullas from various seminaries and schools who while sitting in the comfort of their mosques and homes are fanning the war of hatred against all those who they consider to be kafirs (unbelievers)," said Shiraz.

"But Abbajaan if that be the case, then why can't the respective governments of those countries where these so called moralists and followers of the faithful have made their bases get them all eliminated once and for all,"'said Sherry.

"It is easier said than done my love because in most cases it was the same government that had spawned the growth of these so called radicals in their own country and in their immediate neighbourhood to further their own political interests. But they have now totally lost control over them, and Pakistan is no exception to this damn madness either," said a highly upset Shiraz.

Chapter-4

A New Avatarni for India in the Making

While the after effects of the Luxor massacre was still being felt all over the world, in Pakistan, Nawaz Sharif and his government was getting ready to take on the country's Chief Justice and the judiciary with an unprecedented move that would shock the nation.And though the plan to oust Chief Justice Sajjad Ali Shah had taken root in late August, 1997, but it was put into effect only on the morning of 28th November. In a well orchestrated secret operation. Mian Shabaz Sharif, the Chief Minister of Punjab and the younger brother of the Prime Minister having ordered his party stalwarts to make it by road from Lahore to Islamabad, he together with Senator Saifur Rehman flew down and landed at the Islamabad airport at the unearthly hour of 3 AM that morning. And though the ISI chief Lt General Nasim Rana had got wind of it and had informed the COAS General Karamat, but like a good soldier the Army Chief not wishing to interfere in the tussle between the judiciary and the politicians decided to wait and watch.That very morning, when the politicians stormed the highest court of the country and ousted the Chief Justice, Salim Rehman literally hung his head in shame.

"I am afraid it will now be the political power and the street power that would rule Pakistan," said Salim Rehman in disgust while informing Shiraz over the telephone the shameless manner in which the operation was carried out.

At around the same time, while Pakistani politicians from the ruling party were coercing and intimidating the judiciary, in India parts of the interim report of the Jain Commission that had been leaked to the press had got the Congress on the warpath again. The Jain Commission that was inquiring into the conspiracy aspect of Rajiv Gandhi's assassination had indicted the DMK for tacitly supporting the LTTE. The DMK was part of the ruling coalition at the Centre and when the report at the insistence of the Congress was tabled on the floor of the Parliament and it was confirmed that the Jain Commission had in fact held the DMK responsible for supporting the LTTE, the Congress demanded the immediate resignation of all the DMK ministers in Gujral's government. But for once Gujral stood his ground and the Congress had no other option but to withdraw support. And after the short lived Gujral government fell on the 28th of November, 1997, a day that also coincided with the ousting of the Chief Justice of Pakistan, Unni casually remarked to Monty.

"Well now that the mid-term elections scheduled to be held in February-March next year have been announced, I think the stink from the Bofors gun if it is raised again by the emerging Bharatiya Janata Party and its allies during their campaign, may will seal the fate of the Congress once again. And the so called mammoth Jain Commission report that the Congress has used to destabilize the country not once but twice in the fiftieth year of our independence only proves the point that it will be the Soniaites in the party who will be now probably calling all the shots, and they will ultimately anoint Rajiv's widow as the next Congress President,'"added Unni.

"And in any case Sitaram Kesri who started his political career in the Congress as a drummer boy and an announcer and who was elected to the Lok Sabha only once and that to on a Janata ticket many years ago is now already a spent force. His only contribution to the party as a treasurer for 16 years till he was elected President in January 1997 was to ensure that the party coffers were always full and now that Sonia Gandhi is being pushed to take over the mantle, he too like Narasimha Rao will be drummed out I guess,'"said Monty.

"But all said and done India I am afraid for decades to come we will unfortunately now be ruled through dirty coalition politics and where sadly the interest of the party will overshadow the interest of the country. And that indeed will be a real tragedy," concluded Unni.

As the year 1997 came to a close, and while the political bosses from various major parties in India went hunting for like minded political partners that would bolster their chances of forming a coalition government at the centre, in Pakistan the Nawaz Sharif government to strengthen its own stranglehold in the National Assembly ushered in a new pliable President. On 2nd December,1997 in the wake of the complicated battle between the judiciary and the Prime Minister, President Faroukh Leghari had put in his papers, and on 16th December, when the ruling Pakistan Muslim League nominated Senator Rafiq Ahmed Tarar, a retired Chief Justice to that exalted chair which was now though only ceremonial in nature, Arif Rehman very candidly commented to his wife Ruksana that it was rather unfortunate that the man who is known to be an anti-Ahmedia and who is totally against giving equality to women in Pakistan is going to be the next President of this country.

"But you should not forget that Leghari the lawyer from Pirkot village in District Gujranwala is a very close friend of the Prime Minister and his family and that is what really counts today," replied Ruksana Begum sarcastically.

Meanwhile with the Justice Jain report on Rajiv Gandhi's assassination now in the open, the candid confession that was made by the former Home Minister SB Chavan to the commission that the only reason for the erstwhile Narasimha Rao Congress government to block Justice Jain from going beyond 1987 in exploring the sequence of events up to Rajiv Gandhi's assassination was only to save the good name of the Gandhi family, it only added to more factionalism within the Congress party. And the revelation by the same senior Congress leader later when he was questioned in parliament about it, and he said that it was merely for protecting the interests of a certain family, this clearly indicated that the Congress had something to hide.

"'And mind you, this very statement of Chavan has now put the party in real shit. All this while, the Congresswallas who were braying for the Jain Commission report to be tabled on the floor of the house are now frantically trying to avert a debate on the subject in the parliament. The leakage of the report earlier that the DMK were very much to be blamed for being in league with the LTTE and which had led the Congress to pull the rug from under Gujral's feet,because Gujral had stood his ground has now become a big embarrassment for them," said Unni as he lit his new Dunhill pipe that Peevee had presented him with on his return from London.

"Yes and the same report which till yesterday was being flaunted as the Bible and the Gita by the Soniaites in the party to show their loyalty to the widow and specially to those who had raised the issue that all DMK ministers must resign are now caught in a catch 22 situation of their own. Because now there was clear evidence in that voluminous 5,280 page report to establish the fact that successive Congress governments right from Indira Gandhi's time were aiding and abetting the LTTE," said Monty who kind courtesy Unni had gone through each and every page of those 17 volumes patiently

"And mind you with the midterm elections coming up soon, this very report I am afraid will now spell the nemesis for the Congress too," added

Unni, who with Monty's family and some old friends from the media was celebrating his 75th[d] birthday at his own bachelor's pad at Gulmohur Park in South Delhi,

On the 1st of January, 1998, after Rafiq Tarar the dear friend of the Prime Minister and his family was sworn in as the new President of Pakistan, in India with the Congress Party hopelessly losing ground under Sitaram Kesri's inept leadership, and the Bofors gun still spewing fire, the pro Soniaites in the grand old party started seriously lobbying for the lady from Italy to take over the mantle from the old drummer boy of Danapur, Patna.

"Well as I said earlier, Italian or Indian, it is the Gandhi name that counts when it comes to wooing the illiterate masses in this country to cast their precious votes, and it is not at all surprising that among all the senior stalwarts who are presently in that party, nobody has till today raised a finger against her. And it is simply because all these men in the party after Indira Gandhi took over the reins in 1966 have all become totally impotent. There is no spunk left in any of them anymore it seems. Most of them have become glorified 'chamchas'(slaves) and for all of them, their own very survival is now directly related to their obeisance that they are willing to pay to the lady at 10, Janpath,'"said Unni on that last day of 1997, when he as a guest of Monty at the Delhi Gymkhana New Year's Eve Ball ordered for another large Patiala peg of his favourite Old Monk rum with water, and then for the first time in his life at Reeta's insistence got on to the crowded dance floor to usher in the New Year.

"But Uncle, how can somebody whose husband died six years ago can still retain the same government house as a widow. After all she only joined the Congress party only recently and that to as a primary member," said Peevee.

"Well in this game of dirty politics anything and everything is possible my friend and a sinking Congress in order not to lose any more of its fast evaporating credibility has no other option today, but to cling on to her saree, I guess. And mind you it had taken the lady nearly sixteen years after her marriage to finally decide and become an Indian citizen and that was way back in 1983. And it was primarily because that was the time when her mother-in-law wanted Rajiv to join active politics, and though Sonia was personally against the idea in the beginning, but she had to give in because she knew that he was the heir apparent. But it then took the Congress another six years after Rajiv's tragic death to convince her that she and only she as the ex Gandhi Bahu and widow could save the grand old party from further ruin, and now it is only a question of time before she is hailed as the savior and anointed as the next President of the Congress (I)," added Unni.

"Well Uncle, If the Mauryas, the Moghuls, the Khiljis, the House of Windsor and others could rule India dynastically for so many years, why not the Gandhi's. And so what if she is an Italian by birth, she is now an Indian citizen and that too with a surname that of the father of the nation. And if women like Anne Besant and Nellie Sengupta both of whom were also of foreign origin could become President of the Congress party, why not her," said Peevee who was also now an ardent Sonia Gandhi fan.

Sonia, the girl from the small town of Orbassano near Turin in Italy was born on 9th December, 1946 to Stefano and Paulo Manio. Coming from a conservative middle class Roman Catholic family, she had married Rajiv much against her father's wishes. But now with the pro Sonaites in the Congress begging her to lead them, and in view of the midterm elections that was scheduled to be held in March, the 51 year old lady had no other choice it seems. Nevertheless she took up the challenge boldly and whole heartedly. And with Sonia Gandhi's decision to lead the Congress party at the hustings, the BJP and its allies were now gearing up to once again rake up the Bofors and other issues relating to the corruption that the Congress party had been desperately trying to sweep under the carpet ever since Indira, Rajiv and Narasimha Rao were at the helm of affairs. While the Gandhi family in India came in for some bitter criticism by the opposition for their close links with the absconding Qattrocchis, and the millions that the Italian husband and wife team had siphoned off from the Bofors deal, in Pakistan the Bhuttos were also now facing real shit from their opponents

On the 9th of January 1998, when the New York Times reported that the Bhutto-Zardari duo and their associates had generated more than 1.5 billion US Dollars in illicit profits through kickbacks in every sphere of government activity that included rice deals, selling of government land, purchase of military aircrafts from Dassault Aviation, and even from various government welfare schemes, Ruksana Begum and her husband Arif Rehman were shocked beyond belief. That evening they were attending a dinner in Peshawar in honour of some visiting Americans and Pakistanis settled in America. All of them had come with their wives from the USA and were expected to donate a fairly large sum of money for setting up a school for young male orphans who had lost their fathers while fighting the Russians in Afghanistan.

'I wonder what the world will think of us and of these 'Firangis' in particular who have come to donate money for a good cause. After all 1.5

billion US dollars for a poor country like ours is a helleva lot of money, and I think such people should be simply lined up and shot in public," said an agitated Ruksana.

"Undoubtedly so, but unfortunately in Pakistan corruption at such high levels only breeds more corruption at every level, and knowing how justice prevails in this country for such like VIP's, nothing ever will happen to them I can assure you. After all the laws are only for the poor common man on the street and not for them," added Arif Rehman sarcastically as he took a whiff of the delicious mutton biryani that was being cooked in earthen pots over a charcoal fire.

Chapter-5

All the President's Women

That month of January 1998 also had the President of the world's only super power ducking for cover. Bill Clinton, the President of the United States of America had been accused of all things of sexual misdemeanor while in office both as Governor of Arkansas and as the President of the country.

The first salvo was fired by Paula Jones on 17th January, when she accused him of sexual harassment during his Governorship of the state. But the second one on 26th January was even more damaging, when he on live television denied having any sexual relationship with the former White House intern Monica Levinsky. And when this was promptly followed up on the very next day by the American First Lady, Hillary Rodham Clinton who appeared on the 'Today Show' and she said that the attacks on her husband was part of a vast right wing conspiracy, Shiraz on hearing that comment coming from the American First Lady said to Saira rather confidentially.

"You know I have a hunch that Mr Clinton is not telling the truth and with his wife now also trying to shield him, it will only complicate matters more for the first couple, unless of course Clinton is proved right. But if he is hiding the truth, and later confesses that he did have a sexual relationship with Monica, then he will only be asking for serious trouble. With the kind of promiscuity and free sex prevalent in America and in the west, it is nothing very unusual for a person to sometimes have a casual fling without being emotionally involved with some female partner. But if the truth does surface later and it is proved that the President did have sexual relations with these two ladies and which was more than just pecking them with a kiss on their cheeks, then believe you me this will snowball into a bigger scandal than even the Watergate one that surfaced during Nixon's presidency. Having a good time discreetly with a woman and confessing when cornered is one thing, but to tell a blatant lie to the people and that to as the President of the most powerful country in the world is simply unbecoming of the man. And I hope he is telling the truth," said Shiraz

'But who are these girls anyway?"Are they models, film stars or high society call girls. Because for all I know even the two Kennedy brothers John and Bob though they were also married, they too it is alleged while in office had an affair with a sexy and famous Bollywood star and God bless their souls," said Saira.

"Maybe you are right, but in this case the two ladies are ordinary American citizens and having seen their photographs in the Time magazine, I think they are fairly good looking too. As far as Paula is concerned she was born on 17th September, 1966 in Lonoke, Arkansas. According to her story, she on 8th May, 1991 was escorted to a room in a hotel in Little Rock, Arkansas where Governor Bill Clinton was staying and where the Governor had allegedly propositioned her to have sex with him. But whether the act was actually performed or not is a matter of pure conjecture. However, the affair only came to light three years later in 1994, when a journalist David Brock broke the story in the American Spectator magazine. And it was only on 6th May, that very year and with a two day dead line to beat and failing which the 3 year statute of limitations would have been put into effect; Paula filed a sexual harassment suit against Clinton. And now with this latest Monica Lewinsky scandal surfacing, Paula has taken her case to the Supreme Court and she has declared that Clinton had Trooper Danny Ferguson escort her to Clinton's hotel room where Clinton made sexual advances that she rejected. But eventually and as per her statement, when Clinton dropped his trousers and his underwear and exposed his long john to Jones, she simply told the Governor that she had to leave. But how much of that story is really true, it is difficult to tell because there were no eye witnesses to this so called sexual drama,'"said Shiraz as he showed Saira the photographs of both the girls who were making headlines both in the press and in the visual media.

"And what did this Lewinsky girl have to say regarding her affair with the most powerful man in the world?" asked Saira as she poured her husband the usual one large peg of Black Label whisky before serving dinner.

"Well I guess the American President is also a human being and maybe he also has a glad eye for good looking females. It is after all a human trait or else why should Playboy Clubs, strip joints, dance bars and legalized brothels be so very popular all over the world. And especially if you are happen to be the one in power who calls all the shots then it becomes all the more convenient to make such like propositions. And mind you this is in every aspect of human life and profession, and one may call it sexual exploitation or seduction, but the fact is that it is normally a give and take understanding between the two parties. Therefore you take a chance on the quiet, and if it works out then it's all hunky-dory. But if it backfires, then it's just bad luck and one has to simply forget about it, provided ofcourse the girl or the lady concerned does not blow her damn trumpet later. However, this sort of game has to be played very discreetly and very deftly and without the family and the staff coming to know about it. But then some young women and even men try to boast about all their sexual exploits, and that is where I am afraid the trouble starts. I am afraid Monica unfortunately could not keep her affair with the married President a secret and especially if the married man happened to be the President of the United States of America," said Shiraz while Saira added the required amount of soda and ice to her husband's drink.

"But Abbu, who is this girl Monica anyway and how did she get entry into the White House and of all places into the Oval Room. Because the surname Lewinsky sounds very much Russian and I hope she was not planted there by Boris Yeltsin," said an excited Sherry in all seriousness as she and her brother Tojo joined their parents for dinner.

"Well the young 24 year old Monica was born in San Francisco and she does have Russian—Jewish blood no doubt, but Yeltsin has no part to play in this affair I am sure. That Cold War has fortunately ended, but I am afraid this hot war between the President and those who are gunning for him to take his pants off is becoming a little disgusting though. Incidentally, Monica's father is a doctor and the mother an author and Monica not only holds a Bachelor's degree in Psychology from an American college, but she also has a Master's degree in Social Psychology from the prestigious London School of Economics, so I am told,' said Shiraz.

"No wonder then that Miss Lewinsky with her vast knowledge in psychology and with her sexy looks and charms must have really put all of it to good use while working inside the White House," said Saira.

"But whatever it is, if young Monica, first as an unpaid intern and later as a paid intern during the period July 1995 and March 1997 while serving in the White House and later in the Pentagon could have an affair with no less a person than the President of the United States of America who is old enough to be her father, then the best thing for her and for her own future was to keep it under wraps and there was no need for her to blab about it to her co-worker Linda Tripp, who very conveniently spilled the beans," said Shiraz.

"What a spoil sport, but where was the need for Linda to tell the whole damn world about it. Linda I believe had also secretly recorded the telephone conversations between the two love birds and had also convinced Monica to save all the gifts that Clinton had showered on her." And not only that, Linda also advised Miss Lewinsky to keep one of her favourite dresses that was blue in colour safely in her cupboard and not to have it dry cleaned because that blue dress had a lot of tell tale marks on it too,' said Saira.

"Maybe Linda Tripp thought that she could trap Monica into submission and make a bit of money on it on the side by revealing the affair with solid proofs to some literary agent who would be only too willing to buy such a sensational story," said Sherry.

"Yes you could be right, and with a catchy title like 'All The President's Women', I bet it would have become an instant worldwide best seller," said Shiraz jokingly as he gave Sherry the copy of the Time magazine that had Monica's photo inside it. And when Shiraz further added that if by chance the American President is caught lying to his own people, then for Mr Clinton it could well be from the White House to the Dog House," his wife Saira didn't find it at all funny.

On that 26th of January, 1998 when Clinton in a nationalized White House news conference claimed categorically that he did not have any sexual relations with that woman, Miss Lewinsky, Supriya who was waiting to catch a flight to Moscow to take up her new assignment as India's Ambassador to Russia took that statement with a pinch of salt. It did not really matter to her if the President of America was having an affair with X,Y or Z, that was his damn business, but what was bothering her was the big brother bullying attitude of the American government towards the poor third world countries. That day also happened to be Shupriya's forty eighth birthday and she was delighted because the first one to wish her early that morning was none other than her son Peevee.

Chapter-6

Back To Moskova

It was late in the evening on Shupriya's 48th birthday, when the Cuban Airlines flight from Havana landed at Moscow's Shremetyevo International Airport. And as the Black Mercedes with the diplomatic number plate and the Indian tricolour proudly flying made its way through the snow covered streets of the Russian capital, it reminded Shupriya of the days when she first arrived in that historic city as a young Third Secretary.

"You know I never ever dreamt that I would come back here as India's Ambassador,' said Shupriya to the Minister and the Second Secretary who had come to receive her at the airport.

"I think Madam Ambassador with your excellent track record and having done exceptionally good work in Castro's Cuba, you fully deserved it. But Madam let me also tell you that Moscow is no longer the place it was 20 years ago. It is now a haven for the Russian mafia, drug dealers, rapists, smugglers, arms dealers, and the so called business oligarchs who are nothing but Yeltsin's money sharks, and nobody is safe anymore. Gone are the days when a man or a woman could freely walk the streets of Moscow in the middle of the night, or safely take a cab home. But today, male or female, the young and the old, everyone is afraid to walk on a lonely street even during broad daylight for fear of being mugged," said the Minister.

"That is indeed a real pity, but I hope under Boris Yeltsin's second term in office things will turn out to be better in future,"'said Shupriya.

"But the inside story is that the man is very sick and the Russian economy too is in doldrums, and only a miracle can save the Russian rouble from going further down the abyss," said the Minister, who was the number two man in the Indian Embassy.

As Shupriya entered the Ambassador's residence on Ulitsa Obukha, which was part of the embassy premises and where stalwarts like, DP Dhar, T N Kaul and others as heads of mission had stayed earlier with their families, she wondered whether such a big house for her as a single woman was at all necessary.

Next morning, when she with a flourish signed the visitor's book as Yeshwant Kaur Bajwa and took charge of the challenging assignment, she knew that it would not be easy at all. With the erstwhile Soviet Union having disintegrated, Russia heavily in debt, the instability in Chechnya that could well lead to another bloody second round, and with Boris Yeltsin's regular blackouts and failing health, it was more than just a routine diplomatic posting for the good looking Indian lady ambassador. During the first week of February 1998, Shupriya having presented her credentials to the Russian government was pleasantly surprised to receive a bouquet of flowers and a greeting card congratulating her on her well deserved appointment. The sender was none other than her own first cousin Lalima. She having written the biography of both Che Guevera and Fidel Castro was now a well known literary figure in Russia. Finding her telephone number and address on the card, Shupriya immediately rang her up and said.

"Why don't you drop in for some Indian food this evening and we could have a quiet chat on how things are in this country?" Knowing fully well that Lalima had very good contacts with people who mattered in Yeltsin's government, she wanted to find out indirectly from her as to how the common people of Russia were reacting to the deplorable economic and the worsening law and order situation in the country.

"Though I like many others would hate to go back to the old communist rule, but the fact is that the majority are today suffering from hunger and cold in a manner that they had never ever suffered before, and not even during Stalin's dictatorial regime. And it is all because of the wrong economic policies that the erstwhile Communist Party of the Soviet Union followed during their nearly eight decades of rule in this country," said Lalima who surprised Shupriya by turning up in a saree and by speaking to her in fairly good Hindi.

"My God you look every inch an Indian in that saree, but who ever taught you how to wear it, and where did you learn your Hindi?" said Shupriya with a look of admiration on her face as they shook hands and hugged each other.

"Well I have been an active member of the erstwhile Indo-Soviet Friendship Society for many many years now, and don't forget that my late father Arup Ghosh hailed from your country too," said Lalima very proudly.

"Yes of course and you must therefore also visit India sometime and see our beautiful land," suggested Shupriya.

The friendly tete-a-tete that evening proved very useful to Shupriya. She not only learnt a few secrets about the men who were close to the Russian President, but also of the new Czars of Russia, commonly known as the oligarchs.

"But how could these people like Boris Berezovsky, Mikhail Fridman, Viktor Vekeselberg, Alexander Smolensky; Vahid Alakbarov, Vladimir Bogdanov and Vladimir Potanin make such large fortunes, and that too in such a short time and while Russia is still bleeding economically," asked Shupriya as she served some more of that tasty and pungent mustard fish curry that she had cooked in typical Bengali style for her honoured guest.

"Well let me also tell you the truth, because had it not been for this band of noveau rich tycoons and bandits, Yeltsin probably would have lost the 1996 elections. To begin with, most of them were once part of Yeltsin's government or else they were well connected with those in Yeltsin's administration, and it was their strong financial support that got Yeltsin through for a second term and which led to the defeat of the Communist candidate Gennady Zyuganov in the final runoff,'"said Lalima.

"So these are the guys who are the new capitalists of Russia and I wonder what Lenin would have thought about them had he been alive today," said Shupriya.

"Yes if Lenin was alive he would have probably had all of them shot by now," said Lalima who simply hated this handful of oligarchs who have been literary squeezing the country dry.

"And let me also tell you that this man Berezovsky who was a mathematician to begin with had also served in Yeltsin's government. He was close to Yeltsin and his family and therefore knew how to multiply and manipulate his wealth in double quick time. He initially in the early 1990's made his fortune importing Mercedes cars into Russia, and then got into the automobile business, oil and the television channel network, and thereafter there was no looking back for him. The success story for all the others is no different either, and what is still worse is that they are getting richer and richer, while the poor are getting poorer and poorer day by day.In fact Smolensky who founded the largest private 'Bank Stolichny' is in great trouble it seems because the rumours are that the bank may collapse any day. Likewise Fridman who is the youngest of the lot and just 34 years old is already a multi-multi millionaire. Vahid Alakbarov, an Azerbaijani from Baku is now president of LUKoil and Viktor Vekselberg is the chairman of Tyumen Oil, one of Russia's largest oil and gas companies, and so is Bogdanov who is the president of Surgutneftgas, another large oil and gas company. Potanin who is fluent both in English and French and who is heading the United Export Import Bank and who had worked earlier with the Ministry of Foreign Trade of the Soviet Union and was later the First Deputy Prime Minister of the Russian Federation has used his knowledge and contacts very cleverly, and he is also a big tycoon now,' added Lalima a little sarcastically.

"Well I guess corruption is prevalent in every country, and do pardon my saying so, but the politicians in India and some of their cronies in the big business houses and the bureaucrats working and dealing with them are no different either. Yes there are a few in each of these categories who are honest, but honesty I am afraid does not pay anymore," added Shupriya while serving the rasgullas with vanilla ice cream for dessert.

"But how come, being a Punjabi Sikh and a Sardarni at that you love all kinds of Bengali food and sweets?' asked Lalima as she helped herself to another large rasgulla.

"Well let me tell you that there are a lot of Sikhs who have permanently made Calcutta their home and my grandmother was from that city and she loved Bengali food and sweets. Incidentally she was also a great cook and I learnt a few Bengali dishes from her,' said Shupriya very confidently. She was expecting that question and had the answer ready for it. But fearing that there may be more questions on Bengali cuisine, Shupriya immediately changed the subject to the disarmament crisis in Iraq where the United States Senate having passed resolution 71 had urged President Clinton to take all necessary and appropriate actions against Saddam Hussein because of his refusal to end his weapons of mass destruction programs

"But do you think that by threatening Saddam, the dictator will simply give in to the US Senate's demand. Saddam is no fool and he is a hard nut to crack too. Iraq is an oil rich country and that black gold I am told has made him and all his family members' multi-millionaires, if not billionaires, and I am sure Saddam knows what he is up to. After his defeat in the Gulf War in 1999, he with his so called arsenal of WMD's weapons of mass destruction and with the Americans threatening to oust him, he is only trying to protect himself and his regime with better defensive and offensive capabilities," said Shupriya.

"Yes I too feel that the Americans just for the sake of oil are messing up the issue in Iraq. After all it was the Americans who initially made Saddam Hussein what he is today, but America's real enemy if you ask me is not Saddam, but that tall young handsome bearded Arab who with his Al Qaida followers and his many millions of dollars has now found a safe haven in Afghanistan. But that aside and just for my information, tell me who is the richest Indian today, because somebody told me the other day that it is not Dhirubhai Ambani any more. And is it true?"' asked Lalima somewhat abruptly.

"Well if we discount some of the top politicians who avoid paying taxes or refuse to disclose their ill gotten wealth, the richest Indian today is I think Laxmi Narayan Mittal and he is followed by Dhirubhai Ambani and a few others. The very name Laxmi means wealth and he has so much of it that it will probably take weeks and months for the two of us to count them," said Shupriya jestingly

"But what is his profession and how did he manage to accumulate so much of wealth and if I am not wrong I think you did mention that he is not even fifty years old," said Lalima with a look of total surprise on her face.

"Well this enterprising young man was born in the small village of Sudulpur in Rajasthan on 15th June, 1950 and he like Dhirubhai has also come up the hard way. A product of St Xavier's College, Calcutta he like Dhirubhai has a sharp business brain, and today his worldwide steel business is worth billions of dollars," said Shupriya. as she fixed a small Drambuie for Lalima. And as far as the bearded Osama was concerned, Lalima was absolutely right because a fortnight later on 23rd February, 1998, Osama bin Laden and his right hand man Ayman al-Zawahiri and other fanatical Islamic religious leaders co-signed and issued a 'fatwa'. It was a hard hitting religious edict under the banner 'World Islamic Front for Jihad against the Jews and their Crusaders.' The two line edict was like an ultimatum to the Americans and it said that the ruling to kill the Americans and their allies, both civilian and military is an individual duty for every Muslim and who should do it in any country in which it was possible. And it has to be done in order to liberate the Al-Aqsa Mosque in Jerusalem and the Holy Mosque in Mecca from their grip, and also to ensure that all their armies move out of all the lands of Islam, defeated and unable to threaten any Muslim. This is in accordance with the words of Almighty Allah.And though neither Bin Laden nor Al-Zawahiri possess the traditional Islamic scholarly qualifications to issue any kind of 'fatwa', but that hardly mattered. They were now in full control of the Al-Qaida and were bent upon inflicting casualties on Americans and their allies wherever they may be," added Lalima as she took leave of Shupriya.

CHAPTER-7

Back to Bofors

When Shiraz in Paris heard about that strongly worded 'fatwa', he was convinced that it was not just an empty threat. With Bin Laden's growing popularity among the radical Sunni Muslims all over the world, this was now a reality and one that could not be ignored. Enamoured by the striking personality of Osama and his teachings, a large number of young men from Pakistan and the Muslim world had joined the Al-Qaida and such like radical militant groups and more were being regularly churned out from the many madrassas (seminaries) that now dotted the provinces of the North West Frontier and Baluchistan in Pakistan. And a few days later, there was still more bad news for Pakistan from New York. Squadron Leader Farooq Ahmed Khan of the Pakistan Air Force who was arrested in Manhattan on 9th April last year while trying to dispose of 2 kilograms of heroin that he had brought along with him when he came to pick up the arms released by the US was now sentenced to a year's imprisonment and it was a big blot on the good name of the PAF. It was a sting operation by the FBI that had caught him red handed.

"I think the Pakistani Airforce pilot was damn lucky to get only a year, but I am sure this was not the first time that the Pakistani air force pilots in order to make a fast buck have indulged in this kind of shameful activity. This has not only given the country a bad name, but I am afraid the Pakistanis living in the US, and those travelling to that country will now be subjected to more severe and thorough searches, screening and questioning," said Shiraz as Saira got ready to accompany her husband to the cocktail party that was being hosted by the Russian Ambassador in his honour. Shiraz was now Pakistan's Ambassador designate to Russia and was required to take up his new assignment on the 1st of April, 1998.

Meanwhile in India, with the midterm elections round the corner and Narasimha Rao not being given a ticket by the party to contest, the Congress bigwigs were now banking heavily on the Gandhi Bahu. Sonia Gandhi despite her language handicap looked like a fighter who was no less than her late mother-in-law, Indira Gandhi. With attack being the best form of defense, she in her blistering election campaign challenged the opposition to come out with the names of the recipients of the Bofors payoffs.And seeing the audacity of the Gandhi Bahu, Monty called on his old friend Unni at the Press Club to find out what could be the reasons for Mrs Sonia Gandhi's sudden outburst to challenge the opposition on the smoking gun that was still belching fire.

"Though there was no doubt that the old and close family friend of her's and Rajiv's, Octtavio Quattrochi through his AE Services Ltd had got his cut in US dollars on that deal, which was equivalent to a whopping Rupees fifty crores and which was amply proved by the Swiss Bank account documents that were received by the Gujral government, but the reasons for Sonia Gandhi to take on the opposition head on could be attributable to the following factors. Firstly, the pliable former CBI Director R.C. Sharma who had recently retired on 1st January in a statement to the press after Sonia had fired the first salvo very conveniently in Mrs Gandhi's favour had stated that Quattrocchi had no role to play at all in the Bofors deal. And when he further added that the mere payment of money by Bofors into Quattrocchi's account could not be connected to the Bofors contract, it only gave the Gandhi Bahu more handle to beat the opposition with. Sharma it seems was banking that nobody would have access to the Special Investigating Team report on Bofors which was filed by his predecessor Joginder Singh in May 1997, and which had sought the governments sanction for charge-sheeting those who were responsible for the signing of the contract. The very fact that the Gujral government had been sitting on it for more than eight months and Mr Gujral now saying that he cannot disclose the names of the recipients because such a disclosure would prejudice further information from the Swiss about the remaining accounts is only hogwash. And by Mr Gujral reiterating that the Swiss authorities have made this information available to the CBI only for the prosecution of the recipients and that they have prohibited the CBI from disclosing this information in any other form is indicative enough of Mrs Sonia Gandhi's influence on the man, the caretaker Prime Minister of India who was earlier in the Congress. And with the elections due in a few days time, Mr Gujral was now probably keeping all his options open too. Frankly speaking my personal opinion is that all this is being done by him only to gain time and with the fervent hope that the Congress will be voted back to power, but which I feel is very doubtful. Though the two main parties, the Congress and the BJP are fully in the fray, but in this age of coalition politics, I think the BJP and its allies today have the advantage. However, all said and done like all other corruption issues in this country where politicians are involved, this too will die its own silent death, and may the Bofors gun rest in peace, Amen,"said Unni with a sarcastic smile on his face, as he called for another round of drinks.

"But how could Sharma the DG CBI be so damn naïve, when the Swiss accounts amply prove that Bofors paid AE Services which belonged to Quattrocchi 50,463,966'00 Swedish Kroners, an equivalent of 7,343,941.98 US Dollars on 3rd September, 1986. And that to into the newly opened account number 18051-033 in the Nordfinanz Bank in Zurich. And thirteen days later, the AE Services conveniently transferred the bulk of it amounting to 7,123,900 US Dollars from that account to an account held at the Union Bank of Switzerland in Geneva in the name of Colbar Investments Ltd, which is a Panama based company and which was being controlled by the Italian and his wife, Maria. It is all there in black and white, and yet the Gujral government felt that the time was not yet ripe to charge sheet the Quattrocchis who are not even Indians. That is indeed very surprising and it maybe because they were Italians and were very close to the Gandhi family. Therefore all said and done the stinking Bofors issue I am afraid will never ever see the light of day,"' said Monty.

"My dear friend it is all politics and I won't be surprised if tomorrow this coalition government with its narrow majority in parliament in order to remain in power also conveniently sleeps over the issue, now that the elections are over. And let me reveal to you something more. According to one insider, AE Services was itself a subsidiary of the company that called itself Ciaou Anstalt Vaduz and CAV in short. Even according to Myles Stott; who worked for Quattrocchi, he too in his affidavit has clearly stated that the CAV also worked on behalf of Sofna, which was also a strong contender for the howitzer contract and its owners were a mysterious Mr SI Mubarak and his wife Rita. But who they really are nobody knows still, and yet it was they and Major RA Bob Wilson, as CAV's authorized representative who instructed Myles Stott on how to operate AE Services bank accounts. So putting both these factors in mind, it was always a win—win situation for the Italian all the time. So whosoever finally got the lucrative billion dollar contract, whether it was Bofors or Sofna, the AE Services or the CAV as intermediaries would emerge as the final winners as far as the commissions were concerned? And the very fact that the shrewd Italian having had access to that whopping commission for a whole decade and more and he never withdrew anything from it, but simply kept transferring it from one account to another and from one country to another clearly indicates that he was holding these accounts on behalf of someone else. But who that somebody else is we still do not know But my hunch is that it was probably for the late Rajiv Gandhi. And it may not personally be for him or his family, but it could be for the Congress party. Maybe Sonia knows the real truth, and now that she is in the party and on the big high chair, she cannot possibly let her family and the party down. Can she? And with Quattrocchi still sitting pretty in Malaysia under a red alert given by the Interpol, that man too it seems is also now desperate to wangle out of the situation. According to his lawyer Dinesh Mathur, he is now contemplating to move a petition before the Delhi High Court seeking a revocation of the non bailable warrant that was issued against him. And if you think that the gentleman will ever respond positively to a summons from any Indian court, you can simply forget about it. His guilty conscience will never allow him to set foot in India again. And he won't be so damn stupid also to put that damn noose around his own neck and that of those who shared that booty or wanted to share that booty with him. And knowing fully well how slowly the judicial system works in this country, it will carry on and on and on till the cows come home," said Unni with the usual sly and mischievous smile on his face.

"No wonder the information that was gathered by the CBI to implicate Quattrocchi and others that formed part of the CBI's 30 page affidavit has been put firmly in the cold storage because according to the government one of the conditions imposed by the Swiss government was that the papers would be used only as evidence during prosecution and not for any other political purposes. And therefore all these so called bank related documents have been conveniently kept away even from the Indian Parliament.

"But why has the Congress discarded Narasimha Rao who is now complaining that his plight is like that of Draupadi's since everyone watched her being disrobed, but no one helped," said Monty.'

"Well with all the corruption in the government that surfaced during his tenure as the Prime Minister, it would be like committing harikiri for the Congress Party if they gave him a ticket. And in any case the polygot Telegu Brahmin from Karimnagar, Andhra Pradesh who can speak 13 languages fluently has simply lost his voice in the party. Now nearing 80, he I think is a spent force in politics," added Unni

"But whatever it is, credit must be given to him for making a paradigm shift from the socialist based Nehruvian style of economy to a market driven one. In fact it was his and Manmohan Singh's bold free market reforms that pumped in new life in a nearly bankrupt nation," added Monty as he took a friendly bet that neither the Congress nor the BJP would get more than 150 seats, and ultimately it will once again be a hung parliament.

"Done, but this time the BJP will get more than 200, and it's my Old Monk to your Royal Salute at odds of 10 to1,'said Unni as they called it a day.

When the final election results were declared, Unni had won the bet no doubt, but he did not expect the BJP to get 250 seats, while the Congress got only 140 and for the Janata Dal it was a complete washout

"Well let us hope now that Mr Atal Bihari Vajpayee has got a second chance, he will now at least give the country a corruption free government and step on the gas towards more economic and liberal reforms. Having served 41 years of his life as an active parliamentarian and as diehard bachelor for all his 74 years, what he needs to have in his new cabinet is a team of dedicated ministers whom he can implicitly trust upon and they should not play the Hindu and the Hinduvta card anymore. Moreover, he should also not give too much leeway to his adopted daughter Namita and her husband Ranjan Bhattacharya. Firstly they are nobody in the party and secondly because such people at times who take on these extra constitutional authority without responsibility and accountability more often than not only become an embarrassment to the man sitting in that exalted chair, but also to the party,'"said Unni.

"But, I thought you just said that he is diehard bachelor,"

"Yes he is still very much a bachelor, but he also has two adopted daughters and there is nothing wrong with that. Though biologically Namita and Nandita are the daughters of Mr and Mrs BM Kaul who are old friends of Ataljee, but legally I have been told they are now Mr Vajpayee's daughters. And while Nandita whose pet name is Nanni is a doctor, Nandita who is also known as Gunu and who is married to Ranjan Bhattacharya is I believe Atalji's social secretary. And what is still more interesting is that both the young ladies who were born in the Kaul family have their roots in Kashmir and it was from Kashmir that both Atalji and Ranjan Bhattacharya, his adopted Bengali son-in-law who hails from Patna also kick started their respective careers. In 1953, the 29 year old Atal had accompanied Shyama Prasad Mukerjee, the leader of the then Jan Sangh to Kashmir and he was at his mentor's bedside when he went on a fast into death while protesting against the identity card requirement for Indians entering Kashmir that Sheikh Abdullah had imposed upon. And a few decades later Ranjan Bhattacharya who started his life in the hotel industry showed his own mettle, when he at a very young age became the youngest General Manager of the five star Palace Hotel in Srinagar. And he did create a stir when Vajpayee during his short stint of 13 days in office appointed him as Officer on Special Duty in the PMO's secretariat. But I hope now better sense will prevail and Atalji the new Prime Minister designate will keep the foster son-in-law and his adopted daughter Namita who is also a school teacher by profession away from the dirty world of politics," added Unni as Peevee ordered another large pink gin for the veteran informative journalist.

As was expected soon after Mr Vajpayee took his oath of office on 19th March, 1998, the importance of the adopted foster son-in-law and his wife grew in leaps and bounds, as party bigwigs of all shades and colours, businessmen, bureaucrats and others vied for the couple's attention. Seeing the sudden growing clout of Ranjan and his wife Namita, Monty whose export of carpets from Kashmir was the mainstay of his business called on his friend Unni for his expert advice.

"My dear Monty, sycophancy and black money in each and every profession in this country has indeed taken very deep roots, but it is also a double edged weapon. I know that there is nothing better and faster than to climb the ladder of success or have a favour done by approaching the two people who are nearest to the man who is now the Prime Minister of India, but you are too small a fry and I would not like you to venture into it. It is no doubt true that Ranjan in the early eighties as the General Manager of the Palace Hotel in Srinagar for promoting his hotel's business had made a lot of good and influential friends and contacts in the valley, but that was nearly two decades ago and it was part of his job. But today thanks to Pakistan's ISI, it is completely a different and changed situation as far as the Kashmir valley is concerned. The local artisans and carpet weavers are all shit scared of the ISI sponsored militants who in the garb of fighting for Azad Kashmir keep threatening them to stop doing business with India. There is no doubt that Ranjan is also the new Prime Minister's eyes and ears and he is very close to the man, but it is best if he is left alone. If you remember during the long Congress rule it was men like M O Mathai, Yashpal Kapoor, RK Dhawan and Vincent George who rose from the ranks of being mere typists and clerks to positions of awesome power. All of them successfully climbed up the ladder of success both politically and monetarily not simply because they were the blue eyed hard working trusted boys of the men and women of the Nehru-Gandhi family who ruled India, but they also knew and probably know too much. And today the very fact that at 10 Janpath it is still Vincent George the ever faithful who decides on who can meet Sonia Gandhi and who cannot is proof enough that those who wish to wield power require somebody like him and on whom they can explicitly place their trust and have them at the beck and call all the twenty-four hours of the day. And therefore to my mind there is nothing wrong if Ranjan Bhattacharya at 7, Race Course Road, the residence of the Indian Prime Minister decides on who can or cannot meet his father-in-law. After all the young man is now very much a member of the Prime Minister's family and he and his wife Namita have to also look after the Prime Minister's health. Atalji is not young and is suffering I believe with pain in his knee joints, but all the same he still retains his subtle sense of humour all the time," said Unni.

In India as a cohesive bloc of political parties under Vajpayee's leadership joined hands to form the NDA, the National Democratic Alliance and proved its 286 vote majority in a narrow vote of confidence, a jubilant Monty with his wife Reeta and son Peevee celebrated the occasion by seeing the 11 Oscar winning film 'Titanic' on the big screen at the Regal cinema and followed it by a sumptuous dinner at the Zodiac Grill, a restaurant par excellence at the famous Taj Mahal Hotel in Mumbai.

"I must say that the film is a real masterpiece and the director James Cameron is a real genius and I wonder why Bollywood cannot make such kind of movies," said Monty as Peevee placed the order for the drinks and the starters.

"No doubt it is a great film, but the credit should also go to Kate Winslett and the young handsome Leonard DiCaprio who as Jack Dawson simply stole the thunder. They were superb as lovers, but the ending was rather sad and I wish both had lived through that terrible disaster," said Reeta.

"Incidentally Mom let me tell you that he was named Leonard after the great Leonard Da Vinci and it happened on the day when his pregnant mother was standing in front of a Da Vinci painting at a museum in Italy when she felt the boy's first kick and I am not joking,"said Peevee.

"Well then I must say that it was a good million dollar kick, because the young actor today at 24 is already a superstar,'"added Monty rather humourously.

"But I am sure our Deepak Kumar too will soon get the super star status when his new film 'Jhanda Uncha Rahe Hamara,' is released. It is a story based on Subhas Bose's INA where he plays the role of an Indian soldier who becomes a deserter and joins Subhas Bose's army to fight for India's freedom. The film incidentally is scheduled for release in mid April and the chances of it making an entry into the forthcoming Moscow film festival in May is also very much on the cards," said Reeta very proudly.

CHAPTER-8

A Blast Bigger Than Bofors

It was on April Fool's Day 1998, when Shiraz with his family landed in Moscow. For him as a career diplomat this was going to be a very challenging and tough assignment. Though he had served in Moscow earlier, but that was in a completely different era and environment when the country was known as the USSR.Next day in office, when he asked for the roster and the names of the heads of missions of some of the important countries that had embassies in Moscow, he was surprised to learn that the Indian Ambassador to Russia was a lady who was single and a Sikh at that and whose name was Yeshwant.Kaur Bajwa.

"What is she like? Is she the friendly type or is she snobbish and as usual hates anything and everything that is Pakistani," asked Shiraz as the Minister gave him a small brief on the career graph of the lady

"Oh I see, she was till recently India's Ambassador in Communist Cuba and she had also served in the Indian Mission in Moscow earlier too. And it is no wonder that she holds an interpreter's degree in the Russian language," said Shiraz as he also glanced through the briefs of all those who represented the group of powerful G-8 nations.

On 6th April, 1998, six days after being in office, when Shiraz learnt that Pakistan had successfully test fired the liquid fuelled, single stage Ghauri missile that had a range of 1500 kilometers and a payload of 700 kilograms, it got him a bit worried. It was not only a deadly weapon that could easily target Delhi and other such strategic places well beyond the international border, but it could also start another arms race, which neither country could afford. The test was basically to counter India's Prithvi missile that some reports indicated were stored or deployed at or near the Indian city of Jullunder and which was close to Pakistan's border with India. But what was even more worrying for Pakistan was the emergence of the pro Hindu Bharatiya Janata Party that had in its election manifesto clearly outlined its objective of exercising the nuclear option and of inducting nuclear weapons in India's military arsenal.

Pakistan had named the Ghauri missile in honour of Shahabuddin Ghauri, a Muslim warlord from Central Asia who had defeated the Hindu warrior Prithvi Raj Chauhan many centuries ago and who had founded the Ghauri dynasty in Delhi. Pakistan now also believed that since Ghauri was far superior to the Prithvi, it was therefore good enough a deterrent to counter India with and even if India launched a surprise pre-emptive strike, Pakistan was capable of responding to it effectively.

"I think it's a criminal waste of money for poor countries like ours and India to develop weapons like long range missiles and nuclear bombs to confront each other with, when the man on the street does not even get a square meal a day, and what are both the countries trying to prove anyway?' wrote Shiraz in his little red diary before finally calling it a day.

A week later, when the Second Secretary in charge of the Indian Ambassador's secretariat informed Shupriya that as per the latest circular issued by the Russian protocol department to all the foreign missions in Moscow, a gentlemen by the name of Mr Riaz Mohammed Khan had taken over charge from 1st April as the new Ambassador of Pakistan, Shupriya simply wanted to know prior to Moscow where all had the gentleman served earlier, and whether he was a retired military man, a political appointee or another career diplomat like her'

"Well Madam, he is certainly not a General and all I know is that he has come from Paris and has been in the Pakistan Foreign Service since 1973. I have however asked Delhi to send us his career profile. And as regards the previous incumbent, he has gone home after only completing a year and a half. He was suffering from asthma I believe and he just could not stand another harsh Moscow winter," added the Second Secretary.

"Good for him and do brief me on this new man once you get the details from Delhi,' said Shupriya as she approved the list of invitees for the Ambassador's special Baisaki Day party that was scheduled to be held on the morning of 13th of April. She also reminded the Second Secretary to ensure that a 'Dholki' with the dholak was in attendance all the time.

"After all we cannot simply have a 'Baisaki' without doing the 'Bhangra and the 'Gidda' and especially if the Head of the Mission happens to be an ardent Sardarni like me. And also do not forget to mention in the card that the dress code for all except for the Russian staff and guests will be compulsorily and traditionally Punjabi and all the embassy staff and their families with their children must come in full strength for the occasion," added Shupriya with a big smile on her face.

Baisaki day on 13th of April, 1998 that was held on the Indian Embassy lawns was celebrated with great gusto as the men folk, young and old with their children did the traditional vigorous 'Bhangra' in every possible style, and the ladies of the embassy led by Shupriya also contributed heartily with their well rehearsed 'Giddha'. And as the 'Balle Balle's' resounded to the loud beat of the dholki, the more enthusiastic among the guests, which also included a few top ranking Russians also joined in the merriment, while the more enterprising amongst them kept helping themselves to the specially prepared 'Bhang' that went well with all the tandoori dishes and kebabs that were prepared for the gala occasion.

During her long service in various Indian embassies abroad, Shupriya realized that despite the many foreign postings, the staff always missed such kind of fun and homely atmosphere and she therefore had decided that irrespective of the individual's belief in his own religion, all major Indian festivals including Idd and Christmas must be celebrated by one and all. After all India was a secular country and she had to run a team and there was no better way of doing it than this.

While the merriment was still on, the Second Secretary said. 'Your Excellency, the profile of the new Pakistani Ambassador with a few photographs of the man and his family has arrived by the diplomatic mail bag from New Delhi today and you may like to go through them after the party is over. I have kept the folder in your office,"

"Does he look like a Pathan, a Punjabi Mussulman or a Baluchi?. Because the little that I know is that Sindhis generally do not have Khan as a surname," said Shupriya as she thanked all the guests and the staff for making the Baisaki celebration such a grand success.

Later in the day when Shupriya went back to her office which was inside her residence she felt rather tired and decided to call it a day. It was after many years that she had danced so much and she knew that age was also catching up on her,Next morning after her daily ritual of forty five minutes of yoga, when Shupriya read the brief on the Pakistani Ambassador to which was attached a photograph of the gentleman with his family, Shupriya's only comment to the Minister was that the man does have a very pretty good looking wife and two lovely teenage children and now that Moscow has a few golf courses he and his son won't be missing their golf either.

"And I am told that though with his moustache and beard he looks more like a Mullah, but he speaks impeccable English and Russian too. He is also an old Moscow hand and is also very fond of music and especially those of the Sufi kind," added the Minister.

"Well I am sure I will bump into him one of these days at some diplomatic party and of which there are so very many every month and therefore I will reserve my opinion and comments about him till I meet face to face with him," said Shupriya very diplomatically as she closed the folder and handed it back to the Minister.

A few days later Shupriya was delighted, when she heard from Peevee that his film 'Jhanda Uncha Rahe Hamara' (Keep The Flag Flying High) has been selected as the Indian entry at the Moscow Film Festival, and according to him the festival was scheduled to be held from 28th May to 6th June 1998. But what pleased her most was that Peevee too would be a part of the Indian film delegation. This good news was soon followed by an official letter from the concerned ministry and the MEA, the Ministry of External affairs in New Delhi, which stated that since no less a person than the Minister for Information and Broadcasting would be leading the delegation this time, therefore all arrangements for reception, accommodation and transport for all the 10 members of the film delegation must be top class and as per the laid down protocol.

"Well as far at the Minister and the rest of the delegation is concerned they can all be put up in the best five star hotel in the city, but as far as actor Deepak Kumar is concerned he will be my personal guest and will be staying with me," said Shupriya somewhat casually to her secretary as she read through the ten names that also included the Producer-Director of the film and Purnima Devi who as the heroine had made her debut appearance.

'I do beg your pardon Maam, but may I ask as to why is the young popular Bollywood actor being given this special honour and privilege. Is he personally known to you Madam or is he related to you by any chance," asked the Minister.

"'Yes you could say that he is both. And frankly speaking to me he is something much more than just special. I have known him and his entirely family right from the day he was born and his parents besides being related to me are also very close and dear friends of mine, and I think I should invite them too for the festival as my personal guests," said Shupriya.

"I think that is indeed a very good idea, because not only will you have some good company for a change, but it will also give you some much needed rest after the very long hours of work that you put in everyday Madam," said the Counsellor Political who had been assigned the task to look after the delegation and make all the necessary arrangements.

"Maybe it is because I am single and I don't have to worry about family problems, and the office work keeps me happily and fully occupied I guess," said Shupriya as she directed the First Secretary to give a complete face lift to the Embassy premises and to her residence cum office.

While the entire Indian Embassy staff in Moscow were busy making arrangements for the film delegation and for the never ending visits of MP's and MLA's and their families from India who normally throng to Moscow only during the summer season as guests of the Indian government on the pretext of carrying out some stupid study, but which actually is nothing but an excuse to officially spend public money for their foreign jaunts, far away in India the new government of Mr Vajpayee was waiting to stun the world with 'Operation Shakti,' a revered Sanskrit word that not only meant 'Strength.' but it was also the name of the Hindu Goddess of power.

On 20th March, 1998 the second day of his having taking over office Prime Minister Vajpayee had given the go ahead signal in principle. And on 8th April he had summoned Dr Abdul Kalam and Dr Chidambaram to his office and had also formally given them the final thumbs up sign.India's nuclear weapons program began soon after the 1962 Chinese debacle, when the ill equipped Indian army was badly mauled by the Chinese onslaught both in NEFA and in Ladakh. And it got a further kick, when the Chinese carried out their nuclear test at Lop Nor in 1964. Both these events underscored the dire need for India to become strong militarily and thus began India's indigenous program to develop nuclear weapons as a strong deterrent. The program was shelved after Nehru's death, but was revived by Mrs Indira Gandhi in 1968 and it culminated in India's maiden successful nuclear test at Pokhran in the Rajasthan Desert on 18th May, 1974 that was codenamed 'The Smiling Buddha.'

Initially Vajpayee who held office for only 13 days in 1996 had ordered both the military and the scientific establishment at the Bhabha Atomic Research Centre in Mumbai to proceed with the preparation for testing another nuclear device at Pokhran, but it was shelved after his government lost a no-confidence motion in Parliament, and thereafter the two successive governments of Deve Gowda and Inder Gujral decided to observe the moratorium on testing. It seems that Narasimha Rao while demitting his office had told Vajpayee in secret that India was ready to proclaim herself as a nuclear power and he had even handed over a piece of paper to him and on which was written 'Bomb is ready. You can go ahead.' In fact three years earlier in 1995, Prime Minister Narasimha Rao had decided to carry out further tests, but the American satellites picked up signs of preparation at Pokhran and with Bill Clinton exerting enormous pressure on India, the tests were indefinitely postponed. This had brought home the point to the Indian scientists that the next series of nuclear test would have to be carried out in very strict secrecy and without the American satellites getting wind of it. The preparations this time therefore were only known to a closed group of top Indian scientists, senior military officers, the Prime Minister, the Deputy Prime Minister Mr Lal Krishan Advani, the External Affairs Minister Jaswant Singh who was himself an ex army officer and Brajesh Mishra, the National Security Advisor.

The preparations were carried out in four well rehearsed stages, starting from the first detailed briefing to the final countdown. In the first stage, the two main coordinators, Dr APJ Abdul Kalam, the Scientific Advisor to the Prime Minister and Dr R Chidambaram, the Head of the Department of Atomic Energy and Chairman of the Atomic Energy Commission gave out in their briefing the method to be followed in the assembling and dispatching of the weapons to the test site at Pokhran. Simultaneously in order to convince the Americans and others that India was far from carrying out any tests, the Foreign Secretary K Raghunath and India's Defence Minister, George Fernandes kept harping to the Americans that India was still undecided on this very sensitive issue, and they therefore also categorically told them that there would be no surprise testing and that the National Security Council would be meeting soon to discuss the matter. The second stage was the transportation of the devices to the testing site. During the early hours of 1st May, 1998 at around 3 a.m, the nuclear devices were removed from their vaults at the BARC complex in Mumbai and were loaded into four big military trucks. And while India was still fast asleep, the convoy of four army trucks under the command of Colonel Umang Kapur made their way to the Santa Cruz airport where a giant Indian Air Force AN-32 transport aircraft was waiting for them. On that May Day, and before the break of dawn, the aircraft with its precious consignment took off for Jaisalmer, and having landed there, the cargo of explosives devices were once again taken in big army trucks to the testing site at Pokhran. In order to project that the Indian army was carrying out some training exercises in that area, all the civilian scientists were also made to dress up as army officers and that to with proper insignias, but with fictitious new names. Abdul Kalam became Major General Prithviraj and R Chidambaram became Major General Natraj and all the scientists throughout their stay worked in military fatigues and most of the work was carried out after darkness. To ensure that secrecy was maintained at all levels, even the scientists in small groups of two's and three's made it to Pokhran on different days and from different cities of India. The 55 Engineer Regiment of the Indian Army having dug the shafts under huge camouflage nets simultaneously carried out piling of the sand in the form of shifting dunes, so that they merged with the topography of the area.The third stage and the most difficult one were to place the deadly explosive devices in their respective shafts. It was also decided that all the five tests would be carried out on two different days. The first group would consist of a thermonuclear device code named 'Shakti-1, a fission device code named Shakti-2, and a sub-kiloton device code named Shakti-3, and all the devices in that group would be fired simultaneously on 11th May. But this was subject to favourable weather conditions and with the wind speed and its direction being the crucial decisive factors. Ironically the first shaft that was 200 meters deep for the thermonuclear device was named 'White House'. The shafts were L-shaped, with a horizontal chamber for the test device, and the first three devices were placed in their respective shafts on 10th May. And by 7:30 AM next morning, they were all sealed by the Army engineers.

CHAPTER-9

The Buddha Smiles again and so does Allah Talla

On that day of May 1998, it was indeed very hot in the Pokhran Desert, but the critical factor was the wind. The tests were initially timed for 9 AM, but at 8 AM, when the Met officer with the fictitious name of Captain Adi Marzban reported that the wind conditions were not favourable, and that it could send accidental radiation fallout from the blasts towards the nearby villages, they therefore decided to wait. For India any such radiation fallout was simply not acceptable. With the mane of his silver hair sticking out from under his army jungle hat, both Dr Abdul Kalam and Dr Chidambaram sweating profusely from the terrible desert heat waited patiently for the wind speed to fall. Finally early afternoon after the winds had died down, the two keys that would activate the test countdown was given to Dr M Vasudev, the range safety officer. Having verified that all test indicators were normal, Vasudev handed over one key each to a representative from BARC and the DRDO respectively. Both of them together were now ready to unlock the countdown system

It was a tense Monday afternoon for the group of six who had assembled at the Prime Minister's 7, Race Course Road residence as they kept anxiously waiting to hear the final codeword. At 3.45 PM, on that historic day as the massive blast that was equivalent to 5.3 on the Richter scale shook the earth, and the combined force of the three underground blasts lifted an area of the size of a cricket field to a few meters above the ground, there was jubilation all round. And 10 minutes later when the phone rang in the Prime Ministers house; it was time for India to celebrate. Two days later on 13th May, when two more devices of low yield were detonated, India had truly become a nuclear power. The Buddha had smiled again.

It was 2 o'clock in the afternoon of 11th May, 1998 Moscow time, when Shupriya's telephone also rang. It was Delhi calling. And as soon as she got the great news, she immediately called for a meeting of all her senior staff members to brief them on India's stand.That evening, when the Indian Prime Minister told the world press about India's gigantic achievement, alarm bells started ringing in some of the big world capitals and in Islamabad too. The United States condemned the tests and announced that sanctions would follow. The United Nations also expressed their disapproval and Russia although an old friend also conveyed its unhappiness. But the most vehement criticism came from India's immediate neighbours, Pakistan and China. While China called upon the international community to exert pressure on India to sign the NPT, the Nuclear Proliferation Treaty and told India to eliminate its nuclear arsenal, Prime Minister Nawaz Sharif of Pakistan blamed India for instigating a nuclear arms race in the region and vowed that he would soon give India a suitable and fitting reply.

"But do you think we have the bomb and if we do have one then what are we waiting for," said a visibly agitated Saira, when Shiraz told him about India's nuclear achievement.

"Well Pakistan too has been working on it for quite some time and going by Nawaz Sharif's statement I am sure he must be having quite a few up his sleeve too," replied Shiraz nonchalantly. However, in his heart of heart he seemed very pleased with India's achievement, but he now feared that Pakistan too would give India a tit for tat reply.

Shiraz had no doubt that Pakistan already had the bomb and it only needed a reasonably good excuse and India with five massive explosions it seems had now provided it on a platter. As a prelude to conducting the tests, Pakistan very wisely dispatched their senior envoys to various world capitals to highlight Pakistan's stand and to win the world's support and sympathy. This also gave Pakistan the excuse to once again try and internationalize the never ending Kashmir issue in the various world forums starting from the United Nations. It was on the excuse that her very existence was now being threatened by a belligerent and nuclear India.

A week later, when Salim Rehman from Islamabad rang up to say that 'Allah Talla too will be smiling soon', Shiraz knew that the preparations for Pakistan to explode its nuclear devices had begun in right earnest. Though Shiraz was aware that it was bound to happen, since India had now given Pakistan the sanction albeit inadvertently, but he was not sure as to where and when it would take place finally. He had been constantly and both covertly and overtly through his contacts in the PAEC, Pakistan Atomic Energy Commission monitoring the progress from the early 1980's, when hundreds of Pakistani scientists were sent to China and they came back to start the 'CHASMA' nuclear plant with Chinese assistance and where the technique of nuclear fuel was developed. Later another reactor was commissioned at Joharabad in the Khushab district in Punjab for the production of isotopes and heavy water. Between the period 1983 and 1990, 24 cold tests of nuclear devices were carried out in 24 tunnels that were bored on the Kirana Hills site in the Punjab region of Pakistan near Sargodha. This site was subsequently abandoned and cold test facility was shifted to the Kala-Chitta Range. There was no doubt that it was under the Chairmanship of Munir Ahmed Khan who as the longest serving PAEC Chairman from 1972 to 1991 was instrumental in following the path of silently and covertly pursuing the nuclear goal for Pakistan, though credit must also be given to Dr AQ Khan, Dr Samar, and to Afzal Haq Rajput, the man who designed the Khushab reactor. That crucial reactor had the capability to produce weapons grade plutonium to make the nuclear warheads.

According to Shiraz if and when Pakistan did explode a nuclear device then the honour of being the father of the Islamic bomb should rightly go to Munir Khan, though that title could also well apply to the late Mr Bhutto at the political level, because it was he who after the debacle in Bangladesh in 1971 as the CMLA gave the scientists of Pakistan the first green signal. And it was also Mr Bhutto who had declared way back in 1965 that if India builds the bomb. Pakistanis will eat grass or leaves and they would even go hungry, but they would get one of its own and he was not very wrong in his predictions. And now with its economy in shambles, a hungry Pakistan still decided that it would go for it. And the world did not have to wait for long, when on the afternoon of 28th May, 1998 at 3:16 PM. Pakistan Standard Time, Pakistan under the directions of the PAEC successfully carried out five underground nuclear tests at the Chagai test site. The site chosen was the granite mountain of Koh Kambaran in the Ras Koh Range in the Chagai Division of Baluchistan.

While the proud Prime Minster of Pakistan, Nawaz Sharif congratulated the Pakistani scientists and told the nation on television about the country's stupendous achievement, the grand celebrations in Pakistan had already begun. The final yield of the tests that were reported to be around 40 kilotons had got the entire nation in a mad frenzy as they danced through the streets shouting 'Pakistan Paindabad.'Two days later on 30th May, when. Pakistan carried out one more nuclear test, thus making the final score line read 6 to Pakistan and 5 for India, Saira jokingly said to her husband."Even in this business of making deadly nuclear bombs, Pakistan has beaten India."

And while the world powers criticized Pakistan for having carried out these tests in flagrant disregard of international opinion, the Indian Prime Minister reiterated that India wanted peaceful existence with its neighbours and he also suggested that both countries should for their own benefit hold peace talks. However, in the Indian subcontinent the nuclear race between the two nations having got off to a flying start, Shiraz was apprehensive about the ultimate fallout from it. With the Taliban next door sheltering the ever elusive Osama bin Laden in the mountains of Afghanistan, the possibility of a nuclear bomb of low intensity falling into the hands of the dreaded Al Qaida could not be ruled out. Surprisingly on that very day of 30th May, 1998, half an hour before Pakistan was ready to detonate the final device, a massive earthquake shook northern Afghanistan. It was around 6.30 in the morning and Salim Rehman who felt the tremors at Islamabad wondered if Pakistan's last device was even more powerful than the five previous ones that were detonated two days ago.

A few days later Salim Rehman wrote to Shiraz a long letter intimating to him how the final decision was taken by the Nawaz Sharif government, and how the PAEC, the KRL and the Armed Forces of Pakistan working hand in glove together could achieve it in such quick time, considering that India had conducted her tests a little more than just a fortnight ago. According to Salim Rehman, Nawaz Sharif immediately on his return from a visit to Central Asia on 13th May had held a high level conference that lasted for several hours with the top military brass and senior members of his cabinet. The only agenda at that meeting was to discuss India's action and how should Pakistan respond to it. The nuclear blasts by India had indeed taken Pakistan's ISI and other intelligence agencies completely by surprise. Initially there was a mixed response. Some were in favour of exercising caution, but the majority was of the opinion that it was an ideal opportunity for Pakistan to give a befitting reply. The Prime Minister was however in two minds because on that very day President Clinton had urged him not to respond to India's totally uncalled for nuclear tests.

According to Clinton, India had carried out an utterly irresponsible act and in order to ensure that Pakistan did not do the same, he was even willing to provide Pakistan with more arms and economic aid. At the same time he also cautioned Nawaz Sharif that incase Pakistan followed India's example, then the country would be subjected to more economic sanctions and which he knew the country could ill afford. Therefore for Nawaz Sharif it was a catch 22 situation. Because if he gave in to American pressure, he would be considered a lackey, and if Pakistan did not show its teeth then the people would consider him to be a bloody coward and the possibility of another military coup could not be ruled out since all the three service chiefs were unanimous in their decision that Pakistan must test the bomb at the earliest.Two days later on the morning of 15th May, another top level meeting was held to discuss the fallout from the Indian nuclear test, and since Dr Ishfaq Ahmed, Chairman of PAEC was on a visit to USA and Canada, it was Dr Samar Mubarakmand who spelt out Pakistan's preparedness in giving a matching response. The two main points discussed was whether or not Pakistan should carry out the nuclear tests and if so which of the two organizations, PAEC or KRL at Kahuta should be given the overall responsibility. Therefore in principle though it was finally decided that the tests will be carried out, the Finance Minister Sartaj Aziz was against it because the country was going through an economic recession and could ill afford it. However, the Prime Minister remained non-committal and he decided to go along with the majority. Fearing that the PAEC will steal the thunder, Dr AQ Khan speaking on behalf of KRL, the Kahuta Research Laboratory also pitched in to say that his organization was fully prepared to explode the devices within 10 days. And when on the 18th of May, the task was finally given to the scientists of the PAEC because they were the ones who not only had greater experience in conducting the cold tests, but it was also they who had constructed the test site at Chagai, Dr Ishfaq Ahmed felt highly honoured. So finally when the Prime Minister told him 'Dhamaka Kar Dein" (Conduct the Explosions) a disappointed and crest fallen Dr AQ Khan like an errant schoolboy lodged a protest with the Army Chief, General Karamat. To mollify the man, it was therefore decided that the scientists from KRL too along with the PAEC would be involved in the final preparations.

On 19th May, two teams comprising of 140 scientists, engineers and technicians on two separate Boeing 737 PIA aircrafts left for Chagai. All the nuclear devices in sub-assembly form were flown from Rawalpindi on a giant C-130 Hercules transport aircraft that was escorted by four F-16 fighter aircrafts armed with air to air missiles. The pilots of the F-16's were also secretly told to shoot down the C-130 just in case it tried to fly out of Pakistan air space. After the C-130 touched down at an airport in Baluchistan, the devices were taken to the test site where they were individually assembled in special rooms that were located along the one kilometer long tunnel that had been prepared under the mountain Koh Kambaran in the Ras Koh range. On 25th May, the tunnel was sealed by personnel from the Pakistan Army Engineer Corps, the Frontier Works

Organization and from the SDW, the Special Development Works, which was a military unit that was raised primarily for this very task 20 years ago. The sealing of the tunnel was completed by pouring 6000 bags of cement into the shaft and by 27th May, after all the cement in the heat of the desert had finally set in, the moment of truth had arrived.

The American intelligence agencies that had been monitoring the progress from their satellite eyes in the sky were not in the least surprised. On that very day, President Clinton rang up Nawaz Sharif again and talked to him for a good 25 minutes imploring him to call off the tests, but it was already a bit too late. For the Prime Minister of Pakistan there was no other choice, because he knew damn well that his own political status and survival now depended on the success of the blasts, and succumbing to American pressures would not only be politically suicidal for him, but the possibility of another army coup could not be ruled out either. And in order to ensure that the nuclear tests were carried out as planned on the 28th of May, the Pakistani military high command late on the evening of the previous day had sounded a very high priority nationwide alert. It was all a part of a grand deception plan to create a scare and to make doubly sure that the Pakistani leadership did not succumb to international pressures. That evening Pakistan's DGMO made some urgent telephone calls not only to all the Corps Commanders, but also to the Prime Minister's secretariat and the Pakistan Foreign Office warning them that there was an imminent danger of an attack by Israeli and Indian jet fighters on Pakistan's nuclear and missile sites. Quoting a source from Saudi intelligence, when the DGMO informed all concerned that the intended targets were the Kahuta uranium enrichment plant and the long range Gauri missile sites, the Pakistan Defence Forces and the Foreign Office immediately swung into action. While the Pakistani F-16 fighters scrambled and took off to protect the test site in Baluchistan, a Mirage squadron was made to standby, while the ground based air defence units took up their positions in and around Kahuta. And by dusk all Pakistani radar stations were also put on high alert.

Meanwhile the old hotel that housed the Pakistan Foreign Office suddenly became a buzz of hectic activity as they frantically contacted their missions in Beijing, Moscow, London, Washington and in some other important European capitals and directed them to immediately warn the respective host country of the impending attack. At an unearthly hour of one o'clock in the morning the Indian High Commissioner was also summoned and warned of the dire consequences. Nawaz Sharif personally called Clinton and Tony Blair to tell them about the so called intelligence report. Not to be left behind Ahmed Kamal, Pakistan's permanent representative to the United Nations also informed Mr Kofi Annan, the UN Secretary General about the very serious threat to his country. And while the bluffing game by Pakistan continued throughout the night, the Indian armed forces were also put on high alert and their missile units also took up their battle positions. In the pre-dawn of 28th May, 1998, when Pakistan cut off all communications with the outside world and all military and strategic installations in the country were put on maximum alert, it was more than evident that Pakistan was all set to become the first Islamic nuclear nation in the world.

On that bright clear sunny day at Chagai after everybody including the civilians and the military had been evacuated from 'Ground Zero,' all the top scientists of Pakistan from an observation post that was ten kilometers away waited with baited breath. For them the day of reckoning had arrived and they could not let the country down. With prayers to Allah-Tallah on their lips, when the ten men at the observation post felt the tremor and saw the black granite rock turning chalk white, they knew that the kind and merciful Allah had answered their prayers. Mohammad Arshad, the young Chief Scientific Officer who had designed the triggering mechanism and who had been given the honour to push that nuclear button at 3:16 PM had become a national hero. Those 30 seconds of wait after the button was pushed seemed to be the longest for all those who had worked so hard and for so long on the project. As the earth on the Ras Koh Hills trembled, it was undoubtedly Pakistan's finest hour. A few hours earlier the Indian High Commissioner to Pakistan, Satish Chander was summoned by the Pakistan Foreign Office. Giving the excuse that Pakistan had very credible information that India was planning to attack Pakistan's nuclear installation by dawn, the Indian High Commissioner was taken completely by surprise. And when he was further told that Pakistan was ready to retaliate and that New Delhi must therefore be immediately informed to desist from any such irresponsible act, it was evident that Pakistan was not willing to take any chances.

Chapter-10

Moscow Interlude

While Pakistan was celebrating their newly acquired nuclear status, the ten member film delegation from India landed in Moscow. On that very evening in order to welcome the delegation, Shupriya in their honour threw an informal party at her official residence. Knowing the crazy popularity of the Bollywood stars both at home and abroad and with the young and the old alike, she very wisely had also invited all the officers who were posted in the mission, together with their families and children for that informal gathering.

"I think D.K. (Deepak Kumar) with his Dilip Kumar style kiss curl, Rambo features and the cute dimple on his right cheek is undoubtedly a lady killer. In fact with his height and physique he looks more like Dharmendra and who undoubtedly is the most manly hero and handsome that Bollywood has ever produced and who even today at 63 can give the likes of Shahrukh, Salman and Sanjay a run for their money," whispered the middle aged wife of the Political Counselor to her husband as they with their two teenage girls posed for a photograph with the Indian matinee idol.

"And it is now our turn next,"said the First Secretary's eight year old little daughter, as she with her autograph book in hand and with her parents and grandparents in tow walked up to the actor for a group photograph with him.

"I must confess that I never knew that you were so very popular, and now that the two senior most citizens have requested you for an old song from any Hindi film of yesteryears, you simply cannot or should not refuse them,"said Shupriya who also very much wanted Peevee to sing and she had even arranged for a big Yamaha key board and an electric guitar for him for the occasion.

As Peevee walked up to the mike, there was stunned silence all around. And when he with feelings sang the old Kishore Kumar number "Ye Sham Mastani' from the 1970 hit film: Kati Patang,' there were tears in Shupriya's eyes. That particular song was also her late husband Shiraz's favourite and it was the one that he had serenaded her with after their Gurdwara wedding in September 1971. Pretending that something had gone into her eyes, she quickly excused herself and went to the toilet to wipe away those tears. As the shouts of encore and one more please echoed across the well manicured lawns of the Indian embassy, Peevee obliged with another Kishore Kumar number.But this time it was a much livelier song with a fast beat that had the entire audience tapping their feet and clapping joyfully. It was the age old favourite 'Eena Meena Deeka.'from the film Aasha. The word 'Aasha' meant hope and Shupriya now prayed and hoped that her one and only son Peevee should win the best actor award at the film festival.

As the fifteen day film festival came to a close, there was good news both for Pakistan and India. Whereas the Pakistani film 'Mere Watan Ke Logon' a story of a poor young migrant orphan boy who came to Pakistan during partition and rose to become Pakistan's first civilian Mohajir Prime Minister won the best picture award, the best actor prize however went to India's Deepak Kumar for his role as Captain Param Veer in the film 'Jhanda Ooncha Rahe Hamara'. And though some felt that the Pakistani film in which the Prime Minister of Pakistan kept harping that he wanted genuine peace with India and kept trying to convince his countrymen that the best solution for the subcontinent would be the reunification of all the three countries, India, Pakistan and Bangladesh as one federal entity, some considered it to be more of a propaganda film. Shiraz however, was of the opinion that it could be a viable option, provided all the three nations were ready to sincerely shake hands and let bygones be bygones. According to him, if the United States of America with its many ethnic and migrant population of various castes, creeds and religions could live and exist peacefully together and become a strong nation, why couldn't the United States of India be a reality.?

The awards presentation ceremony on the 6th June, 1998 at Moscow's famous Bolshoi Theatre was indeed a glittering affair as the celebrity crowd gave a standing ovation to all the award winners. And later during the cocktails as the champagne with caviar was being served, Shupriya for the first time was formally introduced to the Pakistani Ambassador and his wife. When she congratulated Pakistan for winning the best picture award, the intonation and her manner of speaking took Shiraz completely by surprise. And for a few seconds he simply just kept staring in amazement at her.

"I think Deepak Kumar too deserved his award and the Indian film was a close second I believe," said Shiraz very diplomatically, while proposing a toast to his daughter Sherry who had turned 19 that day and was waiting eagerly to be introduced to the Indian Bollywood star.

"I am afraid that may not be possible today, because immediately after the award ceremony Deepak Kumar had to leave for the airport to catch his flight back to India. Tomorrow is the mahurat, the inaugural ceremony of his next film and he had promised the producer that he would be back in time for it," said Shupriya as a disappointed Sherry looked at her father and took a sip of the bubbly champagne.

"Anyway a very happy birthday to you and do enjoy yourself,"added Shupriya as she excused herself and called out softly to her secretary to get the staff car ready for the drive back to the embassy.

During the journey back to her residence, when Shupriya remarked to the Second Secretary that the Pakistan Ambassador seemed to be the friendly type alright, but he was not all that handsome as was made out to be in the photograph that was sent by New Delhi, the Second Secretary was in full agreement with Her Excellency. But when Shupriya further stated that photos could be at times quite deceiving, and the Second Secretary who was still a bachelor remarked promptly.

'Yes Madam, I do quite agree with that, but there is no doubt that his wife and daughter are indeed very good looking and the photographs sent by Delhi I am afraid do not do full justice to them either."

On hearing that comment, there was a smile on Shupriya's face.'Well I must acknowledge that you do have good taste young man, but for heaven's sake do not create a diplomatic scandal while I am still sitting on this chair," said Shupriya in jest as Peevee called up from the airport on his mobile phone to say a final goodbye to his Mom number 2.

That night Shiraz just could not sleep. He kept tossing around in bed thinking about the Indian Ambassador who resembled Shupriya not only in her diction and mannerisms, but also in her looks and features too. 'May be and as they say God at times does create two people with similar features and traits, but Shupriya had died 27 years ago, and even if she was reborn she wouldn't be all that old," thought Shiraz as he took a tranquilizer and chased it down with a neat small peg of Napoleon cognac.

Next morning at the breakfast table, when Saira remarked to her husband that the Indian Ambassador though she was nearing fifty was still very attractive and elegant, Shiraz promptly said. "But so is our own Malheeha Lodhi and who as our Ambassador to the United States has been a great success." Shiraz was feeling guilty and wondered if he had talked in his sleep thinking about Shupriya.

"I agree and while Dr Malheeha is a divorcee and has one son by the name of Faisal, the Indian Ambassador I am told is still single," said Saira

"Maybe as a Sardarni she could not find an equally intelligent Sardar," said Shiraz in good humour as he pecked Saira on her cheek and left for an important meeting at the tall and imposing Russian foreign ministry building that was located in the heart of the city on the inner ring road that in Russian was known as the Sadavoy Kaltso.

In mid June, Karim Malik with his wife Mehmuda arrived in Moscow on a week's holiday. They were on their way to Kenya and looked forward to a better life after having spent nearly two years in awful Khartoum. This was going to be Karim Malik's last posting before proceeding on retirement, which was due in June 2000.

"Once you all settle down in Nairobi, we will visit you in early August because I want to go on an African safari and maybe if permitted we could also do some wild life hunting together," said Shiraz as the two cousin sisters Mehmuda and Saira got busy in the kitchen.

"Oh that will be just great Abbu and you must buy me a gun too." said an excited 15 year old Tojo as he got ready to go for his golf practice at the Moscow City Golf Club.The young boy whose only aim in life now was to become a professional golfer was now a single digit handicapper. Only last week having won the 'Moscow Hopes Junior Tournament' his handicap had been reduced by one to lucky seven.

'We can all play Golf at the Karen Country Club golf course in Nairobi too, but provided you give me at least 13 strokes because my handicap is still at 20,'"said Karim as he wished Tojo the very best of luck.

A few days later at the dinner table, when Salim Rehman rang up from Islamabad to say that the Swiss investigating Judge Danial Devaud had rejected an appeal seeking review of the June 2 indictment orders that was passed against the three Swiss nationals who were involved in the money laundering that they had carried out on orders and on behalf of Benazir Bhutto and her husband Asif Ali Zardari in the now famous Cotecna and SGS scam, Mehmuda seemed to be the happiest person.

"I only hope that now at least our politicians will wake up and ensure that the greedy couple who had so blatantly swindled and robbed their own country of millions of dollars will be punished in a manner that would serve as an example to others,"said Mehmuda.

"I would even go one step further and recommend very strongly that they should be shot in public," said Karim Malik.

"Oh these damn crooks with their big money power know how to wangle their way out and believe you me as time goes by and like in the Bofors case in India, this too I am sure will die it's natural death,"said Shiraz as he poured Karim Malik some more of the legendry Romanee Conti wine that he had brought from France. And while they were still enjoying their drinks, Arif Rehman from Peshawar rang up to give the good news that the government had approved Salim Rehman's appointment as the next Ambassador to India.

"Though the firm date of his reporting was yet to be announced, but most probably it would be in early October, when the present incumbent retires," added Arif Rehman.

"That is really wonderful news and now we can all go for a holiday to him in Delhi and visit the famousTaj Mahal at Agra, and Salim Chisti's Dargah in Ajmer," said an excited Saira as she booked an immediate call to congratulate her dear brother. And when Salim Rehman came on the line and said that he was going to celebrate his appointment by going to see the World Cup football finals that was already in progress in France, Karim Malik however, cautioned him to be very careful and to avoid all matches in which the American team was scheduled to play. According to Karim Malik's information that he had gathered from a reliable source in Khartoum, there was every chance of the Al-Qaida or the AIG, the Armed Islamic Group of Algeria disrupting the event with a suicidal attack. As per the French intelligence sources, the key dates for such an attack were Monday 15th June, Sunday 21st June and Thursday 25th June, when the US team in group 'F' would take on Germany, Iran and Yugoslavia respectively.

But luckily for the French police, the arrest of Abu Hamza a senior AIG operative in May had given them ample time to discover the bizarre plot. Fearing for his life, Hamza had spilled the beans, and as a result of which, the Belgian, German, French, Italian and Swiss police in simultaneous raids had swooped down on suspected supporters of the AIG and the GIA, the Group Islamic Army in their respective countries. Among the hundred and more suspects apprehended and questioned were Sheikh Abdullah Kinai, an Arab-Afghan who was close to the GIA leadership and Tayeb al-Afghani who was one of Osama's lieutenants in his Al-Ansar base in Afghanistan. While in Khartoum, Osama within the Al Qaida umbrella had not only sheltered the GIA, but he had also supplied them with arms and funds. With Saudi Arabia, Tunisia and Morocco having also qualified for the world cup, infiltrating these elements into France as spectators seemed ideal for the conduct of such a deadly strike.

"Osama or no Osama, I am still going to be there for the semi-finals and the finals provide my favourite team Brazil makes it to that level," said Salim Rehman.

"In that case best of luck to you, but I am going to cheer the home team who with Zidane as the star player are in excellent form," said Shiraz.

"Alright in that case just for old time sake let's have a friendly bet. If Brazil lifts the cup then you will pay for my airfare both ways, and if France reaches the finals and emerges as the winner against Brazil then I will pay both for your and Tojo's fare from Moscow to Paris and back. And Inshallah hoping that would be the final line up, I will see you in Paris on 11th July," said Salim Rehman very confidently.

"I think you are being rather too optimistic in predicting both the finalists, but nevertheless the bet is on," replied Shiraz.

On the 4th of July, 1998 on America's Independence Day Shiraz again bumped into the Indian Ambassador at the American Embassy cocktail party. The main topic at that party was the Russian government's bold decision to give the last Tsar of Russia, Nicholas Romanov II and his family a befitting burial with full state honours. Though the Russian Orthodox Church was not in favour of it because they doubted the authenticity of the last remains of the Russian royal family since it was a mass murder that was committed 80 years ago, but Yeltsin it seems was more than keen to restore the status of the last Tsar and his family. According to Yeltsin, the Tsar, his wife and their little children had committed no crime and the Romanovs after all were very much a part of Russia's history. That evening at the cocktail party, though Shiraz tried his best to make polite conversation with the Indian Ambassador by showing off his vast knowledge of Tsarist Russia and their endeavour to expand the Russian empire into Afghanistan and India during the last century, but Shupriya it seems was not the least interested. She was rather keen to have a word with the American, British and the Japanese Ambassador's since all the three countries had imposed severe economic sanctions ever since India became a full-fledged nuclear nation.But at the the fag end of the party, when it was time for everyone to leave, Shiraz on the pretext of saying goodbye to the Indian Ambassador asked her very casually if she was from Delhi and about the college and university that she had studied in.

"Originally our family was from Sheikupura, Punjab till partition drove us out from there, and with my father being a public government servant, my education was at various schools and colleges all over India,' said Shupriya very confidently. She was always apprehensive that someone someday may well ask her such like leading questions, and she therefore as Yeshwant Kaur Bajwa was always well prepared to answer them.

That evening after the cocktails, when Shiraz reached home, he kept thinking about his own Shupriya. He just could not believe that there could be so much similarity between two people and had Shupriya lived she too would have been of the Indian Ambassador's age. Late that night with no sleep at all in sight, Shiraz helped himself to a night cap and then went inside the bathroom to look at the little girl's photograph that was inside the locket around his neck. Realizing that her husband was still wide awake, Saira asked him whether he was feeling alright.

'Nothing to worry about my love and I think it is the prawn cocktail that has slightly messed up my tummy," said Shiraz as he closed the locket and went back to bed.

At breakfast next morning, when Saira served him only curd and rice for his upset stomach and asked him what kind of conversation took place between him and the Indian Ambassador, Shiraz promptly cooked up a story and said that it was with regard to the protocol to be followed during the formal burial of the late Tsar and his family that was scheduled for the 17th of July, and for which a large number of Ambassadors and their wives from the Diplomatic Corps were planning to attend.

"In that case I feel we should also represent our country,' said Saira excitedly as she checked on the calendar whether 17th July would be a weekend.

CHAPTER-11

Football, Fatwas and Fireworks

Whether it was his intuition or his vast knowledge of the game, Salim Rehman was dead right. On 7th July, 1998 in the first semi-finals, when Brazil beat Netherlands in a penalty shoot out, and on the very next day France defeated Croatia in the second semi finals, Salim Rehman who was already in France called up Shiraz and said that he was waiting for him.

On 11th July, Shiraz and Tojo arrived in Paris by the Air France flight from Moscow. The city with its snarling traffic was in a very high festive spirit and it took Shiraz more than an hour and a half to reach the hotel. In the many cafés and restaurants of the beautiful city, the only topic being discussed was football and only football, and who would eventually lift the coveted cup. Brazil undoubtedly was the favourite, but the French combination was no less powerful either. Not only did France top its group with three clear wins, but the well knit team had also advanced very convincingly into the finals.

On 12th July, with all roads leading to the 80,000 capacity Stade de France in the suburb of Saint—Denis, Tojo sporting the French colours and the mascot Footix, a cockerel in blue holding the ball in his hand couldn't just wait to get to his seat. 'Vive Le France' shouted Shiraz loudly as both the teams lined up for the grand finale. When the Moroccon referee Sayed Belgola blew his whistle for the final kick-off, the jam packed stadium exploded in a mad frenzy. With the French and their European supporters rooting for France, Salim Rehman flanked by Shiraz and Tojo felt a little out of place. It was the first time ever that a host nation was playing the defending champions, and it was a golden opportunity for France to become the seventh nation in the world and the first host nation to win the tournament ever since Argentina achieved that honour in 1978. France was also the home of the founder of the world cup, Jules Rimet and they literally went hell for leather from the very word go. In the 27th minute, when the tall Zidane converted a corner with a header and then followed it up again a little later with another delightful header, Brazil did not look like the team that it was a week ago. Their star striker Ronaldo was absolutely off colour that day'. He it seems had a fit on the eve of the match and looked like a novice on the field.

"But I wonder why they could not keep him on the bench, when they very well knew that he was not mentally and physically fit," said a disappointed Salim Rehman, when France put another nail on Brazil's coffin by scoring a third goal during the second half stoppage time. At the final whistle when the score read France 3 and Brazil 0, Shiraz too could not believe it. France had undoubtedly outplayed Brazil that day and that night as the celebrations in France carried on till next morning, Salim Rehman very sportingly wrote a cheque for Rupees 20,000 and gave it to Shiraz. It was the price of the two Moscow-Paris-Moscow air tickets.

"Arre Salle Sahib mere ko tere Bahen se jutte padhenge agar maine ye cheque kabool kiya. Behtar toh ye hoga agar tuh apna return ticket cancel kar ke aur issi paise se ek Paris to Islamabad via Moscow air ticket kharid kar humare saat Moscow chal. Saira bhi khush ho jaegi aur hum bhi.'.

(My dear brother-in-law I do not want shoes raining on me from your dear sister when I get back to Moscow. If she comes to know that I have taken a cheque of 20,000 from you there will be hell to pay. Therefore the best thing for you to do will be to cancel your return ticket and buy a new ticket with that money from Paris to Islamabad via Moscow. It will not only surprise Saira, but she will feel happy too)

When they returned to Moscow, Saira was indeed very surprised and to celebrate the occasion she for dinner that evening got busy in the kitchen. She knew her brother's taste for authentic frontier food, and by the time dinner was ready, she had rustled up four different kinds of lamb dishes and one of veal too.

"I wish I too could accompany you all to St Petersburg, but I have to be back in Islamabad to attend a very important conference on the 16th of July that is being chaired by the Foreign Minister and it pertains to the measures to be taken by all our missions abroad to tighten our belts." said Salim Rehman as he helped himself to a few more of the delicious 'Chapali Kababs,' that Saira had served as starters.

"So the fallout from the nuclear blasts is now going to be felt by our stomachs also, and the Prime Minister I believe has also directed that there should be no ostentatious and grandiose parties anymore,"added Shiraz as he poured another stiff Black Label for his dear brother-in-law.

"Yes that is right, and with the imposition of emergency from the very day we exploded those devices, it has only added to our many problems and miseries," said Salim Rehman as they all moved to the dining table.

With the Yeltsin government having decided to finally give the last Tsar Nicholas II and his family a dignified Christian burial in the magnificent St Peter and Paul Cathedral in Leningrad, which was now once again renamed as St Petersburg, Shiraz and Saira were all set to fly to the old capital the next day. Since this was going to be a very historic occasion, they had decided that they must witness it live and pay homage to the man and his family who were brutally murdered in Yekaterinburg 80 years ago.

On the 17th of July, 1998 to the poignant sound of the church organ, when the earthly remains of the last Tsar of Russia and his family together with those who had faithfully and loyally served them till the very end were finally laid to rest in that beautiful cathedral, there were tears in the eyes of the 50 odd relations of the Romanovs and others who had gathered there from all over the world on the solemn occasion. Also present was President Yeltsin and a large number of high ranking personnel from the Diplomatic Corps.On that day as Shiraz in a black suit and Saira in a jet black saree stood silently with the others, and witnessed the proceedings, there was moistness in their eyes too. The Russian President, Boris Yeltsin was given the honour to place the first wreath and he did it very dignifiedly. Watching the event live on television in Moscow, Shupriya was surprised to see the Ambassador of Afghanistan A.V. Assefi with his First Secretary G.S. Gheyrat also present at the funeral. Having made a note of it, she asked the Counselor Political to include it in the Embassy's monthly confidential report to New Delhi.

And while the old people in Russia prayed in the churches for the souls of the last Romanov family to rest in peace, Shiraz on 5th August, having heard that the Iraqi disarmament crisis had taken a turn for the worse and that Saddam had officially suspended all cooperation with UNSCOM teams, he with his family landed in Nairobi. That evening he wondered whether America would once again flex its muscles in the Gulf region and discussed the issue with Karim Malik.

"I do not know why the hell the Americans are hell bent to humiliate the Iraqi strongman and this will only generate more hatred against them. As it is the Al Qaida head honcho Bin Laden has been constantly issuing fatwas and warning the Americans of dire consequences if they don't get out from all Arab lands, and I therefore will not be surprised if he and his diehard radical militants just to prove that they can if required strike anywhere and at anytime against the Americans carry out another Khobar type suicide bombing," said Karim Malik

On the very next evening having visited the many important tourist spots of Nairobi, which included the Nairobi National Park, the Museum, the Snake Park and the Giraffe Centre, both the families got busy packing for the five day safari that would first take them to the famous Tree Hotel inside the Aberdare National Park. This was the same hotel where the present Queen Elizabeth of England had once stayed as a Priness and a young bride and that was in February 1952. And it was while she was there with her husband Prince Phillip that she heard that her father King George the Sixth had died and that she had been proclaimed as Queen Elizabeth 11.

"I am sorry but there will be no hunting of wild animals since it has been banned by the government, but all the same we will carry our 12 bore guns for our own personal safety," said Karim Malik.

"But Chachajaan can't we go bird hunting, at least," said a disappointed Tojo who with his father was looking forward to some real excitement in the jungles of Africa.

"I am afraid this is not the season, but if you come again in September-October or in February-March I will take you to the Kiboko Region which is a four hour drive from here and there you can shoot jungle fowls, partridges, quails, water fowls, sand grouse and what have you. And we can also stay in a tented camp and have a barbecue with camp fire every evening," added Karim Malik while presenting Tojo with his first Winchester air-gun

"Let me also remind everybody that there is no requirement to get up very early tomorrow since our scheduled time of departure in the big hired four wheel drive Pajero is at 10 o'clock in the morning, But all the same don't be late," said Karim Malik as he on a big tourist map of Kenya indicated to Shiraz the many beautiful wild life parks and sanctuaries in that country.

It was around 10:30 in the morning on that Friday of 7th August, 1998, when the Pajero passed by the Indian Embassy in Nairobi, and seconds later a massive explosion shook the entire city.

"My God what was that?"" said Saira as the Pajero slowly made its way through the crowded street. But by the time they reached the next main crossing, there was panic all around.

"The American Embassy which is close by it seems has been blasted by a car bomb," said the policeman on duty at the cross roads, as he desperately tried to regulate the heavy vehicular traffic and the large crowd of people who were fleeing in all available transport from the scene of the devastation. And noticing the manner in which the people were running helter-skelter, Shiraz realized that it was no ordinary bomb and said."'I think we must under such tragic circumstances cancel our trip and try and do some rescue work."

"Yes, and I think you are damn well right and we could use the Pajero to ferry the injured to hospitals," said Karim Malik as he wheeled the car and drove towards the roundabout on the Haile Sellasie Avenue and the Moi Avenue junction where the American Embassy was located. And while their families with the entire luggage got into two taxis and headed home, Shiraz and Karim drove on to the devastated site and was surprised to see the American lady Ambassador Prudence Bushnell already there organizing the rescue work. Providence had saved her life. because at the time of the blast she was in the nearby Ufundi Co-operative Bank building holding a meeting with Joseph Kamotho, the Kenyan Minister of Trade. According to one eye witness the bomb was so very powerful that the yellow Mitsubishi van that had been used for the purpose was catapulted high into the sky. The deadly bomb had devastated the American Embassy building and it was a scene that Shiraz and Karim would never ever forget. Lying on that important road crossing and roundabout were scores of dead men, women and children and most of them were poor innocent Kenyans. Whether they were local Kenyans of African origin or Indians, Pakistanis who had made Kenya their home or whether it was the 'Goras' who once ruled that country for so many years, it made no damn difference as the locals also joined in the massive rescue operations. And while it was in progress, the news arrived that a similar bomb at about the same time had also devastated the American Embassy building at Dar-es-Salam, the capital of neighbouring Tanzania. Coincidently that 7th of August was the 8th anniversary of the arrival of American troops on Saudi Arabian soil and at the end of the day, while the casualties in Nairobi was a staggering 212 people dead including 12 Americans and nearly 400 injured, in Dar-es-Salam it was comparatively much less with only 11 dead and 85 injured.

"Looking at the manner in which the two simultaneous bombing were carried out, it was indeed a very well planned operation, and it seems that probably the Al-Qaida was behind it," said Shiraz.

"Possibly yes, but so far nobody has claimed responsibility. It is also possible that it was a revenge killing by Osama who narrowly escaped death when a massive explosion flattened the Jalalabad Police Station on the morning of 19th March, last year and which took away the lives of more than 50 people and injured nearly 150. And like Prudence it was once again providence that had saved the Al Qaida leader. He had he left the building only minutes before the explosion occured," added Karim Malik as he drove another half a dozen injured people to the nearby hospital.

Next day while the entire world mourned the death of the many blast victims, and an angry American President Bill Clinton vowed to find and punish the perpetrators of the heinous crime, Karim Malik having paid so much of money in advance for the African safari, and in order not to disappoint little Tojo decided to go ahead with the event.For all of them driving through the dense jungles with their experienced Kenyan guides, sometimes sleeping in tented camps, meeting the locals, observing the wild life and appreciating the varied flora and fauna, it was indeed a memorable experience as they spotted the many wild animals including the famed African lion and the leopard.

And on that 8th of August, as the rescue operations at the bombed out American embassies was still in progress, in Afghanistan the Taliban at Mazar-i-Sharif, the largest city in the north went on a mad killing spree and senseless rampage. For the next two days the Taliban driving their pickup trucks up and down the narrow streets simply kept firing away on anything and everything that moved. Even the animals on the streets were not spared. It was an indiscriminate slaughter of the worst kind and the most to suffer were the Hazaras, an ethnic Shia group whom the Taliban regarded as non Muslims. A year ago the Hazaras had rebelled against the Taliban and now Mullah Niazi who conducted that beastly massacre openly declared from the city's central mosque that either the Hazaras accept to become true Muslims or they should leave Afghanistan for good.

Meanwhile the bombing of the two American embassies in East Africa had also got the FBI and the CIA on the hunt for the killers who had masterminded those dastardly and cowardly acts. According to one credible source even as early as mid-1994, the Al Qaida then based in Sudan had been secretly sending small numbers of men to establish dormant cells in East Africa under the garb of setting up offices in the name of 'Help Africa People.' Moreover, East Africa was always considered by the US authorities as a low risk area, and this was despite the fact that the American Ambassador to Kenya had been constantly asking the State Department to upgrade security at their existing premises.

By the beginning of 1998, the Al-Qaida cells in Nairobi and Dar-es-Salam it seems had become active. On 4th August, while Abdullah Ahmed Abdullah and Mohammed Rashid Daoud Al-Owhali carried out the reconnaissance of the American Embassy in Nairobi, another team carried out the same mission in Dar-es-Salam. Whereas the Nairobi team decided to ram the deadly explosive laden truck at the rear of the embassy building because of less security in that complex, Hamden Khalif the suicide bomber in the Dar-es-Salam blast decided to attack headon with his truck bomb. On 7th August, a little after 10:30.A.M.the dare devil suicide bombers accomplished their respective tasks at both the capitals, but Al-Owhali had left the scene prematurely. He had chickened out at the last minute. He had in a hurry thrown the grenade at the Embassy security staff that were manning the gate, but had panicked and had run away from the scene as his buddy Jihad Mohammed Ali got ready to detonate the deadly bomb manually. Al-Owhali was therefore only wounded and was later arrested from a hospital.

On 14th August, after his return from Nairobi, Shiraz on Pakistan's Independence Day and as courtesy and protocol demanded also invited the Indian Ambassador for cocktails at the Pakistan Embassy that was located on 17 Sadovaya Kudrinskaya. With the new Indian government under Vajpayee showing signs of possible rapprochment with Pakistan, Shiraz thought it would be a good idea if he too extended his hand of friendship and trust to his Indian counterpart in Moscow. Moreover, Shiraz was also keen to find out a little more about the lady since her resemblance to Shupriya was constantly nagging him. However, Shupriya giving the excuse that she would not be able to make it because of some previous engagement had dutifully sent back a polite note with a bouquet of flowers congratulating Pakistan on its 51st Independence Day. When the note signed by her as Yeshwant Kaur Bajwa in her own hand was received by Shiraz, he was further taken aback because even the hand writing was so much like that of Shupriya's.

"I think this coincidence is a bit too much and I must one day confidentially find out the real truth," thought Shiraz as he safely kept the note in his diary. Since the very next day was India's Independence Day and the Indian Embassy traditionally held an at home only on the country's Republic Day, Shiraz nevertheless to reciprocate the Indian Ambassador's gesture sent a bigger bouquet of flowers with an identical note to her.

Two days later on 17th August, when the most powerful man in the world confessed to the American people that he did have an improper relationship with Monica Lewinsky and admitted that he had misled the people, it undoubtedly came as a bombshell to many. And on the same very day, when the Russian rouble was further devalued and it further lost its value against the American dollar resulting in many Russian banks collapsing and millions of Russians losing their entire hard savings, Shiraz very aptly remarked to Saira.

"You know while the Bill Clinton-Lewnsky affair was a private one and one that made him fall from grace, but the fall of the rouble is even more disgraceful since it has ruined the lives of millions of Russians. And while some Americans are braying for Clinton's impeachment, the former Russian Tavarishes(Comrades) are cursing Yeltsin for making them paupers."

"Yes it is indeed rather sad that the Russian economy has collapsed like a pack of cards and now I am afraid there will be more people taking to crime on the streets. The country that was once a super power is now unfortunately being ruled by the new oligarchs and the mafia," added Saira as she rang up her mother Ruksana Begum in Peshawar and congratulated her on her 73rd birthday.

And while Russia was struggling to save the country from an imminent economic collapse, the United States of America on 20th August, unleashed 'Operation Infinite Reach.' And while their deadly cruise missiles bombarded Afghanistan and Sudan as a tit for tat against the embassy bombings, Shiraz wondered as to where would all this finally end. According to Salim Rehman, one of the prime embassy bomb suspects and master mind of the Nairobi bombing Mohammed Sadiq Odeh had been arrested when he landed at Karachi on 7th August on a false passport. He was a Jordanian who had joined the Al Qaida in 1992. A hard core Osama loyalist, he had also trained the Somali forces of the warlord Mohammed Farrah Aidid and was a much wanted man by the Americans.

"But why must all these guys have to land up only in Pakistan every time. Can't they find any other country as a safe haven?' said an angry Aasma to her husband Salim Rehman, when she saw the telecast of the gruesome devastations that the American cruise missiles had inflicted on the villages in the Khost and Jalalabad areas of Afghanistan.

"That's indeed a very good question, but your guess is as good as mine. And It may be due to the magnanimous hospitality and culture that we as Pathans always offer to our revered guests," said Salim Rehman jokingly as he called up Shiraz to find out what was Russia's reaction to the American cruise missile attack.

"They have no doubt condemned it outright but not all that strongly, and the Russkies have therefore very diplomatically termed it simply as a dishonourable act by the Americans. But most of the other major European nations and especially England have supported the US strikes," said Shiraz as he replayed the video recording of the cruise missile attack on Afghanistan and Sudan for his wife Saira to see.

Though the target in Sudan was the Al Shifa pharmaceutical factory that the Americans alleged was a front for the manufacture of a deadly nerve gas and was linked to Osama Bin Laden, but in reality the Americans had erred in their judgment. It was in fact a full fledged pharmaceutical factory that produced most of the medicines for the Sudanese people. Whereas in Afghanistan, no less than 75 cruise missiles had landed near four training camps at Khost and Jalalabad with the hope that they would get Bin Laden and his coterie of advisors who were expected to attend an important meeting that day at the Zawar Kili camp near Khost, but that proved again abortive as far as Osama was concerned. Though there were some 25 militants from various countries who had died in that deadly attack, but Osama escaped unhurt and was safe. Like a cat with nine lives, Bin Laden was expecting a massive retaliatory attack and had quietly moved out from there and into the vast wilderness at the nick of time.

On that very night of 20th August, 1998 at Islamabad at around 10 PM, when General Karamat the Pakistan Army Chief was playing host to General Joseph Ralston the American Vice Chairman of the Joint Chiefs of Staff Committee, and the American General kept checking the time on his watch, it did seem something very unusual. And when he suddenly informed his host that soon some 60 American Tomahawk cruise missiles would be entering Pakistan airspace, it took General Karamat totally by surprise. The Pakistan army chief had no idea till then that those missiles were on their mission to destroy the four identified Osama Bin Laden's camps inside Afghanistan and on the Afghan-Pakistan border. It seems that the American General was not only cautioning the Pakistan army chief not to mistake them on the Pakistan radar screen for Indian missiles, but he was also directly sending a message to the Pakistani government that America would not tolerate any safe haven being given to the Al Qaida and their associates from across the border. Though taken aback by this sudden revelation, there was little that a stunned General Karamat could do at that moment. And with that began America's involvement in Afghanistan and war against Osama Bin Laden and his Al-Qaida.

Chapter-12

A World Caught In the Web

On 7th September, 1998 after the deadly cruise missile strikes on Khost that was carried out by the Americans on 20th August and while the CIA was still busy finding out whether they had got their man, the ever elusive Osama Bin Laden, in a small café in America two young Americans named Larry Page and Sergei Brin who had become close friends at Stanford University while studying for their respective doctorates were celebrating their new found global success.They had on that very day given to the world the magic word called 'Google'. That evening on hearing that new word from his father, Tojo looking a bit puzzled asked.

"But Abbu what is meant by 'To Google'. Is it by chance a new variation of the googly ball that is bowled in cricket, or is it just another American slang meaning to gargle."

"No my son, it is neither of the two, this 'Google' is going to be much more than just a bowling action or that of making bubbles in the mouth. It is a search engine that will soon with the click of the mouse on the computer revolutionize the world of learning. Hence the verb 'to google' means to search the web. And with this fascinating new tool that the two American whiz kids have invented, the world one day will literally be in your palms and I mean it literally," said Shiraz. Therefore on that very evening in order to ensure that his son learnt more about the world than just golf; Shiraz presented Tojo with his first laptop computer.

On 29th September, 1998 when the United States Congress passed the 'Iraq Liberation Act' that stated categorically that the United States wanted to remove President Saddam Hussein from power and replace the present Iraqi government with a democratic institution, simply because they suspected Iraq's capability to produce weapons of mass destruction, an angry Shiraz retaliated by saying.

"I don't know why Uncle Sam has to behave every time like the world's top cop. This will only further help Osama and those like him to intensify the already ongoing hate campaign against the Americans. I do agree that Saddam and his sons are also responsible for the misery that they have brought on to their own people, but Iraq is a sovereign independent country and only the Iraqis have the right to decide their own fate and future. This is jingoism at its worst and mind you America will have to pay very heavily for it, if they venture into another war against the Iraqi strongman who has been very cleverly playing into the sentiments of his own people, the radical Muslim militant groups like the Al Qaida, and especially those who are still Bil Laden's ardent supporters. Osama is not only accusing America for ruining Iraq's economy, but the U.S. also of trying to widen the divide between the Sunnis and Shias in what was once known as Mesopotamia," added Shiraz.

"May be Bill Clinton wants to divert attention from his affair with Monica that is hogging the limelight both in the American and International media? And now that the UNSCOM has still not found anything substantial as proof to nail Saddam down on the WMD front, Clinton is probably simply trying to save his own skin by blaming it all on Saddam,"commented Saira somewhat derisively.

In the month of October, while Clinton was still waiting to sign on the dotted line and make the 'Iraq liberation Act,' a full-fledged law, Salim Rehman with his family landed in New Delhi. The day happened to be 2nd October, Mahatma Gandhi's birthday and a public holiday in India. As he with Saira and 19 year old daughter Nadia and 14 year old son Shabir in the Pakistan Ambassador's Mercedes limousine with the Pakistani flag fluttering in the late autumn breeze made its way to the Pakistani Embassy at Chanakyapuri, young Shabir Rehman who ever since childhood had been told that India was a country of only Hindus who hated the Muslims was surprised to notice the many mosques in the Indian capital. As the car passed by another big mosque on the outer Ring Road he said.

"But Dad I think there are many Muslims here too, but are they Sunnis like us or are they Shias?'

"There are not only Sunnis and Shias in this country, but there are also a large number of Memons, Ismailis and Ahmediyas too. And with its huge population today, India has a very large number of Muslims also. It also has some Christians, Jews, Sikhs and Parsis, but all of them combined together are still considered to be part and parcel of the minority community in this country. And that is one and possibly the only reason why the BJP who have been promoting Hinduvta during their election campaign have now come to power," added Salim Rehman as the big black limousine got on to the beautifully maintained diplomatic enclave of New Delhi.The enclave, which was also known as Chanakyapuri was the most posh area of India's capital city and where most of the important foreign embassies were located including that of Pakistan. The well maintained locale with its beautifully manicured lawns and gardens on both sides of the broad avenue was the pride of the capital.

On 7th October, 1998 no sooner had Salim Rehman settled in his chair, when the news arrived that the Pakistan Army Chief, General Jehangir Karamat had put in his papers and General Pervez Musharraf had been appointed as the new army chief. It was supposedly a fall out from the remark that General Karamat had made two days ago about the need for the army to be given a key role in the country's decision making process. According to another reliable source, it all started during the Corps Commander's conference on 19th September, when Lt General Ali Quli Khan and Lt General Khalid Nawaz had allegedly and indirectly criticized Nawaz Sharif's autocratic and erratic style of governance and his inability to check the pathetic economic deterioration that was ruining the country. And as a result of this, when Nawaz Sharif nominated Lt General Perwez Musharaf to take over as the new chief, both Quli Khan and Khalid Nawaz, the two senior most Corps Commanders resigned in disgust. Lt General Ali Quli Khan was the senior most and a hot contender for the top slot and many felt that he had been wronged.Therefore in order to show his solidarity with the top brass, when Salim Rehman's cousin Lt Greneral Aslam Rehman Khan also submitted his resignation a few days later, it hardly mattered. Though he still had only another month and a half more of service to go before being officially superannuated, some intellectuals in Pakistan however felt that Nawaz Sharif by appointing Musharraf had perhaps acted a bit too hastily. There was no doubt that the army in Pakistan ever since the country got its independence always played a major role in the country's decision making process, and what General Karamat had expressed was only an opinion. It seems that the outgoing chief had only suggested for the establishment of a National Security Council that he felt should consist both civilian and military decision makers in order to tackle the many difficult issues facing the country, but this had annoyed the Prime Minister who asked for an explanation from him and that was that.

And on that 12th of October, 1998 after appointing General Musharraf as the new Army Chief, when the Prime Minister under his new powers simultaneously replaced Lt General Nasim Rana the head of the ISI with his own man, Lt General Ziauddin Ahmed Butt who was the Adjutant

General, and that to without consulting the new chief, that sudden move by Nawaz Sharif did not go down well with the army's top brass.Therefore to counter that move, General Musharraf immediately promoted his own man, the DDG ISI, Major General Mohammed Aziz as the Chief of General Staff. Lt Gen Aziz as DDG was in charge of Afghan affairs and that of the Harkat-ul-Mujaheedin who were being trained in camps in Afghanistan to undertake operations in Kashmir. The DGMI, the Director General Military Intelligence came directly under the CGS and Musharraf very wisely transferred the Afghan Bureau out of the purview of the ISI and placed it now under the DGMI.

The Americans too were now building up pressure on Pakistan and seeking their help to influence the Taliban to hand over Osama Bin Laden to them. There were also reports that the Saudi Intelligence Minister, Prince Turki-al-Fazal had only a few months ago met with the Taliban leader Mullah Omar and that some secret deal had been worked out to handover Bin Laden to Saudi Arabia. There was also an unconfirmed report that Lt General Nasim Rana was also present at that meeting, but after the deadly cruise missile attack by the Americans on 20th August, Mullah Omar it seems had changed his mind.

The sudden resignation of General Karamat and other very senior serving Pakistani officers and the reshuffling of important portfolios in the top echelons of the army also came as a big surprise to Shiraz. He was also aware that Nawaz Sharif was under tremendous pressure from the Bill Clinton government, but he it seems was now once again caught in a difficult Catch 22 like situation. The aim of appointing Lt General Ziauddin Butt as the head of the ISI by Nawaz Sharif was primarily to compel the Taliban to throw Bin Laden out of Afghanistan since his presence in that country was highly detrimental to Pakistan' interests. It was after all Pakistan that had created the Taliban and the Americans now wanted the full cooperation of the Pakistan ISI and the I.B. They wanted that both the Pakistani intelligence agencies in close cooperation with the FBI and the CIA must capture Osama alive from his hideout in Afghanistan and then have him flown to the US in Kansi style to stand trial for the two African embassy bombings. And failing which the US would keep delaying the lifting of the sanctions that was now economically and militarily bleeding Pakistan to death. But Osama was now a God like figure not only to the Pashtuns of Afghanistan, but also to those in Pakistan, and Mullah Omar too had given him a cult like status. Both the Taliban and Osama's Al-Qaida were now on the road to becoming powerful Frankenstein's and Nawaz Sharif was now in a dilemma on how to rein the two in. Besides having his own man heading the ISI, Nawaz Sharif also appointed Colonel Iqbal Niazi, a retired army officer who was the Principal staff Officer in the Prime Minister's Secretariat as the Additional Director General of the Intelligence Bureau.

"Well now that we have another Mohajir like the late Zia-ul-Haq as the army big boss, do you think he too will play mischief if the Prime Minister keeps humiliating the big guns in the armed forces," said Saira as Shiraz explained to her as to how and why General Karamat decided to put in his papers.

"On 5th October, 1998 in a speech at the Navy War College the General had said that Pakistan could not afford anymore political unrest or the destabilizing effect of polarization, vendettas, and insecurity driven expedient policies. He also stated that the political mandate given by the people had to be translated into Institutional strength or else the country would have a permanent election campaign environment in the country and he therefore proposed the setting up of a National Security Council to act as an umpire and a supreme arbitrator over the nation's affairs. And I think he simply spoke his mind and I personally do not find anything wrong with it. But our politicians felt that it would be a supra-constitutional measure and Nawaz Sharif thought it was a scathing attack on his government," added Shiraz as he poured another small whisky into his glass and gave a short resume of the new army chief General Pervez.

"Yes he is a Mohajir no doubt and that too from Old Delhi and his service profile is also fairly impressive. The General was commissioned into the regiment of artillery in 1964 and as a subaltern saw action in 1965 in the Khemkaran, Lahore and the Sialkot Sectors. On 28th December 1968, he married Sehba. They were blessed with a daughter on 18th February, 1970 whom they named Ayela and on 17th October 1971was born their only son whom they named Bilal in memory of Musharraf's best friend Captain Bilal who while serving with the SSG in Bangladesh and erstwhile East Pakistan was killed during the operations. During the 1971 operation Musharraf too as Captain had served in the SSG. As a Lt Colonel he commanded two self propelled artillery regiments and later commanded the artillery brigade of an armoured division and the 25 Infantry Brigade at Bhawalpur. After attending the National Defence College and the Royal College of Defence Studies in London, he took over as GOC 40 Infantry Division at Okara and later served as Director Military Operations.During his tenure as the DGMO, he conducted two important GHQ level exercises. 'Exercise Tri Star' at the tri service level was primarily conducted to give the senior service officers and select civilians in the planning and conduct of joint military operations, while 'Exercise Zarb-e-Mujahid' was conducted to test the concept of establishing a Field Army HQ and to work out modalities of quickly deploying a number of division size formations to their operational locations. In 1995, Musharraf was promoted to Lt General and commanded the strike corps at Mangla and today he is the Chief. He never expected to become the chief though and considers himself to be very lucky indeed. He was Nawaz Sharif's choice and was third in overall seniority. Lt General Quli Khan was his course mate and the sword of honour winner from the 29th PMA course and in spite of being the senior most, he was quietly sidelined. Musharraf I am told is also fond of military history and loves his golf too. And as regards to your query whether the new chief might play mischief if Nawaz Sharif who has a brute majority in the assembly tries to interfere in the postings and promotions of senior officers then my answer to that is Musharraf will not take things lying down either and that's for sure. As it is he was very upset, when the Prime Minister without consulting him appointed Lt General Ziauddin Butt as DG ISI," said Shiraz.

Soon after taking over as COAS, General Musharraf's first visit to a field formation was in the high altitude area of the NLI, the Northern Light Infantry and the Siachen Glacier in Kashmir. That was on the 21st of October. 1998 and when during his address to the troops he spelt out that despite the induction of armour and other heavy weapons into the Kashmir valley by the Indian army, the Indian soldiers were finding it very difficult to curb the heroic freedom struggle of the Kashmiris, it indicated to Shiraz that 'Operation Tupac' would probably now be given a bigger boost. And when this was further substantiated by the 'Dawn' of Karachi' on 8th November and some other Urdu papers of Pakistan that the Taliban had set up 28 secret training camps for training volunteers for fighting against the Indian army in Kashmir, and that 1,350 volunteers were already under training, that was reason enough for Shiraz to recheck the authenticity of these news reports. The news papers also quoted one Maulana Mohammed Qasim, who described himself as a leader of the 'Lashkar Hyder', a new organization and who had vowed to take the battle to a new level in Kashmir. Putting two and two together, Shiraz was therefore apprehensive that this trained mercenary force may well be the precursor to a major operation in Kashmir and that to in the not too distant future. He also knew that Musharraf having commanded troops in Siachen was upset when the Indians had recaptured the Quaid Post, and being the outdoor adventurous commando type, he was therefore quite capable of undertaking a clandestine operation of this nature in the name of Kashmir freedom fighters in that high altitude desolate region and where it would be least expected by the Indians. While he made a note of this in his little red diary, the BBC news channel announced that an Indian economist had won the coveted Nobel Prize.

Chapter-13

To Lahore and Back

Born on 3rd November, 1933 in Shantiniketan he was named Amartya, meaning the 'immortal one' by none other than Rabindranath Tagore, the bard and poet who was the first Indian to win the Nobel Prize. Sen's ancestral home was in Wari, Dhaka and Amartya started his college education from Presidency College Calcutta and later moved to Trinity College, Cambridge and from where he did his doctorate with flying colours. At the age of 23, he was appointed Professor and taught economics at Jadavpur University. And by the time he was 30, he became a visiting Professor at the prestigious Massachusetts Institute of Technology in Boston. Later he also taught at the London School of Economics and at Harvard. By virtue of his work on poverty index, famines, and in eonomic sciences, he became the sixth Indian to be awarded the coveted Nobel Prize.

Meanwhile in Bangladesh on that same 8th of November, while the newspaper Dawn of Pakistan covered the story of the Taliban setting ups secret training camps to fight for Kashmir, Kazi Gulam Rasul, a Judge of the District and Sessions Court at Dhaka gave his verdict and declared that all the 15 officers who killed Mujibur Rehman and his family would be shot to death by a firing squad in public. Sheikh Hasina the daughter of the slain leader and others who revered the father of the nation no doubt felt vindicated by that verdict, but the saddest part was that only three of those officers, Lt Colonel Syed Farook Rehman, Lt Colonel Sultan Shariar Rashid Khan and Lt Colonel Mohiuddin Khan were present in the court that day, while the rest were sentenced in absentia because most of them were still in hiding abroad. Soon after the verdict, Sheikh Hasina went to her late parent's house in Dhanmondi, which was now a national museum and Fazal Rehman who also happened to be there with a visiting foreign delegation from Japan felt rather sorry for the poor lady who was orphaned on India's independence day 23 years ago.

Lt Colonel Farook Rehman, who had masterminded the coup d'etat on 15th August, 1975 had finally run out of luck. Two hours later Major Bazlul Huda's luck also ran out as the Bangladesh air force plane from Bangkok landed at Dhaka. Following his extradition from Thailand, he had been handed over to the Bangladesh authorities.

As the year 1998 came to a close, there were war clouds again gathering in the Middle East. On 31st October, when a defiant Saddam Hussein in response to America's 'Iraq Liberation Act' announced that Iraq would no longer cooperate with the United Nations weapon inspectors, it gave America and her allies the one and only excuse that they were looking for to topple the Iraqi strong man by force. In mid November, when the American President Bill Clinton ordered air strikes on Iraq, and Saddam very cleverly agreed to unconditionally cooperate with the UNSCOM, and which resulted in the American air strikes being called off at the last minute, Shiraz in Moscow who was monitoring all these developments very closely breathed a sigh of relief. But a few days later on 20th November, when a court in Taliban controlled Afghanistan declared the accused Osama Bin Laden was a man without a sin as far as the embassy bombings in Kenya and Nairobi were concerned, Shiraz realized that Pakistan now had no other option but to deny that the Taliban was their own creation.

"I think we have messed up the whole issue. In the early 1980's, when the Russians occupied Afghanistan, it was we who actively collaborated with America to help the Afghans oust the Russians from Afghanistan and mind you Bill Laden had contributed very generously with money, material and also man-power to achieve that goal. And today he is America's most wanted man and we are being pressurized to get him out from Afghanistan and hand him over to the damn Americans." said an angry Shiraz as he read the confidential policy letter on the subject that was issued by the Ministry of Foreign Affairs in Islamabad.

"But please do not mind my saying so, but the Americans have always treated us like a' Rhakel,' a mistress of convenience and they have been using us as and when required, and once they are satisfied, they simply dump us back into the gutters. It all started during Ayub's time, when Pakistan joined CENTO and SEATO and the Americans in order to spy over Russia used Peshawar as a base to fly their U2 spy aircrafts. Later when Yahya took over, the Nixon administration used us as their broker and courier so that they could become friends with China. And when we were badly cornered in Bangladesh, all that the Americans did was to first pay a little lip service to our request for help and in order to please us they simply carried out a maritime exercise by moving their Seventh fleet into the Bay of Bengal and nothing more. And later, when General Zia-ul-Haq, the Mullah General took over the country, they used us very cleverly to fight their proxy war against the Soviet Union in Afghanistan. And once that was over, we were once again forgotten. And now they are trying to use us again to fight their dirty war against terror," said an equally upset Ruksana Begum who with her husband Arif Rehman did a short twenty four hour stopover at Moscow, while they were on their way to London. Arif Rehman had suffered a sudden black out recently and he wanted to consult a renowned Harley Street cardiologist.

Meanwhile in the US, during that month of December, the Lewinsky affair once again took centre stage as the House Judiciary Committee began its impeachment hearings against President Clinton. On 16th December 1998, exactly a day before the full House was to vote on the four articles of impeachment, Clinton launched renewed air strikes against Iraq. And on 19th December, when the full House approved two out of the four articles accusing the President for perjury and obstruction of justice, history was created and Clinton thus became the first elected President of the United States to be impeached. However, the Senate trial to remove the President from office was yet to begin.

The four day massive bombing of Iraq code-named 'Operation Desert Fox' that was carried out from 16th to 19th December 1998 on the orders of President Clinton only added more fuel to the Iraqi disarmament crisis. On 31st October, the President had signed into law H.R. 4655. It was also known as the Iraq Liberation Act. The Act appropriated massive funds to Iraqi opposition groups in the hope of toppling Saddam Hussein and replacing his dictatorial regime with a democratic one. Strangely the dates for carrying out the bombings coincided with the dates of the impeachment hearings against the American President, and Shiraz wondered whether both Saddam and Clinton would soon be stripped of their powers. There was no doubt that the Monica Lewinsky episode had the House Judiciary Committee literally holding the American President by his balls, but for Mr. Clinton to order the massive cruise missile attack on Iraq, while the United Nations Security Council was still debating the veracity of the two reports that had been submitted by the IAEA and UNSCOM was nothing less than xenophobia and chauvinism, thought Shiraz. According to his information, both these reports by the respective weapon inspectors were tabled on the 15th and were still being discussed on the 16th by the Security Council, when the deadly bombs started raining on Iraq. And whereas

Mr Mohammed El Baradei, the Chairman of the International Atomic Energy Commission (IAEA) in his letter had categorically stated that Iraq had provided the necessary level of cooperation, Mr Richard Butler on the other hand in his UNSCOM report had stated that not only was there a lack of full cooperation, but there was also a lack of disclosure and efforts at concealment by the Iraqi authorities. Since both the reports were contradictory in nature and was still being debated by the members of the Security Council, Shiraz felt that the air attack both by the US and Britain was totally uncalled for.

As the new year of 1999 began, there was a welcome thaw in the Indo-Pak relationship. This was consequent to the 23rd September, 1998 meeting between Nawaz Sharif and Vajpayee during the annual United Nations General Assembly meet in New York and where both the prime ministers expressed their earnest desire for peace and harmony in the subcontinent. With both countries having realized the strength and the danger of having nuclear weapons of mass destruction in their respective arsenals, they therefore decided to offer one another the hand of peace and friendship.

"Thank God that at last some sense has gone into the heads of the politicians on both sides, and I sincerely hope that Nawaz Sharif's initiative to extend an invitation to the Indian Prime Minister to visit Lahore by road in February will yield some positive results," said Saira.

"Hopefully yes, but I still have my doubts. Nonetheless it was a statesman like gesture by our Prime Minister and I hope he has the backing of the men in uniform and of the Kashmiris who are on both sides of the line of control. Because all said and done Kashmir still remains the core issue and with a mutual give and take, and if both sides agree to a well delineated international border, then only a proper road map could be drawn and cooperation on all other bilateral issues like trade, commerce etc could then follow," said Shiraz as Bill Clinton's looking happy appeared on the CNN channel. He had been spared the ignominy from being removed from office because neither of the articles could get a simple majority during the Senate trial.

On 26th January, 1999 though it was a holiday for the Indian Embassy, Shiraz rang up the Indian Ambassador and congratulated her on India's Republic Day. That very evening, when he met her at the 'At Home' that was being hosted by Shupriya and told her that Pakistan was eagerly looking forward to Prime Minister Vajpayee's visit to Lahore and that the people of

Pakistan were waiting to give him a rousing welcome, Shupriya smiled at him and said.

"Yes and If both sides have the will then the same bus service could be further extended northwards towards Gilgit and southwards right down to Kanyakumari also.We have always been a peace loving country and we genuinely want friendly relations with all our neighbours."

"'So do all of us,' said Saira while congratulating the Indian Ambassador on the beautiful peacock blue Benarasi silk saree that she was wearing for the occasion. At one moment of time Shiraz wanted to find out if it was also her birthday that day, but seeing the people crowding around her, he thought it would be very undiplomatic and therefore gave up the idea.

That evening after the party, the Indian Ambassador's maiden name Yeshwant Kaur and her surname Bajwa also kept playing on Shiraz's mind. Moreover her fluent Bengali while she was talking to the Bangladeshi Ambassador was also quite intriguing. At the same time Shiraz also felt as to how a person who died 28 years ago could still be alive. Yes the possibility of rebirth and reincarnation was always there and maybe soon after her death she was probably born in a Bajwa family from Calcutta, but then she would now be just 26 or 27 years old and here was this lady who was probably nearing her fifties thought Shiraz as he helped himself to a neat cognac and dozed off to sleep.

While India and Pakistan looked forward to the start of the bus diplomacy between the two countries, on 8th February, 1999 India's 'Thinking General' Sundarjee at the age of 69 died at the army hospital in New Delhi. On 10th February, as the General's body on a gun carriage followed by a funeral cortege of over a hundred vehicles slowly made its way from 6, Baird Place to the Brar Square crematorium in Delhi Cantonment, Shiraz who had tuned in to listen to the All India Radio live broadcast of the funeral service was reminded of his days as a young captain in the Indian army when he while courting Shupriya used to very frequently visit the many lovely gardens and parks in the neat and well laid out cantonment of India's capital city. As the twelve year old General's grandson lit the funeral pyre, far away in Rawalpindi, General Musharraf, the Pakistan army chief was giving his final touches to his ingenious plan that would soon light the skies over the mighty Himalayas.

The 20th of February, 1999, was a red letter day for both Pakistan and India as the Indian Prime Minister with his entourage in the bus for peace crossed the Wagah border to a tumultuous welcome by Nawaz Sharif and the people of Pakistan. When the television cameras of the world media zoomed in on to the two leaders as they warmly shook hands and embraced one another with a big smile, Shiraz who with his family was watching it alive on TV much to the delight of Saira and daughter Sherry sang 'Ye Dosti Hum Nahin Thodhenge.' It was the hit song from the 1975 Indian block buster film 'Sholay.

"But the word 'Sholay' I am told also means a spark and I only hope this spark lights up the candle of peace and not the guns on both sides," said Saira in jest as she noticed the popular Indian actor Dev Anand alighting from the bus. And as the camera zoomed away from the evergreen film hero to the cheering Pakistani crowd, an observant Saira remarked.

"But have you noticed that the military top brass of Pakistan are nowhere to be seen, and I wonder why. I hope they are not annoyed with the Prime Minister's initiative to mend fences with India?"'

Unknown to Shiraz and Saira and to the high powered members of the Indian delegation who were being feted and entertained lavishly that day, General Musharraf it seems was busy with his own secret and private agenda. And while the talks for peace and progress by the two political leaders were still being evolved, the Pakistan army chief had already finalized his plans to set in motion 'Operation Badr.' It was to be a covert military operation across the line of control in the Kargil Sector of Jammu and Kashmir.

On 21st February, after both the leaders had signed the historic Lahore Declaration, which categorically stated that besides intensifying the efforts by both countries to resolve all issues, including that of Jammu and Kashmir amicably, the two sides would also reduce the risk of accidental or unauthorized use of nuclear weapons, Shiraz felt that a good beginning had been made and hoped that the guns would now remain silent forever. But it was not to be so.

Chapter-14

War Clouds Over Kashmir Again

No sooner had Vajpayee reached Delhi and the world leaders applauded the historic declaration, Pakistani troops from the SSG the Special Service Group in mufti, paramilitary forces from the Northern Light Infantry and irregulars from Islamist groups like the Lashkar-e-Toiba and Harkat-ul-Mujahideen were getting ready to give the Indian army and its people a real big surprise. According to one reliable source, the new Pakistani army chief shortly after having taken over charge had convinced the government the need to construct bomb proof bunkers all along the (LOC) the Line of Control and the Nawaz Sharif government had already sanctioned Rs 7.6 million for the construction of such solid underground shelters in the first phase to the LOC in the Northern Areas of Gilgit and Baltistan. But according to the threat perception by the Pakistan army top brass, this area was always given low priority and Shiraz wondered what could be the reason for the Northern Areas now being given more importance. Shiraz was also aware that General Musharraf had accompanied Nawaz Sharif on a visit to Siachen on 29th January, 1999 and at a press conference had also reiterated that there was zero chance of a war with India and he had further added that he was not talking about winning a war because to him winning a battle meant winning Kashmir. Putting two and two together, and with more road development activity being undertaken in that desolate area, Shiraz was now apprehensive that Pakistan may well in future develop clandestine operations from that thinly held Indian sector.

Shiraz was also aware that India had pumped in a lot more forces not only to tackle the growing ISI sponsored insurgency inside the valley, but it had also sealed most of the existing entry points along the LOC leading to the valley. Moreover, the deployment of Indian troops and the Pakistanis along the LOC in the Northern Area was always generally very thin on the ground and with very large gaps existing between the various defensive positions on the Indian side; it was therefore highly vulnerable to infiltration. Consequently, Shiraz was also of the view that though this was a low priority sector, but in future it may well be used as a point of ingress and major infiltration by the ISI trained Pakistani Mujahideens into the Kashmir valley.

Taking the historic Lahore Declaration as a good excuse, Shiraz rang up the Indian Ambassador on the very next day and requested if he could call on her officially at any time during the coming week in order to discuss certain issues informally. Since these were issues that could mutually benefit both the countries in the long run, therefore to begin with Shiraz suggested that an Indo-Pak friendship society should be set up in the two big cities of Moscow and St Petersburg. Both these big metropolitan hubs had a fairly large number of students and people from the Indian and Pakistan business communities and by setting up such a society it would give them an opportunity not only to interact more freely with one another, but it would also add to a good confidence building measure. Subsequently cultural evenings and friendly games like cricket, hockey, kabaddi, badminton, table tennis and football etc could also be introduced and these would also help in creating mutual trust and understanding between the peoples of the two nations that history had so cruelly separated them. It would also help those who felt homesick at times to feel more at home in each other's company. However, all these confidence building measures of course were subject to getting a final approval from their respective governments. But for Shiraz the real reason to have an informal tete-a-tete with the Indian Ambassador was to find out a little more about the lady and her family background. Yeshwant Bajwa's striking resemblance to Shupriya and especially her hand writing and fluency in the Bengali language was still bugging him.

The meeting was fixed for the 8th of March at 11 A.M. That day also happened to be the 'International Woman's Day' and very thoughtfully Shiraz arrived at the Indian Embassy dot on time with a beautiful bouquet of 34 red roses.

"But why 34 and not 30 or 40," asked Shupriya as she received the visiting ambassador outside her office.

"I know it is an unusual number, but it was way back in 1965, thirty four years ago that the then erstwhile Soviet Union had declared the day as a national holiday and it was in honour of those women who sacrificed their lives and contributed so much in the war against Hitler and Nazi Germany. And not only that Madame Ambassador, it was also on the 8th of March,1857 while India with patriots like Mangal Pandey, a Hindu foot soldier at Barrackpur near Calcutta was preparing to throw the British out of India, the last Moghul Emperor, Bahadur Shah Zafar on that very day many years ago had pitched in with his Moghul army to join the freedom struggle," added Shiraz as Shupriya directed her personal assistant to send in the tea, coffee and biscuits for the guest.

"Well, to begin with, I must admit that though the Lahore declaration has sparked off an unprecedented euphoria of goodwill and understanding by the moderates on both sides and hopefully one that could eventually lead to a much desired lasting peace in the troubled subcontinent, but do you think that the radicals like the Jamait-i-Islami and others like them in Pakistan who had vehemently protested against Mr Vajpayee's visit will allow that to happen," asked Shupriya as Shiraz added one more cube of sugar to his black coffee.

"But your Prime Minister had also very rightly said that we must put aside the bitterness of the past and together make a new beginning and I therefore personally feel that the only way of achieving this would be by placing more trust in one another. And if we have to achieve that aim then the best way to do it would be by promoting more interaction at the grass root level and which consequently would I am sure promote genuine goodwill between the two sides," said Shiraz.

"Yes, I too feel that it is high time that both India and Pakistan looked at each other as true friends and not as bitter enemies. But both sides must first curb and stop the half baked religious fanatics who in the name of Ram and Allah keep spreading hatred on both sides of the border," said Shupriya.

"Undoubtedly so, but for that we have to first educate our illiterate masses by giving them an opportunity to become literate and that can only be done if both the governments genuinely promote at the grass root level a proactive educational policy. And failing which I am afraid the so called radical Mullas and Pundits will keep taking our ignorant and uneducated masses for a ride," said Shiraz while proposing a common cultural evening program at a neutral venue in Moscow as part of the forthcoming 'Baisaki Day' celebrations that was due on the 13th of April.

"Not a bad idea at all, but to begin with I think it would be better if the student community from both the countries studying in Moscow and Lumumba universities join hands and informally take this social event as a common venture," said Shupriya as she thanked the Pakistani Ambassador for his visit.

Having realized that this being his very first official visit it would have been very stupid of him to ask the lady any personal questions, Shiraz therefore decided to keep them for some other informal opportune moment.

Following his informal meeting with the Indian Ambassador on 8th March, Shiraz was surprised to read a confidential report that was sent by Islamabad. The report stated that at a press conference held at Muzzafarabad in Pakistan Occupied Kashmir on 2nd March1999, Zafar Iqbal of the Lashkar-e-Toiba, the militant wing of the radical Markaz Dawa Al Irshad had categorically stated that he had personally invited Osama Bin Laden who had been asked by Taliban to leave Afghanistan to join in the freedom struggle against the Indian army in Kashmir, and that his organization would welcome Bin Laden with open arms if he decided to do so. According to his source of information in Islamabad, Shiraz also came to know that General Musharraf had called on the Prime Minister on 12th March, 1999 to discuss the security situation and this was followed later on that same very day with a visit by Mr Sharif to the headquarters of the ISI for discussion with the DGISI on the same subject. The Pakistani army chief it seems was of the opinion that as far as the Lahore Declaration was concerned, the Kashmir problem should in no case be linked to other issues, and during the discussion with the ISI officers, Mr Sharif had assured them that despite the Lahore Declaration, his government would continue to provide political and moral support to the Kashmiris.

A fortnight later on 2nd April 1999, when the Prime Minister visited the Pakistan GHQ for detailed discussions with the army chief and the top brass that lasted for a good eight hours, and which finally resulted in the proposed reorganization of the (JCSC) Joint Chiefs of Staff Committee, and the setting up of a nuclear command and control authority, it was evident to Shiraz that the hawks in the army led by General Musharraf were not too happy with the overtures that were being made by the the Nawaz Sharif government to placate India. Shiraz had also heard that some secret talks to resolve the Kashmir imbroglio was also being held by Niaz Naik a personal representative of Nawaz Sharif with BK Mishra, who was a close confidante of Mr Vajpayee.But what was still more worrying to Shiraz were the belligerent noises that were being openly made by some of the radical militant groups in Pakistan. On 9th April, in an interview to the newspaper "The Nation" from Muzzafarabad, Zaikur Rehman Lakhvi the so called Amir of the Lashkar-e-Toiba had openly declared.

'We are extending our network in India and we have already carried out attacks on some Indian installations successfully last year. But now we will set up Mujahideen networks across India and prepare the Muslims of India to join in our struggle. Our Lashkar volunteers in Kashmir have been successfully targeting the Indian army and we will continue to do so till our aim of liberating Kashmir is fully achieved.'

Meanwhile the ballistic missile race between India and Pakistan had also got off to a fresh start, when on 11th April, India successfully launched Agni-II from a new launching site at Wheeler Island in Orissa. The IRBM, Intermediate range ballistic missile capable of carrying both conventional and nuclear warheads had a range of 2,200 kilometers and with its solid propulsion system it could be launched also from a mobile launcher.

To warn India that they were not lagging behind in missile technology and trajectory, Pakistan too on 14th April successfully tested their two stage Gauri-2 rocket from the Tilla Firing Range near Jhelum. The Pakistani IRBM also had a similar range and when Pakistan followed it up on the very next day with the launch of a 600 km range Shaheen surface to surface short range ballistic missile, both the American administration and the United Nations Secretary General Kofi Annan seemed quite upset with the developments in the Indian subcontinent. They felt that the current arms race was completely out of step with the recent political developments between India and Pakistan and the Lahore Declaration. And on that same very day of 15th April 1999, while Pakistan hailed the successful launch of the Shaheen missile from the Sonmiani base near Karachi, the Ehtesab Bench of the Lahore High Court convicted Benazir Bhutto and her husband Asif Ali Zardari on corruption charges and sentenced each one of them to undergo five years imprisonment and to pay a fine of 8.6 million US dollars. The court also ordered their disqualification as members of parliament, as well as confiscation of their property. When that news made headlines in the Pakistani press, Ruksana Begum it seems was not too happy with that verdict.

"I think the corrupt husband-wife duo who had squeezed the country to the last drop by making more than a billion have been left off rather lightly. For their shameless indulgence in emptying the coffers of the nation at the cost of the poor masses of Pakistan, they if you ask me deserve to be shot in public, if not hanged from the nearest lamp post," said an angry Ruksana as her husband Arif Rehman helped himself to another small whisky.

"But take it from me Begum Sahiba and knowing the way how corruption has permeated in all walks of our life and society including the judiciary, the duo I am sure will appeal against the verdict and the case will carry on and on till the cows come home," added Arif Rehman in disgust as the telephone rang. It was a call from his daughter Saira in Moscow giving the happy news that she with her husband and family would be coming home in early May on a month's home leave and thanks to her cousin Lt General Aslam Rehman (retired) they were all planning for a grand family outing and get together on the banks of the mighty River Indus in Northern Kashmir.

Though the historic Lahore Declaration was still fresh on the minds of the people of both India and Pakistan, and serious hush-hush efforts were being made in secret by Niaz Naik and BK Mishra to find a genuine and lasting solution to the Kashmir problem that would be acceptable to both the sides, in that month of April far away in Northern Kashmir, the Pakistani military high command had already launched 'Operation Badr' in right earnest. And not only that, on 20^{h} April, Mr P Ravindranathan an attaché in the Indian Mission in Islamabad was also brutally beaten up by three Pakistanis. The incident took place at Lahore where Ravindranthan was on liaison duty with a group of Sikh pilgrims from India who were on a visit to the Gurudwara Dera Sahib. As a result of this the Pakistani Deputy High Commisioner in India was called to the External affairs Ministry and a strong protest note was handed over to him. And though Pakistan conveyed its deep regret and assured the Indian High Commissioner Mr G Parthasarathy that the matter would be thoroughly investigated, Monty's son-in-law Paddy who was posted in Islamabad however felt that this was a clear indication that not everybody and certainly not the fundamentalists in Pakistan were happy with the Lahore Declaration.

At the same time in India, with the AIDMK chief Jayalalitha threatening to withdraw support to the BJP led NDA government, it looked that Vajpayee's days were once again numbered. The rumblings within the Congress too had started surfacing more openly after Sonia Gandhi was elected as Congress President in 1998 and it now gained further momentum when a group of senior party leaders started questioning her foreign Italian background. When a few senior party members like Sharad Pawar, PA Sangma and Tariq Anwar challenged her right to lead the party and her future aspirations to become India's Prime Minister, the lady had even offered to resign, but the majority wanted her to continue. After all to them the Gandhi surname was equal to ten Pawars, Sangmas and Anwars put together. And the matter got further complicated after the AIDMK withdrew support to the Vajpayee led coalition government and the President of India KR Narayanan also gave his sanction to prosecute the former External Affairs Minister, Madhav Solanki for obstructing the probe in the Bofors payoff case.

With strong rumours in the air that the Congress led Sonia Gandhi would soon topple the Vajpayee led government, the two important cases that were directly related to Bofors scandal and which were still pending with the Prime Minister's Office were suddenly activated. The first case pertained to the prosecution of Gopi Arora, SK Bhatnagar, Win Chaddha and Quattrocchi in the Rs 64 crore kickback cases, while the second pertained to Madhav Solanki for obstructing the probe. Solanki on an official visit to Switzerland in 1992 had delivered a letter by hand to his Swiss counterpart, and in which he categorically requested the Swiss authorities to go slow on the Bofors investigation. Wanting to find out a little more in detail on what would be the final outcome of the ongoing and never ending mudslinging between the BJP and the Congress on the Bofors issue, Monty once again called on his old friend Unni at the Press Club of India.

"Take it from me my friend that though Sonia Gandhi wanted to resign as the party president following the rift within the Congress because of her foreign Italian blood, but her departure would have ruined the political aspirations of those who always toed the Gandhi family line. And mind you the Gandhi name is still very much a vote catcher and the party simply cannot afford to kill the goose that lays the golden egg. And with the Vajpayee government having fired the next salvo to once again rake up the Bofors scandal, all that will happen is that Sonia and her coterie within the Congress will ensure the fall of the Vajpayee government and it will lead to another general election in the country. And the 'Aam Aadmi' of this poor country will keep on singing,';Goosey Goosey Gander, where shall I wander,' said Unni very confidently.

And no sooner had Unni finished his brief summing up of the current political situation in the country, when the news arrived that the Vajpayee government had fallen and it had been reduced to a caretaker status, pending fresh elections in October.

Chapter-15

Back Stabbed Once Again

Early during that month of May, 1999, while the political battle in India between the BJP and the Congress gathered momentum, and the rift within the Congress on the issue of Sonia's Italian blood further divided the party, in Pakistan a small group of ambitious army generals led by their own chief watched with glee as their well trained large infiltration force in small groups of thirty and forty having cleverly, clandestinely, covertly and surreptitiously crossed the LOC, the Line of Control in the Kargil and Batalik Sectors occupied the many posts that the Indian army had vacated during winter in the Muskoh, Dras, Kargil, and the Batalik Sectors in Northern Kashmir. The well planned and brilliantly executed large scale intrusions into this thinly held Indian defensive sector had been carrying on for the past two months and probably even more, but the Indians were blissfully unaware of it. The Pakistanis it seems had very cleverly violated what was always regarded as a gentlemen's agreement between the two sides and had taken full advantage of the sense of complacency and goodwill that had set in among the Indians after the Lahore Declaration. It was an unwritten understanding that troops from both sides would not occupy the snowbound high altitude features in their respective sectors during the harsh winter months that lasted from mid September to mid April, and this was being strictly observed ever since the LOC in that sector was delineated in 1972.

But it seems that both the 121 Infantry Brigade Group of the Indian army that was responsible for the defence of that vital long 150 kilometer sector, and the Indian intelligence sleuths who were responsible to provide tactical and battlefield intelligence had been caught napping. And it was only on 3rd May, 1999 after two local shepherds Tashi Namgyal and Tsering Morup having noticed the presence of some men with long beards, dressed in black salwar kameez and wearing white snow jackets on a ridge in the Kaksar-Batalik area reported the matter to the army authorities at Kargil, that led to the wake up call for the Indians. With that vital input from the two locals, the long winter slumber of the 121 Infantry Brigade Group led by Brigadier Surinder Singh was rudely awakened. The very existence of well armed Pakistanis sitting pretty on the Indian posts and defensive positions that were widely stretched all along the long brigade defended sector was totally beyond the comprehension of the Indian army higher commanders who were responsible for the sanctity of the LOC in that area.

The 121 Independent Brigade Group of the Indian army with its headquarters at Kargil had four infantry battalions and one BSF,(Border Security Force) Battalion to guard the entire sector. On learning about the intrusion in the Kaksar-Batalik sub-sector, a small recce patrol led by the young Lieutenant Saurav Kalia from the 4th Battalion of the Jat Regiment was sent out on 6th May to check and report on the intrusion. But when those six, including their leader went missing and more patrols were dispatched on subsequent days to look for them, and they were fired upon by the Pakistanis, only then did the Brigade realize that the LOC had been grossly violated. There was no doubt that the Pakistani infiltrators were holding the heights on what was clearly Indian territory, but that too did not ring any alarm bell on those who were responsible for the defense and sanctity of that area. And it was only on 9th May, 1999 after the Pakistani artillery blew up the Indian army underground ammunition dump at Kargil that everybody woke up to the grim realities of the situation. The Pakistanis had not only occupied the heights across the LOC in that sub-sector, but in all the other adjacent sub-sectors also

It was also during that second week of May that the entire Rehman clan including Shiraz with his family who had arrived from Moscow on a month's home leave were all enjoying their long weekend at Murree. But on the next day, when they were getting ready to depart by road for Skardu via Gilgit and they were suddenly told that for reasons unknown all vehicular traffic except that of the military to Gilgit and beyond had been suspended till further orders, they were taken completely by surprise

"I hope it is not a fall out of the ham handed manner in which the ISI arrested Najam Sethi, Editor of the Friday Times two days ago from his own very house. The poor man I am told was later taken for interrogation by the ISI for his alleged links with the Indian RAW, but the manner in which it was done was rather shameful and shocking. Not only was he dragged out of his room and beaten, but his wife Jugnoo's hands too were tied, and she was locked up in her dressing room," said Salim Rehman's wife Aasma.

"That my dear I think is rather farfetched and with the civil authorities now confirming that the Northern Areas have also been put under army rule, there is probably more to it than meets the eye," added Salim Rehman.

"But all the same this has ruined our trip to Gilgit and Skardu and our stay at the 'Shalimar' on the banks of the River Indus that everyone of us was eagerly looking forward too,"said Shiraz. He had planned to celebrate his daughter Sherry's 21st birthday on the 6th of June with some spectacular fireworks and a sumptuous family dinner on board a specially decorated barge on the River Indus, and he felt sorry that it had to be cancelled now at the last minute. Retired Lt General Aslam Rehman had even arranged for a local song and dance troupe from Gilgit to perform for them on a floating raft.

On that morning of Sunday 9th May, while the artillery barrage that the Pakistanis had unleashed on Kargil had the locals running helter skelter for cover, Monty had landed at Srinagar to inspect the consignment of carpets, shawls and woolen scarves that were to be exported to Germany.

Unaware to the locals in the valley of what was happening at Kargil, it was business as usual in Srinagar that day. But two days later, when large groups of locals from Kargil and Drass kept arriving at Srinagar, and there were more rumours that a warlike situation was developing in that area and that Pakistani jihadis/infiltrators having crossed the LOC at a number of places had occupied a large number of Indian posts that had been vacated during the long winter months, Monty simply refused to believe it.

Infiltration by small Pakistani Mujahideen groups with the backup of artillery fire through the large porous gaps across the LOC was a routine affair and the locals of that area who are mostly Shias must be exaggerating thought Monty as he rejected one particular consignment of carpets that on inspection were found to be slightly defective.

"Please do ensure that the consignment is exactly as per the laid down specifications that were given to you both in size, colour, design and as per the required knots per square inch and I will again come back a month later in mid June to collect them,"said Monty as he settled the old outstanding bill with the supplier.

Two days later on 13th May, when Monty was on his way from Srinagar to Ganderbal to collect the 'Shatoosh' and 'Pashmina' shawls from his supplier there, his private hired car was stopped by the Indian military and civil police at a check point that had been recently established on the outskirts of Srinagar city and on the National Highway 1 A. This was the only vital strategic road that connected Leh to Srinagar via Sonamarg, Baltal,

Zoji La Pass, Drass and Kargil. Surprisingly and luckily the pass had been opened for traffic only a couple of days earlier and the Indian army it seems had already started sending reinforcements into the affected sector. he vital mountain pass at Zojila normally opens for traffic in late May or early June, but the God of nature it seemed had come to the rescue of the Indian army at the nick of time. Noticing the formation sign of the 8 Infantry Division on a convoy of olive green military vehicles that had lined the road, Monty was now convinced that everything was not all that hunky-dory as was being made out to be by a group of young officers who proudly said they were only waiting to get at the throats of the Pakistanis who had intruded into that cold desolate area.

According to the local refugees retreating from those areas, the Pakistanis sitting on the heights overlooking the strategic NH-1 A were now targeting the road with impunity both with direct and indirect artillery and mortar fire every day. Not only had they occupied the Indian posts across the LOC, but the Pakistanis in order to direct the fire had also established artillery observation posts on them. And as the Pakistani long range artillery guns kept pounding the towns of Drass, the second coldest inhabited place in the world and Kargil, the flight of the locals that had started initially with a trickle from those areas had now become one of mass exodus. When Monty tried to find out a little more of what was happening from the military police officer who was regulating the traffic at the check point, he was politely told not to ask any questions and to go back to Srinagar.

That evening of 15th May, on his return to Srinagar, Monty in order to find out a little more of what was actually happening at Drass and Kargil, decided to call on an old acquaintance of his. The gentleman, a superseded full Colonel was not only an ex Sanawarian, but he was also a contemporary of his late foster brother Shiraz Ismail Khan. They were both together in school and in the National Defence Academy at Kharakwasla, and the Colonel as a re-employed officer was now on the staff of the 15 Corps Headquarters at Badami Bagh, Srinagar. This was, the very formation under Northern Command that was totally responsible to maintain the sanctity of the LOC in the valley and in northern Kashmir, including the Kargil and Ladakh sectors.

"Frankly speaking everybody here at the headquarters is a bit confused, because the daily situation reports that are being received from the 121 Independent Brigade Group at Kargil and the Headquarters 3 Infantry Division at Leh are still rather sketchy. There is no doubt that the Pakistanis have violated the LOC in that sector, but the quantum of force that the

Pakistanis have sent into the area, and whether they are Mujahideens, jihadis or regular Pakistani troops, or are a composite force of all three elements put together is however still not yet very clear. There has also been a large number of sporadic clashes between the two sides, when own patrols tried to probe further, and off late the Pakistanis have also considerably intensified their artillery bombardment of the NH 1A," added the Colonel as he pointed out to Monty on the map, the alignment of that strategic road that at very many places ran very close to the LOC.

"Maybe they want to cut of this vital life line that connects Srinagar to Leh, and if they do succeed in doing so then I am afraid Ladakh will be isolated,"said Monty.

"Well not really, because we also have an alternative life line that runs through Manali via the Rohtang Pass, and we can if required also temporarily maintain Ladakh by air if need be. Moreover, I don't think that the matter is all that serious because the Army Chief, General Ved Prakash Malik is on an official visit to Poland and the Army Commander, Northern Command; Lt General Hari Mohan Khanna has also proceeded on annual leave. And as far as the 15 Corps Commander, Lt General Krishan Pal is concerned, he thinks that this is a localized affair and will be taken care off soon by ousting the Pakistanis from there. In fact he conveyed the same to Mr George Fernandes too I am told when the Defence Minister visited Kargil on 13th May," said the Colonel very confidently.

"But I only hope it won't be a playback, or a repeat of the 1962 Chinese incursion into erstwhile NEFA and to which Pandit Nehru also reacted very confidently by saying that the army has been ordered to throw them out and the rest as you know is now history,"said Monty as he before leaving thanked the forced bachelor host for his gracious hospitality and presented him with a pure 'shatoosh' shawl for his wife.

"I think you have made my wife Archana's day in absentia, and she will be simply delighted with this beautiful gift. And mind you, ever since we got married in 1972, she has been constantly pestering me to buy her a shawl like this one, but I simply could not afford it. I still have another two daughters who have to be married and I only have another year left to serve. Incidentally the elder one is already engaged to a young Captain from the Jammu and Kashmir Rifles who is presently serving with the Ladakh Scouts at Leh and needless to say you and the family must come for the wedding reception that is scheduled to be held at the AVI, the Arun Vaidya Officers Institute at Noida on 26th May," said the happy Colonel as he proudly showed Monty a few snaps of the handsome couple that were taken during the engagement ceremony.

"'I must say that they do make a delightful pair and as the saying goes a perfect made for each other couple too. But just in case I miss out on the wedding reception, let me drink a toast to their future health and happiness,"said Monty as he did a quick bottoms up with his mug of beer and got into the hired car.

"Jaldi Chalo, (Drive Fast) or else I will miss the Indian Airlines evening flight back to Delhi," said Monty to the driver as he checked his watch for the correct time.

It was however on 19th May, 1999 and a good two weeks after the first intrusion by the Pakistanis was detected that the UHQ, the United Headquarters in Srinagar convened an emergency meeting. This was the apex body of the organization that was responsible for managing the security in the state of Jammu and Kashmir and was chaired by none other than the Chief Minister of the state, Farouk Abdullah.That day the entire security establishment at Srinagar starting from the 15 Corps Commander to the Joint Directors from the (IB) Intelligence Bureau, the RAW, the Research and Analysis Wing, the Chief Secretary, the Home Secretary, DG Police, IG BSF, the Divisional Commissioner and the Deputy Commissioner Srinagar were all present in full strength. Unfortunately neither the army nor the IB and the RAW were still clear about the magnitude of the infiltration that the Pakistanis had made in the Drass and Kargil sectors, and the intelligence inputs were therefore still rather sketchy. Moreover, the sudden movement of Indian troops from the valley to the Drass and Kargil sectors had created large gaps in the counter insurgency deployment in the valley and the fact that this could be taken advantage off by the Pakistanis therefore could not be ruled out either.

And it was only on 21st May 1999; after Squadron Leader Perumal in his Canberra aircraft carried out a detailed photo reconnaissance of the area that had been intruded upon by the Pakistanis did the Indian army realize what they were up against.The intruders were not only occupying the heights in strength, but they were also well armed and well stocked. Though his aircraft was hit by a Stinger missile and was badly damaged, the brave pilot had carried out his mission successfully and with one engine in flames had also managed to land back safely at Srinagar. And on that very day in order to bring home to the Indians that the intruders were there to stay, the Pakistani also opened up with vengeance with their long range artillery. Their aim was to blow off parts of the road, the only vital lifeline to Drass Kargil and Leh from Srinagar, and thereby delay and prevent the reinforcements in men, material and artillery that the Indian army was now frantically pumping into that widely intruded sector.

Travelling in one of the vehicle convoys as a convoy commander was the young Captain from the Jammu and Kashmir Rifles who had recently been engaged to the eldest daughter of the re-employed Colonel who was Monty's friend in Srinager. He was bringing the much needed ammunition from Leh to replenish the dump that had been blown up by the Pakistanis at Kargil. After delivering the ammunition he was scheduled to proceed on two months annual leave and go home to get married. But luck it seems was not on the young officer's side. In such like situations risks had to be taken and the young officer was willing to take it. That precious consignment of artillery ordnance was vital for the troops to keep engaging the enemy. On seeing the convoy approaching Kargil, the Pakistani guns had opened up with heavy artillery and mortar fire. The young intrepid officer was leading the convoy in a jeep and in order to ensure that the drivers did not panic or stop their vehicles on the road, he got out from his vehicle and though under heavy artillery and mortar fire kept directing the traffic. Urging the drivers to press on the accelerator, he kept his cool. But late that evening as he stood on the winding mountain road braving the enemy fire, one of the shells landed very close to him. In spite of bleeding profusely from his head and shoulders, he kept directing the traffic till the last vehicle safely went past the danger area. Though he was rushed to the nearest field hospital and the army doctors working in a make shift underground operation theatre tried desperately to save his life, but they simply could not. Early next morning, his body in a bag was airlifted in a chopper to Srinagar and from there it was flown in an IAF aircraft to Delhi. Instead of going for his own marriage, he was now going home for his own funeral.

The encounters between the two sides, which till then were being termed simply as minor border skirmishes had suddenly become a major issue. On 24th May 1999, Farouk Abdullah with his Chief Secretary Ashok Jaitley and the Director General Police, Gurbachan Jagat flew to Delhi, and on the very next day the Cabinet Committee on Security Affairs decided that enough was enough and the Pakistanis who had occupied nearly 1500 sq km of Indian Territory had to be thrown out at any cost.

The next morning 26th May, with the Indian Prime Minister Atal Behari Vajpayee giving the green signal to the three service chiefs, the battle for Kargil had begun. Codenamed 'Operation Vijay'(Victory)for the ground operations by the army and 'Operation Safed Sagar" (White Sea) for the air operations by the Indian Air Force, the valiant officers and men of the two services despite the firm directive by the government not to cross the LOC decided to show the world the stuff they were made off.

On that 26th May, 1999 as the Indian Air Force fighter jets and helicopter gunships got ready to pound the Pakistanis on the heights that were illegally occupied by them, the infantry battalion of the 18th Grenadiers from the 59 Infantry Brigade of the 8 Mountain Division that had been inducted from the valley relentlessly kept attacking the Tololing mountain. At 16,000 feet, the bare naked peak that overlooked the Drass town was a vital feature that had to be taken back from the enemy, but it was all in vain.

And on the next day 27th May, when the Indian fighter jets and helicopter gunships went into action, both the Pakistani military top brass and the Nawaz Sharif government were also taken completely by surprise. By clandestinely occupying the Indian posts, Pakistan had no doubt presented India with a fait accompli, but they had least expected that kind of a violent and aggressive response from their old adversary. On learning about the air strikes, Shiraz who was still on leave from Moscow decided to call on retired Lt General Aslam Rehman who had settled in Islamabad. The General had commanded the Rawalpindi Corps and Shiraz wanted to find out a little more of what the Pakistani army was really up to.

"Well the little that I know is that this was till now a very hush-hush operation that was planned by the present army chief General Musharraf, his CGS, Lt General Mohammed Aziz Khan who is himself a Kashmiri, Lt General Mehmood Ahmed, the 10 Corps Commander who is responsible for the defense of Kashmir,and Major General Javed Hassan, the GOC FCNA, the Force Commander Northern Areas, and the man who is now directly responsible to carry out this clandestine operation. Surprisingly not even the other two service chiefs from the Pakistan Navy and Air force, nor the other Corps Commanders were fully aware of what was happening in that sector till after the balloon went up. Even the DGMO, Lt General Tauqir Zia was brought into the picture at a much later stage. This was primarily to maintain strict secrecy and all information therefore was shared by this group of four and that too strictly on a need to know basis," said Aslam Rehman as his wife Farzana asked the 'Abdar" (waiter) to wheel in the drinks trolley with the snacks.

"However, I must add that the Pakistan Air Force Chief, Air Chief Marshall Parvaiz Mehdi Qureshi and his senior officers from the Operations Branch I am told were conveyed indirectly on 12th May about the clandestine operations taking place inside Indian occupied Kashmir in the Kargil Sector. And this happened during a top level briefing on the so called 'Kashmir Contingency' that was given by none other than Lt General Mehmud Ahmed, the GOC of Pakistan's 10 Corps at his headquarters in Rawalpindi and which was attended by a few senior air force officers from the CAS's operations and planning branch.

During that briefing, the flamboyant 10 Corps GOC sporting his trademark camouflage scarf had openly admitted that his forces were already in occupation of some of the strategic heights that the Indians had vacated, and that besides having the Stinger missiles on those heights, he had also with the help of the MI-17 choppers from the Pakistan Army's Aviation Corps deployed artillery guns and ammunition on those newly occupied high mountain tops. And though Air Commodore Salim Nawaz and Air Commodore Abid Rao who attended that briefing were a little apprehensive about the capability of the Stinger missiles to take on the Indian Air Force single handedly, but Lt Gen Mehmud was so very confident that it would remain a limited localized conflict that he smilingly told the air force officers that there was no need for the Pakistan Air force to butt in." added Aslam Rehman.

"But was the Prime Minister Nawaz Sharif kept in picture, or was it just an act of bravado by the flamboyant new chief?" asked Farzana.

"Well looking at the scale of operations, I am sure the group of four must have taken the Prime Minister into confidence at least. And I am told that since the army chief had convinced him that the army was not being involved directly, and that it was the so called 'Mujahideens' and Kashmiri freedom fighters who were being sent in, the Prime Minister thinking that the move would once again internationalize the Kashmir issue had therefore it seems had agreed to it. In fact this kind of a scenario in the Kargil sector was also discussed twice earlier. It was during general Zia-ul-Haq's tenure, but he had turned it down both the times. Zia feared that it could lead to another full scale war with India and Pakistan was not prepared for it. One must also remember that though' Operation Tupac' was Zia's brainchild, he also did not want India to react violently. His overall long term aim was to keep the Indians and the Indian army bleeding over the Kashmir issue, and to continue doing so till such time it reached the crescendo of a major civil uprising in the valley. And only thereafter would the Pakistan army step in to deliver the final knockout punch," concluded Aslam Rehman as he poured Shiraz another stiff Black Label.

"But don't you think that this military operation that has been undertaken so soon after the Lahore Declaration will only backfire on us.

Because as far as the Pakistan Foreign Service officers are concerned, we have been kept totally in the dark. Moreover, the so called 'Mujahideen Force' I am told also consists of a fairly large number of foreign Muslim mercenaries from various Arab countries and some of whom I believe also have close links to Osama Bin Laden's Al-Qaida too. And instead of internationalizing the Kashmir issue, this stupid action I am afraid will not only brand us as belligerent aggressors, but it will also give us the unholy tag as sponsors and promoters of international terrorism," said a visibly worked up Shiraz.

"May be he is right, but in that case Nawaz Sharif should have put his foot down. According to the rumours that are making the rounds at the ladies kitty parties in the various clubs and officers messes in Rawalpindi, Nawaz Sharif was only brought into the picture a month or so after the Lahore Declaration was signed and during that briefing both his Defence Secretary, retired Lt Gneral Iftiqar Ali Khan and retired Lt General Majid Malik who was also earlier the DGMO and CGS and who is now a member in Sharif's cabinet, both I am told had strong reservations about the implications that would follow, but the Prime Minister it seems was looking forward to his own glory and fame, and he therefore went ahead with the plan," said Farzana.

"But I think that this is all hind sight and the planning for an operation on such a large scale must have begun as soon as the Indians withdrew from those heights last September, or possibly soon after Musharaff took over as chief in early October 1998. Moreover, for such kind of large scale infiltration taking place on a 150 km wide front requires tremendous logistical back up and detailed planning. But I must give full credit to the planners who had achieved it without letting the Indians get a wind of it whatsoever.Tactically the operation undoubtedly has been a great success, but the question now is what next!?" said Shiraz as he helped himself to another large Black Label.

That evening as he recalled Mr Vajpayee's famous words from his poem 'Aab Jang Na Hone Denge'(We will not have any more wars) that the Indian Prime Minister had recited at Lahore, Shiraz knew that India had once again been stabbed in the back. Repeating those lines softly to himself ('Bharat-Pakistan padosi, saath saath rehna hai, Pyar karen ya vaar karen, donon ko hi sehna hai. Jo hum pur guzri, bacchon ke saang na hone denge. Jang na hone denge.) (Both Pakistan and India must remain as peaceful neighbours. What we have both suffered should not be passed on to our children. We must not fight wars.) But looking at the manner in which both sides were escalating the issue, Shiraz therefore wondered whether the fourth round was now in the offing. It also brought home to him the famous saying that in peace the sons bury their fathers and in war the fathers bury their sons and that night he prayed that no more young lives should be lost on both sides in this misadventure that the Pakistan army had now undertaken.

As the casualties on the Indian army kept mounting, so did the pressure on the Vajpayee government by the Indian armed forces. The General Officers now desired that the policy of restraint must end, and the troops must be allowed to cross the LOC at least in the Kargil sector so as to enable them to cut off the supply lines to the intruders. Surprisingly on that very day of 26th May, when Prime Minister Vajpayee gave the green signal to the Indian army to launch "Operation Vijay' and to the Indian Air Force to launch' Operation Safed Sagar' the Pakistan army chief, General Musharraf who was on a visit to China felt very happy with the success of the operation. Feeling on top of the world, the flamboyant General in order to know how things were actually going on the ground had rung up his buddy Lieutenant General Mohammed Aziz, the CGS of the Pakistan army. Unfortunately and unknown to both of them the telephonic conversation between the two top most high ranking Pakistani officers was simultaneously also being secretly recorded, and they never expected that it would soon fall into the hands of the Indians

Unperturbed by the aerial bombing that the Indians had resorted to in the intruded sector, General Musharaff and General Aziz were both confident that with the latest appeal that Kofi Annan had made to both the countries to sit and talk,Pakistan's aim to once again internationalize the Kashmir issue would soon be achieved. The CGS in his conversation had also categorically reiterated to the Nawaz Sharif government that the Pakistan army was in full control of the situation and since they were holding the militants by the scruff of their necks, they could regulate their actions whenever and wherever required, and therefore as far as the Pakistan government was concerned there was no danger at all of an all out war with India.

Meanwhile on 27th May, on hearing the news that the Indian Air Force had gone into action in Kargil, Monty called on his old friend Unni at the Press Club to find out what the hell was happening. During that air attack the Pakistanis it seems had shot down two Indian aircrafts. The first one a MIG 21 that was being piloted by Squadron Leader Ajay Ahuja was hit by a stinger missile and though the pilot had bailed out, he was shot dead as he came parachuting down. In the second case it was a MIG 27 that was being piloted by Flight Lieutenant Nachiketa. He had successfully engaged the enemy on the Batalik heights. In this case however after the pilot had bailed out, he was captured alive by the Pakistanis and was now being used as good propaganda material by them. Parading the Indian officer on PAK TV, the Pakistanis were now telling the world that the present conflict in Kargil was part of India's nefarious game plan to suppress the freedom aspirations of the Kashmiris through military might, and Pakistan would therefore continue to support their Kashmiri brothers in their struggle against the repressive policies of the Indians.

"But tell me if the Indian army has now admitted that the infiltration was in a very large scale and that it is still carrying on, and that the strength of the infiltrators was nearly a thousand or more, then this must be a gigantic intelligence failure on our part. But I wonder what could be the aim of the Pakistanis to suddenly give so much importance to this area, which was always a relatively dormant sector till now," said Monty as Unni ordered a chilled Kingfisher pint beer for his guest.

"Yes I agree that it was indeed a massive intelligence failure by not one, but by all the intelligence agencies in the country, including the IB and the RAW and one should not only blame the army for it. Though everybody is accusing each other, the fact remains that we were badly and literally caught with our pants down.I think the euphoria of the bus ride to Lahore had lulled everybody into a state of deep slumber and Pakistan took full advantage of it. We must not forget that Pakistan is still smarting at the loss of the Siachen Glacier to India and their aim this time therefore is to give it back to us by cutting off the strategic road that links Srinagar with Leh. And by holding on to the heights at Mushkoh, Drass, Kargil, and Batalik, and by further intensifying the militancy elsewhere in that area, they could now try and compel India to back down in Siachen. This would not only alter the alignment of the LOC, but it would also bury the Simla Agreement for good and thus automatically put the Kashmir issue back on the international arena and agenda, And mind you this operation is not being done in isolation, because off late, the tempo of infiltration across the LOC leading to the valley has also increased substantially in other sectors too," said Unni as he called for another large gin with bitters for himself.

"Well in that case it could well lead to a fourth round and if it does escalate to that level then with both the countries now armed with nuclear weapons, it would be sheer disaster," said Monty.

"No doubt that is a possibility, but it is most unlikely under the present day scenario because the Pakistanis have been constantly harping that they are in no way involved and that it is the so called Jehadis and the Kashmiri freedom fighters who are responsible for what is happening in Indian occupied Kashmir," said Unni.

"Well they had said the same thing when they clandestinely pushed the Pathan tribesmen into Kashmir in October 1947 to do their dirty job, and then again in 1965, when they pushed in the so called Mujahids, and there was no denying the fact that the Pakistan regular army was very much a part of those ill fated operations," said Monty.'

"You are absolutely right and believe you me this time too it is going to be no different either, because as per the latest intelligence reports,the infiltrators are a heady mix of Mujahideens, foreign Muslim mercenaries and also regulars from the Pakistan Northern Light Infantry, but the Pakistani government as usual will be the last one to admit it," said Unni with a grin as the barman poured him another large gin and sounded the final bell.

On 28th May 1999, while Pakistan was celebrating 'Yaum-e Takbeer' (Day of Thanks Giving) the first anniversary of their nuclear tests, the Vajpayee government in India was getting ready to launch its diplomatic offensive to tell the world. what Pakistan was really up to That day the Indian Air Force suffered another major reverse when one of their MI-17 helicopter gunship that was being piloted by Squadron Leader Rajiv Pundir while engaging the enemy at Tololing was shot down by a stinger missile and the entire crew of four met their death when the helicopter nosedived into the Tololing Nullah But three days later on 31st May, when the Indian Defence Minister George Fernandes goofed up by telling the press that India was also considering the option of giving the infiltrators a safe passage to get out of Indian territory, it not only put the Vajpayee government in a very embarrassing situation, but it also drew a great deal of flak from retired high ranking Indian Generals, Admirals and Air Marshalls. Reacting to that, the Indian Prime Minister immediately told the nation that it was a war like situation and India would throw the intruders out if Pakistan did not withdraw them unilaterally, and there was no question therefore of giving the intruders a safe passage.

Though the success of downing the Indian aircrafts was being celebrated by the Pakistanis, there was surprisingly no reaction by the Pakistan Air Force and Shiraz wondered why. And it was only a fortnight later when he with his family was returning to Moscow that he came to know the real truth.It was primarily because the PAF top brass it seems was still ignorant of the gambit that Musharraf had undertaken and they were not kept in full picture at all of what was happening in Kargil. Moreover, having categorically stated publicly to the world that Pakistan was in no way responsible for the Mujahideens crossing the LOC they had washed their hands off the entire affair and therefore, it would have been rather foolish of Pakistan at this stage to escalate the crisis and more so when they were sitting pretty on those commanding heights. They were also confident that the Indian army in spite of their artillery and air power would not be able to dislodge them from there in the restricted time frame of three to four months that was now available to the Indian military high command before the onset of the severe winter. And if Pakistan could hold on and consolidate on all those posts till end September, then victory would surely be theirs and India perforce would then have to come to the negotiating table.

But that was not the only reason why Pakistan was shy of retaliating directly because. Shiraz also came to know that with Pakistan's external debt having reached a severe crisis level, the country therefore economically was not in a position to sustain a long drawn out war with India. Moreover, with the Americans, the French and the European nations putting pressure on Pakistan to diffuse the crisis and telling them to respect the sanctity of the LOC, the Nawaz Sharif government was now badly again caught in a 'Catch 22' situation. If he succumbed to foreign pressures, it would call off the bluff and he would not only be branded as a lackey of the west, but the military in Pakistan too would never forgive him. And if he continued holding the heights then the possibility of India continuing with the air strikes from within its own territorial jurisdiction and striking elsewhere could not be ruled out either. Therefore to placate the Americans and the West Europeans, Pakistan on 3rd June as a goodwill gesture released and handed over Flight Lieutenant Nachiketa, and followed it up on 10th June by returning the mutilated dead bodies of Lt Saurav Kalia and five others of the 4th Jat Battalion who were declared missing since 6th May. There was no doubt that the young officer and his five comrades had been brutally tortured before being killed in cold blood and this had only further angered the Indians.

But Pakistan it seems had also grossly under estimated the fighting spirit, the raw courage and bravery of the Indian infantry soldier, as more infantry battalions with close air and artillery support started taking the enemy head on. With the tide slowly turning against them, Pakistan on 12th June, 1999 dispatched Sartaj Aziz their Foreign Minister for talks with his counterpart in Delhi. But the suave Indian Foreign Minister and ex army cavalry officer Jaswant Singh was in no mood to relent. He told Sartaj Aziz very firmly that the intruders must first withdraw before any talks could take place.

But unknown to Sartaj Aziz and much before the break of dawn on 13th June when Colonel MV Ravindranath, the commanding officer of the 2nd Rajputana Rifles radioed to the GOC 8 Mountain Division, Major General Mohinder Puri that he and his troops were on top of Tololing, the Indian army's march to victory had begun. And at 0800 hours on that very morning of 13th June 1999, when the news arrived in New Delhi that the 2nd Rajputana Rifles Battalion and the 18th Grenadiers had captured the mighty peak, there was jubilation in the Indian camp. With the road to final victory having begun, the Prime Minister of India too arrived on the battlefront to personally congratulate the troops.

Two days later on 15th June, with President Clinton urging Nawaz Sharif to pull out off Kargil and praising India for the restraint shown in not crossing the LOC, Pakistan's gamble it seems had now landed them in real thick soup. With the Indian Foreign Minister's visit to Beijing, and Brajesh Mishra the National Security Advisor's visit to Cologne to brief the Chinese and the leaders of the G-8 nations respectively, Pakistan's credibility and their continuous denial that they had no hand or role to play in the entire operation had now been fully exposed. Even China an old friend and ally of Pakistan was not keen to tow the Pakistani line any longer.

Vajpayee's letter to President Clinton that Brajesh Mishra had handed over at Cologne stating that India's patience was wearing thin had spurred the American administration to further tighten the screws on Pakistan. And on 20th June, when the gallant JCO's and Jawans of the 13th Jammu and Kashmir Rifles led by their two highly motivated young company commanders Capt Vikram Batra and Captain Sanjiv Jamwal, who were only 25 and 24 years old respectively got on with the act, it took the Pakistani high command completely by surprise. The 13 JAKS after a bitter fight and without losing a single soldier had captured Pt 5140 and this was considered nothing short of a miracle. It seemed that with the battle cry of 'Durga Mata Ki Jai' (Victory to Goddess Durga)' on their lips and firing frontally from their hips, they had completely mesmerized the enemy. Giving them very close support, the Indian artillery with their devastating and accurate fire from their Bofors guns and multi-barreled rocket launchers had literally got the enemy by their balls. They not only pinned the enemy down, but they systematically destroyed the bunkers that they had clandestinely occupied. When their Commanding Officer, Lt Colonel Y K Joshi came on the wireless set to congratulate his valiant officers and men, the one popular liner 'Dil Mange More' by a jubilant Captain Vikram Batra from atop the 17,000 feet high peak said it all. The Indian army was now braying for more enemy blood and as more reinforcements kept arriving in the battle field zone; both in terms of fire power and bayonet power, the morale of the Pakistanis were now slowly sinking into their boots. As the Indian Air Force and the Indian artillery with their Bofors guns and Russian multi-barreled rocket launchers with impunity kept plastering and pounding the enemy day in and day out, it was now only a question of time for the Indian army to throw all of them out.

As the determined infantry soldiers and young officers of the Indian army leading from the front kept climbing the high barren features using mountain ropes and crampons to get at the enemy, the others elements using the air and long range fire power kept cutting off the enemy's vulnerable supply lines in the rear. Cornered from all sides, the Pakistanis sitting on those posts were now at their wits end. Some of them were now openly cursing their superiors for abandoning them in the wilderness. The very presence of Major Iqbal, a regular officer and others from the Northern Light Infantry who died bravely defending Pt 5140 only added to Pakistan's miseries. Their repeated claims and bluffs that the Pakistan army had nothing to do with the operation had been blown wide open. With the capture of Tololing and Pt 5140, which was the Indian army's first and top most priority, the direct threat to the Srinagar-Leh highway and to Drass was now very much reduced. But all was not over as yet. Pakistanis were still sitting pretty on Tiger Hill, a massive feature that overlooked Drass and at Jubar in the Batalik sector and both these heights had also to be captured irrespective of the cost.

On 29th May, Major Mariappan Sarvanan the young 27 year old company commander from the 1st Bihar Battalion had led the way, when he without any artillery support attacked Pt 5203 on Jubar in the icy cold Batalik Sector. But he unfortunately could not secure or capture it. And though he had reached the very top, he was ultimately gunned down by the enemy. However by sacrificing his life at Jubar, the brave young officer had set an example of raw courage to those who would now avenge his heroic death.

After Drass, the Batalik-Yaldor area was now the Indian army's next priority sector. Besides the capture of Jubar which was now on top of the list and for which the artillery guns and the multi-barreled rocket launchers from Drass had now been re-deployed in that sector, there was also now a threat by the Pakistanis to isolate the southern part of the Siachen Glacier and it was to the credit of Major Sonam Wangchuk of the Ladakh Scouts who in a race against time to reach Chorbat La had beaten the Pakistanis to it.

Upset by the adventurism of General Musharaff and his gang of four that had landed Pakistan in real shit, internationally, politically and diplomatically, Shiraz who was back in Moscow kept praying that the conflict should not escalate into a full-fledged nuclear war. With Musharaff now holding total charge as Chairman Joint Chiefs of Staff Committee and the keys that could trigger off a nuclear holocaust, anything was possible. But in his heart of hearts Shiraz was also happy that the Pakistanis sitting on those heights were now getting it back in royal style from the Indian artillery and the Indian air force.

"I sometime wonder where was the damn need and the frightful hurry for the Nawaz Sharif government and his military generals to put us in the bloody mess that we are now in. And come to think of it this so called bravado by the men in uniform to send in the so called Jehadis to once again do all the dirty work for them has not only exposed Pakistan to international ridicule, but it has also given the Indians the long handle to beat us with. And as a result of which we in the Pakistan diplomatic corps are being looked upon by others as bloody fools now," said an angry Shiraz to his wife Saira as his 16 year old son Tojo came into the room to give the sad news that in the Cricket World Cup match that was being played at Old Trafford in England, the Indian team had also beaten Pakistan convincingly on the cricket field.

And while India rejoiced at Pakistan's defeat on the cricket field, the Indian military high command got busy preparing their plans for the capture of Tiger Hill, Jubar and other key features that the Pakistanis across the LOC were still holding on to. The sudden visit of General Anthony Zinni, the Commander-in-Chief of the United States Central Command and Gibson Lampher, the Deputy assistant Secretary of State to Islamabad in the third week of June it seems had also spurred the Indians to get on with the job. The two high ranking Americans had arrived with a terse message from President Clinton for Nawaz Sharif and General Musharraf to immediately call off the hostilities and to pull back all the infiltrators to their own bases and to maintain the status quo ante of the LOC. The American General had also held intense discussions with the Pakistani army chief, General Musharraf and the mechanics of a negotiated withdrawal from Tiger Hill, Batalik and other features that were still held by the infiltrators was also discussed it seems. Soon thereafter, when Lampher with Niaz Naik landed in Delhi for talks with Brajesh Mishra and Vajpayee and there were strong rumours of Nawaz Sharif heading for Washington to have one to one talks with Clinton, the Indian government however made it very clear that there would be no talks or any negotiated settlement till such time Pakistan withdrew from all the posts and areas that they had occupied across the LOC clandestinely and illegally.

Meanwhile the Indian Intelligence Bureau had also on a tip off had apprehended Dil Fayaz a staff member of the Pakistan High Commission in New Delhi. He was found at the Hindon Air Force Base near Ghaziabad with incriminating documents and as a result of which he was declared persona non grata by the Indian government and had been asked to leave the country by 5th July. As a tit for tat and within 24 hours of India's action, Pakistani government intelligence goons also retaliated by forcibly abducting Mr NR Doraiswamy, a staff member in the Indian Mission at Islamabad. Doraiswamy was pulled out of his official car while he was leaving his house for his office and later was also badly beaten up. This was not the first time that a Indian High Commission official had been physically attacked in Islamabad and as a result of which Paddy and Dimpy with their little daughter Simran had to be doubly careful.

On 2nd July 1999, the US Congress had further tightened the screws on Pakistan, when the House Foreign Relations Committee adopted a resolution calling for suspension of all IMF, World Bank and Asian Bank loans to Pakistan unless Pakistan withdrew the Mujahideens who had occupied areas across the LOC at Kargil. On that very day Lampher with Niaz Naik had presented to the Indian government a withdrawal formula, but India had out rightly rejected it on the plea that it did not want any third party mediation. Unknown to most Pakistanis and Indians, the back channel diplomacy between India and Pakistan to amicably resolve the Kashmir issue had started even before Vajpayee made his historic visit to Lahore. Mr Vajpayee's special emissary, Mr RK Mishra had made at least three trips to Pakistan and where he was given the red carpet treatment, but with the Kargil episode all that had now gone up in smoke.

And on 3rd July, while Nawaz Sharif was on his way to Washington, the 8 Sikh and the 18 Grenadier Battalions of the Indian army were getting ready to have their own 4th of July celebrations atop Tiger Hill. They were a part of the new brigade that had been inducted into the Drass sector. At 1730 hrs on 3rd July, when a full fledged and coordinated artillery attack with the Bofors guns and the multi-barreled rocket launchers began to pound the enemy defences on Tiger Hill, the enter media who were watching that spectacle for the first time and that to live realized the devastation the Indian gunners were capable of inflicting on the enemy. And while the Indian artillery kept the enemy's face down, the gallant young infantry officers and soldiers of the Indian army kept moving closer to the enemy objectives. Unmindful of the danger of coming under their own artillery fire, they kept asking for it till they were less than a hundred yards away from their respective objectives. And then at well past midnight on that 4th July morning, when the battle cries of 'Bole Sonehal' of the 8 Sikh's echoed loudly across the mighty Himalayas, the real battle for the capture of Tiger Hill had begun.

The Sikhs with their megaphones had been tasked to put in feint attacks from the eastern and southeastern flanks in order to deceive the enemy and they did it very cleverly throughout the night. Fearing it to be a brigade size attack that was developing from that flank, the Pakistanis on Tiger Hill panicked and kept asking for reinforcements and artillery fire on the Sikhs. In the meantime young Lieutenant Sherawat of the 8 Sikhs leading his troops from the front had also kept the enemy engaged from the western flank. This flank had to be also secured in order to prevent enemy reinforcements coming in from that direction. And while all these actions to deceive the enemy was taking place, the troops of the valiant 18 Grenadiers under the two young officers, 22 year old Lieutenant Balwan Singh and Captain Sachin Nimbalkar were on their way to surprise the enemy from a direction that they least expected. They were tasked to lead the two assault parties across a sheer massive rock face and they were determined to do it.

As the Ghatak (Commando) Platoons of the 18 Grenadiers led by Lieutenant Balwan Singh and that of Captain Nimbalkar made their way independently from two different directions using ropes to get to the top of the objective, everybody was praying for their safety. The Indian army had no doubt taken a great gamble, but it was a calculated one. Tiger Hill had to be taken at any cost and the Indian army was now all set to do it. It was no doubt a deadly approach and its success depended entirely in not letting the Pakistanis getting any wind of it till the leading troops had made it to the very top.

Throwing all caution to the wind and with the young intrepid Grenadier Yogendra Singh Yadav and his brave Platoon Commander Lieutenant Balwan Singh leading the way, the platoon slowly and steadily made it half way across the deadly obstacle, Till then it was all good going, but then suddenly all hell broke loose as the Pakistanis opened up with machine guns and rocket fire and followed it up by lobbying grenades. Though his Platoon Commander was hit, and he himself was badly injured in the hand, but a determined Grenadier Yadav realizing that many more lives would be lost if the enemy machine gun nests were not silenced, he therefore continued climbing the rock face. And despite being hit by a hail of bullets, on the groin and shoulder, the valiant soldier finally silenced the two enemy machine gun nests by lobbying grenades into them. Then as the war cries of 'Bharat Mata ki Jai' and 'Bole Sonihal' echoed across the mountains that dotted the long jagged ridge line, it was time once again for the celebrations to begin. Finally after a bitter hand to hand fighting and warding of the many ferocious counter attacks by the Pakistanis, when the wireless sets at the headquarters of the 56 Mountain Brigade and 192 Mountain Brigade crackled to give the good news to their respective Brigade Commanders, the time was 0530 hours on the morning of 4th July. Not to be left behind, Flying Officer Gunjan Saxena had also created history that day. The young Indian Air force lady helicopter pilot had flown into the combat zone to drop vital supplies to the troops fighting in the Dras and Batalik Sectors. At 24, she too was a hero or rather a heroine.

"I am sure even the Americans could not have celebrated their 4th of July with such awesome fireworks," said one of the staff officers who had sat up all night monitoring the operation minute by minute

"Yes Sir, you are absolutely right and I think it is also now time for Nawaz Sharif and his Generals to face the music and the fireworks not only from the American President, but also from their own people," said one of the correspondents who too had sat up the whole night writing his exclusive report on the magnificent achievements of the Indian army.

By now the battle for Batalik too had reached a do or die stage for the Indians. Here again the aim was to maintain strict secrecy till the assaulting infantry began their attacks. But that was not to be as the Pakistanis with regular troops were well entrenched on the heady heights of Khalubar, Jubar and Kukarthang. Moreover, the Muslim Company from the 22 Grenadiers of the Indian Army that had been sent earlier to capture Khalubar was now trapped in that area. With no more time to waste, and with time running out for the Grenadier company who were without food, water and ammunition for the past 96 hours, Colonel Lalit Rai, the brave and enterprising Commanding Officer of the 1/1 Gurkha Rifles who was tasked to capture Khalubar by a night attack decided to take the risk and attack the feature in broad daylight. Climbing by day under heavy fire, the sturdy Gurkhas however kept going on and on. And though he himself was very badly wounded, the Commanding Officer refused to be evacuated. And as darkness fell, the stocky nimble footed Gurkhas kept the momemtum of attack going as they with vengeance fell upon the enemy. Leading them was the young Lieutenant Manoj Kumar Pandey who with his platoon and battle cry of 'Aayo Gurkhali' had charged into the blazing enemy gun fire. Though severely wounded, Lt Pandey refused to stop and having silenced the enemy machine gun with a grenade, he crawled from bunker to bunker and kept motivating his men to get at the guts of the enemy. At one stage using his khukri, he even managed to kill the two Pakistanis who had temporarily checked his platoon's advance. And it was only after Khalubar had been captured, that the brave young officer breathed his last.

Elsewhere in the Batalik sector, the 1st Bihar Battalion to avenge the death of the brave Major Sarvanan had in a do or die effort also captured Jubar, while the 12 Jammu and Kashmir Light Infantry Battalion got the better of the enemy at Point 4812. In all these actions no less a role was played by the magnificent Indian Air Force and the Indian artillery gunners, Both of them had played a sterling part not only in pulverizing and destroying the well fortified enemy bunkers on those heights, but they also successfully interdicted and destroyed the supply lines of the enemy in the rear with impunity.

With both Batalik and Drass now totally under control of the Indian army, the focus now shifted in ousting the enemy from the Mushko Valley. The ridge line overlooking the lush green valley was in the hands of the enemy and with its numerous nullas and rivulets, it was being constantly used as a major route of infiltration by the ISI backed Pakistani militants. The Pakistani army's logistic base at Gultari was not very far from the LOC in that sector either, and Pakistan had been taking full advantage of its close proximity to the LOC.

The area around Gultari according to one intelligence report was also the main concentration area of the so called Pakistani trained infiltrators for induction into the area that was now occupied by them. And with the restrictions not to bomb and cross the LOC, for Brigadier Rajesh Kumar Kakkar and his troops from the 79 Mountain Brigade, the task of capturing the key feature Point 4875 therefore had been made all the more difficult. Standing at nearly 17,000 feet, it not only gave the Pakistanis a clear view of the strategic Srinagar-Leh highway, but it also dominated by observation the Indian gun positions and camps in that area.

As the Indian Air Force Mirage 2000 fighters kept pounding the peaks around Mushkoh and the enemy supply lines to the rear, the artillery guns were getting ready to support the attack by the infantry. Soon after last light as the three pronged night attack by the troops of 13 JAKRIF, 17 Jat and 2nd Nagas got under way, the 155 mm Bofors Howitzers and the 105 Field Guns kept plastering the enemy defences on Point 4875. Once again leading from the front were the young infantry officers of the Indian army. They had been tasked to capture that vital peak and it had to done well before sunrise the next day.

Tasked to capture the Whale Back feature first, a determined Captain Anuj Nayyar from 17 Jat and his men shouting their the war cry of 'Jat Balwan Jai Bhagwan' under a hail of enemy automatic fire charged on to the enemy. Motivating his troops to keep up the momentum of attack, the young officer though being seriously wounded kept leading from the front. He was aware that it was only on his success would the troops of the 13 JAK RIF under the command of Captain Vikram Batra that was attacking from another flank will be able to capture and secure the prized objective. Captain Vikram Batra, the young officer who after his heroic feat that led to the capture of Point 5140 in the Drass sector a fortnight ago and who had proudly that day declared "Dil Mange More' (The Heart Wants More) to the young and brave TV reporter Barkha Dutt was once again in the thick of it. Though he was down with fever and fatigue, the spirited young officer from 13 JAK RIF who had earlier been ordered to rest by his Commanding Officer, Lt Colonel YK Joshi had volunteered to lead the attack.

And while he with his troops under heavy enemy fire kept climbing and firing at the Pakistanis, young Rifleman Sanjay Kumar from the same battalion in a rare show of raw courage and guts while crawling under heavy enemy automatic fire kept neutralizing the enemy bunkers and machine gun nests till he was hit very badly on his chest and forearm. Meanwhile Captain Vikram Batra who was now known by the nickname Sher Shah on noticing that his men who had reached the top of Point 4875 were being subjected to very heavy fire from a Pakistani machine gun nest that was sited across a ledge, he decided to go for it himself. Crouching forward under the cover of darkness and while it was still snowing, he slowly crept towards the blazing machine gun and finally silenced it by lobbying a grenade on it. But there were still some other enemy machine guns on that ledge that had to be silenced too and young Batra without caring for his own life led a ferocious charge straight into the guts of the enemy. Shouting the battle cry of "Durga Mata Ki Jai' as he and his men got closer to the enemy, he unsheathed his bayonet and they all then took on the enemy with their bare hands. As the Indian soldiers came charging with their bayonets, the Pakistanis seeing the ferocity of the attack started retreating. But there was still one more enemy machine gun that had to be eliminated and silenced and the brave Captain Batra took that too in his stride. Leading from the front the young bachelor officer by doing so had saved the life of a married soldier comrade who he knew had a wife and children back home. But unfortunately having captured the objective, a rocket fired by the enemy got young Batra on the head and he was no more.

The brave young officer from Palampur in Himachal Pradesh by his heroic actions even in death was an epitome of courage and determination. Both Captain Vikram Batra and Rifleman Sanjay Kumar with their unprecedented acts of bravery and courage had created history not only for the battalion but also for the Jammu and Kashmir Rifle Regiment and the Indian Army. The country would soon honour them with the nation's highest gallantry award, the Param Veer Chakra. It was a unique and rare feat by the 13 JAK RIF, an infantry battalion of the Indian army that had earned not only two Param Veer Chakras in one single action, but a plethora of Veer Chakras too.

Not to be left behind, it was now the turn of Colonel Badola's 2nd Naga Battalion of the 79 Mountain Brigade to show the Pakistanis the kind of stuff that they were made off. The sturdy men from the hills of Nagaland had been tasked to capture and destroy the enemy's mortar position that was sited well in depth. The platoon that was led by Captain Dipankar Sehrawat on the night of 7th/8th July having stealthily made their way across the mountain had descended close to the objective, but found it to be heavily guarded. Nonetheless, the brave Nagas with their deadly war cry of "Jai Durga Naga" attacked the position with their weapons and hatchets that were locally known as 'dahs' and the enemy soon fled leaving behind their mortars, which the Nagas now happily brought back as prized war trophies.

And finally when the Indian Para Commandos cut off all the enemy supply lines to Kaksar, and the infantry cordoned off the Pakistanis that had occupied the heights in and around that feature, it seemed that the game was up for the enemy. And as the Indian artillery and the air force kept playing merry hell into them, the enemy's morale was now in their boots. Isolated from their bases they were now not only short of rations, but their holding of ammunition too had reached a crisis level, and it was now only a question of time before Kaksar too would be in Indian hands. But fortunately that was not to be as the enemy now decided to quit the battlefield and give a walk over to the Indians in that sub-sector.

Having suffered severe military reverses in all the sectors that they had intruded into, and with the President of America on 4th July during his meeting at Washington with Nawaz Sharif having convinced the Pakistani Prime Minister that it was time for Pakistan to see reason and pull back to their own side of the LOC, the stage was now being set to enforce a ceasefire and to permit the Pakistanis to retreat peacefully. But the Indian army having wrested the initiative from the Pakistanis and having pushed them back across the LOC was now very keen to cross the LOC and occupy the dominating heights on the other side. The aim was to preempt any such intrusions in the future, but unfortunately the government policy forbade them to do so. At one stage fearing that the Indian army may well cross the LOC and push towards taking the rest of Kashmir, General Musharraf without informing the Pakistani government had even ordered Pakistan nuclear tipped missiles ready to be launched towards India and especially on strategic military targets inside Kashmir. And when President Clinton on the 4th July confronted Nawaz Sharif and asked him whether he knew how close and advanced was the threat by Pakistan to start a nuclear war in the subcontinent and Nawaz pleaded ignorance, even Clinton was surprised. He reminded the Pakistani Prime Minister of how dangerously the US and the USSR had come to a nuclear confrontation in 1962 over the Cuban crises, and he sternly warned Pakistan not to ever mess with nuclear weapons. At that crucial meeting an angry Clinton had also accused the Pakistan ISI and the Sharif government of doing sweet nothing to help the US catch Osama Bin Laden and other Al Qaida leaders. And when Clinton categorically stated that the ISI instead was not only working hand in glove with the Al Qaida boss and the Taliban in fomenting terrorism and actively supporting the terrorists in Afghanistan and in India, Shiraz just could not believe it. This had been conveyed to him by his counterpart in Washington DC and he wondered what would happen if a Muslim fanatical organization like the Al Qaida ever got hold of such a deadly and destructive weapon. And while the Pakistanis suffered one reverse after the other both militarily and diplomatically, the Pakistani intelligence agents on 5th July abducted another staff member of the India diplomatic staff in Islamabad. Mr Yograj Vij was literally beaten at his very own doorstep before being abducted by more than a dozen armed intelligence operatives.

Realising that the Pakis were very bad losers, the suave Indian High Commissioner in Islamabad Mr G Parthasarathy not only cautioned all staff members to be doubly vigilant, but he also sent a strong note of protest to the Pakistan foreign office. Partha as he was affectionately called by his friends was a seasoned diplomat. He had also served in the Indian army as an officer for five years before joining the India Foreign Office. His first foreign posting was in Moscow as a Third Secretary during the Brezhnev era, and he was also India's Ambassador to Myanmar, Australia and Cyprus. He had already served a tenure in Pakistan earlier from 1982 to 1985, when he was posted as the Consul General in the Indian Consulate at Karachi and he knew how to deal with the Pakistanis.During that period of General Zia's rule he had also established good relations with Benazir Bhutto while she was under house arrest at Karachi.

On the night of 9th July 1999, when the Pakistani DGMO, the Director General of Military Operations Lt General Taukir Zia rang up his Indian counterpart Lt.General Nirmal Vij on the hot line and conveyed to him that Pakistan wanted to pull out from Kaksar by early next morning and subsequently also from other areas, it was evident that Pakistanis had not only lost the battle on the ground at Kargil but it had also been badly bruised politically and diplomatically both at home and abroad.The sudden come down by Nawaz Sharif to pull out completely had not only infuriated his countrymen, but also the many militant organizations that they had been nursing and using in their long drawn out proxy war against India. Though the casualty rate on both the sides during the 42 day intense border conflict was rather heavy, but the fact remained that Pakistan had been beaten once again both militarily and diplomatically by the Indians. And on 16th July, when the final day of withdrawal arrived and Pakistan requested for another 24 hours to pack up and leave, Monty who was celebrating India's victory at Kargil with Unni at the Press Club aptly remarked.

"Having taken Vajpayee on a bus ride, I hope the Pakistanis will keep their word. Because they never ever do so and I won't be the least surprised if the gang of four led by General Musharaff in an act of frustration lets loose their arsenal of nuclear weapons on us."

"Well one never can say, but one thing is for certain that the gamble that was taken by Pakistan has come as a good payoff for the ruling caretaker Vajpayee government, and with general elections due in October, he and his BJP will now be riding high and the party will definitely cash in on it,"' said Unni while predicting that though Sonia Gandhi was now at the helm of the Congress, but the rumblings and disillusionment within the party that had already begun was bound to affect their chances at the polls.

"For some of them to have an Italian and that to a lady as the party boss and whose only qualification is in having the Gandhi surname was not only a matter of national disgrace and shame, but it also showed how headless the Congress had become. The very fact that they could not choose from one of the old veteran stalwarts and experienced leaders from the many who were and still are a part and parcel of the Congress high command for so many decades only goes to prove that most of them are either incapable or are totally incompetent or they too have skeletons in their cupboards that Sonia is aware off," said Monty.'

"I think spunkless and spineless would be more apt," added one of Unni's friends who too was a veteran journalist but who it seems had one too many for the day. And on the very next day, when the news arrived that Arun Singh, who was once Rajiv Gandhi's very close friend, buddy and advisor and who had resigned from Rajiv's cabinet on the Bofors issue and had become a recluse was now back as an advisor and as a Special Executive Assistant to the Vajpayee government, it took the Congress and Monty also completely by surprise.

CHAPTER-16

A Gamble That Failed

Though the enemy withdrew to their own side of the LOC, but they like cowards also played it very dirty. Unable to vanquish the Indians on the battle field, the enemy while withdrawing had placed at random anti-personnel mines and booby traps at various places and on the tracks leading to those heights. And on some posts they had even booby trapped a few bunkers. As the Indian soldiers started reoccupying their posts, the casualties from mine blasts and booby traps also kept increasing and ultimately the sappers with anti personnel mine detectors had to be brought in. The deadly anti personnel mine, the size no bigger than that of a shoe polish tin had maimed quite a few and seeing them being evacuated with one leg or a hand missing had only furthered angered the Indian troops.

'Humme sirf ek mauka aur de do aur hum un sub ka sir katke pesh kardenge. Jaise ke Thakur ne kiya tha Gabbar Singh ko Sholay mein aapne lathon se. Aur hum bhi unko lath mar mar ke unko unki Nani yaad deladenge,' (Just give us one more opportunity and we will cut off and bring back their heads as war trophies. And like the handless Thakur in the film Sholay who showed what his mighty legs could do to dacoit Gabbar Singh, we too will kick the enemy in such a manner that he will forever remember his grandmother) said a young soldier to the group of correspondents who were waiting to interview those few unlucky ones who had survived the battle of the heights. Though the young soldier had lost both his legs in a mine blast, the young soldier's morale was still sky high and the very fact that he was still smiling as he got into the waiting chopper to be evacuated was proof enough for the media to project to the world that the Indian Army was second to none.

"But I must also give full credit to the Pakistanis in the way they took us on. It was not easy going at all for our gallant young officers and soldiers and the Pakistanis were very well prepared to face us. And had it not been for the International pressure they would have probably fought on and they would not have called it off so very abruptly. In fact from most of the posts that they had occupied on our side of the LOC and were still holding on to, they withdrew from them rather reluctantly," said one of the Brigade Commanders who had been in the thick of it ever since Tololing was captured.

"And full credit must also be given to those on the enemy side who had planned and executed this operation so very brilliantly," said another Indian Brigade Commander. And though we lost the gallant Captain Vikram Batra, our fighting Sher (Tiger) during the capture of Peak 4875 in the Mushkoh Valley, but Pakistan also produced one braveheart too during the battle for Tiger Hill.'Captain Karnal whose middle name was also Sher and surname was Khan literally fought like a wounded tiger till the very end. He had launched not one, but three counter attacks to dislodge us from Tiger Hill and at one point he nearly did so. The last and final attack that Captain Karnal Sher Khan, the officer from the 12th Battalion, Northern Light had put in till he was mowed down by a hail of bullets spoke very highly of the officer's motivation and courage, and if I was his commanding officer I would strongly recommend him for the 'Nishan-i-Haider.' which is the equivalent of our Param Veer Chakra', said one of the Commanding Officer's whose troops at Tiger Hill were witness to those ferocious enemy counter attacks.

Though the short low intensity conflict between the two sides on those massive cold mountain ranges and peaks was unprecedented in the annals of military history, the rat-a-tat of gun fire and the pounding of each other's defenses by the artillery still carried on intermittently even after the Pakistanis had withdrawn from all the occupied areas in the Kargil sector. Commenting on the heavy price that both the countries had been paying over Kashmir ever since both the nations became independent countries, Shiraz while discussing the matter with his family said.

"It's a real pity that the Line of Control invariably keeps getting out of control every time there is a move to settle this long standing Kashmir dispute peacefully. And mind you there is no military solution to this unless both the countries are prepared to bleed to death militarily, politically and economically. To me at least it seems that the politicians on both sides including the Generals who presided over Pakistan's destiny in the past and even those who are at the helm of affairs today in Pakistan are simply obsessed with Kashmir. For all of them Kashmir was and still is a mindless fixation and a fire they all want to keep eternally burning for their own damn selfish ends. Because right from the days of the Nehru-Liaqat talks in the early 1950's, to the signing of the Tashkent agreement in 1966 by Ayub and Shastri, followed by the Bhutto-Indira Gandhi talks in Simla in 1972, and now the Sharif-Vajpayee declaration at Lahore, no progress whatsoever has been made to resolve this never ending contentious issue once and for all. And as a result of which both the countries are still suffering. There has not only to be a give and take by both the sides, but also the will and determination to do it benevolently. Because every time the matter is put on the rails, somebody or the other tries to derail it, and it is all back to square one again. And according to my information, the secret talks that had been initiated by Nawaz Sharif and Vajpayee through their nominated representatives after the Lahore Declaration was signed was really making good and steady progress, and the possibility of an international border running through Kashmir was very much on the cards. But the Pakistan army generals had to go and screw it all up. The masterminds of this military operation were probably driven by the belief that their nuclear capability provided the necessary protective shield to the country, but it misfired and the operation fizzled out like a dirty wet firecracker. And what was still worse is the fact that Nawaz Sharif at his meeting with Clinton not only swore complete ignorance about the operation, but he also tried to put all the blame on his generals. And as a result of all this the blame game between the politicians and the generals has already started making the rounds in the gossip circles of the high and the mighty in Islamabad. And not only that, a strong rumour that is currently making the rounds in the diplomatic circuit in Moscow is that Nawaz Sharif was not only admonished by Bill Clinton for violating the LOC, but he was also accused of not reining in his army chief who after the utter humiliation and debacle in Kargil was fearing that India might carry their offensive across the LOC and he had even ordered the nuclear tipped missiles to be ready for action if need be. The American President I believe also took Sharif to task for Pakistan's reluctance to bring Osama Bin Laden to justice and he also mentioned that in spite of making tall promises to get Bin Laden, the ISI instead was hand in glove with the Al-Qaida and the Taliban in supporting terrorist activities in Afghanistan, India and elsewhere too. Therefore having been badly cornered, Sharif finally at the end of the meeting agreed not only to announce a Pakistani withdrawal from Kargil, but also for the restoration of the status quo ante on the LOC. And this I believe was on condition that Clinton should take a personal interest in the resumption of India-Pakistan talks on Kashmir, and Pakistan in turn would reciprocate by intensifying their hunt for Bin Laden in Afghanistan. There was no doubt that Mian Nawaz Sharif having received a rocket from the Americans had already initiated his back door diplomacy. He had even I believe secretly dispatched Niaz Naik, his think tank in a private specially chartered aircraft to Delhi to meet Mr Vajpayee, and the retired former Foreign Secretary did convey to the Indian Prime Minister that Pakistan wanted peace. But by then, the Indian troops had recaptured most of the strategic heights and were going hell for leather to rout the Pakistanis. Seeing the euphoria that was being created by the dare devil Indian soldiers, the Indian political leaders were therefore in no mood to listen to Pakistan peaceful overtures," added Shiraz as he pointed out to his son Tojo and daughter Sherry on a world atlas, the high mountainous areas where the recent skirmishes between the two sides had taken place.

"But Dad if all that you just said is really true, then the army top brass including the army chief, General Musharaff is also equally to be blamed for the fiasco. And it seems that the only saving grace for agreeing to withdraw is Pakistan's tenuous claim that the intruders were all Mujahideens and freedom fighters and not the men in regular Khaki uniform. And now that the Indians have the dead bodies of Captain Karnal Sher Khan, Captain Imtiaz Malik, Naik Inayat Ali who are all from the Northern Light Infantry and a few others like them, how long do you think the world will believe our story," said Sherry as she read out a few extracts from the cover story titled "The Pull Back and Beyond" that the Indian magazine 'Frontline' had published in its issue dated 30th July, 1999 and which Salim Rehman had sent from New Delhi in the diplomatic mail bag.

A few weeks later, when another bunch of Indian magazines and periodicals arrived by the diplomatic mail bag from New Delhi and Shiraz saw the photograph of the President of India, K R Narayanan presenting the Param Veer Chakra medal to the late Captain Vikram Batra's father on India's 62nd Independence Day, he felt both proud and sad. He was proud because his old regiment, the Jammu and Kashmir Rifles had been awarded not one but two Param Veer Chakras for the same operation, which was a unique record in the annals of free India's military history, and he was sad because the 'Dil Mange More' brave officer from Palampur, Kangra was no more. However, an article with a photograph of the handsome Indian film star Deepak Kumar in another magazine had caught his daughter's fancy. The rising film hero it seems was very lucky to have survived without any major injury a deadly train accident In India that took place soon after midnight on 1st August 1999. That night the Avadh Assam Express at 1.45 a.m. had collided with the Delhi bound Brahmaputra Mail and in which over 300 people had died and more than 600 were injured. The terrible ghastly accident had taken place near Kishanganj railway station, which was an area where the militant 'Bodos' were very active. But this was not of their doing. It was in fact a human error by the railways, and it was only providence that had saved Deepak Kumar. He was returning from a commercial advertisement film shoot of a new rugged four wheeler station wagon vehicle that was being shot in the dense jungles of Northern Assam with a horde of domesticated elephants. The SUV vehicle was being compared to a giant elephant walking tall and with ease through the cross country jungle trail. Luckily for Peevee, the Brahamaputra Mail first class air-conditioned bogie that he was travelling in was somewhere in the centre of the long rake and the impact had only derailed it. Nonetheless and like a true hero and inspite of being injured, he too had joined in the rescue operations.

Meanwhile in Moscow while going through the many magazines and periodicals that Salim Rehman had sent, Shiraz noticed that though most of the Indian magazines were still hailing the courage and bravery of the young Indian officers and soldiers, a few also gave prominence to the Indian tennis duo of Leander Paes and Mahesh Bhupathy. Following their win in the French Open, the two Indian tennis stars had also won the doubles crown at Wimbledon, which was the Mecca of lawn tennis. That was also on the 4th of July, after the Indian army had recaptured Tololing.

The August 23rd, 1999 issue of the 'Outlook' with a photograph of Rahul Gandhi sitting next to a girl in mini pants and watching the cricket world cup at Edgbaston in England had also caught Shiraz's eye. There were some unconfirmed rumours from the Pakistani High Commissioner in London that the young man was dating some Colombian girl and the girl holding the vodaphone cutout in her hand in that photograph looked like a Colombian alright.

"I only hope he is not seriously courting her. As it is the poor Italian Bahu with the Bofors stink left by the Quattrochhis still prevaling at 10 Janpath is finding it hard and difficult to lead the Congress party to victory in the coming elections, and the induction of a Columbian Bahu into the Gandhi family I am afraid will only spell more disaster for her," said Shiraz as he showed Saira the photograph.

"I think these media people only create such rumours for publicity. For all you know they may be just good friends,"'said Saira.

"Yes, I also feel that there is nothing wrong in dating a Columbian as long as she does not have any connection with the infamous Medellin drug cartel. As it is one Italian connection with the Quattrochis was bad enough, and another Colombian one may well spell the death knell of the Gandhi's politically and that would really be sad,'"said Shiraz with a mischievous grin on his face, as he noticed Arun Singh's photograph on page 40 of the India Today, 12th July issue. The former bum pal of the late Rajiv Gandhi from Doon school who fell out with his friend and Prime Minister on the Bofors issue had been appointed by none other than Mr Vajpayee as a special executive assistant to the external affairs minister.

"I am sure this must have irked poor Sonia and my gut feeling is that the Bofors gun will once again become a major issue of mudslinging in the forthcoming elections in India," added Shiraz as he helped himself to some delicious 'Chapali Kebabs' that his daughter Sherry had prepared as snacks to go with her father's Black Label whisky. And hardly had the dust settled on the Kargil front, when India on 17th August 1999 shot down a Pakistani naval aircraft in the Rann of Kutch area. According to the Indian version, the Atlantique, a Pakistani naval surveillance aircraft was on a secret spying mission and was therefore shot down when it intruded into Indian airspace. While the Pakistanis maintained that it was on a routine training flight and it was a provocative action by India that resulted in the deaths of 16 innocent Pakistani servicemen, the Indians kept reiterating that the aircraft was on a spying mission. Surprisingly it was also on this very day that India also announced her proactive 'Draft Nuclear Doctrine' that called for the pursuance of a credible minimum nuclear deterrence that would envisage the establishment of a triad of aircraft, mobile land based missiles and sea based assets. The force levels however were not quantified. In the aftermath of the Indo-Pakistani nuclear tests in May 1998, Pakistan did make a comprehensive 'Strategic Missile Restraint' proposal to India, but India it seemed were still in the process of studying that proposal.

Consequently Pakistan's humiliation at Kargil had also led to more intensified and deliberate attacks not only on India's para-military and military outposts in the heart of the Kashmir valley, but also on innocent Hindu civilians even in such far off places like Doda in the Kishtwar District of Jammu and Kashmir. The dare devil storming by the militants of the BSF residential complex and headquarters at Bandipur in the Kashmir valley, that was followed by an attack on a Rashtriya Rifles army post in Chak Nutnusa, and the recent gunning down of Colonel Balbir Singh, the Commanding Officer of the 4th Rashtriya Rifles in a well planned daylight ambush, followed by an audacious attack on a brigade headquarters at Tregam, and the attack on a BSF camp at Rajouri all in quick succession had no doubt introduced a new element of daring in the militants. The very fact that they were now openly targeting army camps and were willing to engage them in fierce gun battles only suggested that there was now a streak of strong fanaticism in them. The intelligence reports also indicated that not only were they heavily armed with rocket launchers, universal machine guns and shoulder fired Stinger missiles, but they were also well trained in the use of sophisticated long range signal equipment. They were also highly motivated now and were ready to fight to a finish if need be. This was definitely not there earlier in them and this sort of 'Jehadi' dare devil suicide actions had now got Shiraz very worried

On learning that a large number of them were foreign mercenaries who had also fought against the Russians in Afghanistan and that the sudden impetus in their activities was a fall out from the humiliation that they had suffered in Kargil, Shiraz now wondered whether there was any link between the Pakistani militant Mujahedeen groups like the Lashkar-e-Toiba and such like others that were trained by the ISI and those from Bill Laden's Al-Qaida camps in Afghanistan.

It was strongly rumoured that before launching the Kargil operation, General Musharraf had also sounded Nawaz Sharif about the requirement of actively involving the so called Bill Laden Brigade on this venture and therefore the presence of these foreign mercenaries of Arab, Afghan and other West Asian origin fighting Pakistan's proxy war in Kashmir, and being paid and compensated for very heavily both in cash and in kind to die as martyrs and fedayeens' therefore could not be ruled out.But Shiraz's biggest worry was that in order to promote Bin Laden's call for total Islamization and Talibanization of the world, this heavily armed, highly motivated and well trained army of diehard fanatical mercenaries may one day point their guns towards Pakistan and terrorize the entire world too. He had no doubt that the ISI which was a state within a state in Pakistan had also systematically spread its tentacles far and wide into India, Bangladesh and Nepal. And the possibility of these groups being used to spread a campaign of terror in India and elsewhere was now very much on the cards.

Moreover, with the BJP, the Hindu oriented political party in India steadily gaining ground, the likelihood of a well orchestrated anti Muslim propaganda campaign by the ISI to spread communal disharmony and violence during the coming elections in India was also a distinct possibility. With all these factors now playing on his mind, Shiraz very much wanted indirectly to warn his Indian counterpart in Moscow, but the present deteriorating relations between the two countries forbade him to do so. He felt that it would be taken as another ploy by the Pakistanis to hoodwink the Indians.

Meanwhile the sell out by Pakistan on the Kargil war had also drastically brought down Sharif's popularity among the masses and had led to serious dissatisfaction among its own people, the military and the various militant groups that Pakistan had been nurturing and using in its long drawn out proxy war against India. But the Indian victory on the other hand had created an unprecedented euphoria of giving the military man in uniform his due. The people of India not only hailed the courage of the young Indian jawans and officers who had sacrificed their lives with astonishing feats of bravery on those dizzy and difficult heights, but it also hailed the mature manner by which the caretaker Vajpayee government had steered and handled the situation both nationally and internationally. There was also no doubt that the military and diplomatic victory over Pakistan had also sent Prime Minister Vajpayee and his Bharatiya Janata Party's popularity soaring sky high. And with the election fever catching up in India and the saffron flag and the lotus symbol now emerging as front runners, a demoralized Congress party that had so far been accusing the Vajpayee government of serious intelligence failures and for the loss of territory was now therefore forced to apply and adopt new poll strategies. The party had been constantly downplaying the Kargil war and the time had come for the Congress President of Italian origin to do some serious thinking on the subject.

According to a national opinion poll that was conducted by 'Outlook' magazine in late August 1999, though it was a two horse race between Vajpayee and Sonia, and coalition politics had come to stay, the BJP and its allies were way ahead of Sonia's Congress and her partners. For Sonia the Congress party chief a safe seat was a must and the Congress had already started the so called 'cat and mouse' game to mislead the opposition.The choice for her was either to stand from Amethi in Uttar Pradesh, her late husband's constituency, or from Bellary in Karnataka from where her late mother-in-law was elected. And when it was finally decided that the battle royal would take place at Bellary between Sushma Swaraj, the 'Swadeshi Bahenji' of the BJP taking on the 'Videshi Bahu' from the Congress, even the bookies were unwilling to give any odds.("Arre Bhai donon mein se koi bhi jeet sakta hai lekin rigging nahin hona chahiye,'(Between the two ladies it is difficult to predict a winner and either of them could win provided there is no rigging) said the bookie to Peevee as he placed his bet for an overall BJP win in the forthcoming general elections.

"Lekin agar Sonia Gandhi ki vajai, koi, Sonia Banerjee ya Sonia Sharma ya Sonia Gupta hoti to woho shahed kabhi maidan mein nahin aati aur jeet to dur ki baat hai. (If instead of Sonia Gandhi, if it was some Sonia Banerjee or Sonia Sharma or Sonia Gupta, then there was no way that she would have one}. But this Sonia happens to be a Gandhi and for the masses the name Gandhi still counts, and with her now leading the party, the Congress party is very heavily depending on her to turn the tables on the BJP," added the Bookie as he handed over the betting receipt to Peevee.

During that month of August 1999, while Pakistan was still finding excuses for the debacle at Kargil, the Nawaz Sharif government had also stepped up the enquiries against Benazir and her husband Asif Zardari. Both of them had been indicted for stealing more than a billion U.S. dollars from the country's coffers and the Pakistan Court had also ordered the freezing of their property in Pakistan which was estimated to be worth some 3 million rupees. And though Zardari was already behind bars inside the Karachi Central Jail, Benazir was roaming free and she in her Toyota Landcruiser with her trademark white scarf over a head was a regular visitor to the jail. A stash of confidential documents that had been stolen from a Geneva based lawyer who was very close to the Bhutto's had given Hassan Waseem Afzal the head of the NAB, the National Accountability Bureau enough material to indict the wealthy couple. The stolen documents clearly indicated that Zardari had moved millions of dollars outside Pakistan and had stashed them in secret bank accounts in England, Switzerland and also in the United States of America. And according to one reliable source all this had been done by floating shell companies in various off shore safe havens, like the Virgin Island, Panama and in the Isle of Man. Not only did the couple have millions of dollars in their banks, but they also owned huge properties in some of the most posh areas of the world and the 131 hectare Rockwood Estate in Surrey was only one of them. And all this was done while Benazir was in power and while Pakistan was sliding deeper into international debt. Surprisingly, the trusted Swiss lawyer did not even report the loss of the stolen documents to the Swiss police, and when the account under the name of Bomer Finance was revealed it was like a bombshell. According to the Pakistani investigators, this offshore company that was run by the Zardaris had on record the details of who will get how much and that too percentage wise. The notings like the infamous Martin Ardbo diary in the famous Bofors scandal case was written in the lawyer's own hand, and it clearly mentioned 50% to AAZ, Asif Ali Zardari and 50% to BB meaning Benazir Bhutto. This was the duo's spending money and it was from this account number 552343 that was held in the branch of the Union Bank of Switzerland in England and from where the purchase of that wealthy necklace for Benazir was made on 13th October, 1994.

And while the Pakistani 'Aam Aadmi' (commom man) on the streets were shouting slogans against Benazir and Asif Zardari, in India the politicians from all parties were wooing the 'Aam Aadmi' to vote for them in the forth coming general elections.

In early September, with the elections in India barely a month away, Monty who had become an ardent Vajpayee and BJP supporter therefore in order to find out the projected seats that the NDA, National Democratic Alliance were likely to get in the 13th Lok Sabha, decided to call on Unnikrishnan, his old friend and guide at the Press Club. That evening dear Unni was in really high spirits as he came out with some interesting stories and facts about the cat and mouse game that the Congress party had played to find a safe seat for the Italian born Gandhi Bahu.

"The Congress bigwigs in order to ensure Sonia's win had kept the matter top secret and even on the penultimate day for the filing of nominations, nobody was sure from where would she fight the elections. And to ensure her defeat, the BJP too did not disclose till the last moment as to who would oppose her. The party wanted a mature and seasoned politician and the BJP head honchos were therefore keeping a close tag on the whereabouts of Rajiv's Gandhi's poor widow. Like the 'Great Game', this cat and mouse game however was being played in typical Indian style. And it all began when Sonia Gandhi with her personal secretary, Vincent George, the Congress Party General Secretary. Ghulam Nabi Azad together with their security entourage on the evening before the last day for filing of nominations boarded the Indian Airlines commercial flight from Delhi to Hyderabad. Waiting for them at the Hyderabad airport was a seven-seater chopper with a flight plan to fly them to Cuddapah. But when the flight finally took off for Bellary instead and the BJP got early wind of it, they too decided to fly in the lady with the big red circular bindi on her forehead. Next day afternoon when Shushma Swaraj's helicopter also landed at Bellary, the battle of the Indian Bahu against the Italian Bahu had begun in real earnest,' said Unni giggling away and gently tapping the bartender on the shoulder to pour him his last large Old Monk rum.

"But you haven't yet told us how many seats will the BJP and her allies will get or are likely to get,'" asked Monty as he too ordered another chilled beer.

"Well, with the success at Kargil still ruling the waves, I think it will be somewhere around 320 plus minus 10 for the BJP and their allies and therefore my own prediction is that the BJP on its own steam will definitely go past the double century mark for the first time. But what is seriously bugging me is that after coming to power, the sacrifices that were made by our valiant soldiers and officers like Captain Vikram Batra, Lieutenant Manoj Pandey and others like them who gave their today for our tomorrow will as usual be lost to history and soon be forgotten," said Unni somewhat despondently.

"Yes, it is indeed a real pity that the many sacrifices by the young jawans and officers of our gallant Indian Armed Forces who are the sentinels of our nation are only highlighted and played up by our politicians and their political parties only in times like these, and it is done only for political gains. But thereafter they are quietly forgotten and put into the dustbin of history. Needless to say that this is the only organization in this country that is not only totally apolitical and secular, but it is also the best disciplined and the most dependable entity in this entire country. Incidentally, this is also the only force whose members take an oath on joining the Services to even die for the nation if need be. Besides guarding our long land and sea frontiers and the skies above, they are also the ones who come to the rescue of the government and the civil administration in times of national calamities and crisis whenever they are called upon to do so, and they do it most willingly, sincerely and very efficiently,' said Monty.

'But the most unfortunate part is that when it comes to giving them their just dues they are more often than not treated like unwanted parasites and orphans. And it is all because they have no significant voting power, no unions and they cannot open their mouths while in uniform. They are therefore taken for a ride every time by the politicians, the 'Babus' in the Defence ministry and the so called bureaucrats from the IAS. And as a result of all this, the armed forces are no longer a service that the young and educated look forward to. And not only is there a tremendous shortfall in the intake of the officer cadre in all the three services of the army, navy and the air force, but they are also not getting the right kind of young leadership material any more. The very fact that they are being constantly and systematically downgraded in status in the order of precedence that the government draws up from time to time only proves my point. By simply honouring a few of them with the so called category of 'Seva Medals' like the PVSM, AVSM, VSM during peace time and doling out a handful of gallantry awards on every 26th of January parade at the 'Rajpath' is simply not good enough. These awards I am afraid will not give them back the status and the honour that they once enjoyed and which they still deserve. And mind you it is not just the poor pay and perquisites that is keeping the bright young men away from this noble profession, it is the clever and systematic manner by which the 'Babus' the politicians and the mandarins in South Block have been sidelining them. For the men in uniform it is 'Izzat, Imaan and Iqbal' that is respect, honour and pride that matters the most and not just free rations, canteen facilities and rail travel concessions. And my only fear now is that if this state of the affairs continues and they keep getting this kind of step motherly treatment, then I am afraid the services that we all once prided upon and on whose dependable shoulders rests our own very safety and survival both from foreign intervention and internal dissension may well one day let us down very badly," added Unni as he with pride and sorrow drank a toast to the gallant Indian Armed Forces.

"Yes, I think you have summed it up very well and the government must now sit up and take stock of the situation. And though I have been told that the people of India and some corporate houses have contributed around Rupees160 crores to the National Defence Fund, but how much of that will actually go towards the welfare of the disabled soldiers and the families of those who sacrificed their lives at Kargil is a million dollar question. Because the contribution to the Army's Central Welfare Fund is not even 2 crores and if one compares these figures to the 400 hundred crores that were spent on the Cricket World Cup related campaigns, it is indeed a national shame. What the army wants besides cash are shelters for the widows, jobs for their dependents, education facilities and hostels for their children, artificial limbs, motorized wheel chairs and jobs for soldiers who have lost their limbs. But above all what these gallant men in uniform and their families need is the "Izzat" (honour) and a salute from the nation for the sacrifices made by them. For the soldier it's the pride and honour that comes before death and defeat and that is what the regimental spirit in the Indian army is all about. But unfortunately our so called 'Netas' (Politicians) and the senior mandarins sitting in their plush air-conditioned offices in the imposing South and North Blocks of the capital have no time for the men in uniform once the battle is over,' said Monty as he sadly narrated to them the manner in which his own foster brother Major Shiraz Ismail Khan a Param Veer Chakra winner, the nation's highest gallantry award who sacrificed his life during the 1971 war with Pakistan had been quietly forgotten by the people of this country.

"There are only a handful of such brave and courageous soldiers who have been given this unique honour, but they unfortunately have no place even in our children's history books. And that is indeed a pity. And incidentally, let me also tell you that the PVC medal was designed by a foreign lady. She was not only a good painter and an artist but she also had a very deep knowledge of Indian mythology, Sanskrit and the Vedas too. Eva Yvonne Linda Maday-De-Maros, the daughter of Russian mother and a Hungarian father was born on 20th July, 1913 in Switzerland. In the winter of 1929 and while on a skiing holiday at Chamonix, she met Vikram Ramji Khanolkar, a dashing handsome young cadet from the Sandhurst Military Academy in England. While teaching Vikram ice skating, they fell in love. She was only 16 then. Later they got married and when she came to India, she became more Indian than most of us and was given the Indian name of Savitri Bai. Soon after Indian became independent, she was asked by the then Adjutant General, Major General Hiralal Atal to design India's highest gallantry medal, the Param Veer Chakra. Taking inspiration from the mythical Rishi Dadich who donated his thigh bones to the Gods to make a Vajra, a thunderbolt to kill the evil Britasur and also the sword called Bhawani from the legendary Mahratta King Shivaji, Savitri Bai designed the medal. Coincidentally, the first PVC was awarded to her own daughter's brother-in-law, Major Som Nath Sharma. Her daughter was married to a Sapper officer of the Indian army who was Major Som Nath Sharma's younger brother." And having said that when Monty raised a toast to all the gallant twenty one Param Veer Chakra winners of India, all those who were present in the Press Club that day happily said cheers.

Monty was about to order a fresh round of drinks, when he heard Peevee's loud voice across the bar. He had arrived unannounced to present a cheque of Rupees ten laks to the Adjutant General of the Indian Army. It was going to be his personal contribution for the welfare of the war widows and the children of those soldiers who had sacrificed their lives at Kargil. But it was on condition that the name of the donor would not be made public.

"I sincerely wish there were more such generous people like you who genuinely care for the welfare of our brave Indian army Jawans, because I know quite a few of our filthy rich people who contributed a paltry sum of a couple of thousands only. But they did it primarily to see their names in the list of donors in a widely read English newspaper," said Unni very sarcastically while raising a toast to the martyrs of Kargil.

During those early weeks of September, while the politicians and the political leaders of India went full throttle to garner the support of the masses with their usual basket full of false promises of shelter, water and a brighter and better India, in Pakistan the causes for the debacle and the defeat at Kargil at the hands of their arch enemy India which led to their shameful withdrawal had got the military and the Nawaz Sharif government at loggerheads. They had now within their own respective forums kept blaming each other, and the public too including the rank and file in the armed forces had started asking some very embarrassing questions of what happened at Kargil. And the most vituperative amongst them were the militant groups led by the Mullahs. While some accused Sharif for being a spunkless coward who had bowed down to American pressure, others questioned the Pakistan army chief's wisdom of undertaking an operation that could not be sustained militarily and politically. And while Musharaff kept telling the men in uniform that the order for the withdrawal had come from the Prime Minister and therefore it had to be obeyed, Nawaz Sharif on the other hand blamed his Army Chief for venturing on an operation where having sent his soldiers to occupy those dizzy heights, he didn't know how to get them down. For Nawaz Sharif, the man who defied the Americans and who detonated the nuclear bomb a little over a year ago, and who to the masses had become a hero, had now suddenly found himself in a very tricky situation. Not only was the Kargil adventure a political failure for him, but he was also afraid of being ousted by the military.

Though tactically and militarily the operation was a success initially, but politically for Pakistan and for Nawaz Sharif in particular it was a veritable disaster. The pullout had not only made the top brass in uniform very unhappy since it was done without extracting the pound of flesh and without negotiating any concessions from India, but the common man on the street too was disillusioned by the manner in which the Nawaz Sharif government had been lying to the people. Having been repeatedly told that the infiltration into Indian occupied Kashmir was the handiwork of the Mujahideens and Jehadis of Kashmiri origin; they were shocked, when the body of Captain Karnal Sher Khan draped in a Pakistani national flag was returned by India through the International Red Cross. And though Pakistan had not sent anyone to New Delhi to claim the dead body, but it did admit it was that of a Pakistani officer and a hero at that who had been awarded the Nishan-e-Haider. And though this was the first time that a person hailing from the land of the Pathans had been decorated with Pakistan's highest gallantry medal albeit posthumously, but the people of that province felt cheated. And it was on that very day while Captain Kamal Sher Khan's body was being laid to rest that Shiraz through his new Miltary Defence Attache who had recently been posted came to know a little more about 'Operation Badr."

As per the Defence Attache's version, the Pakistan army chief and his CGS Lt General Mohammed Aziz had only obtained an 'In Principle' concurrence and without any specifics from Nawaz Sharif to launch the operation with the so called Jehadis. And in order to keep it top secret the Pakistan army also undertook certain steps to maintain the vital element of surprise. As a deception plan they very wisely did not induct any new units or fresh troops into the selected operational area and no new administrative bases were created for the intrusions The additional artillery units that were inducted in that sector in July-September 1998 and which were involved in the exchange of fire during that period were not de-inducted and were redeployed in that sector with additional lethal ammunition. Once the intrusions began piecemeal in late February and early March, no leave of absence was granted to the intruders, and the reserve units and formations into the FCNA were only moved once the battle with India was joined.

"That's news to me and I must say that it was indeed a very well thought out and well executed plan. And the well thought out deception plan did catch the enemy on the wrong foot also, however it's after effects unfortunately has recoiled on us very badly. But all the same it has also had its effect on the current political scenario in India too,"said Shiraz

And while the Indian subcontinent was heading for some major political changes and upheavals, Shiraz in Moscow was surprised to learn about the fast deteriorating health of Boris Yeltsin, the President of Russia. Only a few were aware about the man's love for hard liquor, but at times the manner in which he conducted himself at public functions and gatherings was not only lewd and shocking, but sometimes it also veered on sheer eccentricity. There was no doubt that he was a very sick man, but his heavy drinking bouts were only adding to his many major medical problems. And though Yeltsin had survived another attempt at impeachment in the month of May for his several unconstitutional activities, his style of functioning had hardly changed. And on 9th August 1999, when Yeltsin for the fourth time fired his Prime Minister Sergei Stepashin and his entire cabinet and chose an Ex KGB man to fill the slot, it took everyone by complete surprise.

With the ugly head of revolt again surfacing in Chechnya and the series of apartment bombings that had recently taken place in various cities including the capital Moscow, the confidence of the people in Yeltsin and his government had been shaken very badly. The first bombing was that of the 'Manezh' the newly opened underground big shopping mall under the Red Square and close to the Kremlin. That was on the evening of 31st August 1999 and Shiraz and family were indeed very lucky to have escaped unhurt. At around 8 PM, when they were waiting to go down in the elevator, a massive explosion like an earthquake shook the area around. Soon thereafter on September 4th, 9th, 13th and 16th massive blasts shook the cities of Buynaksk, Moscow and Volgodonsk. They were so very powerful that it resulted not only in the deaths of hundreds of innocent people, and devastation of high-rise buildings, but injured many more. And for Mr Putin the ex KGB man who had just taken over as Prime Minister, it was like a challenge and a warning by the militant Muslims of Chechnya that more such bombings would follow if Russia continued to use its military might against the poor innocent people of Chechnya.

The little known Vladimir Putin, an ex KGB man was born on 7th October, 1952 to ordinary working class parents in Leningrad. His paternal grandfather Spiridon Ivanovich Putin it is believed had worked for Lenin and his wife Nadeshda as a cook and later had even cooked for Comrade Stalin. After graduating from Leningrad State University in International law in 1975, Putin joined the KGB and from 1985 to 1990 was stationed in Dresden, in erstwhile East Germany. Following the collapse of East Germany, Putin returned to the Soviet Union and on 26th March, 1997 was appointed Deputy Chief of Presidential Staff by Boris Yeltsin. On 9th August, 1999, he was appointed acting Prime Minister and seven days later on 16th August, when the State Duma approved his appointment as the new Prime Minister of Russia, it created a new record of sorts as he became the fifth one in eighteen months to hold that post. Virtually unknown to the public, the ex KGB man with the Yul Brynner looks was a much married man with two young daughters. He had become the favourite of an ailing Mr Yeltsin who was now also on the lookout for a suitable successor to the Russian Presidency.

"I hope this Mr Putin will now 'put in' his very best and put out the reign of terror, corruption and lawlessness that has engulfed this country ever since Gorbachov was ousted from his seat," said Saira a little poetically when the telephone rang. It was a call from her brother Salim Rehman who had come to Islamabad from New Delhi on some official work and he wanted to speak urgently and confidentially to Shiraz on an important official matter.

"I may be wrong, but do keep this to yourself. According to a reliable source in the Prime Minister's secretariat there are strong indications of Nawaz Sharif soon doing another 'Karamat' with the present army chief. It seems that he is not at all happy by the manner in which the Kargil episode had backfired on him politically and he is therefore on the lookout for someone who would be more pliable and dependable. It therefore has to be an army chief of his choice and one who would foot the bill as an ally. Though Musharraf was chosen by him for the top slot, but he now fears that the same man may one day topple him like Zia had done to Bhutto. Likewise most of the top army brass too I believe are not very happy in the manner in which the government has been trying to put the blame on the men in khaki for the debacle at Kargil, and the cowardly manner in which Nawaz Sharif succumbed to pressures from the United States," said Salim Rehman.

"But let us only hope that things do not come to such a pass, because it would be downright stupid and foolish to get rid of another army chief just because the Prime Minister does not like his damn face, and one who has been in the chair for not even for a year. And I am sure the army which has always been the kingmaker in Pakistan politics will not take it lying down either," said Shiraz while requesting his brother-in-law to keep him posted in case there were any further developments on this very sensitive and delicate issue.

"I think this blame game over the Kargil fiasco between the politicians in power and those sitting in the opposition together with the army generals who are now openly blaming Nawaz Sharif for not taking advantage of the sacrifices that were made by the Pakistanis on those dizzy heights will only further lead to more anarchy in the country," said Saira who having overheard bits of the telephonic conversation between her husband and her brother had also put two and two together.

"Yes, there I fully agree with you and the fallout from this will only embolden the hands of the various militant groups like the Al-Badr, the Laskar-e-Toiba and the Harkat-ul-Mujahideen, who with the backing of the Pakistani army and the ISI had been used extensively in this operation and whose sacrifices were no less either. And if the reports by some of the western correspondents that the infiltrators were a mixed force of not only Pakistanis, Afghans, Arabs and Kashmiris, but it also had a few British Muslims are to be believed, then I am afraid things are only going to get only worse for the country. Moreover, if it is also true that quite a few who volunteered for the Jihad are also linked to Bin Laden's Al-Qaida, then the day is not far when the world will look at Pakistan as a terrorist state and the possibility of these very groups 'Talibanizing' Pakistan in the near future therefore cannot be completely ruled out,' said Shiraz whose fears about a possible confrontation between the Generals and the Prime Minister was further confirmed, when he in order to find out a little more rang up retired Lt General Aslam Rehman in Islamabad.

"Well it may not be hundred percent correct, but I do believe that during the recent Corps Commanders conference that was held a few days ago in mid September, the army chief it seems had expressed his serious doubts about Nawaz Sharif's competence in running the country and the Corps Commanders generally were in agreement with him also. And the matter I believe has now got further complicated after Lt General Tariq Pervez the Corps Commander of the Quetta Corps confidentially conveyed this to his cousin Raja Nadir Pervez who is presently is the Minister of Communications in the Nawaz Sharif government, and who in turn had sounded the Prime Minister. According to another inside information, the Quetta Corps Commander had also indirectly warned the Prime Minister that if any attempt was made to remove General Musharraf then the army would surely strike as they would not take the removal and the sacking of two army chiefs within a span of one year very kindly So at this very moment it is a kind of a cat and mouse game that is being played in secret by the Prime Minister and his loyal henchmen on one side and the top army brass on the other. And let us only hope and pray that the matter does not get aggravated further by some stupid and irresponsible actions by both the sides," said the retired General.Officer.

A few days later, when some armed army personnel from the 111 Independent Brigade Group located at Rawalpindi together with some armoured cars were seen deployed near the GHQ, and a few infantry columns were seen patrolling the areas around the Prime Minister's house and the National Assembly building, it looked as if the army was getting ready to strike. But in reality it was only sounding an indirect warning to the Prime Minister not to mess with the army. Therefore fearing that another military coup could be in the offing, Nawaz Sharif quickly decided to warn the Americans in advance, and this he did by quietly dispatching his younger brother Shahbaz Sharif to Washington.

On reaching Washington, the dapper younger brother and Chief Minister of Punjab having convinced the State Department that the army was threatening the democratically elected government of Pakistan, and that the Prime Minister who had willingly responded to President Clinton's call to withdraw from Kargil was now on the verge of paying a heavy price for it had got the Clinton administration worried. But when Shahbaz Sharif simultaneously also offered and promised the Americans that Pakistan would henceforth not only take a tougher stand against the Taliban regime in

Afghanistan, but it would also in cooperation with American Special Forces and their own Special Service Group will try and get Osama.Bin Laden dead or alive, the Americans fell for it. And in order to keep that crucial meeting of Shahbaz Sharif that was held on the 17th and 18th of September,1999 with the Americans a secret, and not to let the Pakistan army get wind of it, even the Pakistan Foreign Office was not consulted and nor were they kept in picture. Therefore on the 20th of September, when the Americans responded positively by sending out a clear message that Washington earnestly desired democracy to prevail in Pakistan, and that it would oppose any extra constitutional authority interfering in the affairs of the state, Shiraz knew that the warning from America could not have come suddenly from out of the blue. And when Shiraz also came to know from a colleague of his in Islamabad that the Americans in private had also sounded the Prime Minister to patch up and reconcile his differences with his army chief, it was evident to Shiraz that the matter was now really very serious. Shiraz was also aware that though the Prime Minister had full constitutional authority to dismiss and appoint a new chief, but it could not be done arbitrarily. After all the army chief was no ordinary Tom, Dick and Harry in uniform, but a well respected and a powerful man in the country, and therefore to topple him without a convincing and genuine excuse would only mean buying trouble.

That evening while discussing the matter with his wife Saira and daughter Sherry, when Shiraz in all seriousness remarked that Pakistan was heading towards another disaster unless the present imbroglio of distrust and suspicion that currently existed between the Prime Minister and his Army Chief was quickly resolved, Sherry who till then had no clue of the prevailing political situation in Pakistan simply blurted out.

"I think as far as Pakistan is concerned beggars cannot be choosers and either way one is as bad or as good as the other I guess. And whether they dress up in military uniforms or in dapper civilian clothes, all of them finally tend to become dictators," added the young lady. For her the change from democracy to dictatorship and vice versa had become a cycle in Pakistan politics and it simply did not matter to her anymore.

On the very next morning of 21st September 1999, when Nawaz Sharif noticed the deployment of troops with headphones and wireless sets around his official residence, he naturlly became worried and he therefore immediately asked for an explanation. But the justification that was given by the army authorities did not exactly convince the Prime Minister. Claiming that the army had reliable intelligence of a likely terrorist attack against the

Prime Minister, and that the troops from the 111 Brigade were therefore only reviewing their procedures of protecting him had got the Prime Minister thinking. But this had only made Nawaz Sharif even more nervous. Fearing a repeat of how his first government in 1993 had been toppled because the military had lost confidence in him, he was now convinced that the only way of his continuing in office was to sack the present chief and have him replaced by his crony, Lt General Ziauddin Butt, the very man whom he had personally selected as the DGISI.

Though the General Officer was from the Corps of Engineers, but it was only on his own personal request that General Karamat had given Ziauddin Butt the command of the reserve corps at Gujranwala. Sharif was also aware that this was a pre-requisite for any future chief. Moreover, Ziauddin Butt after Musharraf was also now the senior most Lt General in the Pakistan army and it suited him fine. And though Sharif very well knew that removing General Musharraf would no doubt be a rather risky affair, nevertheless he had now decided that it had to be done, but it had to be done in a very subtle and clever manner.

And while Nawaz Sharif in Pakistan was looking for excuses to oust General Musharraf and strengthen his hold on the country, in India the battle for the ballot had also gained added momentum. Riding on the victory at Kargil, the BJP like the Congress had also roped in the best of the 'Gurus' from the advertising world to do all the thinking for them and thus enhance their brand equity that was required to win the elections. Therefore for India elections had now become a commercial proposition.

Ever since !989, when Rajiv Gandhi got his friend Arun Nanda's advertising agency Redifussion to do the campaign for the Congress party, and which ultimately led to his thumping victory, the use of these 'Gurus' had now become the norm. Heading the NDA camp was the demure and elegant Tara Sinha and she was ably supported by Shunu Sen and Sohel Seth. And the Congress Party had requisitioned the services of Rajeev Desai and Sam Balsara. And with Kargil adding another dimension of patriotism among the people of India, and with the BJP having now tasted power, the party had therefore now decided to put Hinduvta and Swadeshi on the back burner and had put the main focus on the people's comfort factor, on the high stature of Mr Vajpayee, and the economic boom that had surfaced in the past few years

With a whopping campaign budget of Rupees 15 crores in the kitty, and with the young and dapper Promod Mahajan, the Minister for Information and Broadcasting heading the campaign operation, and with the suave and eloquent Arun Jaitley as the party's spokesman, Monty was convinced that the NDA would romp home as the winners. He was also of the opinion that the Congress strategy of blaming the BJP for the Kargil war and telling the people that a multi-party government like the NDA would only add more miseries for the country's illiterate masses would only backfire on them.

Chapter-17

The End Game Begins

To begin with and to allay all fears and doubts from the mind of General Musharraf that he would complete his full three year tenure as army chief, Nawaz Sharif decided to promulgate the order promoting the General from acting chairman to full time Chairman of the Joint Chiefs of Staff Committee. But at the same time he also set the ball rolling for his ouster by having him tailed and by having his telephonic conversations secretly monitored. But unfortunately for him, Musharraf too had kept his eyes and ears open. So when he learnt that some of his top Generals were hobnobbing with the Prime Minister, he therefore in order to prove that he would not brook any indiscipline in the army and in the chain of command from any quarter whatsoever, he immediately had them transferred to less sensitive posts and appointments. This therefore gave the Prime Minister an excuse to now put his own plan into action.

On the plea and pretext that the transfer of Lt General Tariq Pervez and Lt General Saleem Hyder, the two Corps Commanders in quick succession was detrimental to the morale of the army and that it had created an impression that there was a wide gap between the government and the military, Nawaz Sharif now waited for the day to strike. Angry at the manner in which his few friends in the army were slowly and steadily being sidelined by the chief, he had therefore decided that it was time to act and act fast.

Aware of the fact that General Musharraf with his wife would be away on an official tour to Sri Lanka during the second week of October to witness the golden jubilee celebrations of the Sri Lankan army, Nawaz Sharif therefore decided that the change of guard must take place while Musharraf would be away from the country. The ideal time to strike therefore would be while Musharraf was high in the sky enjoying his flight back from Colombo. Not only would he be kept ignorant of what was happening at home and on the ground, but he would also be presented with a fait accompli that he would have to jolly well accept. Confident of the fact that by then the new chief would be in the chair and the other Corps Commanders would have also automatically fallen in line, Nawaz Sharif with his son Hussein Nawaz and a trusted handful of his close confidantes including the army chief designate were now all set to begin the high powered toppling game. Moreover, to keep the Americans in good humour and to project to them that Pakistan was serious in getting Osama bin Laden for them, Sharif on 7th October, 1999 even dispatched Lt General Ziauddin Butt, his ISI chief to meet the Taliban strongman Mullah Omar. But Mullah Omar it seems was in no mood to heed Pakistan's tall request. Not aware about the second channel that the Pakistan army had kept open with Mullah Omar not to entertain General Ziauddin, the ISI chief was not only given the cold shoulder, but he was also told categorically that there were no terrorist training camps of extremists inside Afghanistan that were being sheltered by his own people from the Taliban.

Like in the case of 'Operation Badr', this operation to oust Musharraf also had to be kept a very closely guarded top secret by the Prime Minister till the final official announcement of the new chief by the government duly approved by the President on paper was made and officially announced on Pakistan TV. The key factor however was to maintain the surprise to the very end and to catch the army completely off guard, and not to give the Generals loyal to Musharraf any time whatsoever to react. Therefore to avoid all suspicion and to ensure that the government was functioning in its normal routine manner, a clever cover plan was put into effect by Nawaz Sharif.

On 10th October1999, while General Musharraf was away in Colombo, Nawaz Sharif with his son Hussein Nawaz, his speech writer Nazir Naji and the man who would eventually succeed Musharraf as the army chief took off on their planned flight to Abu Dhabi for a meeting with Sheikh Zayed Bin Sultan. And it was on this flight that the final plot was hatched between the Prime Minister and Lt General Ziauddin Butt. Then again on the morning of 12th October, the day General Musharraf was to return from Colombo in the evening, the Prime Minister in order to avoid the conspiracy being leaked out, he with his small entourage that included his son, his speech writer, and the Chairman of Pakistan TV, Pervez Rashid took off for Multan from Islamabad.Since this was being projected as a political meeting, the Prime Minister very wisely did not take Lt General Ziauddin Butt, the DGISI along with him this time. The conspirators were on their way to the small town of Shujabad near Multan where Nawaz Sharif was scheduled to give a political speech. And while Nawaz Sharif was busy lecturing the locals, the pilot and the crew of the VIP aircraft were told to go and relax inside the airport lounge. And while the crew members were away having their tea and biscuits, the Prime Minister's speech writer Nazir Naji while sitting in the aircraft got busy in translating from English into Urdu the speech that was handed over to him by Hussein Nawaz, and which his father Nawaz Sharif was scheduled to deliver on Pakistan TV to the nation that very evening after the ouster of General Musharraf. And though the word dismissal of General Musharraf was very diplomatically and cleverly kept out from the draft, the contents however included the reasons why a new man had to be given this very important job. A couple of hours later, when the VIP aircraft returned to the Chaklala military airbase and the Prime Minister who had earlier instructed his Defense Secretary, Lt General (Retired) Iftikhar Ali Khan to receive him there got into the car for the drive back to the Prime Minister's residence, it was only then that Nawaz Sharif disclosed his hand. His decision to appoint a new chief took the Defense Secretary completely by surprise and though the Defence Secretary suggested that the Prime Minister may like to discuss the issue with Musharraf first before sacking him, but the Prime Minister was simply unyielding. And no sooner had Nawaz Sharif reached his official residence at Islamabad, the ball was immediately set rolling. Saeed Mehdi his Principal Secretary who was already privy to the plan got on with the job to prepare the necessary papers for the change over and by tea time the notification was handed over to the Prime Minister for his approval and signature. The two line notification simply read as follows.'It has been decided to retire General Pervez Musharraf, Chairman Joint Chiefs of Staff Committee and Chief of Army Staff with immediate effect. Lt General Ziauddin Butt has been appointed Chief of Army Staff with immediate effect and promoted to the rank of General.' But one more formality was required to be completed before the final orders were issued and that too was completed by the time tea was over. The notification was required to be signed and approved by the President of Pakistan who in order to avoid a controversy very wisely and cleverly only wrote 'seen' on the minute sheet and having signed it gave it back to the Prime Minister.

With all legal formalities having been completed on paper, it was now time for the ceremonies and celebrations to begin. At 4.30 PM sporting his new badges of rank of that of a full General and army chief, when a very happy General Ziauddin kept smiling at the PAK TV cameras that had been summoned for the occasion to record and broadcast the news with his pictures, he had no idea that his promotion would soon change the destiny of the entire nation. Not only would his tenure as an army chief be one of the shortest in world history, but it would also land him and the

Prime Minister and other conspirators behind bars. And while the pipping ceremony and the celebrations with the distribution of 'ladoos' and sweets to hail the new army chief was still in progress at the Prime Minister's residence, the Pakistan International Airlines Flight 805 from Colombo was already airborne with General Musharraf and his wife on board.

At around 4 PM, while the flight from Colombo with 197 passengers and crew that included a very large number of children from the International School who were returning to Karachi after taking part in an inter school competition soared towards the sky, little did they all know what was in store for them As soon as the experienced Captain Sarwat Hussein at the controls switched off the seat belt sign and a very efficient and smiling cabin crew rolled in the tea and snack trolleys, the happiness in the face of the little children was there for everyone to see. And when the army chief also waved out and smiled at them, little did he know that he was no longer holding that coveted appointment and chair.

At 5 PM, while the news bulletin on PTV went on the air to announce the appointment of the new chief, the two senior Generals, Lt General Aziz Khan the CGS and Lt General Mehmood Ahmed, Corps Commander 10 Corps at Rawalpindi who were fiercely loyal to Musharraf were busy enjoying a good game of tennis. And it all started when both their mobile phones that were lying by the side of the tennis court kept ringing continuously.

Fearing that these two Generals would not take Musharaff's sacking lying down, the new chief Gneral Ziauddin had purposely kept the news of his promotion a secret from them. He however, had on taking over charge called up the others in the chain of command including Lt General Syed uz Zafar, the senior most Corps Commander at Peshawar who in Musharaff's absence was also acting chief of army staff. Unluckily for General Ziauddin, when Lt General Zafar on getting the news about Musharraf's sacking immediately passed it on to the CGS and to Lt General Mehmood and also informed them that the news was already on TV, the two Generals decided to act without any further delay. Winding up their game of tennis they immediately on their mobile phones got in touch with their staff officers. Thereafter the 10 Corps Commander having passed the necessary instructions to his staff officer Major Nissar, an officer from the Punjab Regiment to get the news item off the air at once, the two Generals sped home and after having got into their military uniforms in double quick time, they made a bee line for their respective offices. Meanwhile the legendary 111 Infantry Brigade that had spearheaded such like bloodless coups in the past also, they too got into the act. The CGS having talked to all the Corps Commanders called for an urgent meeting of his senior staff. They were all of the firm view that the change of army chief by the Prime Minister, while the present incumbent was out of the country was not only unethical and highly improper, but it was also a downright insult to that high rank. The Corps Commanders were also now convinced that it was time for Nawaz Sharif to be shown the door

As Major Nissar with a small contingent of armed soldiers barged into the PTV headquarters at Islamabad and ordered the staff to immediately block any further announcement of Musharraf's sacking, the terrified staff members meekly obliged. And when the six o'clock evening news bulletin made no mention at all of Musharaff's sacking and the appointment of the new chief, Nawaz Sharif who was eagerly looking forward to that broadcast again knew something was amiss. Delegating his Military Secretary, Brigadier Javed Iqbal to rush to the studio and to personally find out what was happening; he now looked a little worried. The Prime Minister was apprehensive that any further delay of that important announcement would not only confuse the issue further, but it would also give the army an opportunity to question him on this sudden change of guard at the very top. Therefore the one and only thing that was now playing on his mind was how to face the crisis once Musharaff was back on home turf. On the advice of his new chief that if Musharraf was kept out of the country, the army would have no other option, but to accept the change over, Nawaz Sharif in order to save his own skin and administration acted rather foolishly. At around 6 PM having got Aminullah Choudhury, the Director General Civil Aviation on the hotline, he personally ordered him to ensure that flight PK 805 did not land anywhere in Pakistan. Coming from the Prime Minister's own mouth, Chowdhury not only immediately ordered the closure of Karachi airport, but also that of Nawabshah, the alternate airport that was located 250 KM's east of Karachi.

Though ignorant of the fact that such a stupid order had been given by the Prime Minister of the country, the top army brass and Brigadier Sallahuddin Satti, the Brigade Commander 111 Brigade with his troops were also now getting ready to bring Pakistan back under military rule. As a desperate Nawaz Sharif tried to save his government, he was not aware that the drills for a bloodless coup by his own military had already been set in motion. And while the runaway lights at the Karachi airport were being switched off and three fire engines were on their way to block the main runaway, Brigadier Javed Iqbal who had been directed by the Prime Minister to rush to the PTV station at Islamabad to ensure that Musharraf's sacking and the appointment of Ziauddin Butt was back on the air, on arrival at the TV studio he found himself in a rather piquant situation.

It was around 6.15 PM, when he with a few armed men from the elite Punjab Police that was part of the Governor of Punjab's and Prime Minister's younger brother Shahbaz Sharif's elite guards reached the PTV headquarters control room, the Brigadier was surprised to find Major Nissar with his armed soldiers already there. And when the Brigadier ordered the junior field officer and his men to lay down their arms and they downright refused, it seemed that a shootout was imminent Not knowing whose orders were to be taken cognizance of, Shaista Zaid the PTV newscaster was aghast to see what was happening. Brigadier Javed was accompanied by Pervez Rathore, the man who was in charge of the Prime Minister's security and that did matter. But luckily better sense prevailed on both the sides and it was only after Major Nissar handed over his pistol to the Brigadier and he and his party were locked up in a separate room, that PTV once again at the end of the 6 PM bulletin announced the retirement of General Musharraf and the appointment of the new chief.

Seeing the news back on the air, Nawaz Sharif breathed a huge sigh of relief and immediately got in touch with Shahid Abbassi, the Chairman of Pakistan International Airlines. The Prime Minister was making doubly sure that come what may, Flight PK 805 did not land anywhere in Pakistan. He wanted the aircraft to be diverted either to Muscat or to any other friendly country in the Arab world or in the Gulf Region, and it had to be done without assigning any specific reason to the pilot of the aircraft.

Meanwhile at the GHQ in Rawalpindi, when the officers monitoring the same news heard that Musharraf's sacking was once again back in the air, they too smelt a rat. Taking no further chances they therefore at once dispatched another Major with a few armed soldiers to the PTV headquarters. And when the armed Punjab Elite Police at the gate refused them entry, the enterprising Major soon came back with a few more truckloads of troops.

"Stop us if you can now,' said the proud Major as his men while given the police some exclusive expletives in Punjabi like 'Salle Madher Chod and Bahen Chod' climbed over the gate and stormed the building. Realizing that they were now completely out numbered and out gunned, the police force meekly watched and offered no resistance whatsoever.Though by 7.15 PM, PTV was once again off the air, but a few enterprising journalists with their cameramen in tow who had gathered there by then had captured the dramatic scene alive.

And while a desperate Nawaz Sharif using all his powers was trying to keep the aircraft from landing anywhere in Pakistan, a bewildered and confused Captain Sarwat Hussein who was now in constant touch with the air traffic control at Karachi kept wondering why he was not being permitted to land, and why the ATC kept asking him about the aircraft's fuel position and about the number of passengers on board.And it all started soon after Captain Syed Sarwat Hussein, the son of a retired Pakistan Air Force and a senior pilot of the PIA with 25 years of service made his first contact with the ATC, the Air Traffic Control at 6 PM and PF 805 was cleared to land at the Qaid-e-Azam airport at Karachi. But at around 6.15 PM, when the aircraft PF805 reached 'SAPNA'; an imaginary position in the sky and the aircraft started its descent as per the clearance given by the ATC, everything seemed quite normal. But immediately thereafter, when the pilot, his co-pilot Akhmal Shami and the radio engineer Aamir Malik heard over the radio net about the closure of the Karachi airport and that the Karachi ATC was now directing all aircrafts to land either at Sukkur or at Nawabshah they were completely taken by surprise. And few minutes later, when Captain Sarwat Husssein the pilot of the aircraft was curtly told that the alternate airport for flight PF 805 was also closed for landing, he wondered what could be the reason for this sudden change of plans,

Though ignorant of the fact that simultaneously a series of conversation between the Prime Minister, the DG Civil Aviation Authority and the Chairman PIA had been instrumental in not granting him the permission to land, Captain Sarwat now had an uncanny feeling that the presence of General Musharraf on board could be the only possible reason for the Karachi air traffic control's constant refusal to permit his aircraft to land at Karachi or at Nawabshah. And at 6.40 PM, when the ATC again contacted PK 805 and asked him to report his fuel position and reiterated that the Nawabshah airport was also closed for landing, Sarwat Hussein therefore decided to have a word with Brigadier Nadeem Taj, the staff officer accompanying the Army Chief. Requesting the Brigadier to come inside the cockpit, when Sarwat Hussein confidentially told him about the problem, and Brigadier Nadeem in turn came out and beckoned the Chief to come to the galley, even the cabin crew had no idea of the imminent danger that the aircraft was in.

A few minutes later having conveyed to the control tower that the aircraft had only one hour of fuel left, and that there were 197 souls on board, the Captain invited Musharaff into the cockpit of the Airbus 300. And when he conveyed to him that the aircraft was not being permitted to land anywhere in Pakistan, a visibly angry Musharaff became suspicious. But he was still not sure that it was all because of him. So when he asked the Captain what were the other options available and the pilot on seeing the lights of the Indian city of Ahmedabad in the distance suggested that as an alternative, Musharaff was simply livid, "Over my dead body,", said the visibly angry army chief. The fact was that Shahid Abbassi, the Managing Director of Pakistan International Airlines together with Rana Maqbool the Inspector General Police of Sind on orders from Nawaz Sharif had already taken over the control of the Qaid-e-Azam international airport at Karachi. To them the orders were not to let the aircraft land anywhere in Pakistan and when the pilot told them that with the current fuel position, the Airbus could only land in India, Rana Maqbool even had the audacity to tell the pilot "OK then land there if you wish.'

Desperate to find out what was happening in the country, both Musharaff and Brigadier Nadim then tried to get in touch with the GHQ and the Corps Headquarters at Karachi on their respective mobile phones. But when they found that they could not get through, they knew that something was radically wrong. And when a quick thinking Captain Sarwat having got the relevant telephone numbers from the General tried to get the calls through on the PIA net and found that too had been blocked, he became a little nervous. The time was now nearing 7 PM and the aircraft had only 45 minutes more of fuel left.

"Godammit, declare an emergency and crash land the aircraft at Karachi if need be," said an angry Musharaff as he once again tried to get through on his mobile with his Corps Commander at Karachi. But it was all in vain. Meanwhile it seems that at the other end, and on the ground, a desperate Nawab Sharif, the DGCA and the Chairman PIA had miscalculated their options. They were now not only aware that the aircraft did not have the necessary fuel to go to Muscat or anywhere else in the Middle East, but they also now feared that if the plane did crash land then it would be they who would not only be accused of cold blooded murder, but of also hijacking the aircraft.

Then suddenly, when the pilot was told by the ATC that he could land at Nawabshah, a much relieved Captain Sarwat immediately climbed up to save some more of the precious fuel. To him it seemed that better sense had prevailed, but in reality the plane was only being diverted to be refueled and then flown to Muscat. The orders from Nawaz Sharif were very clear. On landing at Nawabshah the aircraft would be cordoned by the armed police and nobody would be allowed to disembark. And once the refueling was completed, the pilot would be ordered to take off and fly to Muscat or to some other airport in the Middle East.

And while this tense and desperate drama on board the PK 805 was unfolding itself over the skies of Pakistan, at Islamabad the army having by now taken into custody the Prime Minister Nawaz Sharif and his co—conspirators in a bloodless coup was now getting ready to ensure that the aircraft with the Army Chief would land safely at Karachi and nowhere else.

The first contingent of armed troops under an army Major had already reached the Prime Minister's residence around 6.30 PM, and seeing General Ziauddin with some other senior officers from the ISI standing near the porch, the Major ordered them to surrender. After some initial hesitation and later on seeing more troops converging towards the Prime Minister's residence, General Ziauddin finally gave in.

While PK 805 was on its way to Nawabshah, the army authorities at Karachi who were waiting for the Chief's arrival having got wind of what was happening at Islamabad had by now also taken over control of the airport. And though Brigadier Abdul Jabbar on arrival at the Karachi control tower ordered the ATC to bring the aircraft back to Karachi, but the ATC however decided to first check back with their big boss. And it was only after Brigadier Jabbar threatened Aqeel the General Manager ATC that he will finish all of them if his orders to get the aircraft to land at Karachi was disobeyed, a frightened Aminullah Chowdhury realizing that it would be foolish to disobey the Brigadier finally buckled in. He now knew that it was all over and therefore had no other option but to ensure that the aircraft landed safely at Karachi.

It was already nearing 7.30 PM,. when Major General Malik Iftiqar Ali Khan Shah, the G.O.C. Infanrtry Division at Karachi also arrived at the control tower. And having identified himself he told Captain Sarwat to turn back and head for Karachi. But General Musharraf was still not sure of the true identity of the man and he therefore asked for the Karachi Corps Commander Lt General Muzaffar Usmani who was a good friend of his to come on the line. But with both time and fuel running out, and with the Corps Commander waiting inside the VIP lounge to receive the Chief, it was now a question of touch and go. And it was only when Iftiqar told the Chief over the radio of all that had happened during the last couple of hours and Musharraf was somewhat convinced that the man was telling the truth, a much relieved Captain Sarwat Hussein and his crew now got ready to do a safe landing at Karachi. However, to further check back on the identity of the caller, the General officer was also asked to give out the names of the Chief's two pet dogs. And when he confidently said 'Dot" and 'Buddy,' there was now a smile on the chief's face as he gave the pilot the thumbs up to land at Karachi. And as the aircraft kept losing height and the lights of Karachi and that of the runaway came into view, Sheba Musharraf, the wife of the Chief with tears rolling down her eyes kept praying. Till then neither she nor the passengers on board knew the kind of ordeal that they had been subjected to by Pakistan's corrupt and ambitious Prime Minister, Nawaz Sharif and his cohorts.

At 7.47 PM, when the aircraft finally landed at Karachi and Musharraf waited for Lt General Usmani to come on board, Captain Sarwat Hussein checked his fuel gauge and breathed a bigger sigh of relief. He hardly had 10 minutes of fuel left. Minutes later as the staff car with the Chief's four stars and the flag sped away from the tarmac; Pakistan was once again under military rule.

This was the fourth military bloodless coup in the country's 52 year old history and existence and surprisingly none of the passengers including the many school children who were on that flight knew how close they were to death that evening. They were not even aware of the drama on board the PK 805. An hour later, when the passengers were finally allowed to disembark, the big smile on the pretty faces of Yasmin Beg, Farzana Khalid and Zenab Bibi, the three air hostesses on board said it all. On that momentous 12th October evening, the old PIA motto 'Great People to Fly With' had literally stood the test of time.

And on that very evening as Pakistani troops in the capital Islamabad rounded up the Ministers of Sharif's cabinet from the Ministers Colony, while others detained all Sharif's key supporters in the other big cities and ordered them not to leave the country, Shiraz who had returned from the Moscow Golf Club after a good game of 18 holes with his son Tojo was surprised to learn from his wife Saira about the coup in Pakistan. In his absence, her cousin Lt General Aslam Rehman Khan had telephoned and had given Saira the sensational news Therefore in order to find out as to how and why it happened; Shiraz immediately rang up the senior retired General officer.

"Well to be very frank with you I think Nawab Sharif had totally under estimated the popularity of Pervez Musharraf and having got rid of General Karamat and Admiral Bukhari last year, he thought he could pull this one off too. Unfortunately he had not only chosen the wrong man as his replacement, but the crude manner in which both he and General Kwaja Ziauddin went about with their plans to get rid of Musharraf had now got both of them into very deep trouble. If Sharif thought that by dispatching Musharaff to Muscat he would have got his way, then I am afraid he has not learnt anything from history. After all the army in Pakistan is not a mercenary army. It is a mighty force to reckon with and looking at the manner in which the common man on the street has hailed the ouster of Nawaz Sharif and his corrupt government, it only goes to prove that the people of Pakistan still look up to the man in uniform for justice and fair play," said Aslam Rehman as he gave Shiraz a detailed account of the sordid drama that led to the bloodless coup.

"Like General Zia-ul-Haq the man who had sent Zulfi to the gallows, I hope Musharraf won't do the same to Nawaz Sharif too, because if he does so, then the Pakistan army will not only have the dubious distinction of hanging two democratically elected prime ministers, but nobody in future would like to take on that job either," said Saira jokingly as Shiraz poured himself a large neat peg of some rare old malt Scotch whisky.

"Well you never can say with these army blokes, but whatever has happened is certainly not good for the country and if you look at history then this General too might stick on to the chair till the cows come home," said Shiraz as he enjoyed the 12 year old Glenfiddich single malt whisky and kept wondering of what would now happen to Nawaz Sharif and his co-conspirators.

And it was only at 10.15 PM that eveing that the PTV once again came back on the air, but only to announce the dismissal of the Nawaz Sharif government. However, a few hours later, when at that unearthly hour of 2.50 AM in the morning while most of Pakistan was fast asleep and General Musharraff in his military uniform addressed the nation, Lt General Aslam Rehman and his wife Farzana who had kept awake to hear what the new boss of Pakistan had to say, both of them were quite surprised by the Chief's short and sweet speech. Having briefly explained to the people the ordeal that he and the others in the aircraft had undergone, and how close to death they all were, he simply informed the nation that it was only as a last resort and to prevent any further destabilization of the country, that the Pakistan army had moved in.

Till late that evening and ever since the time the army took over control of the PTV, the only message that was being relayed as a continuous strip at the bottom of the screen was that the Nawaz Sharif government had been removed and that the Chief of Army Staff would soon make an important announcement. This only added to more confusion, because the people of Pakistan were still ignorant of what was actually happening and who had staged the coup. And later that night and till such time General Musharaff's face finally appeared on the TV screen, the PTV in order to keep the viewers entertained had kept showing a documentary on monkeys in the wild. And on seeing that, Ruksana Begum very wisely commented.

"I think the military is once again back to their monkey business, but let us hope and pray that at least this time General Musharraf remains true to his word and does not hang on to power like all his predecessors did. But that I know is like asking for the moon. Because once these men in Khaki usurp power they normally keep holding on to it come hell or high water."

"I think you are damn well right and if that happens again then I am afraid the country is doomed forever. It is not that the military Generals have no brains, but the fact is that we cannot and should not become a 'Banana Republic,' said her husband Arif Rehman while switching off the TV.

Early next morning in Moscow, when Shupriya also learnt about the bloodless coup by the military in Pakistan and that General Musharaff had taken over charge of running the country as the CEO, she was not in the least surprised. After the Kargil fiasco, and with the blame game that was still being played out in Pakistan between the men in uniform and the politicians, she knew it was coming, but she didn't expect it to happen so very soon.

"I only hope the Pakistani commando chief and as promised by him, he will try and bring more stability not only to his country but also to the subcontinent. And with Pakistan having lost face both politically and militarily on the Kargil issue let us also hope that the General has learnt his lessons too. It has once again been amply proved that the Kashmir issue can never be settled with military might or through the proxy war that the Pakistanis have been orchestrating for the past five decades and more," said Shupriya as she briefed all the senior members of the embassy staff on the military takeover in Pakistan.

"But Madam Ambassador, let us also not forget that irrespective of whosoever has wielded power in Pakistan, whether it be a democratically elected government or the military, the core issue for all of them has always been Kashmir, and my fear now is that having got a bloody nose in Kargil, the ISI which is controlled by the military may well with vengeance also shift their focus in using the militant groups like the Lashkar-e-Toiba, the Hizbul Mujahideen, the HUJI (Harkat-Ul-Jihadi Islami), the Jaish-e-Mohammed and such like others more actively against us. I fear that not only will these militant groups increase their nefarious activities inside the valley, but they will also now go all out to strike against our own strategic targets that are located far in depth and deep inside our own country," said the Indian Defence Attache as he gave out a small resume on the character of the man and on whose hands now rested the fate and future of Pakistan.

"Well let me tell you ladies and gentlemen that this 1964 batch Mohajir gunner officer whose hearty appetite during his cadet days at the Pakistan Military Academy at Kakul, and whose parting of the hair in the centre was always much talked about is a very shrewd and ambitious man. He is not only very intelligent and a very highly respected officer in the Pakistan army, but he is also a go getter and a risk taker. He is professionally very brilliant and competent and with his very sharp intellect, he is also capable of taking quick decisions. Frankly speaking, I as a military man and that too from the infantry cannot but complement him in the manner in which the Pakistani operations in Kargil was planned and executed by him. It is however, another story that it ultimately failed in its aim to cut off Saichen and Ladakh and to internationalize the Kashmir issue once again. Nonetheless, it did give the Indian army and the nation a severe jolt. The man with his penchant for military history is also very clever and very calculative too, and therefore he must not be taken lightly. To say that he is ambitious will be a gross understatement and therefore henceforth whatever he says or does must be very carefully analyzed and assessed. With his subtle sense of humour and good command over the English language, he can also be very friendly and diplomatic when he wants to, and therefore one should not get convinced and get carried away with whatever he says now or in the near future. Moreover, in his long military career of 35 years as an officer he has had five miraculous escapes from death. The first one was during the Indo-Pak war in 1965, when an Indian artillery shell scored a direct hit on his artillery battery position. Then in 1972, as a commando in Gilgit he was all set to go on leave by air, but on that very morning two of his jawans died in an avalanche and he decided to stay back. The same very Fokker aircraft that was to take him to Rawalpindi crashed on the high mountains and was never found. His third brush with death was when he was commanding an artillery brigade and was selected by General Zia-ul-Haq to become his military secretary. He was asked to be ready to move at short notice, but Zia finally selected Brigadier Najeeb and that poor fellow with his boss died in the C-130 tragic air crash near Bhawalpur. The fourth time was as a Corps Commander Mangla. He had gone by road to Rawalpindi on some official work and an aviation officer who was returning by his helicopter to Mangla offered to fly him back. Musharraf would have no doubt preferred it, but at the last minute he was invited by a dear friend of his for a meal and did not take the pilot's offer. That helicopter too unfortunately crashed on its flight back to Mangala and there were no survivors. And the last and final call was as you all know on his recent flight back from Colombo. Had the flight 805 remained airborne for another 10 minutes then maybe there would have been no Musharraf today," concluded the Defence Attache as he displayed through the overhead projector a few snaps of the Pakistan army chief and his family, including this two pet dogs Dot and Buddy.

"I must say that our Defence Attache is keeping a very close tab not only of the man who now rules Pakistan, but also that of his family and his dogs too," said a smiling Shupriya in good humour as she had a closer look at those photographs.

CHAPTER-18

The Pink Rose Drama

A few days later, when the Pakistan Foreign Office dispatched the curriculum vitae of the country's new CEO, together with all his achievements, including, his preference for food, drinks, cigarettes, hobbies and choice of books, magazines etc etc to all the heads of their missions abroad, Shiraz was no doubt impressed. Besides having an impeccable record of service, the General was also very well read and was an eloquent speaker too. A typical army man and a Mohajir at that, he had never ever dreamt that one day he would preside over the destiny of Pakistan. Allah it seems had destined his future ever since he as a young boy with his family migrated from Delhi during partition. And now Nawaz Sharif it seems had given him this unique honour albeit by default, when he completely miscalculated the General's popularity in the army and messed up the whole affair by dismissing him in absentia.

That very day Shiraz also received a confidential letter from retired Lt General Aslam Rehman Khan that gave out in typical military style the drama that was played out at the Prime Minister's residence at Islamabad on that fateful 12th October evening by some of the serving senior general officers and top politicians of the country who were virtually ruling the country as dictators.

According to the retired General Officer, the real drama started at 3 o'clock in the afternoon on the 12th of October 1999 after Nawaz Sharif with his entourage landed at Chaklala airport from Multan and was met by his Defence Secretary, the recently retired Lt General Iftikar Ali Khan, and by his Principal Secretary Saeed Mehdi. As they got into the PM's car and while they were on the way to the PM's house, the Defence Secretary was told to issue an important government notification immediately. The notification pertained to the immediate retirement of General Musharraf and the appointment of Lt General Ziauddin Butt the DG ISI as the new Chief of Army Staff.

On arriving at the PM's house, when the Defence Secretary after having considered the serious implications that might follow, expressed his inability and requested for the order of the notification to be given to him in writing, the anger on Nawaz Sharif's face said it all. Accusing the Defence Secretary of being a bloody coward, a visibly livid and upset Nawaz Sharif then passed on the task to his Princpal Secretary to have the needful done at the earliest. And In order to ensure total security and to get the notification ready before Musharraf landed on Pakistani soil, Nawaz Sharif together with his Principal Secretary and Brigadier Javed Iqbal his Military Secretary therefore decided to use the good old time honoured method of simply substituting new names for the old ones. After all it was only a year ago that General Karamat was shown the door. And once the order was ready, the Prime Minister having signed it took it to the President for his approval and authentication. Not willing to be a party to this unethical way of dismissing the army chief, the President simply wrote the word 'seen' on it and returned the noting to the Prime Minister. With all the formalities over, a smiling Nawaz Sharif then returned back to his residence cum office where the television cameras and the crew from the Pakistan TV were waiting to capture live the formal announcement of the new army chief. With secrecy being the key word and as the TV cameras panned the formal ceremony, the Prime Minister took two single stars off his military secretary's uniform and added one each to Lt General's Ziauddin's existing rank of that of a Lieutenant General. And by so doing Nawaz Sharif thought that he had bestowed upon the new army chief the rank of a full four star general. But he did not apprehend the terrible turmoil that extra star would cause and which would rock the nation. While the photo shoot was still in session and as Nawaz Sharif shook hands and congratulated General Ziauddin on taking over command of the Pakistan army, a couple of Lt Generals who otherwise would not have made it as Corps Commanders were waiting in the wings to take over their new important portfolios that they had been promised to them. They had all been handpicked and selected by the Prime Minister and the new chief to replace those who were fiercely loyal to Musharraf. With all the formalities over, all of them now eagerly waited for the announcement to be made over Pakistan TV on the 5 'clock evening news.

No sooner was the announcement made over the TV and in order to ensure Musharraf's removal and Ziauddin's appointment was accepted legally, the Defence Secretary was asked to. return to his office and formally issue the notification. But by the time the announcement was to be made on the six o'clock news again, the army had already swung into action and soon thereafter, the units of Brigadier Salauddin Satti's 111 Infantry Brigade had sealed off both the Prime Minister's and the President's houses. And though the TV station at the end of the 6 PM broadcast did mention in brief once again about the new change of guard, but thereafter both the radio station and the TV station went off the air and were totally under the control of the forces loyal to Musharraf. And with all television broadcasts totally blanked out, the sudden emergence of the 'Pink Rose' on the blank TV screens and with martial music playing in the background had made Nawaz Sharif very jittery indeed. His only hope now it seems was to somehow keep Musharraf from landing anywhere in Pakistan. Seeing the Pink Rose on the TV screen in his office, and the presence of the DGMO, the CGS and the Corps Commander Rawalpindi Corps in the GHQ, the Defence Secretary having put two and two together quietly shelved the idea of issuing the legally required notification.

At around 6.30 PM that evening, Lt Col Shahid Ali the Battalion Commander of the battalion from 111 Infantry Brigade that had been tasked to seal of the Prime Minister's residence, together with some armed soldiers arrived at the main porch of the Prime Minister's bungalow. All of them were surprised to find General Ziauddin Butt with his new badges of rank and Lt General Akram also in uniform standing there posing for photographs. Flanking the duo were Brigadier Javed Iqbal, the Prime Minister's military secretary and Saeed Mehdi, the PM's principal secretary. Guarding them was a field officer, a major and two SSG commandos. An armed vehicle escort party both from the police and the ISI were also waiting to escort the four stars plated new Chief's staff car to the General Headquarters at Rawalpindi. Lt General Akram who was still an hour ago the Quarter Master General had just been elevated to take over as the new CGS. Another new appointee Lt General Salim Hyder had been elevated to take over the Rawalpindi Corps from the Musharraf loyalist Lt General Mehmood. Lt General Hyder had been earlier stopped at the gate and was refused entry by Lt Col Shahid's troops. And though this led to a verbal altercation between the two, but Lt Col Shahid firmly stood his ground. General Ziauddin and the Prime Minister it seems had it all worked out. They wanted the Generals loyal to them to take over charge of those two vital appointments before Musharraf's plane landed at Karachi. But it was not to be. Meanwhile at the General Headquarters, the DGMO, Major General Shahid Aziz had also set the coup ball rolling at Lahore and Karachi, the two most important cities of the country. Till now the men in uniform still had no idea whatsoever of the drama that was being played out in the air and over the skies of Karachi and Sind and which were on the orders of none other than the Prime Minister of the country.

A few minutes later, as an armed Lt Col.Shahid having deployed his men around the porch of the PM' house walked towards General Ziauddin, he was sternly warned by Lt General Akram and Brigadier Javed Iqbal to keep his troops away and to let the new Chief's convoy proceed to the General Headquarters and failing which the Prime Minister's guards and others would have no other option but to open fire. But a calm and determined Colonel Shahid said that he was only obeying orders from the very top and he politely asked General Ziauddin and Brigadier Javed Iqbal to order the guards to lay down their arms instead. Thereafter it was a touch and go situation and at once stage it seemed that a bloody bloodbath would follow. And it was only after the plucky Colonel told them that his full battalion had surrounded the Prime Minister's house, and that it would be foolish of them to start a firefight that the tempers cooled on both sides. Soon thereafter, when another armed platoon arrived on the scene, the two Generals realized that it was all over. And when the guards at the PM's house laid down their arms and the SSG commandos also switched sides, the new chief and his supporters knew that it would be suicidal to offer any further resistance. They were now quickly huddled back into the house and put under arrest. And once all their mobile phones were seized from them and they were left totally incommunicado, the second phase of arresting the Prime Minister and his cohorts began.

At around 7.30 PM, as Lt Col Shahid with his men walked into the family wing and arrested the Prime Minister, his brother Shahbaz and others who were seated around them, there was pin drop silence. Meanwhile at Karachi airport the Corps Commander Lt General Usmani, anxiously waited for flight PA-805 to land. At around 8.30 PM with the Pakistan Army having taken complete control of the country, when the Rawalpindi Corps Commander Lt General Mehmood Ahmed in his military uniform walked in to inform a crestfallen Nawaz Sharif that it was thanks to him the country was now once again under martial law and that General Musharraf and his wife would soon be on their way to Islamabad, Nawaz Sharif knew that for him and his government it was all over.

On board the aircraft to Islamabad, Musharaff got busy writing his short speech in his own hand. Before going to the studio at that unearthly hour of 2 AM on the morning of 13th October, the General who was still in his civilian clothes borrowed a flak jacket from an SSG commando and with his civilian trousers safely hidden away under the rostrum, he at 2.30 on that early morning addressed the nation. And as 'the 'Pink Rose faded away from the TV screen and General Musharraf with all humility told the people of Pakistan as to why and how he and the army had to perforce step in, and that to most reluctantly in order to save the nation, retired Lt General Aslam Rehman and his wife Farzana who were watching the live broadcast at that unearthly hour of the morning only hoped and prayed for a new and better dawn for Pakistan. They were also quite surprised to learn about Nawaz Sharif allegedly having used his intelligence agency to bug the telephonic conversation between General Musharraf and Lt General Mohammed Aziz that took place during the operations in Kargil and when Musharraf was on an official visit to China. According to one source, the tapes were deliberately passed on to New Delhi as proof of Nawaz Sharif's innocence as far as Kargil was concerned.

Three days earlier on 10th October 1999, the death of Lt General Gul Hassan Khan, the man that Bhutto had made Chief after the debacle in Bangladesh had greatly saddened Aslam Rehman and his wife Farzana. For Lt General Aslam Rehman, Gul Hassan Khan was the epitome of what all officers as gentlemen should always be. The man who loved his men more than his Black Label whisky and for whom the only prayer mat was his love for soldiering and who hated everything ceremonial had died unfortunately as an unsung hero. After his final retirement Gul Hassan Khan had moved into a nondescript two room suite in the GHQ Artillery Officer's Mess in Rawalpindi. While the General who sincerely loved the army so dearly spent the rest of his retired life in a simple and humble manner, other senior generals who had served under him were now living in big opulent villas on the prestigious Golf Road. He was also lonely because his Austrian wife after visiting him at the hospital had gone back to Vienna and Sher his only son who was seventeen years old was studying in the United States. Nonetheless, the General's subtle sense of humour was very much in evidence even in his last days. When people and friends came with flowers to see him all he would say with his wonderful smile was, 'What the bloody hell for, isn't it still a little too early?' And on that day after the funeral, while driving back home as as the car went past retired General Aslam Baig's palatial bungalow on Golf Road, Aslam Rehman sarcastically said to Farzana."I sincerely wish they were more such honest and upright Generals like Gul Hassan Khan in the Pakistan army."

"Yes, I wish so too, but thanks to the late General Zia-ul-Haq's rigid policies of promoting 'Mullaism' in the armed forces, that kind of high caliber officers like Gul Hassan Khan I am afraid we will never get anymore," added Farzana.

"Yes and Gul Hassan was not only fair minded, he was also never afraid to call a spade a spade. For instance, on one particular occasion he simply wrote a one line annual confidential report on one of his lazy incompetent subordinates and it aptly brought home the message to the concerned officer. He simply wrote on his confidential report.'The Bloody Chap needs a kick up his bloody arse,' said Aslam Rehman with a big smile and then added a bit sarcastically that he sincerely wished Gul Hassan was there to write some more similar ones on the likes of the Generals and Politicians who while in power have looted the nation at will.

Chapter-19

The Blooming of the Lotus

On that early morning of 13th October 1999, while the pink rose on the Pakistan Television screen heralded the return of the country back to military rule, in New Delhi the blooming of the lotus had finally created political history. Having won 303 seats in the 543 seat Indian Lok Sabha,(The Lower House of Parliament) the BJP led NDA coalition with its stable majority and without the support of the AIADMK were now all set to bring in a new era of democracy and prosperity to the nation. It seemed that at last the lotus, the holiest of flowers for the Hindus and the symbol of creation of mankind and the election symbol of the BJP, the Bhartiya Janata Party had finally bloomed in all its pristine glory. That morning as Mr Atal Bihari Vajpayee, the old and witty bachelor from Gwalior took his oath of office as Prime Minister of India for the third time, Monty and Peevee hoped and prayed that with the comfortable majority in the Indian parliament, it would be a long fruitful innings for the experienced and veteran parliamentarian.

Though Shiraz was happy that a democratically elected government had taken office in India, he was however quite upset in the manner in which the new Pakistani army chief had started his innings as the Chief Executive Officer of Pakistan. What shocked him the most was the undue haste with which General Musharraf pardoned and freed Major General Zahirul Abbassi and a few others from jail? These were the very men whose close links with the deadly militant Jehadi leaders from the HUJI, the Harkat-ul—Jihadi Islami had been clearly established when they plotted together to take over Pakistan in a bloody coup against the Benazir government. The very fact that Abbassi had planned to eliminate not only the Prime Minister of the country, but also all the military top brass during the Corps Commanders conference that was scheduled to be held on 30th September, 1995 was good enough to get him a seven year jail term. Both he and his brother officers and conspirators had been found guilty by a general court martial and Brigadier Mustansir Billah who was the brain behind the plot was awarded the maximum of fourteen years. But this sudden change of heart to free Abbassi therefore did come as a surprise to many and Shiraz was no exception.

"I wonder where was the frightful hurry to release the disgraced General Abbassi,"said Shiraz to his wife Saira as he read out the details of his release in a Pakistani newspaper.

"Maybe the new chief wants the blessings of the Mullah's and Abbassi who is supposed to be a devout Muslim could be used as a good conduit for this very purpose," said Saira.

However what worried Shiraz the most was the rapid mushrooming of the many Jehadi organizations in the country. Since the late 1980's a large number of these had sprouted all over Pakistan and Shiraz was apprehensive that these very militant groups that were the tools of the Pakistan army and the ISI may well one day become a damn nuisance and a big headache to the same military who had now once again taken over the country. He was aware that a United Jihad Council had only recently been formed with seven member organizations, and that included the two big players, the Hizbul Mujahideen and Tehreek-ul-Mujahideen, These two organizations with the help from the ISI were very active in Kashmir, but the Jihadi Council's ultimate aim it seems was in due course to create and establish a theocratic Talibanised Pakistan. And if that ever happens then the country Shiraz felt would be doomed.

With the military and the ISI providing these Jihadis with the deadly lethal arms,ammunition and sophisticated signal equipment, these Jehadis may well be initially used not only against India, but also against those who were not followers of Prophet Mohammed in their own country. And if they were not kept under a tight leash and control, they may in times to come may well become a rogue state within the state and that would be really sad not only for Pakistan, but also for the Pakistan military and for neigbouring India that has a very large population of Muslims too, thought Shiraz as he studied the growth of some of these more active organizations and made notes in his little red diary. According to one report there were now more than 20 such organizations that were active in Pakistan, but Shiraz was only interested in finding out a little more of the three most important ones from that lot.

The HUJI had been set up in 1979 by two Deobandhi religious bodies. This was at the outset of the Afghan war. The initial objective was to organize relief camps for the Afghan Mujahideens. But gradually with the help of the ISI and the CIA they started recruiting and training these Mujahideens to fight the Russians. In 1992, HUJI with active support from Bin Laden had also set up shop in Bangladesh and had been now using Bangladesh as a platform not only to foment insurgency in North East India, but to also promote terrorist activities in certain other areas of India too. This was the same organization that had supported Major General Zahirul Abbassi in his failed attempt to establish Islamic rule in Pakistan.

The LeT(Lashkar-e-Taiba) which belonged to the Ahle Hadith School was set up by Hafiz Saeed in 1986. With its headquarters at Muridke, 32 km from Lahore on the Gujranwala-Lahore Road, it was now a deadly force to reckon with. On the pretext of conducting social welfare activities by running a large number of schools, hospitals and clinics, the LeT has been largely successful in indoctrinating the young minds of the Pakistanis. It emphasized the arming of minds before arming the youth physically for terrorist activities, noted Shiraz.

The Harkat-ul-Mujahideen was founded in 1985 to fight against the Soviets in Afghanistan and to organize humanitarian relief operations for the Afghan refugees in the North West Frontier Province. It now had four training Camps in Afghanistan and though a thousand strong it now also had many Arab and Afghan veterans who had fought against the Russians. Moreover, it had now also developed strong links with the Al-Qaeda. One of its leaders, Maulana Massod Azhar was presently serving a jail sentence in India for terrorist and secessionist activities in the Indian state of Jammu and Kashmir, and Pakistan from time to time had been asking for his release. There were also now strong rumours of a split within the organization and a new breakaway group calling themselves as Jaish-e-Mohammed (JeM), the Army of Mohammed was likely to surface soon wrote Shiraz as he helped himself to another large scotch on the rocks. And while Shiraz in Moscow got busy in finding out a little more about these so called Jehadi organizations from other sources that included his colleagues and juniors from the ISI who were posted with cover appointments at the Pakistani Mission, far away in India the long drawn out Bofors drama had once again entered a very crucial stage.

With the BJP led government now firmly in the saddle, the CBI, the Criminal Bureau of Investigation having finally concluded its investigation had on 22nd October, 1999 filed charge-sheets against five of the accused. The list included Mr SK Bhatnagar, who was the Defence Secretary when the deal was struck, Mr Quattrocchi, the wily Italian wheeler-dealer who was also once a very close family friend of the Gandhi family and was the one who through his so called AE Services had very cleverly got the Bofors their billion dollar arms contract. And there was Mr Win Chadha, Bofors long standing agent in India who was now based in Dubai and Martin Ardbo, former President of AB Bofors who had very cleverly struck that deal. All these four men were all alive and therefore could be prosecuted. But the name of the fifth accused, Rajiv Gandhi because he was no longer alive however appeared in column 2 of the said charge-sheet and that was what had set the cat among the pigeons. So when Judge Ajit Bharihoke the Presiding Judge of the Special Court for CBI cases recorded his opinion that there was sufficient prima facie material on record to proceed against all the five accused and directed that a non-bailable warrant be issued against Quattrocchi and summons against the other four, it not only sent shock waves and shivers down the Rajiv and Sonia loyalists within the Congress party but it also shook the President of the party who was none other than Sonia Gandhi, the wife of the fifth accused. Therefore with the late Rajiv Gandhi also indirectly in the dock, it was once again battle stations for the Congress party.

Following the age old dictum that attack would be the best form of defense, the party under their new leader immediately decided to go on the offensive. With Sonia Gandhi leading from the front and her cronies in the party and in the Parliament ably supporting her, the otherwise quiet and sedate Sonia now went on the warpath by proclaiming in Parliament that her party would never tolerate the framing of an innocent man who was not in a position to defend himself. And while all her loyal camp followers started twisting facts ludicrously and that too with preposterous theories in order to save the good name of their departed leader, to Monty and Unni, it was nothing but a 'grand tamasha' in the Indian Parliament. Both of them were more than convinced that knowing the low level of integrity and honesty among the majority of the Parliamentarians, and the snail's pace by which the judiciary functioned in the country, the Congress as before would simply keep fooling the illiterate masses with their own fairytale version of the Bofors scandal. And with three out of the four main accused safely ensconced outside India and the fifth one in heaven, Monty was dead sure that ultimately nothing would come off it.

That evening as they discussed the issue over a drink at the Press Club of India and Monty wondered as to why the Hinduja brothers had been left out of the said charge-sheet, Unni having ordered his fourth and final large peg of Old Monk rum simply said.

"Well though the Swiss authorities have released the names of the three Hinduja brothers, Srichand, Gopichand and Prakash as being among the seven appellants, but the CBI unfortunately have not as yet received the second set of papers from the Swiss authorities. And it will be those set of papers that will go to prove their 3 percent cut on the deal and which AB Bofors had credited into their three coded accounts that were named Lotus, Tulip and Mont Blanc respectively. And though the Swiss Department of Justice and Police have rejected the various appeals that were made in three successive levels of Swiss courts by the Hindujas who were desperately seeking to block the transfer of those papers to India, my gut feeling is that by the time these papers arrive, the brothers for fear of being charged and convicted may well even change their nationalities.In fact according to one reliable source Srichand Hinduja has already applied for a British passport and the brothers having established good and friendly relations with Mr and Mrs Blair at10, Downing Street and with Mr Keith Vaz, the British Minister of Indian origin in Mr Blair's cabinet, it should therefore not be very difficult for him to get one out of turn. And because of their generous offer to contribute very handsomely towards the construction of the Millennium Dome in London, I therefore will not be surprised if Mr Srichand has the passport in his pocket already. And if that be the case then getting him here in India to face the Bofors music will definitely be a far cry for Mr Vajpayee's new government," addded Unni.

"Well in that case with one million pounds as contribution towards the dome, this must be the world's costliest passport issued to Mr Srichand Hinduja and as such it should therefore go into the Guinness Book of Records," said Monty with a big naughty grin on his face, when his mobile rang. It was Peevee on the line and when he informed him of his unexpected and sudden arrival in Delhi and that he wanted to meet his father very urgently, Monty was very surprised.

"Dad there is something very confidential and important that I need to discuss with you in private immediately. I am in room number 1401 at the Le Meridian and please do come as soon as you can. And please for heaven's sake do not tell Mom about my presence in the city as I will not be able to meet her. And moreover I have to catch the first available flight back to Mumbai either late tonight or early tomorrow morning."

"But please first tell me what 's up son, because you sounded very worried over the telephone," said Monty as Peevee opened the door of his hotel suite and having quickly touched his father's feet took him straight to the bedroom and locked the door.

"Well it is not that I am afraid, but the fact is that I am being constantly threatened on the telephone by some unknown hoodlums from Mumbai's underworld and I need your help very badly.They want me to heed to their advice and the diktat of their Mafia boss and they want me to sign on the dotted line for a one film contract as a hero. The movie I have to come to know is being financed by some Indian underground Don from Dubai and the 'Bhai' desires that it should be done under his own specific terms and conditions. And which according to his cronies would mean that I should not only agree to do the film at half my rate, and I must also accept half of that amount in 'petis' meaning hard cash.Moreover, since this is strictly going to be a one to one gentleman's agreement between the 'Bhai' and I, there would therefore be no requirement of signing any legal papers for the contract. I have also been warned not to discuss this with anybody and they want me to give my consent within the next twenty hours and failing which they also cautioned me to be ready to face their wrath. And to ensure that the Don was serious about the deal, the last caller indirectly also hinted to me but without mentioning any specific names as to how the founder of one big music company had been dispatched directly to heaven not too very long ago, and that too in broad daylight while the poor chap was on his way to pray at a temple in Juhu. He was obviously referring to Gulshan Kumar," added Peevee as he dialled room service and ordered for two chilled beers and a plate of cheese fritters.

"Well I guess these are some of the hazards that you big filmy-wallas have to perforce face in Bollywood and therefore one has got to simply live with it I guess. But since the party and the 'Bhai' concerned have not asked you to shell out a big sum as protection money, that itself goes to show that the Bhai is probably keen not only to produce the film but he will also once the film is completed be its main distributor. I therefore feel that to keep them in good humour you should tow their line. But do so very discreetly, because in most such cases and as far as payments are concerned these Dons I have been told generally honour their word. However, in order to ensure that you are not being duped or conned, you must after giving your consent insist on directly speaking to the Don in person. Because it is well nigh possible that some third party using the Don's big name may be trying to rope you in and con you at half of your ongoing price. But when you do make that call please do ensure that no one is listening in and you should therefore make that call incognito from either from some public telephone booth or from some friend's cell phone and not from your mobile or landline. And also do remember always to keep your mouth shut on such like shady deals and offers that you will now be getting from time to time," advised Monty as he quickly finished his beer and made his way home.

With the cold blooded murder of producer Mukesh Duggal and the music baron Gulshan Kumar. and also the recent daring attempt on the life of Rakesh Roshan, the ex film star turned producer, these extortion and criminal activities by the Mumbai's underworld goons had no doubt shaken Bollywood very badly. And though the Government of Maharashtra had recently enacted the tough legislation called Maharashtra Control of Organised Crime Act or MCOCA 1999 in short to curb the rise in the extortion racket that had gripped India's financial capital, but as far as the tinsel world of Bollywood was concerned the big players it seems had no other option but to keep the Dons happy and to tow their line, albeit very unobtrusively.

For Peevee, alias Deepak Kumar whose code name 'Mauna' the clean shaven was given by the Dons, this arrangement it seemed was far safer and better. It was better to work for less money than to die for more. With the liquid cash with these Dons in abundance and with no documentation whatsoever of money changing hands legally such deals were therefore also safe from scrutiny by the income tax sleuths and revenue authorities, and some of whom were no less than the dons when it came to making easy money thought Peevee as he called the Don from a secluded telephone booth in the Muslim dominated area of Mahim to give his consent. And a fortnight later on 7th November,1999 at the 'Muhurat', the most auspicious date and time when the first shot of the Don's film titled 'Himmat Na Har' was about to be shot, Peevee's cell phone rang. It was a call from the Don in Dubai thanking him for being so very nice and cooperative

"I must say that they have their moles everywhere or else how the hell did he know about my whereabouts," thought Peevee to himself as the clapper boy got ready to start the proceedings for the first shot. The story of the film revolved around the high jacking of a large passenger aircraft by three heavily armed terrorists from the People's War Group on board an Indian Airlines flight from Hyderabad to Delhi. The pilot had been forced to fly to Khatmandu in Nepal and their demand to the government of India was for the release of their leader and 10 others who were being held in an Indian jail. In the film, Peevee as the hero was required to play the role of that of the Captain of the aircraft and the story focused on how he and his crew members after a tense 96 hour ordeal finally managed to outwit the hijackers. As per the Director of the film, most of the shooting was scheduled to be carried out in and around Hyderabad, Delhi and

Khatmandu airports, and for which necessary permission had already been taken from the respective governments and the concerned airport authorities.

Later that evening after the shooting schedule for the 'muhurat' was over; Peevee wrote a long letter to his Mom Number 2 in Moscow and requested her to join the family for a week's get together at Khatmandu that was being planned during the shooting of the film in late December, 1999.

"I will be shooting for a new film at that location and the idea is to ring in the new millennium with Mount Everest in the background," wrote Shiraz while enclosing a few photographs of him dressed as the dashing captain of the aircraft. And on receiving the letter from her son, Shupriya (Yeshwant Kaur Bajwa) immediately applied for a month's leave from mid-December to mid January. She always dreaded the bleak ice cold Moscow winter and looked forward to spending a well earned holiday with the family in India.December was also the festive season in India and it was going to be a grand get together for the entire Bajwa family to ring in the new millennium. During her holidays she also decided to spend most of her time on a book that she was writing and which was titled 'Moscow Then and Now'. Basically it was a comparison of what life was like in Moscow for the working class and the common people during the communist regime in the early sixties and seventies and what it was now. According to her, some of the powerful new Tsars of Russia were the same old erstwhile young followers of Leninism and Marxism, but with the advent of 'Perestroika' and 'Glasnost', the country had now become a haven for the new Mafia and the Oligarchs of Russia. And with rampant corruption abounding in every sphere of life and with the brutal contract killing of rival gangs on the increase, even Moscow the capital was not at all safe. And the worst part of it was that some of these hoodlums had now become the most powerful Mafia bosses of the country.

Most of the information about these Russian mobsters that was gathered by her was from her cousin Lalima. Now in her late fifties, the spinster, half Russian and half Bengali Indian was a very reliable and safe source of information for Shupriya. With Lalima's influential contacts in the government, and with some erstwhile friends in the old KGB who had become hoodlums, and a few new rich oligarchs who always liked to show off their ill gotten wealth, Lalima was a treasure trove of information. Being totally disgruntled with those at the helm of affairs in her Mother Russia, Lalima was now only too willing to tell the world of her country's miserable plight. No longer were the Russians proud of their achievements and of their country and its sudden dramatic fall from a super power to that of a third rate nation had made her indeed very sad. And now the meteoric rise of corrupt and greedy politicians, mobsters and oligarchs had also made her a very bitter person, as she narrated to Shupriya as to when and how it all came about.

According to Lalima, the actual breakthrough for most of the criminal organizations inside Russia surfaced initially during the economic disaster of the early 1990's and which was followed by the mass emigration of Russians to the west and to Israel. Desperate for dollars and other hard currencies, many former government workers and officials therefore had taken openly to organized crime and many of them were former KGB agents, sportsmen and veterans of the Afghan and Chechen wars. They were now all out of work and they therefore willingly joined the organized criminal gangs to make a quick buck. Prominent among the gang leaders were Semion Mogilevich who was popularly known as Don Semyon. He was born on 30th June, 1946 and the wily Ukranian was also known as 'The Brainy Don' because of his business acumen and of his having had a college education with a genuine university degree in economics. He had made his millions in a secret deal in 1994 with the tacit connivance of the Chairman of Inkombank. And despite the collapse of the bank in 1998, he was now a very influential figure too. Born into a middle class Jewish family, the Don with his top lieutenants had moved to Israel and was now involved in the worldwide smuggling of drugs, weapons; prostitution and money laundering.And within the big cities and towns the criminal mafia gangs were generally identified from the various neighbourhoods that they operated from. The main amongst them were the Moscow based Solnetskaya Brotherhood that was led by the mobster Sergei Mikhailov.This was followed by the Dolgoprudenenskaya outfit named after the Moscow suburb of Dolgoprudny, and the Izmailovskaya gang that operated from the Izmailovo District of Moscow.

Sergei Mikhailov also known as Mikhas was born on 7th February, 1958 and he had started his life as a waiter and had worked in several restaurants in Moscow. In 1984, the 26 year old Mikhas was convicted on charges of fraud and theft and was awarded six months rigorous imprisonment and was sent to the dreaded Gulag. There he made good contacts with other Russian gangsters including those who were the members of 'Vor V Zakone,' the Russian Mafia. Back from the Gulag, Mikhas had his own gang which he named after his neighbourhood in Moscow. Pretty soon his Solnetskaya gang with their arms deals, drug operation, prostitution and money laundering became the biggest and the most dreaded criminal organization in the country. Though he was arrested in 1989 on extortion charges, but at his trial, when the key witnesses refused to testify, he became once again a free man and started expanding his empire. After the collapse of the Soviet Union and with a better playing field for diehard criminals like him, he with other Russian Mafia bosses with their money power not only quickly gained control of the politicians, but also of the various important government resources including those of oil and gas. With Russia in total chaos, Mikhas also got into the banking business, opened casinos and also the lucrative luxury car dealership business. His organization had even taken over the local Vnukovo airport in Moscow. From his plush headquarters on Leninsky Prospect, his gang not only controlled prostitution, gambling, and drug deals, but he also had a big hand in various illegal arms deals and that to on a massive international scale. In 1994, he sent his henchmen all over the world to expand his business and he himself decided to go to Israel. Israel had become a popular place among the Russian mobsters who were Jews. This was primarily because of the rule that Jews from all over the world were at liberty to return to the Holy Land and they could not be refused entry even though they were on the run from the law in their own country. Mikhas was not a Jew, but like many other non Jewish Russian mobsters, he had faked his passport and entered Israel as a returning Jew. In 1995, with his billions, Mikhas moved to Switzerland. Operating from his castle in Geneva,he lived like a king, till the Swiss authorities arrested him a year later for massive money laundering in drugs and weapons and for breaking the Swiss law that prevented foreigners from buying property. But such was his authority and power that in 1998, the Swiss authorities were forced to set him free because the Russian government refused to cooperate, and moreover, fearing for their lives, quite a few witnesses for the prosecution at his trial had turned hostile. On his return to Russia, Mikhas in July 1999 even had the audacity to sue the Geneva Canton for the loss of income suffered by him during the two years that he had spent as an under trial prisoner in Geneva.

Not to be left behind, Leningrad which was now back to its old name of Saint Petersburg had it share of Mafia gangs too. Prominent amongst them was the Tambov Gang led by Vladimir Kumarin and the Malyshev Gang led by Alexander Malyshev. These gangs with their muscle and black money power and government contacts were now virtually not only controlling industrial empires within the country but even abroad. Prominent amongst them was Viktor Anatolivich Bout. Born on 13th January, 1967 in Dushambe, Tajikistan, Bout was a graduate from Moscow's Military Institute of Foreign Languages. He could fluently speak six languages and he had also served as a translator with the Russian army in Angola. But after the collapse of the Soviet Union and finding himself jobless, the clever Russian soon took to gun running. According to one reliable source, Victor had been during the Afghan civil war in the early nineties regularly supplying tons and tons of lethal arms and ammunition to various warring Afghan groups. Initially operating from his palatial mansion in Ostend, Belgium, the wily gun runner had now shifted base and was operating from Sharjah, in the United Arab Emirates. And the UAE with its strict bank secrecy laws and free trade zones was not only a major financial centre, but it was also a paradise on earth for such like enterprising arm dealers and money launderers. The man was not only airlifting and selling large quantities of arms and ammunition to the Taliban in Afghanistan, but also to all the warring factions in trouble torn Africa. With most of the deadly assault rifles, grenades and missile launchers and ammunition coming from various factories in Bulgaria, and with a fleet of commercial aircrafts to carry out these illegal deliveries at his disposal, Mr Bout was now a man to reckon with. Moreover with his high level contacts with the UAE royalty and his political connections worldwide, he was now considered almost untouchable by the various law enforcement agencies that were gunning for him. Besides supplying small arms to rebels in small African countries, the ex Russian commando had now graduated in also supplying helicopters, armoured vehicles and even anti aircraft guns and missiles to all those who were willing to pay for them.

"By God, you have really opened my eyes. And if it is true that these Russian Mafia gun runners just for the sake of making easy money are even willing to supply lethal weapons to the Taliban in exchange for drugs, then the matter is really very serious. Because on the same analogy they may be also supplying arms and ammunition to Bin Laden's Al-Qaida and other such fanatical organization of which there are now many in the Indian subcontinent. And therefore the abortive arms drop near Purulia in India a couple of years ago may not have been the only one of its kind. India is a very big country and with its long coastline, it is also highly vulnerable to such like smuggling activities from across the high seas. A striking example of this was the landing of weapons, explosives and ammunition on the Konkan coast near Mumbai in early 1993 and which subsequently led to the series of explosions that rocked the city on that dreadful day of 12th March 1993.' said Shupriya while inviting Lalima to accompany her to India.

'I would have loved to my dear, but it is too short a notice for me. Moreover I have a series of important lectures scheduled to be given on the controversial subject of whether communism as visualized by Lenin and had he lived for two decades more would have ever worked in the 20th Century.

You see I have been invited by some very prestigious German, Polish and Hungarian universities to give these lectures to the post graduate students of political science in their respective countries at the commencement of the new millennium which is only six few weeks away, and I am eagerly looking forward to it. And in any case it now too late for me to postpone or cancel them. Therefore this time you have to give me a raincheck, and maybe I will take on the offer to vist India sometime next year,"said Lalima while presenting her with the 'Order of Lenin' that her late father Arup Ghosh was awarded with posthumously after the Battle of Berlin in May 1945.

"But what will I do with it,' said Shupriya looking rather urprised.

'Well simply find a pride of place for it in the Indian Embassy and don't forget that my late father after all was an Indian citizen,' said a smiling Lalima.as she kissed Shupriya goodbye.

That evening as she lay in bed with the Order of Lenin by her side, Shupriya just could not imagine how life for her had once again come full circle. The late Arup Ghosh was her uncle and her mother Mona's eldest brother. He was the eldest among the four children that her maternal grandfather Debu Ghosh had produced. And though Shupriya had never met him or any of her other three uncles because all of them had died before she was born, she nevertheless had heard stories about them from her late mother and father, Ronen and Mona Sen. Late that night feeling very homesick, Shupriya took out the photograph in uniform of her late husband Shiraz Ismail Khan and that off her son Peevee dressed as an airlines a pilot. And when she compared the two, she just couldn't believe her eyes. There was so much of similarity between them that they actually looked more like twin brothers.

Chapter-20

Some Sordid Untold Facts

While Shupriya was looking forward to her holidays with the family in India, the Pakistani Ambassador Riaz Mohammed Khan (Shiraz Ismail Khan) had also been hurriedly summoned by the Pakistani Foreign office at Islamabad for an urgent important meeting. With the trial of the ousted Prime Minister Nawaz Sharif scheduled to begin on the 19th of November at the anti-terrorist court in Karachi, there was a need to brief all the senior Pakistani Ambassadors who were posted in all the G-8 countries as to why the military had to take over the country.

The charges against Nawaz Sharif were indeed very serious and it included criminal conspiracy, kidnapping, attempted murder and hijacking. Pakistan's economy was also in doldrums and an unbiased justification was required to ensure that the economic and other aid from these rich countries did not dry up. On that Friday of 19th November 1999, when Nawaz Sharif and his co-defenders were brought to court in military armoured vehicles and the whole world watched it live on television, for Arif Rehman and his wife Ruksana Begum it was another day of shame for Pakistan.

"I don't think that even during Stalin's purge and rule, diehard criminals and culprits were ever brought to court in armoured vehicles that were escorted by no less than 20 other vehicles of armed paramilitary forces. Even a notorious hard gangster and killer like Al Capone and the Bonny and Clyde duo in America were not given this special privilege and I don't know why we had to make it such a worldwide spectacle of it," said Ruksana Begum.

"I guess it is all a publicity stunt or maybe the military was apprehensive that supporters of Nawaz Sharif's Pakistan Muslim League may create problems on the streets and the military I guess was not prepared to take any chances." said Arif Rehman.

"Well let us hope it is a fair trial," said Shiraz as he walked in with a magnum bottle of Black Label for Arif Rehman and a big bouquet of roses for his mother-in-law. He had arrived unexpected, and his sudden appearance was a source of joy to the elderly couple. Late that night while they were discussing the colossal amount of money the Sharif family had made after they joined the political bandwagon under the late General Zia-ul-Haq's patronage, and that to in one single generation spanning just two decades, Arif Rehman the former seasoned diplomat came to the conclusion that despite the serious charges leveled against the deposed Prime Minister, the man would in all probability be sent into exile. According to him there was reliable and authentic information that the Royal Saudi Government and other oil rich Muslim nations in the Gulf region had already started putting pressure on General Musharraf and with the Pakistan economy in shambles that could be the right answer. After all we do depend a lot economically on these oil rich Gulf countries,", added the elderly retired diplomat.

"You are right and we cannot afford to hang another Prime Minister, because that would be terrible for our image Chachajaan,"said Lt General retired Aslam Rehman Khan as he with his wife Farzana walked in with another bouquet of flowers. Aslam Rehman on hearing from Shiraz that he would be in Peshawar only for one night had therefore driven all the way from Islamabad to be with the family. When the discussion veered on to what would be the fate of those politicians and businessmen who had been recently arrested by NAB, General Musharraf's newly formed National Accountability Bureau on charges of corruption and embezzlement of billions of dollars, from the country's exchequer, Ruksana Begum with her subtle sense of humour simply added that though the acronym NAB sounds great and apt for the occasion, but in the long run and knowing how justice works in this country, these shameless diehard crooks will I bet simply have the last laugh and get away eventually. Why even the military Generals like Aslam Baig, Fazle Haq and quite a few others while in uniform had amassed millions, but nothing happened to them either."

"Yes you do have a point there, but unfortunately the rot has spread like cancer in all departments of public life in this blessed country, and its indeed a pity that as yet no exemplary punishment worth the name has been dished out to these crooks who are only masquerading as so called do gooders, 'netas' and leaders,"added Shiraz when the news on the CNN television channel surprised everybody.

That evening in the United States, John Carpenter became the first ever millionaire on a game show. The young man from Hamden, Connecticut who was born on Christmas Eve, 1967 and who ironically was a collection agent in the U.S. Internal Revenue Service had actually collected his personal one million dollars at the popular American game show 'Who Wants To Be A Millionaire'. And so very confident was he of giving the correct answer to the million dollar question and which was who among the four American Presidents Lyndon Johnson, Richard Nixon, Jimmy Carter and Gerald Ford appeared on the television series "Laugh In', that the contestant John Carpenter in order to add a little more pep to the show decided to use the lifeline of 'Phone-a-Friend'. He had reached the final question without the use of any of the three life lines and when he asked for his father to come on the phone, there was pindrop silence inside the auditorium. And when Regis Philbin the master of ceremonies and the quiz master of the show told John that he had only 30 seconds to give the answer and he immediately started the countdown, John's wife Debbie silently said a prayer. And when John got through to his father and simply told him 'Hi Dad, I don't really need your help, but I just wanted to let you know that in a few seconds from now I am going to win a million dollars,' everyone watching the show thought that he was joking. But with just seven seconds to go when a confident John Carpenter simply said that his only and final answer was Richard Nixon, there was a look of bewilderment on Philbin's face. However, in order to keep the suspense going, Philbin decided to keep a poker face. And after a few agonizing seconds when Regis declared that Richard Nixon was indeed the right answer and conveyed to John's wife Debbie that she would definitely be going to Paris for a second honeymoon, the crowd inside the jam packed auditorium burst into an unprecedented loud applause for the man who had just created history.

"Well my dear if John Carpenter made his first million in a straight forward quiz contest then it is legitimately acceptable. But in this country when most of these corrupt politicians siphon off millions from the poor and that too shamelessly without batting an eyelid or being quizzed about their sources of income, that's downright cheating and they therefore only deserve to be shot in public, "said an angry Ruksana Begum as she bid all of them a very goodnight.

Over breakfast next morning, when the question of what would happen to Lt General Ziauddin Butt, the disgraced former boss of the ISI who had aspired to become the Chief, the consensus of opinion was that he should be tried by a court-martial and be given at least a life term.

"'But you never know that man. And I won't be the least surprised if he in order to save his own damn skin, he like Aminullah Chaudhuri the ex director of civil aviation may also turn approver,' said Shiraz as he helped himself to another 'Aloo Ka Paratha."

But what really startled Shiraz while they were driving back to Islamabad with Aslam Rehman at the wheel was the bizarre story that Aslam narrated to him. It was about a good looking, highly educated Muslim lady with a master's degree in English. She was from a respected Karachi Memon family and in 1978 during General Zia-ul-Haq's regime was instrumental in exposing a deadly spy ring of a dozen Pakistani nuclear scientists and engineers who wanted to sabotage the country's aspirations of becoming a nuclear power. The expose came to light when the lady narrated her heart broken story to a senior military officer from the ISI who was then posted in Karachi. This spy ring that was working under the aegis of the American CIA actually wanted to sabotage the project and if that was not possible then they were to try and indefinitely delay Pakistan's ability to produce the nuclear bomb. But thanks to the lady, all those who were involved in this bizarre spying game had been nabbed in the nick of time. The lady concerned was a college lecturer and the one and only motive for her to share this secret with the ISI was to seek revenge against her ex lover. She had madly fallen in love with Rafique Munshi, a nuclear scientist who was then working at the Karachi Nuclear Power Plant (KANNUP). With the lure for American dollars and luxury style living, Rafique with a few others who were also working in that complex had been secretly passing highly classified matter to a western consulate at Karachi. But known to only a few this unsung jilted girl by telling her sad love story to Brigadier Imtiaz Ahmed who was then a Lt Colonel heading the ISI at Karachi had out of sheer vengeance saved Pakistan's nuclear project plans from being derailed. This was the same Brigadier Imtiaz of the infamous 'Operation Midnight Jackal'fame and the man who with the help of the ISI had later got Nawaz Sharif to power for the first time and was subsequently rewarded with the post of Director Internal Security in the Nawaz Sharif government. But thereafter he had got into the bad books of Benazir Bhutto and when Benazir made a comeback, she promptly had him sent to prison.

The first clue about the spy ring came when Colonel Imtiaz by chance or rather by luck noticed a red Mazda car with a Pakistani number plate entering a foreign consulate in Karachi and that too in a great hurry. When later that car was traced to the Tariq Road Mazda showroom and it was found that it had been rented out to one Rafique Munshi who resided in a suite in the MPA hostel, located in Garden East at Karachi and that he was a scientist working on Pakistan's nuclear project plant at Karachi, Colonel

Imtiaz became a little suspicious. He therefore through his ISI agents in the sprawling big city kept a discreet watch on that man and on his contacts and whereabouts. Earlier the lady concerned had contacted Colonel Imtiaz but she was hesitant to tell him what she knew about her lover boy who had jilted her so very badly. But finally when Colonel Imtiaz advised her to take it off her chest because it was badly affecting her mental health, the lady finally spilled the beans.

Not only was Munshi her class fellow at the Karachi University, but he had also promised to marry her. But when Munshi secretly started courting a white skin memsahib who was working with the foreign agency and the Muslim lady found out that he was cheating on her, she could not take it anymore. For the sake of easy money, Munshi was also selling classified secret documents on the country's nuclear project to this powerful foreign country. In fact Munshi the key player in this spying operation was actively playing the role of an agent allegedly between the American CIA and the Pakistani scientists and engineers who were working on various nuclear projects inside Pakistan.

Then on one fine day and with the tacit connivance of the lady lecturer, Colonel Imtiaz with the help of a key making expert had somehow managed to open the safe in Munshi's apartment wheh the gentlemen was away on duty. And when he found dozens of highly classified secret documents, he discreetly photocopied them. They were all related to Pakistan's nuclear sites and installations. And though the iron safe was also stacked with American dollars, Colonel Imtiaz in order not to arouse any suspicion that the safe had been broken therefore did not touch them. Finally after working on the man for nearly a year, Colonel Imtiaz caught him red handed at Hawkes Bay, Karachi when Munshi was in the process of handing over some more classified documents to the foreign agent in exchange for hard cash.

On being grilled by the ISI, they soon had the names of a dozen other officers. They were all on the payroll of the foreign secret agency and they had all been tasked to sabotage the nuclear sites by developing long term technical snags in them, thereby delaying indefinitely Pakistan's projected nuclear program to produce the bomb. When the DG ISI, General Riaz Mohammed informed General Zia that the concerned foreign agency was based in Washington, Zia just could not believe it. He nevertheless got in touch with the American President to express his deep concern. But to keep the Americans in his good books and to extract some more largesse from the super power, the President of Pakistan at the request of White House decided not to make the matter public. However, the Pakistani scientists who were involved in this bizarre game of selling their country were tried in a court of law and all of them were sentenced to life imprisonment. Rafique Munshi in fact was initially sentenced to death, but on the recommendation of an influential political leader of Sindh whose political support General Zia very badly needed at that time, it was commuted to a life term for him also.

"I sincerely hope what you just narrated to me is gospel truth and if that could happen two decades ago in General Zia's time when the Russians were breathing down our damn necks in Afghanistan, then I am afraid it would be even worse if our scientists for the lure of easy money decide to pass on these secrets to the radical Islamist organizations like the Al-Qaida, the LeT and such like other fundamentalist outfits that are mushrooming not only in Pakistan and Afghanistan but also in India, Bangladesh and in the whole wide world including the UK and USA where the younger generation of Muslims are being thoroughly indoctrinated in the name of Allah to save Islam. And not only that, they are also being mentally tuned and motivated to become suicide bombers by these so called half baked and semi literate and self appointed Muslim clerics," said Shiraz with a look of disgust in his face, as he took out the latest photograph of his wife and children from his wallet and showed it to Farzana.

"I must say that your daughter Sherry is a real stunning beauty and I think it is time that we started looking for a good match for her 'said Farzana.

"'But Jaani, she is only 20 plus and in this modern age and with her cosmopolitan background I think we should leave that decision to her. And I am sure that when the time comes to choose her own partner, she will choose the perfect gentleman. And keeping her deep interest in music in mind, I think someone like another Zubin Mehta in the making would be ideal,'"added her husband Aslam Rehman as he too had another good look at the photograph.

"Yes I also agree and even if though he is a Zorashtrian, I won't in the least mind. I won't even mind even if he is a Muslim from India, provided of course he is as good looking and talented like Amjad Ali Khan, the great sarod player. But certainly not a Kashmiri Hindu music maestro like Shiv Kumar Sharma, the versatile Santoor player, though he like Amjad is a very handsome man too,", added Shiraz very cleverly.

"But frankly speaking, I do not know why do we in every matter have to be so very anti Indian an anti Hindu. I think that is being rather unfair and parochial, because when it comes to watching Bollywood movies and listening to Hindi filmi songs, both our older and our younger generation of Pakistanis; including the teenage girls and boys and their young mothers and fathers still prefer to watch the aging Amitabh Bachchan, Dev Anand and Dharmendra on the silver screen, But at the same time they also like to watch upcoming heroes like Deepak Kumar, Akshaye Kumar, and beauty queens like Madhuri Dixit and Aishwariya Rai also. And mind you all of them are Hindus. And given the opportunity and a choice, all of them I bet would prefer to watch the Bollywood stars than their own Lollywood heroes and heroines."added Farzana.

"Well as far as good looks and acting talent is concerned, I think if given the opportunity, our very own Reema Khan and Babar Ali and Shaan from Lollywood can also give the Bollywood stars a good run for their money,"said Shiraz while expressing his desire to see the diamond jubilee hit movie 'Munda Bigra Jaye' starring Reema Khan and Babar Ali.

"In that case we can see it tonight sitting at home in our own little home theatre,' said Aslam Rehman.'

"I think that is a splendid idea and I therefore suggest that you pack your bags and check out from the Pakistan Foreign Office VIP guest house right now. You only have another 48 hours in Islamabad before you fly back to Moscow and we could do well with a little more of your lively company,"said Farzana.

"I think that is indeed a brilliant idea and with such a juicy spy story coming from your husband about the jilted lover that had been kept top secret for so long, I would love to hear some more of such Pakistani James Bond stuff. After all Aslam Bhaijaan too had done a fairly long stint with the ISI when he was posted to the Embarkation Headquarters at Karachi, and that was the time when most of those sophisticated clandestine arms and ammunition for the Afghan Mujahideens came in big ships from the American CIA channels during the Russian occupation of Afghanistan. And keeping that in mind, I am sure he will be able to throw some more light on the unholy nexus that existed between the drug lords, the CIA, the ISI in particular and the Pakistan military top brass in general,' added Shiraz.

That evening after having made himself comfortable at Aslam Rehman's palatial bungalow, Shiraz over a bottle of some rare malt scotch whisky on the rocks and some delicious 'chapli kebabs' that Farzana had specially made for him, asked Aslam quite candidly whether the Pakistan army during the Soviet occupation of Afghanistan had collaborated with the American CIA in drug running and vice-versa, and whether the senior Pakistan scientists having successfully detonated a series of nuclear bombs a year ago could be trusted with their loyalty to the country.

"Well frankly speaking both are very difficult and tricky questions to answer, but there is definitely a ring of truth in them alright. The Americans are no saints and neither are we, and at that time it was a question of helping the Americans out in making the Russians bleed at the hands of the Mujahideens, and in the same manner as the Viet Cong in Vietnam with massive Russian arms aid had done to the Americans. Moreover, Pakistan's economy was in doldrums and we needed financial aid from the Americans and the World Bank. And in that context, the unholy nexus that existed between some of the big time drug lords, the moles and the secret agents in the CIA, and their counterparts in the ISI including some very high ranking military officers in the Pakistan army was not a well kept secret either. And quite a few of them on both sides of the fence without mentioning any names of course did make quite a killing."

"Well I guess till now making a fast quick buck by the politicians, the bureaucrats, the bankers and the privileged men in military uniform in this country was considered to be part of their perks. But now with the promulgation of the NAB, the National Accountability Bureau and with the NABO, the National Accountability Bureau Ordinance having already come into effect from 19th November, 1999, General Musharraf hopefully will come down heavily on these bastards who shamelessly and systematically have been cleaning up the country's coffers. On 22nd October, Lt General Syed Amjad Hussein, the Commander Strategic Command at GHQ was appointed to head this important bureau and he is already on the job. As the Chairman of the Accountability Cell he has been given very wide powers and has been tasked to establish and implement the parameters and mechanisms to effectively recover the billions that these bastards have looted and to also give exemplary punishment to those found guilty," said Aslam Rehman.

"Well let's hope that General Musharaff will keep his word because the Ehtesab Act of 1997 was also enacted by the Nawaz Sharif government to rein in corrupt people, but it was nothing but a sham and eyewash. It was tailor made to prosecute his own political rivals, and particularly the PPP, while at the same time it was also meant to protect him and his colleagues from any such scrutiny," added Farzana.

"But all said and done, these so called earlier ordinances and acts were not made applicable to members of the armed forces, but I am happy that this new one, the so called NAB will be applicable to any person who has served in and retired or resigned from the three services, or has been discharged or dismissed from the Armed forces of Pakistan and for that I will give General Musharaff full credit,. And it would have been even better had he also included those who are now serving too. It seems that the serving members of the Pakistan Armed Forces and members of the judiciary for some reason best known to the Chief Executive have been exempted," said Shiraz as he helped himself to another large malt whisky.

'Well, looking back at this country's 52 years of inglorious existence, wherein we had a few short lived democratic governments in the chair and some long spells of military rule, but nothing has really ever changed, or will change in the future either. Promises are only made to be broken, and I am afraid the law in this country is only enforced on the poor and the down trodden 'janata', the common people of this Godforsaken land, and not for the rich and the famous,' said Farzana rather sarcastically.

And no sooner had Farzana concluded her diatribe, when suddenly from the front door smartly marched in Vovka, Major Samir Aslam Khan. The handsome field officer from the First First Punjabees had come to give the good news that he had been selected to attend the Command and General Staff Course at Fort Leavenworth in the United States

'Then that calls for a grand party, Bhiaya and since Riaz Jijaji will be leaving for Moscow the day after, you must therefore give us a treat tomorrow. And I want to have dinner at the Diva Lounge where the mushroom sizzler is simply out of this world, 'said Nasreen, smacking her lips.

Aslam Rehman's only daughter Nasreen was 17 and she was now in her final year at the prestigious ISOI, The International School of Islamabad on Johar Road. Like her mentor Benazir Bhutto, she had made up her mind to go to Radcliffe, which only recently had become part of the Harvard University, in Cambridge, Massachusetts.

That evening after a late dinner and after all the other family members and servants had gone to bed, Aslam Rehman and Shiraz over some Cointreau liqueur seriously discussed what could or would be the future of Pakistan under the present CEO and Army Chief, General Pervez Musharraf, and whether he would stand by his promise to bring back democracy and civilian rule as soon as normalcy was restored.

'Well being a straight forward guy who always calls a spade a spade, and in view of what he has been repeatedly stating in public that he would get rid of all corrupt politicians and others who have been looting the country systematically and bring in a new look government of honest, patriotic and hardworking people, it all sounds very honky-dory no doubt. But whether he will be able to deliver is another million dollar question. His intentions may be very good and noble, but in a corrupt ridden Pakistan, this may not be all that easy. Till now the general public no doubt has hailed him as a savior, but to maintain that euphoria he must set an example by quickly acting against all those political crooks and their henchmen, be they civilians or men in uniform. Till date at least I have never seen any of them behind bars, except for Zardari. But that was also because of political vendetta. And now is the time when we must act quickly and ruthlessly and ensure that these so called leaders, 'netas', and crooks if found guilty are not only debarred from active politics and public life, but they should also be put behind bars," said Aslam Rehman as he poured some more Cointreau into Shiraz's small crystal liqueur glass and then gave a detailed monologue as to why and how Pakistan after the Soviet invasion of Afghanistan in 1979 became a stooge and a crony of the Americans.

According to Lt General Aslam Rehman Khan, it all started after General Zia-ul-Haq seized power in 1977. Professing to be a true dedicated Muslim and a firm believer in the teachings of Prophet Mohammed and the Holy Koran, which the officer from the famous Guides Cavalry no doubt was, General Zia unfortunately in order to make himself popular both with the common masses, the Mullas and with the other ranks in the Pakistan Armed Forces went hammer and tong to enforce the Sharia law and which in turn resulted in what we now call Zia's so called Islamaization of Pakistan. The idea may have been very noble but some of the self appointed Mullas of the country thinking that they were the chosen ones to now enforce it, felt that it was time for them to also show their damn authority with muscle power. And as a result of which quite a few of them in the name of Islam and with the help and aid from the Zia government started opening 'madrassas'(seminaries) anywhere and everywhere inside the country.

'Though these 'madrassas' were supposed to be a place of learning, but quite a few of them soon became centers of fanatical power to promote 'Jihad: And once Zia launched Operation Tupac in Indian Occupied Kashmir and the Russians also landed in Afghanistan, these same very 'Madrassas' soon became the prime recruiting areas for the Mujahideen fighters not only from Pakistan and Afghanistan, but from other Arab countries also. And with the massive arms aid happily coming from the American CIA who were only too willing to supply the Mujahideens with all the weapons and ammunition to bleed the Russians to death, and with the Saudis willing to pump in tons of their oil money for the same cause, Pakistan in general and the North West Frontier region in particular soon became hosts to a large number of Muslim fanatics and mercenaries from all over the world. But no sooner were the Russians and their Communist puppet government ousted from Afghanistan, and the Soviet Union disintegrated, America once again and as usual started treating us like a pariah state. And the day the Russians were kicked out by the CIA and the ISI sponsored Mujahideens, the infighting between the various Afghan warlords to gain total control of the country began and it steadily grew in momentum.Pakistan and the United States also made the stupid mistake of initially supporting the Taliban and now the same damn Mullah Omer's Taliban with the tacit support from Osama Bin Laden's Al-Qaeda has therefore become a bloody headache not only for both the countries, but also to the entire damn world. And I am afraid the creation of this fanatical monster in the near future will only add to our miseries. As it is the world is branding us as a terrorist state and very rightly so because a very large number of them who were recruited in the name of Islam and Allah from various countries as mercenaries and Mujahideens to fight the Russians are now with the Taliban and the much dreaded Al-Qaeda which America too now fears. And what is still worse is that our own ISI and the Pakistan Army are not only giving these same very terrorists the wherewithal to fight the proxy war for us in Kashmir, but it is also providing them with a safe haven in our own country. And as and when things go wrong, the pressure from the United States on Pakistan to get Osama Bin Laden and such like terrorists dead or alive is automatically also stepped up. And when it comes to such a situation, we not only plead our ignorance of their existence, but we also secretly and quietly push them back into Afghanistan. In fact our present policy of recognizing the Taliban regime is full of pitfalls,' said Aslam Rehman in all seriousness as he poured a wee bit more of the Cointreau into Shiraz's liqueur glass.

"'But I believe Lt General Fazle Haq who was a very close confidante of General Zia-ul—Haq, he too had as Governor of the Northwest Frontier Province during the Soviet occupation of Afghanistan made pots of money," said Shiraz as he once again clinked glasses with Aslam Rehman.

'There is absolutely no doubt about that. In fact he as the de-facto overlord of the Mujaheedin Jihadis he had very cleverly allowed the setting up of hundreds of heroin refineries in the province and very soon it became a very lucrative business. With the drugs for arms campaign, Fazle Haq very smartly used the same vehicle convoys bringing the unmarked CIA weapons from Karachi to return back with tons of heroin and which eventually found its way to the international market. And mind you though it was way back in 1982, that General Fazle Haq was listed with the Interpol as an international drug trafficker, but nobody could touch him because he was considered at the same time to be a good asset for the American CIA. Thereafter Fazle Haq, the ex Guides Cavalry officer very ingeniously moved the heroin money through the now defunct but notorious BCCI, the Bank of Credit and Commerce International and by the time Zia died, he had conveniently made his millions. However, he did not live long to enjoy his ill gotten gains because a few years later he was gunned down and killed by an assassin," added Aslam Rehman as he took out an old photograph from an album in his library cum study room and said.

'You know my father and his very close friends were right when they told us when we were young that it would have been wiser and better had India remained as one country.'And when Aslam Rehman handed over some of the old photographs for him to see who those close friends were of his late father Major General Gul Rehman, Shiraz was taken totally by surprise.Below one photograph was the caption 'The Three Musketeers-IMA February 1935.' And in another group photograph there was Colonel Ismail Sikandar Khan with the entire family. That was taken in Lahore soon after partition and when Aslam Rehman was only seven years old. Looking at those two familiar photographs that he had seen being proudly displayed on the mantelpiece in his foster parent's home in New Delhi, Shiraz's thoughts went back to Bibiji. For him the grand old lady was more than a mother. That night as he went to bed, he wondered whether he would ever get reunited with his foster brother Monty and his family again.

Next morning at breakfast, in order to find out a little more of what actually happened at Kargil and how the operations from Pakistan's side was kept such a well guarded secret, Shiraz very frankly asked Aslam.

'But tell me Bhaijaan for a clandestine military operation of such big magnitude, the Prime Minister Nawaz Sharif I am sure must have been kept fully in picture by General Musharaff. But it seems now that he is in the docks, Sharif is vehemently and openly denying it and is putting the entire onus of the debacle on the Pakistan military, which I think is ridiculous and highly unfair, isn't it,?" added Shiraz as he congratulated the cook for the delicious breakfast of 'makki di roti 'with 'sarson da saag' that was served to him on a pure silver platter.

"Yes on that score too I fully agree with you, and to say that Nawaz Sharif did not know a damn thing about the operation at all is all bloody humbug. Nonetheless, credit must be given to our selective and clever military planners. The first and most important thing that was done to support the winter operation was to declare Army rule in the Northern Areas. And once that was enforced, it automatically and completely isolated the area from the rest of the country and automatically all access to the area was denied to all media, both national and international. And that is why if you remember even we were not allowed to visit Gilgit and Skardu last summer. Thereafter, to speed up the logistic operation, extensive use during winter was made of helicopters, snow mobiles and animal transport. A large number of forward helipads close to the LOC were also constructed for this very purpose, and it paid off handsomely. Even during the build up and subsequent occupation of the Indian defenses, all troops taking part in the thick of winter and which included mostly those from the Northern Light Infantry, the SSG, the Chitral and Bijaur Scouts and the Mujahideens Groups, they were all the time kept ignorant of the exact aim and motive behind the operations. They had also been ordered to carry out the operations only in the local tribal attire. And to doubly ensure that the details of the operations remained confined to the local inhabitants of that area, only the troops from the Northern Light Infantry Battalions who were all basically from the Gilgit and Baltistan area were selected for the main task of occupying those strategic heights that the Indians had vacated. So much so that in order to tell the world that the operations were conducted by the so called 'Mujahideens', the troops were not even allowed to wear their official oval shaped identity discs. But it seems that some of them without knowing the grave implications did carry their uniforms and certain other identity documents like pay books, personal letters and photographs with them. But the game was finally up when some of them were captured by the Indian army, and when both the world and the Indian media played up the matter in royal style, we looked like bloody fools. And what was even worse is that we still kept denying our involvement. Orders therefore were now given to all, including the officers not to carry any identity documents. The saddest part was that not only did we as professional soldiers kept flouting all military norms and traditions, but we even refused to accept the dead bodies of our valiant officers and soldiers including those of Captain Karnal Sher Khan and Havildar Lalak Jan who were both later decorated posthumously with the Nishan-i-Haider, Pakistan's highest gallantry award. And to put it very bluntly the Northern Light Troops were simply used as cannon fodder and it was they who ultimately had to pay the price of sacrificial goats in that military debacle," concluded Aslam Rehman when at that late hour the call bell suddenly rang. And when Aslam Rehman opened the door, and was pleasantly surprised to see his younger brother Fazal Rehman Khan, it was time for more celebrations.

Chapter-21

'Operation North By North East'

Fazal Rehman Khan, the handsome and suave senior officer from the Bangladesh Foreign Service and who also happened to be Aslam Rehman's younger brother had come from Dhaka for an important meeting with the Pakistan government regarding the tentacles that the ISI and the Al-Qaida were now spreading to build their bases in and around Bangladesh and along its long porous border with India. The ISI it seems was especially interested in creating trouble for the Indians in the strategic narrow 20 kilometer wide Siliguri corridor belt. This narrow corridor that linked the Indian peninsula to Assam and other Indian hill states in the North Eastern Region was therefore always considered, militarily, economically and politically very important to India. According to one report, the Muslim population in that vital belt had suddenly shot up by more than 150 percent in the past few years and this had naturally got India worried. There was also reliable information that the arms and ammunition that were being supplied by the ISI to the ULFA, the United Liberation Front of Asom were primarily meant to create problems for India, and these clandestine supplies to the secret ULFA camps inside Bhutan was being regularly routed by the ISI through Bangladesh.

"It seems that the leaders of this militant separatist group are hell bent upon having their own damn independent state of Asom, but with the ISI's covert involvement, it is also creating problems for us too. The 2nd June, 1999 blast at New Jalpaiguri station in the narrow vital Siliguri corridor that killed10 and wounded more than 80, and which was followed by a much more severe blast in August at Gasian railway station in the North Dinajpur area of West Bangal that killed over a hundred no doubt did send a few cheers among the ULFA leaders and their ISI handlers, but soon thereafter, the arrest of Raju Chakroborty and Dilip Burman, the two ULFA activists and their subsequent confession to the Indians that the ULFA was having very strong links with the ISI and that the ISI was openly operating from inside Bangladesh has now got us in a real mess with India. And when the arrested persons told the Indian intelligence sleuths that one Lt Colonel Masud Rana from Pakistan ISI had often met Anup Chetia, the ULFA General Secretary in the up market area of Uttara Dhaka, that input became even more embarrassing for us. And though we have officially and categorically denied our involvement with the ULFA movement and the ISI, but India thinks otherwise. Moreover, with some recent reports that the Al-Qaida and the ISI with the help of Bangladeshi Mullas are luring the young Muslims of Bangladesh to become Jehadis and terrorists and are asking them to join the militant Mujahideen Groups in Kashmir and Afghanistan to fight against all 'Kafir's,' the so called unbelievers, this trend is also rather disturbing. And mind you all these developments in no way augur well for the countries of the entire subcontinent and that includes Pakistan too. And let me also tell you that Osama's Al-Qaida set up is also now fairly active in Bangladesh too. In fact the Dhaka based HJAI, the Harkatul Jihad Al Aslami, which is an active Islamist fundamentalist organization and which is financed by Bin Laden had during the Kargil war called for a massive recruitment of some 5000 volunteers to go and fight for their Kashmiri brothers. And not only that, the HJAI has also spread its tentacles to Murshidabad in West Bengal for the recruitment of such like volunteers to create trouble for India too,' added Fazal Rehman while showing them a copy of the secret meeting of the HJAI that was written in Bengali and which was held on 11th June, 1999 at Cox Bazaar. 'And surprisingly the Pakistan ISI is also actively supporting the activities of the HJAI. And mind you if this sort of jingoism is allowed to continue, then I am afraid it will soon become a monster in the making, and I won't be the least surprised if these very Jihadis with the backing of the Mullas, and on the pretext of preaching that Islam is in danger, may one fine day start calling all the shots in Bangladesh too," said Fazal Rehman as Aslam poured him a double Cointreau.

"Well all this is certainly news to me. And what surprises me even more is that only 28 years ago these same very Bangladeshi Mullas and their followers had welcomed the Indian army with open arms to throw out the Pakistanis. And I therefore tend to fully agree with Fazal Rehman's assessment that these very half baked Mullas may well become the Frankensteins of their respective countries. As it is Pakistan is being indirectly branded by the United States and her western allies as a terrorist state, and if we don't rein in these so called militant groups and their Mullah leaders soon, we will be only asking for trouble. As it is the Kargil fiasco has created a big rift between the so called Jihadis, the army top brass and the deposed Nawaz Sharif government, and the militant hawks amongst these Jihadi groups are now not only asking for more sophisticated arms and ammunition to seek revenge, but they also want to step up the ongoing proxy war not only inside Kashmir, but also deep within India, I am told," said Shiraz as he looked at Aslam Rehman for his comments and reaction. Shiraz had very cleverly broached the subject and was keen to find out if the Pakistan ISI was hand in glove with the big Jehadi groups like the LeT, Laskar-e-Taiba and the Hizbul-Mujahidden who were allegedly being guided and trained by the ISI to carry out terrorist attacks on strategic targets deep inside Indian territory.

"Well I won't say that you are very much off the mark, but the fact remains that the ISI ever since it was created has grown from strength to strength and there is no doubt that it is now a state within the state. It is therefore undoubtedly today a very powerful potent force and with the army always having a stranglehold on it, there is every possibility of these Jehadi organizations with the covert connivance of the powers that be, may well be used in the near future to carry out some sensational terrorist activities and operations against our perennial adversary across our eastern borders. One must not also forget that the humiliating withdrawal from Kargil that was carried out under the orders of the Nawaz Sharif government has not been forgotten by the Pakistan military and the Jihadi groups that took part in those operations. Not only did we have to shamefully vacate the area, but in the bargain we also suffered very heavy casualties. Politically and diplomatically it was a gigantic disaster and both the Pakistan army and the Jehadi groups are therefore now looking for ways and means to give it back to India, and that to in a very big way,"added Aslam Rehman as he bid Shiraz and Fazal Rehman a very good night and invited both of them for a round of golf at the Rawalpindi Golf Club early next morning.

"That will be really great and we might also bump into some old friends and colleagues at the golf course. But we must all truthfully declare our present handicaps because we are going to play fairly high stakes", said Fazal Rehman who was also now an avid golfer.

"That suits me fine because I am also now playing to a steady fourteen handicap,"said Shiraz as he gulped down the rest of the liqueur and retired to his room. Maybe I should send a warning note about the ISI's sinister plan to use the dreaded terrorist outfits like the Let and the Hizbul Mujahideen for the likely attacks against important strategic targets in India thought Shiraz as he changed into his night suit and sat down to write an anonymous cryptic note for the Indian High Commissioner in Islamabad. However, on second thoughts and fearing that it would be a very risky and difficult task to deliver the same at the High Commissioner's residence or at his office, because both the places that were located on the G-6 and G-5 Areas of the Diplomatic Enclave at Islamabad were very highly guarded and were under twenty hours strict surveillance by Pakistan's intelligence agencies and cameras, he therefore shelved the idea for the time being and burnt the note. Moreover the main entrance to the Indian Chancery building was only some 300 meters from the Pakistan Foreign Office check post on the U.N. Boulevard and it would therefore be foolish of him to try and even get close to it without being noticed or observed. Maybe on my return to Moscow, I will try and warn India's lady ambassador indirectly, thought Shiraz as he hit the sack.

Next day morning having completed the first nine holes, as they all sat down for a sumptuous breakfast at the Rawalpindi Golf Club, Shiraz very diplomatically asked Fazal Rehman whether the present Bangladesh government that was being led by Sheikh Hasina's Bangladesh Awami League Party was aware of an abortive military coup that had allegedly taken place in May 1996 coup and which was only a month before she and her party were re-elected back to power. And also whether the ISI had any hand in it.

"Well as far as coups and attempted coups are concerned, Bangladesh like Pakistan is certainly not lagging behind and the little that I know is that in no way was the ISI involved. But what happened in that month of May 1996 is very much a fact. Lt General Abu Saleh Mohammed Nasim, the one legged 1971 war hero who had been appointed Chief of Army Staff by Khaleda Zia's Bangladesh Nationalist Party in 1994 did attempt a coup, but it misfired very badly. At that time there was an interim caretaker government at the centre and it all started on the 19th of May, 1996, when the President of the country, Abdur Rehman Biswas ordered the retirement of two senior army officers who it was believed were politically hobnobbing with political parties. But General Nasim simply refused to comply with that order. And when President Biswas sacked him the very next day and the army chief then followed it up by sending soldiers to take over the state radio and television stations in Dhaka and elsewhere, the matter got further aggravated. But General Nasim instead of bowing out gracefully, decided to take up cudgels and the matter became very serious when he as the army chief ordered the army units stationed at Bogra, Jessore and Mymensingh to march to Dhaka. But luckily, there were some senior serving generals who decided to remain loyal to the President and to the Constitution. And one amongst them was Major General Immamuzzaman, the General officer Commanding the 9 Infantry Division at Dhaka.Realizing that the military coup could lead to further destabilization of the country and especially so because of the general elections was around the corner, the GOC 9 Infantry Division quickly took some effective and timely actions that eventually led to the downfall of the chief. To begin with, he not only removed all the boats and ferries that the Jessore and Bogra garrisons would eventually require to cross the River Jamuna at the Aricha Ghat near Dhaka, but he also sent his formations to establish strong blockades on the roads leading to the capital from Mymensingh and Chittagong respectively. And when the GOC of the 33rd Infantry Division at Comilla and a few others also decided to remain staunchly loyal to the Constitution, the game for General Nasim was up, and subsequently with his arrest, the so called coup became an instant cropper,"added Fazal Rehman, while reminding Shiraz and Aslam Rehman of their current winnings and losses after the first nine holes.

Having enjoyed their wholesome continental breakfast, when the three of them got ready to tee off again from the tenth marker, Shiraz, in order to find out a little more about the ISI's penchant to perennially create problems for India asked. "But Aslam Bhai is it true that during the Khalistan movement in India, and more so after Mrs Gandhi's gamble to send in the regular Indian army troops and tanks inside the Golden Temple, the ISI became hyper active to support the disgruntled militant Sikhs in setting up their Independent State of Khalistan. But did they succeed in any manner?"

"Well soon after the Russians withdrew from Afghanistan in 1987, the ISI besides continuing to fan trouble for the Indians inside Indian occupied Kashmir under 'Operation K', they also spread its tentacles deeper into Indian Punjab and subsequently launched another aggressive plan that was code named K2. It was called the Kashmir Khalistan Front and it aimed at the Balkanization of India by forging strategic alliance not only among the Punjabi and Kashmiri militants, but also from those Muslim fundamentalist elements in that country who were also known to be staunch Pakistani sympathizers and supporters And thus with the supply of lethal weapons and training, and by conducting thorough indoctrination of some disgruntled young Indian Muslims, the Student Islamic Movement of India, known as SIMI was born," said Aslam Rehman as he got ready to take his tee shot.

But when his ball slowly rolled from the fairway into an out of bounds area, Shiraz jokingly remarked. "I am sure this too must be of ISI's doing, since these spooks love to operate in out of bound areas only."

"Well I hope I will not follow my elder brother, but then one never can say," added Fazal Rehman as he made a few practice swings with his number one wood. But with the very narrow fairway on the tenth hole, when Fazal Rehman's tee shot also followed the same path, Aslam feeling rather happy about it remarked rather subtly. "Well now that it has been confirmed by my dear brother Fazal Rehman that the ISI has launched 'Operation K-3', the third proxy war in the North Eastern part of India, I am positive that the sleuths and operatives from the DGFI, the Director General of Forces Intelligence of Bangladesh must be having their hands full too. After all, the office of the DGFI that was set up by the late President Ziaur Rehman was exactly on the same lines as that of the Pakistani ISI, and there is no doubt that both these agencies must be playing a very active part in those out of bound areas also."

"Well, If that be the case then I for one will not play the tee shot with my driver, because with the ISI and the DGFI snooping around, it will be far safer for me to use the number three iron," said Shiraz in jest as he got ready to take his tee shot. And as they kept playing the second nine holes, Shiraz was surprised to learn how deep the DGFI and the ISI's involvement were in creating trouble for India in the North East. Both these intelligence agencies that were led by very senior general officers in their respective countries with active support from some political parties like the Freedom Party and the JEI, the Jammat-i-Islami of Bangladesh were not only providing the ULFA and the Bodo rebels with arms training, but they were also acting as the conduit for the supply of arms and ammunition to all these militant groups. According to one reliable source, a certain Colonel Farouk from the Freedom Party had visited Pakistan in 1991. And acting as the conduit between the ULFA and the ISI, he was paid a huge sum of four hundred thousand US dollars to procure sophisticated arms from Pakistan for the ULFA militants. Thereafter the ISI in order to keep its firm hold on the ULFA, it also promised them with more arms, ammunition and training of their cadres in Pakistan, provided they engaged in sabotaging India's oil refineries, railways and other such vital installation in that region. And according to Fazal Rehman not only the ISI officers in the Pakistani Mission in Dhaka, but also the ISI officers who were stationed in the Pakistan Embassy in Khatmandu were both supplying the ULFA cadres with money and fake passports. Besides training the ULFA and the Bodos, even other insurgent groups like the NSCN, the National Socialist Council of Nagaland from the Issac—Muivah faction were also being trained in secret camps inside Bangladesh. Therefore as far as Aslam Rehman and Fazal Rehman's assessments were concerned, the year 1999 had seen a manifold increase in the Pakistan's proxy war against India, and Shiraz was now afraid that having gained success, the ISI may well increase their nefarious activities even further.

Later that evening as Shiraz accompanied by the two Rehman brothers, Aslam and Fazal made his way to the Islamabad International airport to catch his flight back to Moscow via London, he was quite impressed with the display of Pakistan's mighty fire power on both sides of the road leading to the airport. Earlier while returning from Rawalpindi, Shiraz had noticed the well lit gigantic brown fibre glass model of the dusty Chagai Hills, the feature where Pakistan had carried out its successful nuclear tests. And now when he noticed the giant replicas of the mighty Gauri Missiles in their green and gray camouflage paint shining majestically against the backdrop of the Marghalla Hills and with the country's motto of 'Faith-Unity-Discipline' written boldly on big white stones, he only hoped and prayed that these weapons of mass destruction should remain as models only. And as far as the country's motto of 'Faith-Unity and Discipline' was concerned, the less said the better he thought.

The 28th May of 1998 in Pakistan had been dubbed as 'The Yum-I-Taqbeer', the Day of the Greatness of Allah. And for the first time when that giant fibre glass model was lit up, the mammoth jubilant crowd that had assembled there to see the splendid spectacle literally went berserk. They not only punched the air with gusto, but they also with their deafening cries of' Pakistan Paindabad' and 'Allah Ho Akbar' had hailed the country's magnificent achievement. But with the army now back in power, and the corrupt Nawaz Shariff government having been disgraced and dismissed, that euphoria had all but evaporated, thought Shiraz.

While on the flight to Moscow, Shiraz was surprised to learn that the United States government despite their earlier classic carrot and stick approach towards the Taliban government in Afghanistan to hand over Osama Bin Laden, had now once again managed to get the stringent economic sanctions passed by the United Nations Security Council against that beleaguered poor country. With the Taliban's refusal to hand over Bin Laden and his cohorts, the Americans were now offering not only a reward of five million dollars for his capture, but a similar large amount was also being offered for the capture of his number 2 man, Al-Zawahiri and that of Mohammed Atef, who was Osama's military commander.And in order to further ensure that no further economic development takes place in that landlocked country, the American government had also forced the American oil giant, UNOCAL to pull out from Afghanistan. The UNOCAL as the head of a consortium had already signed an agreement to build a gigantic oil and gas pipe line from Turkmenistan to Pakistan via Afghanistan, and that Shiraz felt was rather unfair. Aslam Khan had also once casually mentioned to him that when Nawaz Sharif was still in the chair, there was a secret plan that was mooted by the United States government to jointly use a specially trained squad from both the countries to capture Bin Laden. And though this plan had the tacit approval of the Pakistan government, but it was shelved soon after General Musharraf came into power.

"I wish the plan had been carried out. But this kind of sheer big brother bullying attitude by the Americans towards the third world poor nations is simply disgusting and unacceptable. And the Americans cannot, and must not be allowed to use the United Nations forum to punish the weaker nations at their own whims and fancies. As it is the Americans with their pro-Israeli and anti-Muslim policies have antagonized a large number of economically backward Muslim countries, and if this trend continues, then I am afraid some diehard fanatical followers of Islam may seek bloody revenge on them," wrote Shiraz in his little red diary.

Though Shiraz felt happy to be back with his family in Moscow, he was also very concerned in the manner in which the Russians were determined to crush the revolt in Chechnya. The second round had already begun in October 1999, and the Russians having been badly humiliated in the first round were now hell bent to teach the Chechens a bitter lesson.

And in November, when at the recent meeting of the heads of states of the Organization for Security and Cooperation in Europe, the flamboyant American President Bill Clinton while pointing a finger at a sick Boris Yeltsin openly accused him of waging an unjustified war against Chechnya and asked him to halt his deadly bombing of innocent civilians, a visibly angry and upset Yeltsin had simply walked out of that conference. And it once again looked that the Cold War between the Russians and the Americans would erupt again. But luckily Prime Minister Putin on realizing that the confrontation with the Americans would not only prove unproductive, but it would also be foolish, he therefore decided to play it down. He had not forgotten that during the war in Kosovo, Yeltsin too had strongly opposed NATO's involvement, but luckily the Russians did not intervene there. But the Chechens with their fanatical Muslim blood in them were good fighters too. But what Shiraz was more afraid of now was the growing nexus between the hard line Chechen Muslims and Bin Laden's Al Qaida.

"I think that Russia's rather ambitious, but inconclusive foray into Afghanistan to suppress the Afghans by military power two decades ago, and which resulted in the deaths of so many innocent men, women and children was a bad gamble. And now this latest military venture to subjugate the Chechens by their mighty fire power will only result in more bloodshed and hatred,"noted Shiraz in his little red diary. Later that evening, when his wife Saira and daughter Sherry suggested that they as a family should get away from the harsh winter of Moscow and usher in the new millennium in Los Angeles with their brother Tojo, Shiraz immediately agreed to the proposal. With his love and passion for golf, Tojo with his single golf handicap had been offered a scholarship by the UCLA, the University of California at Los Angeles and he had gladly accepted it. And since he had won quite a few local amateur tournaments, he in order to improve his game and to make some more pocket money had therefore taken up golf coaching on weekends for the young aspirant beginners at one of the more prestigious golf club in Los Angeles.

Chapter-22

Heading East and Heading West

On 18th December, 1999, while Shupriya headed East and landed in India to usher in the new millennium and to be with her son Peevee and Monty's family, Shiraz with his family headed West from Moscow and arrived at Los Angeles to cheer Tojo who was taking part in an important golf tournament that included both professional golfers as well as promising amateurs.And while Shupriya that late evening on landing at Delhi was shocked to learn about the assassination attempt that was made that day on Chandrika Kumaratunga the President of Sri Lankan, Shiraz on landing at Los Angeles was surprised to learn that the assassin had missed his target by a whisker.

The attracrtive and charming lady who was the daughter of Mr and Mrs Bandaranaike and whose both parents were once Prime Ministers of that country was lucky to escape death, when a diehard suicide Tamil Tiger bomber detonated a powerful bomb while the lady after addressing a final election rally at the Colombo Town Hall premises was walking back to her car. The blast not only claimed the lives of 36 people including her driver and two bodyguards, but had injured many others too. But Mrs Kamaratunga was indeed very lucky. She only lost her vision in her right eye.

Born on 29 June 1945, and with a degree in political science from the prestigious University of Paris, she had joined the Sri Lanka Freedom Party in 1974. In November 1994, on being elected as President she appointed her mother Srimavo Bandarnaike as the Prime Minister. In 1960, when Chandrika was not even fifteen, her mother had created history when she became the world's first woman Prime Minister.Unfortunately Chandrika's husband, the late Vijaya Kumaratunga, a popular filmstar and poliitician had also been assassinated. He was shot dead outside his residence on 16th February, 1988 by Lionel Ranasinge. The assassin had been commissioned by the JVM-the Janatha Vimukti Peremunar, a Marxist organization. Shupriya had met the charming husband and wife team in 1987, when she was posted in Colombo and wondered whether the LTTE would make another attempt to get rid of her. Her father Mr Bandaranaike too had been assasinated.

While Monty was there at the Palam airport to receive Shupriya, a handsome Tojo with a putter in hand was all smiles when his parents with his sister Sherry walked into the arrival louge at the Los Angeles International airport. Tojo had decided that come what may, he would one day turn professional and he therefore wanted to test his skills in the company of some of the well known professionals in that game. Though commonly known in golfing parlance as a Pro-Am tournament, it also had some of the country's famous professional golfers also taking part in it. With some good luck and good putting, Tojo had just made the cut by one stroke, and on the fourth and final day which happened to be a Sunday, when he noticed all his family members among the many spectators cheering him, his morale really went sky high. And finally when he completed the tournament as an amateur with a minus one overall score, the most delighted person was his father. This was also the first time that Tojo had breached and carded one below on that particular 288 par golf course.

"Well I guess that calls for a special prize from me and though it is only 500 dollars to start with, nevertheless it should encourage you to earn in millions in the years to come, provided you become a dedicated professional golfer like the great Jack Nicklaus and Arnold Palmer. And that mind you requires very hard work. Jack Nicklaus who is also known as 'The Great Bear' became the US open champion at the young age of 22 and you are going to be only 17 on the coming New Year's Day," said Shiraz as Saira not to be left behind added another 500 to her son's kitty.

"That was indeed very creditable, but mind you there is another young golfer by the name of Tiger Woods from Stanford University who in 1996 at the age of 21 turned professional and is now already creating waves," said Sherry while hugging his brother.

"Yes I know he is an Afro-American and is the only son of a Lt Col in the US army who had also served in Vietnam. And now that Tojo has been invited to play at the Chester Washington Golf Course on the 31st of December which happens to be a Friday, and since the course is located close to the Los Angeles International airport, we might as well tag along with him and usher in the new Millennium Eve with his 17th birthday at the nearby Renaissance Los Angeles luxury hotel," said Shiraz.

"Yes Papa, it is a long weekend too and we could also make a trip to some of the famous film studios of Hollywood, and maybe with luck we may bump into my favorite movie star the young and handsome Johnny Depp," said Sherry somewhat excitedly.

"But do you know that the guy Depp is totally tattooing crazy and on the last count he had nearly half a dozen of them all over his body. And by the way and not so very long ago he was arrested for brawling with the paparazzi outside a famous restaurant in London. He had gone there with his new girlfriend, the French actress and singer Vanessa Paradis, and therefore my dear sister right now I am afraid you don't stand a chance," said Tojo somewhat teasingly.

While Shiraz with his family enjoyed the salubrious Californian winter weather, for Shupriya it was going to be a grand family reunion at Khatmandu, the capital of Nepal. Monty's son-in-law Paddy after completing just two and a half years in Islamabad had only recently been posted there as First Secretary in the Indian Embassy and with Peevee's plan to celebrate the New Millennium on the lap and shadows of the mighty Mount Everest, all of them on the morning of Sunday the 19th of December descended on the Nepalese capital by the Indian Airlines flight from New Delhi. Besides some foreign tourists and a few young newly married Indian couples going on their honeymoon to Nepal, the flight was otherwise full of people from Bollywood. They were going there to shoot the final climax scenes of the movie 'Himmat-Na-Haar' (Don't Lose Heart) that had Deepak Kumar (Peevee) in the main role of a pilot and captain of a hijacked commercial aircraft. And the locations selected included the areas in and around the Tribhuvan International Airport at Khatmandu

With the knowledge of the film shooting already in the air, a very large number of young and old local Nepalese men, women and children and also some Indians who had settled in Khatmandu had gathered at the airport to welcome the film stars. And as soon as the hero of the film, Deepak Kumar got out of the aircraft, he was greeted with thunderous cheers. Some of them had even brought trumpets, bugles and drums to sound the fanfare and a few were also seen doing the Nepali Khukri dance as Deepak Kumar with his bodyguard walked into the arrival lounge.

"My God, I hope they don't mob you and your heroine, because the manner in which they are dancing with their sharp Khukris it could well lead to a serious accident and you better be careful," said Monty while noticing the poor security arrangements at the airport. Besides a couple of policeman with their ancient 303 Enfield Rifles on duty, the place in general and the departure area in particular was in a state of utter chaos as passengers jostled with their luggage and tried to make their way to the handful of check-in counters for the departing flights. 'Luckily for Shupriya, Peevee, Monty and Reeta, waiting for them near the VIP lounge was Paddy with his wife Dimpy. As diplomats with red passports they were a privileged couple and very wisely they whisked all of them away from another exit that was normally used by the airport staff. As the Indian Embassy car with its diplomatic number plate made its way through the busy streets of Khatmandu, Dimpy requested her brother Peevee to spare at least some time from his hectic shooting schedule so that they could all as a family spend Christmas Eve and Christmas Day together at the picturesque tourist resort of Pokhra.

"It is long holiday weekend and to cut down on travel time we will therefore be doing the trip to Pokhra by air and not by road. Moreover, 26th December happens to be a Sunday and on the 27th we can all be back to work again," added Dimpy.

"'Well it all depends on the producer and the director. As it is they have overshot the budget, but to ensure that I make the trip with you all, I will request them to reschedule my shooting dates and if required I will also compensate them by cutting down on my contract amount," said. Peevee as he hugged his sister and presented her with a diamond studded bracelet.

"Now whatever is this for?" said a delighted Dimpy while thanking and hugging her brother.

"Does one have to have a reason to present a gift to one's only dear sister," replied Peevee as he took out another expensive gift from his pocket for Paddy his only brother-in-law. It was a beautiful Bretling chrono-matic wrist watch. And finally when he took out from his suit case a giant size 'Winnie The Pooh' a stuffed toy that could also talk, and it suddenly said 'Hey Simran, I am your new friend,' Peevee's four year old niece was so very thrilled that she immediately lifted the two feet tall and chubby Winnie in her arms and smothered him with kisses.

Very early on the morning 24th December, 1999 and after four days of hectic film shooting schedule, when Peevee joined the other family members at the Khatmandu airport to catch the Necon airways flight to Pokhra, little did anybody know that for the many Indian tourists returning by the Indian Airlines flight 814 to Delhi that afternoon, it would be a traumatic nightmare that would last for several days. Travelling on that ill fated flight that day was the film producer's younger brother. He had been tasked to return to Mumbai and meet the other financers of the film and get an additional rupees thirty five lakhs released immediately, and off which at least fifty percent was to be in hard cash. Having seen the earlier rushes of the film, the big time film distributers were keen that the film should be released both in India and abroad on 26th January, 2000 to coincide with the celebrations of India's 50th Republic Day.

Though it was only a thirty minute flight to Pokhra, but it was worth it as they all enjoyed the breathtaking view of the snow capped Annapurna Mountain range till the small aircraft landed safely at its destination. The most fascinating among the eight mountains of that range was the awesome Fishtail Mountain, and as Peevee got busy taking photographs with his zoom lens camera, Shupriya simply kept watching her son. Looking handsome in his grey flannel trousers and a black leather jacket covering his massive shoulders, he looked a carbon copy of his late father, Major Shiraz Ismail Khan. But fearing that he would be mobbed by the local Nepalese who simply loved Hindi movies and their stars, Peevee before deplaning had cleverly covered his head and face with a monkey cap and with the high collar of the leather jacket covering half his face and his Rayban dark glasses shielding his eyes, he very confidently made his way with all the others through the arrival lounge to the waiting chauffeur driven chartered minibus. But to his bad luck one of the co-passengers, a local Nepalese from the First Gurkha Rifles of the Indian army who too was on that flight gave the game away. He was coming home on annual leave and when he requested for a photograph with him and without the monkey cap, Peevee had no other option but to oblige. Soon it was the turn of the many cab drivers as they made a bee line to mob Peevee. And it was only after they reached near the lakeside for the boat ride on the beautiful Phewa Lake that there was some respite for the popular actor.

That afternoon, after indulging in some authentic Nepalese cuisine that was kind courtesy the Nepalese Havildar from the Indian army who insisted on giving all of them home cooked food as a picnic lunch on the boat, Peewee was surprised to learn about the large number of Gurkha soldiers from Nepal that the Indian army had on its roll including the pensioners. Not only were there seven full fledged Gurkha Regiments in the Indian army, but there were also a very large number of pensioners and war widows who were being very well looked after by the IEWON, the Indian Ex-Servicemen Welfare Organization in Nepal.

On the next evening and before they all departed for Khatmandu, Peewee donated a sum of Rs50,000 for the welfare of the disabled Gurkha pensioners of Pokhara. And he was pleasantly surprised when Shupriya too donated a similar large sum towards the war widows from that area.

"That was indeed very nice and thoughtful of you, but do you also have some link with the Indian army, like I do. After all my grandfather Lt Colonel Daler Singh Bajwa was from the Jammu and Kashmir Rifles and that regiment also has Gorkhas on their rolls," said Peewee.

"Well in a way yes because I too am now a Bajwa,' said Shupriya as Monty quickly butted in to add that one very close relation of Mom Number two who died during the 1971 war against Pakistan was also a highly decorated soldier and that regiment too had a complement of Gurkhas, but they were all Indian domiciled like that of his grandfather's regiment.

After visiting a few temples at Pokhara, when they caught the flight back to Khatmandu it was nearing 3.30 in the afternoon. And at around 4P.M. when the small aircraft landed at the Nepalese capital, they were surprised to find that the Indian Airlines flight 814 to Delhi whose scheduled departure time was at 3.30 was still in the process of checking in passengers. And when Peevee noticed that the film producer's brother, was still waiting to board the aircraft, Peevee waved out to him and in colloquial Punjabi said 'Oye Bharkurdar, paise leke jaldi aiyo wapas, nahin yahan toh pura kaam thap ho jayega.' (Dear Friend, please do return back soon or else all work will come to a standstill here, little did Peevee realize then that the ill fated flight to Delhi would in a way bring the new Vajpayee government to its knees?

Though it was Christmas Eve that day, but having had a very tiring trip to Pokhra, they all decided to spend the evening at home, instead of going to the Yak and Yeti for the dance and dinner that they had earlier planned for. "But only on one condition that there will a no cooking at home please," said Peevee as he called up the manager of the Chimney Restaurant at the five star Yak and Yeti Hotel and ordered for a special meal for seven that included besides two tandoori chickens and some sheek kebabs for starters, his favourite Chicken a la Kiev, a Smoked Bekti and a Savor Rack of Lamb with some rolls of garlic bread. And with the sun going down early in winter, Paddy by 6.30 PM had also got his bar fully organized. But when he had just about finished serving everybody their first drink, and was about to say cheers, the telephone rang. It was an urgent call from the Third Secretary in the Indian embassy who conveyed to him that the Indian Airlines flight IC 814 that had taken off at 4.30 PM from Khatmandu for Delhi had been hijacked. According to him and as per the latest input, the aircraft had tried to land at Lahore, but when the Pakistanis refused permission, the aircraft finally landed at Amritsar and was still there when last reports came in,

."But who do you think is behind this bizarre air piracy and what could be the motive, "asked Peevee as he tuned in his transistor radio to find out if the B.B.C.had something more to add to it.

"Well since the aircraft first tried to first land at Lahore, it could well be the handiwork of some ISI aided militant group from Jammu and Kashmir," said Reeta.

"But why did they have to come all the way to Khatmandu to pull this off," asked Dimpy.

"I think we can only come to know the truth once the hijackers list their demands. But since the ISI is now also fairly active in Khatmandu, and keeping in view that the security at the Tribhuvan airport is nothing much to write home about, I won't be very surprised if Reeta's hunch comes true," said Monty.

"Well whatever it is, I only hope and pray that the passengers and the crew of the aircraft are all safe," added Shupriya while helping Dimpy with the starters.

"And it is also rather coincidental that while a reel life movie on the very subject of an aircraft hijacked by militants is being shot at this very location, a real live hijack drama is also being played out on an aircraft that had taken off from here only a couple of hours ago," said Paddy as he tried to contact the Indian Airlines office in Khatmandu for the names of all the passengers and their nationalities who were on board the IC 814. During that entire evening and late into the night, when they all kept tracking the progress of the hijacked aircraft over the various news channels, it all seemed very confusing. And it was only on Christmas Day morning that a clearer picture emerged

The aircraft was hijacked twenty five minutes after it took off from Khatmandu at 4.30 PM, and on being been denied permission to land at Lahore, it landed at Amritsar at around 6.45 P.M instead. But an hour later it took off again from Amritsar and went back to Lahore and landed there at 8.20 PM. Twenty minutes later at 8.40 PM it took off again from Lahore, and at around 11 PM, when Kabul denied permission for the aircraft to land at the Bagram airport, it headed towards Dubai and landed there at the Al Minhat Air Force Base at 1 A.M on Christmas Day morning. At Dubai, the hijackers released 27 hostages, mostly women and children and the dead body of a passenger by the name of Rupin Katyal, and it took off again. Finally at around 8.30 on that cold Christmas morning after the aircraft landed at Kandahar in Afghanistan the hijackers started making their demands. It seems that they were now in friendly territory and were now demanding not only the release of their leader Maulana Massod Azhar and thirty five other militant terrorists who were in Indian jails, but also 200 million U.S. Dollars in cash and the coffin of a dead terrorist by the name of Sajjad Afghani.

"But after the aircraft landed at Amritsar and while it was there for over an hour, why could not we take some action to ensure that it did not take off again. After all the Raja Sansi airport at Amritsar is also a military airport,"'said a visibly upset Peevee as they all met at the breakfast table.

"'It is easier said than done my son, but don't forget there were 170 innocent men, women and children including the crew on board and their lives could not be risked. Moreover, the airport is manned by civilians and the local police and they are not trained for such kind of operations I guess. And don't also forget that the hijackers were a desperate lot and were well armed and they had already killed one innocent passenger,"'added Monty as Dimpy served all of them a simple breakfast of parathas and dahi.

'And I believe he was newly married too and had come to Khatmandu with his young bride for his honeymoon, and one can imagine what the poor girl must be going through right now," said Reeta.

"Yes, that is rather tragic and I am also wondering what would be the poor film producer brother's plight since he was also on that same flight. And I sincerely hope he comes back soon with the money or else the movie will not be ready for release on 26th January as planned, and which also happens to be Mom Number two's fiftieth birthday," added Peevee as he reloaded his plate with two more giant size parathas and some homemade delicious hot mango pickle to go with it.

"Well looking at the tall demands made by the hijackers, this may well become a very tricky affair for the new Vajpayee led N.D.A. government. I think it is a typical 'Catch—22'situation for them. If they give in to the hijacker's demands, it will be considered as a weak and spunkless government. And if they don't, then those who are not directly affected will give them a pat on the back for taking the hard line. But the families of those who are affected will cite the example of Rubaiya, the daughter of Mufti Mehmood the ex Home Minister in the erstwhile VP Singh government and they will create hell for the Prime Minister and his cabinet colleagues. And mind you, Rubaiya was only one single individual who was taken hostage and was released in exchange for five Kashmiri militants way back in December 1989, and that was a decade ago. But here we have over a 170 people including a handful of foreigners who have been taken hostage and whose lives are now in real danger," said Shupriya who genuinely felt that the need of the hour for the government was to get in touch with the Taliban government in Afghanistan and seek their support and help.

"But we have not yet recognized that government, so why should the Taliban help us,"said Peevee.

"I agree, and though to date only Pakistan, Saudi Arabia and the UAE have given them official recognition, but that country economically is facing a lot of hardships and we could on that pretext at least open a dialogue. There are also indications that the Taliban government is desperately seeking recognition from other nations and that includes India too,and we could therefore on that pretext also take advantage of it and request them to act as a mediator." said Shupriya.

'But I don't understand as to why these militants who are also terrorists are still languishing in our jails as guests of the government of India. Since they had waged a war against the country and had without showing any remorse wantonly and brutally killed many of our brave jawans and other innocent civilian people, the bloody bastards should have all been eliminated once they were caught," added Peevee in anger as he watched on the television screen the dead body of the young Rupin Katyal being off loaded at the Delhi airport. A special aircraft sent by India had brought back Rupin's dead body, and the 24 women and children that the hijackers had set free at Dubai.

Chapter-23

A Disastrous Christmas and Ramzan Week

For Mr Vajpayee, and his cabinet colleagues, the hijacking of the Indian Airlines flight IC-814 by the terrorists on Christmas Eve had come as a rude shock, and the tall demands made by the hijackers on his 75th birthday had got him extremely worried. The aircraft with the hostages were in a country where there were no diplomatic ties or representation by India, and the pressure from the kith and kin of those whose loved ones were trapped inside had also started mounting on him and on his two month old NDA government.

"I think this is one birthday and that too in his diamond jubilee year Mr Vajpayee will never forget,"said Peevee while announcing to his family about the sudden change of plans. Due to financial and other security constraints following the hijacking of the Indian Airlines aircraft, the shooting of the final climax of the film at the Khatmandu airport had now to be cancelled. And since both the Producer and the Director of the film were now looking for a new location in India, Peevee therefore suggested that it would be better if all of them returned back to Delhi at the earliest. Moreover, with all Indian Airlines flights to Khatmandu being cancelled till further orders, Peevee recommended that they should all make it back by road in some reliable hired private transport.'

"But what about you and I hope you will join us too," said Shupriya.

"Maybe I will after a few days when the unit finally packs up from here and returns to Mumbai," said Peevee.

"'Well whatever it is, you will have to be with us to usher in the new millennium as promised. After all Mom Number 2 has come all the way from Moscow at your invitation and you just cannot let her down now, shooting or no shooting,"'said Reeta rather firmly.

"I won't promise but I will definitely try my level best and we will celebrate it in Delhi maybe."said Peevee as he touched the feet of all the elders and wished them a safe journey.It was very early on the morning of 26th December and with no definite news as yet about the fate of the hostages, Monty with his wife Reeta and Shupriya left for Delhi by road in an air-conditioned Qualis. And after making brief halts at Gorakhpur and Lucknow for meals, they reached Delhi well after midnight. But what surprised Monty was that the Vajpayee government even after 48 hours was still indecisive. The government it seems still did not know where to begin and how to go about tackling and solving the crisis. According to the latest news only Mr Erick de Mul, the United Nations Resident Coordinator for Afghanistan had held some talks with the Taliban Foreign Minister, but no positive move this way or that way had been made by the Indian government. Meanwhile the relatives of those being held as hostages had all converged at Delhi and they had even gate crashed into India's Foreign Minister Jaswant Singh's press conference. Some of them were so very worked up with the incompetence of the government to have the hostages released, that they openly declared that they simply couldn't care a damn and even if the government had to give up Kashmir for the sake of getting back their loved ones, the government should do so. And when Jaswant Singh the Foreign Minister suggested that the Government had to keep the nation's interest in mind, one of them very rudely said in Hindi "Bhaad mein jaye desh,aur bhaad mein jaye desh ka interest (To hell with the country and to hell with the national interest.)

"I hope the government pulls up it socks fast, or else we might mind find Mr Vajpayee and his senior colleagues being 'gheraod' (encircled) by these people, and I won't blame them because if I was in their situation, I would have probably done the same," said Reeta.

"'I don't think the government is sitting idle and I am sure they realize the extreme gravity of the situation and they will do something to resolve the issue," said Shupriya.

"But those hijackers are ruthless ruffians and they have already given an ultimatum that they would start killing more people if their demands are not met by 2 PM on Monday the 27th, and it is already early morning of the 27th today and time is running out fast," said Monty.

On the afternoon of 27th December,1999 and just before the deadline could expire, with the sudden arrival in Kandahar of Mr A.R. Ghanashyam, the Counselor Commercial and a senior diplomat who was serving in the Indian High Commission at Islamabad, there was now a ray of hope. Having held talks with the Taliban government, the hijackers had extended their deadline by another three hours. And a little later, when a relief aircraft from

Delhi with a high level negotiating team also landed at Kandahar, it was evident that it was the hijackers who were now calling all the shots.

The hijackers it seemed had threatened that if India failed to meet their demands they would not hesitate to start killing the 156 hostages on board. And on the very next day, when the hijackers reiterated their demand for the release of 36 of their comrades together with the 200 million dollars and the coffin of Sajjad Afghani, together with the threat that they would blow up the aircraft with all the hostages inside if all their demands were not met, it was all back to square one. However, on the same very day, there was some respite for the crew and the passengers, when the hijackers permitted three cleaners inside the aircraft to clean up the filth that had accumulated inside the toilets. They were not only stinking, but it was also affecting the hygiene and health of those who were cooped up inside the aircraft and that included the hijackers too. And there was something more to cheer about also after the Indian Airlines technicians had repaired the faulty A.P.U. the Auxiliary Power Unit and the air-conditioning inside the aircraft was once again functional. That morning the hostages were also provided with breakfast. But that did not cool the nerves of the relatives of the passengers as they scuffled with the police outside 7 Race Course Road, the Indian Prime Minister's residence. And it was only on that 27th December evening that the high level seven member negotiating team from India led by Mr Vivek Katju, the Joint Secretary in the Ministry of External affairs made their first face to face contact with the leader of the hijackers, Meanwhile the Taliban government forces with machine guns, rocket launchers and tanks had surrounded the two aircrafts and they had also warned the hijackers that killing of hostages would simply not be tolerated by them. Late that very evening, Monty in order to get some more detailed information of what the Indian government's final stand would be in working out a deal drove to the Press Club of India to meet his old friend and veteran journalist Unnikrishnan.

"Well all I can say is that India is left with a Hobson's choice. Luckily the response by the Taliban government to end the ordeal I must say has been quite positive and even encouraging upto now and this perhaps may force the hijackers at the most to tone down the demands," said Unni as he ordered a chilled beer for Monty and another large Patiala peg of Old Monk Rum for himself.

"But who do you think is the brain behind all this?" asked Monty as they clinked glasses

"Well, since the hijackers have landed in the Taliban leader Mullah Omar's own home turf and backyard and the Taliban government's initial response towards India has been fairly positive so far, I therefore feel that we can safely rule out the Al-Qaida's involvement and hand in this. And to my mind this I think is the brain child of Pakistan's ISI. Don't forget that Pakistan is still smarting from the ignominy of their disastrous Kargil misadventure and now that General Musharaff and his military generals are in power, they therefore in order to keep the Jehadis happy and to keep the Kashmir pot boiling must have given their final approval. And I won't be surprised if the ISI in order to show their support to the militants in the ongoing proxy war in Kashmir have directly aided and used a group of such like Jehadis to hold India to ransom and to demand for the release of their own 36 comrades who are languishing in Indian jails," said Unni.

"However, I think the only mistake the hijackers committed or should I say miscalculated was that they overlooked the fuel requirement that was needed for the Air Bus 300 to fly them non-stop from Khatmandu to Kandahar. And when they ran short of fuel, they thought that by landing at Lahore the Pakistani government would willingly refuel the aircraft and they would still make it to Kandahar or Kabul by last light. But Pakistan in no way wanted to get directly involved. So the next best option was to land in nearby Amritsar and demand for the refueling of the aircraft from the Indian authorities, and this they did by threatening to kill the passengers. And it was as a result of this that young Rupin Katyal lost his life. But when India kept them hanging for a fairly long time at Amritsar, the hijackers fearing that the Indian commandos may well storm the aircraft, they probably lost their nerves and at gun point forced the pilot to head for Lahore again. And while it was taking off from Amritsar, the aircraft's wing tip very narrowly missed the fuel tanker that was carrying the Punjab Police commandos. They had been tasked to deflate the tyres, but they unfortunately arrived a bit too late. And the very fact that the pilot landed safely at Lahore was also nothing short of a miracle. The aircraft was not only running desperately low on fuel, but the Pakistani airport authorities were also not willing to play ball They not only warned the pilot not to land, but they also switched off all the runaway landing lights. But despite all the handicaps and a desperate fuel situation, the brave and experienced Captain Sharan took a calculated risk and made a spectacular force landing at Lahore," added Unni.

"But how many hijackers are on board and have they identified themselves and to which Jehadi group do they belong to ?" asked Monty.

"Well they have not yet given their real names and that I am afraid they will never disclose and therefore all the five hijackers are using some fictitious names and titles like 'Chief,"Doctor', 'Burger' 'Bhola' and 'Shanker'. However, looking at the profile of the militants whom they want India to release and particularly that of their leader Maulana Masood Azhar it is quite evident that they are all from the notorious 'Harkat-ul-Ansar,' and I won't be the least surprised if the hijackers are all Pakistanis,", concluded Unni.

On the morning of 28th December,1999 with the hijacking entering its fifth day, Peevee also reached Delhi. It had now been decided that the climax scene of the movie would be shot first at an old airfield near Jabalpur during the second week of January 2000 and finally at the Begumpet airfield at Hyderabad. This was suggested by the airport authority of India because the Dumna airfield at Jabalpur was seldom being used for commercial activity and it had the required infrastructure for the shoot. This would also give the film unit the required time to put up all the sets and the mock ups that would be essential for the final climax scene at Hyderabad.

"I pity and wonder what those poor hostages must be going through. Being cooped up inside the Airbus 300 for over four nights and five days and with the constant fear that the hijackers will not spare them if the Indian government does not give in to the demands, it must be really terrible and scary for them. And the sooner a deal is made it will be better for all of us. The families of the passengers too are also getting exasperated and the delay in getting them back safely is also reflecting badly on our political leaders and the mandarins in the External Affairs and the Home Ministry," said Peevee.

"There I fully agree with you, but it is also a very tricky situation. Because if we totally give in now to all the demands, then next time they will be asking for even more and there will be no end to it. And now that Mr Jaswant Singh, the Foreign Minister and the PMO's office are directly dealing with the problem, and they are I believe in direct contact with Mr Muttavakil, the Taliban Foreign Minister,I am sure something positive will be worked out in the near future and one that will be acceptable to both the sides,"said Shupriya.

Though she did not know about the new deal then, but Shupriya was dead right because late on that evening of 28th December, the final deal was struck and the hijackers had toned down their demands considerably. In exchange for the aircraft, the passengers and the crew, the hijackers were now demanding the release of only three dreaded terrorists and it included their leader Maulana Masood Azhar, Mushtaq Ahmed Zargar and Ahmed Omar Sheikh.

Like the Airbus 300 that ran out of fuel at Lahore, Maulana Masood Azhar during his clandestine visit to the Kashmir Valley in February 1994, while travelling in a car had literally also run out of fuel near Anantnag. He had entered the valley via Bangladesh and Delhi on a forged Portuguese passport with the new name Essa Bin Adam Issa. On 11th February, 1994 while returning from a clandestine meeting with a fellow terrorist at Matigund village, near Anantnagh when the car that he was travelling in got on to the national highway to Srinagar, it suddenly spluttered to a halt. And when the faulty fuel gauge showed that the fuel tank was empty, Azhar together with Sajjad Afghani and Faroukh Ahmed their bodyguard took an auto rickshaw to the nearest petrol pump, which was at Khanabal. On the way they suddenly bumped into a Border Security Force armed road patrol. Azhar's bodyguard not knowing where to hide his weapon panicked and fired at the patrol party and escaped. But Azhar and Afghani were both caught and arrested. Azhar's brief case not only contained the forged Portuguese passport, but it also had 1200 US Dollars in hard cash and an Indian Airlines ticket for the flight back to Delhi on the 13th of February. And had it not been for that faulty fuel gauge, Azhar probably would have been a free man thought Monty. That the man being a Pakistani citizen was further confirmed in June 1996 by none other than retired Major General Nasrullah Babar. The ex Rimcollian who was then the Interior Minister during Benazir's rule had officially written to the Indian High Commissioner in Islamabad asking for the man's release on humanitarian grounds. And later again in December 1997, when the Pakistani High Commission in Delhi sent a formal Note Verbale to the Indian Ministry of External Affairs claiming Maulana Masood Azher to be a Pakistani national and requesting for Consular access to him, it was evident that the man was no small fry. The second person by the name of Mushtaq Ahmed Zargar whose release the hijackers were demanding was a Kashmiri from Srinagar. He was a diehard militant who had been trained by the ISI. He was nicknamed 'Latram' because he frequently used the word 'Latram-Patram 'which literally meant talking nonsense. The young man was not only a known ruthless killer and a kidnapper for ransom, but he was also responsible for forcibly recruiting young Kashmiri Muslim boys to join the so called Jihadis. He was arrested in May1992. And as far as the third terrorist Ahmed Umar Sayed Sheikh was concerned, he was a British national and the main fund raiser for the organization. He was the one who had organized the kidnapping of four foreign nationals from a hotel in Paharganj in New Delhi to secure the release of his leader Azhar Masood. Luckily on a tip off from a reliable source all the four foreign nationals were rescued in the nick of time from a hideout in Saharanpur by the Indian police, and on 31st October, 1994, Ahmed Sheikh was arrested. As regards Sajjad Afghhani was concerned, he in September1999, while serving his jail sentence inside the Kot Bhilawal jail in Jammu tried to escape with his other terrorist inmates. He was however caught while trying to getaway through a tunnel that they had dug and was shot dead. Ironically, he was buried at a graveyard, which was not far from Chief Minister Faroukh Abdullah's residence in Jammu. Earlier the hijackers had demanded for his coffin, but now that demand too had been dropped by the hijackers.

The next two days of 29th and 30th December were crucial for the Vajpayee government. It had to doubly ensure that the deal made would be honoured in letter and spirit by the hijackers and that they would under no circumstances renege on it or raise any further demands. The three terrorists who were to be released were located at three different jails in the country and they were to be flown to Kandahar for handing over to the hijackers who wanted to ensure through physical identification that they were not being hoodwinked. Moreover, the deal had to be kept a well guarded secret from the general public and the media till the very last moment of its final execution.

On 30th Dec, 1999 evening, a twin engine executive jet took off from Delhi for Srinagar on a very important top secret mission and by the time it landed there, it was already dusk. On board were Mr A.S. Dulat, the Chief of RAW, the Research and Analysis Wing of the Government of India and a few other intelligence officers. Dulat had been tasked by the Indian government to meet Mr Faroukh Abdullah, the Chief Minister of Jammu and Kashmir and persuade him to release two of the three terrorists who were in jails in his state. Though Dulat was the first outsider to head RAW, but he was a very capable officer from the Intelligence Bureau and had done good operative work in Jammu and Kashmir and also while serving in the Indian Embassy in Nepal. Though it took a fairly long time to convince the Chief Minister, but finally Dulat did manage to do so and at the unearthly hour of 1A.M. the Jail Superintendent of the Srinagar jail was woken up. At around 3 A.M on that New Year's Eve frosty cold morning, three bullet proof jeeps with armed police escorts drove Mushtaq Ahmed Zargar from Srinagar to Udhampur and by the time they reached there, it was already nearing sunrise. Without wasting any more time, the terrorist was put into a waiting helicopter that immediately took off for Jammu with Captain AS Kahlon, the State Government's helicopter pilot in control. Waiting for him at the Jammu airport was Zargar's leader and mentor Masood Azhar. Azhar had earlier been brought to the airport from the Kot Bilawal prison in Jammu. Minutes later they were huddled inside the executive jet and were flown directly to Delhi. On landing there, they found the third terrorist Ahmed Umar Sayed Sheikh waiting for them. Soon all three of them were on board the special Indian Airlines Boeing aircraft and they found themselves in the company of none other than India's suave and articulate Foreign Minister, Jaswant Singh.

In order to ensure that the hijackers would stick to their side of the deal and incase important decisions had to be made on the spot, Jaswant Singh therefore had wisely decided that he would go himself to Kandahar and bring back the hijacked aircraft with the crew and the passengers safely by that very evening. All the beleaguered passengers and crew had very bravely and calmly faced the terrible ordeal for eight long days and Jaswant Singh wanted to reunite them with their families before the turbulent and eventful 20th Century was finally over.

Born on 3rd January, 1938, in a well to do Rajput family from Jasol, a village in the Barmer District of Rajhastan, Jaswant Singh was educated at the famous Mayo College at Ajmer, a prestigious school that in the good old days of the British Raj was primarily meant only for the wards from India's princely families. Born in the desert, he was a person who liked outdoor life and though he wanted to go for higher studies to Oxford or Sorbonne, the family could not afford it. He therefore like a true Rajput joined the National Defence Academy in 1953 and in 1957 was commissioned into a Cavalry regiment of the Indian Army. He was a forceful debater and an excellent horseman who loved playing polo and in taking part in horse shows and pig sticking competitions. But in November 1966 after nine years of meritorious service he quit the army voluntarily in order to join politics. But it was no cake walk for a 28 year old young man and a political novice at that to make his mark in national politics and that to in a party that had strong leanings with the RSS, the Rashtriya Swayamsewak Sangh and of which though he was never a member. Nevertheless, the bigwigs in the BJP, a party that was formally launched in 1980, saw the tremendous leadership qualities in him and very soon he was in the inner circle of the privileged few.

During that turbulent Christmas week and Ramzan month, while the rest of the world was enjoying the holiday season and were eagerly looking forward to the start of a new millennium, Jaswant Singh on that fateful 24th December afternoon had become a proud grandfather of a little girl. He was however on that day extremely busy contacting his counterparts all over the world for help and to bring to an end the miseries of the passengers and crew on board the ill fated flight IC 814. The ratio of setting free 3 three dreaded terrorist for 161 innocent passengers and crew had been constantly playing on his mind. But right or wrong the decision had been taken collectively by the government. The government had also considered the option of conducting a raid by trained commandos from the N.S.G. the National Securiy Guard. They were to be sent with the negotiators and others on the relief plane that had taken off for Kandahar on the 27th December afternoon, but with the possibility of the plan being exposed prematurely; the risk could not be taken. Only a handful of people were aware that Jaswant Singh's younger son like a true and brave Rajput immediately on hearing about the plight of the passengers and the agony of their families had volunteered to be taken hostage in exchange for those in the aircraft. And now that his father was going to Kandahar, he too had volunteered again to go with him. But there was no need for that now, since the father was confident that the deal would be honoured by both the sides and without any further bloodshed

With the Taliban now acting as the chief referee, there was now a ray of hope for Jaswant Singh as the special aircraft with the three terrorists on board took off from Palam, New Delhi. It was during this very month that the Holy Koran was revealed and Jaswant Singh was confident that both the Taliban and the hijackers would honour the deal. It had been decided that on landing at Kandahar, the three prized terrorists would first be handed over to the Taliban authorities and under a Taliban escort they would then be taken to the hijacked aircraft for identification by the hijackers. Thereafter all the passengers would be allowed to deplane. And once the deplaning drill by all the passengers and crew was completed, only then would all the three terrorists be handed over by the Taliban to the hijackers.

It was 4 o'clock in the evening, when the Boeing 737 carrying the Indian Foreign Minister and the three terrorists landed at the barren dilapidated Kandahar airport. Thanks to the Taliban who had earlier got the hijackers to give up the demand of the 20 million dollars and the dead body of Sajjad Afghami since they were considered to be against the tenets of Islam, and especially so that being the month of Ramzan, Jaswant Singh was confident that there would be no hiccups. As the door of the aircraft was opened by the flying attendant, it was now time for the Taliban leader as the referee and mediator to conduct the final swap over. As the three terrorists came down the aircraft ladder, Jaswant Singh was surprised by the cheering and embracing that followed on the tarmac. The released prisoners were being felicitated by their own kith and kin. They had been specially brought from Pakistan to identify them. And as the joyous shouts of victory for the hijackers echoed across the hills, the five men who had successfully carried out the hijacking were also welcomed as heroes.

On that evening of New Year's Eve, when the cold winter sun went down over the horizon, the long and scary eight day miserable ordeal for the crew and the passengers of IC 814 was also finally over. As the transfer of all passengers to the other two aircrafts began, Muttawakkil, the Foreign Minister of Afghanistan in the presence of Jaswant Singh announced that all the hijackers had been given only 10 hours to leave Afghanistan.

On that auspicious Saturday morning of 1st January 2000 with the dawn of the new millennium while the crew and passengers of IC 814 in India celebrated their reunion with their near and dear ones, in Pakistan the five hijackers with the three released terrorist heroes broke their Ramzan fast with some mouth watering frontier food. It was the New Year's millennium feast for all of them. On the previous evening also, the Taliban officials had treated them to a delicious 'Iftar' meal. And thereafter they were driven to the Pakistan-Afghanistan border and from where they simply disappeared. There was therefore no doubt in anybody's mind that this daring successful hijack of the Indian Airlines flight could not have been carried out without the tacit support and involvement of the Pakistan ISI.

It was on the afternoon of 24th December, when a Pakistani Embassy car with the diplomatic number plate 42CD14 had arrived at the Tribhuvan airport in Khatmandu. And minutes later after getting out from the car, and flouting their diplomatic passports for easy entry, Mohammed Arshad Cheema, the First Secretary in the Pakistan Embassy at Khatmandu with his assistant Zia Ansari, who was carrying a bag had entered the VIP lounge. Waiting for them was one of the hijackers. He was a transit passenger who had arrived earlier by the PIA flight, PK 806. The man was then handed over his ticket on flight IC—814 and the bag that contained weapons, explosives and arms. As a result of this the bag therefore did not go through the routine security check at all. Thereafter the duo from the Pakistan Embassy quickly left the airport.

In October 1998, the same Arshad Cheema had also handed over a packet containing 20 Kg's of the deadly RDX explosives to a Sikh militant who unfortunately for Pakistan was caught and had confessed. For the Pakistani ISI, Khatmandu in particular and Nepal in general had become a major hub for making contact with illegal drug dealers, gun runners and also with disgruntled elements of young Muslims from the Indian subcontinent who were willing to spy and work for the Pakistan ISI. With tourism and smuggling being the two most lucrative economic activities in that country and with security being given very low priority, big Mafia Dons like Dawood Ibrahim and Chotta Shakil also now had strong bases in that landlocked Himalayan kingdom.

A few days after the crew and passengers were released, the Indian sleuths from the Intelligence Bureau and the RAW got into the act. And it did not take them very long to find out how the hijacking was planned and executed. According to one reliable source, the hijacking of the aircraft was initially planned for the 27th of December, but it was later advanced by three days. The air tickets for the hijackers were booked by three separate travel agencies under fictitious names that were given to them by their handlers. The two executive class tickets in the names of A.A. Sheikh and S.A. Qazi were booked by Himalayan and Gurkha Travels respectively, while those of Z. Mistry, R.G.Verma and S.A.Sayeed in the economy class were booked by Everest Tours and Travels. Initially they were all booked on the 27th December flight from Khatmandu to Delhi, but on 13th December all of them had them altered for the same flight on the 24th.

While on board the aircraft, the hijackers had started addressing each other only with their code names of Chief, Doctor, Burger, Shanker and Bhola respectively. The real identity of the five hijackers was however established only a few days later after four of their accomplices were arrested in Mumbai. And this came about after the Indian intelligence officials intercepted a telephone call from Pakistan to one Abdul Latif in Mumbai on the night of 29th December. The caller had directed Abdul Latif to make an anonymous call to a certain TV correspondent in London and to convey to him that if the demands of the hijackers were not conceded, then they would blow of the aircraft with all the passengers and the crew inside. The 'Chief', whose real name was Ibrahim Akhtar hailed from Bhawalpur, while the 'Doctor' was Shahid Akhtar Sayeed, 'Burger' was Sunny Ahmed Qazi and', Zahoor Mistry was 'Bhola' All of them were residents of Karachi while the fifth, Shakir who called himself 'Shanker' was from Sukkur in Sind. All five of them were Pakistani citizens and they were diehard followers of Masood Azhar, the founder and leader of the dreaded Harkat-ul—Mujahideen. The freeing of the three dreaded terrorist was indeed a big victory for the Muslim fundamentalists of Pakistan and a sad defeat for the Indians at Kandahar. But with that it also became very evident that the state sponsored terrorism from Pakistan had now not only been given added impetus andmomentum, but it had also a reached a menacingly high level as far as India was concerned.

CHAPTER-24

Marching Towards A New Millennium

On that 1st of January 2000, at the break of dawn of the New Millennium that was being celebrated all over the world, Peevee true to his promise returned to New Delhi in a chartered private aircraft to be with his family and Mom number 2. But it was only for a day because he had to be back in Hyderabad on the very next morning for the shooting of the final climax scene of the film 'Himmat Na Haar.'

"And though most people in the world celebrated the dawn of the new millennium on 1st January 2000, but technically speaking and as per the Gregorian Calendar, the honour and distinction to herald the birth of the 21st Century and that of the new millennium should rightly have gone to the first day of the year 2001. And that is because the first century began from 1st January in the year 1 AD and the second century commenced from the year AD 101 and so on and so forth. And therefore the third millennium should logically start from 1st January 2001," said Peevee as he very deftly opened the Dom Perignom champagne bottle to usher in the year 2000. He was hosting a gala lunch party for his family at 'Daniell's Tavern', a restaurant par excellence in Hotel Imperial, the luxury hotel on Janpath, in the heart of New Delhi.

"Let's drink to the stars,"said Monty with a big smile as he stood up and raised a toast to God Almighty to herald in a better and a more peaceful world for Peevee and his generation and for the generations to come. After all Peevee was now a super star and Monty was only quoting from the words of none other than Mr Dom Pierre Perignon, the French monk who more than three centuries ago as the principal cellar master in a Benedictine Abbey in France had mastered the art of making that sparkling and bubbly white wine from red grapes and which was now known all over the world as champagne. And that evening, when Shupriya in honour of Peevee hosted a dinner at the 'Dumpukht" Restaurant in Hotel Maurya where authentic Frontier and Avadi food was indeed a specialty and which she knew was

Peevee's and Monty's favourite, she was also reminded of her late husband Shiraz who was also very fond of such kind of food that was cooked in earthen pots. But as a young Captain in the Indian Army it was beyond his means to regularly patronize such five star restaurants. And the only other place where he could afford such kind of equally tasty food and that to at one fifth the cost was at "Karim's' near Jama Masjid in Old Delhi. And the only time when Shiraz took Shupriya to Karim's was on 26th January, 1971 on her 21st birthday. That day also happened to be India's 21st Republic day and it was made all the more memorable because it was on that day that Shiraz had secretly proposed to her.Quietly taking out the small dainty silver ring band from her purse that Shiraz had presented her with on that day, she discreetly put it to her lips and said a prayer for the safety and well being of their only son Peevee. Besides the photograph of Shiraz in uniform, this was the only other memento that she had safely and secretly preserved.

"A penny for your thoughts, Mom Number 2," said Peevee with a smile while noticing the sudden moistness in Shupriya's eyes.

"Yes, I was thinking of you my dear. Because in another few hours from now you will be back to your busy shooting schedule in Hyderabad and we will all miss you," said Shupriya as she handed over the wine and menu card to Peevee and requested him to do the needful.

That night Shupriya just could not sleep at all. She knew that in another few days time she will back to work in Moscow and it could be months before she would be able to get to see her only son again. At 4 o'clock in the morning, there was a knock on Shupriya's door and Peevee was surprised to see that Mom Number 2 was still wide awake. Peevee had come to bid a final goodbye to her.

"Come on go to sleep now and I will call you as soon as I land in Hyderabd,"said Peevee as he touched her feet. On that early morning, while on his return flight to Hyderabad by the executive private charted jet, when Peevee learnt from the pilot that Captain Devi Saran and the crew of flight IC-814 were all from Hyderabad or rather they were based in the old Nizam's capital, it came as quite a pleasant surprise to him. And finally while shooting for the climax scene of the film, when Peevee was told by the Producer's younger brother in a little more detail of what actually happened inside the aircraft during those frightful chilling eight days, he was simply stunned.

"You know boss, initially for the first twenty four hours and till the aircraft landed at Kandahar, all the hijackers were in a deadly murderous mood to kill anybody and everybody. We were flying over Lucknow and they hijacked the aircraft while the cabin crew was still in the process of serving the passengers with the evening tea and snacks. At Amritsar airport the hijackers became very panicky and jittery, and it was more so when there was an unusual delay by the Indians to get the oil tanker to refuel the aircraft. And in order to prove to the pilot Captain Devi Saran that they meant business, they not only killed Rupin Katyal, but they also assaulted a few others male passengers with sharp knives. Fearing the possibility of the aircraft either being stormed by the Indian commandos or of the tyres being deflated to prevent its taking off from Amritsar, the hijackers at gun point forced the pilot to take off and land at Lahore again. And during those first eight hours and till the aircraft landed at Dubai which was around midnight it was the most agonizing for all the passengers. And the mood of the passengers only started cheering up a bit after the hijackers permitted the 24 women and children to be off loaded at Dubai.That also gave the rest of the passengers and the crew a little hope that they too would eventually soon be set free. But it was all very short lived. But once the aircraft landed at Kandahar and there was a lot of delay by India in not responding to their many demands, the mood of the hijackers once again became restive and menacingly aggressive. And it was only after the first group of negotiators from India arrived on 27th December evening and there was hope of some deal being worked out that the mood of the hijackers started gradually and slowly mellowing down. Seeing the discomfort of the passengers, the hijackers on 28th December permitted the aircraft flight engineer Anil Jaggia to repair the faulty auxiliary power unit. And with the air-conditioning being restored, they even allowed the crew to serve the passengers with breakfast. One of the hijackers even offered his leather jacket to Anil Jaggia while he was carrying out the repairs in that cold Kandahar weather," added the Producer's brother as he dug into his wallet to take out a piece of paper.

"And what happened thereafter friend," asked Peevee while directing the makeup artist to get ready to put the required amount of dark red paint on his face for the next shot. The sequence to be shot was a fight on the aircraft between the pilot and the hijackers and as a result of which blood had to be shown dripping from the hero's face and lips

"However, on 30th December, the mood of the hijackers once again became sour and they were very angry when there was a complete stalemate in the talks. Then suddenly late on New Year's Eve morning, when the hijackers heard that India had agreed to set free the three dreaded terrorists, the mood of the hijackers from being hostile suddenly became very friendly, helpful and jovial too. According to the passengers and crew the nicest of them all was 'Burger'. Once when Burger asked all the honeymooners on the plane as to what they would name their first born, and most of the ladies gleefully responded with the name Burger, the armed hijacker holding a gun in his hand was indeed very thrilled. By and large they were all very courteous and at times they were also very caring and helpful too, especially to the ladies and children," added the Producer's brother as he showed Peevee his prized boarding card that he had taken out from his pocket and kept as a souvenir.

'But I must say that you and the other men folk were very lucky because had the Vajpayee government not relented it could have led to many more deaths. But thereafter what was mood like of the hijackers, asked Peevee.

"On 31st Dec, when the people finally started getting down from the aircraft, Burger who had earlier presented a passenger by the name of Pooja Kataria with a shawl on her birthday became somewhat sentimental and apologetic. There was moistness in his eyes too as he shook hands and apologized to the passengers for all the inconvenience caused. But full credit must also be given to Captain Devi Saran and his magnificent crew. He was not only a crack pilot, but he was also a very mature and level headed man. The conduct of the Co-pilot Rajendra Kumar and the entire cabin crew that included the air hostesses, Kavita Mukherjee, Kalpana Mazumdar, Rajni Shekhar, Sapnarani Menon, Tapa Debnath, and the Flight Purser Sateesh during those grueling eight days was also exemplary. They not only kept their cool all the time, but they also did not lose their nerves under those trying conditions as they carried on doing their duties with the gun on their heads," said the Producer's brother, as Peevee's make-up man finally got him ready for the next shot.

On that 31st of December,1999 while the drama on the hijacked flight IC 814 at Kandahar ended with exchange of pleasantries between Burger and all the passengers, in the United States a bizarre plot to bomb the busy Los Angeles International Airport on Millennium Day had been timely unearthed by the United States Immigration and Customs officials. Born on 19th May, 1967, Ahmed Ressam, the 32 year old Algerian Muslim in 1994 had entered Canada on a forged French passport. When questioned by the immigration officials at Montreal airport, he had pleaded for mercy and claiming that he would be prosecuted if he was deported to Algeria, he had promptly asked for political asylum as a political refugee. But when he did not show up at the hearing for the grant of political asylum, his application for refugee status was declined and cancelled and a warrant for his arrest had been issued instead. Meanwhile in order to avoid deportation,

Ressam quietly went into hiding in Canada.Thereafter he obtained a false passport using the name Ben Norris, and in April 1998 travelled to attend an Al-Qaida training camp in Khaldan, Afghanistan. After nearly six months of intensive training at the Khaldan camp and having gained his skills in the handling of weapons, explosives and in bomb making, he returned to Canada.

On 14th December, 1999 Ressam with his rented car boarded the ferry boat M.V. Coho at Victoria Island, Canada for his entry into the United States. According to rules, all passengers travelling from Victoria to the U.S. entry port at Port Angeles were required to be first pre-cleared by the U.S. Immigration Authorities at Victoria and then on landing at Port Angeles were required to be inspected by the U.S. Custom officials. Ressam surprisingly had no problems with the U.S. immigration authorities at Victoria, but at the U.S. port of entry while he was being questioned by the Custom authorities, he became very nervous. And when he was asked a few searching questions of his place of birth, his education and his family, he suddenly panicked and attempted to flee. He was immediately arrested and physically searched. When the Custom officials found a legitimate Canadian passport, but it was under a false name, they became even more suspicious. And when the rented car was subjected to detailed scrutiny, Ressam's bizarre game was up. Stashed in the wheel bed of his rented car were more than 100 pounds of deadly explosives, and concealed in the well of his spare tyre were four sophisticated timing devices. The subsequent detailed interrogation by the F.B.I. gave out the full story. In 1992, when the Civil war in Algeria broke out, Ahmed Ressam had moved to Paris. In 1994, using a doctored French passport and with his face crudely stuck on it, he had landed at Montreal and sought political asylum. Thereafter he went into hiding and in order to avoid deportation became Benni Antoine Norris by using a forged baptismal certificate. After his training at the Khaldan training camp, he flew from Peshawar, Pakistan to Los Angeles via Soeul to do a close reconnaissance and a dry run of the Los Angeles International Airport. In order to check and find out how much time it would take normally for the security officials at the airport to locate any unclaimed baggage, Ressam had placed an empty suitcase inside the airport complex and waited patiently. When he noticed that it took a fairly long time for the airport security officials to locate it, he was convinced that he could not only safely do the job, but he could also quietly and easily get away from the devastated site. But to his bad luck, the Canadian Mounted Police had timely tipped off the U.S. of his disappearance. And this was after they discovered bomb making material in the Motel Room in British Columbia where Ressam had stayed before boarding the ferry at Victoria. Motivated by Al-Qaida's strong resolve to punish the Americans and to promote the cause of ushering in a worldwide Muslim Caliphate, Ressam had planned to bomb the Los Angeles International airport on Millennium Day.

Later when Shiraz learnt about this sinister plot from his counterpart in Washington D.C. it came as a shock to him. The very fact that the Al-Qaida training camp at Khaldan was training fanatical Muslims from all over the world to spread terror and target the Americans on their own very soil was not only very disturbing for him, but the deadly manner in which it was timed to take place on Millennium Day at the busy Los Angeles International Airport was simply horrifying. On that morning he and his entire family were at the golf course which was nearby to the airport. They were there as spectators to cheer Tojo who was taking part in a prestigious golf tournament that day. And later on that very evening they were all at the Renaissance Luxury Airport Hotel celebrating Tojo's 17th birthday. The luxury hotel on the boulevard road was only a stone's throw away from the bustling airport and the very fact that the airport was to be targeted by a fanatical deadly Muslim bomber on that very day had got him thinking.In 1993, the Al-Qaida had targeted the World Trade Centre in New York which was on the east coast, but the American west coast too it seems was now under the scanner of Bin Laden and his fanatical followers, thought Shiraz as he tried to find on a world map the exact geographical location of Khaldan and its proximity to the Pakistan

The hijacking of the Indian Airlines flight IC 814 to Kandahar was also playing on his mind and Shiraz wondered whether the Al-Qaida had a hand in that also. There was no doubt in his mind about the ISI's involvement in pulling off such a well planned operation. And he was fully convinced that by themselves and without the active support of the ISI, the five hijackers could not have pulled off such a sensational act of air piracy to free Masood Azhar and the other two terrorists out from Indian jails. Shiraz was also aware about the ISI's direct involvement with the Taliban in setting up training camps both for the Harkat-ul-Mujahideens and the Al-Qaida recruits, and he was now afraid that this unholy growing nexus of highly fanatical Muslims from all over the world in the volatile Pashtun dominated areas of the North West Frontier and Afghanistan may soon get Pakistan the dubious award of becoming the world's most terrorist infested state.

On his way back to Moscow, Shiraz decided to spend a few days with his in-laws at Peshawar. On 10th January morning, Shiraz with his wife Saira and daughter Sherry boarded the Cathay Pacific flight from Los Angeles to Hong Kong. At Hong Kong airport they got into PF-893, the PIA bi-weekly direct flight to Islamabad, and by early evening of the next day, they were in Peshawar. While on the flight, Shiraz was shocked to read in an Indian weekly magazine about the shameless exploits of one Mr Ashok Agarwal, a senior investigator and a Deputy Director in the Enforcement Directorate from the India Revenue Service. He together with his close friend and accomplice Abhishekh Verma, the playboy son of Mrs Veena Verma a Congress Member of Parliament and whose husband the poet Shreekant Verma had helped the late Mr Rajiv Gandhi to brush up his Hindi had been regularly and through blackmail extorting huge sums of money from very well to do Indian businessmen. Agarwal who had a first class degree in engineering with his many influential contacts amongst senior politicians and senior bureaucrats in the capital had it seems become a terror. He knew that most Indian businessmen were flushed with black money both at home and abroad, and one simple phone call from him or even a fax message from his directorate was enough for the victims to cough up with his big demands and which at times even ran into a couple of lacs, and in some cases even into millions.

But his luck it seems ran out after Mr S C. Barjatiya, a rich Delhi businessman with pots of money who was being blackmailed by the duo saw through the game and lodged a complaint with the police. He had been threatened with a FERA case by Mr Agarwal. The Foreign Exchange Regulation Act was like a noose for those who violated it, but one stupid fax that was sent by the duo to Mr Barjatya had given the game away. And on 2nd December 1999, when Abhishek Verma confessed before a magistrate, Agarwal was now on the run. Finally when Agarwal who was absconding was found in a hotel in Saharanpur and was arrested, the game was up for him and his jet-setting socialite friend Abhishek Verma also. But by then the duo had made their millions. Among their many victims were Mr Ashok Jain, the publisher of the influential Indian newspaper, the Times of India and Mr JK Jain, a former Rajya Sabha member and the owner of Jain T.V.

But having read in detail the well written and informative article in the magazine, Shiraz as however skeptical about its final outcome. As far as both India and Pakistan were concerned, the rich and the famous with their big money power and political contacts in both the countries always got away with such crimes. And what seemed even more ironical is that the self made millionaire extortionist was picked up from an obscure hotel in Saharanpur that was named Taj Hotel. The 1985 batch officer with that crowning glory it seems had within a span of his fourteen years of service amassed more than Rs 2500 million.

The sudden arrival of their son-in-law with his wife and daughter at Peshawar came as a pleasant surprise to Arif Rehmnan and Ruksana Begum. It was also Arif Rehman's eightieth birthday that day and the entire Rehman clan had congregated there to wish him. It was like a mini reunion for the entire family. Arif's son Salim Rehman with his wife Aasma and daughter Nadia and son Shabir had arrived from New Delhi that very morning. His eldest nephew, the retired Lt General Aslam Rehman with his wife Farzana, son Major Samir Rehman and daughter Nasreen had arrived a day earlier from Rawalpindi to organize the birthday party. And so was the case with Karim Malik and his wife Memuda. They too had arrived a day earlier from Lahore. Mehmuda was Arif Rehman's one and only niece, but the couple had come minus their two siblings. Their married daughter Tarranum was in the U.S and their son Javed was at Oxford. And then all of a sudden late that evening, when the cake cutting ceremony was about to begin walked in merrily Fazal Rehman with his wife Samina, daughter Sameera and son Shafiq, it took everyone by complete surprise. And with that the family of three generations of the Rehman family was more or less complete. Fazal and family too had flown down from Dhaka without giving any prior notice and like Shiraz they too wanted to give everybody a real surprise.

At dinner that evening, when Shiraz informed them about Ahmed Ressam's bizarre plot to bomb the Los Angeles International Airport on Millennium Day, and that the Muslim bomber from far away Algeria was a diehard Al-Qaida product who was trained in the Khaldan Camp in Afghanistan, Aslam Rehman was not at all surprised. According to Aslam, the camp came into existence during the Soviet occupation of Afghanistan. It was initially a camp where ethnic Afghans with help and support from the CIA and the ISI had been armed and trained to fight the Russians. Thereafter, with Bin Laden's presence in Afghanistan and with his strong financial support; it had now become a multinational training camp for young Muslim Jehadis from all over the world. Besides Ahmed Ressam who had now been dubbed by the Americans as the 'Millennium Bomber', even Ramzi Yousef the man behind the World Trade Centre bombing in 1993 and his close associate Ahmed Ajaj were both trained in this very camp, added Aslam Rehman as he at Shiraz's request quickly drew on a paper napkin the outline map of Afghanistan and the rough location of the camp at Khaldan vis a vis Afgahnistan's international border with Pakistan.

But what surprised Shiraz even more was the information that Fazal Rehman came up with that evening. According to Fazal Rehman, the Al-Qaida had recently and only a week ago had held a summit meeting at Kuala Lumpur, the capital of Malaysia. The secret meeting commenced on the 5th of January and ended on the 8th, and according to his source, the summit was well attended by representatives who were mostly from the Middle East, South East Asia and the Arab world countries. However, his source claimed that the elusive Osama Bin Laden, the handsome Al-Qaida leader was surprisingly absent from that summit.

"'But how can one be so very sure. And for all you know he may have been there in some disguise and incognito. After all he is very much a wanted man by the Americans," said Aslam's son Major Samir Rehman.

"But what is still more surprising for me is why the summit was held of all places at Kuala Lumpur. Because as far as I know the Muslims of Malaysia are quite modern, progressive, and they are not all that fanatical," said Shiraz.

"Well at least let's thank Allah that it was not held in Karachi or in any of the other big cities of Pakistan. As it is General Musharaff is under heavy pressure from the Americans. They want us to sincerely help them in capturing the ever elusive Bin Laden and his henchmen, but that I am afraid is not going to be an easy task. Bin Laden has the full backing of Omar Abdullah and the Taliban and we at this stage just cannot change sides. After all it is we who with the full tacit support of the CIA and the ISI had created this monster called Taliban, and we have to unfortunately live with it now," said Arif Rehman, the veteran diplomat as all the family members got up to sing "He is a jolly good fellow'.With Arif Rehman now eighty years old and his wife Ruksana Begum touching seventy five, they were not getting any younger. It was already nearing midnight and it was already well beyond the bed time for both of them.

It was on 15th January 2000, that Shiraz with his family returned to Moscow. It happened to be a Saturday and it was the 'Army Day' in the Indian Army. It was on this day 52 years ago in 1948 that the command of the Indian army was handed over to an Indian officer. On that day General K.M. Cariappa became the first Indian Commander-in-Chief of the prestigious Indian Army. It was also a day when people paid homage to the Indian officers and soldiers who had sacrificed their lives for the nation.

On the drive to the embassy from the airport, Shiraz very vividly remembered the Army Day celebrations of 1971 in New Delhi. On that day after the grand parade that was held in New Delhi's sprawling army cantonment parade ground, he had sneakily picked up Shupriya on his scooter from the university and they first went for lunch to Karim's. After a sumptuous lunch they spent the whole afternoon at the Surajkund Lake, which was only 20 kms from the heart of Delhi. It was also on that auspicious day that Shiraz wanted to propose to her, but he had forgotten to bring the silver ring band that he had bought the previous evening from Cooke and Kelvey. The small ring with the satin case was left in the pocket of the trouser that he was wearing that previous evening. While thinking about her, Shiraz very discreetly kissed the locket that had little Shupriya's photo inside and he silently prayed for her departed soul to rest in peace.

Shiraz was however not aware that on that very morning of 15th January 2000, Shupriya with Monty and Reeta had gone to the 'Amar Jawan Jyoti' memorial at India Gate to pay homage to his departed soul. This was an age old tradition, and the 'Army Day' parade only began after the homage was paid to those gallant officers and soldiers who had become martyrs while fighting the enemy, by the Indian army chief.

On that 15th of January, Shupriya too boarded the late night Air India International flight 6536 from Delhi to Moscow and she was back on her desk the very next morning. It was now time for her and her staff to prepare for the 50th Republic day celebrations in Moscow and she earnestly desired that the Golden Jubilee commemoration should not only to be a grand success, but something that the privileged diplomatic community of Moscow and the bigwigs in Putin's government would forever remember. She of course did not want it to be on a very lavish scale, but at the same time she wanted the best as far as Indian hospitality and cuisine was concerned. Therefore to cut down on the overall cost, she decided to be very selective as far as the guest list was concerned. And the venue that she chose was the historical Metropol Hotel in the heart of Moscow. The luxury hotel that was constructed in 1903 was situated in the close vicinity of the famous Red Square and opposite the grandeur of the Bolshoi Theatre, it was once the hotel for the Russian nobility. After the revolution this Art Nouveau palace like structure had also served for sometime as the home of the Bolshevik leaders. In 1991, after the Russians had dumped Communism as a way of life for good, the old majestic hotel was fully renovated and was reborn again as Moscow's first international five star luxury hotel. This was the same very hotel that Shupriya had stayed for a few days, when she first came to Moscow as a young Third Secretary. It was still a well known hotel then, but since it was totally state controlled, the service and quality of food was nothing much to write home about.

The selection of the guests by her for that occasion was not at all an easy task. Besides the many VIP's to be invited from the list of Russian politicians and the very senior government officials from the various ministries that the India Embassy regularly and routinely dealt with, there were also more than a hundred foreign embassies in Moscow. Moreover, the number of officers who were posted in the Indian Embassy starting at the Third Secretary level together with their wives was also fairly large in number. Space wise too, Hotel Metropol's biggest conference cum banquet hall could accommodate a maximum of 300 people only. Keeping all these factors in view, it was therefore finally decided that the Heads of Mission of all the G-22 nations together with their lady wives must be invited. And since India was very much a member of that group and was hosting the party, the number of invitation cards that was required to be sent was therefore automatically reduced by one. The second list of the invitees included the Ambassadors and their wives from all the countries that bordered India, which included Pakistan, Bangladesh, Nepal and Sri Lanka. The third list of invitees were the heads of mission with their wives from those countries, both big and small where the Indian working community was very large in size and where the volume of bilateral trade between the two countries was sizable too. There was no doubt that India's hard currency reserves had made a quantum jump ever since the Indian economy was liberalized a few years ago, and the Indians working abroad had been handsomely contributing towards it. In addition to the above list of invitees, Shupriya also decided to invite Lalima and a few other very distinguished Russians from the fields of art, culture, literature and music. And they were particularly those who had notably and significantly contributed towards the bonding and promotion of Indo-Russian friendship.

That gala evening at India's 50th Republic Day anniversary celebrations in Moscow was indeed a grand affair. The various types of colourful fruit mocktails with pure coconut water as the base that were served to the guests duly compensated for the lack of alcoholic drinks at the party. This was in strict accordance with orders that the government of India had issued on the subject and it categorically stated that only soft drinks will be served on such occasions. And as far as the snacks were concerned there were more than a dozen to choose from. For the non-vegetarians there were chicken tikkas, mutton sheek and buti kebabs, koliwada fried fish, garlic pepper prawns, crab meat cutlets, followed by mouth watering kathi-kebabs. And for the vegetarians there were mini idlis with chutney, various types of Indian pakoras, aloo-tikkis with mint sauce, crispy samosas, dhoklas, followed by cheese and dumaloo stuffed kathi-kebabs.

That evening Shupriya, dressed in a bright Magenta coloured heavy silk Benarasi sari with a light make up on her face and a Shirley Mclaine hair style to go with it looked very elegant and charming as she with other senior officers and their wives got ready to receive and welcome the distinguished guests. Though she had turned 50 that day, she did not look her age at all. She had maintained her stunning figure by regularly doing the Yoga exercises that she had learnt from a qualified yoga teacher during her probationer's training at the National Academy of Administration in Mussouri.

Once the party got going, Shupriya as the chief hostess went around meeting all the distinguished guests. It was only to ensure that all of them were being well looked after. And when she met the Pakistani Ambassador, Riaz Mohammed Khan (Shiraz), and he very wittily and aptly remarked.

"Well Madam Ambassador, with so many delicious snacks and especially the delicious chicken tikkas and the mouth watering sheek kebabs making the rounds so very frequently. I think there will be no need for all of us to have dinner tonight."

"That was indeed very kind of you to say so your Excellency, but both your wife and you must keep some space for the mutton 'kathi-kebabs'. that will be coming up soon," said Shupriya while complementing Saira for the lovely torquise blue 'gagra-choli' dress that she was wearing. Earlier while welcoming them, when Saira presented her with a beautiful bouquet of fifty yellow roses, Shupriya was quite taken by surprise. According to Shupriya, the yellow rose was always universally considered to be a rose that signified friendship, but it is also considered to be a sign of jealousy. And at that moment while graciously accepting the roses, when the Pakistani Ambassador also wished her many happy returns of the days, both Shupriya and Saira were both astonished. However, this fact was is no state secret, since the date of birth was very much in the Madam Ambassador's dossier that was being maintained by the Pakistan Foreign Office in Islamabad and a copy of which was with the Pakistani Embassy in Moscow. But the name on it was Simran Kaur Bajwa.

"Thank you for the good wishes," said Supriya with a smile as she made her way to the first couple from Bangladesh who being Bengalis were enjoying the delicious garlic pepper prawns and the crab meat cutlets.

On his way back to his residence, when Shiraz inadvertently remarked to his wife that the Madam Ambassador from India had a striking resemblance to someone he once knew fairly closely, Saira very sportingly held her husband's hand and said.

"Well darling whoever she may have been, she must have been very beautiful too." Then suddenly realizing that it was indeed rather stupid of him to have mentioned it to his wife, Shiraz quickly changed the subject.

That night while lying in bed, Shiraz kept thinking about Shupriya. He just could not get over the fact that two people could have such astounding similarities including their dates of birth. At the party, he had even quietly heard her speaking in fluent Bengali to the Bangladeshi couple and her intonation and mannerism of speech dumbfounded him. Moreover, it would have been Shupriya's 50th birthday too had she been alive. Shiraz had earlier also noticed the uncanny similarity in her hand-writing. However, next morning all those thoughts vanished from his mind, when the Pakistan Defence Attache presented a confidential note on the recent reshuffling of important portfolio's that General Musharraf on taking over as CEO had recently carried out in the higher echelons of the Pakistan army. Along with that was also attached a small brief on each of the affected officers. As per the noting, Lt Gen Mahmud Ahmed, Corps Commander 10 Corps at Rawalpindi had been appointed as the new D.G.I.S.I. replacing the disgraced General Ziauddin Butt. The posting of Lt Gen Aziz the C.G.S. who had earlier been tipped to take over 10 Corps from Lt Gen Mehmud had been cancelled, and the Command of that prestigious and important corps was now given to the recently promoted Lt General Jamshed Gulzar Kiani. Lt General Mehmud Ahmed like General Musharraf was a gunner officer and a regimental colleague of the army chief. Commissioned in 1964, both had served in the 16 Self propelled artillery regiment. In October 1995 having commanded the 23 Infantry Division at Jhelum, he was posted as the DGMI, the Director General Military Intelligence at the GHQ and in June 1998 on promotion to Lt General became the Commandant of The National Defence College. In October 1998, after Musharraf was appointed army chief, Mehmud was given the command of the prestigious Rawalpindi X Corps and was directly instrumental in staging the coup that brought Musharraf to power. A product of Lawrence School, Ghoragali, he was also fairly close to Musharraf.

Lt General Jamshed Gulzar Kiani was also commissioned in 1964 in the Baluch Regiment and after the Bangladesh war was posted as a Major to the ISI headquarters at Karachi. In 1975, with his expertise in intelligence, he was promoted Lt Col by Zulfiqar Ali Bhutto and was posted as Security Officer at the very sensitive and secretive establishment that was known then as E.R.L, The Engineering Research Laboratories at Kahuta. In 1987, on being promoted Brigadier, he served as a principle intelligence officer at the GHQ and was instrumental in gathering information for the newly formed SSG base at Khapalu in northern Kashmir. This base at the height of over 6000 meters in that very year had been used to launch an attack on the Indian post at Bilafond La in the Siachen Glacier, but the attack failed with heavy loses to the Pakistanis. In 1996, Gulzar Kiani was promoted as Major General and was posted as Additional DGISI. At the time of the coup, he was the DGMI at GHQ and his taking over command of X Corps on promotion did create a few ripples in the top echelons of the Pakistan army.

Lt General Mohammed Aziz Khan was commissioned into the Punjab Regiment in 1966. He was born on New Year's Day, 1947 in the village of Dhar Dhrach near Pilandri in the erstwhile Princely State of the Maharaja of Jammu and Kashmir and what was now known as Azad Kashmir. Earlier it was he who had been tipped to take over the X Corps from Lt Gen Mehmud Ahmed, but since he was basically a Kashmiri Patan, there was strong opposition from the Jamaat-e-Islami and the Jamaat-ul-Ulema, and as a result of which his posting order had been abruptly cancelled and his taking over a Corps was held in abeyance. As a Brigadier, he had commanded the Infantry Brigade in the high altitude Siachen Area and later had also served as a Deputy Director in the ISI. On promotion to Major General, he commanded the FCNA, Force Commander Northern Areas. In October 1998 and in spite of his being fairly junior, Musharaff on becoming chief appointed and promoted him to the coveted post of that of the CGS, Pakistan army. According to one reliable source he was given this appointment so that with his knowledge and expertise of the terrain and that of India's deployment pattern of regular troops in the Northern Areas, he could therefore ably assist the new chief in the planning and execution of 'Operation Badr', which was Pakistan's well calculated gamble in the Kargil sector, but which unfortunately resulted in a bloody fiasco. General Aziz was also a key man that had brought Musharaff to power. Besides the small brief on the above officers, there was also a short resume on Lt General Mohammed Yusuf Khan Qainkhani, Corps Commander II Corps at Multan and Lt Gen Muzaffar Hussein Usmani, Corps Commander V Corps at Karachi and both of whom were considered very loyal to Musharaff, Born on 10th February 1948 at Sargodha, Lt General Yusuf Khan was commissioned in 1966 into the Guides Cavalry. As an armoured corps officer he had also commanded a Tank Battalion in Saudi Arabia and later the Armoured Division of Pakistan's Strike Corps. In June 1998, he was promoted Lt General and was posted as the MS, the Military Secretary at GHQ. In October 1998, when Musharaff took over as chief, he was posted to Multan as Corps Commander II Corps. He was man who was known for his hawkish comments and for his was very anti-Indian outlook.

Lt General Muzaffar Hussein Usmani was also commissioned in 1966 in an Armoured Infantry Battalion and like Yusuf Khan he had also commanded an Armoured Infantry Battalion in Saudi Arabia. As a Brigadier, he commanded a Mechanised Brigade and as Major General an Infantry Division. Prior to taking over the Karachi Corps, he also commanded the Bhawalpur Corps. He was also a key figure during the 12th October coup and he was the one who made sure that Musharaff's plane rom Colombo landed safely"at Karachi and nowhere else.

"Well the manner and the speed with which he has started shuffling them around, it looks as if General Musharraf is wary about those very Generals who had whole heartedly supported him in ousting the corrupt and ambitious Nawaz Sharif. And to me it seems that even as the army chief and the CEO of the country, he is not too very sure in distinguishing friend from foe. And I won't be very surprised if this cycle of changing the top commanders at short notice continues till as long as he is in the chair. Moreover, if you notice unlike Musharraf, most of them are very religious minded Muslims," said Shiraz to his Number 2 in the embassy as the Defence Attache got ready to brief both of them about the role and manner in which the Fauji Foundation functioned in Pakistan. This was at the request of Shiraz who had learnt that the foundation had recently been given a sudden big boost by the army chief and as CEO.

The Fauji Foundation which was primarily meant to find employment for the retired army personnel had now not only become big business, but it had also become a source of second employment and income for the men in uniform. With over a thousand serving and retired officers that included hundred plus Lt Generals, Major Generals and their equivalent in the Pakistan Navy and the Air force on its roll, it now also had a stranglehold over the country's fledging economy. The number of Army Brigadiers and their equivalent in the other two services, both serving and retired were a staggering figure of 160 and Musharaff after taking over had not only inducted them in high civilian posts in various ministries inside the country, but also in Pakistani missions abroad. From producing fertilizers, edible cereals and corn, the Fauji Foundation was also now controlling oil terminals, power, gas, sea-ports, the national aviation and the shipping corporation of the country. The foundation had also in a very big way gone into real estate, housing, leasing and even into producing cement. The Defence Housing Authority besides constructing houses for the servicemen, was now also into establishing clubs, restaurants and hotels for the defence personnel. The entry fees to all these recreational institutions had also been heavily subsidized for the men in uniform. Whereas the entrance fees for the defence service officers to the Creek Club and the Marina Club at Karachi had been pegged at Rs 25,000 for the man in uniform, but for the civilians it was a mind boggling sum of Rs 6, 00,000.

"I think that with the military men in uniform now holding the monopoly in running the very diversified 'Fauji Foundation' in all important fields of commerce and trade in the country, we need not go begging to the World Bank and to the United States anymore,"said Shiraz somewhat sarcastically as his number 2 in the embassy gave out a chuckle and added that he had made a big mistake of not joining the Pakistan Military Academy when he had the golden opportunity to do so and that to when he had been selected on sheer merit.

"Yes you should have become a 'fauji', a military man and had you done so in 1970, you would have been at least a Major General if not a Lt General by now and maybe a future chief in the making too," added Shiraz in good humour.

Chapter-25

'To Nab or Not to Nab'

After having got a low down on the functioning of the Fauji Foundation from his Defence Attache, Shiraz on his own decided to do a little discreet investigation on the progress made by the newly appointed NAB, the National Accountability Bureau that was being headed by Lt General Amjad Hussein Syed. The General had been especially selected and appointed by General Musharraf to look into all major corruption cases in the country.

The NABO, the National Accountability Bureau Ordinance had come into force from 16th, November, 1999 and the Chairman and his office for the purpose of inquiry and investigation had even been empowered to arrest the proclaimed offenders if need be. To facilitate the NAB to unearth money laundering and the colossal amount of black money that had been stashed away inside Pakistan and in banks abroad by the big time players, all banks were directed to notify to the NAB within one month of all such dubious high value transactions. The NABO was also empowered to disqualify a corrupt individual for 21 years from not only being an election candidate of the assembly but also from holding any public office. Possession of assets which could not be accounted for was also made an offence of absolute liability.

The NAB on 17th November, 1999 no doubt had arrested some of the top loan defaulters and it included a blend of politicians-cum-feudal lords, rich and influential businessmen, retired senior officials of the armed forces and former bureaucrats. And though most of them were big and prominent names in their respective professions, but the root cause of all this Shiraz felt was the official patronage that was always being given to all such corrupt practices by those wielding power. And he therefore concluded that it would ultimately be an exercise in utter futility unless the politics of corruption, coercion and misuse of power was effectively countered by long term institutionalized strict measures rather than by resorting to political witch-huntings and gimmicks that surfaces time and again with the change of governments.

The NABO was amended on 3rd February, 2000 and besides arrest and investigation, it was now also given prosecution powers. The military regime thereafter launched an intensive drive against loan defaulters and though they were given one month's grace period to return the loans with the accumulated interest, but the amounts were simply mind boggling. Besides others, at least 589 former and suspended parliamentarians were defaulters to the tune of nearly Rs 10 billion. And that was only the tip of the iceberg. And though the military regime was impartial in drawing up the list of those arrested which included several federal ministers like Anwar Saifullah, and Faisal Saleh Hayat, it also included the Chief Minister of Punjab Mr Manzoor Wattoo, Air Marshall Viqar Azim, and Admiral Mansoorul Haq, the former Pakistani Naval Chief who was still an absconder. And knowing very well that corruption was a top-downwards phenomenon with the state itself providing the opportunities for all sorts of corrupt practices to flourish including those relating to bank loans, allotment of plots and issuing of postings, allocation of funds, appointment of commissions etc etc, Shiraz was of the firm opinion that ultimately nothing would come out of it. But all the same he was quite baffled by the names of the many high flying culprits that had been unearthed and exposed by the NAB. As per Pakistan's Finance Minister Shaukat Aziz, out of a mind boggling Rs 146 billion that was due from the loan defaulters, only Rupees 8 billion had been returned to the kitty during the one month grace period that was given to all the defaulters. And according to Mukhtar Nabi Qureshi, the Acting Governor of the State Bank of Pakistan there were nearly 325 defaulters whose amounts were over Rupees 100 million each and which itself amounted to Rupees 75 billion of bad debts. Leading the pack of top defaulters who did not give back a penny during the grace period were Yusus Habib, the owners of Mohib Textile Mills, Saifur Rehman, Sadruddin Ganji, the Tawakkals, ARY Gold and a few others. Besides these, there were those from all the main political parties who were leaders of the PML ANP,PPP,MQM, and it also included one of Pir Pagaro's disciple, and a number of ex-cronies of Benazir's husband, the ten percent Asif Zardari.

The list of defaulters who had been hauled up was like a veritable who is who of Pakistan included the Legharis, Saigols, Khokars, Rehmans, Farooqis, and other such prominent and well known families of the country. According to the Chairman of ADBP, the Agricultural Development Bank of Pakistan, the major defaulters were the recently suspended members of the Pakistan Senate, the National Assembly and those from the Provincial Assemblies and their close relatives who numbered 263. Besides these so called recently suspended 'Netas', there were another 326 such like political bigwigs and their relatives from the previous assemblies who were yet to cough up the large loans that were given to them. But what was still more revealing to Shiraz was that some major government organizations like the Pakistan Steel Mills were big defaulters too.

"I really do not know where this country is heading for economically, if this is the state of affairs where the law makers themselves have shamelessly and openly looted the exchequer," said Shiraz as he read out the names to his wife Saira of a few well known and financially well connected people who were also close friends of theirs.

"But finally in the long run and I can guarantee you that though General Musharraf today has promised to root out corruption in this country, but in the end nothing will happen to these diehard crooks. In fact with their colossal ill gotten money power these same bunch of political crooks with their cronies and goons will be in action once again when all this euphoria about the military justly ruling Pakistan becomes one of despair in the years to come," said Saira as their daughter Sherry walked in with the copy of Umar Saliya's statement. Umar Saliya, the President of Small Traders Chamber and Cottage Industries of Pakistan had categorically stated that the corruption in the CBR, the Central Board of Revenue was causing a financial loss of a staggering Rs 450 billion each year and out of which Rs 150 billion through bribery was being pocketed by the tax authorities who were giving undue benefit of Rs 300 billion to these so called big and politically well connected unscrupulous businessmen crooks. And when Sherry very aptly pointed out that the politicians were not the only people with unlimited greed, and that the military and the civil bureaucracy were no less greedy when it came to making a fast buck, both Shiraz and Saira were in complete agreement with their daughter.A fortnight later and at his own request, when a close friend of Shiraz who was assisting the NAB chief General Amjad Hussein Syed sent him a list of Pakistan's nuveau rich billionaires and millionaires who had looted the country's exchequer and who were being investigated, it was like the who is who of the Pakistani elite. And what was more glaring was that the amounts that were looted by them were not in terms of rupees but in US dollars. Heading the list of 17 billionaires were Asif Ali Zardari, Nawaz Sharif, Anwar Saifullah and it also included the late General Fazle Haq, Lt General retired Zahid Ali Akbar, Retired Captain Gohar Ayub, Retired General Aslam Baig, Retired Major

Aftab Sherpao and Retired Brigadier Imtiaz. There were even two former bureaucrats, Salman Farooki and Ahmed Sadiq who overnight had become billionaires. The list also included the names of Humayun Akhtar Khan and Ijasul Haq, both sons of former Pakistani Generals. Humayun Akhtar was the son of General Akhtar Abdur Rehman who was the DGSI during Zia ul Haq's regime and Ijasul was the late General Zia-ul-Haq's son and both the families were closely related too. And among the top bureaucrats, Ahmed Sadiq, was Benazir Bhutto's Principal Secretary when she was the Prime Minister of the country and it seems he too made his big pie during that period.

"It seems that the 17 billionaires and 15 millionaires that have so far been unearthed by NAB have more precious foreign exchange in their own banks than what Pakistan has in its fast depleting foreign exchange reserves," said Shiraz while handing over the list to his wife Saira.

"But take my word for it all these big crooks with their money power will one day go scot-free and as time goes by some of those who are in military uniform now and who are presently presiding over the destiny of the country will in times to come also join the looters league," said Saira very confidently.

A week later in early March, when Saira's cousin retired Lt General Aslam Khan with his wife Farzana visited Moscow as the honoured guests of the Pakistani Ambassador and his wife, they too became a part of the diplomatic cocktail circuit.

"I must admit that besides spending so much of time in the office every day, sometimes these cocktail parties in the evenings does become a pain in the neck. But one cannot help it I guess, because it is considered a duty and it is bad manners if you refuse the invitation, and especially if the occasion happens to be the national day of that country and more so if it is also a Muslim country," said Shiraz as they all got ready to go for the cocktail party that was being hosted by the Ambassador from Mali. There at the party while talking to a senior diplomat from the host country, Shiraz was surprised to learn that Mr AQ Khan the Pakistan nuclear scientist had a couple of years ago visited some West African countries including Mali. And the only purpose of visiting Timbuktu for Dr AQ Khan was to oversee the construction of the Hendrina Khan Hotel. Surprisingly the hotel was named after his wife Hendrina and Shiraz wondered from where all the money came from. During that trip AQ Khan with a group of nuclear aides and senior Generals from Pakistan had also visited Niger, a country that has considerable uranium deposits. Shiraz also learnt that AQ Khan had earlier visited Khartoum and the Al-Shifa factory that had been bombed by the Americans in response to the Al Qaida bombings of US Embassies in Africa. Therefore that evening after the party, when they returned home and in order to check back whether what he had heard about AQ Khan's visit to West Africa from Mali's number two man in Moscow was true or not, Shiraz asked General Aslam Khan if he was aware of such a visit.

"Yes a high powered delegation led by AQ Khan did visit these countries, but I am not sure what were the real purpose of those visits. AlI that I can deduce is that since late 1970's, Niger had been a major supplier of yellowcake uranium to Pakistan,and this could be one good reason for Mr Khan to visit Niamey the capital of Niger. And regarding the Hendrina Khan Hotel in Timbuktu and from where the money came from, your guess is as good as mine. And as far as the visit to Khartoum, the capital of Sudan is concerned, the possibility of establishing a three way link up between Bin Laden's Al Qaida set up that was earlier based at Khartoum, with the Pakistan ISI and the Sudanese government could be the only reason that I can think off. And don't forget that Bin Laden was not only treated as a VVIP by the Sudanese government while he was there, but he also made tons of money in Sudan through the various government sponsored road construction work that was given to him and his company," said Aslam Rehman.

"But I only hope that Dr AQ Khan who is one of Pakistan's renowned nuclear scientists and who some consider to be the father of the Pakistani nuclear bomb is not hobnobbing for monetary gains with the Al-Qaida Supremo and his friends in the Islamic world so as to help them in producing an Islamic nuclear bomb. Because if that does happen then it will be a disaster not only for Pakistan but also for the whole world," said Shiraz.

"Well, let's hope not. And now that you have said that it could be for monetary gains, I won't be surprised if Dr Khan is selling nuclear secrets from his vast knowhow and expertise of how to make such deadly bombs for such rogues and for such rogue countries. Because by doing so he will soon be able to build not one such hotel, but a chain of such Hendrina Khan Hotels all over the world. And even if the NAB does manage to nab him, he will simply implicate the big bosses in the government, and thanks to our corrupt system they will all live happily ever after,"'said Farzana as Aslam Rehman helped himself to a tot of Napoleon brandy. Later that night, when both Aslam Rehman and Shiraz got into a serious discussion about Pakistan's hobnobbing with the Taliban in Afghanistan and of Pakistan not being able to help the US government in getting hold of Bin Laden and his cohorts, Shiraz was surprised to learn from Aslam as to how successive democratically elected Pakistan civilian governments together with the help from the ISI and the Pakistan army after the death of General Zia-ul-Haq kept blowing hot and cold over this very sensitive issue. According to Lt Gen Aslam Rehman, when Benazir Bhutto in 1993 was the Prime Minister of the country, she with the help and support of Major General Nasrullah Babar, her Minister of the Interior and General Musharraf who was then the Director General of Military Operations at the General Headquarters, decided to secretly support and arm the Taliban. Simultaneously they also decided to unleash the forces of fundamentalism to step up the proxy war against India in Kashmir. With that aim in mind Musharraf and the ISI therefore took the help of the several Islamic organizations that had mushroomed by then in Pakistan. One of them was the MDI, the Markaz Dawa Al Irshad that was founded several years earlier by the followers of Bin Laden and whose military wing was known as the LeT, the Lashkar-e-Toibaa. Another such powerful fundamentalist organization was the Harkat-ul-Ansar and which later became known as the Harkat-ul-Mujahideen. These two main fundamentalist groups were therefore asked to supply volunteers who would be trained and armed in camps inside Afghanistan and thereafter would be required to fight as guerrillas our proxy was inside Indian occupied Kashmir. Subsequently, when Osama Bin Laden with his Al Qaida set up from Khartoum was welcomed with open arms by Mulla Omar and his Taliban followers in Afghanistan, it became even more difficult for Pakistan to convince the one eyed Mulla Omar to hand over the Al Qaida Supremo and his top henchmen to the Pakistani government. And the only time it came close to getting Bin Laden out of Afghanistan and hand him over to Saudi Arabia was in early 1998, when the Saudi Intelligence Minister Prince Turki-al-Faisal made a secret deal with Mulla Omar. But later during the third week of August, when Turki in the presence of the Pakistan DGISI Lt Gen Nassem Rana was about to finalize the deal, the Americans unfortunately let loose their cruise missiles on Afghanistan and that was the end of that. With an angry Omar Abdullah vehemently denying that he had never made any deal whatsoever to hand over the fugitive Bin Laden to Saudi Arabia, both Turki and Nassem Rana had to return back empty handed. Moreover the CIA it seems was not aware that before those deadly cruise missiles landed on their designated targets to get rid of Bin Laden and his henchmen, the much wanted man had been very cleverly tipped off by none other than the Pakistani ISI to find refuge somewhere else," said Aslam Rehman as Shiraz poured him a little more brandy into his hot coffee.

"By God and when I learnt about this it was news to me too. And the irony of the whole affair was that at one time not so very long ago both the CIA and the ISI were strongly backing the Taliban to come to power in Afghanistan. And at one stage the CIA even provided to Pakistan secret satellite information about the large cache of arms and ammunition that the Russians had left behind in Afghanistan These Soviet trucks with arms and ammunition were hidden in big caves and having found them, it gave a much needed boost to the Taliban fighters to soon get rid of their many rivals in the civil war that had erupted in Afghanistan soon after the Russians left that country," added Aslam Rehman.

"About the huge quantity of arms and ammunition being left behind by the Russians I do not doubt that at all, but from where the hell did the Taliban get those tanks, artillery guns, anti tank missiles and aircrafts to defeat their opponents," asked Shiraz.

'This may surprise you my dear, but ironically it was a Russian arms wheeler dealer by the name of Victor Bout who first made a killing by arming Afghanistan's Northern Alliance and then he switched sides and started selling tanks, weapons and arms to the Taliban and to the Al Qaida also. Formerly Bout worked for the KGB, but after the collapse of the Soviet Union he shifted base to the UAE, the United Arab Emirates and he now operates the world's largest private weapons transport network from Sharjah. The enterprising Russian arms merchant after the Taliban captured Kandahar in late October 1996 in one single deal had delivered 40 tons of Russian weapons to the Taliban and pocketed a cool 50 million US dollars as his profit. According to one very reliable source Mr Bout was even now freely trading with the Taliban and this was being done on behalf of the ISI and our own government in Pakistan. I have also been told in secret that a huge deal is now being worked out by the ISI with some dubious arm dealers from Ukraine to supply the Taliban with a very large number of Russian T-55 and T-62 tanks, and the responsibility of safely delivering them to the Taliban is being given to Mr Bout who is now also known as the 'Merchant of Death,' said Aslam Rehman.

"Oh no, I just cannot believe all this. This must be all CIA propaganda that is being carried out by their department of disinformation to blame everything on the Russians and on us,and it maybe because our government is not putting enough pressure on the Taliban to handover Osama Bin Laden to us," said Shiraz.

"Maybe you do have a point there, but the fact still remains that Pakistan it seems does not have the heart or the will to curb fundamentalism in the country. They simply want to use these so called 'Jehadis' to promote its war by proxy against India and to somehow get Kashmir. They even export them to other countries like Bosnia and Chechnya to show their solidarity with the Muslims of those countries who are fighting for their own independent Muslim nationhood. In fact in early 1993 and according to the testimony of Lt General Javed Nasir who was then the DGISI, not only was a Pakistani vessel containing ten containers of arms and ammunition for the Bosnian Muslim army intercepted in the Adriatic Sea, but a month or two later Pakistan also airlifted a large number of sophisticated anti-tank guided missiles to the Bosnian Muslims who were literally fighting for their very own survival," said Aslam Rehman as Shiraz took out a photograph and added.

"But tell me Aslam Bhai, how is it that a person like Saeed Sheikh whose handsome face you see in this photograph and who is a British citizen of Pakistan origin and a student of the prestigious LSE, the London School of Economics, how did he become a diehard Jehadi. And I believe he had in April 1993 also made a trip to Bosnia that was sponsored by the 'Convoy of Mercy', which was nothing but a front of the newly formed militant Islamic fundamentalist group Harkat-ul-Ansar and which in 1997 changed its name to Harkat-ul-Mujahideen, and that was only because the U S State Department had named the former as a terrorist organization. In fact I was told that after his trip to Bosnia he had moved to Afghanistan and on receiving his training at camps that were run by the Al Qaida and the ISI in that country, he was sent to India to befriend and kidnap innocent western tourists and which he did, till he was caught and put in jail by the Indians. And now after the recent hijacking of the Indian Air Lines flight to Kandahar, he is once again a free man."

"May be it is the lure of easy money and it also could be attributed to the high doses of indoctrination that such young educated Muslims get subjected to from time to time by the so called Mullahs in the mosques and who on the plea of preaching that Islam is in danger motivate them to sacrifice their lives and even become Fedayeens if need be. And according to one CIA report the ISI it seems is currently funding the HUM, the Harkat-ul-Mujahideen to the tune of 60,000 US dollars per month," said Aslam Rehman.

"But in a poor country like Pakistan where is all this money coming from?" asked Shiraz as he too helped himself to another cognac.

"Well initially it was the BCCI, the Bank of Credit and Commerce International which as we all know was founded in 1972 as a small merchant back by Agha Hasan Abedi, a Pakistani. Thereafter with the blessings of the then head of the CIA George H W Bush senior and Kamal Adham the Saudi Intelligence Minister it was turned into a worldwide money laundering machine and it soon became the fastest growing bank in the world. But it was not just a bank, it was also the main hub for global intelligence operations and with its mafia like enforcement squads, it was soon able to solicit business with all major terrorist, rebel and all such like underground organizations in the world. And the intelligence thus gained was then to be shared by the so called friends of the BCCI. But by doing so it soon created the small merchant bank into the biggest clandestine money network in the world. Operating primarily out of the bank's offices in Karachi, its enforcement arm was soon dubbed as the 'Black Network.' With its sophisticated spy equipment and techniques, together with bribery, extortion, kidnapping and sometimes even murder the 1500 odd employees of this black network would stop at nothing to further the bank's aims and the ISI too had a hand in this big pie. In 1984, when I was with the ISI and I was posted to the Embarkation Headquarters at Karachi, it was the BCCI and its Black Network that took over effective control of the Karachi port. With bribery and intimidation it dominated the Pakistan's Custom Service and with that also the flow of arms and ammunition to the Mujahideens who were being funded by the CIA and the Saudi Government to fight the Soviets in Afghanistan,"'said Aslam Rehman with a lot of authority as he too poured himself another small cognac. And realizing the Lt Gen Aslam Khan was in the right mood and that he was keen to reveal a few more state secrets, Shiraz added another small cognac into the General's goblet and then asked. "But tell me Bhaijaan was there also a strong link between our government, Dr AQ Khan's nuclear network and the BCCI ?,"

"Of course there was and it first surfaced on 11 July, 1991 when retired Brigadier Inam-ul-Haq was arrested by German authorities in Frankfurt and where he spilled the beans. And he was arrested just one week after BCCI was shut down worldwide. Four years earlier in 1987, the US intelligence agency in a sting operation was about to arrest Brigadier Haq for trying to buy nuclear components that were meant for Pakistan's nuclear program, but before they could swoop down upon him, the CIA it seemed had tipped of the Pakistani government and a low level associate of the Brigadier was apprehended instead.The CIA had long known that the Brigadier besides being close to the ISI, was also one of AQ Khan's trusted key procurement agents. Earlier in another clandestine operation some 12 years ago in 1987-88, the Luxembourg and London branches of the BCCI had financed a shipment of nuclear materials out of the Untied States. So you see it was a fairly close link between the government, the AQ Khan network and the BCCI, which the popular Time magazine had once dubbed as the world's sleaziest bank," said Aslam Rehman.

"I must say that you are a wealth of information and knowledge and in fact you should write your memoirs and I can bet you that it will be a best seller,"'said Shiraz somewhat seriously as he prodded Aslam Rehman to tell him as to how the Taliban and the Al Qaida with Afghanistan's meager financial resources has been able to not only procure sophisticated arms and weapon, but also food, oil and other essential requirements from abroad, and it was still continuing to do so.

"Well it all started from 1996, when the Taliban and the Al Qaida took full control of the Ariana Airlines, which as you are aware is the National Airlines of the country. Thereafter passenger flights became fewer and practically redundant and cargo flights carrying drugs, weapons, and gold from Afghanistan to the Emirate of Sharjah and to Pakistan became the order of the day. While large quantities of drugs are still being flown from Kandahar to Sharjah every day, the returning aircrafts bring back a large quantity of arms and ammunition, kind courtesy Mr Victor Bout who operates with impunity from Sharjah. While Afghan taxes on opium production are paid in gold and thereafter when the gold bullion is flown to Dubai, it is then laundered into cash. It is as simple as that," said Aslam Rehman

"But just tell me as to how could the ISI warn Bin Laden about the cruise missile strikes on the six designated Al Qaida camps inside Afghanistan that took place on 20th August, 1998. And it was not just a few of them, but a massive 66 such cruise missiles that I believe had pulverized and devastated those camps,"asked Shiraz.

"I am not quite sure, but I believe that in order to pin point the target, the US military were constantly tracking Bin Laden's satellite phone. And according to one reliable source, when in May 1998 a replacement battery was given to the Al Qaida boss, a sophisticated tracking beacon was also placed inside that very phone. The US however did give us about ten minutes advance notice before those cruise missiles flew over our air space and this was done primarily to ensure that the missiles wouldn't be misidentified as enemy missiles and then shot down by us. But all the same ten minutes was too short a time for Bin Laden to take cover, and my hunch therefore is that he had been tipped off by the ISI soon after the car bombings of the US embassies took place in Nairobi and Dar-e-Salam on 7th

August, 1998. Apprehending that the Americans would retaliate drastically against the Al Qaida, it is therefore quite possible that the ISI had warned him timely to move out to some other safe area. And it is also possible that Osama knowing very well about his involvement in the embassy bombings, decided to shift base and play the cat and mouse game with the Americans. But there is also a strong rumour floating around that Lt General Hamid Gul, the former ISI head who is also very anti American had allegedly warned Bin Laden fairly well in advance of a possible missile strike on the Al Qaida camps in Afghanistan,"' said Aslam Rehman.

"But why then is the ISI and the Pakistan government not cooperating fully with the CIA and the American government to once and for all get rid of this damn fugitive who has become a bloody nuisance for us. And as days go by he is not only becoming a pain in the neck for all of us, but also a bloody pest to the whole wide world," said Shiraz.

"Well that is a million dollar question and my gut feeling is that we require his presence and that of his Al Qaida fighters to continue our war of proxy against India in Indian occupied Kashmir," said Aslam Rehman.

"But by giving Mr Bin Laden protection, aren't we antagonizing the Americans and the western world. Moreover, what are we really gaining from all this. The Al Qaida to my mind is no less an evil than the LeT and, the HUM, and all of them together with the ISI are hand in glove in only fostering and promoting diehard fanaticism and fundamentalism and which not only is detrimental to Pakistan's interest, but it could well become a many headed monster that would soon be very difficult to control,"said Shiraz.

"On that score I hundred percent agree with you, but the problem is that Pakistan is now in a serious Catch 22 situation. On the one hand having recognized the Taliban government of Mulla Omar in Afghanistan, we cannot now simply turn our backs on him, and at the same time we have to keep playing ball with the Al Qaida Chief, the LeT, the HUM and the United States administration and try and keep all of them happy and in good humour all at the same time. Moreover, we have to also keep the Kashmiri 'Kangri', the eternal fire of liberation burning perpetually inside the belly of Indian occupied Kashmiri premanently and to do that we need all these fundamentalist organizations to do all the dirty work for us. And with President Clinton who is due to visit India and Pakistan shortly, I am afraid the ISI may well use these fundamentalist outfits to carry out some sensational killings of non Muslims in the valley and conveniently attribute the same to the so called atrocities being committed by the repressive Indian

Security Forces and try and again internationalize the Kashmir issue," said retired Lt Gen Aslam Rehman while calling it a day.

Though it was fairly very late that night, nevertheless Shiraz meticulously before going to bed made some notes in his little red diary on the gist of all the conversations that he had had with Aslam Bhai that evening. That night he even wondered whether he should indirectly warn the Indian Ambassador in Moscow about the likelihood of a major attack by militants on non Muslim civilians in the valley and which was most likely to coincide with Mr Clinton's visit to India, but on second thoughts and not knowing for sure where that attack would take place at all, he shelved the idea.

Aslam Rehman was dead right. On the night and just hours before President Clinton was to land in Delhi on 20th March, 2000 and was to be given a hearty welcome that was to be followed by the formal and traditional ceremonial guard of honour, the ISI backed Lashkar-e-Toiba militants, most of whom were hired Muslim foreigners dressed in Indian army uniforms butchered in cold blood 35 innocents Sikhs from the village of Chitisingh Pora. This was one of the largest Sikh populated villages in the Anantnag District that was located in South Kashmir and it was the first killing of its kind against the Sikhs of the state. With the mass exodus of the Hindu Kashmiris from their homeland in the valley, this was an entirely new phenomenon. Earlier the militants were targeting the Kashmiri Pundits, the Hindus and the Hindu labourers who were working in that state, but it now seemed that the militants with Pakistan's backing were now embarking on ethnic cleansing of of both Hindus and Sikhs from the valley and with the aim of turning Kashmir into a single Muslim religion entity. Already over some three lakh Kashmiri Pundits had lost their homes and had left the valley for good, and now it looked that the one lakh Sikh population of the state will have to bear the brunt of the militant's gun fire also and be forced to find refuge elsewhere. And though the Pakistani propaganda machine through their television networks promptly and squarely blamed and attributed the killings of the 35 Sikhs to the trigger happy Indian armed forces, but the cat was soon out of the bag, when the Indian media channels and the Indian intelligence agencies visited the bloodstained and demoralized village.

In such villages in the area where militants were known to hide, a periodical search by the Indian security forces was nothing new. But what was new was the sudden burst of rapid gunfire from the so called 'soldiers' amidst cries of 'Bharat Mata Ki Jai' and 'Jai Bajrang Bali. Initially they had lined up the village folk for an identification parade, but when their leader in his broken Hindu and Urdu started addressing them, the locals knew that they were not Indian soldiers but militants masquerading in Indian army uniforms. And as soon as the deadly carnage that was unleashed by the militants was over and they simply faded away into the darkness of the night and into the nearby forest, the truth was out of the bag.

And while the villagers of Chitisingh Pora were mourning the losses of their near and dear ones, in New Delhi, Mr Bill Clinton, the President of the United States of America who was staying in the Maurya Sheraton luxury hotel that had been converted into a veritable Fort Knox was getting ready to leave for Dhaka. For four days before the arrival of the American President, American aircrafts had made umpteen sorties to India ferrying the men and machines that were needed for Clinton's security. And the one and only song that was on the lips of the hundred marines accompanying him was 'I see like a hawk. I buzz like a bee. I am Mr Clinton's securiteeee.' Even Mr Richard Celeste, the lanky silver haired American and the Ambassador to India admitted that security today was of a very major concern not only to India and to the US, but to the whole world, and when he added that it was time to check this growing menace of terrorism from becoming a monster, everybody agreed with him. For India and the Americans, the security of the US President on Indian soil was of prime importance to both the countries. By constantly making use of their many satellites in the sky that had powerful electronic eyes, they therefore kept a nonstop vigil of every step that Clinton took during his visit to the Indian subcontinent. Besides the hordes of men from the American secret service tailing him every minute, the Americans had also brought a trained Labrador dog to sniff for explosives The Maurya Hotel was so heavily and sophisticatedly bugged that even a slight whisper anywhere in the hotel premises could be picked up from the many hidden microphones that were located inside the five star complex. Besides the American Air Force-1, which was equipped with the state of the art communications and radar systems, six choppers were always kept ready and in standby mode at various nearby helipads to whisk the President to the safety of his Air Force-1 Jumbo Jet. One special helicopter was like a flying hospital and it was equipped with life saving drugs and equipment. So tight was President Clinton's security that there was hardly any movement planned by road for him.

"I sincerely hope nothing untoward happens during his five day visit to our country," said Monty's wife Reeta as she called up Peevee in Mumbai and told him to be careful when the President visits the city on 24th March. "Oh please don't worry Mom because while Mr Clinton enjoys his short sojourn in India's financial capital with his favourite chicken tikkas, I will be on my way to Chennai for the shooting of my new film which is based on the life of Prabhakaran and his Tamil Tigers. And though I know that the film after its completion may not be passed by the Indian censor board for screening in India, for reasons well known, but all the same I have to fulfill the terms of my contract with the film producer. However, I am a little surprised that the American President's visit to the famous red light district of the city, and which I believe was also very much on the cards and which was primarily to announce a major initiative on aids research has now been called off. Personally I think it was in a way good, because with the Monica Lewinsky affair still quite fresh on everyone's mind, it would have been a major embarrassment for the handsome saxophone playing Clinton who is also being accompanied by his young daughter Chelsea and his mother-in-law Dorothy Rodham, if one of the many whores opened that sensitive topic again," said Peevee.

Peevee now nearly 28 years old was a superstar in Bollywood and when Shupriya heard that he was the hero of the film titled 'The Tamil Tiger' and that it was based on the life of the LTTE Supremo who was responsible for killing Rajiv Gandhi, she too was really very worried. Shupriya was however happy that the American President's visit to India had passed of very peacefully and that the Vajpayee government had successfully created a climate of friendship, better understanding and further cooperation between the two nations and specially so in the fields of foreign trade of which the US was India's largest trading partner, and also in the field of technology where the Americans today were world leaders. And as far as the short five hour stopover visit to Islamabad on the 25th of March was concerned, Shupriya felt that it was probably to tell Pakistan that America still needed them and at the same time also to try and diplomatically and politely twist Musharraf's and Pakistan's arm to take things seriously and to stop and prevent the notorious ISI from financing, arming, training and supporting the growing terrorist activities that were emanating from that region and which also included those of the Taliban and that of the Al Qaida in Afghanistan. There was no doubt that President Clinton was very much aware of this growing nexus between the ISI, the Taliban and the Al Qaida, and according to one senior American diplomat in the US embassy in Moscow, the President had also once commented that though the US was trying to work with Pakistan to diffuse tensions in the Indian subcontinent, and that the two nations had been allies during the Cold War, but the very fact that Pakistan directly and indirectly supported the Taliban, and by extension the Al Qaida, it was therefore of great concern to him and his administration. And not only that, when Clinton also said that the Pakistani intelligence service had also used some of the same camps that Bin Laden and Al Qaida did to train the Taliban, and that some of the insurgents who fought in Kashmir at Kargil were trained in these very camps by the ISI, it did not come as a big surprise to Shupriya. But when she was told by the same diplomat a few weeks later that Clinton while giving his nod to use the cruise missiles against Afghanistan that took place on 20th August, 1998, was also very apprehensive of the fact that if the Pakistan's ISI found out about the planned attacks in advance then it could well warn the Taliban and the Al Qaida, his hunch it seems was very right. Because ultimately the whole exercise was in total futility when the Americans found out that their prime target Bin Laden and his top lieutenants had escaped the massive onslaught and that to without a scratch. There was also no doubt now in Shupriya's mind that Pakistan's new military regime like all the previous democratically elected governments before, they all wanted Bin Laden and his organization the Al Qaida and the Taliban to survive. But what Shupriya now feared was that the very nexus that was now spawning the rapid growth of fundamentalism within Pakistan may one day become the very nemesis of that politically unstable country. For India, a politically stable Pakistan was the prime requirement of the day for bringing about peace, prosperity and progress in the subcontinent and Shupriya sincerely hoped and prayed that General Musharraf and his new government would move positively in that direction.

On 23rd March, 2000 and as protocol demanded, when Shupriya attended the at home that was hosted by the Pakistani Ambassador Riaz Mohammed Khan (Shiraz) on Pakistan Day in Moscow, she found that His Excellency the host was not only in very high spirits, but he was also trying to be a little more familiar with her. And when he tried to find out a little more about her father and forefathers and from where they originally came from, she was somewhat a little surprised.Because such kind of personal questions normally at such parties and especially between the heads of missions are not asked. And when she was about to leave and the Pakistani Ambassador jokingly said to her. "Well I sincerely hope Your Excellency that President Clinton who visited the Ranthambore Tiger Sanctuary today could spot a few tigers and his visit earlier to village Nayla to see the milk cooperative being effectively and profitably run by the village women folk who were all decked up in their traditional colourful Rajhastani costumes also must have been a big hit," Shupriya simply smiled and said very diplomatically. "Yes I guess so and all I can say is that President of the United States is thoroughly enjoying his stay in India and like the good old Macdonald advertisement, I think he too is simply loving it. And I sincerely hope that his brief five hour stopover in Pakistan will be a success too."

That night after Shiraz returned to his residence, he was still very confused. Some of the mannerism of the Indian Ambassador and especially her body language that evening were so much like that of Shupriya's that at one stage he even thought of addressing her by that name. Even the entry that was made by her in the visitors' book in her own hand, and the style of writing including the signature was very much like that of Shups. He remembered quite distinctly that Shups always dotted the letter 'i' with a small roundel on top of the letter instead of the usual dot and it was no different today when she wrote the words 'With best wishes and signed her name Yeshwant Kaur Bajwa below it.

Therefore in order to find out a little more about her antecedents, Shiraz decided to discreetly check back on the little information that he had with difficulty gathered from India's lady ambassador that evening. All that she had told him was that her forefathers were from the town of Sheikhupura, which was now in Pakistan and that her parents had migrated to Calcutta during partition to her maternal grandmother's house which was in old Bhawanipore and where she was born. But with such scanty information, Shiraz also knew that it would be a very difficult to ferret out more information about the lady and her forefathers, since there may have been many more Bajwas from Sheikhupura who had migrated to India during partition, and as far as Calcutta was concerned there were a large number of Sikh families who had made Bhowanipur their home from the time Clive defeated Sirajuddaulah at the Battle of Plassey. And the only other piece of information that he had gathered from her earlier was that her late father was a government officer and because of his various postings she had been educated at different schools and colleges all over in India. Therefore he thought that the only way he may be able to find out a little more about this particular Bajwa family was from either the data and records pertaining to Yeshwant Kaur Bajwa that may be available at Pakistan's Ministry of Foreign Affairs, or from some of the old devotees who regularly visited the Sikh Gurudwara that was not far from Calcutta's famous Kali Temple at Kalighat and which was close to the busy intersection of Rash Behari Avenue and S P Mukherjee Road in South Calcutta. But since the second option seemed a little farfetched and also fairly difficult, he therefore decided to write a confidential letter to one of his close friends in the foreign office at Islamabad and with a request to send him a photocopy of Yeshwant Kaur Bajwa's complete dossier.

Chapter-26

Scams Galore

And while Shiraz anxiously waited for Miss Yeshwant Kaur Bajwa's dossier to arrive by the diplomatic mailbag from Islamabad, Shupriya was busy visiting the Indian Consulate General's office in St Petersburg. She wanted to find out as to how bad was the crime situation in that city since one Indian businessman had been badly beaten up recently and robbed by some hoodlums.

'Well Your Excellency, despite the rise in prices in the black market of all essential commodities, and the steady increase in the crime rate in the city and which is mainly attributable to the powerful cartel of Russian mafias who are operating from the Tsar's old capital, the crime rate is not very alarming and the historical sites of this magnificent city and its many museums holding priceless treasures of art and artefacts touch wood have not been vandalized as yet. And though the city was devastated during the Second World War, the pride of the thousands of Russian, men, women and children who had kept the Germans at bay for nearly three years, 872 days to be exact and who did not let the city fall into Hitler's hands and who had sacrificed their lives defending the city for their motherland was solid testimony of their patriotism that was in their blood. And even today the people of this great city are very proud of their heritage. And this will be amply evident when you visit the Leningrad Mass Graves Cemetery at Piskariovskoy and the impressive War Memorial on Victory Square,' said the young Indian Consulate General as he showed her some pictures of both the popular tourist sites of that historical city.

Early next morning and before sunrise when Shupriya visited the beautifully laid out and well maintained mass graves cemetery at Piskariovskoy she was moved to tears. While the strains of martial music rented the air and she read the names of some of them who were only in their early teens but who had gallantly sacrificed their lives for Mother Russia, she was reminded of her late husband Shiraz Ismail Khan. Thinking about him she placed a wreath in memory of the man whom she loved so very dearly and prayed for his soul. On her return from St Petersburg, Shupriya very carefully went through the detailed report that had arrived in her absence from the Indian Ministry of External Affairs. It was regarding the recent visit of the American President to India and she was very happy that the new NDA government led by Mr Vajpayee besides discussing some very strategic issues with the Clinton administration and which included that of effectively curbing the growth of terrorism, it also highlighted the desire of both the countries to expand trade and strengthen the economic ties between the two largest democracies in the world. This was the second ever visit by an American President to India and having come barely two years after the Pokhran and Chagai nuclear blasts and not even a year after the Kargil war and the military coup in Pakistan, it therefore reflected a paradigm shift in the post Cold War foreign policy of the United States. However, on the home front things were not looking all that rosy for the NDA government. And though Prime Minister Vajpayee's coalition government was speeding up economic reforms in the country by privatizing some of the loss making government owned corporations and by going in for free market restructuring, but what irked Shupriya the most was the blatant manner in which the politicians and others were indulging in making a solid quick buck for themselves through corrupt and sleazy deals. It was indeed a shocking revelation not only for Shupriya, Monty and Peevee, but also for the general public in India when scam after scam that took place during the long Congress rule were now regularly being highlighted as articles in the press by Unni the veteran journalist.

'First there was the infamous 1974 Maruti Scandal, where Prime Minister Indira Gandhi's son Sanjay Gandhi was awarded the license to produce Maruti cars by the government even before the company was even legally formed. Then came in 1976, the notorious Kuo Deal where the government owned Indian Oil Company entered into a large contract with a fictitious Hong Kong based oil firm and which led to a huge loss to the exchequer. This was followed by the 1981 stinking Antulay Trust affair, when the Chief Minister of Maharashtra made a whopping 30 crores for his so called trust. And when that was quietly brushed under the carpet, it was the 1986 shameful Bofors gun deal where a person no less than the Prime Minister of the country Rajiv Gandhi with his Italian connection allegedly made a killing. And while the Bofors scandal was still being probed came the 1991 Telgi fake stamp paper scam wherein a half educated counterfeiter by the name of Abdul Karim Telgi swindled a staggering Rupees 43,000 crores allegedly in connivance with some top political leaders of Maharashtra. And while those fake stamp papers were still being unearthed, the 1992 Harshad Mehta Securities Scam rocked the country. The great Big Bull in close collaboration with senior officers of nationalized banks, stockbrokers, bureaucrats and politicians had siphoned off a cool 4000 crores. Two years later in 1994, the Sugar Import scandal only made matters worse, when Kalpanath Rai the then Food Minister in the Congress government blatantly and willfully cleared the import of sugar at higher prices which resulted in Rs 650 crore loss to the government, The year 1996 was of course the year of all scams. It started with the great Hawala swindle that involved top ranking political leaders from all parties allegedly receiving kickbacks from the Jain brothers who were big time hawala brokers. And this was followed by the Telecom scam where Sukh Ram the Union Communication Minister from the Congress party for monetary gains showed undue favour to a Hyderabad firm for the supply of telecom equipment while coolly ignoring those who had tendered far lesser amounts. Soon thereafter came the Urea Deal where a group of businessmen who were close to Prime Minister Narasimha Rao and his son in close cooperation with the Managing Director of the government owned National Fertilizers Limited made a cool Rs133 crores from a deal that involved the import of two lakh tonnes of urea, which never arrived in India. And finally came the 'Charaghotala' or the great Fodder scam, where the ex Chief Ministers of Bihar, Jagannath Misra and Lalu Prasad Yadav allegedly in collusion with other state officials pocketed a staggering sum of Rs 950 crores by cooking up false bills to provide feed, medicine and animal hiusbandry equipment to vast hordes of livestock that physically never existed. And mind you all these last four scams took place in 1996, when Prime Minister Narsimha Rao from the Congress party was sitting on the hot seat" added the aging correspondent and writer as he lit his new Dunhill pipe that Peevee had presented him with.

'Yes and the saddest part is that all these massive scams of looting the national exchequer took place during the last two decades of Congress rule. And if you count the 1995 JMM bribe scandal where the Narasimha Rao government allegedly paid Rs 30 lakh each to all the Jharkhand Mukti Morcha Members of Parliament in order survive the 1993 no confidence motion against his government in parliament, and the tricky pickle affair wherein one Lakhu Pathak a businessman is said to have paid Narasimha Rao and his so called god man crook Chandraswami a bribe of Rs 10 lakh in exchange for a paper pulp contract, then it just goes to show as to how deep, how very corrupt and how bloody shameless are our politicians and the political parties that they represent. In fact the entire political system as of today in this country has been so badly contaminated from top to bottom by these corrupt politicians from the grand old party, that it has now become more of a money laundering machine for most of them," said Monty somewhat disgustedly.

"That's true no doubt, but as a an ardent supporter of the saffron led NDA government if you think that things will change for the better and that such like scams will subside and those who were responsible for the earlier scams will be suitably punished, then all I can say is that you and I are living in a fool's paradise. These shameless so called political' Netas' of all hues, shades and sizes, and no matter how much they already have, and irrespective of to which party they belong, they will always crave for more and my gut feeling is that in times to come such scams and that too in greater magnitude will only keep increasing," said Unni as Monty decided to celebrate the day with a quiet dinner at 'The Oberoi Maidens'. And while they were all enjoying their drinks with the mouth watering starters at 'The Spice Route', the speciality restaurant of the heritage hotel, Unni recounted a few more such dirty and lurid cases.of corruptions that had given the country a very bad name.

And while Monty and Reeta were much impressed by Unni's investigative journalism, Shiraz's friend in Islamabad was busy tracing out the confidential dossier on Miss Yeshwant Kaur Bajwa. And though It did not take very long for his friend in the Pakistan foreign affairs ministry to trace out the dossier, but it did take a little time for him to have it cleared with the concerned secretary in the ministry and have a certified photocopy made and sent to Moscow.And by the time it arrived by the diplomatic mailbag on Shiraz's desk, it was already end April. However, the document was only a brief three page dossier of India's high profile lady ambassador and it only had her date of birth 26th January, 1950, the higher education qualifications of the lady, her date of commission from the Lal Bahadur Shashtri Academy in Mussouri, and the rank and appointments that were held by Miss Yeshwant Kaur Bajwa during her long career in the Indian Foreign Service and the countries that she had served in. But there was nothing very revealing as far as her upbringing, education and family background was concerned. While the education qualification column simply read Post Graduate and interpreter in Russian language, the column under permanent place of residence was shown only as Bhowanipur, Calcutta but with no street name or house number to amplifly it. However, under the column 'NOK', next of kin and though it mentioned that both parents were deceased, but it did have the name of one MS Bajwa as a first cousin, but no residential address was given of the next of kin either. Shiraz's foster brother Monty too had the same initials M S and Bibiji's name was Simran Kaur, but how could Shupriya as Yeshwant Kaur be Monty's first cousin, and moreover he had never heard about Monty having a first cousin by the name of Yeshwant Kaur either thought Shiraz as he put the dossier into his locker and for the time being forgot about it. Shiraz however decided that at the next chance meeting with India's lady ambassador and whenever that maybe, he would diplomatically try and find out a little more about this first cousin brother of her's and who as per dossier was her next of kin also. Moreover, the same date of birth of both Yeshwant Kaur and Shupriya, together with the initials M.S. and the surname Bajwa as Yeshwant Kaur's first cousin is what kept bugging him now.

And while Shiraz debated in his mind on how to find out a little more about this cousin brother of India's lady Ambassador and what he does for a living, the news arrived that Nawaz Sharif the ousted Prime Minister of Pakistan had been sentenced to life imprisonment on two specific charges. The first charge was that of hijacking the PIA flight from Colombo to Karachi and the second charge was that of terrorism. On the other two charges of attempted murder and kidnapping, he had however been acquitted. But what surprised Shiraz the most was that all the other six of Mr Sharif's co-defendants, which also included his younger brother Shahbaz, the ex governor of Punjab had all been acquitted of all the charges.

Later on that very night of 6th April, when Shiraz's mother-in-law Ruksana Begum rang up her daughter Saira in Moxcow and told her about the drama that took place that morning inside the courtroom when the verdict was announced by Judge Rehmat Jafri, Saira felt sorry for the Sharif family. A convoy of armoured personnel carriers had brought the ousted premier and his co-accused to the court in Karachi that morning and there was heavy security all around. Initially Mr Sharif's wife Kulsoom sitting inside the court quietly kept softly reading kalimas from the Holy Koran, while others waited for the moment of judgement to arrive. At around 11.30 A.M. when the Judge asked all the accused to be ushered in, Sharif who was wearing a white salwar kameez with a black waistcoat looked fairly calm. But when the Judge within ten minutes acquitted all the others except Nawaz Sharif and sentenced him to two terms of life imprisonment, practically all his family members including his wife and Shahbaz started weeping and some others who till then were counting prayer beads and were reciting holy verses suddenly jumped up from their seats and kept shouting 'Nawaz

Sharif Zindabad'. As Sharif was being taken away, several of the women wept and kept beating their chests. And though Sharif kept telling them to have patience, there was near pandemonium inside the courtroom. The only plus factor was that the judge did not give him a death sentence. Because had he done so then Pakistan would have had the dubious distinction of having two of its democratically elected prime ministers hanged from the gallows, thought Saira while handing over the telephone to Sherry who also wanted to talk to her loving grandmother.

And while the members of the Sharif family in Pakistan were still reeling under the impact of the severe life sentence that was given to the ex-prime minister, Shupriya during the last week of May 2000 arrived in New Delhi for a week's official visit to the capital's imposing South and North Blocks. Interacting with senior bureaucrats and colleagues in the various ministries, she was indeed glad to learn that Mr Vajpayee's NDA coalition government during its first six months in office had done well to re-invigorate the country's economic transformation and growth by promoting pro-business and free market reforms that were initiated and started by the previous Narasimha Rao led Congress government, but which had got bogged down after 1996 due to the successive unstable hot-potch coalition governments in the centre and the 1997 Asian financial crisis And though the Vajpayee administration were also now getting brickbats from various unions and government workers in the various public sector undertakings for their aggressive campaign to privatize government corporations that were basically loss making and inefficient, the general mood of the man on the street however was that of hope and prosperity, and it showed as more and more foreign capital investment progressively came into the country.

Thanks to the BJP's dependence on coalition support, the Vajpayee government was also wise in not yielding to pressure from its ideological mentor, the RSS and the hardliners from the VHP, the Vishwa Hindu Parishad. They were not only keen to enact the Hinduvta agenda and build the Ram Janmabhoomi Mandir at Ayodhya, but were also determined in the repealing of Article 370 which gave special status to the state of Kashmir and for the enactment of a uniform civil code that would be applicable to the adherents of all religions in the country.Luckily the mass surrender of more than 500 insurgents and armed rebels in the Indian state of Assam on 4th April, 2000 also came as a blessing in disguise for the Vajpayee government. That also indicated that the rebel separatist movement had lost its popular support in that state. On that day the surrender ceremony that took place at Ranghar, the old 13th century amphitheatre that was used by the Ahom tribe, the main ethnic group in Assam, it brought both hope and joy for the younger generation. This was also the very place where the dreaded ULFA was founded 21 years ago. And when 532 insurgents laid down their arms in front of the Governor, retired Lt General S K Sinha, it was another feather in the cap of the Vajpayee government. Since the beginning of the year a large number of rebels from India's north eastern states had been surrendering in trickles, but this was a windfall that took even Prafulla Kumar Mohanta, the Chief Minister of the state completely by surprise.However, this certainly was not the end of the insurgency movement in Assam, as the senior militant leaders of the banned ULFA had now started setting up training camps inside Bangladesh. The ULFA has been fighting for an independent Assamese homeland and their firebrand leader Paresh Barua was not the one who would give up so very easily.

And while the surrender by the rebels in Assam boosted the image of the Vajpayee government, the visit of Mr LK Advani, the Indian Home Minister to the Kashmir valley during the first week of May and his offer to open a meaningful dialogue with the All Party Hurriyat Conference, which was an umbrella body of 27 militant and secessionist group in that trouble torn state was also taken as a positive move by the people of India. They felt that the Vajpayee government was moving in the right direction to bring back the much needed peace to the Kashmir valley. George Fernandes the Indian Defence Minister and Brajesh Mishra the National Security Advisor through their interlocuters had already made contact with some of the more important Hurriyat leaders. But as a result of this Ahmed Zargar the Al Umar Mujahideen leader who was one of the three 3 militants who was released in exchange for the IC 814 passengers had also given an ultimatum that he would kill the Hurriyat leaders if they dared to negotiate with their Indian counterparts. Though some of the pro Pakistani elements in the Huriyat were in constant touch with the Pakistani Ambassador in Delhi and Yasin Malik was one amongst them and they were asking for a three way dialogue on the Kashmir issue, but the Vajpayee government had categorically ruled that out. There was no question of getting Pakistan on India's negotiating radar and table. But what irked Shupriya was the manner in which the BJP was trying to take forward the Hindu nationalism movement through the backdoor. Mr Murli Manohar Joshi, the Education Minister from the BJP at the centre together with other leaders like Mr LK Advani who were indicted in the 1992 Babri Masjid demolition case for inciting the Hindu mob to pull down the old mosque were now planning to promote their brand of Hindu nationalism through the official state education apparatus by making vast changes in the existing school curriculum.

Besides attending the high level three day conference on the new government's foreign policy that was organized by the Ministry of External Affairs for some of the heads of the more important Indian missions abroad, Shupriya also interacted with all the concerned ministries and departments including that of the Ministry of Defence, which were dealing with the Russian government and which had a direct bearing on the foreign trade and security of India. All the three Defence Services, the Indian Navy, the Indian Air Force and the Indian Army were still highly dependent on Russian arms and equipment and the Kargil War necessitated the early replenishment of some critical equipment of arms and spares that were vital to India's defence needs. The Russians were past masters in this game because when it came to replenishing such supplies of spare parts they invariably hiked their prices with the excuse that since such like arms and equipments were outdated and were no longer under production or in the pipeline, and therefore it was not possible for the Russians to supply the same at the old rates. Shupriya was also well aware of how very corrupt the system had become after the collapse of the Soviet Union, but there was little that she or the Indian government could do about it. These spares and equipment were vital for defending the country from external aggression and they had to be procured at any cost. There were also strong rumours that certain Indian agents acting as brokers with strong political connections at the right places were back into the game as middlemen to promote the purchase of arms and equipment from abroad. And a case in point was that of the Soviet aircraft carrier 'Admiral Gorshkov', which according to one Russian source, the Russians were now willing to sell to India. Though it was originally named as 'Baku", the Kiev Class aircraft carrier had been renamed as Admiral Gorshkov soon after the collapse of the Soviet Union. Commissioned in January 1987, the ship after a boiler room explosion in 1994 was finally decommissioned in 1996, but was now being offered to the Indian Navy.

A day before Shupriya was to return back to Moscow and in order to give everyone a surprise, Peevee flew down from Mumbai unannounced to be with her and the family.' Deepak Kumar' the actor that day was busy shooting for his new film at a studio in the Film City at Mumbai. It was a story about a young Sikh NRI from England who had come to India with his parents in search of a bride. Since the boy's parents were looking for a girl from a very rich Sikh family, the story revolved around the evils of the dowry system in India and how some young innocent Sikh girls after marriage and while staying abroad were being physically and mentally abused and exploited by their husbands and their greedy parents. And since Peevee wanted to travel incognito and he had to make it direct to the airport from the studio, he therefore flew with his makeup on and decided to make his entry into the house dressed up as a handsome Sardar bridegroom complete with the five K's and that included the kirpan also. For his role in the movie, Peevee had grown his natural beard and moustache and with the saffron polka dotted turban adorning his head, he looked every inch a handsome and aristocratic gentleman from a princely Sardar family. So very effective was his make up that even his fellow passengers and the crew on the flight did not recognize the popular actor. And as soon as he took his window seat in the executive class, he asked for an extra pillow and having fastened his seat belt soon fell off to sleep. He had been shooting in the studio since early morning and was dead tired by the time the unit packed up for the day.

To make his arrival look even more officious, Peevee before taking off from Mumbai had instructed his secretary to inform his parents about the arrival of a dear friend of his from Mumbai who was from a rich erstwhile princely family of Punjab and who had consented to finance and produce a feature film that was based on the life of Maharaja Ranjit Singh, the Lion of Punjab. And since the friend was expected to drop in that very evening, Peevee desired that he should be well looked after and his father Monty should discuss the film script with the financier cum producer and check for its authenticity.

On his arrival at Palam airport, Peevee hired a brand new chauffeur driven Mercedes limousine. But when he reached home and rang the bell and found Mom Number 2 at the door, he became a little nervous. He thought that the servant would open the door and he would then posing as the Yuvraj of Pipli carry on with his act. Nevertheless, when he introduced himself to Mom Number 2 and with a poker face said very politely in Punjabi that his name was Paramveer Singh and that he was a very dear friend of Deepak Kumar, even Shupriya was fooled. But as soon as they were seated on the sofa and Shupriya noticed the familiar gold cufflinks that she had presented Peevee with on his last birthday and which had the especially designed initials 'PV' very artistically engraved on them, she became a little suspicious. She knew that even Shiraz her late husband was very fond of playing such practical jokes, but for her son to come home dressed up as a Sardar and that to from a princely family was too much of a coincidence she thought. But thereafter when she asked him a few questions of how and where she met the popular actor Deepak Kumar and from which princely state he was from and Peevee in his tenor voice kept fumbling while giving the answers, a smiling Shupriya simply patted him on the back and said. "You can fool everybody else my son, but you simply cannot fool your own mother can you?" Hearing those words and the laughter, Reeta who was busy in the kitchen came running and quickly added."Yes, Yeshwant is absolutely right and a Bajwa with or without the beard and the turban will always remain a Bajwa and as mothers we can make out instinctively whether it is the real Bajwa or Bajwa the actor." Having realized that she should not have uttered those words that had come automatically to her because she was Peevee's real mother, Shupriya quickly changed the subject and said.

"Well now that you are playing the part of a young handsome Sikh who is looking for a life partner in reel life, why dont you look for one in real life too?'

"I think it is a bit too early to think of that, but all the same if you all have somebody nice and homely in mind and she is willing to smilingly face the mad mad world of Bollywood and the roller coaster life with its ups and downs that the Bollywood stars often have to face with, including the juicy gossips that the media often comes out with between the heroes and heroines of the tinsel town, then I certainly wouldn't mind. But having tied the knot she should not later back out with the usual excuse of boredom and by declaring to the whole world that my dear husband is always so very busy running around trees and singing to his heroine that he has no time for me and my family, then that I feel would not be fair. Don't you think so?"

"Yes in a way you are right, but there are exceptions too and one of them is Sharukh Khan, who is married to Gauri,' said Shupriya.very confidently.

'But please do not forget that it was a love marriage. And though the boy was a Muslim and the girl a Hindu,their parents were very simple and broadminded too. Moreover Sharukh's father Mr Mir Taj Mohammed was a freedom fighter and the girl's father was an army officer and that too from the infantry which is known as the 'Queen of the Battle'. And if I am not wrong he was I think from the Sikh Light Infantry, and for all you know their forefathers probably came from the same stock, And there is nothing wrong if a Muslim wants to marry a girl whom he loves and if she happens to be a Hindu so what," said Peevee

Hearing that coming from her own son, Shupriya lovingly put her arm around him and declared very proudly. "Yes there is nothing wrong in that at all and if you have any such Muslim girl in mind, you will have my blessings too."

"And our blessings too and to satisfy both the parties we will solemnize the wedding in the presence of both the Granthi and the Kazi," said a beaming Monty as he popped open a bottle of sparkling white wine and poured them into the four champagne glasses.

"Thanks to Yeswant Kaur's noble thoughts and Peevee's promise to soon tie the knot, let us all therefore drink to the good health of the Bajwas.' said Monty loudly as they all clinked glasses.

Next morning, when Shupriya boarded her flight to Moscow, little did she realize that her son Peevee would soon meet his match and that it would be a beautiful and talented Muslim girl not from India or elsewhere, but from Pakistan?

The month of June 2000 saw most of India's top Bollywood stars in London. They were all there for the International Indian Film Academy Awards.This was the first of its kind ever to be held and the venue for the spectacular event was none other than the newly constructed Millennium Dome. Unfortunately Peevee could not make it because on that day of 24th June he was busy shooting the climax scene for the film 'The Tamil Tiger'. The location was a village near the town of Jaffna in Sri Lanka and since he had already committed himself to the producer of the film, he could not even take a day off to be in London fot that gala event. However he did manage to see a video clipping of the historic event a few days later, and with the indomitable Indian superstar Amitabh Bacchan leading the pack, it was indeed a magnifent show. Though the film "Hum Dil De Chuke Hai Sanam' won the best picture award, Peevee however felt that the award should have gone to the film 'Sarfarosh' and in which his favourite actor Naseerudin Shah's performance in a negative role was simply outstanding. Despite having lost an opportunity to see London and be among the many stars from India, Peevee was now looking forward to his trip to France in the second week of July. He had been selected by an international advertisement company to feature in a promotional commercial for an Indian sparkling wine and it was required to be shot in location in one of the many vineyards in northern France.

CHAPTER-27

The Plot Thickens

It was on 25th July, 2000 at the Charles de Gaulle airport in Paris, while Peevee was waiting to catch his Air France flight to Mumbai, he was pleasantly surprised by a smart young lady who approached him for an autograph and then said.

"Do pardon my bad manners, but aren't you Deepak Kumar the Bollywood hero who won the best actor award for the film 'Jhanda Uchha Rahe Hamara' at the film festival in Moscow? And what brought you to Paris?"

"Yes that's right, I did get that award in Moscow and I was in Paris to shoot a commercial film for a wine grower in India. The gentleman is now making sparkling wine in the country and he wants to give it a little French flavour I guess. But who are you and how did you know that I was given that award?" asked Peevee with a big smile as he shook hands with the pretty young lady and autographed the best seller book that was in her hand.

"Well after the award ceremony in Moscow, I was very much there at the cocktails that evening and I wanted to personally congratulate you, but you were missing from the party. And I was later told by someone that because of some important commitment that had to be honoured by you, you had to catch the flight back to India on that very afternoon." said the enterprising and charming young lady

"Well I must say you are not only very well travelled, but you are also well informed too. And judging by the title of the book that you are currently reading and with your good looks, you could well be a contender for the heroine's role in the next James Bond film," said Peevee with a impish smile on his face

.

"Oh thank you very much indeed for the compliment, but acting is not in my line. I like to read books and especially spy stories that are related to contemporary history and conflicts. And this particular author Robert Harris is my current favourite and I must say that 'Archangel' is a real masterpiece. It is set in modern Russia and it's all about a secret black notebook which is believed to be Stalin's secret diary and which reveals a lot of what happened during Stalin's repressive reign," said the young lady, when suddenly there was an important announcement over the airport's public address system." Ladies and Gentlemen we regret to inform all passengers that due to some administrative and technical problems, all flights have been temporarily delayed for a while and please wait for an important announcement that will soon follow."

"Well now that we both have to wait a little longer for our flights to take off for our respective destinations, why not we do a little more of chin wagging over a cup of good fresh coffee maybe," said Peevee as they both made their way to the nearest coffee bar.

"Well now that you know me only by my screen name, let me tell you that my real name is Paramveer Singh Bajwa and I am actually a shaven Surd. But what is your good name and which part of India do you come from and what were you doing in Paris?" said Peevee somewhat a little excitedly while ordering for two large cappuccinos.

"Well though my official name is Shezadhi Riaz Khan, but to all my friends I am popularly known as Sherry and you may call me by that name also if you so wish to. And by the way I am not from India but from Pakistan and I had come to Paris to complete my diploma in classical western music and that to on the concert grand piano. And now I am on my way home to my parents who are presently posted in Moscow," said the charming young lady while not wishing for security and other reasons to disclose to Peevee that she was the daughter of the Pakistan Ambassador to that country.

"Oh that's rather interesting and now that I know you are a well qualified musician, pianist and a music teacher too, maybe someday you will give me the pleasure of listening to some of your recitals on the piano that those great Russian and European composers like Tchaikovsky, Wagner, Bethoven and Mozart have given to this world and to which sometimes I also listen too," said Peevee as they talked about those great legendary music masters.

"In that case I will no doubt be highly honoured, but you will have to first reciprocate by inviting me to Bollywood to see the shooting of one your films. However, with the present strained relations between the two countries getting a visa I know will be a big problem I guess," said Sherry somewhat nonchalantly as they shook hands.

"Well in that case I could always invite you either to the US or Canada, or to Switzerland or even to nearby Dubai or for that matter to Singapore maybe, because these are some of the popular locations and hotspots where we love to shoot our blockbusters. However, it has to be on one condition though and that is much that I would love to have your presence at the shoot as my personal honoured guest, but I just cannot risk doing that. And that is simply because in this wicked celluloid world of films, the media only wants a chance to cook up juicy stories. And mind you it is not only in Bollywood, but in Lollywood and Hollywood too, where the damn media and the Paparazzi more often than not get on our damn nerves. They are only waiting for an opportunity to spread gossip and rumours about the stars and their private lives. And it gets even worse when they deliberately twist facts and then try and add more colour to it by splashing a few photographs of who is going around with whom and why and where. Therefore with your good looks and being a Pakistani at that, the media will only play it up. And it may well soon become the talk of the town. Hence one has to be very discreet and careful in such matters. Thus to be on the safe side and if and when I do invite you for a film shoot, you will have to be there not as my personal guest, but as one of the many ardent fans of mine. And if that suits you, then you are most welcome. But once the shooting is over we could of course discreetly meet over a nice drink in some secluded cafe and be far away from the maddening crowd and autograph hunters. And incidentally there may be an occasion for me as a private individual of course to visit Moscow, Petersburg, Volgograd and a few other historical places in Russia in the near future too and when I am there I will definitely get in touch with you,"said Peevee as they exchanged their personal cell phone numbers.

"Yes that will really be great and I too will look forward to it," said a beaming Sherry when the announcement over the public address system at the Charles De Gaulle system shocked all the passengers who were eagerly waiting for their flights to take off.The Air France flight 4590 to New York that had taken off a little earlier from the Charles De Gaulle International Airport had crashed. It was a Concorde flight that was charted by the German company 'Peter Dielmann Cruises' and all the 100 passengers who were mostly Germans and who were looking forward to be on board the cruise ship MS Deutschland for their 16 day long cruise to South America from New York together with the 9 crew members had all perished. The aircraft had plunged into an area that was near Hotelissimo Les Relais Bleus Hotel at a place called Gonesse which was not very far from the airport. And as a result of which 4 people on the ground were also killed.

"Oh my God, and I sincerely hope it wasn't sabotage by some extremist group," said Peevee to Sherry as the next announcement for all passengers travelling to Moscow to board the aircraft was made.

"Yes and I also hope it is not one of those sickening Jehadi groups and I really feel very sorry for the families of those who have perished. But I guess one cannot fight against fate and God's wishes,"said Sherry while bidding bon voyage to Peevee.

"Bon Voyage to you too and I will look forward to meeting you again,"said Peevee as he took a few photographs of Sherry with his new mobile phone camera.

And though the findings of the air crash was ultimately attributed to a fairly large piece of titanium strip that was on the runaway and that had punctured one of the Concorde's tyres on takeoff', but it was a piece of the hot rubber tyre, which on impact had fractured the fuel tank and that had led to a fire in engine number two. As a result of that the crew was unable to retract the landing gear and the aircraft soon went totally out of control. The crash also spelt the death knell of the Concorde. It was the beginning of the end of the fastest flying passenger aircraft in the world and which would soon now also go out of service

Realizing that it would be rather unwise on his part to talk about his encounter with the beautiful, young and talented Pakistani lady with others including his family members, Peevee decided to keep the matter to himself. There was no doubt that he was smitten by the lady's good looks and wide knowledge, but to pursue a close friendship with her at this stage of his career he felt was not the answer But he did not mind being friends with her though.

While on his way to Mumbai from Paris, Peevee stopped by for a day in Delhi to be with his parents. It was as usual a surprise visit by him, and in order to celebrate the occasion, Monty invited a few of his close friend for drinks and dinner. The hot topic that evening was the sudden resignation of Mr Ram Jethmalani, the Law Minister from Mr Vajpayee's government and the arrest and immediate release of the fiery Shiv Sena leader Mr Bal Thackeray im Mumbai. Born on 14th September, 1923 at Shikarpur in Sind, Pakistan, the ace Sindhi criminal lawyer was some kind of a genius. At 17 he had not only completed his LL.B, but he soon also joined the bar. He moved to Mumbai after partition and though he had two wives and four children, but that did not deter him from reaching the pinnacle of success in the legal world at a fairly young age. With his in-depth knowledge of criminal law and with his razor sharp skills of cross examining witnesses he had fought a number of high profile cases including that of defending Mr Gandhi's killers, some well known gangsters and smugglers and even a scam tainted character like Harshad Mehta. And though he was now 77 years old, he was still a fighter who spoke his mind out and who did not hesitate to criticize even the high and the mighty in the country and elsewhere.The reason for asking for his resignation it seems was because of a personality clash between the Law Minister and the Attorney General of India Mr Soli Sorabjee. Earlier with his brash handling of the lawyer's strike, Mr Jethmalani had antagonized the legal fraternity. And now with the Chief Justice of India, Mr AS Anand feeling aggrieved for not being consulted on the appointment of the MRTP Chairman, the matter had come to a head. The Monopolies and Restictive Trade Practices Act was an act against unfair trade practices and it was introduced in 1969. According to one reliable source, Mr Jethmalani's induction into the Vajpayee cabinet was at the insistence of Mr L.K.Advani, but the ace lawyer it seems never enjoyed Mr Vajpayee's confidence. The decision to ask him to resign was made on 22nd July, when the Law Minister was on his way to Pune to address the Symbiosis Law College and it was conveyed to him by Mr Jaswant Singh. And Mr Jethmalani without batting an eyelid on reaching Pune immediately put in his papers. Peevee somehow always had a very high regard for the brilliant lawyer and though some considered him to be some kind of a maverick, but to Peevee he was the best criminal lawyer in the country. And while the men in black debated the adverse comments on the Government's doublespeak on the Srikrishna Commission report that was made by the Supreme Court and its non implementation due to lack of collective cabinet responsibility as was stated very firmly by the Chief Justice of India, it only brought to the surface the disharmony and discord that existed at the top most level of judicial administration in the country.

And as regards the arrest and release of Mr Bal Thakeray was concerned, it was more of a tamasha. After the Shiv Sena leader was arrested and produced in the court under section 153(A) of the Indian Penal Code for his inflammatory writings in his paper Samna which dated back to the communal riots of 1993, there was a smile on the faces of many of his adversaries. But when he was promptly released by the concerned magistrate because the Mumbai police had taken six long years to make the charge sheet and the case had legally become time barred, there was jubiliation in the Shiv Sena camp. Monty and Reeta were in Mumbai on that day. They had gone to look for a new tenant for their flat at Cuffe Parade. On 27th July 2000, after the tension in Mumbai had evaporated and Monty had found the right tenant, Reeta expressed her earnest desire to her husband to take her on a pilgrimage to the famous Amarnath caves in Kashmir.

"Sure my love," said Monty as he promptly booked two tickets to Srinagar via Delhi by the early morning Indian Airlines flight on 29th July. It happened to be a Saturday that day and the short 5 day trip to Srinagar would also give Monty the opportunity to check on the progress of his various export orders of Kashimir handicrafts and artefacts that were to be delivered by end September. Late in the afternoon of 1st August, after Monty had reviewed all his export orders, he with Reeta in a hired car left for the Amarnath Base Camp at Pahalgam.The pilgrimage to the famous Shivling on top of a high mountain was an annual event that attracted over lacs of devotees every year from all over India and the world. Since the journey from the base camp to the holy caves could be very tiresome and time consuming by foot, they had initially planned to do it on horseback with some of the the other elderly devotees in the tented camp. But later on the advice of some friends and to save precious time they decided to do it independently by starting very early next morning. They therefore instead of staying in the crowded camp decided to stay in a decent hotel that also provided better groomed local hired ponies. It was around six in the evening, when they reached Pahalgam and checked in at the Hotel Senator Pine-n-Peak. Situated on the banks of the fast flowing River Lidder, the small picturesque town was steaming with pilgrims. Like every year, a special tented camp had been erected for them at a place that was a little away from the town and everybody seemed to be in very high spirits that evening. For better security of the area, soldiers with arms were also deployed near the camp. Since they had to get up very early next morning, Monty and Reeta decided to have and early dinner and go to bed. But suddenly at around 7 P.M. while Monty and Reeta were enjoying a drink sitting in the second floor balcony of their room that overlooked the river, the rat-a-tat of rapid machine gun fire was heard. Initially everyone in the hotel thought that the pilgrims in the camp were probably celebrating with fire crackers. Soon thereafter there was commotion inside the hotel as the word spread that armed militants had attacked the pilgrim camp and a fierce firefight was in progress.

"Thank God that we finally decided not to stay at the base camp." said Reeta to her husband as both of them joined the others in the restaurant to find out what was happenning. That night the firing continued sporadically for a few hours and it was only early next morning that they learnt that 21 people who were mostly Hindu pilgrims had been killed and 30 others were injured. Those killed also included two militants. Most of the casualties however it seems were as a result of the shootout between the militants and the soldiers who were guarding the camp. Because of the prevailing darkness some pilgrims it seems were unluckily to have been caught in the crossfire. Next day with curfew having been imposed and the pilgrimage to the sacred caves cancelled by the authorities, Monty and Reeta kept sitting in the hotel. And on the 3rd of August, when the curfew was finally lifted they decided to return to Srinagar and catch the flight back to Delhi. On the flight they were shocked to learn that on that very night of 1st and 2nd August, 2000 the militants had not only targeted the innocent pilgrims at Pahalgam, but they had also brutally killed a very large number of innocent Hindus in various other parts of the state. Most of them were poor migrant labourers and workers, and according to one report a total 105 people had been massacred by the militants on that dreadful night.

"This must have been a very well planned and deliberate operation, and the perpetrators could very well be an ISI sponsored militant group who are opposed to the Hizbul Mujahideen's recent ceasefire declaration," said Monty to a senior army officer who was also on the same flight to Delhi that afternoon.

"'I guess you are right, but something positive can only be achieved if the government allows us a more free hand in dealing with these bastards. And the only way we can do it is by taking the bull by the horn and attacking the many militant camps that are across the LOC and inside Pakistan Occupied Kashmir," said the high ranking General Officer who was seated next to Monty in the executive class. It seemed that the General Officer was thoroughly disillusioned with the government's peace initiatives and policies. According to him, after the defeat and debacle at Kargil, the new military regime in Pakistan had not only stepped up their sponsored militant activities inside the state, but there was also now indications that the proxy war on Kashmir unleashed by Pakistan through the various Jehadi groups may well now be extended to other parts of India as well.

"Yes, and though Mr Vajpayee has been extending his hand of friendship by announcing the continuation of the ceasefire in the state, but it is simply not working it seems. Moreover, Pakistan is hell bent in creating a fear psychosis for the Hindus residing and working in the state as has been seen in the recent spate of militant kilings both against the men in uniform and against the people on the civvy street," said the newly promoted Lieutenant General and who surprisingly was also a coursemate from the National

Defence Academy at Kharakvasla of Monty's younger foster brother the late Major Shiraz Ismail Khan, PVC.

"Yes, and I am sure my brother too would have been a Lieutenant General today and probably he too would have felt the same way as you do," said Monty as Reeta also butted in to say very proudly that had he lived, Shiraz Ismail Khan would have definitely become the first Muslim Army Chief of India.

Though the wanton killing of innocent pilgrims by armed fanatical Muslim militants up north at Pahalgam in Kashmir hogged the headlines, in the south the dare devil kidnapping of the popular Kannada film actor Rajkumar on the night of 30th July by the ever elusive dacoit Veerapan came as a rude shock to his many fans. The Kannada matinee idol and the winner of the prestigious Dadasaheb Phalke award had been taken hostage from his own ancestral farm house at Gajanur. The village located in Tamil Nadu's Erode district was only 4 kilometers from the Tamil Nadu-Karnataka border and the farm house of his was inside a forested area. At around 9 PM that evening Veerapan with his men in pouring rain had stormed the house and having done that he coolly escorted the 72 year old actor and a few others out of the house and took them deep inside the forest. In all his years of banditry this was Veerapan's most high profile hostage and it now had both the governments of Tamil Nadu and Karnataka in a tizzy.

The kidnapping of the veteran actor and singer also came as a shock to Peevee who admired the man's acting and singing talent. In fact in order too improve upon his own histrionic ability, Peevee had seen some of his hit films like 'Krantiveera' and 'Swayamwara', and he too now prayed for his safe home coming. Veerapan the dreaded sandalwood and ivory smuggler who had killed more than a hundred people including some senior policemen eversince he became a dacoit more that twenty years ago was a dangerous man and he was somehow always one step ahead of the security forces. Though he carried a reward of a few crores on his head, he somehow managed to always give the police and the Indian intelligence agencies the slip.

On 12th August, despite the heavy monsoon rains while the massive hunt by hundreds of armed policemen both from Karnataka and the Tamil Nadu police force was in progress to capture the ever illusive Veerapan and rescue the popular Kannada matinee idol, Peevee landed in Bangalore. He had come for a commercial photo and video shoot for a new brand of hard liquor that had just been introduced in the market with the catchy name of 'Bottoms Up'. But it could be advertised only as a sparkling soda, because advertisements of liquor products were not permitted by the government. The location for the shoot was the swimming pool of the Leela Palace luxury hotel and for the shot, Peevee was required to be dressed up as a deepsea diver.The shot was suppose to show Peevee opening a bottle of 'Bottoms Up' soda at the bottom of the ocean and while having a large swig from it he through the hundreds of sparkling colourful bubbles had to say the one line dialogue 'Bottoms Up even at 20,000 leagues under the sea is always as bubbly as ever.' However by the time the shooting finally got over it was nearing midnight and having had a very tiring day wearing that heavy sea divers outfit, Peevee got into a pair of jeans and a designer tee shirt and walked into the hotel's Library Bar for a drink. His entry no doubt initially created a flutter, but by the time the barman served him with his large black label whisky, all eyes were on the television screen. He was unaware of the fact that a Russian nuclear submarine ship with its entire crew of 118 officers and sailors had sunk in the Barents Sea that very morning. The nuclear submarine K-141 Kursk that was named after the Russian city of Kursk where the biggest tank battle in military history was fought during the Second World War was an Oscar—II Class nuclear powered cruise missile submarine that was commissioned into the Russian Navy's Northern Fleet after the fall of the Soviet Union. It was the largest submarine ever built and it had successfully tracked the United States Sixth Fleet in the Mediterranean during the Kosovo War last year. The submarine was out on an exercise to fire dummy torpedoes at another Russian battlecruiser and the probable cause for the accident was due to the failure and explosion of one of the submarine's hydrogenperoxide filled dummy torpedoes.This was an unprecedented disaster for the Russians and Peevee felt sorry for the families of those whose sons had perished in that tragic undersea calamity. He thought that it was rather ironical that on the very day when he was doing an advertisement for the 'Bottoms Up' brand of liquor dressed up as a deep sea diver, the big Russian submarine had to go down to the bottom of the sea.

And while the state governments of Tamil Nadu and Karnataka intensified their efforts to capture the brigand Veerapan and rescue the famous actor, a war of words had erupted between the governments of India and Pakistan. Following the many massacres of Indians in the valley, the Indian government warned Pakistan to stop aiding and abetting the militants in Kashmir. And though Sherry too was aware of the fast deteriorating relations between the two countries, she nevertheless on 14th August, Pakistan's Independence Day rang up Peevee's from her personal cell phone to find out about his plans to visit Moscow, Peevee was no doubt pleasantly surprised with that call, but he was stuck for an answer. With Mom Number 2 as India's ambassador to that country and with the existing strained relations between India and Pakistan after the Kargil war and the recent massacres in Kashmir, it would not be ethical on his part to date a Pakistani girl and certainly not in Moscow he thought. Therefore giving the excuse that with his many shooting schedules that had been lined up for the next couple of months it would not be possible for him to come to Moscow in the near future, he asked her whether it would be possible for her to make a short trip to Australia instead.

. "'I'll tell you what, since I will be shooting with a few well known Bollywood stars and starlets in a yet to be titled blockbuster film, why don't you make it to Sydney instead. The film unit will be there for a week or so from 3rd October, but I intend reaching Sydney on 30th September so as to be in time to witness the gala closing ceremony of the Summer Olympiad that is scheduled to be held on the 1st of October, and maybe we could both witness it together. And thereafter if you still want to see the longish dance item number which will be shot outdoors in a giant open air stage and with the backdrop of the famous Sydney Opera house and the Sydney Bridge, you are most welcome to do so, but as a fan and as a spectator only. However, before the actual shooting commences we could also spend a couple of days in each other's quiet company if you so wish."

"Thank you very much for the invitation and the offer, but I won't promise you anything right now because I too have certain compulsions. However, I will definitely try and be there if I can on some excuse or the other but only if I can convince my parents," said Sherry somewhat optimistically.

A fortnight later on 27th August, 2000 Shiraz, Saira and Sherry had a near close brush with death again. That day happened to be a Sunday and all of them had gone to the 7th Heaven restaurant in Moscow. Known in Russian as the 'Cedmoy Neba' restaurant, it was a revolving restaurant that provided a panaromic bird's eyeview of the city. Perched high and roughly midway to the top of the famous 540 meters Ostankino television tower, the monument was also one of Moscow's top tourist attractions. Designed by Nikolai Nikitin and completed in 1968 to mark the 50th anniversary of the Russian October Revolution, the tall tower till 1976 was the tallest in the world. A little after 7 PM that evening and after the first round of drinks with caviar and cheese balls as starters were served to them, there was a fire alarm. For a while everybody thought that it was a joke since there was no fire or smoke visible anywhere inside the restaurant. But a few minutes later, when they saw flashes of light and smoke above the restaurant and on the higher reaches of the television tower, they knew that it was something serious. Luckily with everyone following the evacuation drill without creating any panic, all those who were in the restaurant and at the observation tower at that time, managed safely to reach the base. When Shiraz saw the huge crowd that had gathered by then to observe the fire that was raging above the place where they had been sitting till a few minutes ago, he put both his hands to his eyes and thanked Allah. The fire was due to a short circuit in the wiring and as a result of which not only three people had died, but all television and radio signals were disrupted in and around Moscow. Luckily the breakout of the fire was quickly observed by the maintenance staff and though it took more than 300 fire fighters and emergency staff to bring it under total control but the damage done was enormous.

Late that night evening, when Sherry informed Peevee about her narrow escape and assured him that she would definitely try and meet him in Sydney, Peevee too prayed to the Sai Baba of Shirdi. Only a fortnight earlier on 8th August, 2000, Sherry was lucky to escape death once again, when a bomb at around six in the evening exploded in a very busy underground pedestrian walkaway near the busy Pushkin Square which was in the heart of Moscow. The walkaway linked two major streets and three subway stations and it was only five minutes before the blast that Sherry had made her way through that subway to board the metro at the Pushkinskaya station. According to Moscow's Mayor Yuri Luzhkov, 7 people had been killed and over 90 were injured and according to the Mayor this was the handiwork of the Chechen militants.

And while Peevee looked forward to meeting Sherry in Sydney, on the 6th of September, 2000 there was news that Bofors, the last wholly owned Swedish arms manufacturer had been sold to an American arms maker that was known as United Defense.And coincidentally it was also around this time that all the world leaders were meeting for the United Nations Millennium conference in New York. Because it was in October 1985 at the United Nations during the Heads of Countries conference that Rajiv and Palme had first met and the deal on the Bofors gun took its roots.

"I think that with the Bofors now safely in American hands, it will be even more difficult now to get hold of that clever Italian fugitive and crook Octavio Quattrochhi and Ardbo the big Swede. And with Octavio being the prime player on that notorious deal and who was once very close to

10, Janpath, it will now be even more difficult to get to the bottom of that ever smoldering scandal." said Monty as he with Reeta and Unni drove past Number 1 Race Course Road on their way to the Delhi Gymkhana Club for their usual Sunday afternoon drinks followed by the excellent buffet.

"Yes you do have a point there, and since this scandal which I believe has now become a big money game for those involved, I therefore won't be the least surprised if those actual beneficiaries from this infamous dirty deal and their close partners even buy off those who matter in the present government and in the CBI. It is now no longer a question of the Rupees 50 odd crores that were paid off as bribes by Bofors to seal the deal, it is now a question of the credibility and the political survival of the Congress Party and their leader at 10 Janpath, also,"said Unni.

"But I don't understand as to why both of you always and every time we pass either Number 7 Race Course Road or 10, Janpath you have to discuss this very sordid topic only. Since you both say and agree that nothing finally will come out of it, then where is the point in flogging the dead horse," said Reeta somewhat angrily.

"I think she is absolutely right and from today no more Bofors please," said Unii somewhat apologetically while ordering another extra large gimlet for himself.

"But Sir, why don't you try a Bofors Barrage cocktail"instead,' said one of Unni's junior colleagues from the Press Trust of India, who had overheard the discussion and who was also enjoying his drink at the bar that day.

"And pray what kind of a coctail is that,", asked Reeta while Monty invited the gentleman to join their table.

'Oh it is a very heady cocktail mix Madam and where the base is half a pint of good Italian red wine kind courtesy Mr Q, and to which is added a large peg of Old Smuggler English whisky, thanks to the Hinduja Brothers, a Patiala peg of Indian Sea Pirate rum with compliments from the Chadda family, and is topped up with some chilled Swedish beer from Mr Ardbo. And in order to give it a little more kick and some black colour you could also add a dash of CBI bitters and finally garnish it with some 10 Janpath Congress grass and the government of India's sour grapes," said the gentleman while ordering another large Vodka with soda for himself.

"Wah Wah, that's some deadly cocktail indeed. But the problem is and as the popular saying goes who will make the bloody horse drink. As it is with all the horse trading that goes on to keep mouths shut, and with our politicians always being power drunk, it is not going to be all that easy my friend," said Unni while raising a toast to the utter incompetence of the CBI to crack the Bofors code.

"Yes earlier it was called the Congress Bureau of Investigation, but today it is the Corruption Bureau of India and tomorrow with coalition governments coming and going at the centre it will probably be the Condescending Bureau of Inactivity," said Monty as the warning bell for the last drink was sounded.

A fortnight later on 29th September, 2000 when Monty with his family and friends were once again enjoying their drinks and dinner at the Delhi Gym, the news about Narasimha Rao and Buta Singh's conviction was the main topic that everybody was discussing at the club. That day both of them had been convicted by the CBI special judge Ajit Bharihoke in the infamous Jharkand Mukti Morcha bribery case. It was a case against the former Indian Prime Minister Narasimha Rao and his Home Minister Buta Singh that had been filed under the Prevention of Corruption Act, 1988 and it related to the alleged bribing of Opposition MP's in the India Parliament in order to defeat the 28th July, 1993 no confidence motion against the then Congress government of Mr Narasimha Rao.

"Well for once atleast the court has given the two big Congress devils their dues, but some of those other devils who took those bribes have been unfortunately acquitted and it is simply because of the Supreme Court ruling of 17th April 1998 that stipulates that MP's taking bribe to vote in Parliament enjoyed constitutional immunity against prosecution. And that unfortunately is a rather sad commentary on how we run our country. Those devils not only escaped punishment, but they were also rewarded with hard cash and if this trend continues then god save our country from these hard boiled crooks,", said Unni.

"Yes it is rather sad and unfortunate that the Lokpal Bill that was first introduced by Mr Shanti Bhushan way back in 1968 to fight corruption at all levels is till pending to be passed by the Indian Parliament. And mind you it was passed in the fourth Lok Sabha in 1969, but it could not get through the Rajya Sabha. Thereafter upto 1998 it was introduced six more times but was never passed. And the reason is very obvious because our ministers including our prime minister and members of parliament, some of whom are very corrupt do not want to come under its perview. Bcause if they do so they will be putting the noose around their own damn necks," said Monty.

"But do you think they will ever go to jail? My Foot.They will I am sure go in appeal and as in every other case where politicians had been convicted, they will ultimately go scot free. As it is in this particular case all the key witnesses among the 100 odd that deposed in the court had turned hostile. And with the big black money power that these politicians have in their pockets, they can always buy their own freedom. And as far as the Lokpal Bill is concerned these same very politicians will ensure that it always remains a nonstarter," said Reeta somewhat mockingly, when her mobile rang. It was from Peevee informing her about his forthcoming trip to Sydney.

Meanwhile in Moscow on that weekend, Shiraz with Pakistan's Defence Attache as his partner was busy taking part in an inter embassy four ball golf tournament. Having lost very narrowly to the American foursome, when all the teams gathered at the 19th hole which was also the club house for cocktails and for the prize distribution ceremony, Shiraz was very surprised to learn from his own Defence Attache that General Musharraf before leaving for New York to attend the United Nations millennium summit had carried out another major reshuffle of some of his top military commanders.

According to the Military Attache, Lt General Aziz Khan who was the Chief of General Staff in Rawalpindi had been appointed as the new Lahore Corps Commander and his place had been taken by Lt General Yousuf Khan who was commanding the Corps at Multan. And while Lt General Khalid Maqbool who was commanding the Lahore Corps had been appointed as the new chairman of the NAB, the previous chairman was shifted to command the Multan Corps.

"I think General Musharaff enjoys shuffling around his top commanders and I wonder why. If you recall, soon after taking over as chief he had shuffled the pack by appointing those close to him in important key appointments and posts as corps commanders and principal staff officers. Thereafter on taking over as the CEO, he sent those whom he distrusted packing home, while those whom he implicitly trusted were given some more important portfolios, both in the government, in the Fauji Foundation and in the armed forces including that of the DGISI and NAB. And now within a spate of not even a year, he has reshuffled the pack again. I therefore feel and I may be wrong though, but it could be because he is feeling a bit insecure sitting on that hot seat and maybe he is afraid of being ousted by one of them." said Shiraz.

"Well Sir, as a junior serving officer I don't think it will be proper on my part to comment on my seniors and definitely not on the CEO who is also the army chief. But my own gut feeling is that he wants to probably inject new blood into the whole damn system and make it more people friendly and efficient," said the Defence Attache somewhat diplomatically.

"Well I hope so too. And now that he has represented the country at the UN summit in New York which was held from 6th to 8th September and where a record number of heads of states attended, I guess he must have also bumped into Mr Vajpayee at some formal get together or the other. And it would have been very wise and statesmanlike for both of them if they had firmly shaken hands and let bygones be bygones," said Shiraz.

"Maybe they already have Sir," said the Defence Attache as he helped himself to another soft drink. Thanks to late General Zia-ul-Haq, this Brigadier too had become a staunch Muslim. As a young officer and while serving in erstwhile East Pakistan during the Bangladesh crisis he had been quite a boozer and a heavy smoker. But in 1978, when General Zia added the Islamic flavor of 'Mullaism' to the men in uniform, he had become a complete non-drinker and a non-smoker.

A few days later, when Shiraz came to know that Pakistan was allowing the Taliban to use Pakistan territory in the frontier region for the conduct of military operations, and as a result of which the American state department and the US Ambassador in Islamabad were very upset, he too was of the firm opinion that Pakistan by helping the Taliban was unnecessarily digging its own grave. According to one secret cable that was sent by the U.S. Department of State on 26th September, 2000 to the US Embassy in Islamabad, Pakistan was not only providing the Taliban with funds, fuel, war material and technical assistance, but also with military advisors and trained man power to enable the Taliban to take full control of Afghanistan.

"I do not know why we are so stupidly supporting the Taliban in Afghanistan. And I have been told that not only are we sending a large number of our young people to fight their dirty civil war in that country, but by doing so we are also jeopardizing the security of our own nation. This unholy nexus between the Taliban and Pakistan is also antagonizing the Americans whose support both economically and militarily we badly need. And I am afraid that one fine day these very jihadis whom we are now arming and training will turn the same very guns on us," said Shiraz to his wife Saira, as Sherry very diplomatically poured another large single malt whisky with ice for her dear dad and having pecked him on his cheek very candidly asked if she could go to Australia for a week.

"But why all the way to Australia my love. Do you have a boyfriend there?' said Shiraz jokingly.

"Well not exactly Abbu, but I might bum into one because a lot of my old friends from Pakistan, France and the U.S. have gone there to witness the Olympic Games at Sydney and I want to be there with them for the gala closing ceremony that is scheduled to be held on the 1st of October. Moreover, I am also very keen to attend a classical music festival that is also going to be held in Sydney at the beautiful opera house immediately after the games,' said Sherry very convincingly as she waited for the nod from her father.

"Well it is alright with me provided your mother agrees, 'said Shiraz. "And it is alright with me too provided she stays with our High Commissioner in Australia," said Saira.

"But Meri Jaan, my love the Pakistan High Commission is in Canberra, while the games are been held in Sydney. However she can stay with our Consulate General who is located in Sydney,' said Shiraz.

"That's one option, but Canberra is not too far away from Sydney either and she can always commute from there by train or by bus,"said Saira.

"Agreed Mama, but please leave the choice to me," said Sherry rather excitedly as she lovingly hugged her. And before she could change her mind, she therefore asked her father to ring up the Pakistani Consul General and request him accordingly.

Sherry too it seems had been badly smitten by the handsome Indian Bollywood actor. Off late she had been secretly and constantly in touch with Peevee on the mobile phone and she was now looking forward to meeting him again. Since he was a shaven Surd and a very popular Indian at that, she knew that she too had to be very careful and discreet. After all her father was now a very senior career diplomat and she was afraid that with the military back in power in Pakistan, her going around with an Indian film star could well become a source of embarrassment both to her, to her family and to her country. In another year or so, her father would also be in the run to become Pakistan's Foreign Secretary and her involvement with Deepak Kumar could well mar his chances, thought Sherry. Therefore in order to keep the affair a secret from her parents and from the military rulers of Pakistan, she knew that she had to be very careful and extra cautious too

Soon after Sherry got the nod from her parents and her father had booked her on the first available flight to Sydney, she immediately called up Peevee and informed him about her flight number and her expected time of arrival at the Sydney Kingsford Smith swank international airport.

"Oh that's simply marvellous and don't you worry I will be there at the airport to personally receive you. And although you are cutting it very fine, but nonetheless do ensure that you arrive well in time at Singapore to catch the connecting Quantas flight to Sydney from there. However, you may not be able to recognize me since I have had to perforce grow a moustache and a beard for the song and dance item number that will be shot for the blockbuster film," said Peevee while wishing Sherry a very comfortable flight.

"Please do not bother about picking me up from the airport, because the flight is expected to land at an unearthly hour of 2.30 A.M. in the morning Australian time and moreover, the Pakistan Consulate General in Sydney who is a dear friend of my father will be personally there to receive me. And since he will be coming in his official car with a diplomatic number plate, and since I will be staying with him, I think it will be more prudent and wise for both of us not to be seen together at the airport. However, we could meet at some unobtrusive place for lunch and then go for the closing ceremony of the games from there," suggested Sherry

"Well as you please and if that suits you then it is fine with me too. But do call me up once you land in Sydney. Your ticket for the closing ceremony is with me and as suggested I will scout for a nice cosy little place on the outskirts of Sydney for our lunch date. And if it is not asking for too much, may I request you to come casually dressed in jeans or pants, and not in salwar-kameez or in a sari. And that is because I do not want you to look like a Pakistani or like an Indian and I am sure you must have guessed the reason why," said Peevee as he wished Sherry a comfortable flight.

Since the long song and dance item number for the film shoot was based on the brotherhood, international integration and bonding of the various Indian communities with their host nation Australia, it therefore required that the entire Indian cast had to be dressed in their traditional Indian costumes and dresses for the shooting of that catchy and fast number. And Peevee being basically a Sikh had therefore very cleverly opted to appear as a rustic village Sardar, because he did not want to be recognized and identified as Deepak Kumar the actor while moving around with Sherry in and around Sydney.

Though Peevee was still not aware that Sherry was the daughter of the Pakistan Ambassador to Moscow, but it was now evident to him that her father was probably serving in the Pakistani embassy there and that to in some senior rank or else why should the Pakistani Consulate General in Sydney bother to pick her up at such an unearthly hour from the airport. It was early on the morning of 30th September, 2000, when Peevee landed at Sydney and he discreetly checked in at one of the not so sophisticated guest house which was well away from the airport and the city centre. It was one of those vintage homely guest houses that usually catered for middle class western tourists and it was located outside the sprawling city limits of Sydney. It also had a nice small restaurant that served good continental and Italian food. It was previously a big country house that once belonged to a rich Irish joint family from Belfast, but it kept changing hands and its present owner was an old retired colonel from the Australian army. The three floors with its many rooms had been converted into a fourteen room homely hotel by its enterprising owner and his Italian second wife. The hotel with its inherent privacy also had a nice sprawling garden with an outdoor bar and where one could relax on a deck chair while enjoying the not so hot sun with a book and a glass of chilled beer. The big double room that Peevee had selected was at the far end of the topmost floor of the building and it also had a private big open verandah as an open air sit out. By and large the room was tastefully furnished with antique furniture and it also had a nice big bath cum toilet attached to it. The room overlooked the beautiful Australian countryside and by car it was only 20 miles from the city centre. In order to remain mobile, Peevee had hired a chauffeur driven private car from the airport for the whole day and that morning while he caught up with some much needed sleep after the long jet lag, he eagerly waited for Sherry's telephone call. Peevee however before dozing off to sleep did glance through the morning papers to check the final medals tally, and though the Americans had once again walked away with the largest number of gold medals, but what surprised him was the manner in which China was emerging as a future contender for the top honours. With a grand tally off 28 gold, 16 silver and 14 bronze, it was number 3 in the overall standings. And as far as India and Pakistan were concerned it was once again a pathetic show. While India got one bronze medal in women's weigtlifting, Pakistan could not even manage that.

It was around 11 that morning, when Sherry finally contacted Peevee on his private mobile phone. She was speaking from some small wayside café that was not very far from the main Olympic stadium and she wanted Peevee to come and pick her up from there as soon as possible. Sherry had told her host that she was going downtown to meet up with all her other friends from America and from there she would go with them to witness the grand finale of the Olympic Games and return home late after dinner.

"Just hang around and I will be there in half an hour to pick you up," said an excited Peevee as he gave the chauffeur the address of the café and asked him to step on the gas.

"My God you are simply looking gorgeous and with your westernized English accent and dress, and who will ever think that you are a Pakistani," whispered Peevee as he softly nibbled her ears with his lips and very chivalrously opened the car door for her to get in first

"Thank you so much for the compliment and I must say that with the moustache and beard, you also resemble my father quite a bit. But where are we going?, And remember we have only another three hours to get back to the stadium," said Sherry as Peevee presented a set of mascots of the Olympic Games as souvenirs to her and instructed the driver to go back to the guest house. The three cute little mascots aptly named as Syd for Sydney, Millie for Millennium and Olly for Olympics was designed by Mathew Hattan and they were all based on native Australian animals. And as a result of this all the three mascots were an instant hit both with the spectators and the athletes.

"Oh just don't worry. First we shall have a sumptuous Italian lunch with some good wine as promised by me to you on the telephone and thereafter we shall see what we do. Maybe we could enjoy witnessing the grand closing ceremony on the TV screen and in the quiet comfort of the hotel room with a bottle of champagne followed by a candle light dinner if you so agree. And though I know that watching the closing ceremony live while seated inside the stadium would be an experience by itself, but I don't want to take any chances. In fact I would like to spend as much time with you alone as I can," said Peevee as he gently squeezed her hand and lovingly pecked Sherry on her cheek.

"Well I am not one of those crazy athletic types either, but my deadline tonight is 10 P.M.sharp and I must be home by that time because I have lied to my host. I told him that after the closing ceremony, I will be having early dinner with my friends and I also promised him and his wife that I will be positively home before the clock strikes ten. Moreover, if I am not back by that time, not only will my host be worried, but my parents if they do call up on the landline and they don't find me there, it could well lead to an embarrassing situation for all of us. And though I am very much an adult and can take good care of myself, but you know how parents are, don't you?" said Sherry as she kept tightly holding on to Peevee's hand.There was no doubt that both of them now really cared for one another. And the fact was that they had actually fallen in love it seems.

That evening as the superb closing ceremony of the Sydney Olympiad came to a close and as a grand finale to the games a massive fireworks display lit up the clear sky over the magnificent Sydney harbour and the beautiful Sydney Opera house, Peevee passionately kissed Sherry on her lips for the first time. Thereafter they held each other in a tight embrace and as they kept kissing each other all over the face and the neck, they knew that they were madly in love with each other. And while softly kissing her forehead, when Peevee confessed that he could not live without her, there were tears of both joy and sorrow in Sherry's eyes.

"Oh how I wish we could be together forever darling, but that is not possible I guess," said Sherry as she gently stroked Peevee's long hair, while he rested his head on her heavy breasts

"But pray why not darling and who and what is there to stop us. I know that you are a Pakistani Muslim and I am an Indian Sikh, but so bloody what. We are both adults and we are both human beings and if we really love one another, nothing in the world can stop us from being united in holy matrimony. And for that you don't have to become a Sikh nor do I have to convert myself to become a Muslim. And all we have to do is to get our blessings from our respective parents and have a simple court marriage and it is as simple as that. And to hell with what people have to say,'"said Peevee as he once again embraced her tightly and kissed her on her lips.

'Well it is not as simple as it sounds my love and it is a little complicated too. My father happens to be a very high ranking senior government officer, in the Pakistan Foreign Service and he simply will not agree to it. And though he is very broad minded and a wonderful man whom I deeply respect and love but he is also currently our Ambassador to Russia and no way will he or my mother agree to my marrying a shaven Sikh and that to an Indian and a superstar from Bollywood, As it is after the Kargil war the relations between the two countries has further deteriorated very badly and with Pakistan now once again under military rule, a proposal like that will not only kill my father's career, but I too will be declared a kafir by the Mullas. And don't be surprised because if the radicals find out about our relationship, they may well kill not only me, but my whole family too, and they will not spare you either," said Sherry in all seriousness as she kept holding on tightly to Peevee's hand.

On hearing that Peevee wasn't very surprised. He knew that Sherry did have a point in what she had just stated and that to so very frankly and convincingly. And he therefore feared that with the radical Islamists in Pakistan slowly gaining the upper hand, her life and that of her family could be in real danger if their secret relationship was ever discovered.

"You know it may sound rather like a strange coincidence to you, but it is also gospel truth. You see I too have a dear aunt in Moscow and she also happens to be India's ambassador to that country. She is still single and being my father's only cousin, she too is very close to my mother and my late grandmother. In fact she I was told was brought up in our house by my grandmother and I too love her very much. Unfortunately not only my aunt, but my father and mother too had lost both their near and dear ones fairly early in life and I therefore did not have the privilege of getting spoilt by my grandparents. You see I was born well after they had all left for their heavenly abode. And I have also been told that when I was a little toddler, I became so very fond of my dear aunt that I often addressed her as mom also. And even now I sometimes lovingly address her as my mom number two," said Peevee as their lips met again in a passionate kiss

"Yes and I have met her too, but only once. And that was during the award ceremony at the Moscow film festival and I must say that even at this age, she is really very stunningly beautiful too," said Sherry as she too kissed Peevee passionately on his lips. And while they lay in each other's arm, Sherry suddenly checked her watch.

"I think it is getting a little late and maybe we should go down to the restaurant for our candle light dinner," whispered Sherry as Peevee got up and poured some more champagne into her glass.

"But maybe we could have it served in the room or in the open air verandah outside. Frankly speaking I would like to be alone with you for a little longer my darling," said Peevee as he put his arm around Sherry and escorted her to the verandah.

"As you please, my love," said Sherry as she held her dark lipstick stained champagne glass close to Peevee's lips for him to also take a sip from it.

"Since I am also free tomorrow and you have nothing to do either, maybe we could go and spend the day at some exclusive seaside resort which is well away from the city," said Peevee as he poured the rest of the champagne into his glass and quickly got on to the internet on his laptop to search for an ideal place to go to for the next day's outing.

"I think that will be simply wonderful darling and when I get home tonight I will cook up another convincing story for my hosts. I will tell them that I have been invited by a group of friends whom I had earlier met in Paris when I appeared for my music exams there and whom by chance I had bumped into at the stadium today. And to allay all fears and doubts from my host's mind, I would like you to therefore come personally and pick me up from his residence. After all we did meet for the first time in Paris, didn't we love," said Sherry with a playful smile on her beautiful face.

"It seems you have been reading far too many of that James Bond stuff and therefore from today since we have bonded so very well and nicely together, I am going to call you 'Jaanemann' my beloved' and you can call me not Vagabond, but Mega Bond from the word megastar if you so desire,' said Peevee in a lighter vein as they passionately kissed again.That evening while dropping Sherry back to the Pakistan Consulate they had decided that come what may they will discreetly carry on with the affair and hopefully wait for an opportune moment to tell their respective parents about their desire to get married.

Early next morning, when Peevee went to pick up Sherry and as planned was introduced to the Consul General and his wife simply as Mr Mega Bond from Paris, the elderly Pakistani couple never realized that the handsome young man with his fair complexion, moustache and beard was none other than the Indian superstar Deepak Kumar. With his fair complexion and beard they took him to be a French musician. On the way to the seaside resort, when Peevee showed Sherry the massive sets and stage that were being erected near the famous Sydney Opera House for the next day's shoot of the much awaited song and dance item number for the blockbuster film, and Sherry very casually conveyed to him that the possibility of the entire Pakistani consulate staff including the Consul General with their families may very well be there to witness the Indian stars in action, Peevee became a little nervous.

"My God what have we done? What if the guy and his wife recognize me performing on the stage? It will be disastrous for both of us. Though I will be made to look like a rustic Sardar complete with turban and lungi to lead the 'Bhangra' group, but you never can say," said Peevee.

"Yes, it was a big mistake and I think it was very stupid of me to have asked you to pick me up this morning from his residence. I am really sorry my love because it never struck me that you were going to be on stage tomorrow. But don't worry my darling I think we can still pull it off," said Sherry sounding a little optimistic but also a little upset

"But how, because turban or no turban, this damn moustache and the beard that I especially grew to camouflage myself in order to be with you may now let me down," said Peevee

"Don't worry my love. After all you are a great actor and therefore Consul General or no Consul General of Pakistan, you will have to live up to your great reputation not only tomorrow, but also in the days to follow and while you are here in Sydney with the entire film unit. Moreover, if you so desire your makeup artist I am sure will be able to do wonders to make you look completely different while you still remain a Sardar. You can always ask him for a new set of moustache and beard while getting rid of this one tonight," said Sherry as she ruffled his hair very lovingly

"By Jove darling, you are a real genius I must say. And being an ardent fan of mine you will have to also come and cheer me up. But you must come dressed up in a simple traditional Punjabi salwar-kameez suit and without any makeup whatsoever. And that is because I do not want anybody else to cast an eye or to make a pass at you. Needless to say that our film producers and directors are always on the lookout for fresh new pretty faces like yours on the silver screen and I don't want them coming anywhere near you. You are mine and you are mine alone,"'said Peewee as he drew her closer and softly kissed her on the cheek.

"Ya Allah and I must say that you are simply confidence personified. And for all you know with your new make up even I may not be able to recognize you from among the many stars who will be performing on the stage with you tomorrow," said Sherry somewhat jokingly.

"Well let us hope for the best, and even if you don't recognize me as a star that really won't in the least matter to me. Because I want you to only recognize me as your future life partner and as a true friend and a trustworthy life's companion,"' said Peevee in all seriousness as he halted for a minute to check his bearings from the tourist map. A little while later, when he got off the main road and drove straight towards the beautiful, small but exclusive seaside resort that was tucked away under the large clump of Norfolk pine trees, Peevee knew that he had selected the perfect spot to propose to his one and only Sherry. Located to the north and only an hour's drive from Sydney, the 'Kims Beach Hideaway Luxury Resort' was the ideal getaway place for lovers. With its spacious lavish bungalows and luxurious spa villas on the Toowoon beach front, it provided the absolute privacy that Shiraz desired. Peevee had booked the most expensive deluxe beach spa villa for the day on Nine Beach.The villa was not only very spacious but it also had its own private pool, jacuzzi, sauna and a spa too. And to ensure complete confidentiality and to keep away from the prying eyes and the zoom lens cameras of the Paparazzi and the media, Peevee had also hired a self driven four door old Qualis station wagon with tinted glasses. And with his beard and golf cap covering his head he that morning looked like a younger version of Peter Ustinov. Sherry had also come very appropriately dressed for the occasion, but she had no idea that Peevee would propose to her that day. Since it was supposed to be a day picnic by the seaside, she had worn an ankle length fawn coloured silk skirt with a dark brown crochet knitted top and a multicoloured scarf to go with it. And with an oval shaped golden coloured hat covering her head, she looked every inch like a super model from the popular Vogue fashion magazine.

"While it is still nice and warm under the Sun, therefore let us go for a swim first and have our breakfast later," said Peevee while presenting Sherry with two swimming costumes of two different sizes with matching caps

"I must say my Megabond thinks of everything my darling because water has all been my first love," said Sherry as she pecked him on his cheek and quickly went inside to change into the orange polka dotted two piece swimsuit.

Then as they held hands and their lips met and they waded slowly into the clear waters of the blue Pacific Ocean, it was like the scene from the old movie classic "Farewell to Arms". Based on the book that was written by Ernest Hemingway and starring Rock Hudson and Jennifer Jones in the lead roles, it was a love story of a British nurse and an American soldier on the Italian front during World War 1.The author himself had served as an ambulance driver in that war but he had to return home early after he was seriously wounded on the battle front.

After a good swim and a heavy breakfast of eggs on toast with fried liver that was served to them inside the cozy little cottage, when a dead tired Sherry after a nice hot foam bath got back into her picnic dress, Peevee very quietly stood behind her and watched her as she sat in front of the dressing table and continued to apply a little lotion to her flawless dainty hands and shapely legs. But no sooner had she finished applying a modest make up to her beautiful face and she turned around to ask Peevee whether she was looking presentable or not, Peevee very gallantly knelt before her and holding the expensive heart shaped diamond studded broach that he had brought with him all the way from Mumbai, said to her very humbly.

"And though they say that diamonds are forever, but they can only be so if they are firmly secured by a heart of gold. And today I want to be that heart of gold because I want you forever my love." Then as he gracefully pinned the broach on to her crochet knitted top and kissed her tenderly on her forehead, Sherry was really touched by that dignified and loving gesture of his. In fact she was so overwhelmed with those words that she literally had tears of joy running down her cheeks.

"I wish we could get married right now and at this very moment my darling, but we are both helpless I guess. Nevertheless, be rest assured that I will never ditch you and Allah Talla a time will come when no heaven on earth will be able to stop us from becoming man and wife," said Sherry as she too tenderly kissed Peevee on his forehead.That afternoon as they lay naked in bed and Peevee made love to her for the first time using a condom, Sherry also let herself go. And thereafter as their hands kept probing each other's nakedness and they kept kissing each other passionately in a tight embrace, they simply wanted more and more. And by the time they got into the car for their long journey back to Sydney, it was well past sunset.

"Though we may not be able to meet alone soon, but I must see you at the film shoot tomorrow. And maybe we could plan to be alone together once the shooting schedule finally gets over hopefully by 10th October as scheduled," said Peevee.

"But I don't think that will be possible my love, because my return ticket is for the 5th of October and I must be back in Moscow in time. On the 10th my parents and I will be leaving for Islamabad to attend the marriage ceremony of my cousin brother Vovka whose his real name is Samir Rehman Khan and he is a Major in the Pakistan army and is the only son of my father's first cousin, retired Lt General, Aslam Rehman Khan," said Sherry as she wiped away the swelling tears from her eyes and got ready to be dropped off. And a little later as Peevee parked the car a little away from the Consul General's residence and told Sherry that he would definitely try and see her in Moscow in March or April next year after completion of all his existing shooting dates that he was legally bound to honour, that lovely million dollar smile was back on Sherry's face.

"That will be wonderful my darling and you must not come just for a few days with your big filmi crowd, but all alone and at least for a month if not more. And till then let this beautiful relationship remain a well kept secret between the two of us,", said Sherry as she once again passionately kissed Peevee and as a token of good luck presented him with a miniature copy of the Holy Koran that she always carried with her in her ladies purse.

That night Peevee just could not get any sleep at all. All the time he kept thinking about Sherry and wondered what future was in store for them and whether they would be able to get married at all and have children of their own.Early next morning, when Sherry rang up to say that she together with a few other Pakistanis from the consulate would be very much there by mid afternoon to see him and the other Indian Bollywood stars rehearsing and performing the mega dance number for the blockbuster Bollywood film, Peevee was thrilled. And when she further added that the Consul General and his wife were simply not interested, Peewee breathed a huge sigh of relief. But when she said that she would be there only for a short while because she did not want to become a source of distraction to him while he was shooting, Peevee was both happy and sad. He was happy because he would once again see her in flesh and blood and sad because he would probably have to wait till next morning or maybe the next afternoon to see her again

"My God just look at the huge crowd. I didn't know that the Bollywood stars are so damn popular and crazy in Australia also," said the visa officer from the Pakistan Consulate to Sherry as they both showed their red diplomatic passports to the Australian police authorities and thus managed to get a little closer to the scene of action. The film unit had booked the entire Forecourt open air theatre for the dance extravaganza.The Forecourt was very much a part of the iconic Sydney Opera House complex that overlooked the magnificent Sydney Bridge and the Sydney harbour. Located at Bennelong Point and surrounded by the Sydney harbour from three sides, the magnificent Opera House designed by the Danish architect Jorn Utzon in modern impressionist style was also a grand tourist attraction as Shupriya took a few pictures and surveyed the crowd.

"'Yes that's true and most of the crowd as you can see is from the subcontinent and one just cannot make out the difference of whether they are from India, Pakistan or Bangladesh. And surprisingly there are quite a few white skin and Negroes too," said Sherry as she tried to focus her eyes through her dark glasses to spot Peevee, but Peevee was nowhere to be seen. Then suddenly, when the portly film director who was standing next to the dance director and the cameraman loudly shouted on the megaphone for everyone to keep quiet and for the unit to get ready for the opening shot, the sporting crowd immediately obeyed. And a minute or so later when the director followed it up with the standard word of command of' music, action and roll camera, there was complete silence as the long boom of a giant crane that was holding Peevee like a flying bird in the sky appeared from nowhere. And when Peevee who was dressed like a typical rustic Sardar in his colourful lungi, kurta and turban circled the area and waved out to the crowd, he was spontaneously greeted with a big applause. Seconds later to the rhythm of the pre-recorded lilting Punjabi folk music, when Peevee landed on the giant stage like a trapeze artist, it was only then that all the action began.

With the opening shot having been approved by the director, it was now the turn of the dholkis and the junior artists to come on the gigantic stage. To the typical haunting Punjabi folk music and the lilting beat of the two dozen dholkis, when the 'Balle—Balles' of the 100 hundred odd junior artistes consisting of both young boys and girls doing the graceful Bhangra and Giddha in their multicoloured traditional Punjabi dresses and costumes entered from the many wings of the beautifully decorated stage, it was simply a riot of colours. And as they with their well coordinated rhythmic steps joined the hero in that mega dance number, and the smoke from the many coloured smoke candles of red, blue, yellow and green from various directions drifted slowly upwards from the gigantic stage, the scene was indeed very breathtaking. Then with every Punjabi and Urdu couplet as the other Bollywood stars first in pairs and then in groups of four came romping on to the stage in traditional Indian costumes to join the others, the mammoth crowd simply went crazy.

And it was only after half a dozen retakes of that dance number, when there was a short break that Peevee finally spotted Sherry in the crowd. And though she was dressed in a simple plain white cotton salwar kameez and with no makeup whatsoever, she still looked strikingly very beautiful. In order not to make it look very conspicuous, Peevee went a little closer to her and while signing a few autographs for some of his keener fans, he blew a flying kiss in her direction and then followed it up like a good circus artist by blowing kisses all around with both his hands.Having stood there for over two hours, and with Peevee being very busy with his shooting schedule, Sherry was also tired and she finally called it a day. And it was only around midnight, when Peevee rang up from his mobile phone that they could at least speak to one another for a while in complete privacy.

"My God, I never knew that film shooting could be so very boring and so very tiring for you guys, but I must say that you are a very good dancer too my love," said Sherry as she lovingly smacked her mobile phone with her lips.

"Well that's what we are paid for my darling and on the sets it is the director who is the boss and it is he who calls all the shots and we have to simply follow his directions, good or bad, And I wish I could see you right now my love," said Peevee as he too blew her a kiss over his mobile.

"Yes time is fast running out for us my darling. Tomorrow is my last day in Sydney and my flight to Moscow via Singapore is a little past midnight on the 5th morning and I want to see you desperately too, even if it is just for an hour or so," said Sherry somewhat pleadingly.

"Yes, I also want to see you too and hold you tightly in my arms. Maybe we could plan it for tomorrow, when the unit gets a longish lunch break. I will make an excuse that I have an upset stomach and that I need to rest for a while. Then I will quietly get back to my hotel room and wait for you. I will however be only able to tell you the exact time of our meeting at the hotel once the director makes up his mind to give the unit the much needed long lunch break. And incidentally I am staying at the Park Hyatt Sydney which is located close to the Central Business District and the hotel overlooks the iconic Sydney Opera House. But we will first meet at the 'Harbour Kitchen and Bar Restaurant', which is the hotel's specialty restaurant on the waterfront and you should be there around two in the afternoon and not before that. And in case if I get delayed, I will send you an SMS accordingly. And just to make it look more officious and convincing, I will therefore, before leaving the hotel tomorrow morning tell the staff at the reception counter that I will be expecting a local reporter from 'Film Ink", the popular Australian film magazine and that she will be coming to interview me personally sometime in the afternoon and you will have therefore to play it up accordingly my darling. Therefore do come armed with a few copies of that popular magazine, a note book and a decent camera around your neck. And also do remember that like all good press reporters, you must come a little shabbily dress and once again with no makeup whatsoever. An old pair of jeans and a plain simple top with a zero power reading glass over your beautiful big eyes will be ideal I think, and I will see you at the restaurant tomorrow,"'said Peevee as he blew her another kiss.

"That sounds more like a James Bond or an Alfred Hitchcock movie setting my love and as soon as I get your SMS I will be there as directed eagerly waiting for you at the restaurant. I know that right now you must be dead tired and you therefore need to get some good sleep and I will see you tomorrow definitely my darling," said Sherry as they wished each other a very good night.

It was only at around 3.30 in the afternoon of the next day when Peevee managed to sneak away from the sets, and by the time he could get back to the hotel it was already 4 o'clock. He had however managed to send the SMS to Sherry well in time and also had time to change from the lungi-kurta dress to something very casual. Quickly collecting the room key from the reception desk, he made a dash for the rstaurant and finding Sherry sitting there alone in one far corner, he said rather loudly for all the others to also hear. "I guess you must be the correspondent from Film Ink and do please pardon me for being a little late. But I can only give a maximum half an hour or forty five minutes at the most for the interview and since I have to change and rush back to the sets, may I request you to conduct the interview and the photo shoot in my suite and where my secretary can also be of some help and assistance to both of us."

"That suits me fine," said Sherry somewhat coyly as they shook hands and quickly made their way to the elevator. And as soon as they were inside the magnificent suite on the top floor that overlooked the harbour and the iconic Sydney Opera House, Peevee like a new bridegroom lifted Sherry up bodily with both his arms and while kissing her passionately on her lips carried her to the big, warm and soft double bed. Seconds later they were caressing and undressing each other.

"Oh my God how I wish we could be together like this forever," whispered Sherry softly into Peevee's ears as they lay naked in bed and made passionate love in the missionary position. Soon thereafter they were eating each other out in the classical sixty nine pose. Finally when they climaxed again simultaneously with Sherry sitting on top of him, it was time for Peevee to rush back to work again.

"I must say that though we met only for an hour today, but it has really been an hour of total bliss and I will really miss you terribly my love,"'said Peevee as they both quickly got dressed

"And I will miss you too my love and I will look forward to meeting you in Moscow in March or in April next year as promised by you. But you will have to come for a holiday only and not on business. And let us hope and pray that by then the leaders and the people of both our countries will realize that political and military brinkmanship does not pay. And that the future lies in bringing about a lasting peace in the subcontinent. And this sort of blame game, belligerency and jingoism over Kashmir must end once and for all," said Sherry as she took a few pictures of Peevee.

"Yes you are absolutely right my love. That princely state unfortunately has been the root cause of all our problems ever since the day we got our blessed independence, and it is high time we resolved it amicably and justly. And to do that it has to be a fair give and take attitude from both the sides," said Peevee.as he too took a few pictures of Sherry with his new cell phone camera. And when he told her that his paternal grandmother was from a place called Rawalakot and which is now in Pakistan held Kashmir, Sherry was pleasantly surprised.

"Well it's indeed rather a strange coincidence, because my father also comes from the same area of Kashmir that you're late grandmother came from. He is from a village near Philandri while you grandmother according to you is from Rawalakot and surprisingly both the places are now in what the Indians call POK, Pakistan Occupied Kashmir," said Sherry as they kissed for the last and final time that day.

r.

.

Chapter-28

The Son of a Gun called Bofors

It was very early on the morning of 10th October, 2000, when Peevee still sporting his big beard and moustache landed at Palam airport. Dressed as a typical Sardar and with a turban over his head and in order to remain incognito, he quickly took a cab home. So good was his make-up that even the Sardar cab driver did not recognize the Indian superstar. And not only that, even the private security guard at his Defence Colony residence refused him entry into his own father's house and he was made to wait outside the gate till Monty had to personally come and escort him inside. As usual this was also a surprise visit and both Monty and Reeta were delighted because a week ealier their daughter Dimpy with her husband Bharat and their only grand daughter Simran had arrived from Khatmandu to spend the Dusshera and Diwali holidays with them. The festival of Dusshera which fell on 7th October was celebrated by the Delhites in the presence of the Prime Minister Mr Vajpayee with grand fireworkers at the traditional Ram Lila grounds and the family really enjoyed the event.

Peevee's sudden arrival that morning from Sydney had no doubt set the house and the neighbourhood abuzz, but what really set the tongues wagging that day were the startling headlines in some of the leading newspapers. A day earlier on the 9th of October, a damning charge sheet on the Bofors rip off had been filed by the Central Bureau of Investigation in the Delhi Court of Special Judge Ajit Bharihoke and it clearly and in no uncertain terms indicated that the Hinduja brothers were very much a party to that nefarious deal and it also clearly stated that they too had been paid a sum of 81 million Swedish Kroners by Bofors as their commission. And that this money had been paid in three installments into the three Swiss Bank accounts of the Hinduja's during the months of May and July 1986 and which was only a few months after the deal was signed by the then Rajiv Gandhi government. That morning at breakfast,when the family very seriously discussed whether the Hindujas who had been named in this new charge sheet together with the Quattrocchis and the Chaddhas and others like Mr SK Bhatnagar, the former Defence secretary and Mr Ardbo of Bofors who had been named earlier in the previous charge sheet that was filed by the CBI exactly a year earlier in October 1999 would all be brought to book for their underhand deals in getting the Bofors company the billion dollar gun contract, Monty was very candid in stating that ultimately nothing will happen to nobody and that as time goes by, the son of a gun called Bofors will die and get buried under its own weight of sheer bureaucratic and political helplessness, while the Hindujas, the Quattrocchis and the Chaddhas would keep enjoying their handsome commissions for the next couple of generations atleast.

"You all don't seem to realize realize that these big time crooks if they open their big mouths and if they spill the beans as to how and why they became initially part of the deal and how subsequently they also became part of the government cover up, it could spell the death knell of not only the Congress party but also of 10 Janpath. All these guys on paper may be on the run from the Indian judiciary, but don't forget that there are also a lot of highly placed and influential politicians and bureaucrats in this country who are running along with them to keep them all safely out of our jail's reach. This is politics my friend and who knows may be the same people who got the kickbacks on this deal are today willing to share a part of their loot with any government and political party that is in power at the centre,"added Monty while ordering another stuffed gobi ka paratha for his son.

"I think Dad is very right and looking at the manner in which the CBI has been changing colours like a chameleon, it has become totally a mug's game now. Well all the same, I think this so called son of a gun can now fire both ways as far as the Congress party is concerned. And it is for the simple reason that both the key figures are Italians who are holding the trigger. One is the Congress party president of Italian origin and the other is the wheeler dealer fugitive who is still on the run. And God forbid if they ever decide to open their big mouths then it may not only backfire on them personally, but the Congress party as a political entity I am afraid will also be up the gum tree," said Peewee as he helped himself to another giant size gobi-ka-paratha.

"'Yes and maybe that is why the party is probably so very keen to keep Mrs Sonia Gandhi happy and at the helm of affairs. And had Mr Sten Lindstrom the key Swedish investigator in the Bofors case been given a free hand to uncover the truth, he would have probably done so long ago. And it was only the tremendous pressure from India that not only led to the closing down of the investigation by the Swedish prosecuter, but it also led to the Swedish National Audit Buieau sending out a half baked version of its inquiry to India and where all the relevant parts containing the critical payment details were conveniently blanked out by them. And even today Mr Swen Lindstrom feels that a few leading questions to Mrs Sonia Gandhi and to Mr Quattrocchi on how this murky deal was contracted could blow the lid off the Congress party. And that reminds me of a poignant question that was raised by the investigative reporter Chitra Subramanium many years ago when she said. "Well if the Gandhis are not involved, why can't they simply ask their friend Ottavio to testify in India and clear their names," said Unnikrishnan the veteran journalist with a mischievous smile on his face as he too joined them for a sumptous breakfast.

"Yes that indeed is a 64 million dollar question, but I guess there is too much at stake for both the Congress President and her party and they will have to therefore keep ensuring by hook or by crook that Mr Ottavio Quattrocchi never ever lands up again on Indian soil," said Monty.

Two days later on 12th October 2000, evening, when the CNN reported that an US naval ship the USS Cole that had harboured at the Yemeni port of Aden to refuel had allegedly been targeted by the Al-Qaida and that 17 Americans sailors had been killed and 39 were injured and some of them very seriously, Monty who with Unni had gone to see off Peevee to the airport was shocked.

"I think Mr Osama Bin Laden is hell bent on getting the Americans where ever they maybe and whether it is on land, sea or air it hardly makes any difference to them it seems," said Monty as they on reaching home switched on the CNN news channel to get more details of the attack. According to the news channel it was one of the deadliest attacks against an armed United States naval ship. The ship under the command of Commander Kirk Lippold was in the process of refueling at Aden, when at about 11.18 in the morning a small craft approached the port side of the US Destroyer and soon thereafter there was a deafening explosion. The blast hit the ship's galley where the sailors were lining up to be served their lunch. According to another source, a similar attack was planned on the US Navy Destroyer SS Sullivan at Port Aden on 3rd January 2000. It was to be part of the Al Qaida's millennium attack plots, but the small boat carrying the heavy explosives because of over weight had sank before it could reach its target.

And while the deadly bombing of the USS Cole was hogging the headlines in America, in India, when the same Special Judge Mr Ajit Bharihoke in the JMM case of bribery for votes in parliament found the then Prime Minister of the country, Mr Narasimha Rao of the Congress party guilty and sentenced him to a term in jail, it came as a rude shock to the Congress High Command. And when the learned Judge further added very categorically that the best way to discourage corruption in public life and particularly in high places was to award exemplary punishment to the high ranking public servants so that a strong message is sent to the society, there was a glimmer of hope for the people of India. The people on the street were also very happy with the verdict. But as far as Monty and Unni were concerned, corruption at high places to remain in power had become a rampant and incurable desease in India and it was very difficult now to stem the rot that had set in. Such like scams were now being regularly and shamelessly exploited, aided and abetted by the so called 'Netas' (political leaders) of the country. According to Unni, political morality had reached its all time nadir and putting one Mr Rao behind bars or a dozen of them would make little or no difference to the power and to the money hungry corrupt politicians of India today.

"Alright politics apart, but tell us why there has still been no reconciliation between the Bachchan and the Gandhi families who were once thick as thieves. And if I am not mistaken I think it was Amitabh who on that chilly morning of 13th January, 1968 was the one who received Sonia at the Palam airport and escorted her to his father's house when she arrived in India to get married to Rajiv," said Reeta as she also joined her husband and Unni for a dosa lunch at the good old Madras Café on Connaught Place.

"That's another 64 million dollar and which I am afraid only the two parties concerned can truthfully answer. But it is still very sad no doubt. In the late sixties and before Amitabh became a superstar I often spotted them on the India Gate lawns enjoying their ice cream. Those days Rajeev used to ride an old Lambretta scooter and one day I think I even saw Amitabh pushing it. To Rajiv's children, he was their beloved 'Mamu".(Uncle), but then soon after the Bofors and the HDW submarine scandal surfaced in parliament things started going a bit awry for both of them. And I personally feel that it was the world of murky politics that ruined their relationship and Amitabh was only being made a scapegoat. And mind you after Rajiv was assassinated, it was Amitabh who took charge of the funeral arrangements. A couple of years earlier at the launch party of Amitabh's 'Khuda Gawah' in a Delhi hotel it was still all very honky-dory as Rajiv happily posed with him and Sridevi for photographs, and a reserved Sonia Gandhi watched the proceedings from a distance," said Unni while ordering for some more of that mouthwatering 'rasam'.

"Well whatever it is that had caused the split, it must have been a very serious issue. But let us hope and pray that things will improve and they will be friends once again," said Reeta.

"Well to me it doesn't seem so and atleast not for the present. Because if there was a chance of some reconciliation it could have been last year, when Amitabh's son Abhishek debuted in the film 'Refugee' and I believe an invitation was also sent to Sonia but it was a no show by her," added Unni as he insisted in paying the bill.

"In any case I think as President of the the Congress (I) Party and with her chamchas and the coterie of Natwar Singh, Fotedar and others earnestly urging her to contest for re-elections that is due to be held on the 12th of November, and with the inner bickerings growing within the party because of her being a foreigner, she probably does'nt have the time io go to movies. Afterall she too has now taken refuge in India permanently,"said Reeta a little sarcastically.

And while they were discussing whether Abhishek had the capability to emulate his illustrious father who was now still the most sought after superstar in Bollywood, there was a call from Peevee from Mumbai on Monty's mobile informing him that there was again pressure being brought on him by the goons and cronies of Mumbai's underworld to cancel his dates for a movie that is currently being shot in Film City and to make himself available for another film that will be financed by the Don who is based in Dubai. And since there was a serious threat to his life if he refuses to follow the diktat Peevee therefore asked Monty whether he should ask for police protection.

"Don't be a bloody fool. By seeking help from the police you will not only be cutting your own feet, but you will also be ruining your own damn career too. There is no doubt that a section of the film industry is married to the mob and I also know that the mob money power has become quite a factor in Bollywood. But you must play it real cool and try and see how best you can keep both the parties happy. Maybe you could reduce your price and work overtime. In any case if you need any financial help from this end I am always there," said Monty as Reeta seeing the anxiety on her husband's face asked her if everything was alright.

'I think your'ladla beta' (darling son) is becoming a bit too popular in Bollywood, but there is nothing to worry about. He only called up to say that because of his busy schedule, he will not be able to make it next week to Delhi for Diwali," lied Monty very comvincingly and while putting up a poker face. And on 29th October, 2000 while Peevee im Mumbai agreed to the 'Don's diktat, in New Delhi a dapper Jitendra Prasad from the Indira Congress Party threw in the gauntlet to challenge Sonia Gandhi for the post of the party president. Born on 12th November 1938, the 62 year old suave politician from Uttar Pradesh who was a product of Sherwood College Nainital and Colvin Talukdar College, Lucknow was more than convinced that the party was worse than better off eversince the lady from 10 Janpath had taken over the reins in1998. On that there was no doubt because the Congress vote share had plunged dramatically He was also firmly of the view that coteries do not serve the interest of the party and like cancer it only slowly eats into the vitals and destroys it. But for him to take on the present boss of the party who besides being Rajiv's widow, also had the big Gandhi name tag behind her was not at all going to be easy and he very well knew that. But the challenge from him did scare the wits of the Sonia coterie and so much so that her close advisors like, Arjun Singh, Natwar Singh and ML Fotedar fearing that taking Sonia to file her nomination papers at the Congress Party Headquarters on 24 Akbar Road may lead to an ugly situation because there were still quite a few stalwarts within the party who had already shown their disapproval of her being of Italian origin, they therefore giving the lame excuse that her going there could pose a security risk for her made her file her nomination papers from 10 Janpath itself. With the battle lines now firmly drawn, it initially looked that it would be a close fight, but finally it turned out to be no fight at all. And as the election date grew nearer, quite a few of the sycophants from the Sonia group openly pointed out that the party was a family concern and therefore the magic of the Gandhi name to lead the party must carry on. Predictably therefore on 15th November, 2000, when Ram Niwas Mirdha the Central Election Authority Chief at the party headquarters announced the final results, Sonia had romped home with flying colours. She had secured a whopping 7,448 votes, whereas Jitendra Prasad got a measly 94. It happened to be a Wednesday that day and on that evening, when Monty met up for his usual weekly tete-a-tete with Unni at the Press Club, all that Unni had to say about the Congress Party Election was.

"Well I am afraid that from now on no veteran from within the party will dare to raise a finger at Soniaji or at the Gandhi family. The family unfortunately has become not only there Mai-Baap, but for all those who want to remain in their good books, they I am afraid will have to eat from their hands too. After all they have all now become now the chamchas and slaves of what is now widely considered to be India's defacto royal family."

"That is no doubt true and it only goes to show that there is no spunk left in these senior veterans and that indeed is a pity. And whatever little spunk was shown by Jitendra Prasad will also now dry up among those who are in the middle and lower rung of the organization. The name Gandhi for the Congressmen unfortunately has become the political mantra for the grand old party and with that name tag the party I am afraid will soon become a one woman show. This reminds me of the famous words of Dev Kant Barua who during Indira Gandhi and Sanjay Gandhi's's hey days during the infamous emergency had said 'India is Indira and Indira is India', and today with the sycophancy level wihin the party reaching shameful limits, the slogan could soon be 'Sonia is India and India is Sonia. Take it or leave it," said Monty with a sense of sheer disgust.

The month of November 2000 saw three more new Indian states being carved out from Madhya Pradesh, Uttar Pradesh and Bihar. Whereas Chattisgarh became the 26th, Uttaranchal became the 27th and Jharkhand the 28th respectively. And after three months of endless criticism of the Tamil Nadu and the Karnataka government for the inability of their police force to nab the ever illusive dacoit Veerapan and rescue the respected matinee idol from his clutches, there was even more embarrassment for the two governments, when the old veteran actor Rajkumar walked free from the clutches of his captor. On 15th November, when a smiling and and happy Rajkumar came out of the forest unharmed, Peevee was indeed very happy.

That month of November was also really hectic for Peevee as he in order to keep both the Dubai Don and the old film producer happy regularly kept doing two full shifts a day. The sixteen to eighteen hours of work under the arc lights was no doubt back breaking, and the only consolation was that since both the films were being shot in two adjacent studios inside the Film City in Goregaon, Mumbai, he did not have to waste time commuting through the mind boggling traffic of the city. His newly acquired air conditioned luxury caravan had become his second home and his only consolation was that he could atleast speak in complete privacy to his beloved Sherry atleast once everyday.

It was very late on the night of 30th November, 2000 and while Peevee was busy talking to his lady love in London, when Sherry conveyed the news to him that another young nineteen year old beauty queen from India by the name of Priyanka Chopra had become Miss World 2000.

"My God I must say that you Indians are churning out international beauty queens by the dozens eversince Sushmita Sen and Aishwariya Rai hogged the limelight in 1994. And I must say that this one too is very good looking and she like Sushmita also has a million dollar smile,"said Sherry while informing Peevee that she was very much there on the scene at the Millenium Dome that evening to witness the crowning ceremony of the 50th Miss World Pageant.

"Well you too could have given Miss Chopra a very close fight had you participated In the pageant too as Miss Pakistan," said Peevee lovingly to his beloved Sherry as he blew her a kiss over his mobile phone.

"Thank you for the compliment my love, but there were a total of 95 of them and all of them were equally good looking and had I taken part I would have probably been eliminated after the very first round itself." said Sherry somewhat humbly.

"Now don't try and be modest, but what the hell are you doing in London? asked Peevee as he poured a stiff cognac for himself.

"Oh I am here in London to take part in a classical musical festival and I will be back in Moscow by the middle of next month. And I do hope that your visit to your Mom number 2 in mid April as planned still stands,"asked Sherry.

"Yes, for the time being there is no change in the program, but there is every possibility of it being delayed by a month or two. And that is because of some important commitments that I had to perforce make to some key captains ot the Bollywood film industry and which I have to honour come hell or high water. Because if I don't then there may be a big problem," said Peevee while instructing his secretary to get hold of a copy of the Femina magazine that had covered the last Miss India contest.

In 2000, India had scored not only a grand double but a grand treble too, as Lara Dutta walked away with the Miss Universe crown, and Diya Mirza too bagged the Miss Asia Pacific title. The pair of Lara and Priyanka had brilliantly emulated the feat of Sushmita and Aishwariya when they too had bagged both the coveted beauty crowns in 1994. This was a sort of a record that no other country had ever achieved before. And what was still more revealing was that in a span of just six years India had produced seven winners and which included two Miss Universe titles and five Miss World titles. And a few days later, when Peevee saw the photograph and also read the short biodata of the newly crowned Miss World 2000 that was splashed across most Indian newspapers, he was no doubt very impressed with her good looks, fabulous figure and above all by her very captivating smile.

"I think she will be a great hit if she becomes a film star too," said Peevee to the veteran film director as he got ready to take the next shot.

"Well it is a question of luck I guess, but plain good looks don't always make stars. She must have some acting talent on the stage too," said the director as the cameraman zoomed in to take a close up of Peevee.

"Well if she could be on the world stage for the competition and with her good looks, complete poise, supreme confidence and well thought out intelligent answers floor the jury for the Miss World crowm, I am sure that if rightly guided and handled by a good an experienced director like you, she could one day become a Bollywood movie star also,' said Peevee while requesting the director to pack up the unit a little early that day since he had to attend an important filmy party and where the main financier from Dubai was expected to be the chief guest.At that filmi party that evening, when Peevee also came to know that the new Miss World who was born on 18th July, 1982 at Jamshedpur and that she was the daughter of an army doctor, he indeed felt very proud. But what struck him the most was that having studied for a while in the John F Kennedy High School in Massachusetts; she wanted to either become a software engineer or a criminal psychologist. And not only that, the tall and beautiful girl with Mimi as her nickname had a flair for writing poetry and short stories too. And according to another close admirer of her's she could sing fairly well also.

"Maybe the Miss World Crown will make her now change her ideas," thought Peevee as the film producer who was hosting that lavish party poured another large Blue Label whisky into the financier's glass.

At that party grand Peevee also came to know that prior to the Miss World pageant, the same magnificent Millenium Dome in London where the glamourous event was held had been targeted by some dare devil criminal gang. The gang wanted to steal the 12 rare diamonds that were on display there and it also included the priceless millennium star. And had they been successful it would have been the world's biggest daylight dacoity and robbery. But luckily the London Metropolitan police had been timely tipped off and the great diamond robbery was foiled at the last minute. On the morning of Tuesday 7th November, 2000 the gang of four armed men with smoke bombs, ammonia, a sledgehammer and a nail gun had smashed their way through the perimeter fence and the gates of the Millennium Dome while using a stolen heavy duty JCB Excavator. Having done that, they headed straight for the vault where the rare diamonds were kept. But while they attempted to smash their way into the display case using the sledgehammer and the nail gun, all four of them were immediately caught red handed by the police who were waiting for them. The operation was aptly code named "Operation Magician' and Detective Superintendent John

Shatford with his flying squad officers disguised as cleaners, and with their guns hidden inside their bins did their magic that shattered the dreams of the five criminals and which also included the speed boat driver. The gang had planned to escape after the heist by a high powered speedboat that lay in anchor on the River Thames.

And while Priyanka Chopra, the army doctor's's beautiful daughter was hogging the headlines in all the leading newspapers and magazines of India, another journalist son of an army officer was getting ready to expose some of the high and the mighty in the Indian Defence Ministry and also a few prominent 'Netas' and leaders of the many political parties in the country for their corrupt practices. Meanwhile at Lahore in Pakistan the stage was also being set to deport Nawaz Sharif and his family to Jeddah, Saudi Arabia. The Saudis it seems had struck a deal with Musharraf on condition that Nawaz Sharif and his family would live in exile in Saudi Arabia for a period of 10 years. But before being deported he would not only forfeit 500 million rupees worth of his property in Pakistan, but he would also be barred from taking part in political activities for the next 21 years.

On the 9th of December 2000, while Lt General Aslam Rehman and Farzana were waiting at the Lahore airport to catch the PIA flight to Dhaka, they were surprised to see the heavy security arrangements both insde and outside the airport. Besides the heavily armed guards from the police and the army, there were also some SSG commandos on top of the control tower. They were all deployed to see the safe exit of the entire Sharif family from Pakistan. And as Nawaz Sharif with his wife Kulsoom and some 18 other family members that also included his father Mian Mohammed Sharif and younger brother Shahbaz Sharif boarded the special Royal Saudi aircraft, Lt General Aslam Rehman was not at all surprised. He was however critical in the underhand manner in which General Musharraf had allowed Sharif and his family to get away. It reminded him of the day in 1958, when General Ayub Khan also forced President Iskandar Mirza at gun point to quietly leave the country and seek assylum in London.

Aslam Rehman and his wife Farzana were now looking forward for a relaxing holiday with Fazal Rehman and his family in Dhaka. The two brothers and their wives had not met for quite sometime and moreover Farzana who had never been to Dhaka earlier wanted to see for herself the land and its people who were very much a part of Pakistan earlier. And while on the flight, when Farzana pointed out that with Sharif's ouster from Pakistan, three of Pakistan's leading politicians including, Benazir Bhutto and Altaf Hussein were now all in exile and that Mr Asif Ali Zardari since

1996 was still in jail on serious corruption charges, Aslam simply smiled and said.

"Well if that trend continues then one day General Musharaff may also have to seek exile elsewhere. And in any case now that Benazir, Sharif and Altaf have made their many millions and which are all safely stacked in banks abroad, they and their families will definitely not suffer financially for sure. And now that they are out of the country and in safe havens abroad, the possibility of all of them ultimately joining hands is also very much a possibility. And later with pressure from the United States and the Saudis they could also force the military to bring back democratic rule in the country. But at the moment with Musharraf firmly on the hot seat that possibility is a bit too far fetched though. Nevertheless, the very fact that Musharraf under pressure from the Saudis was made to buckle and give Sharif his freedom only proves the point that all the big talk that was given earlier by our CEO that no one found guilty of serious crimes and however high and the mighty they maybe will be spared was simply hogwash," said Aslam Rehman as the pretty airhostess served them with some more of that aromatic hot coffee.

The flight to Dhaka was indeed very pleasant and they were surprised to see the entire Fazal Rehman family present at the Zia International airport to receive them with big bouquets of flowers. Fazal Rehman at 56 and his wife Samina who was nearing 50 both looked younger than ever and their daughter Sameera who was around 25 was really a beauty. A rare combination of beauty and brains, Sameera was now waiting to get her doctorate in economics from Harward University. And as far as their son Shafiq was concerned, he was soon going to be 18 and like his father was planning to join the Bangladesh Foreign Service after his graduation.As the two brothers and their wives tightly embraced each other and Sameera waited patiently to present the bouquets of tuberoses to her favourite aunt and uncle, Shafiq with his new Nokia mobile phone camera merrily clicked away. That evening over some good rare single malt Jura scotch whiskey and plates full of delicious fried fish and kebabs to go with the drinks, the hot topic for discussion was the much awaited judgement by the High Court on the fate of Mujib's killers. Judge Kazi Golam Razul the District and Sessions Judge in his verdict that was given on 8th November, 1998 had given 15 of them the death sentences, while five others were acquitted. Thereafter on appeal the case had been referred to a two Judge High Court Bench and the judgement from them was expected to be announced soon.

"Well I think it was a very heinous and barbaric crime and the guilty must be sent to the gallows at the earliest,"said Samina.

"My God, don't tell me that it took more them a quarter of a century to dish out justice in such an important case and where non other than the 'Bongobodhu,' the father and the founder of the nation with most of his family members were mercilessly gunned down by those handful of Bangladeshi army officers," said Sameera who was born a day prior to the horrific massacre. That 15th of August, 1975 also happened to be India's Independence Day. It was also the month and the year when DP Dhar who was one of the main architects of giving the Bangladeshis their much loved freedom died and thanks to Madame Gandhi and his son Sanjay the infamous emergency was also declared in India.

"Yes, and it is unfortunately so because nobody it seems was interested in bringing the guilty to book till Sheikh Hasina who was one of the few survivors became the party president and who is now our prime minister, and it is she who took up the issue very seriously," said Samina.On the very next morning all of them visited the Mujib family house in Dhanmondi which was now a museum and a tourist attraction, and there Fazal Rehman narrated to them as to how the perpetrators of that dastardly crime had carried out that shameful act.

On 14th December, 2000, the two judge High Court bench of Dhaka delivered its judgement, but it was a split verdict. While Judge ABM Khairul Huq upheld the trial court verdict, Justice Ruhul Amin confirmed the death sentence against only nine of the fifteen, and he gave life imprisonment to one and acquitted the remainng five. And as a result of this, the case was now referred to the third bench of the High Court.

"Well if it carries on like this then I am afraid the main culprits will never be brought to book. As it is most of them are abroad and knowing their hatred for Mujib's family they may even try to eliminate Sheikh Hasina too." said Aslam Rehman.Late that night and after a sumptuous dinner of authentic East Bengal cuisine that was meticulously prepared by Samina and which included five varieties of fish preparations including the mouth watering 'shorshe ilish', a dish of smoked hilsa with mustard seed paste, the two brothers got into a serious discussion whether the current Islamic resurgence in both Pakistan and Bangladesh was good or bad for both the nations.

"Well I think it is rather sad, but it is definitely true that the first seeds of Islamization of Bangladesh and Pakistan were sown by non other than Zulfiqar Ali Bhutto and Mujibur Rehman respectively. And it was only later and after General Zia ul Haq ousted Bhutto that it got a bigger boost. In the case of Pakistan, both Bhutto and General Zia ul Haq in order to remain in power had to pander to the diktats of the Mullas and that was why we always called Zia the Mulla General. Whereas in Bangladesh, fearing that the Mukti Bahini and the erstwhile Mujibnagar government that was led by Tajuddin Ahmed were becoming a bit too powerful inside his regime, Mujib perforce had to take effective steps to assert Bangladesh's independent identity by distancing himself and his country from India. And with the passage of time and as you can see today both Pakistan and Bangladesh have become staunch Islamic republics. And don't also forget that it was Mujib himself who attended the summit of the OIC, the Organization of Islamic Countries summit conference that was sponsored by Bhutto and was held at Lahore in 1974. Moreover both General Zia-ur-Rehman and General Ershad in order to seek political legitimacy had to also lean towards Islam because both in Pakistan and in Bangladesh, Islam is a very important political weapon." said Aslam Rehman

"But I am afraid this so called Islamization is getting us nowhere near Allah. Instead it is only fostering more radicalism within the community and which is leading to more bloodshed in both the countries,"said Samina.

"Yes I guess she is very right because even in Bangladesh today the most vocal Islamic fundamentalist slogan is surprisingly 'Amra Hobo Taliban, Bangla Hobe Afghan' which when translated means, we will be Taliban and Bangladesh will be Afghanistan,"said Fazal Rehman as he poured another large single malt in his elder brother's glass.

"My God if that ever happens then we are doomed," said Sameera as she put a few more fried tiger prawns in hot garlic sauce on her uncle's plate.

"But I don't think it is all that serious, but one thing is certain and that is whoever wants to come to power in Bangladesh and wants to survive, then the first golden rule is that he or she must maintain a certain distance from India and secondly continue to foster and maintain the Islamic identity of this country,"said Fazal Rehman.That night after everyone else had called it a day, the two brothers got into a more serious discussion on the subject of Islamic resurgence in Bangladesh and the growing strength of the HUJI-B, the Harkat-ul-Jihad-al-Islami of Bangladesh. According to Fazal Rehman, the Islamic resurgence of the country began with the resurfacing of the Jamaat-e-Islami, the party that was once hated by the Bengalis for their collaborative role during the country's liberation war. And it was only able to return to the political scene after the assassination of Sheikh Mujib in1975. The party was now also getting a lot of financial backing from the

Rabitat-al-islami in Saudi Arabia and other such organizations and was also running a wide network of Madrassas, Ibnsena hospitals and Islamic banks in the entire country.

"Ironically the Jamaat-e-Islami is now being led by Ghulam Azam. The ex student leader from Dhaka University who had openly collaborated with the Pakistan army during the 1971 liberation war and was also actively involved in the killing of a large number of Bengali freedom fighters and intellectuals. And I am not kidding because I saw it all happen with my very own eyes. During the war Ghulam Azam moved to West Pakistan and even from there he kept directing his deputy Abbas Ali Khan to get the Razakars cracking in the elimination of the Bangladeshi freedom fighters. A similar group, Al Badr was also launched by the Islamic Chatra Shibir, which is the student's wing of the Jamaat-e-Islami. And today unfortunately the Jamaat-e-Islami is the third largest political party in Bangladesh," reiterated Fazal Rehman as he poured a little more of that Napoleon Cognac into Aslam's fluted liqueur glass.

"Yes, I guess you are right and the return of the Jamaat to the land and its people where they were once hated has therefore had far reaching ramnifications too. In fact it has been instrumental in reviving old linkages between Pakistan and Bangladesh and with both countries now promoting a fundamentalist agenda which is both anti-Hindu and anti-India; it is definitely not a good sign. This will not only create more bad blood between the Hindus and Muslims in all the three nations, but it will also result in more sectarian violence and killings in the entire subcontinent. As it is Dr Taslima Nasreen's book titled 'Lajja' (Shame) which was published in 1993 and which told a story of how a Hindu family in Bangladesh was persecuted by Muslims was not at all taken well by Muslim fundamentalists all around the world, and some have even put a big reward for her head. And as a result of which the young 38 year old doctor turned writer is still on the run," said Aslam Rehman.

"Well that is a different story I guess, but what is really bothering me is the stupendous rise and growth of the HUJI-B. It was formed only eight years ago in 1992 with the active aid of Osama Bin Laden and it now has six well established camps in the country. Its primary base is the southeastern region that borders Myanmar and it is headed by Shawqat Osman alias Maulana Farid. According to one reliable report more than 30 Bangladeshi Mujahideens had died in the war against the Soviets in Afghanistan and after the Russians left, those Bangladeshi Mujahideens who survived became the founders of this fundamentalist organization.Their sole aim is to foist

Nizam-e-Mustafa or Islamic rule in Bangladesh. On 23rd February, 1998 the HUJI-B's link with Osama was further cemented, when Fazlul Rehman the leader of the Jihad Movement in Bangladesh and of which HUJI-B is a party signed the official declaration of Jihad against the United States,"added Fazal Rehman

"Well this is really food for thought and with Mr Osama Bin Laden still at large and the Americans hankering for his bloody blood, the Al Qaida's tentacles I am afraid is growing larger by the day. And with poverty, illiteracy and corruption pervading in almost all Muslim countries of the world, this together with the LeT and others such like diehard jehadi groups could soon become the most dreaded terrorist organization in the world and if it is not one already,"said Aslam Rehman as he wished his younger brother a very good night.

Exactly a week later on 22nd December, 2000 when two diehard Lashkar-e-Toiba Jihadis stormed and attacked the high security target of India's famed Red Fort in Old Delhi and killed two Indian soldiers and a civilian, it came as a shock to both the Rehman brothers.The historical Red Fort not only houses a strong military garrison, but it is also an interrogation centre and the attack came the day after the Indian government on the occasion of Ramzan extended its current unilateral ceasefire in Kashmir by a month.

"I am afraid that this kind of ISI sponsored attacks and that to inside the heart of India's capital city by the LeT who I believe have also claimed full responsibility for it is definitely not going to get us Kashmir and that is for sure. And General Musharaff must excercise more effective controd over these so called sipahis and soldiers of Allah. Because if it is not done now and these so called Jihadi groups are further encouraged to fight Pakistan's proxy war against India, then I am afraid one day these same very fanatical organizations led by the Mullas will start calling all the shots and they will make Pakistan the epicentre and capital of worldwide terrorism. As it is our country's economy is in shambles and with the Americans breathing down our necks to get hold of Bin Laden and to hand him over to them, we are simply losing whatever little credibility that we have in calling ourselves Pakistan, the so called land of the pure," said a highly agitated Farzana.

"Yes and I think that Farzana Bhabhi is hundred percent right because this sort of so called fidayeen acitivities in the name of Islam by the self styled Mullas is not only giving Pakistan and the entire Muslim world a bad name, but they are also spawning a new breed of both educated and uneducated young Muslims with the lure of big money and a so called guaranteed passport to heaven. And they are doing it by motivating them to voluntarily becoming martyrs and to willingly embrace death. And unfortunately it is the revered Kalimas from the Holy Koran that the Mullas are always quoting to them and which they guarantee and preach will get them this salvation in heaven. But unfortunately this is nothing but a method of Islamic indoctrination and that too without knowing the true indepth meaning of those Kalimas. Salvation in Islam as a true Muslim is through human works of doing good to the people and it is not by killing humans just because they are not Muslims,"said an highly agitatated Samina while reciting loudly in Persian the first Kalima that says that there is no diety other than Allah and that Prophet Mohammed is his servant and messenger.

"Yes and I think Samina is absolutely right. In the Talim-ul-Haq or in the teachings of Islam, the religion of Islam stands on the five main pillars of the Kalima and these are first and foremost the 'Kalima Tayyibah' that Samina has just recited and which every good Muslim must believe in. Then comes the Kalima Shahdat (Testification) or the Sallat' which means to pray or say the namaz five times a day. Therafter comes the 'Kalima Tamjeed '(Glorification of Allah) and the 'Zakaat' which requires the Muslim to contribute and share a percentage of his wealth for the benefit of the poor and the needy. It is followed by the 'Kalima Tauheed' which means believing in the unity of Allah and in the 'Saum' which requires all of us to fast during the holy month of Ramzan. And finally it is the 'Kalima Radhe-Kufr' or the disproving of Kufr and seeking protection from Allah by performing the Haj. And therefore from childhood we had always been taught that Islam is a religion of peace and it is the true and perfect religion which teaches us all the good things about this world and the hereafter.But unfortunately today the word 'Imaam' which actually means firm belief in Allah is being wrongly used by some of our worthy Mullahs and preachers to take revenge on those whom they call 'Kafirs' or the so called non-believers. And that is indeed very sad,"said Aslam Rehman.

And while the two Rehman brothers with their families in Dhaka were enjoying the hospitality of some of the rich and the famous of that crowded city, inside the office of the Tehelka website in New Delhi, the stage was being set to send the Vajpayee led NDA government into a mad tizzy. It was going to be an unprecedented brave and fearless sting operation that would take the wind out of those who were going to be targeted.Having started his career with India Today, Tarun Tejpal the young and dynamic 37 year old journalist son of an army veteran in March 2000 had started 'Tehelka.

com.' It was an online independent news and views channel that focused in bringing home to the general Indian public on how bribery, chicanery, and bum sucking could buy people that mattered. The enterprising young team of Tehelka journalists led by Tarun Tejpal had already exposed the high and the mighty of Indian cricket, when they successfully showed to the people of India and the world as to how match fixing was done purely for monetary games.Cricket was no longer a gentleman's game any more,when India's captain Mohammed Azharuddin together with Ajay Sharma, Ajay Jadeja, Manoj Prabhakar and the team's Physiotherapist Dr Ali Irani were charged with having links with bookies and were banned forever from playing the game. The match fixing scandal was further substantiated recently when the Delhi police intercepted a telephonic conversation between Sanjay Chawla, a big bookie and the South African cricket captain, Hansie Cronje who admitted to throwing away matches during the 1999 Pepsi Cup and who also named Mohammed Azharuddin, Ajay Jadeja and Salim Malik of Pakistan of being very much a part of this bloody racket.

On that afternoon Saturday of 23rd December, 2000 when Shiraz read about Salim Malik's active involvement with the bookies for fixing matches and the attack by the LeT on India's Red Fort on the previous day, he made a few more coded entries in his little red diary of Pakistan's future intentions of using the many militant groups that the country had spawned for stepping up the proxy war against India. And while he was doing that the sad news arrived that Noorjehan, the Malika-e-Tarannum (Melody Queen) of Pakistan had died after a prolonged illness at Karachi. The lady from Kasur whose real name was Allah Wasai and who started her singing career at the age of six and who began life as a child artiste in Hindi films way back in the early thirties had really become a living legend in her lifetime. The great artiste that she was had been suffering from protracted illness and had been undergoing dialysis for the past one year.She was taken to hospital in a serious condition by her son-in-law, the equally well known Pakistani hockey centre-forward Hasan Sardar and where she died at the age of 74. When Shiraz conveyed the sad news of Noor Jehan's passing away to his wife Saira and daughter Sherry, little did he know that in India his foster brother Monty and his own son Paramveer Singh Bajwa whose existence he was not even aware off together with the large film fraternity of Bollywood were also mourning the loss of the great Pakistani star who had started her acting career with Bollywood when she was still a teenager. It was in the film "Khandaan' in 1942 where Noor Jehan as the young heroine and a dashing Pran as the hero made their film debut.

And while the loss of the great artiste was being mourned in the Indian subcontinent, Tarun Tejpal's Tehelka team through a series of well planned out sting operations was getting ready to launch 'Operation Westend' and one that would severely rock the nation. Simultaneously to keep the Kashmir pot boiling, a young suicide car bomber on 25th December, Christmas day literally once again rocked the Headquarters of the Indian Army 15 Corps at Srinagar. Post the Kargil War debacle, Pakistani trained militant groups in order to seek revenge had been progressively stepping up their attacks against the Indian army camps in the Kashmir valley. And since it was the 15 Corps Headquarters that had spearheaded the Kargil operations, it had therefore become the militant's prime target. It first came under attack on12th September, 1999 and then again on 3rd November, 1999 when 10 people including the Indian Defence Public Relations Officer, Major Purshottam was killed. On 19th April, 2000 the first human bomb attack had taken place there and at that time another young militant had driven an explosive laden car right upto the main gate of the heavily guarded Badami Bagh army cantonment, and the massive explosion had resulted in eight persons being killed on the spot and another seventeen injured. A few minutes after the explosion on that Christmas Day, the Union Defence Minister George Fernandes also landed in Srinagar. The explosion at Badami Bagh Cantonment that morning no doubt had brought home to the Defence Minister that though India was observing a unilateral ceasefire, the militancy in the valley was still being actively sponsored by Pakistan through their many proxy outfits like the Jaish-e-Mohammed, the Lashkar-e-Toiba and others. It was also evident to him that it was being actively supported by pro Pakistani sympathizers from within the valley itself. But Mr Fernandes had no idea then that in another two months time and thanks to TTT, Tarun Tejpal's Tehelka, a bigger explosion would soon rock his own Samta Party, the BJP and the RSS supporters of the BJP government.

Meanwhile the increase in militancy in Kashmir and the daring suicide bomb attack at Badami Bagh and that to despite Mr Vajpayee's,the Indian Prime Minister's recent announcement of one month's extension of the unilateral ceaefire in Jammu and Kashmir had got Shiraz in Moscow really worried. According to his own perception it seems that General Musharraf's military regime was still smarting over the failure of 'Operation Badr' in Kargil and this was probably one way of avenging the humiliation that they had so badly suffered both politically and militarily at the hands of the Indians.

CHAPTER-29

Into The New Millennium

And while Pakistan lauded the courage of the Badami Bagh suicide bomber, Monty at the request of Peevee with a suitcase full of hard cash landed in Mumbai from Srinagar and was shocked to see the tension in the faces of some of the top Bollywood stars. The financial capital of India was agog with rumours about the mafia targeting the lucrative film industry. There was a serious threat to Peevee's life also and it had been made by a gang of extortionists who were working for some new overseas based Don and Monty did not want to take any chances. It was only 10 'Petis' and which in Mumbai's underworld parlance amounted to rupees ten lacks and which was not a very big amount keeping in view that big stars were now asking for huge sums and the cost of film production were now running into many many crores of rupees.A few days after the slush money had been paid by Peevee, there was more bad news for the film industry of Bollywood, when Nazim Hassan Rizvi the producer of the yet to be released film that was ironically titled 'Chupke Chupke-Chori Chori (Silently and Stealthily) was nabbed in a secret police operation for allegedly plotting attacks on film stars and diverting mob money into films. The film starring Salman Khan, Preity Zinta and Rani Mukherjee was scheduled for release on the 28th of December 2000, and there was high expectation of it doing well at the box office. According to the police, the main financier of the film was Bharat Shah who was basically a big diamond merchant and therefore, when both Rizvi and Bharat Shah were booked by the Mumbai police under the Maharashtra Control of Organised Crime Act 1999, a lot of eyebrows were raised. But what was even more revealing was the FIR, the first information report that was filed by the police against Rizvi. As per the FIR, Rizvi had not only planned to kill Rakesh Roshan and his handsome young son Hrithik Roshan who was now also a rising star in Bollywood, but he had also threatened Ratan Jain of Venus Music.The police also claimed that the dubious plan also had the backing of gangster Chotta Shakeel, the Dubai based right hand man of Dawood Ibrahim, the Bombay Don who was now living in Karachi. There were also unconfirmed reports that both the Abu Salem gang and the Chota Shakeel gang who were rivals in this murky business of extorting money from the film world and the Bombay builders lobby were also hand in glove with the very people who were suppose to be the guardians of law and order in the state and in the country. It was not even a full year since the actor and director Rrakesh Roshan was targeted by the underworld, when on 21st January 2000 evening he was shot at as he came out of his office in Santa Cruz. Luckily for him the the two shooters were poor shots. One bullet got him on his arm and the other only grazed his chest. But all the same it was an attempt on his life alright.

"I think it is high time Peevee gave up this dangerous and higly unsafe profession of acting in Bollywood films. It is simply not worth it and instead he should join Monty in his export business and which thanks to liberalization is doing fairly well now,"said Reeta over the phone to Shupriya. Reeta had read about the arrest of Nazim Rizvi which had made headlines in some newspapers and she wanted to convey it to Shupriya. However, she was not aware of the so called protection money of ten lacs that Peevee and her husband Monty had paid to the underworld goons who were becoming a real menace in the financial capital of India.

"Maybe he should join Monty in his business, but will he? I don't think he is cut out to do that kind of work. And having made a big name in the tinsel and glamour world of Bollywood, his quitting films at such an young age will not only upset his thousands of fans, but also the producers and financiers who have and still are investing so much money in him. Needless to say that Bollywood and the builders lobby in Mumbai together with some of the more corrupt politicians and policemen of the city have also played an important part in the growth and clout of the underworld. And I guess we have to live with it. And if I am not wrong these so called Mafia gangs today are a convenient conduit for money laundering and for promoting the hawala racket that is flourishing in the country today," said Shupriya while promising to have a word with Peevee at some opportune time.

On that New Year's Eve of 31st December 2000, while Shupriya sat at home and kept worrying about her son's safety and career in the murky world of Bollywood, Shiraz with his entire family was enjoying a long weekend at one of the exclusive dachas outside Moscow. Located at Zhukova, the once exclusive retreat for the members of the mighty Soviet politbureau, the dacha was now a property of a nuveau rich Russian mobster and Mafia leader who had converted it into a mini palace and a resort for the rich and the famous. Later that evening they went for the New Year's Eve Ball that was being held at Tzarskaya Okhota.(Tsar's Hunting Lodge). It was a comparatively new elite restaurant that was located nearby and which primarily catered to the high ranking government officials and ministers, foreign diplomats and ofcourse the nuveau rich Russian mafia leaders who now had millions to throw around. Behind its carved doors and watched by armed security guards who were dressed as Boyars, it was now considered to be one of the most sophisticated hangouts for the rich and the famous from all over the world.Noticing the car parking lot jammed with Mercedes 600's, Lexuses, Jeep Cherokees, Audi's and BMW's, Shiraz could'nt help but remark to his wife Saira that had it not been for Gorbachov, this place from the outside would have probably remained as a nondescript country house for the high and the mighty of the erstwhile leaders of USSR to have their weekly flings. And so very highly rated was the place now that even President Boris Yeltsin took President Jacques Chirac of France for a meal to this very restaurant and that was not very long ago either.

"Well to me it looks that the days of the Romanoff Tsar dynasty and of their Counts and Countesses are back again in Russia," said Saira as she glanced through the big names that were in the rich leather bound visitors book of that restaurant.

"Yes, and the present décor together with the many well dressed middle aged men in traditional tuxedos and with so many lovely young Russian ladies in long designer evening gowns dancing on the floor, it reminds me of the scene from the film 'Dr Zhivago' where the lecherous Count Komarovski makes an indecent pass at the beautiful Lara,' said Shiraz as he cautioned his beautiful daughter Sherry to be careful of the middle aged man who was standing near the bar and who simply kept staring and smiling at her.

"By God, this damn place is even more expensive than Alain Ducasse's restaurant in New York and the Gordon Ramsay in London, and even the Du Palaise Royal in Paris is cheaper than this place," said Tojo as he looked through the beautifully bound menu and the wine card. And a little while later at Shiraz's request, when the band started playing 'Lara's Theme' and before anybody else could approach his beautiful daughter, Shiraz quickly led her to the dance floor and beckoned his son and wife to join them also. With that old nostalgic and haunting music ringing in his ears, it was indeed an evening to remember. And later, when Shiraz requested the band to play that old and fast 1960's Russian super hit song (Naash Coced-Our Neighbour) that had been made popular by the singer Edita Pexha, the stamping of the feet and the clapping of hands had practically everybody on the floor.

And when Shiraz joined the band and he also started singing with them in Russian, everyone too sang in chorus with him.

"By God Dad, I never knew that you could sing so well and that too in Russian," said Sherry as she affectionately hugged her father and requested the band to play her parent's favourite number'OverThe Waves'. And as Shiraz and Saira gracefully guided across the floor doing the traditional waltz, Sherry thought about the day when she with Peevee would visit the place as a lovey dovey couple. She was looking forward to their meeting in Moscow during the coming spring season, and the trendy restaurant being a liitle away from the city, would be an ideal and comparatively a much safer place for the love birds to pass their time in each other's company thought she. And while she was looking at the photograph very secretively of her sweetheart that was on her mobile phone, there was a miss call. On checking the number there was a smile on her face as she quickly made her way to the ladies wash room to ring the caller back. "A very very happy New Year to you my love," said Peevee as he loudly smacked the the phone with his lips a couple of times.

"Thank you my love and I also wish you and your family a very happy and prosperous New Year too. And though here in Moscow we still have another two and a half hours to usher in the year 2001, you must be already celebrating it. And I was just thinking of you only, when the miss call came. We as a complete family are celebrating the occasion at one of the new exclusive restaurants which is outside the city and I am missing you terribly my darling. My brother Tojo who is now a professional golfer also arrived from California two days ago to be with us on this festive occasion. But where and how are you ushering in the New Year?' asked Sherry as she too smacked the phone with her lips.

"Well, you will be surprised if I tell you that I am presently resting in my caravan inside Mumbai's Film City. The film director has given us a half an hour break from the shooting schedule and that was only because he was not very happy with the lighting of the set. And therefore my ushering in the new millennium will probably be on the sets tonight," said Peevee when the clapper boy came to inform him that the cameraman and the director were ready to take the next shot.

"Will call you again tomorrow my darling and let us hope that the year 2001 brings you and your family great joy and happiness too," added Peevee as he once again gave the mobile phone a good and loud smack and instructed his makeup man to add a little more gel to his hair.

The first day of January 2001 was the first day in the first year of the 21st Century and also that of the 3rd millennium, and Peevee sincerely hoped that it would be lucky for him, his family and for his beautiful Sherry too. It was already morning on that New Year's Day, when the unit finally packed up from the studio and soon thereafter Peevee first called up his father and mother in New Delhi and then followed it up with a call to his Mom Number 2 in Moscow to wish all of them a very happy New Year.

On that New Year's Day, Calcutta also became Kolkata. Calcutta was the anglicized name that was given by the British Raj to what was then British India'a capital city. But for the Bengali Moshai it was always Kolkata and the ruling Communist Party Marxist government in West Bengal felt that the name change for Calcutta like that from Bombay to Mumbai and Madras to Chennai was long overdue.Next day morning Reeta too was not very surprised to see the name change of the capital of West Bengal. But what caught her immediate attention was the write up about the elaborate preparations that were being made for the Maha Kumbh Mela at Allahabad. And though she was a Punjabi Hindu and her husband a Sikh, nevertheless she very lovingly said to Monty.

"You know darling this is one historic event that we must not miss, because as per the planetary configuration January 2001 is a very auspicious month in this year's Hindu calendar and the Maha Kumbh only comes once in 144 years."

"Alright if you so desire we will go, but only for a day or two to have a dip at the Sangam, the confluence of the two holy rivers Ganga and Yamuna and I hope it will clean our body and soul for good,"said Monty somewhat casually as he narrated to Reeta the origin and importance of this great Hindu festival. "I may be a Sikh but I do believe that the informal assembly of ascetics and yogis that used to take place at the Kumbh Mela served as a kind of Hindu parliament. And in the 7th Century even Hueng-Tsang the renowned Chinese Buddhist traveler attended the fair with Emperor Harshavardhan. However, my only request is that we must finish the bathing ritual well before sunrise and though I know that it will be very cold this time of the year, but with millions of people from all walks of life waiting to take a dip at sunrise I am afraid the water will then get highly polluted and we cant take a chance on that,"said Monty.

"Fair enough and in that case let us make it to the fair on the auspicious day of Paush Purnima which falls on 9th January and it is also happens to be a Tuesday, my weekly fasting day," said Reeta.

Though the two day trip to the Maha Kumbh Mela at Allahabad by road for Monty and Reeta was no doubt a bit tiring, but none the less it was enjoyable also as people from all walks of life and from all parts of India mingled with each other to share their joys and sorrows. It was like a mini India and the best part was that everybody was so well disciplined for a change. The Indian and the Uttar Pradesh government as the organizers had no doubt done a tremendous and splendid job, and by the time the six week mela ended, no less than 60 million people had a dip in the holy river and there was no major untoward incident whatsoever.

And on that 9th of January 2001 evening at the Maha Kumbh Mela, while Reeta and Monty had kept their fingers crossed and prayed that there should be no repetition of what had happened during their tragic Amarnath yatra, far away at a place near Peshawar, the former Pakistan Army Chief Aslam Beg with the former head of the ISI, Lt General Hamid Gul were attending the Darul Uloom Haqquaina Islamic Conference. At that meeting that was being attended by 300 Muslim leaders who were representing various Islamic groups, it was unanimously agreed and declared that it was the religious duty of Muslims all over the world to protect the Taliban government in Afghanistan and the Saudi dissident Osama bin Laden, the man that the Taliban was hosting as a revered guest and whom they considered as a great and well respected Muslim leader and warrior. On the very next day, when Arif Rehman Khan rang up his son-in-law Shiraz in Moscow and in the course of general conversation with him casually mentioned about the large gathering of leading Muslim clerics at the Islamic conference near Peshawar, and also that of the presence of some of the top retired army brass that included General Aslam Beg, the ex Pakistan army chief and Lt General Hamid Gul the ex DG ISI at that conference, it did not come as a surprise to Shiraz. But it definitely was a cause of worry because both Aslam Beg and Hamid Gul during their tenure as army chief and as DGISI had strongly advocated and had used a large number of Muslim mercenary Jehadis from different Muslim countries to fight their proxy war in Kashmir and which also got a big boost during their tenures as the army chief and as the DGISI respectively.

General Mirza Aslam Beg was born on 2nd August, 1931 at Azamgarh in the Indian state of Uttar Pradesh where his father was a small town lawyer. He was commissioned into the Baluch Regiment in August 1952. As a young officer he was selected for the SSG, the Special Service Group of the Pakistan army and did his specialized commando training in the United States. As a young major in 1960, he commanded an SSG company that was instrumental in ousting the Nawab of Dir from his princely state in the North West Frontier Province. And this was primarily because of the defiance and belligerence that was being shown by the Nawab against Field Marshall Ayub Khan's' martial law government. He took over as army chief after General Zia-ul-Haq's death in 1988 and like Lt General Hamid Gul he too was always pro Taliban. He was also one of the main architects of Pakistan's strategy of 'strategic depth' which meant that in case of a war with India, the tribals areas in the NWFP and neghbouring Afghanistan would serve as a safe fall back position for the Pakistan army. He was the army chief during the time when Pakistan's top nuclear scientist Dr AQ Khan was blatantly selling nuclear secrets to Iran, Libya and North Korea, and according to one reliable source the General was also very keen to give to Iran, Pakistan's nuclear expertise in exchange for Iranian oil.

And as far as Lt General Hamid Gul was concerned, he as the DGISI after the withdrawal of the Soviets from Afghanistan was one of the main architects in getting Mullah Omar and his Taliban to power in Afghanistan. Born on 20th November 1936 to Mohammed Khan an ethnic Pathan from Sargodha, Hamid Gul was commissioned into the 19th Lancers, an armoured regiment in 1958. As General Zia-ul-Haq's blue eyed boy he commanded the prestigious Pakistan 1st Armoured Division and as Corps commander Multan Corps conducted Exercise Zarb-e-Momin in the winter of 1989 and which was the biggest Pakistan Armed Forces show of military strength after the 1971 debacle. During his tenure as the ISI Chief in 1988, General Gul successfully gathered a large number of right wing politicians and was instrumental in creating the IJI, the Islami Jamhoori Ittehad party under Nawaz Sharif to oppose the left leaning liberal Pakistan Peoples Party of Benazir Bhutto. He also actively backed the Khalistan terrorism in the Indian Punjab and the on going insurgency movement in Kashmir by giving the plea that this was the one and only way to preempt a fresh threat by India to violate Pakistan's territorial integrity. On Benazir Bhutto's taking office as Prime Minister in December 1988, and fearing that the diehard ISI boss could well one day upset her applecart, she promptly had him posted as the Multan Corps Commander. And when the new Pakistan Army Chief Asif Nawaz in August 1991 posted him as the DG Heavy Industries at Taxila and he flatly refused, he was quietly retired from the army. Shiraz was also aware that in 1993, the outspoken and retired General Hamid Gul had personally met Osama Bin Laden and the General was of the firm view that Osama was not a terrorist. Hamid Gul was also thoroughly disillusioned, when America not only turned its back on Afghanistan after the Soviets withdrew from there, but it also began punishing Pakistan with economic and military sanctions for going ahead with its secret nuclear weapons program. So much so that the ex ISI chief openly declared that the Muslim world must stand united to confront the US in their so called war on terrorism and which according to him was nothing less than a war against Muslims. He even advocated to the Muslim world to destroy Americans wherever its troops were trapped on Muslim soil.

Seeing the manner in which some of the retired Pakistani senior officers had blatantly started hobnobbing with fundamentalist Muslim religious leaders, Shiraz was apprehensive that one day the seeds of Islamization that had been sown by the late President General Zia-ul-Haq in the Pakistan armed forces may well spell disaster for those who still took pride in wearing their khaki military uniform, and who earnestly desired that the army should remain truly apolitical. To him the increase in terrorist suicide attacks on innocent Hindu labourers and pilgrims and on army camps inside Kashmir, together with the recent audacious attack on Delhi's Red Fort were clear indications that the Musharraf government and the Pakistan ISI were hand in glove with these so called Jehadi groups who were bent upon taking the proxy war deep inside Indian territory. Fearing that if such daring attacks like that on the Red Fort with suicide squads were allowed to carry on unabated in the future, and that it could well trigger off another Indo-Pak conflict, Shiraz was petrified about the consequences. Moreover, with both sides now having nuclear weapons it would be simply disastrous. And having heard about the sincere efforts that were being made by the Balusa Group to foster better Indo-Pak relations, he initially thought of contacting them.

The Balusa group was set up on the initiative of a Muslim brother and sister team who were originally from the Nizam's state of Hyderabad in India and and who after migrating to Pakistan with their parents at partition were now very influential American citizens, and their sincere efforts to promote genuine peace and harmony between Pakistan and India was being lauded both by the United States and the United Nations. The formation of the group was the brainchild of Dr Shirin-Tahir Kheli, a renowned political scientist at John Hopkins University and her brother Toufiq Siddiqi and it comprised of eminent Pakistani and Indian citizens from various professional fields. Nominated by PresidentGeorge Bush (Sr), Dr Shirin had also served as the Alternate Rpresentative of the US for Special Political Affairs in the United Nations from 1990 to 1993 and that to in the rank of an Ambassador. Named after two adjoining villages in the Punjab Province of Pakistan, the Balusa Group had held its first meeting in Singapore in 1998 and thereafter at Bellagio in Italy in 1999 and the latest one was held in Chennai only two months ago in November 2000. The much married lady whose father had served as a scientist in Hyderabad's Osmania University was born on 24th August 1944 and had earned her PhD degree from the University of Pennsylvania in 1972, whereas her brother Toufik Siddiqi became an active environmentalist and an energy expert. With active support from the United Nations Development Programme and the Rockefeller Foundation, the brother and sister team had brought together a group of emiment and influential Pakistanis and Indians that included army generals, politicians, bureaucrats, academicians and others to discuss ways and means to bring in 'sense and direction' to the Indo-Pakistan relationship that had further deteriorated after the 1999 Kargil War. It was no doubt a well meaning Track II initiative to get India and Pakistan to once again sit across the table and resolve all their outstanding issues amicably, honestly and with a sense of purpose so as to usher in a lasting peace in the troubled subcontinent. The group also emphasisied the futility and the grave risks of militarization, which was not only highly detrimental for the economic progress and well being of both the countries, but could also spelt disaster since both the nations were now equipped with deadly nuclear weapons.

On going through the list of eminent people who were part of the Balusa Group, when Shiraz found that Major General Mahmud Ali Durrani of Pakistan and Lt General Satish Nambiar from the Indian Army were also active members,he gave up the idea of getting in touch with the group. Moreover, he also felt that as a serving Pakistani diplomat it would not only be unethical on his part to give his opinion and advice to this organization independently and that too without informing his own government, but it could also spell great danger to him and his family if his true identity was ever unearthed. Major General Durrani an armoured corps officer from 25th Cavalry and an ethnic Pashtun had retired in 1998 after holding the post of Chairman Pakistan Ordnance Factories Board for a record term of six years. He was Pakistan's Defence Attache in Washington from 1977 to 1982 and had also served as the Military Secretary to President Zia-ul-Haq prior to his taking over command of the Multan based prestigious Pakistan 1st Armoured Division. It was during his command that the trials for the American Abrahms tank took place at Bhawalpur and on that very evening itself when General Zia and other senior Pakistani generals died in that mysterious aircrash, a finger of suspicion was pointed at him also. With the old air crash controversary of who could have done it still in the air, Shiraz did not want to get involved with the Pakistani army general who though he was keen that Pakistan under General Musharraf should take the intiative in opening peace talks with India, however his alleged insistence with President Zia to witness the American tank trials at Bhawalpur was still looked upon with mistrust. And as far as Lt General Satish Nambiar of the Indian army was concerned and though the general officer was eight years senior to Shiraz in service, they had not only served together in the same Indian Division, but they had also done a few army courses together and Shiraz was apprehensive that the gentleman may recognize him. The Bombay born and an alumnus of St Xavier's College Mumbai, General Nambiar was commissioned into the famous Mahratta Light Infantry in Decenber 1957 and was decorated with the Veer Chakra during the 1971 Bangladesh War. The General Officer had also served with distinction as Director General of Military Operations at Army Headquarters and in that capacity had led two important defence delegations for discussions with his Pakistani counterparts. In the joint meeting that were held in April 1991 at New Delhi, he negotiated an agreement on the exchange of information between the two countries on the conduct of military exercises and aircraft flights in the proximity of the border, as also communications between naval vessels at sea. And in September 1991 at Islamabad, he negotiated an end to hostile actions between the two countries on the Line of Control in the Poonch Sector. He was appointed by the Government of India as the first Force Commander and the Head of Mission of the UN forces in former Yugoslavia and had the distinction of setting up the Mission under most difficult conditions. On 31 August 1994 he retired from the Indian army as the Deputy Chief of the Army Staff.

On 15th of January 2001, while the units and formations of the Indian army that were deployed in Jammu and Kashmir were celebrating their 52nd Army Day with a Barakhana, thousands of Kashmiris in that state on that very day also voted to elect their candidates in the first ever local panchayati elections that were being held after a lapse of 23 years. And with the elections to the 125 village councils being conducted despite the threat by Islamic militants to boycott it, it was quite evident that the locals were fed up of violence and they genuinely wanted peace. It was also the holy month of Ramzan and the extended ceasefire that had been unilaterally declared by India was it seems welcomed by the majority of Kashmiris in the valley. And on that very day evening, when Shiraz also heard on the BBC that Mr Vajpayee the Indian Prime Minister had met Mr Li Peng, the visiiting Chairman of China's National People's Congress and that both leaders had made substantial progress while discussing the old border dispute, it made him very happy indeed. But his wife Saira was even happier, when she also learnt on that very day that the NAB, the National Accountability Bureau in Pakistan had actually published a list off Pakistan's 44 biggest crooks and thieves. It was like a mini who is who of Pakistan because most of them were big politicians or their immediate relations, high ranking bureaucrats, top notch bankers, politically well connected businessman and also a few from the Pakistan armed forces The list also had the names of Benazir Bhutto, her husband Asif Ali Zardari, retired Admiral Manzoor Ul Haq, the former Paksitani Naval Chief and retired Major General Shujat Bukhari But the only sore point was that though arrest warrants had been issued against all of them, but most of were nowhere to be found and were absconding.

"Mark my words all this is simply hogwash and ultimately all these people who have been systematically looting the country will not only go scotfree, but they and their families will also keep enjoying this ill gotten wealth for the next couple of generations," said Shiraz with a ceratin amount of sarcasm.

"Well let us hope not, or else the credibility of our General Musharaff our country's CEO will take a big beating," said Saira. But Shiraz's joy was however short lived, when on the very next day of 16th January in a dare devil suicide attack, six armed LeT militants stormed the heavily guarded Srinagar airport at Badgam. It took place soon after mid-noon and as a result of which 11 persons including the six militants, three policemen from the CRPF, the Central Reserve Police Force that was on duty guarding the airport and two innocent civilians had been killed, and eight CRPF personnel and one Kashmiri policeman had been badly wounded. The six diehard Lashkar-e-Toiba militants wearing Indian army uniforms having earlier hijacked a jeep of the State Forest Corporation confidently drove up to the main gate of the airport. And on being challenged, they simply alighted and with their automatic weapons and grenades attacked the CRPF post that was guarding the gate. Then a big firefight followed, and while the militants were being engaged, messages were flashed inside the main terminal for everybody to remain within. And as a result of which the main airport building was immediately sealed off. Luckily all the passengers who had arrived earlier by the two incomimg flights had already left the airport and the passengers who were waiting to depart were also in the process of boarding their respective aircrafts. Realising the imminent danger to the two passenger aircrafts, the control tower immediately asked the two pilots to take off. Unknown to Shiraz, his foster brother Monty who had come on a business trip to Srinagar two days earlier had checked in only a couple of minutes earlier for his return flight to Delhi. And it was all thanks to the presence of mind of the airport security chief Ali Mohammed who personally supervised the security arrangements inside the terminal building while the fighting outside was still going on that saved Monty's life and that of a few others who were still at the check in counters at that moment of time. Late that afternoon, when Monty arrived in Delhi and told his wife Reeta about his narrow escape, Reeta immediately drove to the Shri Guru Singh Sabha Gurudwara in Defence Colony and prayed for the well being of her beloved husband. Because this was not the first time, but the fifth time that Monty had escaped death by a whisker. That day was also a Tuesday and a day of fasting for her. Later that evening, when Reeta rang up Shupriya in Moscow and Peevee in Mumbai and told them about Monty's providential escape, they too said a prayer and wondered whether the conflict for Kashmir will ever end.

Four days later on 20th January as Shupriya listened to the inaugural speech of America's 43rd President she was not very impressed. This was the second time in American history that the son of a preceding President had occupied the White House. The first time was when John Quincy Adams became the 6th President of the United States. Born on 6th July, 1946 George Walker Bush who had earlier served as the 46th Governor of Texas and who after his marriage to Laura Welch in 1977 unsuccesfully ran for the House of Representatives had won his Presidential election by a whisker, when he defeated his rival AL Gore the Democratic candidate by just a handful of electoral votes. It was actually 271 to Gore's 266. And with the new millennium that had technically just begun, George W Bush had also created history. He had become the first and only American President with an MBA from Harward to preside over the destiny of the world's most powerful nation. The man who once fondly loved his alcohol and in 1976 before his marriage was arrested for driving under its influence and for which his driving license was suspended, was now a changed man. Thanks to his wife Laura he gave up drinking in 1986. With his grandfather Prescott Bush having served as a Senator from Connecticut, and his father George H. W. Bush having served both as Vice President and President of the United States, and one brother named Jeb still serving as the Governor of Florida, it looked as if politics ran in the Bush family's blood. Nonetheless the 55 year old Texan who portrayed himself as a compassionate conservative and who campaigned on issues like cutting taxes, improving education, helping the minorities and increasing the size of the United States Armed Forces, did not quite realize that somewhere in the high mountain caves of Afghanistan the elusive Al Qaida leader Osama Bin Laden with his henchmen was planning a deadly war on American soil.

When the new President appointed General Colin Arthur Powell as America's first coloured African-American Secretary of State, it was welcomed by the majority of Americans. The retired Commander-in-Chief of the US Armed Forces had not only headed the Joint Chiefs of Staff Committee, but had also served as National Security Advisor during his distinguished service. But on that historic inauguration day General Powell too did not realize that America's deadly enemy the Al-Qaida was actually lurking in his own backyard.

Born on 5th April, 1937 in Harlem in the New York City Borough of Manhattan, Colin Powell who as a young school boy worked in a shop to support his parents had not only earned a bachelor's degree in geology from City College New York, but also an MBA from George Washington University before joining the army as an officer. While serving as a young Captain in Vietnam from 1962 to 1965, he was wounded while out on a patrol when he stepped on a punji stake. During his second tenure in Vietnam as a young Major and while on staff of the 23rd Infantry Division in 1968, when the infamous massacre of Vietnamese civilians at My Lai took place, he felt bad no doubt, but was not very shocked by the incident. In early 1980, when Powell was serving in Fort Carson, Colorado he had a serious clash with his superior General John Hudacheck and even though the General in Powell's efficiency evaluation report had written that Powell was a poor leader who should not be promoted, nonetheless the coloured American who was an officer and a gentleman ultimately proved his superior wrong. The man who held the coveted post of Chairman Joint Chiefs of Staff during the 1990-1991 Gulf War probably never thought that America as the only world power could ever be terrorized.

CHAPTER-30

The Lid is Blown

Soon after the inauguration, while the new President of America and his new Secretary of State seriously deliberated on the subject of how to oust President Saddam and prevent Iraq from becoming a nuclear power, and India was getting ready to celebrate her 51st Republic day, the news arrived that some of the major players in the Bofors payoff scandal had been summoned and they were scheduled to soon appear in courts both at Kuala Lampur and in New Delhi.

Octavio Quattrocchi, the slimy Italian wheeler dealer and an old friend of the Gandhi family was the key man who had primarily brokered the scandalous Bofors gun deal and he was taken completely by surprise, when on 20th December 2000, at around 10.30 a.m. the Kuala Lumpur police knocked on the door of his plush 10th floor office on Jalan Raja Chulan. The man who had successfully evaded arrest since he with his family like a thief fled India on the night of 29th July, 1993, was somewhat caught off guard that morning when the Malayasian police arrived at his office doorstep. And he also looked somewhat shaken and very much perturbed when he was produced first before a magistrate and later in the Malaysian Sessions Court. He had fled India soon after his appeals in Switzerland to disallow Indian investigators to access his Swiss bank accounts were struck down by the Swiss Federal court. Though in February 1999, the then government in India headed by Mr Deve Gowda did send a two member CBI team to Kuala Lumpur with an arrest warrant against the elusive Italian, but they had returned empty handed. And thereafter the CBI had made little or no headway till such time a charge sheet against the Italian and others, who had made the illgotten money on the Bofors deal was filed in a Delhi Court on 22nd October, 1999. Infact it was because of the contempt that Quattrocchi.had shown towards the apex court in India, and also the fact that the Indian Prime Minister Mr Vajpayee was soon to visit Malaysia, that probably prompted the Malaysian authorities to book the Italian. Though the Italian had been granted bail, but his passport had been impounded. On the evening of 22nd of January 2001, after Quattrocchi was produced before a Malaysian court in Kuala Lumpur and the three globe trotting Hinduja brothers who were now naturalized citizens of foreign lands were also produced in the Court of Special Judge Ajit Bharihoke in Delhi on the same day, Monty called on his old trusted journalist friend Unnikrishnan at the Press Club. Monty wanted to find out a little more about the possibility of the wily and shrewd Italian being extradited to India to face trial, and whether all the major players in the long standing 14 year old Bofors corruption case would finally be indicted and lawfully punished.

"I am afraid it is still to to early to tell what will be the final outcome of this old damn sordid drama, but my gut feeling is that it will be the same old story of being so near and yet so far. Though Mr P C Sharma the Special Director CBI and Mr RK Raghavan Director CBI together with Veena Sikri our High Commissioner in Malaysia are leading the Indian charge in the Malaysian capital, but it is not going to be all that simple. Firstly because India does not have a formal extradition treaty with Malaysia, and secondly because the Congress Party President Mrs Sonia Gandhi and her party leaders who though they are now in the opposition will go all out to ensure that not even the ghost of Mr Quattrocchi ever enters India again. Because if he does come back and spills the beans then I am afraid it will be a total disaster not only for the grand old party, but also for the entire Gandhi family. And mind you even after the hearing in the Malaysian court today, the Italian not only denounced publicly that the legal proceedings against him were being politically motivated, but he even openly and categorically stated to the press and to the waiting media that the whole idea was to compromise the political career of his one time friend and the Congress (I) President Sonia Gandhi. Not to be left behind, the Congress Party leaders too have already started accusing the Vajpayee government of vindictiveness and of trying to settle scores with their leader Sonia who was a widow. But everybody also knows about Rajiv and Sonia Gandhi's close relationship with the Quattrocchi family when Rajiv was the Prime Minister of the country, but nobody it seems is keen to open the can of worms again,"said Unni with the usual mischievous smile on his face.

"Well in that case if it turns out to be a no show once again by Mr Quattrocchi, then all I will have to say is that the CBI who today is taking so much credit for this latest development will once again cut a very sorry figure. As it is the majority of the Indians today have little or no faith in the CBI because they only function at the whims and fancies of the political leaders in power and who are also their masters. And mind you it's been a good 14 years when the first salvo was fired by the Swedish press on this shameless scandal and everytime our CBI sleuths gets anyway closer to the real target, either the CBI investigating team is conveniently changed, or the learned judge is transferred," said Monty with a sarcastic grin on his face as Unni gifted him with two passes to witness the forthcoming Republic Day Parade from the press gallery.

On the morning of 26th of January 2001, while the Indian army proudly displayed their military might at the traditional annual Republic Day parade in New Delhi where the President of Algeria, Abdulaziz Bouteflika was the chief guest, far away in the desolate Kutch region of western India a massive earthquake that measured a massive 7.7 on the Richter scale devasted the area. The worst hit areas were the four urban centres of Bhuj, Anjar, Bachau and Rapar where young school children who had gathered that morning inside their respective school buildings to celebrate the Republic Day. And as a result of which large number of them had died. So severe was the earthquake that the shock waves were felt even in faraway Mumbai, Delhi and beyond.

It was around a little after 8.45 that morning, while Peevee was having his bath when he literally felt the ground shaking under his feet and the big French window panes in his Bandra flat started rattling. Later that afternoon, when the television channels showed the terrible destruction that the colossal earthquake had caused, Peevee immediately appealed to all his colleagues and friends in Bollywood to help in whatever manner they could. The very next day, when the banks opened, Peevee very thoughtfully sent a bank draft of Rupees10 lacs but without mentioning his name and status to Anil Mukim the concerned District Collector.This was one of the two most deadly earthquakes to strike India in its recorded history. Monty and Reeta who on that morning were witnessing the impressive Republic Day parade by the Indian armed forces on Rajpath had no idea about the terrible tragedy that had struck the people of Kutch and Gujrat. Not only the dead ran into many thousands, but some hamlets and villages in that region had also been completely obliterated from the face of the earth. On that afternoon after they came to know about the terrible tragedy, both Monty and Reeta.joined a group of concerned citizens who were mostly retired army officers and their wives from Defence Colony. And for the next couple of days they with a few big big trucks in tow went from door to door and from shop to shop collecting blankets, tarpaulins, bedsheets, clothes, dry rations and whatever else they could for the grief stricken and homeless people of Kutch.

A day or two later sitting in his embassy office in Moscow, when Shiraz saw on the big television screen the vast destruction and damage that the massive earthquake had caused, he really felt bad and he therefore sent a letter of condolence to the Indian Ambassador. He was however not aware that the Musharraf government in Pakistan with the help from the Balusa Group was already in the process of opening the track II Channel with Mr Vajpayee's government in Delhi. And on 30th January, 2001 when BBC reported that Pakistan had offered a helping hand to the victims of the devastating earthquake in India and it was followed by an unprecedented five minute telephone call on 2nd February by General Musharaff to Mr Vajpayee to offer his condolences and Pakistan's help in providing emergency aid to the survivors of the Gujrat earthquake, Shiraz thought it was a good statesman like gesture by the Pakistan CEO. But a fortnight later on 15th Febuary, when four Kashmiri stone throwing demonstrators were killed by the Jammu and Kashmir police at a place called Haigam which was 40 km north of Srinagar, and as a result of which the Kashmiri separatists protested violently, it sparked of another week of bloody riots in the valley. The demonstrators were protesting against the death of a Kashmiri while in police custody. And later during that week when five policemen from the Koker Nag police station were ambushed and killed by militants, it was back to square one again. And though the Indian government had once again extended the ceasefire in Kashmir by another three months, but Pakistan and the ISI it seemed were bent upon in keeping the Kashmir pot boiling all the time. Keeping in mind Musharraf's famous words earlier that Pakistan would bleed India to death over Kashmir; Shiraz wondered whether Musharaff's telephone call to Vajpayee and his offer of help to India was simply a publicity gimmick and a ploy to keep the Americans happy. The new Bush government had already started putting more pressure on Pakistan to stop flirting with the Taliban government in Afghanistan and to help America in getting them the ever illusive Mr Osama Bin Laden and who according to the Americans was the mastermind behind the American embassy bombings in Africa and the more recent attack on the U.S.S. Cole in Yemen.

It was also during that month of February 2001 that the two men intrepid Tehelka team comprising of Aniruddha Bahal and Mathew Samuel under the expert guidance of their chief Tarun Tejpal had in complete secrecy kept editing and re-editing the mass of visual and audio tapes that both the reporters had so daringly filmed and recorded for the website channel. It was an unprecedented major sting operation and a journalistic investigation par excellence that would soon shake the Vajpayee government by its roots. The primary objective of this massive sting operation was to convey to the people of India of how deep and dangerous the cancer of corruption at all government levels had reached, and specially so in the Ministry of Defence who were suppose to be the guardians of India's security. And while the Tehelka Investigative team that Tarun Tejpal had given the naughty acronym of 'TIT' was getting ready to blow the whistle in India, the FBI in the United States had finally managed to get hold of one of their their dangerous moles. The clever spy had been for years together passing valuable and high classified information first to the KGB and then to its successor in Russia and the man was also doing it purely for monetary gains. Robert Hansen, the fifty six year old Chicago born American of mixed Danish-Polish and German descent who spied for Soviet and Russian intelligence services for 22 years starting from 1979 was finally arrested on 18th February, 2001 from a park that was near his home in the suburb of Vienna in the State of Virginia while he was in the act of placing a package of highly classified documents at a pre-arranged dead drop. But by then he had already amassed a huge fortune that amounted to nearly 1.5 billion dollars both in cash and in diamonds. And this activity according to some experts was one of the biggest intelligence disasters in US history and it all started in 1979, when Hansen approached the then Soviet KGB head in Washington D.C. and offered his services. His most important leak of information was the betrayal of Dmitri Polyakov whose code name was 'TOPHAT'. Dmitri was a very important CIA informant for twenty long years and was executed by the Soviets in 1988.

However it was only two days later on the 20th of February that the Americans and the world came to know about Hansen's arrest. That evening, when Shiraz learnt about Hansen's spying activities and saw his photograph and that of his wife and six children on the TV screen, he literally had goose pimples. Though he had not really spied for India, but the very fact what could happen to him, his wife and children if he was ever unmasked, now had him unduly worried.

Using the codename of 'Ramon Garcia' with the Soviets and the Russians, Hansen very cleverly had never revealed his true identity and profession ever to his Russian handlers. And it was only in November 2000, when the FBI by paying a former Russian KGB agent who was now a successful businessman the staggering sum of 7 million dollars and with a promise to give him and his family a new identity in the United States that the American sleuths finally got a lead to Hansen. On that day the former

KGB agent had handed over to the FBI the huge bulky file that contained the mole's correspondence with the KGB from 1985 to 1991. The package also contained some computer floppy disks and also an audio tape of a 21 July 1988 conversation between the mole and the KGB agent. With the mole always being referred to only as Ramon Garcia in the tape, the FBI first thought that it was probably the codename of Brian Kelly, a CIA operative who was also under surveillance. But when they played that tape again and it did not match with Kelly's voice, the FBI was once again in a fix. However, one FBI agent Michael Waguespack who had worked with Hansen earlier and who also had listened to that tape did recognize the voice as fairly familiar, but he could not identify or remember whose voice it was. Then while rifling through the files, when the FBI sleuths found notes of the mole using a familiar General George S Patton quote about 'the purple pissing Japanese,' the FBI analyst Robert King remembered that Robert Hansen had often used that same quote also. And while listening to the tape again, when Waguespack confirmed that it was none other than Hansen's voice, the game for Hansen was finally up. And on that 18th of February 2001, when Hansen with a sealed garbage bag full of classified documents was in the process of taping it to the dead drop which was on the under side of a wooden footbridge that ran over a small creek in his home town of Vienna, the FBI sleuths pounced on him and caught him red handed. The American spy with an MBA in accounting and information sytems and who earlier wanted to become a dentist had by his actions betrayed the very agency and the country that he was suppose to protect. At the same time he had also taken some teeth off the FBI, the very organization that was required to defend the nation. Hansen in his many years of spying had unmasked a large number of Russian moles who too had been making quite a few bucks from the American CIA.

And while the FBI was rejoicing in finally having nabbed Hansen, Saddam the Iraqi strongman and his military advisers while reacting to the deadly bombing of Baghdad that was carried out by the British and American pilots at around 20.30 hours Baghdad time on 16th February pledged to fight on to victory against the United States. On that evening, while President Bush who had earlier authorized the strike was on a state visit to Mexico, 24 aircrafts from both the countries had targeted the five air defence centres south of the Iraqi capital and it was done to ensure that the allied aircrafts patrolling the southern no-fly zone were safe from Iraqi anti-aircraft fire. Terming the raid as a Zionist plot, Saddam Hussein it seems was once again preparing to flex his muscles. Since this was the first raid in two years and that to without any concrete provocation, Shiraz was the view that come what may, the Americans and the British it seems were determined to get rid off Saddam and his coterie. But he also feared that such kind of unilateral air attacks against an oil rich and virtually landlocked defenceless Muslim country and that too on a holy Friday and which resulted in the deaths of innocent men, women and children could only lead to more bitterness between the Catholic and the Muslim world. And with Islamic terrorism on the rise, that could be really dangerous.

Chapter-31

Expose Extraordinaire

By the first week of March 2001, Mr Tarun Tejpal's team that had only a year earlier took the pads and the abdomen guards completely off some of India's top cricketers and exposed the myth that cricket was no longer a gentleman's game, it was now getting ready to take the pants off some of India's top ranking politicians, high ranking defence officers and a few others for whom even a bottle of rare whisky or a good looking whore in bed was good enough to sell this country. 13th of March happened to be a Tuesday, an auspicious day for Hindus all over the world and a day when a large number of Hindus also keep a fast. But for Mr Vajpayee's government and for his saffron friends it was going to be a day of reckoning. From early that morning as telephones jingled in the houses of some retired senior army officers, a few retired senior bureaucrats and those who mattered in the media and with invitations to all of them to be present for an exclusive audio-visual presentation at 1.30 PM at the historic ballroom of the Hotel Imperial in Connaught Place, nobody was aware of the explosive bombshell that would stun the Indians and the world that day. It was at the same very venue where in June 1947, fifty four years ago the Muslim League led by Mr Jinnah held its last historic meeting in the capital, and where a group of angry Khaskars who were opposed to the partition of the country attacked and nearly killed Mr Jinnah. And it was now the turn of the TIT, Tarun Tejpal'sTehelka that would attack the Vajpayee government for sleaze and corruption and open the can of worms for the NDA government.

Unnikrishnan the veteran correspondent who knew the potential of Mr Tarun Tejpal the former Managing Editor of the Outlook magazine and that of Mr Aniruddha Bahal who was also with Outlook earlier and who had exposed the Indian cricketers for match fixing, immediately contacted Monty and asked him to be at the Imperial hotel latest by I.P.M that afternoon. And it was at around 12.45 in the afternoon, when Monty joined Unni for a chilled beer at the famous 'Patiala Peg' bar. That afternoon the hotel was bustling with unusual acivity as the large number of important invitees including some politicians kept arriving one after the other.

"I think we are in for something very sensational and the venue too I think is perfect. But the best part is that nobody including your's truly knows what it is all about," said Unni while ordering a chilled Kingfisher beer for Monty and another large Beefeater Gin with bitters for himself.

"Well the manner in which most of the people including the many 'Netas' and media are heading towards the ballroom, I think we should immediately after this drink make a quick move from here so that we too can occupy ring side seats for the Tarun Tejpal's grand show," said Monty as the waiter very carefully poured the rest of the chilled beer into his crested beer mug.And it was only at around 1.30, when the tapes finally began to roll and all the sleazy characters turn by turn came up on the big wide screen, that the grand expose with the codename of 'Operation West End' had everbody glued to their seats. It not only stunned the audience in the ballroom, but also the millions of Indians who saw it live on their television screens that day. Sitting in that historic ballroom the faces of quite a few of the invities who considered themselves as VIP's also went ashen as the well edited journalistic true story that had no trace whatsoever of politics slowly unfolded itself. It not only highlighted how deep corruption, nepotism, greed and decay at all levels had contaminated the system, but it also brought out how easy it was to breach security and film those very people who were primarily responsible for the country's security. It also brought out the fact that there was big money being made not only by the middleman, but also by the political parties, the political leaders and their henchmen. The fictitious hand held thermal camera that was christened 'Lepak' by the enterprising Bahal and Mathew team and which was an item that the Ministry of Defence was looking out for in order to enhance India's night fighting and reconnaissance capabilities had not only opened the eyes of the common man to the level of corruption that some Indians in authority could stoop to, but it had also blinded those who were ready to lend a helping hand in procuring it for a price. Everybody from politicians, to senior defence officers in uniform, to senior bureaucrats, Babus, clerks and arms dealers, they were all eagerly willing to back the non existent hand held thermal camera in order to get the monetary kickbacks. That evening as the entire country kept viewing the sordid and sensational expose on their television screens, Unni and Monty decided to find out a little more about 'Operation Westend.' They were also worried that since the ruling party and some of their well known personalities had been thoroughly exposed by

'TIT', the fall out would not only lead to blatant denials by them, but it could also lead for a tit for tat against Tarun Tejpal and his Tehelka. Though Tehelka did have men like Shankar Sharma of First Global and the Indian superstar Amitabh Bachchan as their first round investors, but the politicians using their clout, muscle power, money power and resources could well ensure the end of Tehelka if they so wished to do so. And all of them were very powerful people too.

And it was only after Mr Geroge Fernandes, the Indian Defence Minister resigned on the Tehelka expose on 15th of March, that Unni and Monty started digging more seriously into the story. And a week later, when they had pieced all the facts together they threw a grand party for some of their close friends and relatives at one of the fancy farm houses at Mehrauli, which incidentally belonged to a well known and highly connected family who were also neck deep in defence deals. The idea of congregating there was to tell everrybody as to how the whole operation was conceived and how meticulously the sting operation was carried out despite the inherent dangers to the enterprising and courageous two man Tehelka team.

It was in August 2000, soon after the cricket match fixing sting that 'Operation Westend' was born. Aware of the fact of that the defence establishment was not a holy cow, Aniruddha Bahal had first floated the idea of exposing the dubious nature of the various kinds of defence purchases that were being made by the defence ministry and with the recent big explosion of an important Indian army ammunition dump at Bharatpur in April it only added to the necessity of doing it in double quick time. And with the infamous fourteen year old Bofors deal still spewing fire in the Indian parliament and in the law courts, Tarun Tejpal and his Tehelka team felt that the time had come for India to be woken up to this sordid game of making money while our gallant jawans kept risking their lives day in and day out while safe guarding and fighting for the country's honour and territorial integrity.

After doing a lot of initial spadework by greasing the palms of some lowly paid civilian section officers and clerical staff in the defence ministry, when the Tehelka team came to know that the Indian army was on the lookout for a hand held thermal camera, the idea struck them and they decided to go and bid for it. Since neither of the team members knew much about the product and its uses, they therefore became a little wiser by downloading whatever they could on the subject from the internet. Then with the help of their own design department they created a sophisticated brochure and that gave birth to West End International, the dummy company from England that would offer the product to the Indian army. Starting at the rock bottom of the graft ladder, they first paid Rupees two thousand to the concerned section officer to seek valid entry into the branch and office of the concerned defence ministry department that was dealing with the subject. And therafter by offering larger amounts both in cash and in kind to their immediate higher ups they kept slowy climbing up the ladder successfully. So much so, that to sell their product, they even landed up at the doorstep of the Defence Minister's residence and even at the office of Mr Bangaru Laxman an Indian politician and a former Minister of State for Railways in the Vajpayee government and who was also now the President of the BJP, the Bhartiya Janata Party. And that man too had to perforce resign after he was exposed and caught red handed while taking a bribe of Rupees one lac from the enterprising sting operators.

The hand held thermal camera which they named Lepak was in reference to the Lepak gun, while the company logo of West End International was taken from a book jacket. Being absolute novices in this game of promoting defence deals, the duo of Bahal and Mathews did make some gaffes too, but so very greedy were the wheeler dealers to make a fast buck that they did not even suspect them to be sting operators at all. To them the defence ministry buyers it was probably a routine response to their inquiry for the product. However walking staright into the tiger's den all wired up and with hidden spycam cameras and tape recorders needed solid guts and raw courage too and that both Bahal and Matthews it seems had in plenty. Because if they had they been caught red handed they could have been charged even with spying for a foreign nation.

That evening, when Peevee who was also enjoying the party came to know that Mathew on being questioned by one agency about who were the bankers of 'West End International' and he had very confidently said that it was Thomas Cook, Peevee simply couldn't help burst out laughing. It seemed that Mathew had not paid much heed to the likely FAQ's that he may be confronted with. On another instance when they were asked about the range of the product and Mathew hurriedly said that it was unlimited and when to that reply of his there was sudden silence, it looked as if the game was up. But when Mathews suddenly realized his mistake and quickly added and said that ofcourse it does blur after a point, the situation was saved at the nick of time. It seemed that to Mathew's interculators the greed to make a quick buck even blindly was so very strong that they did not want to miss out on whatever was being offered to them in cash or in kind.The very fact that two amateurs posing as businessmen and that too with little or no knowledge of defence equipment and hardware could sell an absurd non existent product that would throw egg on the face of the highly corrupt who ran India's defence ministry and also catch them red handed in taking money only proved the point that all political parties, big and small were all in this game of loot and sleaze. Following the Barak Missile Deal scandal, not only was George Fernandes the Defence Minister of India forced to resign, but what was even more shocking was the manner in which underhand money was made in the supply of sub-standard coffins for the soldiers who died for their country fighting the enemy in the dizzy cold heights of Kargil.

A week later Peevee was back in Delhi. He was on his way to Singapore for the shooting of his new film and had stopped by for a day to be with his parents. He also wanted to give them a surprise gift. That evening during supper, when the topic of whether sting operations like that of Tehelka would bring down corruption in India was being discussed, Peevee very candidly said.

"You know Dad, when it comes to corruption in this country, I think all political parties in India of all shapes and sizes, hues and colours, big and small, new and old, national and regional, leftists and rightists, I think they are all the same. When they get power and as soon as they get a glimpse of the Mahatma's smiling face on the Indian rupee or George Washington's face on the American dollar, or Her Majesty Queen Elizabeth's face on the sterling pound, they all just go bonkers it seems."

"Well what Mr Tarun Tejpal of Tehelka has come out with is no doubt very sensational, but our politicians are so very thick skinned and crookedly clever that they will not only deny all the allegations by saying that it was a political conspiracy to tarnish their good name and that of their political party, but they will also vehemently claim that the videotapes were all false and doctored and paid for by their rival party. And I won't be one bit surprised if Mr Bangaru Laxman starts claiming that it was not his hand that had accepted those bundles of cash, but it was that of somebody else like him who had been paid to impersonate and implicate him and his party," said Monty.

"And maybe he will like Diego Maradona also say that it is the hand of God and get away with it too," said Peevee while presenting his parents with the keys of the latest model of the Mercedes Benz luxury car that was now being manufactured in India.

"But mark my words no matter how many' tehelkas we 'machao' and how many scams we unearth, the political party in power will ensure that the agency deputed by them to investigate and inquire into the matter tows the government line only. And irrespective of the fact whether they are from the CBI or from the judiciary or for that matter even if they constitute a JPC, the end result will always be the same. Nothing concrete finally will come out of it ever. And a few glaring and living examples of such scams where the concerned politicians had the last laugh and got away scot free are far too many. Nevertheless I will narrate a few that I have also included in my yet to be published book," said the veteran journalist Unnikrishnan as he too joined them for the joy ride in the Mercedes.

And a week thereafter, when more factual stories of such like murky defence deals started coming out from various cupboards of some well connected nuveau rich middleman and their top political contacts, Monty was reminded.of what Mr Nani Palkiwala wrote seventeen years ago and that was even before the Bofors scandal had surfaced and when Mrs Indira Gandhi was in power. On

16th January 1984, the eminent Parsi Lawyer wrote.

'The picture that emerges is that of a great country in a state of moral decay. The immediate future seems to belong to the doomsayers rather than to cheermongers. We suffer from a fatty degeneration of conscience, and the malady seems to be not only persistent but prone to aggravation. The life style of too many politicians and businessmen bears eloquent testimony to the truth of dictum that the single minded pursuit of money impoverishes the mind, shrivels the imagination and desiccates the heart. The tricolour fluttering all over the country is black, red and scarlet—black money, red tape and scarlet corruption.' Therefore whether it is match fixing in cricket or whether it is fixing defence deals, one thing is for sure, no politician or cricketer will ever go to jail. And I feel sorry for those defence officers in uniform who were targeted and were lured into accepting money, wine, woman and song for their role in this lurid but much needed sting operation. And for all you know one day the same very corrupt and crookied politicians and cricketers will become bigger netas and flaunt the Indian tricolor with even more impunity," said Monty's wife Reeta to her husband somewhat disparagingly as she replayed the finer points of the "Operation West End' tape. She had recorded it for sending it to Shupriya in Moscow.

With Laxman Bangaru the BJP President being shown openly accepting one lac of rupees as token bribe to facilitate West End's prospects in clinching the deal and expecting another 30,000 US dollars later, it had got the BJP in a real fix. And to add to that, when Jaya Jaitly the close aide and confidante of Mr George Fernandes, the Defence Minister of the country and the Samta Party President was shown accepting the two lac bribe, and the party national treasurer Mr R. K. Jain was caught on camera openly talking about accepting bribes of one crore and more from Lt Commander Suresh Nanda, the son of the ex Indiian Naval Chief Admiral SM Nanda who had quit the navy to follow his father's footsteps, some took it as an empty boast. But when Jain reiterated that the same Suresh Nanda of Crown Corporation had paid the Samta Party Rupees one crore in swinging the Rs 250 crore order for the Armoured Recovery Vehicle in favour of a Slovakian company and another one crore for the Barak air-to air and surface-to-surface missile system for the Indian Navy, and further boasted that it was he who as the Samta Party Treasurer had swung the lucrative deal in favour of the Israeli manufacturers, the goose for the Samta Party was nicely and properly cooked. The contract for the Barak missiles and systems was signed on 23rd October, 2000 and it was valued at around 270 million US dollars and the deal had been made despite objections by Mr APJ Abdul Kalam who was the head of the DRDO, the Defence Research and Development Organization. Mr Kalam had categorically pointed out to the government that his organization was well geared to produce such kind of missiles and systems, but the Samta Party it seems was not willing to play ball and miss out on their 3 percent commission on the deal. But what was really even more tragic was the manner in which senior Indian Army officers got nailed. Starting with Lt General Manjit Singh, the DGOS, the Director General Ordnance Service to Major General PSK Choudhary who dealt with the army's requirement of weapons and equipment and Major General Murgai the Senior Director of Quality Assuarance in the Ministry of Defence followed by Brigadier Iqbal Singh who was the Prospective Procurement officer and Brigadier Anil Saigal the Deputy Director in the office of the DGOS, they all unnecessarily sang like canaries to show their so called importance and what they got in return was really nothing to write home about. In fact it was peanuts as compared to what the political parties and their Netas had made. And even Mr L.M. Mehta from the I.A.S. cadre who was the additional Secretary and the number two bureaucrat in the Defence Ministry probably fared only a little better. It seems that for most of them a few bundles of hard cash, a bottle or two of some rare skotch whisky and a couple of pretty young hostesses and call girls to keep them company was more than enough to completely numb their senses. They had not only become a disgrace to the men in unform but a bigger disgrace to their own families and to the nation

The scary and shameful fact that a nonexistent and a fictitious company with a measly budget of only Rupees eleven lacs could buy at will 34 prominent Indians including the president of the ruling party, and those from the Samta Party whose leader was also India's Defence Minister, and that it could also manage to get a trial evaluation letter issued by the concerned ministry was indeed very shocking. And Monty was more than convinced that no matter how high one was in Indian politics, in the Indian government and in the Indian business world, one could always be bought. It was really unfortunate to see that a poor country like India could be sold off at will by the rich and the powerful. And what was still worse is when such like custodians of the nation themselves loot and plunder the country and they go unpunished. The Tehelka tapes also brought out very clearly that systematic institutionalisation of corruption at high places has been on the increase eversince the country got its independence and no government worth its salt was keen to bring in the much need Lokpal bill and neither were they keen to seriously prosecute and punish those who were involved in the murky Bofors deal. And while everybody in the country gave kudos to Tehelka for their superb expose, the Special Judge Ajit Barihoke who since 1996 was conducting the trial in the high profile Bofors pay off, the St Kitts forgery and the Lakhubhai Pathak case and who had sentenced the former Prime Minister Narasimha Rao to three years rigorous imprisonment in the equally shocking JMM bribery case was surprisingly transferred on 5th March as additional rent controller in the Karkardooma courts in East Delhi. And the very fact that it was a one to one swap over between him and Mr RL Chugh it had raised quite a few eyebrows in the country. To some like Monty and Unni it seemed that even the BJP led NDA government was also now dragging its feet on the sensitive Tehelka and the Bofors case.

"But this is only the beginning my friend and with the Hinduja brothers now also being roped in and Mr Ardbo still sitting pretty in Sweden and refusing to come to India, there will be a lot more such like transfers of Judges you will see,'"said Unni very confidently as he with Monty made their way to the Press Trust of India from where the news of the transfer of the Special Judge Ajit Barihoke had emanated.

Meanwhile in Pakistan, the sudden dismissal of Dr AQ Khan from his post as Chairman Khan Research Laboratories by General Musharraf drew very strong criticism from the Muslim clerics, the opposition and from some intellectuals also. There was no doubt that it was American pressure that had made General Musharraf to clamp down on the nuclear scientist who was regarded as a national hero and icon and the father of Pakistan's nuclear bomb. The U S government had become increasingly convinced that Pakistan was trading nuclear weapons technology to North Korea in exchange for ballistic missile technology and therefore they it seems had twisted Musharraf's tail to get rid of Dr Khan. However to save face, General Musharraf soon thereafter appointed AQ Khan to the post of Special Science and Technology Adviser and that to with a ministerial rank. Though some regarded it as a promotion, but it was only to keep a closer eye on the man. And according to one reliable source, Dr AQ Khan's frequent overseas trips as Chairman KRL in PAF aircrafts to countries like Iran, Iraq, Libya, North Korea and to some other African and Middle East countries was indicative enough of his combining nuclear profileration with his personal business interests.

And while the fallout from Dr AQ Khan's dismissal as Chairman KRL became the main talking point in Pakistan, in India theTehelka tapes kept ringing into the ears of the common Indian man on the street. And though the Indian politicians in power tried to parry away the serious charges against them of taking bribes, but it looked as if Mr Vajpayee's coalition government was in for big trouble. And when those who were directly involved in taking those bribes had the temerity to say that the tapes had all been doctored, it was more than evident that corruption in public life had come to stay in India. During that shameful month of March, 2001, while Indian people even in the far off villages of the country were happily stung by the sensational Tehelka blast in India's Defence Ministry and one that had rocked the Vajpayee government; another one was in the offing. And this time it involved some of India's top excise and customs officials including their chief from the Indian Revenue Service who had been systematically looting the country. And it all happened ironically on April Fools Day 2001, when the CBI raided the residence and the offices of 48 high ranking custom officials throughout the country including that of their Chief B.P. Verma, who was the head honcho of the country's Central Board of Excise and Customs.

On that night of 1st April, when the CBI sleuths called on Mr Verma's residence in South Delhi's Andrews Ganj, he did not know what had hit him. He was having a nightcap with his son Siddharth and the pleasure of both father and son enjoying their drinks soon vanished, when they were charged with receiving massive bribes for favours and amassing wealth that was well beyond their known sources of income. While the father kept doing all the dirty work of getting cash for favours, the son acted as his trusted courier and collected the money from those who were being favoured by the Chairman of the CBEC. And it was a telephonic conversation between the Chairman and Mr Vijay Pratap a Chennai based exporter that had been secretly taped by the CBI which led to Mr Verma's and his son's arrest that evening. Verma had told the exporter on the telephone to arrange for the money and that his son would collect the Rupees two crores from a five star hotel in the capital, and in return he would clear the export consignment that had been seized by the customs in Chennai. And the best part was that the consignment contained only rags instead of the specified garments which the exporter had declared as the export item, This had been done to falsely avail of the duty drawbacks which was a concession given under the incentive scheme for exporters. But this had now become a big racket to convert black money that was parked abroad into legitimate white money because the buyer abroad in most of the cases were benami or front companies that were owned by the same export business houses in India. Thus the black money could then be sent back as payment for the duty waived on the export product and that could be anything but the genuine product. In this case it was just rags that had been declared officially by the exporter as garments. But that was not the end of the story, because on that same night besides all the custom officers who had been netted for graft, there was also one mysterious lady by the name of Bhavna Pamdey who had been picked up by the CBI from her one bedroom house in the up market area of Saket in South Delhi. The 31 year old unmarried lady from Haldwani had been listed as an accomplice who allegedly also collected the loot on behalf of Mr Verma from his clients. And during her interrogation, the defiant and arrogant manner in which she replied to the police, it clearly showed that she was not only well connected with the Verma family, but also with a lot of influential politicians and businessmen. So strong was her link with Mr Verma that a copy of the posting orders of Custom Officers to lucrative posts and to important cities were regularly faxed to her residence, and it was alleged that she too was in the chain of getting such postings done for monetary gains. And once those postings were implemented, she would then share the loot with her mentor. And according to one inside source, the cash for such lucrative postinge was not a small amount and it often ran into quite a few lacs.

When this murky sordid story of money laundering and bribe taking with Mr Verma's mug came on the front pages of India's leading newspapers, Monty as usual made a beeline for the Press Club. He wanted to find out from his good friend Unni as to who was this hi-fi crook and how did he manage reach the topmost rung of his profession without being suspected of such like wrong doings. Because as per one of the newspaper reports this sort of thing had been going on for quite sometime under Mr Verma's patronage, but no cognizance was ever taken.

'Well I must say that you have quite hit the nail right on the head because this was not the only time, and earlier too Mr Verma's acts of dishonesty and wrong doings were suspect. In fact during the period 1996 and 1999 there were even three enquiries instituted against him, but subsequently all of them I believe were closed. And in 1993, while he was posted in Calcutta as Customs Collector there was also an investigation against him for an irregular clearance of the import of a Mercedes car by one Mrs Aarti Gidwani, but that too was closed in December 1998 and for that he was only given just a warning by the CVC, the Chief Vigilance Commissioner of India. And on 31st May, 1999 the same gentlemen Mr Verma after being cleared by non other than the Appointments Committee of Mr Vajpayee's cabinet which in addition to the Prime Minister also included Mr LK Advani the Home Minister, and the leader of the opposition in parliament, he was appointed as the CEBC. It seems that from 1999 onwards Mr Verma while serving in Delhi as a Member of the Board had effectively and successfully developed good contacts with top politicians and with big business houses too, or else how could he get on to the drivers seat and amass assets that today are worth a staggering 40 crores. And as the popular saying goes you just cannot clap with one hand. Therefore in other words, the hands of some our politicians too must have gone deep into Mr Verma's big pockets and they too must have made quite a pile from that big loot. And you will be surprised that the Finance Minister, Mr Yeswant Sinha who is also from the BJP was not at all in favour of Verma becoming the CBEC. His choice I believe for that top job was Mr A M Prasad who was also a sitting member of the board and who was senior to Verma, but since the PMO's office was in favour of Mr Verma, he just could not say no, though Mr Sinha was somewhat aware of Mr Verma's nefarious activities and wrong doings. And while Tarun Tejpal's Tehelka with a measly budget of Rupees of just 11 lacs in a spate of just seven months could rip open the sleazy world of politics and corruption in India's defence ministry, it took the CBI and the CVC nearly half a decade to book the CBEC and 48 others in the Finance Ministry who had been systematically looting the nation. Mr Verma had taken over charge only on 1st June 2000 and was due to retire soon, but in 11 months his total assets both movable and immovable it seems had risen by more than 11 times.And what was even more strange was that the note to remove Mr Verma was sent by Mr Yeshwant Sinha to the PMO's office for approval of the Appointment Cabinet Committee on the

1st of March, 2001 and that was a month ago., And it was only after the CBI raided Verma's residence and arrested him on charges of corruption that the file finally surfaced on the Prime Minister's table and he was livid," said Unni as he showed him a picture of that mysterious lady that an enterprising press photographer had taken while she was being escorted to the police station for interrogation.

"My God if this is the way the country is being run, then all I can say is that with the kind of coalition politics that has come to stay, the scams will only get bigger and bigger by the day. And as far as accountability is concerned the Indian army I know for sure will definitely take necessary strong actions against their own officers under the Army Act, but as far as the civilian bureaucrats are concerned they I am afraid will probably go scotfree, or at the most be asked to go home. And as for the politicians who are involved in this sordid drama, they will be made to simply resign and will be asked to lie low for a while till all the dust in both these murky deals and affairs finally settles down for good. And once it settles down, they will be merrily brought back to power and to the money making batting crease for a second innings," said Monty in a disparaging tone as he handed over to Unni an invitation for lunch at his house on the 13th of April.

"But what is the occasion my friend and don't worry I will not get Miss Bhavna Pandey with me," said Unni jokingly as he put the lady's photo back into his satchel.

"Well the 13th of April happens to be Baisakhi Day and with all the Tehelka that Tarun Tejpal and his 'Tit" has created in this country we also wanted to celebrate it with a grand party. Moreover it is also the Sikh New Year and a day when the Khalsa Panth to fight against tyranny and corruption was born," said Monty while taking leave from his close confidante.

Meanwhile on the 6th of April, in Moscow, when Shiraz read in the Indian newspapers that had arrived that evening by the weekly diplomatic mail bag from Islamabad about the arrest of India's Excise and Customs Chief, he was not at all surprised because in the entire Indian subcontinent corruption at such high places had become the norm of the day. And it did not shock him either when on that very day itself the Supreme Court of Pakistan set aside the judgement of Asif Ali Zardari and Benazir Bhutto who had earlier in April 1999 been convicted in the famous SGS Cotecna case and where the duo had allegedly taken huge commissions while awarding contracts to these two Swiss companies that were made responsible for pre-shipment inspection of imports into Pakistan. But what really surprised him was the video tape of the Tehelka sting operation that his brother-in-law Salim Rehman Khan had sent from the Pakistan Embassy in New Delhi. The incriminating videos of the BJP President Bangaru Laxman, and other stalwarts from the Samta Party of George Fernandes who was the Defence Minister of the country taking bribes was bad enough, but to see some serving senior Indian army officers accepting bribes in cash and in kind was more than just shocking. As far as politicians and their cronies were concerned it was'nt a very big deal, since such corrupt methods of making a quick buck had become a part of the system, but for the Indian army officers in uniform willing to make a quick buck in cash, or willing to sleep with a good looking whore and guzzle a couple of bottles of some imported rare free skotch whisky was a disgrace to the profession to which he once belonged. The disclosures made by Tehelka had no doubt tarnished the image of Mr Fernandes and his ministry, but it had also severely battered the image of Mr Vajpayee and his led NDA government. As a result of which the Congress and its allies were screaming mad for his blood and demanding his immediate resignation. But all said and done Shiraz was full of praise for Tarun Tejpal and his team and he wished that some journalist like him in Pakistan should now rip open the high level of corruption in defence deals that the Pakistan Defence Ministry had been regularly indulging in. However on the very next day, there was a smile on Shiraz's face when a fairly senior Pakistani diplomat from the Pakistani Embassy in Washington DC who was also a dear friend of his rang him up and confidentially told him about the progress made by the Balusa Group. Till then he had only an idea of the existence of this group, but when he was told that as a Track II channel the group had the blessings of General Musharraf and that it had made fairly good progress in opening a dialogue between the two governments of India and Pakistan, Shiraz indeed felt very happy. And a few days later when he learnt that General Musharaff had deputed Major General Ehsan-ul-Haq, the Director General Military Intelligence to head a special cell and appointed Lt General Ghulam Ahmed his Chief of Staff in the Chief Executive's Secretariat to coordinate the efforts being made for a possible summit meeting with the Indian Prime Minister and to resolve all outstanding issues bilaterally, Shiraz was simply delighted. However, he was not aware that Musharraf had also set up another task force that was headed by Lt General Mahmood Ahmed the DG ISI and it consisted of retired Lt General Moinuddun Hyder who was the Interior Minister and Lt General Muzaffar Usmani the Pakistani Deputy Chief of Army Staff and where the primary role of this task force was to ensure the complete break up of the PPP, the MQM and the Sindhi nationalists who were becoming a source of headache to the CEO.

"I think our military head of state has finally realized that confrontation with India will not pay, but I sincerely hope that it will be a genuine hand of peace and cooperation and not a publicity gimmick to keep sitting on the high saddle," said Shiraz to his wife Saira as he helped himself to a highball cocktail of whisky with lots of ice and ginger ale and made a screwdriver for Saira and his daughter Sherry.

"Well cheers to that Papa and let's hope the CEO does not screw it all up like the way he did in Kargil. Because having done a Kargil on India earlier, I personally do not trust the Commando General,"'said a smiling Sherry as she thanked her dad for the drink.

"I think you should not talk in that manner against our own head of state. Maybe his intentions are good, but knowing the psyche of our Mullahs and their various militant groups who have a phobia as far as Kashmir is concerned this may not succeed unless ofcourse India allows the Hurriyat conference to also participate in these talks. After all we all have been harping for the last 54 years that Kashmir is the core issue and if that is not resolved, it will be only an exercise in total futility," said Saira

A fortnight earlier on 23rd March Pakistan Day, when Shiraz had met the Indian Ambassador at his official cocktails he did find her a little more friendly than usual and he now wondered whether she too was aware of the track II channel. That evening he even thought of finding out a little more about her Indian upbringing and her family background and whether as a single Sikh lady in such a high profile post in Moscow she felt at ease dealing with the Russians. But since it was a formal evening, he decided to keep it for some other informal occasion. Everytime he saw her he got reminded of his dear Shupriya, and that day was no different either as having reached home quietly went to the loo and kissed the photograph that was inside the old locket. That little talisman it seemed had become like a good luck charm to the ex Indian army allegedly dead hero who was now a top Pakistani diplomat. That night before going to sleep, Shiraz also had an uncanny feeling that with the track II channel making good and steady progress, Pakistan's flamboyant and media loving CEO, General Musharaff may soon try and unseat Rafique Mohammed Tarar from his chair too and like General Zia-ul-Haq had done earlier, he too would probably use the people's consensus to his advantage and appoint himself President of Pakistan. The very fact that the on going secret talks were primarily to lay the ground for an Indo-Pak summit in the near future was indicative enough that Musharraf could not represent Pakistan's interest simply as a CEO, and protocol therefore demanded that he should go there only as the head of state.

The 13th of April 2001 being a Friday, the party at Monty's bungalow in Defence Colony to celebrate Baisakhi was a really boisterous affair. And with Peevee's presence there with the guitar to regale the guests together with his large repertoire of Punjabi 'tappas' and popular Hindi songs, it was all Bhangra and Giddha that day. And with some good wine, chilled beer and the heady 'bhang' flowing like water, the merriment carried on till even well after sunset. Present in that crowd were a large number of old retired Sikh defence service officers from the neighbourhood who were Monty's late father's colleagues and friends and most of them had taken part in all wars since independence. Amongst them was a recently retired and a relatively young Bengali Brigadier who was also from the 4th Jammu and Kashmir Rifle regiment, the same battalion that Monty's father and foster brother Major Shiraz Ismail Khan had served in. The retired Brigadier was a subaltern during the 1971 war and for him Shiraz was always a role model. And being a Delhite from Defence Colony he had always kept in close touch with the Bajwa family. The retired Brigadier only a few years ago was India's Defence Attache in Dhaka and that evening after most of the guests had left, Unni asked him rather candidly that in view of the recent conviction of those army officers who had killed Mujib, whether the present lot of senior serving Bengali Muslims officers in the Bangladesh army were capable of staging another coup to oust his daughter Hasina Begum who was primarily responsible in getting some of those officers who were the main conspirators of that dastardly crime to stand trial. And though they had been convicted with death sentences but they were yet to be hanged.

"Well Sir, the possibility cannot be entirely ruled out because unlike the Indian army which is absolutely apolitical, the Bangladesh army like the army in Pakistan does have an important role and say in the governance of the state. However, one thing is very clear and that is most of them have forgotten the sacrifices that we Indians had made for getting them their freedom. And the saddest part is that quite a large number of them are still very much pro Pakistani. And my fear is that since Prime Minister Hasina is still pro Indian and now that she has finally been successful in getting some of Mujib's killers to face the gallows, but those who are still absconding may take revenge and get her eliminated. And with fresh elections around the corner, together with Khalida Begum's Bangladesh Nationalist Party and the Jaamat-e-Islami accusing Sheikh Hasina of being an Indian baiter, it maybe an uphill task for her and the Awami League to retain power.

Moreover, the claims and counter claims that are currently being made by both the governments on some of the disputed border issues may one day become volatile too and that indeed will be a very sad day for both the countries,"said the retired Brigadier who had also served in the BSF, the Border Security Force as a DIG in the Eastern Sector for a year, before finally hanging up his boots for good.

Chapter-32

Trouble on the Eastern Front

Two days later and whether it was by intuition or otherwise, the retired Bengali Brigadier's premonition had come true. For the first time since 1971, tensions grew between the BDR, the Bangladesh Rifles and the Border Security Force on the Meghalaya-Assam-Bangladesh border, when on the wee hours of that15th April morning three battalions comprising of some 3000 armed men from the Bangladesh Rifles and the Bangladesh army laid siege and forcibly occupied the Indian BSF outpost at Pyrdiwah. Pyrdiwah was a Khasi village and during the 1971 Bangladesh war it was an Indian army training base to train the Mukti Bahini. And though after its liberation Bangladesh staked its claim to it, but it had remained all along a disputed area. The initial skirmish took place, when the BDR personnel tried to forcibly flush out the BSF from their small outpost at Pyrdiwah and it became worse, when three BSF jawans were captured and taken to Dhaka.Thereafter for the next four days both sides retaliated with heavy machine gun and mortar fire. On 18th April matters became even worse, when in the course of border clashes, 15 BSF jawans who had been taken hostage by the BDR from the Boroibari and Kurigram, areas were killed and 3 BDR personnel also died in a firefight. According to one reliable source, Prime Minister Sheikh Hasina who was also holding the Defence portfolio was touring the border areas and Major General Fazlur Rehman the DG BDR probably wanted to show her that his force was no less in taking on the Indians. But such kind of bravado only complicated matters for the poor lady. Well whatever was the reason for the flare up it did cause a lot of heartburning on both the sides. Luckily both the governments managed to diffuse the crisis by announcing a ceasefire on the 19th and by agreeing to restore the status quo ante.

On hearing about the fairly serious border incidents and armed clashes which resulted in the deaths of quite a few Indians and Bangladeshis from their respective para-military forces, Fazal Rehman who had taken over as the Bangladesh Ambassador to Thailand in October 2000 was indeed very surprised. And keeping in view that the country was surrounded on three sides by India; he always maintained that it was in Bangladesh's interest to maintain friendly relations with her big and more powerful neighbour. There had been clashes of a minor nature on the dispute over the Muhurichur Island that had also resulted in gunfire first in 1975, then in 1979 and also in 1985, but this one was of a very serious nature and Fazal Rehmnan feared that it could spark off a bigger conflict unless all border disputes with India were sorted out by both sides through negotiations and by a sincere give and take approach.

"I think such kind of sabre rattling will only worsen matters for a poor country like ours and though I do agree that as an independent nation we should not bow to bullying tactics by India, the fact remains that everytime the government changes in Dhaka our foreign policy also undergoes a radical change and which is definitely not a step in the right direction," said Fazal to his wife Samina as he showed her the grizzly photographs of the BSF personnel who had been killed. The photographs had appeared in one of the leading weekly journals of India and which also highlighted the point that all of them had been brutally tortured by the BDR before being killed.

"I think such kind of brutality needs to be thoroughly condemned and those involved must be severely punished," said an angry Samina who was reminded of the terrible killings and torture that took place between the Pakistanis and the Bangladeshis during those dark days of 1971 and where both sides were equally guilty. Meanwhile in Moscow, Shiraz too was shocked by the sudden belligerence that was shown by the BDR who otherwise were a comparatively docile lot. And being a disciplined force in uniform it was therefore very unlikely that they could be the ones who had so brutally tortured their Indian counterparts thought Shiraz. The villagers on both sides of the border in all the sectors had been living quite peacefully and such disputes had always been resolved through negotiations and not by a show of force.The incident to Shiraz also highlighted the fact that even after almost five years in power Sheikh Hasina and her party was not in total command over her military, paramilitary and intelligence establishments. Moreover her inability to reverse the process of Islamization of the country that surfaced during the two military dictatorships after her father's assassination has been altogether an utter failure. And with the fundamentalist political parties and militant organizations like that of the Jamaat and the HUJI-B gaining ground, there were now clear indications that Islamic rule had probably come to stay in that impoverished part of the subcontinent. Nonetheless, and in order to get a few more inputs and to find out what was the true story behind those skirmishes, Shiraz rang up Fazal Rehman in Bangkok.

"Yes Bhaijaan, the fact that there were serious border clashes are definitely true, but what is not quite true is the torturing and killing of the BSF personnel who had been taken hostage by the BDR. According to one report the BSF while patrolling the area had lost their way and were taken hostage by a large group of Bangladeshi civilians. And it was they who lynched and killed them so very gruesomely. However, the possibility of the Jamaat's hand in this cannot be ruled out either. Nevertheless the incident of torturing the Indians has only added to the animosity of the locals on both sides," said Fazal Rehman while extending an invitation to Shiraz and his family to come and spend a holiday with them in Bangkok. I must tell you that Thailand is a paradise for both the rich and the poor tourists who flock to this place throughout the year. Food and accommodation is still fairly cheap and the Thai cuisine is simply out of this world. Though my favourite is the steamed lemon grass crab legs, Samina prefers the spicy garlic and pepper shrimp and the traditional green Thai curry. And the best part is that while you are here we could wine and dine and play some good golf too in one of the many golf courses in this country and that to without making a big hole in our pockets," added Fazal Rehman as he smacked his lips and. gave the phone to Samina so that she could speak to both Riaz (Shiraz) and Saira and extend her invitation to them also.

As the month of April 2000 came to an end, Sherry who was eagerly looking forward for Peevee's promised visit to Moscow was disappointed. Late on the evening of 28th April, Peevee rang her up to say that Mom number two's plans to visit India suddenly in early May had upset everything. And since he was informed about it only on telephone this morning by her secretary, he had to therefore cancel his confirmed Mumbai-Moscow air ticket by Air India that was scheduled for the 30th of. April. But Shiraz however promised her that he would definitely accompany Mom No 2 when she returns to Moscow, but that could take a little more time.

Shupriya had been summoned by the Ministry of External Affairs for an important high level three day seminar of all Indian Ambassadors who were the heads of mission in all the G8 countries. During the seminar it was expected that the Indian Prime Minister together with other cabinet ministers from the ministry of commerce and foreign trade, finance and external affairs would also address the high powered gathering. With the country's economy showing good growth, the NDA government led by Mr Vajpayee was very keen that more trade opportunities must be created with all these economically powerful nations.

And while the Ministry of External Affairs in New Delhi was busy making all arrangements for the high level seminar, there was high drama in the court of the Special Judge Mr RL Chugh. A month earlier in April 2001, the three Hinduja brothers had moved the Delhi High Court asking for a speedy trial and which had been agreed too. But when they also asked to be given permission to go abroad, it was denied. Thereafter in the first week of May and in order to speed up the trial in the Rupees 64 crores Bofors payoffs case, the CBI had moved the designated court for a separate trial of the three Hinduja brothers and the three others accused that included the Bofors Agent Win Chadda, SK Bhatnagar the former Defence Secretary and the Swedish Company AB Bofors.Therefore as a sequel to that, when Mr Chugh the Special Judge asked all of them to file replies to the CBI plea by the 8th of May, and the battery of eminent lawyers like Ujwal Rana, Arvind Nigam and Y Kaul who were defending the Hinduja brothers in the presence of the three accused pleaded for exemption from appearance on the date fixed by the Judge for the next hearing, and also for the exemption of their clients from personal appearance in the court, the angry Judge remarked somewhat sarcastically. 'On the one hand, you want an expeditious trial and on the other hand you want exemption from appearance?'That evening on learning about it the Judge's caustic remark from one of his old lawyer friend, Unni who had been following the case very closely simply said somewhat acerbically. "Now I guess they will start looking for another Judge. And to me and for obvious reasons I guess it looks that no government is keen to get to the bottom of the whole issue and slowly like most other political corruption scandals in this country, this too will also die its own death, RIP Bofors."

Following the grand success of the seminar, a fabulous sit down formal lunch was hosted by the Exterrnal Affairs Minister on 11th May. The venue was the ballroom of the Imperial Hotel and the guest list besides the concerned cabinet ministers also included the Heads of Mission of the G8 countries and their wives. And it was during lunch that Shupriya came to know that the Prime Minister had not only agreed to honour the Asean treaty, but he had also ensured that Southeast Asia will be kept as a nuclear free zone. Simultaneously the government had also announced the opening up the country's arms production industry to private investors including 26 % foreign capital, and that according to Shupriya was also a step in the right direction. Though the Indian Ordnance Factories were doing a good job no doubt, but with the requirement of more sophisticated arms and equipment for the Indian armed forces and especially so after the recent Kargil war and the Tehelka revelations, opening up of this sector to private players was also considered to be a wise move. Not only would it bring in good clean competition, but India could also become a major arms exporter and thereby earn and save more valuable foreign exchange.

On 12th May 2001 and the day after the seminar ended, both Gopichand Hinduja and Srichand Hinduja were allowed by the Indian Supreme Court to return to the UK provided they give bank guarantees of 150 million rupees each for their bail, while the third brother Prakash who was now a Swiss national was ordered to remain in India. And this was only to ensure that the two elder brothers did not renege on the agreement and they returned to India by 20th August to face trial.The decision to allow the two senior Hinduja brothers tó return to the UK had upset Shupriya. She knew that with their money power and high level contacts in the UK, there was every possibility of them being used to curry favours personal or otherwise by the political parties that mattered in India and it was immaterial whether it was the ruling party or the opposition.Shupriya had earlier applied for a month's home leave after the seminar to sort out some of her personal problems and since that had been sanctioned even before she landed in Delhi, she was now planning to go on a gurudwara darshan to some of the more and important Sikh gurudwaras in the country and also visit the Sai Baba Temple at Shirdi. And though she had Reeta Bhabhi for company to go and pray at the Golden Temple, and at Anandpur Sahib, Patna Sahib, Paonta Sahib and Nanded Sahib Gurudwaras, she however wanted that Peevee should also accompany them to Shirdi.

"But please Mom Number 2 much that I would have loved to accompany both of you on the grand gurudwara darshan tour, but because of the sudden change of plans I have already committed myself to my producers. Infact I have already given them my firm dates for the shoots, and I will only be free from those commitments and shooting schedules on the 10th June which is only two days before you return to Moscow. But don't worry this time I will not only keep you company on the flight, but I will also spend a whole month with you at your Ulitsa Obukha residence," said Peevee with a big smile while promising her that he will definitely land up in Shirdi on 10th June as scheduled and escort both her and Mom number one back to Mumbai.

For Shupriya the visit to all the gurudwaras was a good education on how Sikhism and the teachings of Guru Nanak and the Gurus who followed him were propogated as a religion and how it spread throughout the length and breadth of the subcontinent. She was aware about the history of the Golden Temple and that of AnandpurSahib where Sikhism was born, but she was fairly ignorant about the history and importance of Patna Sahib, Paonta Sahib and Nanded Sahib. But thanks to her Reeta Bhabi, Shupriya by the time she arrived in Shirdi, she knew the full history of the Sikhs and of the many historical gurudwaras that the Sikhs were so very proud off. It was eversince her marriage to Shiraz on 15th September 1971 that the Guru Granth had become her holy book.To her Sikhism was the one and only religion that was capable of unifying the whole world and this was also what the Saibaba of Shirdi had preached. For the Saint of Shirdi it was 'Subka Malik Ek', meaning thereby that there is only one God and he is the Almighty and only he and he alone is the supreme head of all living things. Patna was visited first by Guru Nanak and later by Guru Tegh Bahadur the Ninth Guru in order to spread Sikhism in Eastern India and Patna Sahib was also the birth place of Guru Govind Singh, the Tenth Guru. And and it is from this sacred Gurudwara that the commandment of valiance and fearlessness was first preached by Guru Gobind Singh. Located in the capital city of India's Bihar state it is considered to be the second holiest Sikh shrine after the Golden Temple. Built on the banks of the Yamuna River, the Paonta Sahib Gurudwara located 50 kilometers from Dehra Dun was the place where the 16 year old Guru Gobind Singh first dismounted from his horse to set up camp. It was like a fort with the gurudwara inside from where Guru Gobind Singh engaged himself not only in hunting and training his warrior Sikhs in the martial arts, but he also spent a great deal of his time in literary activities, composing many religious works and heroic poetry including the Jap Sahib. He also filled his Darbar (court) with as many as 52 of India's most talented poets and writers and many of whom came from the ancient city of Benares. He put most of them to work translating the ancient classics of India's literature from the Sanskrit of the Priests and Khatris scholars into the then common languages of Braj or Punjabi, the vernacular languages of the people. The Guru also took many steps to beautify Paonta. And as far as the Gurudwara down south in Nanded was concerned, it was the site where Guru Gobind Singh established his camp in August 1708. Situated in the Indian state of Maharashtra it is also known as Hazur Sahib where Guru Gobind Singh spent the last few days of his life till his death on 7th October. And it was from here that he had passed on the spiritual light of Guruship to the Holy Granth forever when he said. 'The Eternal Father willed and I raised the Panth and hereafter all Sikhs must accept the Granth as their divine teacher and seek guidance from its holy words.'

On 24th May, while Shupriya after praying at the Patna Sahib Gurudwara heard the news in her hotel room that Mr Vajpayee had not only extended an offer of talks on Kashmir to the Pakistani CEO General Musharaff, but that he had also invited him and wife to visit India, it was like a bolt from the blue as far as she was concerned. But at the same time nowithstanding the cordial invitation, India had also simultaneously ended the six month old ceasefire that it had declared unilaterally in Kashmir. However, though the invitation was considered to be a statesman like gesture by Mr Vajpayee, but Shupriya was not very happy with this sudden development. She felt that the very man who planned Operation 'Badr' so very stealthily and deceitfully and which led to the war in Kargil not so very long ago was not only very shrewd, but he was also very smart and calculative too. And the very fact that the logistical and preliminary operations to occupy the posts that were vacated by the Indian troops in Kargil were already in progress while the political leaders of both the countries were in the process of signing the Lahore Declaration in February 1999 to usher in the much needed peace and stability in the subcontinent was clear proof of the man's crafty and devious intentions. Moreover, with the Pakistan aided militancy in the Kashmir valley not showing any signs of receding whatsoever, she was off the opinion that the man just could not be trusted.

Sitting in Moscow Shiraz was also not very optimistic that a plausible and workable solution to the age old Kashmir could be solved by the Indian offer of talks unless both sides were willing to give and take and show a lot of magnanimity and trust in each other. And surprisingly on that very evening of 24th May, 2001, when the BBC announced that there was another major fire in a very big Indian army ammunition depot near Suratgarh which was not very far from the Indo-Pak international border and that the loud explosions could be heard 15 km away, Shiraz did not rule out sabotage by Pakistani agents either. Already there were five such major fires at big Indian army ammunition depots since 28th April 2000 and most of them were located fairly close to the Indo-Pak border and he therefore felt that it could well be the handiwork of pro—Pakistani sympathizers in India's border areas. And he only hoped that he was wrong. He did not want that the offer made by India to be withdrawn because of this fire episode. Shiraz also felt that it would be a tight rope walk for Musharraf if he accepted the offer because keeping in view that the militant groups like the Jaish-e-Mohammed, the Lashkar-e-Toiba, the Al-Badr and the Hizbul Mujahideens had felt let down by the Pakistan army and by the then Nawaz Sharif government for meekly submitting to the diktats of President Clinton to climb down from those heights during the Kargil war, it would therefore be very difficult for General Musharaff now to work out a deal that would be acceptable by these fanatical and fundamentalist Islamist organizations in the country. Nonetheless the very fact that the Indian governemt had invited Musharaff and had offered to hold talks was a step in the right direction thought Shiraz.

And on the 27th of May, when Pakistan formally announced that General Musharraff had formally accepted Mr Vajpayee's offer to visit India and to hold talks to bring about the much needed peace and stability in the subcontinent, Shiraz also felt very happy. That day happened to be the 27th of May and ironically it was also the 37th death anniversary of India's first Prime Minister Pandit Nehru. He was the man and a Kashimiri at that and who unfortunately kept telling the United Nations and the world that India would always respect the will of the people of Kashmir and would allow them to choose their option of joining either Pakistan or India or remain independent. And the worse part was that he kept harping on it even when the Indian Army was on the verge of throwing out the Pakistanis from the entire state in 1948. There is no doubt that had such a plebiscite taken place at that time, the people of Kashmir with Sheikh Abdullah at the helm of affairs would have overwhelmingly opted for India, but it was on the condition that the Pathan raiders and the entire Pakistan army must first get out from the state lock stock and barrel. And it was only when Mr Jinnah realized that his gamble to send the wily Pathans to do his dirty job and get Kashmir on the platter for him had failed, that he ordered the Pakistan army in the veil of Azad Kashmir Forces to keep doing the dirty work for him. Afterall it was India which took the question of invasion to the UN Security Council first and which consequently led to the establishment of UNCIP, the UN Commission for India and Pakistan. And it was way back on 13th August, 1948 that the resolution by the UNCIP was accepted by both India and Pakistan and which clearly stated that both countries must first implement the ceasefire and thereafter through a truce agreement Pakistan must also withdraw all its forces from the territory of the state of Jammu and Kashmir. And once that was completed only then the will of the people would be ascertained. And under those conditions had Mr Jinnah accepted the resolution he knew for sure that he would have lost Kashmir for good. It was like doing Harikiri for him. The bloody atrocities that were committed by the hordes of Pathans were still fresh on the minds of the Kashmiris and more so of those in the Kashmir valley and which was the most important part of Kashmir that Mr Jinnah always wanted. And therefore the next best option for Mr Jinnah was to consolidate on whatever territory was already in Pakistan's hands and keep grabbing more and more. But Shiraz felt that Nehru's first blunder on Kashmir was made on 2nd November 1947, when he in a broadcast to the nation over All India Radio said. 'We have declared that the fate of Kashmir is ultimately to be decided by the people. That pledge we have given, and the Maharaja has supported it not only to the people of Kashmir but the world. We will not, and cannot back out of it. We are prepared when peace and law and order have been established to have a referendum held under international auspices like the United Nations. We want it to be a fair and just reference to the people, and we shall accept their verdict. I can imagine no fairer and juster offer.'And he compounded it further by sending a telegram to the Pakistan Prime Minister Liaqat Ali Khan the very next day and in which he again categorically stated.'I wish to draw your attention to my broadcast on Kashmir which I made last evening. I have stated our government's policy and made it clear that we have no desire to impose our will on Kashmir but to leave the final decision to the people of Kashmir. I further stated that we have agreed on impartial international agency like United Nations supervising referendum.'And to that when Pandit Nehru in his letter dated 31st Dec 1947 to the United Nations said.' But in order to avoid any possible suggestion that India had utilized the State's immediate peril for her own political advantage, the Government of India made it clear that its people would be free to decide their future by the recognised democratic method of plebiscite or referendum which, in order to ensure complete impartiality, might be held under international auspices.'This only further complicated matters for Pakistan, because at that time the majority of the people of Jammu and Kashmir were wholly for joining the Union of India. And in January 1948, when Mr Gopalaswamy Ayyangar who was India's Representative to the United Nations further told the august body that the question of the future status of Kashmir vis-à-vis her neighbors and the world at large and a further question, namely, whether she would withdraw from her accession to India and either accede to Pakistan or remain Independent, with a right to claim admission as a Member of United Nations—all this we have recognized to be a matter for unfettered decision by the people of Kashmir, after normal life is restored to them.This further compounded the matter because an idependent J and K State was unacceptable to Pakistan and this prompted

Jinnah to send more regular troops into Kashmir and to ensure that normal life was not restored. And this was at a crucial time when not only the people of Kashmir were fully with us, but the Indian Army too was in the process of getting ready to throw out all the raiders and the Pakistani army from Kashmir. They had already recaptured Baramulla and Uri and the link up with Poonch had also been established. The Indian army was poised to advance and recapture Muzzafarabad and Domel and the Indian soldiers could have easily done so had Pandit Nehru not dilly-dallied on the issue of plebescite and had given the army a freehand to crush the enemy. And it would have been wholly justified keeping in view that not only was Pakistan refusing to withdraw the Quabailis and their own regular army troops who were masquerading as Azad Kashmir Forces inside that occupied state, but they were also silent on the plebiscite proposal by India.

And while Shiraz in Moscow debated in his own mind of what Pakistan's stand on Kashmir would be at the proposed summit meeting, at the Press Club in New Delhi Unni was of the view that though it was a good gesture by Mr Vajpayee, but it would not be easy going for both the sides as far as the issue of Kashmir was concerned and which was as per Pakistan's CEO the core issue. Unni also felt that it was not completely because of India's initiative that the proposal to hold talks at the highest level was made. There was pressure on both India and Pakistan by the western powers and in particular by America because both the nations were now equipped with nuclear weapons and they were therefore very keen that there should be a proper dialogue between both the countries and they should resolve all issues in a peaceful manner. For Musharraf and Pakistan, the scenario was even more precarious because not only was the country's economy in shambles, but the Americans were also breathing down his neck to dismantle the terrorist network that the ISI was still nurturing both inside Pakistan and Afghanistan and of Pakistan's failure to get Osama Bin Laden for them. Pakistan's economic lifeline was already on a drip and for survival it desperately needed immediate help from international financial institutions. Besides that, Pakistan military regime was also desperate for international legitimacy and especially what happened after the army's Kargil fiasco. Therefore according to Unni the invitation to Musharraf was God sent as far as the General was concerned and he immediately therefore jumped for it.

"But one thing is very clear and that is General Musharraf is not going to appeal to the Mujahideens goups and fighters to stop their operations in Kashmir. And if he does so then he will be openly admitting Pakistan's hand in fostering militancy in Kashmir and that will be a tremendous folly.

Afterall Pakistan has always been saying that it is the people of Jammu and Kashmir who have risen against the unlawful occupation by India of their motherland. And to make that sound more legitimate he will also during his visit express his desire to meet the pro-Pakistani members of the Hurriyat Conference. And and if that meeting is denied by India, then I am afraid there will be no headway in the talks as far as Kashmir is concerened,"concluded Unni.

"By God I must say that you have very logically and correctly analysed General Mushraff's plight. Because though personally he maybe very forthright and willing to arrive at a fair deal as far as J and K is concerned, but he cannot afford to annoy and go against the hawks in his own country, can he?' said Monty.

"That is true, but let me also quote to you of what our late Prime Minister Pandit Nehru had said way back in 1951 and in 1952. On 6th July 1951 while addressing the All India Congress committee he said. 'Kashmir has been wrongly looked upon as a prize for India or Pakistan. People seem to forget that Kashmir is not a commodity for sale or to be bartered. It has an individual existence and its people must be the final arbiters of their future.'Then again on 2nd January, 1952 he further clarified the above statement by stating that. 'Kashmir belongs to the Kashmiri people. When Kashmir acceded to India, we made it clear to the leaders of the Kashmiri people that we would ultimately abide by the verdict of their plebiscite. If they tell us to walk out, I would have no hesitation in quitting. We have taken the issue to United Nations and given our word of honour for a peaceful solution. As a great nation we cannot go back on it. We have left the question for final solution to the people of Kashmir and we are determined to abide by their decision.' And that's not all. On 7th August 1952 Pandit Nehru in Parliament also said and I quote. 'Let me say clearly that we accept the basic proposition that the future of Kashmir is going to be decided finally by the goodwill and pleasure of her people. The goodwill and pleasure of this Parliament is of no importance in this matter, not because this Parliament does not have the strength to decide the question of Kashmir, but because any kind of imposition would be against the principles that this Parliament holds. Kashmir is very close to our minds and hearts and if by some decree or adverse fortune, ceases to be a part of India, it will be a wrench and a pain and torment for us. If, however, the people of Kashmir do not wish to remain with us, let them go by all means. We will not keep them against their will, however painful it may be to us. I want to stress that it is only the people of Kashmir who can decide the future of Kashmir. It is not that we have merely said that to the United Nations and to the people of Kashmir, it is our conviction and one that is borne out by the policy that we have pursued, not only in Kashmir but everywhere. Though these five years have meant a lot of trouble and expense and in spite of all we have done, we would willingly leave if it was made clear to us that the people of Kashmir wanted us to go. However sad we may feel about leaving we are not going to stay against the wishes of the people. We are not going to impose ourselves on them on the point of the bayonet. I want to stress that it is only the people of Kashmir who can decide the future of Kashmir. It is not that we have merely said that to the United Nations and to the people of Kashmir; it is our conviction. I started with the assumpion that it is for the people of Kashmir to decide their own future. We will not compel them. In that sense, the people of Kashmir are sovereign.'

Having quoted from the many speeches that Pandit Nehru had made in the past on Kashmir, Unni very aptly summed it all up by saying. "Well having quoted exstensively from Nehru's speeches and taking into consideration the colossal amount of money and which probably amounts to quite a few trillions that both countries have so far spent and wasted in defending Kashmir till now, and as a result of which a large number of the men in uniform and innocent people including children on both sides of the Line of Control and the international border have been killed, I think the time has therefore come for both India and Pakistan to shake hands and give up their claims for what was once a heaven on earth and which is now a journey to hell and back. Because if this fight for Kashmir continues then I am afraid not only will more blood be spilled on both sides, but economically too it will drain the resources of both the nations. And don't forget that both countries are now armed with nuclear weapons. Therefore let us hope and pray that both India and Pakistan at the forthcoming summit either agree to demarcate the existing LOC as the international border, and failing which they must let it become the Switzerland of the East. I personally think that there is no other region in this whole wide world that can equal the splendour and beauty of that unfortunate land."

Chapter-33

Madness At Midnight

While the people of India and Pakistan were still debating as to what would be the final outcome of the proposed summit talks, on the night of 1st of June 2001 a macabre tragedy of vengeance killings, bloodshed and horror struck the people of neighbouring Nepal and also of those in far away Israel. On that bloody Friday night at the Narayanhity Royal Palace in Khatmandu, Prince Dipendra the heir to the Nepalese throne armed with two automatic weapons in a fit of rage had shot dead nine members of his own family including his father King Birendra, his mother Queen Aishwarya, his younger brother Prince Niranjan and his sister Princess Shruti and he also tried to kill himself. The young Prince who was being groomed to be king since childhood had within a spate of just nine agonizing minutes of sheer madness eliminated most of the royal family. And the mass family murder had shocked the entire world. And three days later the young King who while in coma ruled over Nepal for seventy two hours also succumbed to the self inflicted injuries. After his death when there were also rumours that having shot his father he had even kicked him with his boots, the people of Nepal refused to believe it. If that was indeed true then what made him do that would will probably now remain a million dollar mystery.

At around the same time on that evening of 1st June, 2001, while the members of the Nepal royalty in Khatmandu were being brutally massacred by the young crown Prince, in Tel Aviv the capital of Israel, Saeed Hotari, a lone Palestinian suicide bomber was also getting ready to carry out his macabre plan of killing as many young Israelis as he possibly could. At around 8 PM Israel time on that holy Friday evening, Saeed Hotari dressed in clothes that some orthodox Jews from Asia normally wear stood in line in front of the Dolphinarium discotheque awaiting his turn to get in. And standing with him in that long line were a lively group of young Israeli teenage girls and boys and most of whom had migrated with their parents from the former Soviet Union some years ago.The Dolphin was one of the more popular discos on the Tel Aviv seafront promenade and Hotari had chosen a perfect target. Very close to it was another nightclub called 'Pacha' and where also there were people waiting in line outside to get in. The youngsters from the former Soviet Union had planned a dance party at the Dolphin disco and were looking forward to a great evening, when suddenly at around 8.30 that evening that popular place for the Israelis became a deadly dance of death as Hotari blew himself up killing 21on the spot including himself and wounding another 120, and some of them very seriously too. The young Palestinian suicide bomber before doing that dastardly act had it seems also taunted his victims as he kept banging his drum that was packed with explosives and steel ball bearings and while he kept repeating the words in Hebrew,'Something is going to Happen.' And when it did happen it was a deadly blast that shook the entire Tel Aviv waterfront. Reports indicated that the young Palestinian bomber was linked to the deadly Palestinian militant group called Hamas. The word Hamas, which was the acronym for Harakat-al-Muquawamat-al-Islamiya, meaning the Islamic Resistance Movement had its origins in Egypt's Muslim Brotherhood, and it was founded in Gaza by Sheikh Ahmed Yassin and Mohammed Zahar in 1987. But it had by now a large following and it had also emerged as a strong political rival to Mr Arafat's PLO and whose dominant factor was known popularly as Fatah. Hamas had carried out its first attack in 1989, when they abducted and killed two Israeli soldiers. And the Israelies retaliated immediately by arresting Yassin. It not only sentenced Yassin to life imprisonment, but it also deported 400 Hamas activists including Zahar to South Lebanon which was then occupied by Israel. While in Lebanon, Hamas had built up a relationship with the dreaded Hezbollah. In 1991, Hamas too created its own military branch the Izzad-Din—Al Qassam Brigades and during the 1990's they had also carried out numerous attacks against Israeli civilians and their armed forces including suicide bombings. And in 2000, this became known as the Second Intifida or the second uprising against Israeli rule in occupied Palestime and it had now become more daring and violent as was evident in the Dolphinarium bombing case. But what was even more astonishing was the fact that in Ramallah dozens of Palestinians celebrated the killings of the 21 young Israeli Jews by dancing on the streets and by firing guns in the air and while the father of the suicide bomber kept praising his son as a martyr.

Next day early morning Monty was to catch a flight from the Palam airport in Delhi. He was scheduled to fly to Colombo to finalize an important export order and then from there fly to Mumbai and meet his son Peevee. On reaching Palam airport, when he read the bizarre headline news about the Nepal palace killings and the possible reasons for that ghastly massacre, he thought it was more than what the press had to say. Till then it was all conjecture and with some giving it the jilted love angle story while others were attributing it to too much of alchohol in Prince Depinder's blood. Therefore to find as to what actually happened inside the royal palace and as to what made the young crown prince carryout that insane act against his near and dear ones. Monty called up his son-in-law Bharat Padmanabhan who was the First Secretary in the Indian High Commission at Khatmandu. Paddy however had no clue till then as to why the young Crown Prince had to resort to such a gruesome and deadly act. All that Paddy said was that though the Palace authorities had claimed that the firing was accidental, but nobody in Khatmandu was buying that story. Paddy however said that he would get back to Monty once the full facts were known.

And on that very afternoon, when Monty checked into his hotel room in Colombo and switched on the TV to hear what the BBC had to say about the palace killings, he got another shock when he learnt about the suicide bombing of the Dolphinerain disco in Tel Aviv. "I think the whole world is going bloody mad. First it is a young Hindu crown prince from Nepal who gets into a mad frenzy and kills most of his family members and then tries to commit suicide. And now it is a young Muslim fanatic who blows himself up with a whole lot of young Israeli Jews. And if it carries on like this then I am afraid nobody is safe in their homes also. Its all bloody madness," said Monty to his Sinhalese client.

"I wholly agree with you. And with the diehard Tamil Tigers getting bolder and bolder day by day and with their leader Prabhakaran refusing to see reason, today even in Colombo nobody is safe and one doesn't know when and where they will strike next," said Monty's client as Monty rang up the room service for some nice hot Sinhalese tea and a plate of cheese sandwiches.

On the afternoon of 5th of June, having secured a fairly good export order for his garments, and before leaving for the airport to catch his flight to Mumbai, Monty again rang up Bharat in Khatmandu. He wanted to find out if there were any further developments in the sensational palace killings. And what Paddy told him was indeed really something very shocking. Paddy it seems had got this version from his own source and now that the new King Dipendra after a three day reign while lying in coma was also no more, the story therefore seemed more plausible and authentic. According to that source, the Crown Prince on that night of carnage was dressed in combat fatigues and he was armed with two automatic weapons. And as he walked into the room where his father, mother and others were sitting, he simply opened fire. He first his killed his father with a burst from his automatic rifle and left the room. But when he again came back a second time and his favourite uncle Dhirendra told him that enough was enough, the crown prince shot him dead too. Then he left the room again and when he came back for the third time he simply started spraying the whole room with bullets. Those who were lucky to survive ran for cover. Thereafter as Dipender headed back to his room, his mother and brother ran after him. But now there was now no stopping this mad maniac as he turned around and shot both of them in cold blood also.The entire mayhem though it lasted only for about ten minutes, but it had resulted in the deaths of nine and had wounded five and they were all from the royal family including Princess Ketaki Chester who was the King's cousin, but who had renounced her title. And nobody still knows for definite as to why the young crown prince did it,"said Paddy.

"That is rather surprising and with nobody from the palace staff either being killed or wounded, what were the damn palace guards doing?' asked Monty as he told Paddy to be careful. The Maoist influence in Nepal was on the rise and Monty feared that the brutal killings of the royalty in Nepal could well kick off a civil war.

Soon after Monty landed in Mumbai and when the news arrived that Mr Tony Blair's Labour Party had been re-elected once again with a landside victory over their arch opponents the Conservatives, Monty was not very surprised. In the elections that were held on 7th June, 2001 the Labour Party had won 413 seats out of 659 and the Conservatives could muster only 166. And with that thumping win, Tony Blair became the first Labour Prime Minister in British history to serve a full second consecutive term.

And while the British Labour Party in England was basking in their new found glory, in India Shupriya and Reeta on the 9th June after two hectic weeks of visiting various Gurudwaras, drove down to Shirdi from Nanded, and by the time they reached that holy place, it was already well past sunset. It was a Saturday and both of them were pleasantly surprised to be greeted by Monty and Peevee when they checked in at the Hotel Sun-n-Sand. It was a five star hotel that was near the sacred shrine of that pilgrim city and it provided all the required amenities. The very fact that the Samadhi of an unknown Muslim who lived from 1838 to 1918 had been converted into a sacred temple only proved that India was truly still a secular nation. It was like the tomb of the Unknown Soldier at India Gate where the flame of the eternal soldier is kept always burning. And at Shirdi too it was the Sai Baba's eternal light that preached to people from all walks of life and from all castes, creed and religion that faith and compassion were the only two supreme attributes to reach the state of godlinesss. That night for the first time in her life Shupriya as a mother shared the hotel room with her one and only son. And before falling asleep that night she fondly remembered Shiraz because there was so much resemblance between the father and the son. Next morning they all got up very early to be in time for the daily first morning ritual. Known as the 'Aaarti', this was a daily religious ritual with oil lamps and candles that starts at 5.15 every morning. In the peacefulness of that early morning dawn, when all the devotes sitting at the feet of the Baba sang Hindu hymms and closed their eyes to seek the Baba's blessings, Shupriya realized that if Shiraz had lived he would have soon been 55 years old and they would have all been one happy family. Soon after the 'Aarti 'was over and after a sumptuous breakfast of masala dosas and idli sambhar at the hotel when Monty checked the time it was nearing 7.30. Realizing that it was a Sunday and that the devotees would soon converge from all directions, he quickly asked for the bill. But before they could all get away quietly in Peevee's new Mercedes Benz, a group of young college girls and boys who had come from Pune having recognized the handsome Bollywood actor surrounded the car and demanded for a group photograph with him.

"Sure and with pleasure, but on condition that it will be only one group photograph and no more or else we will be all be late to catch our flight from Mumbai to Moscow,' lied Shupriya very proudly. And as soon as that group photograph was taken and everybody got into the car, Reeta too breathed a sigh of relief.

"Thank God the young crowd was not too demanding and knowing how people get carried away seeing a Bollywood star, we would have been caught in a massive traffic jam and our departure thanks to Deepak Kumar would have been delayed considerably," said Monty too rather proudly as Peevee got on to the main road.That afternoon after a short halt for lunch at a motel near Igatpuri they were back in Peevee's new big four bedroom penthouse on Carter Road in Bandra West. Overlooking the Arabian Sea and costing over a crore of rupees it was no doubt an expensive buy, but keeping in view that it was in Bandra's prime location, Peevee was dead certain that the property was bound to appreciate many more times in the next decade. However, he had no intentions of selling it.That night over some good French wine and some authentic frontier food that Peevee had ordered from Caravan Serai which was one of the very few restaurants in Bandra West that offered various types of kebabs and tandoori dishes and also delicious sea food, and which he knew were Monty's and Mom Number Two's favourite, when the topic once again veered around to his getting married, or whether he had found his lifetime partner, Peevee very diplomatically parried the question by saying.

"But I am only 29 and though I am now some sought of a superstar, but I think it is still too early to even think about it. Even Dilip Kumar the tragedy king of Indian cinema got married to Saira Banu when he was 42 and Saira who was then the beauty queen of Bollywood was practically half his age, so where is the hurry?"'

Then as Peevee helped himself to some more of that rare French Red Wine that Shupriya had presented him with, Monty very wisely said." 'Yes it is true that Mr Yusuf Khan alias Dilip Kumar was 42 when he married the vivacious 22 year old Saira Banu, but as Paramjit Singh Bajwa alias Deepak Kumar are you going to wait that long and look for someone who is 22 and then tie the knot? That I think won't be fair either to you or to her. And let me tell you that the Dilip-Saira marriage did not blossom from a love affair between the two Bollywood stars It was because of certain circumstances and compulsions that was beyond their control and which led them to the alter. And that is what I am told is a fact," said Monty as he too topped his wine glass.

"That's rather interesting and pray may I also know as to what were those compelling circumstances and compulsions," asked Shupriya who had absolutely no clue that Saira Banu was the only daughter of Naseem Banu and that the young lady was in love with the actor Rajender Kumar. Naseem Banu was the beautiful veteran actress of the black and white cinema era and she came into limelight in 1939 with her stirring performance as Malaika Noor Jehan the beautiful wife of the Moghul Emperor Jehangir in the Sohrab Modi hit film 'Pukar".

"Well as we all know and see that with Bollywood being Bollywood, stars do fall in love with each other at times and like it happened in the case of Nargis and Raj Kapoor, Dilip Kumar and Madhubala, Sohrab Modi and Mehtab. And therefore the Saira Banu-Rajendra Kumar affair was no different either. As Bollywood co-stars stars both of them were churning out hit films in the early and mid sixties and consequently they had fallen in love with each other. And the possibility of them getting married was also very much on the cards. But when Naseem Banu came to know about this serious affair, she immediately contacted the tragedy king who was also a good Muslim family friend and when the veteran actress requested him to please talk to Saira and make her understand, the problem was solved. So they got married on 11th October 1966 and as the saying goes everybody lived happily ever after."

"'Well I must say my dear Patiji (husband) that you are not only well versed with Indian history, but with the history of Bollywood affairs too, and if Peevee has some good looking heroine in mind then we will have no objection whatsoever. But it should not follow the great Kishore Kumar's Bollywood love stories of marrying four times four different actresses starting with Ruma Devi followed by Madhubala then Yogeeta Bali and finally ending up with Leena Chandavarkar," said Reeta as she looked approvingly at Peevee for his nod. But Peevee feeling a bit cornered said very tactfully.

"Unfortunately my love affairs with my screen heroines have always been in films and it remained on the cinema screens only. But I need a little more time before I commit myself. Being a Bollywood hero and with such stiff competiton from all the talented and famous Khans like Shahrukh Khan, Salman Khan, Aamir Khan and now we also have Saif Khan, I maybe a nobody tomorrow in this rat race. So please do allow me to establish myself a little more in this so called tinsel world of stars."

"Yes I agree and you do have a point there. Therefore while you have a nice long holiday in the company of Mom Number Two in Moscow but do give it some serious thought, and afterall we too would like to have a 'Bahu'(Bride) and some grandchildren playing in our house soon," said a smiling Monty as he helped himself to some more of the French wine.

That night before going to sleep Peevee called up Sherry in Moscow and once again reminded her that both of them will have to be very discreet while dating each other and he also confirmed to her that he would be arriving in Moscow on 12th June from Mumbai accompanied by his Mom Number Two.

Chapter-34
Moscow Rendezvous

And while Peevee was eagerly looking forward to meeting his sweetheart in Moscow, Shiraz was busy making some very important notes in his secret red diary. The new Pakistan Defence Attaché, who was a senior Brigadier and an artillery missile gunner officer had only taken over charge on the 1st of June. He had been posted from the SPD, the Strategic Plan Division that had been established only in February 2000 at Chaklala and whose main function was to improve the control of nuclear military operations. During his first interview with Shiraz on 3rd June, and to impress His Excellency, he not only boasted about his vast knowledge of nuclear weapons, but he also talked about the quantum of nuclear weapons that Pakistan possessed, and also about their location and capabilities. According to the Brigadier, the entire stockpile of nuclear warheads were hidden in secret underground facilities, and when required it could be quickly assembled and transported to the required delivery system. Needless to say that Pakistan now had both ground and air capability for the delivery of nuclear weapons.

Using a combination of page numbers, selected lines and words and phrases as codes from Leo Tolstoy epic book titled 'War and Peace', which the famous Russian author had written in 1869 on Napoleon Bonaparte's invasion of Russia, Shiraz therefore with meticulously encoded all the valuable information that was given to him by the Brigadier in his secret red diary. A couple of days later Shiraz and all other Pakistan Heads of Mission in the G8 countries were summoned to Islamabad for an important two day conference that was to be held on the 10th and 11th of June. They were required to be briefed by the government on what stance Pakistan was likely to take at the the forthcomimg Indo—Pak summit meet and they were therefore required to follow it up with the countries they were accredited to. But some of the statements that were made by Mr Abdus Sattar, the Pakistan's Foreign Minister on 27th May to the world press on the very day when General Musharraf accepted Mr Vajpayee's invitation to go to India for talks, only showed that Pakistan's entire focus was on Kashmir. And when Sattar said that it was a singular success of the military government of Pakistan to make India unconditionally accept Pakistan's long standing offer for talks on Kashmir, Shiraz knew that the former foreign seretary was a typical bureaucrat who had to say what Musharraf wanted him to say. As a seasoned diplomat. who had earlier served as the country's High Commissioner to India and who was also Pakistan's Ambassador to the Soviet Union before the country broke up, Abdus Sattar had also recently stated that any denial of the Pakistani delegation to meet the executive council members of the Hurriyat Conference would have a negative impact on the efforts to solve the Kashmir issue and that only showed that Pakistan was hell bent on focusing the demand for plebiscite again.

On that late afternoon of 12th of June, 2001 after Shuypriya and Peewee had landed at Sheremetyevo International Airport in Moscow, and while they were waiting at the conveyor belt to collect their suitcases, Shupriya were surprised to see the Pakistani Ambassador collecting his luggage from the adjoining belt. He too it seems. had arrived a couple of minutes earlier from Islamabad by the PIA flight as was indicative by the big tag on his suitcase. And since it was summer, Shiraz that day was wearing a typically white flowing spotless silk Pathani dress with a light woolen jacket. Peevee on noticing the tall gentleman with a well trimmed moustache and beard and with a Rayban sunglass covering his eyes thought he was probably some sophisticated Mulla. He did not know that the man was Sherry's father although he had been introduced to him once briefly during the Moscow film festival presentation ceremony.

"My God in that Pathani dress code the tall gentleman to me looks like some modern Mulla, but I wonder to which mosque does this Imam belong too. And don't tell me that there are also mosques in Moscow too?" said Peevee to his Mom Number two as Shiraz without noticing the presence of the Indian Ambassador quickly walked away with his luggage trolley towards the green channel.

"And by the way son he is not a Mulla at all. He is Riaz Mohammed Khan, Pakistan's Ambassador to this country and as regards mosques in Moscow are concerned, I only know of one and which is known as the Cathedral Mosque. It is also commonly known as the Tartar Mosque and it probably dates back to the time when the Tartar hordes who were Mongol Muslims invaded Russia and some of them thereafter settled in this city too,"said Shupriya as the green light on the conveyor belt came on.

On learning that the man was Pakistan's head of mission in Moscow and whom he had met very briefly earlier, Peevee wondered whether the man would ever accept him as his son-in-law. So far Peevee had not confided to anyone whatsoever about his courthip with Sherry and he was also in two minds whether to confide in Mom Number 2 about his love for the Pakistani girl. Likewise Sherry too had kept it a secret from her parents. Both of them were waiting for an opportune moment and time to make that official announcement. And keeping in view General Musharraf's impending visit to India in mid July, and with both the young lovers being very optimistic about the success of the summit talks, they had therefore decided that on the stroke of mid-night on 14/15 August would probably be the ideal time to announce their engagement. That would be their tryst with destiny.

In order to ensure that they always met quietly and unobtrusively in that sprawling Russian capital, the lovers had mutually earmarked all Mondays, Wednesdays and Fridays starting from the coming Friday of 15th of June as their first meeting day. Those were all week days when both the embassies would be working and there would be less chances of their being seen together. They had also decided that there would no meetings after sunset. All rendezvous would mostly be inside the many beautiful metro stations or at the many railway stations inside the city and it would be as per the timings laid down by them. They would entrain separately and travel to the prearranged destination and if required get off separately also as strangers on a train. And from there they would either take a cab if it was at all required and go to one of the decent restaurants or to a hotel or motel that were outside Moscow's city limits. The idea was to keep as far away as possible from the city and to visit places where the chances of being spotted together by Indians and Pakistanis were the remotest. In order to hide his identity, Peevee once again had grown his hair and beard and with the felt hat covering his head he looked more like a hippy. And as far as Sherry was concerned she had decided that she would be either in jeans or pants. In such kind of dress and with their fair complexion they could easily pass off as Georgians or Armenians.The excuse to be given by both of them for being away from home would either be to visit various museums and places of tourist interest in the city or to a library or for a movie or a theatre performance. And for that both of them had therefore procured good guide books in English and a detailed map of the Moscow metro and the city. And to avoid further suspicion, they had decided to get back home during the daylight hours and within the time slot of 4 to 5 hours at the maximum.

While Peevee at times would also give the excuse that he had been invited by Mosfilm or by the Gorky film studios for seminars, but after being dropped there by the embassy car he would take a cab to the designated metro or railway station for the rendezvous.

Peevee's first three days in Moscow was not exactly boring because Mom Number 2 had a series of informal lunches and dinners lined up for him. The idea was to present the Bollywood star to some of her close friends and colleagues and on one occasion she had also invited Lalima and a few other bigwigs from the Indo-Russian Freindship Society. Her Indo—Russian cousin who was now fairly well versed in Hindi had become a very popular and active member of the Indo-Russian Friendship Society and she still loved those old Raj. Kapoor and Nargis black and white movies that she had seen as a young girl with her late mother Galina Ghosh. And when Peevee learnt about Lalima's family history and that she had never been to India ever, he immediately offered to take her with him as his honoured guest. But Peevee was also yearning to meet the love of his life. Sherry was near and yet so far and though they spoke to each other everyday on their mobile phones but those three days of waiting was like an unending agony for both of them.

On that 15th June Friday morning at 10.30 sharp and as planned both of them in separate cabs reached the big Kievsky railway station and boarded a local train. Their destination was Peredelkino, a small dacha settlement outside Moscow that was made famous by Boris Pasternak the Nobel laureate and the author of Dr Zhivago who had lived there for many years and whose dacha was now a museum. It was only 20 minutes by train and because of its proximity to Moscow the place also had some decent hotels and restaurants. On the plea that they were very tired and that they wanted a double room to rest for a couple of hours, they had no difficulty whatsoever in checking into a fairly decent hotel. In fact the Manager of the small Country Club Hotel that had only nine rooms was very pleased to get a customer who was prepared to pay a full day's tariff just for a couple of hours of stay and that too in American dollars. And no sooner were they inside the room, Peevee held Sherry tightly in his arms and kissed her all over her pretty face. And when he presented her with a pair of diamond ear tops, there were tears of joy in her eyes. This time Peevee had come fully prepared with half a dozen durex condoms and soon both of them were all over each other on the double bed as they made love in all possible positions. And it was only at three in the afternoon feeling very tired and hungry that Peevee finally ordered two club sandwiches and some hot coffee from room service. And at 4.30 PM when the entire love making was finally over, they vacated the room and checked out from the hotel. On the return journey by train they finalised their plans for their next meeting that was scheduled for the coming Monday.

And while Peevee and Sherry in Moscow were making love that day, far away in New Delhi a bizarre Al Qaida plot to bomb the U.S. Embassy on Chanakayapuri was timely averted. The terrorist group had planned to leave a deadly car bomb with a timer outside the busy visa section of the American embassy. According to the the Indian police and some other sources Abdul Raouf Hawas, a Sudanese student had been arrested a couple of days earlier and according to his story Al Safani a Saudi of Yemeni descent who was involved in the bombing of the USS Cole and the US Embassy bombings in East Africa was the master mind behind the plot. There was also a rumour that the car and the explosives were provided by two diplomts of the Sudanese Embassy in New Delhi. That evening when Peevee returned home to his Mom Number 2, and when Shupriya told him about the plot, he just couldn't believe it. There was no doubt that while in Sudan, Bin Laden and his Al Qaida group were hand in glove with Khartoum's Islamic National Front, but the very fact that the Al Qaida network had planned that dastardly bombing on the American Embassy in India came as a rude shock to him.

During the weekend while he with his Mom Number 2 went shopping in Moscow, Peevee eagerly waited for Monday to come. And once again sharp at 10.30 in the morning on that Monday of 18th June, 2001 the two lovers met. This time it was at the Kurski railway station and they boarded the 10.40 local to Podolsk and from there took bus Number 65 to Dybrovitsky. It was a small town just 25 miles outside Moscow and which was once the country estate of the royal Romanov family. Besides the large country house for the royalty, there was also a very beautiful church on the estate and it was completely different in style from the typical onion shaped copula domes of the Russian Ortodox Church. This time they decided to picnic at a beautiful spot inside a wooded area on the nearby riverside and for which Peevee had come fully prepared. Giving the excuse to Mom Number 2 that he was going out on a picnic with some of the Russian actors and staff from the Mosfilm studio, Peevee had brought along with him a few cans of Tuborg beer, a portable tent for two, and a tiffin carrier full of typical Indian food including a full tandoori chicken, gajar ka halwa and the sweet Gujrathi pickle known as 'Chunda.'. And since this was not a regular tourist spot and a comparatively lonely place, they therefore had no difficulty in making love inside the tent.

And as the weeks went by it was only such like place outside Moscow and which were completely off the beaten track that became their regular destinations. And finding suitable accommodation at those places or at places nearby for a few hours was no big deal either, because the lure of the American dollar and the Pound Sterling to the Russians was as good as gold. And though the official exchange rate was 30 Rubles to a US Dollar, but in the black market one could get many times more. By the time the month of June came to an end they had also visited Arkhangelskoye and Borodino. Borodino on the outskirts of the city was the famous battle field where Napoleon Bonaparte in his quest to conquer the world was defeated by the Russians or rather by General 'Winter', because the severe Russian winter that year had forced him to retreat and Napoleon's army thus could not capture Moscow. And Arkhangelskoye with its historical estate and the church of Saint Michael was just 20 miles west off Moscow and both places had good decent hotels for tourists.

In the meantime in Pakistan and as envisaged by Unni, the CEO of the country General Pervez Musharraf on the 20th of June, 2001 using the country's consensus to his advantage had coinveniently eased out President Rafique Mohammed Tarar from his chair and had appointed himself President of Pakistan. And though he in his broadcast to the nation again reiterated his commitment that he would return the country to a true democracy in the near future, Ruksana Begum hearing that said rather sarcastically to her husband Arif Rehman. 'And so did promise Field Marshall Ayub Khan, General Yahya, and General Zia-ul-Haq, but take it from me this guy too will be no different. They all make promises only to break them."

` "Well you are right but now that he has accepted India's invitation to visit that country and hold talks with Mr Vajpayee, this will definitely add to his status and as per diplomatic protocol that I know off, there is no such designation like that of a CEO of a country," said Arif Rehman.

"Well all that I can say of Pakistan's 54 years of existence is that whether we were being ruled by a duly elected Prime Minister from the civvy street or by a General in military uniform, to me it makes no difference because they were all CEO's, the chief exploiting officer of our poor country," said Ruksana Begum somewhat mockingly when the telephone rang. It was from their daughter Saira inviting them to come to Moscow during mid August and to be with them atleast for a fortnight since she and Riaz (Shiraz) were planning to hold a grand reunion for all members of the entire Rehman clan on the mighty River Volga. It would be a seven day sight seeing cruise on a luxury boat and all children and grand children were also required to join them.

"'Well I think it's a splendid idea and if everybody accepts and which I feel they all must, then for us old foggies it will be an excellent opportunity to meet all of them at one place. Afterall at 81 I am not getting any younger, and once we all get on board then we can all sail and sing together that famous popular old Russian Volga Boatmen's song," said Arif Rehman as he tried to sing it in Paul Robeson style much to the amusement of Ruksana Begum. And while Sherry's grandparents started planning for the memorable trip, Sherry was busy planning her next rendezvous with Peevee.

A week later, when Shiraz read in one of the popular American news magazines that one George Trofimoff who was a senior retired American army officer had been convicted by a court in Florida for spying first for the Soviet Union and then for Russia, and that he had been in this spying business for the last quarter of a century, he just could not believe it. Afterall 25 years is a helleva lot of time, and the fact that the Americans had woken up only now after the gentleman had hung his boots as a Colonel in the US Army Reserve way back in 1987, only proved the point that the American intelligence set up had been very casual right from the day Trofimoff reported for duty at Nuremburg in Germany. And that was way back in 1959, when the Cold war was at its peak.Trofimoff was born in Germany in and around 1928 to Russian émigrés and he became a naturalised US citizen in 1953. He enlisted in the US army in 1948 and received a commission in the US Army Reserve in 1953 and after three years of active service was honourably discharged in 1956. And the very fact that he was thereafter employed by the US army as a civilian and was assigned to work in the military intelligence department right from 1959 to 1994 was itself rather intriguing and shocking. Not only had the man served in a senior appointment at the Nuremburg Joint Interrogation Centre in Germany for a very long time and where he was privy to some much classified secret and top secret information, but he also kept selling these with documentary proofs for monetary gains to the Soviet Union and the SVR, the Russian Foreign Intelligence Service. And for those many years neither the CIA nor the FBI had a clue of what the man was upto. And it has now been alleged by the FBI that Trofimoff had not only made a whopping 250,000 dollars and more, but he had also been awarded the Order of the Red Banner for his spying services. And had it not been for Vasili Mitrokin a Soviet KGB clerk who had defected in 1992 to the US and who told the Americans that one of the US interrogation centres was being compromised by a career American intelligence officer, Trofimoff probably would never have been caught. But the man's greed for more money led to his own downfall when Igor Galkin an FBI undercover agent got the better of him. Luring Trofimoff that he would offer him 20,000 dollars or more for some classified information to start with, Trofimoff fell for it. He agreed to meet Galkin at Tampa in Florida and fell into the trap. The very fact that Trofimoff had been awarded a life sentence had made Shiraz sit up. And though as a career diplomat he had till now not indulged in any spying activity as such for India, except for taking down notes from certain classified documents in his little red diary, but the fear that he may one day be unmasked and exposed as an Indian spy indeed was very frightening for him.

And while Shiraz kept pondering whether Trofimoff who was basically a Russian had been recruited and indoctrinated by the KGB even before he became a naturalized American citizen, his daughter Sherry was busy planning for her next date with her Indian matinee idol. In the meantime in the Indian state of Tamil Nadu, on the night of 30th June, Jayalalitha the Chief Minister went on a rampage as she in close cooperation with her new police chief A. Ravindranath in a midnight sweep arrested her arch rival M. Karunanidhi and a few others including the Union Commerce Minister Murasoli Maran and the Environment and Forest Minister T R Balu. Seeing the sordid drama on the television channel of the 77 year old ex Chief Minister of the state being physically manhandled by the police and being dragged and beaten like a common criminal in his own residence, Monty was shocked beyond words. The feud between the two political rivals had started in 1989, when Jayalalitha was assaulted on the floor of the assembly and which resulted in her being roughed up and her saree torn. This time the ball was in her rival's court as she charged the members of the first DMK family with rampant corruption and then as a special thanksgiving flew to Guruvayoor in Kerala to donate an elephant to the diety in that temple.

"The way these shameless politicians fight when they get to that big chair is worse than little kids fighting for a piece of candy. This is nothing short of vendetta and while the state is burning, the buxom madam Chief Minister of the state is away asking for blessings from the Lord Almighty," said Monty somewhat sarcastically to his wife Reeta while reminding her to ring up Peevee in Moscow and to find out whether he would join them on the 4th of July for dinner that is being hosted by him for all his ex Sanawarians friends at the Delhi Gymkhana.

The 4th of July, 2001 happened to be a Wednesday and since it was also America's Independence Day Sherry decided to treat Peevee to some exclusive Russian cuisine at the popular Tsarskaya Okhota Restaurant in Zhukovka Village on the Rublyovo Uspenskoye highway. But before that she also wanted to show him the kind of VIP cottages and mansions that had come up on both sides of that road. On that day she had hired a Mercedes car that Peevee insisted on paying for and as they made their way on the A-105 highway, Peevee was completely bowled over with the kind of luxury apartments that had and were still coming up in that nuveaux rich fashionable area on the outskirts of the Russian capital.

"But where is all the money coming from and who are the owners of such luxury villas and penthouses. Because even in India and in big cities like Mumbai and Delhi and on their outskirts like Khandala and Gurgaon only a handful of individuals can dream of having such opulent houses and live in such grand royal style," said Peevee as he took a few photographs of some of those luxury mansions and houses.

"Well it is the nuveau rich and the oligarchs of new Russia and ofcourse also the mafia who have become not only very powerful but also very rich. And these tycoons are also now well connected to the powers that matter in Russia's own White House. In fact the boss of Lukeoil, Mr Vagit Alekperov who is now a multi billionaire and whose father was a Muslim from Azerbaijaan and his mother an Orthodox Russian and he also has some prime property in this area. And by the way his oil company was the first one to open Russia's first gasoline filling station 26 kilometres outside Moscow and that too with a 17 room motel on the Moscow-Riga highway in September 1997. Though the young Baku born oil magnate and engineer had lost his father who had worked all his life as a simple worker in the Caspian Sea oilfields, but the enterprising Vajit in 1990 became the youngest Deputy Energy Minister of emerging Russia and in 1991 during the dying days of the Soviet Union a small group of Soviet bureaucrats led by Vajit formed Lukoil and thereafter there was no looking back for him. and his close friend Vitaly Schimdt who was also a petroleum engineer. Unfortunately Vitaly Schimdt who had also become an oil tycoon like Vajit suddenly died under very mysterious circumstances in August 1997," said Sherry as Peevee with his new Nikkon camera took a few close up photos of her leaning against the black coloured Mercedes Benz. Thereafter standing near the gate of a big mansion and with Sherry by his side, Peevee requested the driver to take a photograph.

"Well I must say that you are pretty well uptodate with the new oligarchs of modern Russia, but do be careful of them because some of them I believe though they are married they are also fond of good looking girls and women too," said Peevee with a mischievous smile on his face as Sherry instructed the driver to turn around and head towards the Tsarskoye Okhota restaurant.

"I guess all this inside knowledge of what is happening in this country is because of my dear father's love for golf. And he I am quite sure must be getting it all on the 19th hole of the MCGC, the Moscow Country Club Golf Course that was founded in 1987 by Swen Johanson, the famous Swidish Ice Hockey player. And Abbu is there religiously on every weekend to rub shoulders with Russia's new business tsars and others who matter," replied Sherry very confidently as they were guided to their reserved table which was in one far corner of the restaurant.

"And please don't mind but I think your dear father looks like a sophisticated Mulla in his Pathani dress, "said Peevee quite matter of factly as Sherry looked at him with utter surprise till Shiraz showed her the photograph that he had casually clicked with his mobile camera at the Moscow airport.

"My God that really gave me quite a scare, but nevertheless even with that moustache and beard he is still very handsome I think," said Sherry very proudly as the waiter handed over the menu and the wine card to them. The two storied restaurant with its rustic furniture and with portraits and busts of Russia's old royalty all over the place was considered the best for Russian cuisine in Moscow. Stocked with a very good bar, Sherry quickly ordered the starters and a big bottle of Russian pink champaign to go with it. Though it was a working Monday, but there were a lot of Americans from the American Embassy in Moscow in the restaurant that day. And they were all there that afternoon to celebrate the 4th of July. Seated amongst them on a big table was Duff Cooper a Second Secretary in the embassy and whose father was a white American Christian and mother an Indian Hindu Saraswat Brahmin from Bangalore. Duff had met Sherry at a couple of diplomatic cocktail parties and had fallen for her, but Sherry was not at all interested in him. Once at a dance party at the American Embassy, when Duff who had quietly followed her to the ladies rest room tried to force himself on her, Sherry had slapped him hard and since then Duff had held a big grudge against her. Duff was also aware that though Sherry came from a modern Muslim family who were fairly broad minded, but at the same time he also knew that as far was marriage was concerned her parents were very orthodox. And this was what Sherry herself had told him when he tried to probe a little more into her personal life. And she had even told him very curtly that her future husband had to be a Sunni Muslim only and not a half American-Indian like him.

That day Duff had noticed the couple entering the restaurant holding hands and smiling, but Sherry hadn't noticed him at all. And since Sherry and Peevee were sitting in one far end of the restaurant that was well away from the big long American table, she also did not notice Duff since he had his back towards her. However, seeing the young lady walk in with a bearded gentleman, Duff kept discreetly observing them and he it seems was feeling a little jealous. A little while later when Duff saw them kissing and smooching and that too rather passionately, he quietly left the table, and on the pretext of clicking some photos of the interior décor inside the restaurant, he also managed to click a few photographs of the couple in that compromising position. Sherry and Peevee were so very much in love with each other that they it seems were not bothered of who was doing what in the restaurant. Kissing and smooching in public was very common in Russia and it was so also in Europe and in America. Therefore for young couples to show their feelings to one another in this manner at public places was very common and nobody really bothered. Both Sherry and Peevee it seems were in a world of their own that day and they were simply oblivious of what was happening around them. And it could also be attributed to the large bottle of Champagne that Sherry had ordered and which was now nearly more than three fourths empty. And by the time Sherry paid the bill it was nearing five in the evening and it was time for them to go home. And as they walked out holding hands, they found that they were practically the last ones to leave the restauratnt. The group of Americans had already left much earlier.

Duff was under the impression that the gentleman who was kissing and smooching Sherry was probably some nuveau rich mafia leader who looked very much like an Armenian, Azerbajani or a Georgian. And therefore in order to take it out on Sherry, he decided to send those photos with the caption 'Beware—Too much of freedom could spell disaster for your pretty daughter" to her father and mother, but without mentioning the name of the sender at all.

With Peevee scheduled to fly back to India on the 14th of July, the time was now running out for the lovey-dovey couple.There were only four more working week days left for them to be in each other's arms and therefore in order to get more time to themselves, they decided to meet not in far away places that were out of Moscow, but in small nondescript motels, inns, guest houses and hotels that were in nearby suburbs but away from the city centre. On 6th July they spent the whole day at the two stars Altay Hotel that was near the Botanical gardens and the Vladikino metro station. And on the 9th of July it was a nondescript one room guest house in the suburb of Ismailova and which was very close to the Ismailovo Park where Peter the Great grew up. But on the 11th of July, when they checked into a rented posh apartment near Hotel Ukraina which was in the heart of the city they did not realize that they were been trailed and videographed by the Pakistani ISI. It seems that on the morning of 10th July, when those intimate photographs with the date, time and place clearly marked on them were received in a biggish sealed envelope addressed to His Excellency Riaz Mohammed Khan, Ambassador of Pakistan to Russia, the clerk on duty at the reception desk in the embassy as was routine had sent it immediately to His Excellency's secretariat. And since it was not marked secret, confidential or private, the private secretary to his Excellency who had the authority to open such letters did so routinely. And when he saw those revealing photographs, he got a shock of his life.

During that week His Excellency with his wife was away on a tour of duty to Helsinki the capital of Finland, because that country too was also accredited to the Pakistan Embassy in Moscow. And they were only expected back on the morning of 14th July to be in time for the Bastille Day lunch at the French embassy. And since there was no covering letter attached to those photos and only the word mafia written in bold red Russian alphabets and that to on the reverse side of some of those more intimate photographs, the private secretary therefore thought that the Ambassador's daughter may be hobnobbing with some Russian mafia leader or maybe she was mixed up with them. So he quietly and confidentially went and showed them to the Minister who was the number two man in the embassy. And the Minister in order to find out a little more about the gentleman that Sherry was going around, he too immediately put the Visa officer on the job. The Visa officer was actually from the Pakistan ISI and he had been told to go about it very discreetly since it was the young lady's private matter. And with the young lady being none other than the daughter of the Pakistani Ambassador to Russia it had to be therefore handled very deftly. The Russian mafia leaders were big money sharks and the possibility of a rival gang kidnapping her for ransom could not be ruled out either. And if that did happen then it would be a big diplomatic scandal thought the Minister. The ISI agent was therefore told to leave everything else and to discreetly keep a close watch on Sherry and her whereabouts. His task was to find out primarily and with photographic evidence as to who was the man in those photographs, and it had to be done before the big boss and his wife returned from Helsinki.

On the morning of 11th July at around 10 o'clock in the morning as Sherry got into a cab near her residence and made her way to a posh apartment near the big Ukraina Hotel, she had no idea that she was being followed. Sporting a new wig and dressed like a hippy with a backpack and a handyman camera at the ready, the ISI agent had followed her all the way on a second hand BMW motorcycle that he had hired for the entire day from Ad-MoreTours in Moscow. But once Sherry went inside that apartment building all by herself, the agent felt rather disappointed. He was under the impression that she would probably head for some restaurant for the rendez vous with her lover and fearing that this could well be the Mafia leader's apartment; he felt a bit scared and therefore did not try to venture inside. However he took a vantage position outside the building and from where he could keep it under total surveillance. And for him it was indeed a long wait that day but it was definitely worth the effort, when at around 5.15 in the evening Sherry with her loverboy emerged from that big building.Though Peevee sported a felt hat and all the previous photographs that were with the agent showed the target to be bear headed with long hair, but nonetheless the agent knew that he had found his man. And as Peevee got into a cab and made his way to the Indian Embassy on Ulitsa Obukha, the agent feeling mighty happy kept following him. But when he saw the cab stop in front of the embassy building and saw the man being greeted with a big salaam by the Indian security guard on duty, he got a shock of his life. Thinking that the Mafia leader may have gone inside for a meeting with some Indian embassy trade officials since export and import had also become part of their big business, he drove another 50 yards and while sitting on his bike kept a close vigil on the Indian embassy gate. The time was already nearing six thirty in the evening and though it was well past closing time, some staff members in their personal cars and motor bikes were still seen coming out from the embassy gate, but their was no sign of the man that he was on the lookout for. And at seven thirty feeling a bit tired and thinking that the gentlemen may well have taken a lift in some diplomat's car, he returned to his own apartment on Leninisky Avenue.

Early next morning, the ISI man was again back in action again, but this time he was dressed in a safari suit and was without the wig. And for his mobility he had borrowed a scooter from one of his embassy colleagues. But his waiting a little away from the Ambassador's residence and expecting Sherry to come out at anytime was all in vain because it was a Thursday and a rest day for the two lovers. However, in order to check if she was at all at home or not on that day, the gentleman around 5 o'clock in the evening rang the door bell. And when Sherry opened the door, he simply asked her if she had received a separate invitation card for the Bastille Day lunch at the French embassy on the 14th of July. And the reason for his asking for that information was primarily to find out if Madam Sherry would be accepting or not accepting the invitation. Because the information was required by the embassy's protocol department to give a proper formal RSVP to His Excellency the Ambassador of France by evening. Since such formal invitations to Sherry from various missions were now routine because she was considered to be an adult, Sherry therefore was not at all surprised. She however conveyed to the Visa officer that she had not received any such invitation and even if she had she would have declined it. And when Sherry offered him a cup of tea and he refused by giving the excuse that he had to finish some important work to finish before office closing time, Sherry knew that the gentleman was only trying to impress how very sincere and hard working he was.

However after wishing her Khuda Hafiz when the Visa officer went back to the embassy, he in order to find out whether the young lady would at all be going out that evening, he therefore requested the Minister to ring her up and ask her if she would be home in the evening and whether it would be alright for the Minister to drop by for a cup of tea and look her up since her parents were away. And to make it look normal he also requested the Minister to take along with him a few newspapers and magazines that had arrived that day by the weekly diplomatic mail bag. And.when Sherry told the Minister over the phone that she had no intention whatsoever of getting out of the house that evening, there was sanse of relief for the ISI man. But for him time was also running out because he had been tasked to find out the true identity of the man in the photograph before the Ambassador returned from his Helsinki tour and he had now less than 48 hours to complete the mission. He however did manage to take a short video footage of the gentleman while he was getting into the cab near Hotel Ukraina that day, but that was not good enough to identify the person concerned. And though he was weaing a felt hat that evening there was no doubt that he was the same man who was with Sherry at the restaurant on the 4th of July also. On closer examination the face did look a little familiar to him, but the ISI man simply could not place where he had seen him earlier.

For Peevee and Sherry, Friday the 13th of July, 2001 was the last and final day when they would spend their time as lovers in Moscow. And in order to spend maximum time together they had decided to meet a couple of hours earlier than usual. The time fixed was at 8.30 in the morning and in order to save time commuting to and fro, the venue chosen for the final rendezvous was a nondescript and an inexpensive place in the very heart of the city. Popularly known as the 'Bed and Breakfast Vanilla Guest House' it was coveniently located off Tverskaya Street and in close vicinity of the Kremlin, Pushkin Square and the famous Bolshoi Theatre. And Peevee had discovered it while browsing on the internet. But he did not realize that the 13th would prove very unlucky for both of them.

In order to get out from the house early that morning, Peevee had given Mom Number 2 the excuse that he had been invited by a Mosfilm star to his dacha for a duck shoot and since that was going to be followed by a late lunch, she should not expect him back before 7 in the evening. But he had also promised her that he would be well in time for the informal sing-song party that was being hosted by her in his honour on the eve of his departure for India. And as far as Sherry was concerned it mattered little to her as to what time she left home and what time she came back, because her parents were out of town and she was like a free bird. But she was not aware that the Minister on the previous evening had taken the Pakistani security personnel in the Ambassador's house also into full confidence and had told them to keep a close eye on her. The security guards had been told that in view of His Excellency and Madam being away on duty to Helsinki, and with their daughter being alone in the house, they must therefore be more vigilant. And since there was also a possibility of the young lady being kidnapped by the mafia, they must not allow any unknown visitors to enter the premises, and one of them must always be ready to discreetly follow her everytime she went out alone from the house. And if they did find her leaving the house at anytime then they must also immediately inform Mr Iqbal Ahmed the Visa Officer in the embassy on his mobile phone. And for that very purpose the Minister had also now temporarily parked a hired BMW motorcycle with a full tank of petrol for use by the security staff if and when it was required.

It was around 8.15 on the morning of 13th July, while Iqbal Ahmed was having his breakfast with his wife when his mobile phone rang. And telling his wife that it was a very important call from the Ambassador's residence and that he had to go immediately, he left his half finished breakfast and got on to the borrowed scooter. Minutes later he was seen speeding away on the road . . .

"Just keep following the cab and don't loose sight of it. And also keep me continously posted on the route being taken and towards which general direction the cab is heading," said Iqbal.to Rahim Khan who was one of security guards at the Ambassador's residence. And as Rahim Khan on the BMW motorcycle kept following the cab at a safe distance, he also kept his boss continuously posted on the direction towards which Sherry's cab was heading . . .

"'Most likely it is heading towards the city centre Janab because when Missysahiba told us to get her a cab she also told us to tell the cab driver that the destination would be the city centre. And that is because the cab drivers are often very choosy about doing short distances during peak hours. But since it was fairly early in the morning most of them were willing to go to the city centre," said Rahim Khan the burly Pathan who had put on the helmet with the tinted glasses while he kept following the cab on his BMW. A few minutes later Iqbal Ahmed's mobile rang again. It was Rahim and he was now giving a running commentary. "Janab we have now entered the Tverskaya Ulitsa close to the metro station and the cab has stopped to probably ask for directions. Now it has started moving again and it has turned into Bolshaya Bronnaya Street and is heading in the southwesterly direction. It has once again stopped in front of the Alye Parussa food store and Missybaba has got off. She has paid off the cab driver and she is now going on foot along that street. Now she has reached a road crossing just ahead of the foodstore and has turned right into another small street which goes by the name of Kozhinski Perulok. She has once again stopped near the Neverland kids store and is talking to some elderly lady. The old lady is pointing her hands towards something which I can't figure out right now."

"Alright just discreetly keep following her but be careful she should not recognize you. Don't go too close and keep the helmet with the visors on," said Iqbal Ahmed as he too got into Bolshaya Bronnaya Street and raced towards the food store. But by the time he could catch up with Rahim Khan, Sherry had already got inside the small guest house. Rahim Khan luckily had seen her going inside that guest house and he informed Iqbal accordingly.

"Alright you can now get back to the Ambassador's residence and I will keep vigil on her. Maybe she has gone to meet some old college friends of hers who I am told have come as tourists from America to this city and therefore there is nothing to worry about,"lied Iqbal Ahmed very confidently as Rahim Khan bid him Khuda Hafiz and got on to the bike and left.

Though there was a fair lot of activity of young foreign tourists with backpacks going in and coming out of that the small guest house from time to time, but there was no sign of Sherry. And if she was going around with a rich mafia leader as was suspected then this was definitely not the place to be in. Only the day before he had seen her entering the posh apartment near Ukraina Hotel and why should the couple now chose such an out of the way small guest house for their romantic interludes, thought Iqbal Ahmed as he kept waiting and waiting for her to come out with her lover. And while he kept sitting on his scooter on that small side street and kept waiting for

Missybaba to come out with her lover, the ISI sleuth was also now getting a bit impatient. He was also tired of giving the same excuse to the young Russian admirers of his new imported scooter that he was only waiting for a dear friend of his to turn up. There was no doubt that Iqbal Ahmed being a Pakistani in his mid thirties was also feeling a little akward and scared while hanging around that small street. Moscow was very unsafe and with reports of Mafia gangs mugging people even on the roads and side streets, he therefore around mid-afternoon called up Rahim Khan again and told him to have a quick lunch and to meet him outside the Neverland kids store at I P.M. sharp. And when Rahim Khan arrived on his BMW, Iqbal Ahmed briefed him thoroughly. He not only handed over his camera to Rahim Khan to discreetly take photographs of Sherry and her companion, but he also told him to keep the guest house under total and strict surveillance all the time and to inform him immediately as soon as Missybaba came out from that place. And in case he saw any gentleman with long hair and a beard coming out with her or following Missybaba, then he should tag the gentleman on his motorbike and keep him posted on the route being taken by that man and his final destination.

While Rahim Khan kept a discreet watch of the people going in and coming out from that small nondescript guest house, Iqbal Ahmed quickly made his way on the scooter to the nearby Café Pushkin. Having had practically no breakfast in the morning he was feeling famished and he therefore ordered for a thick solyanka meat soup, a vinigret salad and a plate of beef strogonoff. And once the meal was over, he ordered his favourite blinni for dessert. It was nothing but pancakes with honey. With service at lunch time in that popular café being pretty slow, Iqbal by the time he settled the bill it was already nearing three thirty in the afternoon and there was still no call from Rahim Khan. However in order to check that Rahim Khan was keeping proper vigil and that every thing was in order he rang him up instead.

"Arre Tussii Fiqar na karo Janaab mere donon annkhen target pur datti hui hai aur aabhi tak aapke parinde bahar nahin aaye. Mayne ye bhi patta kiya agar koi dusra darwaja hai ussi guest house main aane jane ka, lekin khuda ka shukur hai ek hi main darwaza hai anne ka aur janne ka bhi,'said Rahim Khan very confidently. (Please do not worry and my eyes are glued to the door of the guest house but so far no birds that you are looking for have come out of their nest. And I also enquired if there was another entrance and exit to that guest house but thank God there is only one main entrance)

"Bahut Khoob aur tum wahan hi date raho jab tak main wapas nahi atta. Mein thodh dusra zaroori kaam ke liye ja rahan hun aur wapas ate waqt tumhare liye aur tumhare sathi ke liye bhi kuch shaslik aur kebab lete aaoonga,.'(Very good and keep your eyesight fixed on that door and on my return I will bring for you and your colleague some delicious shasliks and kebabs) said Iqbal Ahmed as he drove to Moscow's Novy Arbat. This was Moscow's most fashionable avenue and where he could also do some girl gazing. It was also a place where one could easily pick up a nice young Russian whore and who he knew would be ready to go to bed even for a few US dollars. But when he suddenly realized that it was nearing 5 PM and that there was no time for having such a quick fling, Iqbal Ahmed quickly picked up the shashliks and kebabs from Kebab House in Old Arbat and made his way back to the Vanilla Guest House. On reaching there he relieved Rahim Khan and he himself once again kept a close vigil on that little guest house. But what he could not understand was as to why Sherry was taking so much of time. Then finally at about 6.15, when he spotted the lovey dovey couple hand in hand coming out of that guest house and noticed that they were walking towards him, Iqbal Ahmed got a bit nervous. Fearing that Sherry would definitely recognize him, he quickly donned his helmet with the visor and made an effort to manually park the scooter a little closer to the Neverland Kids Store which was on the opposite side of the street. And having done that, he briskly with his helmet over his head entered the toy store. But since he could not afford to lose sight of the couple, he waited for the couple to first pass him by. And as soon as they passed by the store, Iqbal with the helmet still over his head came out once again on to the street and sat on his scooter to observe the couples next move. Surprising the gentleman with Sherry who was very tall was still wearing the same felt hat but there was no time or opportunity for Iqbal Ahmed to video film them while they were walking arm in arm towards the Bolshaya Bronnaya Street. Since the road junction from the store was hardly fifty metres away, Iqbal Ahmed kept observing them while sitting on his scooter. But as soon as the couple reached the main road junction and he saw them hailing for a taxi, Iqbal Ahmed got worried. After so much of effort he could not afford now to lose their trail. He therefore while pretending that his scooter was giving some problem, he kept slowly pushing it towards the road junction. Luckily for him it was a busy working day that day and it was also closing time for most of the offices in that area. And as a result of which all cabs with their passengers kept just whizzing past without stopping. Realising that it would not be all that easy for the couple to get a taxi at that hour, Iqbal Ahmed took out a spanner and a screwdriver from the tool box and pretended as if he was busy repairing his scooter. Finally after a long fifteen minute wait, when he saw that he couple had finally managed to flag down a cab, but the Russkie driver it seems was unwilling to go unless he was paid something extra. Then all of a sudden seeing the big smile on the cabbie driver's face, Iqbal Ahmed knew that the deal had been struck. And when he saw the man passionately kissing Sherry on the sidewalk and then opening the door of the cab for her to get in, Iqbal Ahmed also cranked his scooter. And when the cab drove off with only Sherry as the passenger it did not worry him because he knew that she would at this time of the evening definitely go home. But what was bothering him was the identity of Sherry's companion and lover. Time was running out and Iqbal Ahmed only had a couple of hours left to find out the man's true identity and he therefore waited patiently for the gentleman to make his next move. And in order to have a closer look at the man, Iqbal Ahmed therefore decided to walk up to him and ask him for directions if required. But when he suddenly saw the the man crossing the road and with a fistful of greenback American dollars in his hand kept frantically waving out to all the passing cars, cabs and vehicles for a lift, he realized that the man was definitely in some frightful hurry. He therefore started his scooter and kept observing him from a distance. A minute or so later, when a private car, an old 1986 model Volga suddenly stopped and picked him up, Iqbal Ahmed was certain that with that kind of American money to throw around, the man was definitely a member of some big Russian mafia gang and as had been indicated by the anonymous person who had sent those lurid photos to the Pakistani embassy. And as the driver of the Russian made car with the passenger next to him in the front seat stepped on the accelerator, Iqbal Ahmed also kept following it but not too closely. He could never trust the Russian mafia.

But twenty minutes minutes later, when the car turned into Ulitsa Obukha and stopped right in front of the Indian Embassy gate, Iqbal Ahmed once again got a shock of his life. And while sitting on the scooter and a little away from the Indian embassy gate, when he saw the tall gentleman alighting from the car being greeted with a big salaam by the Indian security guard, he checked his watch. It was nearing 7 PM. And while entering through the gate when the man very respectfully doffed his hat to the sentry on duty, Iqbal Ahmed observed that the man not only had long hair but he was also good looking and handsome too. He therefore concluded that the man was definitely not a Rrussian and certainly not a member of the Russian mafia He therefore now feared that the gentleman could be an Indian spy from RAW and who as an Indian diplomat having seduced the Pakistani ambassador's good looking daughter was probably now wanting to use her services as a mole. With those passionate pictures of the couple kissing and smooching, and with what he saw with his own very eyes today of the couple kissing on the sidewalk, there was no doubt in Iqbal Ahmed's mind that the Ambassador's daughter was very much in love with that handsome Indian gentleman. And the very fact that President Musharraf's was about to embark on his historic visit to India on the very next day, and the possibility of the man using Sherry to pass on some highly classified and secret information to the Indians could not therefore be ruled out either. But inspite of all the day's hard work, the fact remained that Iqbal Ahmed had still not been able to yet identify the concerned gentleman. He neither knew his name or his designation. And since it was a desparate situation for him, because the Ambassador was expected back from Helsinki on the very next morning, he decided to take a chance. Therefore throwing all caution to the wind, Iqbal Ahmed boldly walked up to the Indian sentry at the Indian Embassy and said to him very confidently in good Hindi. ('Arre yaar Mafkarna, lekin ye to batao ke jis yuva diplomat sahib ko mere jigri Russian dost ne apne gadi mein yahan tak abhi abhi lift diya, aur usse gate ke andhar jate waqt aapne usse ek bada salaam bhi kiya, unka pura naam aur designation kiya hain. Baat ye hai ke mera gadiwala Russian dost aur mein, hum dono Indo-Soviet Friendship Society ke karyakarte hain aur hum chahate hain ki kaal aakar hum usse officially mille aur unse darkhast karen ke vo hamare agla yuva program mein chief guest ban kar zaroor aanye.)' Please do pardon my asking, but just tell me what is the full name and designation of the young diplomat to whom my good Russian friend just gave a lift in his car and to whom you also gave a big salaam as he walked in. You see both my Russian friend and I are honorary secretaries of the Indo-Russian Friendship Society and we would like to come tomorrow and officialy invite him to be our chief guest for our next function which is directed towards the youth of both the nations." ('Arre kiya yaar tumbhi kamal ke ho. Arre baba jis aadmi ko aap milna chahte ho kal, vo koi altu-faltu aadmi nahin hai, aur nahi toh vo koi Indian diplomat hain. Vo toh India ka Bollywood cinema ka ek mahan kalakar hai aur is waqt woh hamare Rajdoot ka khas personal mehman bhi hai. Kiya aapne kabhi Deepak Kumar ka ṅaam nahin suna?).Well you seem to be quite a clueless character. That man whom you want to meet tomorrow is not an ordinary person and nor is he an Indian diplomat. He is a well known Bollywood cinema star and he is presently the personal honoured guest of our Ambassador. Have you never heard the name of Deepak Kumar? Said the Indian sentry looking quite surprised that the man had failed to recognize the popular Indian superstar. Therefore feeling somewhat embarrassed, Iqbal Ahmed quickly added (Han ji suna toh zaroor hun aur uske bahut sare picture bhi dekha hun, lekin unko is dress, hat aur aissi lambi daari aur muchhon mein maine pehle kabhi koi picture mein nahin dekha. Khair aap ka bahut bahut shukriya aur main kaal subah zaroor aaoonga usse milne) 'Ofcourse I have heard his name and I have also seen a lot of his films, but I have never seen him on the screen in that dress with a hat, and with such a big beard and moustache. Well anyway thank you very much and I will definitely come tomorrow to meet him," said a somewhat confused Iqbal Ahmed who actually had not seen a single film of that Bollywood hero but he had only heard about him and had seen his photographs in some Indian film magazine. However feeling happy that he had finally identified his quarry, he raced back on his scooter to the Minister's house.

"Don't be bloody well crazy and you must be off your bloody rocker. But are are you very sure that the man with the beard and the felt hat is none other than the Bollywood star. Deepak Kumar,"'said the Minister as he once again saw the video footage that Iqbal had taken near the Ukraina Hotel and compared it with the photographs that had been sent anonymously earlier." But Janab this was told to me by none other than the Indian sentry on duty at the Indian embasssy gate and why should he lie to me," said Iqbal Ahmed looking a bit upset with the Minister's sudden outburst.

"Yes you do have a point there and the best and only way to confirm will be to go on the internet and see the actors profile and pictures. And for that I am sure he must also be having his own website. But what is more intriguing is where, how and when did they meet Because one thing is for sure and that is Sherry has never been to Mumbai or for that matter to India ever. And if they have been having their love escapades right under our own damn noses in Moscow and we were completely ignorant of it, then all I can say is that you guys from the ISI posted to this embassy are blind as bats," said the Minister in a gruff and angry tone as he switched on his laptop commuter to get on to the actor's website. That night as the both of them kept surfing on the computer they found without an iota of doubt that the gentleman was none other than the Bollywood star Deepak Kumar. But now they were in two minds whether to inform His Excellency when he arrives from Helsinki next morning or to wait and and see if the Indian spy agency RAW has any hand in this so called affair. Since as a routine a lot of classified official mail was also regularly sent to the Ambassador's residence, they were now keen to find out if RAW was using Deepak Kumar as an agent. And maybe with the lure of big money, glamour and a promise by the actor to marry Sherry, Deepak Kumar in turn was also probably using the girl as a conduit to pass on those classified documents and information to him. Though it seemed to be a a very rare possibility, but no chances could be taken and the only way it could be confirmed was by keeping Sherry under total surveillance both at home and outside.

"Maybe they will meet again at some place either tomorrow or the day after, and once the lovey-dovey rendezvous of the two lovers gets over for the day like it did today, I and my colleagues will lie in wait for them to part company. And once Mr Deepak Kumar goes his own way, I and my team on the pretext of being his ardent fans of his will first befriend the Indian Bollywood star and later mug him. We will then carry out a full body search of the superstar and and if we do find anything incriminating on his person we will charge him with spying and expose him to the world. And moreover since Deepak Kumar doesn't have any diplomatic immunity in this country, it will make our task all the more easier," said Iqbal Ahmed.very confidently.

"But all the same we will all have to be very very careful, because President Musharraf is leaving for India tomorrow and any wrong move on our part on this so called love affair could well jeopardize the entire peace talks. And till such time the talks are on we should lie low and keep the matter to ourselves. And we will only tell His Excellency after we catch Mr Deepak Kumar red handed. May be the two of them are madly in love, but that is their personal business and affair. But if Sherry is found guilty of passing secrets to her lover, then I am afraid even Mr Riaz Mohammed Khan our Ambassador will be in deep trouble too," said the Minister.

Next morning instead of keeping a track on Sherry, Iqbal Ahmed with a forged Indian passport under the false name of Prashant Kumar Verma from Rohini, New Delhi landed up at the Indian Embassy. The time was 9.30 in the morning and being a Saturday he knew that the offices would be closed. To be on the safe side, he also carried with him a neatly typed letter that was addressed to Mr Deepak Kumar personally. It was a proposal for a Bollywood style mega show that was to be held at the Moscow Olympic stadium during the summer of next year and with Deepak Kumar as the chief guest. The letter also stated that since there was now a very large population of Indians, Pakistanis, Shri Lankans, Bangladeshis and Nepalese people working in the country, and since there were also a large number of students from the subcontinent studying in Russia the show therefore was bound to be a grand success and money was no constraint. But when the clerk on duty at the Indian embassy told him that Shri Deepak Kumar had left early that morning for Mumbai, Iqbal Ahmed looking rather surprised quietly took back the letter and quickly made his way back home.He was under the impression that maybe the Indian RAW was now tagging him too. And fearing that their agent Deepak Kumar would be compromised the RAW had therefore whisked him away, thought Iqbal Ahmed.That day was a holiday for him too, but seeing the unexpected development he immediately went to the Minister's apartment and informed him that the lover boy had suddenly left for Mumbai that very morning.

"Thank God' said the Minister as he got ready to go to the airport to receive His Excellency. He and Iqbqal Ahmed had jointly decided that unless they had full proof of classified documents being passed by Sherry to her lover, they would not disclose the affair that was going on between the two love birds to the Ambassador or his family. And definitely not for the time being atleast while General Musharraf was visiting India.

"And what if they are actually in love and it has nothing to do with spying at all, because in that case we will look like bloody fools, won't we ?. Moreover with President Musharraf already on Indian soil to hold talks with Mr Vajpayee, it would be rather untimely to publicise the affair at this sensitive juncture. And on the other hand if the couple, one a beautiful Pakistani Muslim girl and the charming daughter of a high ranking Pakistan diplomat, and the other a shaven off Sikh matinee idol from Bollywood India both decide to tie the knot soon in the near future, and the summit talks also leads to reconciliation and better understanding between both the countries on the core Kashmir issue, then it will not only be a win win situation for both the sides, but it will also add to greater bonding and friendship between the two nations,"said the Minister while once again cautioning Iqbal Ahmed not to disclose the matter to anybody and whosoever he may be.

Chapter-35

Lost And Found

The 14th of July 2001 was the 212th anniversary of Bastille Day in France. It was on that day of July 1789, when the people of France revolted and stormed the famous Bastille fortress prison in Paris while fighting for their freedom. With those three famous words of freedom, equality and fraternity, they had humbled King Louis XVI and his monarchy. And on that afternoon at the French embassy gala party, while Shiraz and Saira hobnobbed with their counterparts from other countries, they were also delighted to have a long and pleasant conversation with the Indian Ambassador. First it was on the subject of how more cultural exchanges between the two countries could add to better understanding of each other's problems. And then it was on the subject of cross border trade and its vast potential that could bring about greater economic prosperity to both the nations. That morning of 14th July,2001 was also the day, when President Musharraf with his wife Sehba and a 63 member high powered delegation from Pakistan had landed at the Palam airport in Delhi for the first ever summit level conference between the heads of two countries following the 1999 Kargil War.

With India playing host to the Pakistani delegation, maybe the Madame Ambassador has been directed by Delhi to be a little more friendly with her counterpart from Pakistan, thought Shiraz as they made their way to the lavish buffet table that displayed a huge spread of delicious salads and mouth watering French cuisine. And with July being a summer month it was unusually hot that day and Shupriya had therefore come elegantly dressed in a light green chiffon saree with a floral design and a matching half sleeve blouse to go with it. And since it was a fairly low cut blouse that was worn just below the navel, it therefore also revealed a wee bit of her still slender waistline. And inspite of her being fifty-one years old, Shupriya with her regular yoga exercises had indeed kept her figure trim and proper.And while they kept chatting, they also collected their dinner plates and being a senior lady Ambassador, Shupriya therefore was given the honour to attack the food first. Seeing the many types of salads that the Indian Ambassador had filled her plate with, Saira who was following closely behind her, very sportingly remarked."Well now I know for sure what the secret of your fabulous figure is. And I wish I could also have that kind of a will power to maintain mine like yours Madame ambassador.

"Thank you very much for the compliment, but my weak point is the sweet dish and I hope they don't have a big spread of that too,' replied Shupriya. And as the two ladies kept heping themselves to the large buffet spread they also kept the finer points of French cuisine.Then at one particular food counter in order to find out what was the item inside the deep round shaped silver entrée bowl, when Shupriya bent down to have a closer look, Shiraz literally got the shock of his life. While Shupriya was in the process of bending down, the back of her blouse had got lifted a bit and Shiraz noticing the two black beauty spots on either side of her vertebrae just could not believe his eyes. This was far too much of a coincidence thought Shiraz as he excused himself and made a beeline towards the bar for another refill of that excellent draft beer.

"Please do keep Her Excellency good company and I will join you both within a few minutes," said Shiraz to his wife as he with his refilled beer mug quickly made his way to the men's rest room. While he locked himself inside the toilet, he took out the small photo that was inside his locket and with tears rolling down his eyes kissed it very tenderly. He simply just could not believe that his Shupriya was alive. And since he was still not hundred percent sure of whether it could actually be her or not, he therefore kept discreetly observing and watching her from a distance. That evening after the party in the French embassy, when Shiraz reached home he kept constantly thinking about Shups. And after analyzing every little aspect of what he had seen, heard and observed that evening and earlier, he finally came to the conclusion that Miss Yeshwant Kaur Bajwa could be none other than Shups, his wife. Her height and features were the same. Her voice was the same. Her handwriting was the same. Her date of birth was the same. Only her hairstyle was different and the surname Bajwa though it was a bit intriguing at first but it now connected her to Monty's family. And it was those two black beauty spots in the middle of her back that had convinced him that she was none other than Shups his wife. And the fact that she was very much alive is what was now constantly bugging him.But nonetheless he was also now frantically keen to find out as to how it could have all happened. Shups with her parents had died in the train expolsion at Allahabad railway station that took place in mid December 1971 and at the fag end of the Indo-Pak war. It was an act of sabotage by some Pakistani agents and it had also been officially confirmed by the Government of India that there were no survivors in that first class compartment. They had even published the names of those who had died and it included the entire Sen family including Shupriya Sen. And even if Shups had survived that terrible blast, there would have been at least some tell tale injury marks on her body. But she had none at all. That night he just could not sleep and he kept thinking about her. He was now desperate to find out the truth and he wanted it straight from her mouth.

The next day happened to be the 15th of July. It was a Sunday and General Musharraf and Mr Vajpayee were to begin their first summit talks at Agra. That morning Shiraz got up early as usual to go for his Sunday golf. But on the way he stopped at a public telephone booth and rang up Shupriya at her residence.

"'Please do pardon me for ringing you up so early in the morning your Excellency, but I need to talk to you very privately and very urgently on something that is very important and confidential. I am calling from a private telephone booth and please do not misunderstand me. This is a very important matter about which and I would like to talk to you personally and in private only. And therefore in order to maintain complete confidentiality and secrecy I am therefore calling from a public telephone phone booth. And please do not get me wrong, but this has something to do with the high level talks that are scheduled to take place at Agra today and I only want to be of some help. So I want you to please listen patiently to what I have to say and do not interrupt till I finish. This pertains to the 54 Indian army officers and jawans who were taken prisoners of war during the 1971 war by Pakistan and who are still being held by us in various prisons. Among other issues this is also one of the points that your Prime Minister is expected to talk about in his opening address today. I know from a very reliable source in our government and also from my Defence Attache who has been recently posted to this embassy that most of these prisoners of war are still very much alive and are languishing in Pakistani jails. And though the Indian government has been repeatedly asking Pakistan for their release, we have been constantly denying it by saying that we do not have even a single Indian POW in our country. But I know for sure that it is a blatant lie. I also know that Pakistan some years ago as a publicity gimmick had also invited the kith and kin of some of these prisoners of war to come and see for themselves and some of them did visit Pakistan with a lot of hope, but unfortunately they all went back disappointed and empty handed.

Incidentally let me tell you, your excellency that I also happen to be the only son and child of an army officer who had served in the British Indian army and my late father too was taken prisoner of war by the Japanese in Burma, and we too never saw him thereafter. I was only two years old at that time and I therefore know the kind of agony and mental torture that my poor mother as a young widow had to go through all her life and till her death a few years ago. I therefore as a human being want to give you some factual information of the whereabouts of these unfortunate people confidentially so that you could then without mentioning the source sound your government and they could then take it up with the Pakistani delegation while the summit talks are still in progress. This is only a humanitarian gesture on my part to reunite those unfortunate families who I am sure must be praying for their return someday And I would also like to mention that though most of those prisoners of war are Hindus and Sikhs, but Pakistan also has one prisoner of war who is a Muslim. He I believe is also a very highly decorated Indian officer and his name according to my Defence Attache is Major Shiraz Ismail Khan, said Shiraz very softly as he waited for Shup's response.

When Shupriya heard that name, she was completely dumb struck and she nearly fainted. For a moment she just did not know how to respond. But after a little pause when Shupriya in all excitement said that she was ready to meet him at a place and time of his choosing during the day today, Shiraz knew for certain that Miss Yeshwant Kaur Bajwa was none other than his loving wife Shups.

"You're Excellency, now that you have very kindly agreed to my proposal, first let me find out a decent, quiet safe place somewhere in one of the distant suburbs of this sprawling city and where we can be alone for sometime. And maybe we could also have lunch together if you so desire. But like me you too will have to come alone and without any aides. Hence to keep this matter only to ourselves we therefore need to be very discreet, And as regards the likely rendezvous, I will now start looking for a suitable place and once I find it, I will get back to you on your mobile phone provided you can trust me with your number,"' said Shiraz.

At around eleven that morning and having played all eighteen holes of golf, Shiraz while browsing on the internet found the restaurant that he was looking for. Then he rang up home and lied to Saira. He told her that being a Sunday there was unusually a very heavy rush at the golf course and since his foursome would finally tee off only at 12.30, she should not expect him for lunch. And in order to keep her in good humour, he also told her that he would definitely be home by 5 PM and later in the evening would take her and Sherry to their favourite restaurant 'Uzbegistan"on Neglinayya Street. After that call to his wife, Shiraz rang up the Indian Ambassador on her mobile phone. Shupriya was anxiously waiting for that call. From the time she received the first call early that morning, she was in a world of her known. The very fact that her husband was still alive had brought back to her all the happy memories as she kept admiring his photo, his many medals of bravery and the little golden locket with a gold chain that had the words 'Allah Ho Akbar' written in Persian on it.

It was 12.20 in the afternoon, when Shupriya's mobile phone rang. again.'Your Excellency we will meet at the restaurant in Hotel Rus Solnichni. This hotel is south of Moscow and in one of the distant suburbs of the city. It is also right on the Warsaw highway and the nearest metro station is Varshavskaya. You should catch the metro from Paveletskaya which is close to your embassy and please be there at the restaurant at 1.45 PM sharp. The hotel is only a couple of kilometers from the metro station and it is a well known landmark and there are taxis available there too. But do please ensure for my sake and yours that you are not being followed.

"All right I will definitely be there around that given time and rest assured I will be alone. And I am looking forward to meeting you,"said Shupriya as she switched off the mobile phone and went looking for a map of the Moscow metro and that of the city suburb where the hotel was located.Soon thereafter she called up her private secretary and giving the excuse that she had just been been invited by Lalima Ghosh for an informal hen party at one of her friend's place, she dressed up very casually and without any make up got ready to go for that very important rendezvous. Making the plea that since it was a Sunday and a holiday, and since it was not an official function, she therefore did not require the official mercedes car with the diplomatic number plate and the national flag, and she therefore asked the private secretary to arrange for a cab instead. It was already nearing 1 PM, when the cab finally arrived and having got inside Shupriya waited till she was given the last big salaam by the sentry on duty at the gate. And only when the cab was well out of the embassy premises, she told the cab driver to quickly head for the nearby Paveletskaya metro station. On reaching the metro station, she not only paid the cab driver the correct fare, but she also gave him a big tip. Then she stood there for a while observing the people around. And it was only when she saw the cab driver taking some new passengers and driving away that she made her way to the ticket booth. Standing in line, she discreetly surveyed the area to check if there were any familiar faces around, and on finding that there were none, she purchased a return ticket and made her way to the designated platform.

Though Russia had changed considerably and the KGB had been disbanded, but the possibility of diplomats being trailed by the new Russian sleuths from the counter intelligence agency department was still very much there. On reaching the designated platform, she walked leisurely to the far end and where she knew that the last bogie would stop. And as soon as the doors opened she got into the vestibule. Then she kept standing for a while. And once the wheels were again in full motion, she kept slowly moving forward through the vestibules towards the first bogie. And as she crossed over from one bogie to the other, she also very discreetly kept observing that nobody was following her. Luckily it was a Sunday afternoon and the metro was generally not crowded. And since her destination was more or less the last metro station on that line and people kept thinning out at every station, it became all the more easier for her to ensure that she was not being tailed.

It was exactly 1.30 in the afternoon, when Shupriya got off at the Varshavskaya metro station, but there were no cabs in sight. Fearing that she would get late for that important appointment she rang up the Pakistani Ambassador on his mobile and told him not to leave the place till she arrived. Luckily after 10 minutes or so she found a cab, but the cab driver was unwilling to go such a short distance. But when Shupriya spoke to him in fluent Russian and told him that she was willing to pay also the return fare and that to in American dollars, the cab driver immediately got down and with a big smile that prominently displayed quite a few of his gold teeth, he very chivalrously opened the door for her to get in and in typical Russian style having said pazhalusta (please) he cranked the engine.

It was a few minutes past the given time, when Shupriya entered the restaurant. Seeing her at the door, Shiraz did not even get up and nor did he immediately wave out to her. He waited for a while to check whether she was being tailed. And when he found that there was no other lone customer entering the restaurant after her, he stood up and waved out to her. Then as she neared the table, Shiraz stood up gallantly and greeted her softly with a 'Walaim Ko Salaam.' (Peace be upon you) And when 'Shupriya immediately also responded with 'Salaam Walaim Kaum,' (And upon you be peace) there was a big smile on Shiraz's face.

"I must say that your Urdu diction is pretty good Your Excellency,' said Shiraz as he helped her to get seated opposite him. It was table for two and it was tucked away in one far corner of the restaurant . . . .

"Well that diction could be attributed to city of Calcutta or Kolkata should I say because it still has a large Muslim population and having grown up there l still have many friends in that city and though some of them are Bengali Muslims but they always greet me in the manner in which you just did Your Excellency. And surprisingly though they are also Bengalis but they don't have that typical rounded Bengali rosshogulla accent when it comes to saying Salaam Walaim Kaum," lied Shupriya as she sat facing the man who she did not know was none other that Major Shiraz Ismail Khan her husband.Then as Shupriya got busy going through the menu card, Shiraz said very softly.

"Unfortunately they only have hard Russian drinks and beer in their bar, and since you are the soft drink type I have therefore already ordered a freshlime soda which is neither salty or sweet for you and a large Stolichnaya vodka with orange juice for myself."

"Well the good old Nimbu Paani has always been my favourite drink right from the day I passed out from school," said Shupriya as Shiraz ordered a mixed plate of pickled cucumber, olives and mushrooms as starters.

"You know I wish the Russians would learn how to make dosas and idli sambhar instead of the blinni (pancakes) with honey, and they should also learn how to make the typical Bengali prawn curry with coconut milk and the spicy shorshe bata fish that I use to regularly relish at a nice Bengali restaurant in London. It was called 'The Bengali Cuisine' and it was located in Brick Lane in the East End of the city. But that was very many years ago when I was posted there as a Third Secretary. But I still miss that kind of food and London really offers a very wide variety of Pakistani, Indian and Bangladeshi cuisine," said Shiraz as he quickly glanced through the menu card and asked Her Excellency if she had ever been posted to London. "Only once Your Excellency and that too was very many years ago," said Shupriya.

'And by way and if you don't mind of course may we address each other today by our first names today and the reason for that is also quite simple. You see we have to show to the people who are seated around us that we are not just old friends or lovers, but we are also a very happily married couple. And by being so very officious with the words excellency with every sentence it may also create problems for both of us. Therefore may I request you to address me only as Riaz while I will address you as Yeshwant. Because one never knows and as the saying goes even walls have ears,"said Shiraz very cleverly and diplomatically.

"Well I guess under the present circumstances we have no other choice, but to pretend that we are husband and wife that I think is asking for a bit too much' isn't it?" said Shupriya as they both drank to each other's health and prosperity. And while Shupriya got busy nibbling away from the various pickled salads, Shiraz kept observing her very closely. And while they kept nibbling away the starters and they talked about the on going Musharraf-Vajpayee talks in Delhi, Shiraz said very softly.

"'Well before I give the details of those prisoners of war that I talked to you about over the phone this morning, may I first tell you something about yourself very confidentially and which I have come to know only recently from my sources in the ISI. According to the ISI your name Yeshwant Kaur Bajwa is not your original real name, but it is the official one no doubt. You were initially a Bengali, but later after marriage took to the Sikh religion. You did your schooling from Sanawar and college from LSR New Delhi. You married a Muslim officer of the Indian army shortly before the 1971 war and that to without the consent of your parents and that same handsome officer was later decorated posthumously with the Param Veer Chakra. And mind you that officer today is very much alive and his name is Major Shiraz Ismail Khan and he is from the Jammu and Kashmir Rifle Regiment. And now that I have told you about your real identity, I am sure you too would like to know in which Pakistani jail your husband is languishing at this moment.'

Hearing all that coming from her counterpart in the Pakistani Embassy in Moscow, Shupriya not only got a rude shock, but she was also stunned beyond belief. But how could the ISI know so much about her and she also wondered as to who could have leaked such vital information to them. The only persons who knew about all this was Monty and Reeta and surely they would'nt ever betray her she thought. Nevertheless she not only kept vehemently denying all those facts, but she also told the Pakistani Ambassador point blank that he was wrong and it was a clever figment of imagination by the Pakistan ISI to cook up such a stupid story.

"All right maybe I am wrong and it is an entirely cooked up story by the ISI, but I also have some solid evidence to prove that what I had just said is the truth and nothing but the truth. And if you still do not believe me then I would only request you to close your eyes for a minute and open it when I only tell you too," said Shiraz.

"Oh please stop playing games and don't try and make a fool of me. I am Yeshwant Kaur Bajwa and I will always remain so," said Shupriya in a somewhat angry and defiant tone.But she suddenly realized that with her husband still languishing in a Pakistani jail it may well be he who had blurted out all that information to the Pakistani intelligence agency during his interrogation.

"Well in that case you don't have to close your eyes at all, and I will present the evidence in front of you right now" said Shiraz as he unhooked the old silver chain that was around his neck and, opened the locket. And even when Shupriya saw that photograph of her's in little Shiraz's arm, she still did not realize that the gentleman who was sitting facing her was none other than her own husband. She thought that probably that locket with the silver chain had been confiscated by the ISI and the agency must have given it to the Pakistani Ambassador to confront her with. But then why should the agency give it to the Pakistani Ambassador and why should they want His Excellency to confront her now with all this and at this stage when the summit talks were already in progress at Agra, thought Shupriya as she again had a closer look at that old miniature photograph. But now that she knew that she had been unmasked, she was also very keen to now know about the whereabouts of Major Shiraz Ismail Khan and therefore she simply asked . . . .

"But where did your Excellency get that photograph from? Because that chain and that locket with the photo inside was presented by me to my late husband on our wedding day and now for heaven sake will you please tell me where is he and is he all right or not,"said Shupriya somewhat in exasperation and as tears kept rolling down her eyes.

"Well to tell you the truth, Major Shiraz Ismail Khan is not only absolutelyy hale and hearty and in fact at this very moment of time he is sitting here right in front of you my dear Shups,'said Shiraz

Hearing him addressing her by that name, Shupriya simply kept looking at him. She just could not believe it till Shiraz told her the whole story of what happened on that fateful night when he attacked the Pakistani petrol dump near Kotli and how he got severely wounded. But somehow he had managed to escape and survive. And it was due to the deep shrapnel wound on his right cheek and the plastic surgery that he had got done subsequently that had changed his facial appearance completely. And in order to hide his real identity, he therefore decided to keep a beard and a big moustache eversince. And it was only after he learnt while he was still in Pakistan that she and the family were no more and that his sudden coming back from the dead and that to with a posthumous Param Veer Chakra would raise many questions, and some may accuse him of being a bloody coward and even a Pakistani agent, he therefore decided to stay back and take on a new identity. And his intention after he joined the PFS was to primarily spy for India as her good old Dablo. Then he met Saira in London and after they got married and had children he gave up the idea of spying completely. But he still keeps making important notes in his secret red diary and may be one day those very notes could be very useful to India," said Shiraz as Shupriya kept looking at him in utter disbelief . . .

And when Shupriya narrated to him her own tragic life story and how her parents were forcing her to get married and what happened on that evening at the Allahabad railway station which compelled her to go back to Monty in Bangalore and change her name to Yeshwant Kaur Bajwa, there was moistness in Shiraz's eyes also. She however did not disclose to him that they have a grown up son.

"I must say that life has come full circle for both of us, but we are helpless I guess. It is like a fairy tale story because we were both suppose to be dead and none of us ever thought or dreamt that life would reunite us again after thirty one long years and that too as the Ambassadors of two different nations who still don't see eye to eye with another. And of all the places in the world we had to meet in Moscow and that to at a time when both India and Pakistan are holding the summit talks at Agra. But I must confess that the locket with that photograph has always been my lucky charm and it will always remain around my neck till I die,"said Shiraz as he tenderly kissed the locket and put it back again around his neck.

"Well I guess though it is an unique case of both being lost and found, but we have to live with this now and you have a nice family to look after too. But if you are ever feel that one day you might get exposed and unmasked, and you need my help, then you can always count on your Shups. To me you will always remain my Dablo and I wish you and your family all the very best in the future,'said Shups in a somewhat choked voice as Shiraz for old time sake softly squeezed her hand.

"Well now that both of us have made it this far in our profession and that to all on our own steam therefore let's hope that the present summit talks at Agra will once again unite both the countries like the manner in which we were reunited today. And as regards those 54 Indian prisoners of war are concerned I will try my best to locate them and get back to you as soon as possible. I had lied to you about them and my only reason for lying was that I wanted to see you alone and to tell you in person that your Dablo was very much alive. And the only way I could do it was to give that subtle hint that Major Shiraz Ismail Khan was a prisoner in Pakistan and which ironically in a way I still am and which is of my own doing though,"said Shiraz.

And while they discussed the prospects of the summit, Shupriya said."But personally I don't think the summit will serve any purpose whatsoever, because neither side is going to budge an inch as far as Kashmir is concerned. And General Musharraf I am afraid though his intentions may be noble and good, but he cannot at this moment of time go against the hawks in his own country and especially those that belong to the fanatical Muslim fundamentalist militant organizations like the Jaish-e-Mohammed, Lashkar-e-Toiba, Harkat-ul-Mujahideen and such like others that the Pakistan military and the ISI have spawned over the years and are now probably repenting for it And whch I am afraid if they are allowed to grow will only be detrimental to Pakistan's interest in bringing about the much needed political and economic stability in the entire subcontinent," added Shupriya.as she drew a sketch of her Dablo with her ball point on the paper napkin and with the words 'dasvidaniya, sevo karoshova', and the two OO's meaning goodbye and all the best presented it to him as a parting memento. And then as she got up from the table she also whispered into Shiraz' ears. "I am afraid I will have to meet you again because I must return to you some of your worldly possessions that I have always cherished and kept in my safe custody all these years. But it will now be at a place and time of my choosing,"

"In that case I shall not say farewell my love as yet and till we meet again,"said Shiraz as he once again tenderly squeezed Shupriya's hand. And as soon she got into the waiting taxi, Shiraz observed that there were tears in her eyes. And as the cab drove away, Shupriya clasped both her hands to her lips and face and kept sobbing silently. Finally when she too looked back and waved out to her loving Dablo for the last time, it was Dablo who had his hands on his lips and over his face and he too was sobbing silently.

And on that late Sunday afternoon of 15th July 2001 in Moscow, while the world had come once again full circle for Shiraz and Shupriya, a day earlier and just a few hours before General Musharraf landed in Delhi, far away on the LOC, the Line of Control in Kashmir violence had once again erupted with a heavy exchange of gun fire between Pakistani and Indian troops, And while both sides accused each other of cross border violation, at Agra the first round of talks between General Musharraf and Mr Vajpayee and between the members of both the official delegations had also concluded. But looking at the manner in which the talks had so far progressed, Unni who was enjoying his daily quota of four large rums with soda in the company of Monty at the Delhi Gymkhana Club that evening strongly felt that the entire exercise was an exercise in futility.

"To begin with Pakistan on the 5th of July and just ten days before the official talks that began today had under strict security arrangements held elections to chose a new legislature in that disputed mountain region which they call Azad Kashmir. But pro-independence and pro-India candidates from Pakistan's so called Azad Kashmir were barred from contesting the elections altogether. At the same time the Pakistan President had also expressed his desire to meet some of the Hurriyat leaders during his visit to India and to which India had responded very strongly by saying that the Hurriyat had no role to play in the summit at all and that it was a complete non-issue as far as India was concerned. But yet I am told that President Musharraf did meet atleast a few of them at the official reception that was hosted by the Pakistani Ambassador yesterday in Delhi in Musharraf's honour. Then to keep the Kashmir issue fully alive, Pakistan in these last ten days have not only provoked India by opening heavy fire on some of our border posts in that sensitive region, but it has also intensified its cross border terrorist activities in some of the more infiltration prone sectors of Northern Kashmir. Only a week or so ago seven heavily armed militants and some of whom were equipped with the deadly AK-56 rifles were killed in the Macchil, Karnah and Bandipur sectors in North Kashmir by our security forces. And with current rumours floating that the Pakistani President is likely to appoint Major General Mohammed Anwar Khan who is the VCGS, the Vice Chief of General Staff and who is likely to retire soon as the new President of Azad Kashmir, it only goes to show that with the present and pre-determined mindset of the ex commando General, these talks will be just hogwash. And the very fact that on the 9th of July Musharraf escaped death for the sixth time when a car that was being driven by one Abdul Aziz drove into Musharraf's convoy only goes to show that he is left with no other choice but to follow the diktat of the many hardliners and hawks in his country. And I am sure now that he is on the hot seat as President of Pakistan he would like to remain there for a while with all its pomp and glory and surely he would not like to dig his own grave by compromising in any manner on Kashmir and which he has said time and again is the only core issue," said Unni as the television channels showed the General and his lovely wife enjoying an exclusive cultural programme at Hotel Jaypee Palace in Agra

"Yes I think the man from Neherwali Haveli in Old Delhi who was only four years old when he with his parents and family migrated to Karachi never in his dreams had ever thought that one day he would return to his ancestral home as the President of Pakistan. And though the man may have come with very good intentions, but unfortunately his intentions as an individual hardly matters. And the irony of this whole exercise in futility is that the very man who as the Pakistani Army Chief was against the Lahore Declaration and who was primarily responsible for the Kargil War is today our honoured guest," said Monty a little sarcastically as Reeta too joined them at the over crowded bar.

"Alright now enough of Indo-Pak politics and let there be one more last round of drinks before we move in for dinner,", said Reeta as she showed them the many photographs that Peevee had sent on his visit to Moscow and to Mom Number 2.

'But who is this young good looking lady dressed so elegantly in jeans and a polo neck sweater standing smartly next to our young hero and in front of a palatial mansion. "said Unni as he took a closer look at that photograph.

"Oh it must be some new found acquaintance or friend in Moscow, but whoever she maybe I must confess that she is a stunning beauty and I think it is worth finding out staright from the horse's mouth as to who is she and if Peevee was interested in her," said Monty as he called up Peevee on his mobile.

'Oye Bharkudhar ye konsi nahin cheez hai jisse tum Moscow mein ishq lada rahe the. Dekhne mein toh photo mein bahut hi khoobsorat hai lekin irada kiya hai. Shaadhi Waddhi karege ya nahin.?' (So who is this good looking lady whom you were wooing in Moscow. She is undoubtedly looks very pretty in the photograph, but what are your intentions. And are you planning to get married or not," asked Monty rather seriously.)On hearing that coming from his father, Peevee was taken completely by surprise. But he kept his cool and asked. "But Papa whom are you talking about?" And when Monty told him about the photograph in which he was standing next to her in front of a huge mansion, Peevee realized that he had sent it by mistake. He however had a ready answer for it. He knew that someday someone who might see her photograph would probably ask him the same question.

"Oh that is a young tourist from Istanbul who had come with her parents. I met her by chance on the tourist bus. The bus was taking us on a sight seeing tour of some of the palatial buildings and modern dachas on the outskirts of Moscow and which are now owned by the new oligarchs of this country. She and her parents had been to India too a few years ago and they had also seen my film 'Sherdil" and they therefore recognized me. So the girl wanted a photograph to be taken with me and I also took one of her's and that was that," lied Peevee with full confidence.

"That sounds convincing all right, but are you going to keep in touch with her,"said Monty as he winked at Reeta.

"Maybe yes and maybe not, and it all depends on the pressure of work which is increasing day by day and I have a lot of backlog to catch up with also. And it is all thanks to my one month's lovely holiday with Mom Number 2," said Peevee as he checked his watch. It was nearing 11 at night and Sherry's call was due at anytime.

On the morning of 16th of July all eyes were on General Musharraf as he held his impromptu press conference at Agra and with that ended whatever little hope there was for hammering out a deal that could have been acceptable to both the sides. The Pakistani General with his answers to questions from the media had literally launched an all out physcological war on India and it no doubt took the Indian delegation completely by surprise. In fact for a few minutes the Indians did not know what hit them as General Musharraf kept very bluntly telling the world media that it was all India's fault. Though Pakistan considered it to be a master stroke, but India felt that it was entirely uncalled for and it was nothing short of hitting below the belt. The man who became the President of Pakistan on 20th June, 2001 under the Provincial Constitutional Order by removing Rafiq Tarar before he was allowed to complete his five year tenure and who in his inaugural speech had declared very firmly. 'I think I have a role to play; I have a job to do here; I cannot and will not let this nation down. And then gave the three reasons for his taking over to be that of constitutional, political and economic failures of the past governments was now once again hogging the limelight. And naturally he could not let Pakistan down at Agra and that to in the very city where the great Moghul Emperors had their capital till Shahjehan decided to shift it to Delhi.

And while both sides spent most of that Monday trying to find a common ground that would finally lead to some sought of a declaration and one that could be signed by both the leaders, it all ended up with no agreement being reached at all. And as a result of which not only was Musharraf and his wife's visit to Ajmer to pray at the dargah of Salim Chisti cancelled, but by late evening the entire Pakistani delegation were also busy packing their bags for the flight back to Islamabad. And once again it was all because of both the countries mad obsession with Kashmir. And as a result of which no real headway could be made and another golden opportunity to bring about a long lasting climate of peace and stability in the subcontinent was lost.

"Did'nt I tell you well in advance that it will be an exercise in futility," said Unni as Monty joined him at the Press Club of India.

"Yes probably things may have turned out a little differently had the Pakistani General not indulged in a public relations exercise. With his sometimes aggressive and sometimes friendly, but at all time maintaining a flamboyant approach while handling the media, he simply cooked his own goose as far as further progress on the talks was concerned. And looking at the loud and glitzy manner in which he spoke at that press conference, that man I think is ideally suited to compere the popular Kaun Banega Crorepati game TV game show. And though the President of Pakistan has extended an invitation to the Indian Prime Minister to visit Pakistan and which I believe Mr Vajpayee has also accepted, but I doubt with the failure of the talks at Agra whether that visit will take place at all. And even if it does it will also I am afraid end up only as a sight seing tour by our very articulate and at times very witty leader from Gwalior," said Monty.

"Well to me whether Mr Vajpayee visits Pakistan or not is a million dollar question. And with no life lines of communication left after all that has happened at Agra in these last two days and with the audience poll in both countries also showing total dissatisfaction, I think it is time again to play the fastest finger first. And therefore my question to both the delegations will be. "Please arrange in chronological order starting with the oldest year first all the wars that so far have been fought by India and Pakistan over Kashmir and also indicate the most likely year when it will be fought again. And the years are 1999, 1947, 1971 and 1965. And as far as the next war is concerned, your guess will be as good as mine, "said Unni as he laughed away at his own joke.

"Really I must say you do have a subtle sense of humour, but my only fear is that with both countries now armed with a big arsenal of nuclear weapons it has to be nothing else but fastest finger first,' added Monty.

"Yes and I think that calls for another drink because you have really hit the nuclear button on its head. And God forbid if that ever happens it will neither be phone a friend or fifty-fifty. It will be simply curtains for both Pakistan and us,"said Unni as he raised a toast tor Monty's sense of humour.

Sitting in Moscow, Shiraz who was following the summit level talks at Agra very closely and with very high hopes was badly disappointed with its final outcome. To him it was a complete no show by both the high level delegations. He had thought that it would atleast bring in the much needed goodwill between the peoples of the two countries and that would in turn foster better economic prosperity and more political stability in the subcontinent that are so very badly needed for the progress of both the nations. He was however extremely happy since it was during the Agra talks that he had finally discovered that his dear Shups was very much still alive. He was also happy because on that Monday of 16th July, 2001 the two Presidents of Russia and China had also signed their first treaty of friendship in more than half a century. And when he saw Vladimir Putin and Jiang Zemin on the television screen vigourously shaking each others hand he realized that it was probably to checkmate the United States missile defence plans.and to boost the bilateral trade between the two countries.

Next day sitting in his office, Shiraz kept thinking about Shups. Maybe we could both at our own initiative and with like minded friends from both the countries start a track 3 diplomacy channel,' thought Shiraz as he made a note of all those people he felt he could tap at his end. This would also give him more opportunities to meet and discuss with Shups the parameters to be worked out for such kind of a backdoor diplomacy and make it move forward if required. To him it was more than evident that the track 2 diplomacy of the Belusa Group had been a failure, but there was still a dire need for both the nations to continue with the dialogue in a peaceful and conducive manner. Therefore to find out if Shups was in agreement with him, Shiraz once again from a public booth late on that evening of 18th July called her up on her mobile phone

"Though the idea sounds rather nice, but I am afraid I can only see and discuss it with you at the earliest either on the 21st which is a Saturday or on the 22nd July which is a Sunday. And now if you can message to me your confidential Moscow mobile number then I can get back to you. And to be on the safe side whenever we get in touch we will henceforth address each other with our old names Shups and Dablo provided nobody else picks up the phone. And if somebody else does pick up the phone then all we need to say very apologetically to the person concerned is 'sorry wrong number and switch off the phone.' Now I hope that is OK with you," asked Shups.

"I think that should be fine, but all the same and till the time we get the group functioning together; we have to be very discreet and careful. Because as career diplomats we cannot and should not be seen together in each others company in restaurants or at other public places, and neither should we be identified as the founders of this group? That you will understand will be suicidal for both of us. And therefore to get the group functioning in a positive manner we have to perforce work and guide all our activities from behind the scene, and that to in a clever and secretive manner. And if possible let us therefore meet on this coming Sunday to work out all the nitty-gritties because that is my day for golf and I can get away from the club in the afternoon by giving some excuse or the other,"said Shiraz while sounding rather hopeful.

"That's fine and I will get back to you soon with the place and time for our next rendez-vous,"said Shups while wishing Dablo a very goodnight.

On the 19th of July night before Shiraz went to bed, he tuned in as usual to listen to the BBC news and was both surprised and shocked to learn that his favourite British author and politician had been sentenced to four years imprisonment for perjury and for perverting the course of justice. He could not believe that the 15th April 1940 born Jeffery Archer, who was once an honourable Member of Parliament, and an ex Deputy Chairman of the Conservative Party and who was made a life Peer in 1992 and who was the author of the best sellers like 'Not a Penny More,Not a Penny Less', 'Kane and Abel', and 'First Among Equals,' would now go to the Bellmarsh Category "A' prison to serve his long sentence.The controversial politician and the ex school teacher who was also a successful sprinter at Oxford and who became an MP in 1969 at the young age of 29 years it seems had now run out of steam. In 1986, he was allegedly involved in a sex scandal with Monica Coghlan, a prostitute, but even then in 1999 the Conservative Party had selected him as their London mayoral candidate for the 2000 election. But thereafter his world well apart, when the News of the World published serious allegations that he had committed perjury in the 1987 Daily Star libel case on the infamous Monica Coghlan affair and which Archer had won. And now Shiraz wondered what would happen to him if he was seen and caught hobnobbing clandestinely with the Indan Ambassador.

It was at 1.30 PM on that 22nd of July, when the two Ambassadors met again. And the rendez-vous this time was the Volga-Volga restaurant on the Leningradsky highway and which was close to the Richnoi Voksal, the last metro station on that line. And with Shups playing host, it reminded Shiraz of her 20th birthday on 26th January 1970, when she for the first time treated him to only bhelpuri, chaat and ice-cream for lunch and that to from some of the local roadside vendors at Bhadkal Lake which was on the outskirts of Delhi and where they had gone to spend the afternoon together clandestinely. And when Shiraz also reminded her as to how she panicked when on the return journey, his scooter packed up before entering Delhi, Shups too recalled that incident very vividly. Shups was already late that day and before leaving home that morning she had told her mother a lie. She had told her that she had been invited on her birthday by Loveleen and some other of her close college friends for a dosa lunch and which was to be followed by a matinee movie. But she had also promised her mother that she would definitely be back home latest by six in the evening and would help her to make all the necessary arrangements for the evening dinner party that was being held in her honour. And it was all thanks to Loveleen whom Shiraz had somehow managed to contact at the nick of time from a nearby wayside telephone booth on that 26th January evening that had saved the day for her.After the phone call Loveleen had immediately gone to Shups house and had told Mrs Sen that after the matinee movie, since all the hostel girls kept insisting that Shups must cut the cake that they had arranged for in the hostel,Shups therefore had no other choice but to accompany them and therefore Mrs Sen should not be unduly worried if Shups was delayed slightly in reaching home.

"Yes that was indeed rather close that day and thank God Loveleen came to our rescue in the nick of time. And luckily I also managed to find a three wheeler just in time to take me home. But it was also thanks to you and your great idea when you told me that I must buy a small cake from any shop that I found on the way and land up home with a atleast a piece of it for my dear Mum and Dad and which is exactly what I did and it had them smiling too when I returned home albeit forty five minutes late,"said a delighted Shups while placing the order for the food. That afternoon over some good continental lunch and after they had discussed in a little more detail about the aim and objectives and other various aspects of the proposed track 3 channel, and the manner in which it should be tackled and progressed, Shupriya took out the small little silver box from her handbag. And having opened it, when she started presenting one by one the items that were inside to her dear Dablo, Shiraz was simply overwhelmed with emotion. As those old medals and decorations came out in strict seniority starting with the 1887 Victorian gold guinea that Lord Curzon had presented to Curzon Sikandar Khan way back in 1892 and which was followed by Naik Curzon Sikandar's Khan Victoria Cross that the great soldier had earned at Loos in France in 1915 posthumouslly, Shiraz kept examining them very minutely. They were not only priceless, but they also had a lot of history attached to them. And when those two old medals were followed by the Mahavir Chakra that his father Colonel Ismail Sikandar Khan' who had adopted him had won posthumously during the 1947-48 Kashmir Operations, and the Veer Chakra that was awarded to Shiraz in the 1965 war with Pakistan, it brought back to both of them some nostalgic memories of their own young days. And finally when Shupriya presented him with the Param Veer Chakra that he as her husband had been awarded albeit also posthumously during the

1971 Indo-Pak conflict, Shiraz was filled with emotion . . . And while Shiraz kept on admiring it, Shupriya said

"But hold on Dablo there is still one more item. And though it is not a medal for gallantry, but it is important all the same as far as you own life is concerned. It is the gold locket with a small gold chain that has the words Allah Ho Akbar inscribed in Persian on it, and which was around your little neck when your father who adopted you found you near the Christian Mission Hospital gate at Baramulla. You had been left there as an abandoned child with a note for the finder by a good Christain Irish Nun. And since you were a Muslim boy you were given the name Shiraz Ismail Khan by your father I was told. Therefore this too rightly belongs to you," added Shupriya as she started putting all of them back into the little silver box which was once her mother's prized possession and which was used by her to store her small quota of paans for the day.

"But that is not fair Shups. And I just cannot accept them just like that. After all you are legally also my wife and that too my very first one. And now that Major Shiraz Ismail Khan historically does not exist anymore, I would like you to keep all these medals and memorablia with you. My taking them back may be a bit risky and it could lead to my being asked too many awkward questions about my past and which could be dangerous. However I will keep that locket with the gold change because I would need all of Allah Tallas's blessings if I have to succeed in my track 3 mission,"said Shiraz.

"But my keeping them is risky for me too. And historically speaking your Shups does not exist either and as Yeshwant Kaur Bajwa I have no right to keep them now. Yes, I have been keeping them secretly all these years, but that was only because of its sentimental value,"said Shupriya.

"Alright in that case I suggest you give them all back to Monty Bhaiya, but for heaven sake do not tell them that I still exist. Because as the saying goes 'Silence is Golden'and I want it to remain that way for my own safety, for your safety and for the safety of Saira and my children,"'said Shiraz as Shupriya asked for the bill.

"Alright till next Sunday then and let us work sincerely to get this track 3 diplomacy channel going. And we will discuss its likely composition over lunch at a time and place of my choosing,"said Shiraz as both of them decided to leave separately and with a five minutes time gap. As soon as Shups got up and left, Shiraz went to the men's rest room to change into his Sunday golf rig.

Chapter-36

Tailing the Bosses and the Shadow Boxing Begins

That day on reaching home, when Saira told Shiraz that so far everybody from the Rehman clan except her brother Salim Rehman had confirmed about their joining the seven day Volga boat trip from Moscow to St Petersburg in August, Shiraz immediately rang up his brother-in-law. Salim Rehman. Salim Rehman had only a month ago and before the Agra summit began had been posted back from Delhi to Islamabad.as an Additional Secretary in the Pakistan Foreign Office.

"Arre Yaar what is your problem? I know that nothing was achieved at Agra but for that you are not to be blamed. I am now also working on a very ambitious plan that could help keep the dialogue going and I therefore need to personally and urgently consult you 'Salle Sahib'. Therefore you must come with Aasma Bhabhi and the children. And no backing out please. This grand family reunion in the New Millenium for all of us may well be the last one with your parents and who today are the Rehman family senior rmost patriarchs After all my father-in-law Arif Rehman Khan and my mother-in-law Ruksana Begum are not getting any younger and I want you to escort and accompany them from Islamabad. We will all be meeting in Moscow latest by 13th August. On the 14th we will celebrate our Independence Day at an exclusive dacha outside the city and where everybody will be accommodated in real royal style and we will all stay there till the 21st morning. And all this is thanks to one of my new found nuveaux rich Russian friend who has very kindly offered me the use of his palatial dacha. On the 21st evening we will all be on board the luxury cruise boat 'Leo Tolstoy' and we will spend seven full days on the mighty Volga leisurely exploring the various historical sites that are situated on the banks of that historical river including the magnificent cities of Moscow and St Petersburg, which was once the capital of Tsarist Russia. And from St Petersburg after the cruise ends on the 27th August morning, I will ensure that all of you will catch your flights back to your own respective destinations. So it is just a question of you getting away from your office for a fortnight and please I do not want a negative answer, said Shiraz somewhat pleadingly.

"OK its done you bum and we will all be there bang on the 13th of August and as scheduled.; And please do also convey our grateful thanks to your friend from the new Russian oligarch circle and I am also looking forward to meeting him too. Only be careful because I frankly do not trust them one bit. Some of them are the ex KGB types and they might even blackmail you for an extra buck or they may even sell you to the CIA and the Indian RAW if it suits their damn purpose. These guys are capable of doing anything and everything under the Sun, and I hope he is not one of those Mafia gun runners who is also is in the lucrative business of exporting good looking females in the ever expanding worldwide Russian flesh trade," said Salim Rehman as he called out to his wife Aasma to start packing and to get everyone ready for the forthcoming Moscow sojourn.

And while Shiraz got immediately busy in making all the arrangements for the grand Rehman family get together in Moscow, his elder foster brother Monty with samples of more export garments, rugs and carpets got ready to make another flying visit to Colombo. And from there he was scheduled to visit to Frankfurt and Berlin. Having landed at the Bandarnaike International Airport on the late evening of 23rd July, 2001 he was received by his old client. From there they went straight to the Full Moon Garden Hotel which was the closest to the airport. Though it was a small two star hotel but since Monty was to catch the Sri Lankan Airways flight to Frankufurt early next morning he did not mind spending the night there, rather than going all the way to the Colombo Hilton Hotel where he otherwise normally stayed. In order to have an early night Monty handed over the three suitcases with the samples of garments that were meant for his Sri Lankan client and after a quick nightcap fell fast asleep. But a few hours later all his plans to leave for Frankfurt and Berlin early next morning were dashed as the deafening loud explosions and the sound of heavy gunfire paralysed all activities in and around the international airport. In a daredevil and surprise attack at 3.30 AM that morning, the Tamil BlackTigers from the dreaded LTTE's suicide squad had infiltrated the next door Katunayake air force base. After successfully destroying the heavy duty electric transformers that plunged the air base into total darkness, they had cut through the barbed wire fencing surrounding the base and had assaulted it with rocket propelled grenades, anti-tank weapons and with automatic rifle and machine gun fire. Their aim it seems was to destroy as many Sri Lankan military aircrafts that they could find parked on the tarmac and they succeeded in destroying eight of them and severely damaging many more, and which included amongst others two MiG-27 fighter bombers, half a dozen Kfir fighter aircrafts and a few helicopters of the Sri Lankan Airforce. As per one estimate there were a total of 14 Black Tigers who had taken part in that dare devil operation and though eight of them had died in the initial attack on the air force base, the remaining six had crossed the runaway and had attacked the commercial aircrafts that were luckily all empty at that time, but were parked next door on the tarmac at the Bandarnaike International Airport. Using explosive charges and anti-tank rockets they destroyed and damaged a large number of Airbuses which mostly belonged to the Sri Lankan Airlines. And while the battle continued for nearly six hours that morning, Monty kept sitting in his hotel room and wondering whether this civil war in Sri Lanka will ever end. His client was absolutely right when he had told him on his earlier visit last month that Colombo was no longer safe. And it was only at around 9 O'clock in the morning, when the hotel manager confirmed that it was all over and that the fighting had stopped, Monty left for the airport. But on reaching there he found all the terminals barricaded and all outgoing flights had been cancelled, while all the incoming flights had been diverted to Chennai and elsewhere. The fighting early that morning had resulted in the deaths of all 16 LTTE daredevils and of six or seven Sri Lankan Airforce personnel. And a total of 26 aircrafts were either damaged or destroyed. At the airport he also came to know that the LTTE had timed the attack to coincide with the rioting and killings that had started eighteen long years ago on 24th July 1983 and which had resulted in the deaths of thousands of innocent Tamilian men, women and childrens. It seems that on the 2nd of July Prabhakaran the LTTE Supremo had also warned that he would resume the attacks unless the Sri Lankan military stopped bombing targets in the north and east of the country. This was no doubt the boldest attack by the LTTE on the Sri Lankan capital and which also signalled the start of the real war between the Sri Lankan armed forces and the Tamil Tigers. Seeing the terrible destruction caused by the deadly attack, and the raw courage of the LTTE suicide squads to attack at will wherever and whenever they liked, Monty decided that it was not really worth visiting Colombo and to do business with Sri Lanka anymore. Twenty fours hours later, when the air services from Colombo were once again resumed, Monty finally caught a flight to Frankfurt via Dubai. It was an Emirates flight and when he finally reached Berlin he was already 72 hours behind time.

While transiting through Dubai, when Monty heard that Phoolan Devi who was once a notorious dacoit and who after serving 11 years in prison was now an honourable member of parliament from the Samajwadi Party had been shot dead as she got out of her car at the gate of her official residence in New Delhi, he knew that it was definitely a revenge killing. The 'Bandit Queen' from the Mallah community who mercilessly and in revenge had massacred the so called high caste 22 Kshatriyas/ Thakurs of a rival dacoit gang in February 1981 for outraging her modesty had fallen prey to the bullets of Sher Singh Rana and his associates. The young assailant who was a Kshatriya had also taken his revenge after 20 long years.

And while Monty was busy exploring the German market for the export of garments, rugs and carpets during the coming Christmas season, in Moscow it was time again for Shiraz and Shups to meet at a new rendezvous. On the afternoon of Sunday the 29th July 2001 and after playing his full 18 holes of golf, Dablo and Shups met again secretly. This time it was an out of the way little restaurant called 'Othdhik' meaning 'Rest' in the Russian language". And it was located in the quaint surroundings of Podolsk. It was the same small tourist spot that Peevee and Sherry had visited a month earlier and which was outside the city limits of Moscow. And Dablo and Shups too had made the journey by the local train. However, they had no idea that the Russian FSB, the Federal Security Service that had replaced the erstwhile dreaded KGB had started keeping a tag on them. It is not that it was illegal for the Ambassadors of the two countries to meet in restaurants, but it was the clandestine manner in which it was being done outside the main city limits that had caught the attention of the sleuths from Bolshaya Lubyanka. And they had therefore decided to keep an eye on them. Initially they thought that maybe the two of them were having an affair, but that was something very personal and it was none of their business. And moreover since there there were no specific indications of them ever meeting inside hotel rooms that aspect was therefore ruled out. Nevertheless, they decided to discreetly and anonymously sound the two concerned embassies, but without mentioning any names or designations of the people involved. And that was primarily because they did not want this affair to surface as a big diplomatic scandal later, and which they knew if given the opportunity the international press and the media would play it up to the hilt. Moreover, Russia always had a very healthy diplomatic and trade relationship with India and they did not want to sour it and especially so after the recent very major arms deal that had been signed by the two countries, when Jaswant Singh the Indian Defence Minister visited the country recently.

On the evening of 31st July, while Shups was busy drafting the key points to be discussed by the members of the proposed Track-3 channel, the news arrived that Prime Minister Vajpayee citing problems of being unable to run a cohesive team of the NDA, the National Democratic Alliance had offered to resign. But because of pressure from his own party and that of the members of his coalition government, he had no option but to continue in office. With the failure of the Indo-Pak talks, the shocking Tehelka revelations that led to the resignation of his Defence Minister, and the recent mutual fund scandal by the Unit Trust of India, the otherwise witty and jovial Prime Minister of India was now a broken man. And though he had said that he had grown old and was unwell, he was not allowed to resign.

For their next meeting which was scheduled for the 5th, the first Sunday of August, Dablo and Shups in order to save time decided to meet at 1.30 in the afternoon at Mama Zoya. It was a fairly popular multistoreyed floating boat restaurant on the River Moscova and it also served very good Georgian food including the delicious grilled lamb, which was one of Shiraz's favourite. The restaurant along the riverside was across the big public park known as Park Kultiri, the Park of Culture and it was located in the heart of the city and close to the Frunzenskaya metro station. But neither Shiraz nor Shupriya had realized that at this particular meeting they would both be on the radar of their respective intelligence agencies also. Being a nice sunny Sunday afternoon, the restaurant was very crowded, but Shiraz having anticipated that had therefore come fairly early after his usual round of golf and had managed to get a table for two in one far corner on the upper deck. And while he sat there enjoying his glass of chilled beer and read the current best seller 'Angels and Demons' which was a briliant mystery thriller that was written by Dan Brown, he also waited anxiously for Shups to join him. But he had no idea that all his movements from the time he came on board Mama Zoya was being observed and videotaped. And when Shups joined him it came as real shock to Iqbal Ahmed. The ISI sleuth had followed his boss incognito on his motorcycle as His Excellency drove out in a taxi from the golf course. And Iqbal Ahmed had zeroed in on him from the photograph that was sent by the FSB and it was more so because of His Excellency's daughter Sherry's involvement with Deepak Kumar, the Indian matinee idol. And Iqbal Ahmed had therefore come to the conclusion that probably the entire family was now in this business of cash for classified and secret documents. That day Iqbal Ahmed had come dressed up as a hippy tourist complete with a big Satya Saibaba like shaped wig over his head and neck and a Sony handycam held firmly in his hand. However, he was not aware that one of the Indian diplomats who was also posted to the Indian Embassy in their visa section and who was also on deputation from the Indian RAW was also discreetly tailing his own big boss.

Mr Omprakash Sharan, a fairly senior officer from the Indian Police Service who was on deputation with RAW as one of the First Secretaries had also like Iqbal Ahmed received a photograph of the couple having their lunch in some obscure restaurant from some anonymous source. And it had also been delivered to him by name a few days ago and without any covering letter. And what was even more surprising was that it was in an ordinary Russian envelope. And he too therefore was taken by complete surprise seeing Her Excellency in the company of the Ambassador from Pakistan. And on subsequent enquires that he had discreetly made through the personal assistant in Madam Ambassador's secretariat, when he also came to know that on the three previous Sundays too, Her Excellency on some pretext or the other had been asking for a normal Russian cab, rather than for her official staff car to go somewhere and that too all alone, he became a little suspicious and he wanted to find out as to what was going on. Therefore on that Sunday morning he too decided to follow her incognito as a touring musician. He was therefore dressed very casually in old torn jeans and a tee shirt that had Michael Jackson's picture with the caption of his hit song 'Thriller' on it. And with an Elvis Presley type wig covering his head and a Spanish guitar slung around his left shoulder and a camcorder hung around his neck, he had stealthily followed her on a motorcycle. And when he too reached the upper deck of Mama Zoya and found Her Excellency in the company of Mr Riaz Mohammed Khan the Pakistani Ambassador, he felt that something was not only very fishy but also very alarming. Therefore he too by pretending to casually survey the area around the big boat and the river had managed to get them both on his video camera. And as both the sleuths from India and Pakistan and without being aware of each other's presence they from a safe distance kept a discreet eye on what was happening at that table, they were stunned when they also noticed that both of them were periodically exchanging certain papers and documents and also making notes. They were seldom seen talking to each other though and most of the time both of them were engrossed in simply reading those papers and documents. It was around three in the afternoon, when the Indian Ambassador left first and the Pakistani Ambassador having cleared the bill left some ten minutes later. Thereafter it was time for both the sleuths to also make their way home and to try and find out a little more about this mysterious and regular Sunday meetings between the two heads of missions that had been now going on for someime.

During that particular meeting at Madame Zoya, both the Ambassadors had given their detailed methodology and plans on how to make the track 3 channel an effective and workable one. And both of them also desired that the plan must not only be flexible and practical, but it should also be acceptable to both the sides as far as the core issue of Kashmir was concerned. They had also submitted to each other the list of eight eminent members from their respective countries who would be the likely members of that high level group and with that was also attached their brief biodata. This group would then form the core team and would deliberate the various issues and on reaching a viable consensus they would approach their respective governments to kick start the dialogue from where it was left off at Agra. And these were the papers and documents that the sleuths from both India and Pakistan had observed being periodically exchanged by the two heads of mission during that meeting. And while both the sleuths were discreetly doing their jobs they however had no idea of each other's presence at Mama Zoya that afternoon.

Dablo and Shups had also decided that since it would take quite a bit of time for them to approach and get the approval of their respective candidates to become active members of the Track 3 channel, and also in view of the fact that Shiraz's close relations from the Rehman family would all be descending in Moscow from the 12th of August onwards for a fortnight, no firm dates of their next meeting was therefore fixed. On that last Sunday meeting at Mama Zoya, Shiraz had also shown Shupriya some photographs of all the family members including that of his in-laws and others who were all part of the big and influential Rehman family and to that Shups had very aptly remarked. "I must say that not only is the big Rehman clan a well-knit one, but all of them are very talented too. And as far as your daughter Sherry is concerned, I thing she is gorgeous and your son Tojo the golfer is very handsome also. And as far as your wife Saira is concerned I think she is a typical Muslim beauty. And though she is from a Pathan family, but to me she looks more like a Kashmiri. And all of you together no doubt do make a very happy and contended family. And may Allah Talla, Wahe Guru, Jesus and Ma Durga protect you all," added Shups as she took leave of Dablo that day. Hearing those lovely and kind words coming from Shups, Dablo had also told her quite frankly. "But no one is as pretty and as understanding as you are Shups. And if I could marry you again and which I definitely can under Muslim law provided you are willing to become Shabnam instead of remaining Yeshwant Kaur the girl I left behind, I am ready to propose to you again right now."

"That is indeed very chivalrous and kind of you, but do remember that you have in Saira a very loving wife and a devoted mother and who has also given you two lovely children. And maybe some day I will also tell you a little more about this girl called Yeshwant Kaur Bajwa and also show you some interesting and fascinating photographs of the Bajwa family that had so lovingly given me shelter, confidence and guidance to become what I am today," said Shups but without mentioning a word that they too had a son and who was now 29 years old. Realising that she may not be able to control herself, Shupriya with her handkerchief wiped the tears that were swelling around her big bright eyes. And as she bid a final farewell to her one and only Dablo, she discreetly also surveyed the area around to ensure that she was not been observed or followed. She however did realize that her Dablo had never in all these years had never forgotten her. But she did not know that her meeting with her Dablo had been videotaped by one of her own staff members.who was from the RAW.

That night before going to bed, Shupriya took out the photograph that Monty had taken on their wedding day on the 15th of September 1971. It was a photograph that showed Dablo dressed as a Sikh Sarder complete with turban and sword and she dressed up as a typical young Pumjabi Sikh bride taking their religious vows around the Holy Guru Granth Sahib.

For the next fortnight or so both the officers from the respective intelligence agencies of Pakistan and India discreetly kept a close watch on the activities of their respective heads of mission. They were still not sure as to why the two of them had met at Mama Zoya and if it was to pass on or exchange certain secrets and confidential documents then that would be the last place that one would have chosen for such kind of spying activity. Not only was the restaurant a popular place on Sundays, but it was also in the heart of the city and where one could be easily identified and spotted. Therefore fearing that these meetings may well be just an informal tete-a-tete between the two ambassadors, and more so since it started soon after the Agra summit, they decided to keep the information to themselves and not report the matter as of now to their respective higher authorities. Afterall both were the highest representatives of their respective countries in Russia and therefore it would be improper to snoop on them in this highly unprofessional manner. And unless they had some definite proof and reason, it would be foolish of them to assume that the two heads of mission were exchanging secrets and classified documents, and why would they. But what kept tickling Iqbal Ahmed the ISI agent's mind was the fact that Sherry had earlier been meeting Deepak Kumar the Indian superstar clandestinely and who just a few weeks ago was the personal guest of the Indian Ambassador and he was staying with her. He therefore thought that maybe both the families were aware of the on going affair between the Indian superstar and the ambassador's daughter and the meetings between the two heads of mission was either to settle the issue discreetly through holy matrimony, or to ensure that the affair did not carry on any further. But then Iqbal Ahmed also thought that if the matter was known to both the sides then where was the need for the two young lovers to meet clandestinely in that small little hotel that was right in the heart of the city. And unless the Madam Ambassador was closely related to the Indian superstar, why should she poke her nose in what was entirely a private affair between two adults.

And while Iqbal Ahmed decided to find out a little more about the Indian Ambassador and her relationship with the Indian matinee idol, Omprakash Saran the officer from RAW also asked the headquarters of RAW and the Ministry of External Affiars in New Delhi to furnish him with more details about Mr Riaz Mohammed Khan, his family and also his career profile.

CHAPTER-37

Rehman Clan's Grand Moscow Reunion

With the intelligence sleuths stationed in Moscow from both the countries still trying to figure out the big puzzle that concerned both their bosses, Shiraz and the entire Rehman clan were enjoying every minute of their memorable holiday in Russia. Starting with Arif Rehman and Ruksana Begum who were the seniormost in the clan, everbody was there. Lt General Aslam Rehman with Farzana being the next senior most had come with their son Vovka Major Samir Rehman, daughter Nasreen who was now 19 and daughter-in-law Zeba. Fazal Rehman with his wife Samina, daughter Sameera and their nineteen year old son Shafiq arrived from Bangkok. Sameera was now engaged to Fazal Rehman's own First Secretary and they were soon to get married. Mehmuda and Karim Malik with their daughter Tarannum, son-in-law Taufiq and their two five year old grand daughters Sakina and Naseema arrived from the U.S. And their twenty four old and only son Javed who was now an airlines pilot with the PIA joined them from Karachi. Salim Rehman and his wife Aasma with their twenty-two year old daughter Nadia and eighteen year old son Shabir had accompanied the two patriarchs. And as far as Shiraz was concerned his family too was complete, when Tojo after playing a major golf tournament arrived from Paris at the very last minute. And with that the last three generations of Haji Abdul Rehman's family from Peshawar and who were still living were complete.

The first couple of days at the palatial dacha with its vast garden and orchard were full of fun and games for the younger crowd and shopping for the mothers, while the elderly men folk discussed and debated the future of Pakistan and Bangladesh. One evening over a drink and barbecue party, when the topic of why Jinnah's dream of a secular Pakistan could not be fulfilled, and why Pakistan after becoming an Islamic country was in such a mess now was being debated and discussed, Arif Rehman said.

"It would have remained secular if Jinnah had lived for another decade. But unfortunately he lived for only a little more than a year after we attained our independence. And though he gave the Muslims of India their own country and though technically the birth of Islam in this country could be attributed to the day Pakistan became an independent nation and a free country fifty four years ago, but Islamism got truly embedded in the functioning of the state from the day Zulfiqar Ali Bhutto was ousted from power and Zia-ul-Haq the Mulla General from the famous Guides Cavalry took over the country. And it was under his military rule and thereafter that the tenets of Islamic fundamentalism took deeper roots in Pakistan. And it was given a further boost, when the US intelligence network during General Zia's rule very cleverly sponsored the growing Islamic fundamentalism in our country and through military and economic aid to the Afghan Mujahideen and refugees they also very cunningly roped us in to fight the invading Russians in neighbouring Afghanistan. And though that too was a war by proxy, but nonetheless it did spawn the growth of many diehard fundamentalist militant organizations within the country such as the Hijbul Mujahideen, the Lashkar-eToiba, the Jaish-e—Mohammed and such like others. And unfortunately this policy that was adopted by the military dictatorship of General Zia was also with a view to undermine the structures of civilian government and the rule of law. In 1984, and soon after the Mullah General through a bogus referendum declared himself as the President of Pakistan and he had the parliament replaced by a bogus consultative assembly, the so called 'Majlis-e-Shoora, Islamism in Pakistan had now come to stay. And though this consultative assembly was composed of scholars and professionals who were appointed by the President of Pakistan, but Zia's only aim it seems was to project himself as a good Muslim, bring in the Shariar law and keep the Muslim clergy happy. And as a result of which there were a spate of arrests, public flogging and imprisonment for those who did not see eye to eye with Zia's policy. But that unfortunately became the rule of law in Pakistan. And therefore for the mess that we are in now, we have only to thank the CIA, General Zia, his military advisors and the ISI," said Arif Rehman somewhat sarcastically.

"Maybe in a way you are right Chachajaan, but one should not also forget that during the Cold War and its aftermath, the repeal of democracy and militarization of Pakistan was one of the prime foreign policy objectives of the US government. And that was primarily because for the United States, Pakistan was and it still is an important geopolitical hub and from where all U S sponsored covert and overt intelligence operations have been launched. And it all started with Pakistan joining the CENTO and the SEATO and the ill fated Gary Powers secret flight on the U-2 that took off from Peshawar during Field Marshall Ayub Khan's military regime, but was unfortunately shot down by the Soviets as the spy plane flew over that vast country," said Karim Malik.

"Yes and I think Karim Mia is right and though President George Bush on General Musharraf's taking over power had said that the guy will bring stability to the country and that his taking over was good news for the subcontinent, but I personally think Bush has spoken a bit too early. After all it was the Americans who had very cleverly got us involved in Afghanistan, and that was soon after the Soviet invasion of that poor country. And the same very Americans are now seeking our active support to get hold of Osama Bin Laden for them. And if I remember very correctly even President Ronald Reagan in his 7th state of the union address in January 1988 had said very categorically that the Afghan freedom fighters, the Mujahideens are the key to peace in that region and America therefore supports it. And now look what is happening and I really do not know why we are supporting the Taliban so very stupidly and foolishly.And there is no doubt whatsoever in my mind that the Soviet-Afghan war was definitely a part of the CIA's covert agenda to make the Russians bleed to death in Afghanistan. And that agenda was first initiated during Mr Jimmy Carter's presidency and which totally encouraged, aided and supported in financing and arming the many Islamic fundamentalist militant brigades to give the Soviets their own Viet Nam. And it was from that damn womb that the Al-Qaida and such other fundamentalist militant groups were born. And it was the Pakistani military regime and the ISI thereafter who played a key and decisive role in those US sponsored military and intelligence operations across the Pak-Afghan border," said Shiraz.

"But I don't think that all Pakistan's ills and failures can be attributed only to the men in uniform. Because even during the short-lived democratically elected governments of Benazir Bhutto and Nawaz Sheriff that ruled the country after Zia's death in 1987, it didn't stop pandering to the US and their interests in Afghanistan. And the Americans were all the time using us as pawns in this new great game that is still being played out in this ever volatile region that is bordering our north western frontiers. And with the US being the only superpower, both the Benazir and the Nawaz Sharif governments had no other choice but to accept the policy diktats of that country and also the economic diktats of the IMF and the World Bank. And the blatant and hungry manner in which our politicians have systematically looted this country left, right and centre for their own personal gains, therefore they too are equally to be blamed for the bloody mess that we are now in,' said retired Lt General Aslam Rehman as Shiraz poured into the General's glass another large peg of that excellent Jura malt whisky.

"Yes in a way you are right too because both Benazir and Nawaz Shariff with the overt and covert help of the ISI also created this monster called Taliban. But in 1978 April, when the PDPA the Peoples Democratic Party of Afghanistan seized power in Afghanistan after a popular insurrection that was directed against the dictatorship of President Mohammed Daud Khan and the PDPA wanted to introduce land reforms, promote education and introduce health programs and it even actively supported women's right in Afghanistan, it should have been allowed to do so. But because the PDPA started leaning heavily towards the then Soviet Union it got the Americans thinking and the CIA's covert operations was therefore intended to undermine and ultimately destroy the PDPA government and curtail the growing Soviet influence in Afghanistan and in Central Asia. And therefore the covert American support to these Mujahedeen and Islamic brigades was meant only to destroy the foundations of the secular PDPA govt. But from the very outset of the Soviet-Afghan war, when Pakistan under the Mulla General and military rule in close liaison with the CIA started playing this game, we should have been more cautious about its fallout. And when Pakistan Military Intelligence and the ISI actively kept supporting those Islamic brigades and fundamentalist militant organizations, we should have realized the terrible mess that we were getting into," said Salim Rehman.

"But the very fact that the ISI has now become a very powerful organization and a parallel government in Pakistan cannot be denied. And the covert war that the Americans began in Afghanistan by using Pakistan as the launch pad was initiated actually on 3rd July 1979, when President Carter signed the first directive that authorized the secret aid that was required to be given to the opponents of the pro Soviet regime in Kabul. And that was very many months before the Soviet paratroopers and tanks descended on the Afghan capital. And mind you it was done in spite of Mr Carter's National Security Advisor, Mr Zbigniew Brzezinski warning to his President that this kind of aid would only encourage and induce a Soviet military intervention in that region. And that is exactly what happened. And this has been certified and corraborated even by Mr Robert Gates who at that time was a Deputy Director in the CIA and who later also became the country's powerful Defence Secretary. And during that turbulent period the ISI was operating virtually as a close affiliate and a staunch ally of the CIA. And no one cannot deny that the ISI played and it is still playing a very central but dangerous role in channeling support to the Al Qaida and other such like fanatical, fundamentalist militant Islamic groups not only in Afghanistan, but also in Pakistan, India and in Bangladesh.'Acting on behalf of the CIA, the ISI was very much involved in the recruitment and training of the Mujahideen and from 1982 to 1992 some 35,000 Muslims from no less than 43 Islamic countries were recruited to fight in the Afghanistan jihad. The many madrassas that surfaced in Pakistan and that were financed by Saudi charities were also set up with US support. And what was still worse was that the same very madrassas with directions from the US government were also told to inculcate Islamic values in all these young students. Thus these camps became virtual universities for future Islamic radicalism. And these young Muslims were not only mentally indoctrinated and highly motivated by the Mullas, but they were also well trained under the auspices of the CIA and the ISI to carry out assassinations and car bomb attacks and to become Fedayeens. And the deadly bomb attacks on the US embassies in Africa and on the USS Cole by the Al Qaida operatives is ample proof of their growing clout in the Muslim world. Ironically Osama Bin Laden, the American bogeyman and on whose head there is now a big American reward was recruited by the CIA in 1979. And I believe that at the very outset of the US sponsored jihad in Afghanistan, the then 22 year old Osama was even trained in a CIA sponsored guerilla training camp. And today while America is desperately trying to hunt and eliminate him, Pakistan with subterfuge is trying to protect and shield him. And if this sort of cat and mouse carries on it will only encourage other such militant groups that are inside Pakistan to side with the handsome Yemeni Arab and that certainly won't be good for Pakistan and the subcontinent where the need of the hour is to maintain peace, stability and tranquility in the region,' argued Fazal Rehman.

"Yes and it all started during President Ronald Reagen's Presidency, when Osama who came from the wealthy Bin Laden family was put in charge of raising money for these Islamic Brigades and all these fund raising operations was coordinated by the Saudi Intelligence that was headed by Prince Turki-al-Faisal in close liaison with the CIA. Thereafter the Pakistani ISI was used as a go-between and the CIA's covert support to the Mujahideens fighting in Afghanistan became a joint CIA-ISI operation. In March 1985, when President Reagan issued the NSDD 166, the National Security Decision Directive, it not only authorized the stepping up of the covert military aid to the Mujahideens, but it also gave its full support to the religious indoctrination of these fighters. And besides supplying and training them with the use of sophisticated weapons, state of the art communication equipment and military satellite maps, the CIA and the ISI head honchos also met regularly at the ISI headquarters in Rawalpindi to coordinate the so called jihad. And with William Casey as the CIA boss in Washington and Lt General Akhtar Abdur Rehman the DGISI in Rawalpindi actively controlling all activities, the NSDD 166 soon became the largest covert operation in American history. The US supplied support package which comprised of organization and logistics, military technology and ideological support for sustaining and encouraging the Afghan resistance movement together with the ISI's active support in arming and training these so called freedom fighters no doubt had forced the Soviets to get out of Afghanistan, but look at the bloody mess that it has now created for us. And on top of that we like bloody fools are still supporting Mulla Omar and his Taliban and which I am afraid may one day backfire on us. The millions of dollars that the US spent to supply the Afghan schoolchildren with textbooks that were filled with violent images and militant Islamic teachings are now being used by our very own Mullas in the many madrassas in the North West Frontier, Baluchistan and Waziristan. And that is now the core curriculum in all these schools. And I know for sure that those very books that were published in the dominant languages of Dari and Pashtun by the University of Nebraska-Omaha to motivate and indoctrinate the Afghan Mujahideens are now being used to motivate and indoctrinate our very own children in those tribal regions, and this could well be a monster in the making," said Aslam Rehman.

"What do you mean it could be, it is already in the making? It is already a big monster and with the Pakistan government and the ISI both now closely cuddling up to it, it will soon turn into a Frankenstein and which will be difficult to control. But that I guess is Pakistan's headache at the moment. But sooner or later with the ISI now actively operating in Bangladesh it may well be a headache for us too. As it is there is a cry by some of the fanatical members of the HUJI-B, the Harkat-ul-Jihad-al-Aslami of Bangladesh in my country and which is openly now declaring.'Amra shob hobo Taliban-Bangladesh hobe Afghanistan' which means that we will all become Taliban and we will turn Bangladesh into Afghanistan," said Fazal Rehman as he helped himself to some more of the delicious barbecue that Saira had prepared.

"But in what manner and why is the ISI poking its damn head in Bangladesh now. And from where and how did the HUJI-B emerge,' asked Shiraz as he too helped Saira in serving the snacks.

"Like most of the other Islamist terrorist groups, the birth of HUJI-B also took place during the Soviet-Afghan War. After fighting the Soviets a group of Bangladeshi Mujahideens who returned home formed this radical outfit and its formation was officially announced at the Jatiya Press Club in Dhaka on 30th April, 1992.Historically, Soviet intervention in Afghanistan in 1979 had stirred the Islamist world and prompted them to launch jihad against it. Getting support from the ISI in Pakistan, the then Reagan administration of U.S.A. and Saudi Arabia, they formed the Harkat-ul-Jihadi Islami. But Bin Laden it seems was not happy with the concept of Bengali nationalism among the Muslims of Bangladesh. Therefore after the withdrawal of Soviet forces in 1989, Bin Laden had convened a meeting of some of his trusted Mujahideens from Bangladesh and advised them to organise the Muslim youths to transform their country into Dar-ul-Islam. In the initial period of its birth, HuJI-B used the favourable regime of Begum Khaleda Zia to strengthen the organisation and recruited both the locals and the foreigners as its members.Although the Madrasas were mostly financed by Arab charities and were the primary source of recruitment of its cadres, Rohingya Muslim refugees from Myanmar, who had fled from their native land allegedly due to religious persecution was another significant source of recruitment. With the assistance of ISI it imparted training to the Muslim Rohingya insurgents from Myanmar and they were also sent to fight against the Indian security forces in Jammu and Kashmir besides providing sanctuary for the northeast insurgents from India. Installation of the Awami League Government led by Sheikh Hasina in June1996 created some set back for the HuJI-B. But formation of an International Islamic Front (IIF) for Jihad against the Jews and Crusaders in January 1998 by Bin Laden of which HuJI-B was also a member made the latter an important militant Islamist organisation of the world. With a view to translate the objective of Al Qaida into action, Osama Bin Laden in association with the terrorist groups from Egypt, Pakistan and Bangladesh announced the formation of IIF and issued a fatwa on February 23 of the same year for Jihad against the USA and called for attacks on all Americans including civilians. With long-term strategy to replace the existing political structure of the world with the Caliphate, his immediate priority was to destroy the USA and its allies. Apart from Bin Laden other signatories of this fatwa included Abdul Salam Muhammad alias Fazlur Rahman, of 'Jihad Movement of Bangladesh' (an activist of HuJI-B), Ayman al-Zawahiri and Rifai Ahmad Taha aka Abu Nasir of Egypt and Sheikh Mir Hamzah, Secretary of the Jamiat-al-Ulema-e-Pakistan. After becoming a constituent of IIF, HuJI-B increased its violent attacks on the Hindu minority, and also on the progressive intellectuals like poets, journalists and liberal Muslims of Bangladesh.With the help of ISI and the patronage of radical Islamists it became easier for the HuJI-B operatives to merge among the Muslim groups in states like Assam, West Bengal, Uttar Pradesh and Delhi and to set up their cells there. Various reports suggest that in addition to its links with Indian terrorist groups like the United Liberation Front of Assam (ULFA), it also maintains links with terrorist groups outside Bangladesh, including Jaish-e-Mohammed (JEM) and Lashkar-e-Taiba (LET) in Pakistan. Calling its members as Bangladeshi Taliban, HuJI-B gradually emerged as one of the most militant Islamist outfits of Bangladesh and it soon became an important link in the chain of the wider net work of Al Qaeda. Prime suspect in 2000 assassination attempt on then Prime Minister Sheikh Hasina, HuJI-B had a history of carrying out violent attacks on secular and progressive intellectuals, writers and journalists. It was also involved in the assassination of a senior Bangladeshi journalist for making a documentary on the plight of Hindus in Bangladesh. Mohammad Salim, the prime accused in the New Jalpaiguri explosion incident in a troop mobilisation train for Kargil War was believed to be an activist of the HuJI-B. And as far as the ISI is concerned, it is hand in glove with such like Bangladeshi fundamentalist groups and their common aim is to create a sovereign Islamic state in India's northeast. There are also very reliable reports that Pakistan nationals owing allegiance to different terrorist outfits have been using Dhaka as a transit point for entering India and Nepal, as well as using it as a safe escape route. The ISI has been instrumental, either directly or through the Pakistan High Commission in Dhaka, to develop a nexus between Indian insurgent groups (IIGs), Islamic fundamentalists and criminal elements in Bangladesh. Besides assisting terrorists in the procurement of arms, ammunition and explosives, the ISI has been arranging meetings of terrorists of different hues to coordinate their activities. The ISI has also been helping IIGs in obtaining weapons and explosives from different places, including Thailand. The ISI has also been using the local media to generate strong anti-India sentiments. The ISI also has plans to appoint Pakistan nationals, trained as *maulvis* in *madrassas* and mosques in Bangladesh,and particularly the ones that are situated on the India-Bangladesh border'. There are also indications that these madrassas and mosques will also provide help and shelter to the ISI operatives in their respective areas. There are also plans to set up jihadi training camps in the areas of Moulvi Bazar and the hill tracts of Chittagong and Cox's Bazar. Top IIG leaders staying in Bangladesh, like Paresh Barua and Ranjan Daimary, have close links with the ISI. Bangladesh has been used as a staging point for sending members of both IIGs and jihadi groups to Pakistan and Afghanistan as well as their infiltration into India. The persons involved in conspiracy of the hijacking of flight IC-814 from Kathmandu in December 1999 had used Bangladesh for their movement to India from Pakistan. The Pakistan Intelligence Officers in Dhaka are becoming increasingly active in carrying out espionage activities against India.It is hardly any secret that the ISI has close links with Bangladesh's Directorate General of Forces' Intelligence (DGFI) and operates openly and freely in that country. It not only helps coordinate the activities of al-Qaeda and fundamental Islamic militant groups like the HUJAI, but actively assists, through organizations like the latter as well as the DGFI, secessionist outfits operating in northeast India. According to an intelligence report, HUJI, which is often called the Bangladeshi Taliban, and which has close links with Al-Qaeda and Osama bin Laden, runs six training camps for ULFA terrorists in the Chittagong Hill Tracts across the border from Tripura in India. The ISI agents based in Bangladesh are also spreading their dragnet in Jambudwip and other parts of the Sunderbans," concluded Fazal Rehman as Sherry announced that food was on the table.

During that delicious meal of tandoori chicken, mutton roghanjosh and fried fish that were served with hot tandoori rotis and buttered nans, when Fazal Rehman said that the general elections in Bangladesh that were scheduled to be held on 1st October would not be a peaceful one, and that the chances of the BNP, the Bangladesh National Party of Khalida Zia with its coalition partner the radical JEI, the Jamaat-e-Islami coming to power was very much on the cards, Shiraz was not very surprised. In July 2001 and soon after Sheikh Hasina's Awami League government stepped down, the cases of sporadic bombing by Islamic militants had been on the rise.But when Fazal Rehman also said that the chances of Sheikh Hasina could possibly also suffer the same fate as her late father Sheikh Mujibur Rehman, and further added that two or more abortive attempts had already been made on her life during these last couple of years and that in one particular case the services of female LTTE suicide bombers had also been requisitioned, it took everyone by complete surprise.

According to Fazal Rehman the matter only came to light after Raju Srivastava an ISI agent based in Nepal was apprehended by the Kolkata police at the Dum Dum airport on 18th May, 2001. He had arrived from Mumbai and was on his way to Khatmandu. And after the Indian sleuths from the Intelligence Bureau and RAW started thoroughly grilling him, he broke down and spilled the beans. According to Shrivastav's story the first meeting to formulate a plan to assassinate ShaikhHasina took place in the apartment of Major Najmul Alam. The former Bangladeshi army officer staying in the posh Bonani Apartments in Dhaka and his brother Najmal Amin had hatched the plot. Najmal's wife was a Tamil Muslim from Jaffna and her mother was an active member of the Women's wing of the LTTE. Simultaneously another group of army officers who were absconding and who had been finally sentenced to death for Mujib's murder on 30th April, 2001 by Justice Mohammed Fazlul Karim were also planning to get rid of Sheikh Hasina. Led by Colonel Munirul Islam Chowhdury the son-in-law of the late Tajuddin Ahmed and Lt Colonel Khondakar Abdur Rashid, the duo it seems had also got in touch with Alain Deloin, a notorious French contract killer. On 6th June, 1999 at a secret meeting at St James Court Hotel in London, both the groups finally decided to give the contract for 10 million dollars to the LTTE suicide bombers though the French killer was only asking for only half that amount. And that was because they felt that the LTTE was more dependable and they normally left no trace. Moreover their features were similar to that off the Bangladeshis and therefore it would be easier for them to mix with the local population and carry out the dastardly act. According to a senior official of Bangladesh's National Secutiry Intelligence that meeting was also attended by Colonel R M Ahsan, a former Pakistani Army officer who was also a frontman for the ISI and who was now running an export-import firm in Karachi. And in case the LTTE plan failed, then the conspirators would put into action the back-up plan which was to activate the 76 Kg of RDX that was to be planted 100 yards from the dias from which Sheikh Hasina was to address the public election meeting at Kotalipara in Gopalgunj District that was scheduled for August 2001.

On 7th March, 2001 another group of Mujib's killers had met at a restaurant in Breda. It was a small town in southern Holland where Lt Col AKM Mohiuddin, who was one of Mujib's killers and an absconder had opened his restaurant.The group had planned to kill Sheikh Hasina before the coming elections.But luckily all the plans failed after the Bangladesh intelligence and the Indian RAW got wind of them in the nick of time. Like in the case of Rajiv Gandhi, the LTTE were planning to use young Tamilian women bombers. Two of them under fictitious names of Sheikh Taslim and Subhalaxmi had applied for visas from the Bangladesh Consulate in Kolkata and a third with the Bengali pseudonym of Mahua without a visa had also managed to infiltrate through the porous Indo-Bangla northeast border. Mahua was required to do the initial recce. But after the other two ladies were apprehended, Mahua too chickened out. And the back-up attempt at Kotalipara also failed when the RDX was discovered by the public an hour and a half before the meeting was scheduled to start. And as far as the Breda conspiracy was concerned and which was also attended by Colonel Shoaib Nasir from the Pakistan ISI, it was thanks to the Dutch intelligence and the Mossad who it seemed had tapped the conversation between Colonel Shoaib Nasir and Brigadier Riaz, the ISI chief of operations that took place on the 9th of March soon after the meeting in the restaurant. And according to that plan either a Palestinian hit man or a mercenary who was based in Europe was required to do the job.

"I must say the lady indeed has been very lucky and let us hope that nothing happens to her before the elections," said Shiraz as Sherry announced that everyone must be ready by 7AM next morning to board the special bus that would take them to Moscow for the grand seven day cruise.That night after everyone had retired to their respective rooms in the palatial dacha, Shiraz sat on the the thunder box in the bathroom and hurriedly made notes in his little red diary. He felt that he must warn Shups about the growing influence of the Al Qaida and the HUJI-B in Bangladesh politics and about their nefarious plans in collusion with the ISI to forment trouble in India. It seemed that Manoj Shrivastav had also told the Indian intelligence sleuths that the recent fires at Indian army ammunition dumps was also the handiwork of the ISI and that there was also a plan to carry out a sensational attack on some important targets inside India in the near future. According to Fazal Rehman there was still a very large number of Bihari Muslims in Bangladesh and who as Pakistanis even after 30 years were still waiting to be repatriated to Pakistan. But Pakistan it seems was not in the least interested. Shiraz therefore felt that these stateless Bihari Muslims were ideal material for recruitment by the ISI and the DGFI. They were all still living in refugee camps in Bangladesh and the Rabita Trust which was established by General Zia-ul-Haq in 1988 with Saudi money and whose aim was to fund their repatriation and rehabilitation could well now be used to fund such like terrorist activities against India.

Chapter-38

Strange But True

On the next morning after the big Rehman family boarded the luxury cruise boat 'Lev Tolstoy' and were heartily welcomed by the friendly Captain and his crew, they were surprised that quite a few amongst them could also speak fairly good English. And during the next two days when they were taken on a conducted tour of Russia's historic capital and the expert guide who happen to be an attractive middle aged Russian lady narrated to them in impeccable English as to when and how the Kremlin was built, all the children were indeed very impressed, but the men folk it seemed were more interested in taking her photograph than listening to her. One of the elderly rich American tourists from California who was a divorcee was so smitten by her beauty and charm that by the time they set sail for St Petersburg, he even wanted to propose to her. But unfortunately for him, the beautiful lady was not only married with two grown up kids, but her husband too was part of the crew and he was the person who was overall incharge of all the entertainment. Nonetheless the husband and wife team made a charming couple and they got on famously with everbody.

Everyday at meal times on board the luxury boat when the entire family consisting off 24 adults and the two minor great grand children from the Rehman clan led by Arif Rehman and Ruksana Begum trooped in and took their seats in the 'Katrina' restaurant, the happiest persons were the chefs, the waiters and the waitresses. And that was bcause with every meal there was also a big tip in American dollars for all of them. On the third day as the luxury boat made its way to the ancient town of Uglich with its many churches, all the children with their parents and grandparents decided to go for a swim in the boat's swimming pool that was situated on the boat deck and was adjacent to the 'Neva" Bar. And while Arif Reman decided to first have a Bloody Mary cocktail and then get into the pool, he suddenly noticed the small gold chain with the locket in Shiraz's hand. It had come out from his purse while Shiraz was in the process of handing it over to him for safe keeping. And when Arif Rehman had a closer look and found the words 'Allah Ho Akbar' written in Persian on it, he simply asked Shiraz from where he got that from.

"Oh I believe that it was around my little neck when a soldier from the Maharaja of Kashmir's army found me lying in an improvised cradle outside the Christian church near the town of Baramulla. And seeing that I was a Muslim he had adopted me. My father who adopted me was a Muslim soldier in the Maharaja's 4th Kashmir Infantry. He was from a village near Philandri and in October 1947 after the Muslim company in which he was serving revolted at Muzzafarbad and they with the Quabailis/ raiders reached Baramulla, he found me outside that church. I think I was just one year old at that time and he thought that somebody had abandoned me. And finding Allah Talla's name on my locket he as a good Muslim took me home and gave me the name of Riaz Mohammed Khan, and which according to him meant 'devotion' lied Shiraz very confidently."

'My God but I just can't believe it. But tell me do you also have a very strange looking birthmark that looks like a quarter moon or more like a waxing crescent moon should I say somewhere on your backside,' asked Arif Rehman.

"Sure I do, but how did you guess it Abbu!" said Shiraz looking quite amazed on being asked so many questions about that gold oval shaped small locket and the birthmark on his bum by his father-in-law.

"Well it may sound rather stupid, but can I have a look at that birthmark of yours, before I draw any further conclusions. And if I am right then it will be nothing short of a miracle I can tell you," said Arif Rehman as he called out loudly to his wife Ruksana Begum to quickly come and see what he had found. But the Begum Sahiba was in the pool and she was taking good care of her two identical great granddaughters Sakina and Naseema and she did not want to leave them alone. So when Arif Rehman walked upto her and showed her the old gold chain and the small oval locket with 'Allah Ho Akbar' engraved in Persian on it, Ruksana Begum's face suddenly lit up.

"Ofcourse and I think this is that same very gold chain and locket with those engraved wordings that your father Colonel Attiqur Rehman had put around little Imran Hussein's neck just before your sister Shenaz and her husband with their only son left Peshawar in that brand new yellow Studebaker car for their second honeymoon to Kashmir. And that was way back in mid October 1947 and they never came back and nor was the car ever found. And your father was heartbroken when he came to know from the same jeweler who made that chain and locket that the family had probably been robbed and killed by the invading Pathan tribesman at some place near Mandir Buniyar while they were returning from Srinagar to be in time to celebrate Idd with the old man," said the Begum Sahiba as she kept staring at her son-in-law. And if I also remember correctly your father had also instructed the jeweler to engrave a small miniature waxing crescent moon and a star on the reverse side of that locket, and if that is also there then this could be none other than late Imran Hussein's. But to locate that one would need a powerful magnifying glass,"' added the Begum Sahiba as Shiraz who had no idea whatsoever and about whom they were talking about asked the young bartender if he with his naked eye could spot that waxing crescent moon on the reverse side of that oval shaped gold locket.

"Yes it is very much there, but since it has slightly faded, it will be therefore difficult for all of you elderly people to spot it," said the young bartender as he with a glass swivel stirring stick pointed out the exact spot to the elderly lady. Seeing the keen interest being shown in that old locket by his in-laws, Shiraz requested the life saver on duty at the swimming pool if he could arrange for a good magnifying glass at the earliest. And by the time it arrived from the boat's map room, and seeing all the hullaballoo that was being created over that old locket, all the other senior members from the Rehman clan also gathered around the bar to have a look at it.

"But there is just one more thing that needs to be seen before I declare that we have today probably found a long lost somebody who is very close and dear to us. But since that cannot be seen in front of all the ladies and chidren, may I therefore request Riaz Mohammed and Salim Rehman to accompany me to the men's rest room please," said an excited Arif Rehman. And while everybody else except the Begum Sahiba thought it to be some kind of a joke, Arif Rehman in anticipation ordered four bottles of the best champagne. And seeing all the excitement around the bar, Sherry with all her young cousins also came out from the pool and asked her grandma.

"But do also tell us what is Big Abbu really upto?"

"May be Big Big Abbu wants to show all of us some magic,'"said little Sakina as her mother quickly put a towel around her.

"No you stupid, Big Big Abbu wants to give all of us gifts and chocolates and he has therefore gone to the rest room to get them," said little Naseema.

"Well all I can say is that it is definitely going to be a miracle and Allah's greatest gift to all of us if what Big Big Abbu has gone to find out turns out to be really true,'"said Ruksana Begum as she closed her eyes and said a prayer. And as all of them waited anxiously around that open air bar for that miracle to happen, the loud baritone voice of Salim Rehman from the men's washroom was heard. He was shouting triumphantly.

"It is him our own Imran Hussein. We have by Allah's kindness found him." Hearing that, Ruksana Begum with tears of joy in her eyes ran to kiss and hug her own nephew and who was now also her son-in-law, while all the others looked with total bewilderment at each other. It was indeed a miracle.The Rehman clan after fifty four years had been reunited with Imran Hussein, the only son of Shenaz and Nawaz Hussein. Shenaz was Arif Rehman's own sister and she was the youngest in the family. And with the loud popping of the champagne corks, when Arif Rehman narrated that tragic story to all the others, everybody was totally dumbfounded and even Shiraz could not believe that he was actually very much a blood related member of the same Rehman clan and that Saira his wife was his own first cousin. Reminding the family that it was time for 'Dhuhr' the afternoon prayer and to thank Allah for that miracle, a misty eyed and happy Ruksana Begum requested all of them to dress up appropriately and congrerate inside the Tchaikovsky Hall which was the main entertainment centre on the luxury boat.

With that grand find of their long lost relative, the seven day cruise to St Petersburg became even more exciting for the Rehman clan. And when Shiraz wondered what would be Shups reaction to that fairytale story, he suddenly realized that he was actually a Pakistani and not an Indian at all. And while Shiraz with his family and relatives were enjoying their cruise on the River Volga, Shupriya in Moscow received a big fat envelope from her Reeta Bhabhi in New Delhi. Enclosed with a personal letter from her were the set of photographs of Peevee's visit to his Mom Number 2 in Moscow. And although most of the photos were those of herself and that of her son with some of the staff members from the Indian Embassy, and a few of the weekend visit to the dacha outside Moscow that was exclusively reserved for the senior members of the diplomatic corps, but there was one photograph that was rather intriguing. It was that of her son standing next to a pretty girl in jeans in front of some palatial house. And though the face looked somewhat familiar, but she simply could not remember where she had met or seen this girl. Maybe it is one of the actors or some actor's wife from Mosfilm, thought Shupriya. But since the matter kept bugging her and the girl was indeed a very beautiful brunette, she therefore rang up Peevee to find out a little more about her.

"Oh she is just a casual acquaintance that I met by chance Maa. And it was on the luxury bus that took us on the conducted tour of the new palatial luxury dachas of the nuveau rich Russians that have come up on the Rubleyev-Uspenskoe highway on the outskirts of the city," lied Peevee very confidently.

Hearing the word Maa coming from her son for the first time, she jokingly asked him if he was in anyway interested in her and where was the girl actually from. "With her jet black hair, sharp features and good figure, she looks unlike a Russian to me and more like an Armenian or an Iranian," said Shupriya.

"Well you are not very wrong and she is a Muslim from Istanbul, Turkey," lied Peevee again.

"But are you both in touch with each other? And so what if she is a Muslim?'

"Yes in a way I am in touch with her, but it is northing very serious,"said Peevee.

'Then I guess it must be atleast a little serious if not very. And if you are really interested then you should not fool around with her. That will not only be morally wrong, but it will be most unlike a Bajwa, the Jat tribe who are known for their, chivalry, honesty and bravery," said Shupriya while requesting him to be careful of the growing nexus between the Dons of Mumbai's underworld and some of the big time film producers and financiers of Bollywood. Shupriya had read somewhere that though the controversial film 'Chori Chori Chupke Chupke' had been finally released in March 2001, but it had also clearly established the stranglehold that Dons like Chhota Shakeel and others now had in Mumbai's tinsel world. And as Shupriya kept wondering of what would be Dablo's reaction if he was told that they had a 29 year old son and who was a mega Bollywood star and still a bachelor, she had no idea about how madly in love was her son with the Pakistan Anbassador's daughter. Meanwhile far away ln St Petersburg while the Rehman clan was being taken around on a conducted tour of that magnificent and historic city, Shupriya wondered when she too would become a grandmother.

On the last and final day of the cruise, when during breakfast the entire Rehman family sang in chorus the old popular Volga Boatmen's song, it took the entire Russian crew totally by surprise. Shiraz had taught all of them to sing with him in chorus the Russian song and they had rehearsed it very well too. And as Shiraz with his guitar in hand lead the clan, and they all simply sang magnificently, the captain and the crew were so very happy and delighted with that excellent performance that they too immediately put up an impromptu show exclusively for all the Rehmans. And as the Russians vigorously sang and danced to the old popular number "Kalinka', the entire Rehman clan led by Arif and Ruksana also very sportingly joined them in the dance And thereafter when a group photograph of the Rehman's with the jovial and burly Russian skipper of the cruise boat standing in the centre was taken by some of the crew members, a loud three cheers for Lev Tolstoy and the crew was given by the entire family. And as they all got ready to disembark, there were tears in the eyes of some of the elderly Russians who were also a part of that magnificent and friendly crew.

"I must say that this wonderful cruise has been the happiest moment of our lives and we wish the Captain and the crew all the very best for the future. Dasvidaniya and Khuda Hafiz (Goodbye and may Allah bless all of you),' wrote Arif Rehman in the boat's visitors book as he once again hugged his son-in-law for that fantastic holiday. The little boy Imran Hussein who was found and was given the name Shiraz Ismail Khan by Colonel Ismail Sikandar Khan, and who later took the name Riaz Mohammed Khan, was now once again being addressed by his own kith and kin as Imran Hussein. Life once again had turned full circle for him and though these last three decades had been a very eventful and a happy one for the seasoned Pakistani career diplomat and the decorated ex Indian army officer, but he never could forget his dear Shups. For the first two years after he decided to stay back in Pakistan it was a roller coaster ride for Major Shiraz Ismail Khan because one false move could have sent him to the gallows. Not only had he killed many Pakistani soldiers but he had also escaped death by a whisker at Kotli and now as they all lovingly started addressing him as Imran Hussein, Shiraz naturally at times felt a little awkward and ill at ease. But that was his real and original name and he was destined to live with it now, atleast as far as the Rehman clan was concerned. Surprisingly Imran was also the name of the Holy Prophet and in Arabic it also meant prosperity and longlife.

On the 28th of August, 2001, when Shiraz with his family returned to Moscow, he immediately rang up Shups. He was eager to tell her as to who he really was and who his biological parents were.

"I know you will not believe me Shups, but there is something I want to tell you in person very urgently. Therefore may I request you to meet me at the same restaurant where we first met, and which is close to the Varshavskaya Metro station. And though it is a Wednesday and a working day tomorrow, but we could meet for a while after office hours and say around 7 O'clock in the evening. And that would also enable us to exchange notes regarding the final composition of our Track 3 channel," said Shiraz in a somewhat excited tone.

"Alright Dablo if you so desire I will be there tomorrow, but it will be only for half an hour at the most. And the way you sounded just now it seems that the Rehman clan's big reunion on board the Lev Tolstoy has enthused some new life and blood into you," said Shups.

"You are dead right and it definitely has but more about that tomorrow when we meet. And please do ensure that you don't have anybody tailing you. As far as I am concerned I have already told Saira that I will be late from office tomorrow since I have an important meeting with some Russian officials at the Russian Foreign Office. And maybe you too could give the same excuse and come in your chauffeur driven official car to the Russian Foreign Ministry office. And we could first meet there and from there slip out quietly and take a cab to the restaurant. That would also be safer and and we would also be able to avoid the peak hour rush on the metro. Moreover it will also give us more time in each other's company. Likewise we will also use the same mode of transport for the return journey back to the foreign office and quietly get into our respective cars and head home safely," said Shiraz.

"Well that sounds more like my real professional Dablo working out his mission plan and don't worry I will be there at the foreign office on the dot at 6.30 PM,'"said Shups as she wished him a very good night.

Next evening when they met and Shiraz told her the fairytale story of who he really was and who his real parents were, and that he was married to his own first cousin, Shupriya was simply amazed. And the best part was that Shupriya's parents and grandparents too had known both Dr Ghulam Hussein's family from Calcutta and the Rehman Khan family from Peshawar very initimately. Her father Ronen Sen, Arif Rehman and Dablo's father Nawaz Hussein, they were all very close friends and contemporaries, and she had heard a lot about them from her parents when she was a young girl. In fact once when Arif Rehman visited Delhi as a member of the Pakistan Foreign office delegation she had also met him and she had even sent a small doll as a gift for Saira. And when Shupriya narrated the incident and how she had requested Arif Rehman that day to hide in the bathroom, it was Shiraz who was now amazed and said. 'My God what a small world'!

That evening instead of going to that far off restaurant, they decided to go to a restaurant called Shokoladnitsa near the Pobedy Park which is also known as the Victory Park. This park was opened in1995 to mark the 50th anniversary of Russia's victory over Nazi Germany and with its war museum it was a tourist landmark for all visitors to Moscow, and especially for those who were interested in military history and Shiraz was one of them. As they took their seats in one far corner of the restaurant and Shiraz heard a bugle playing the 'Last Post' he was reminded of the heart rendering story behind that unforgettable touching tragic song which is now played at military funerals. And as he narrated that heart rendering story to Shups there were tears in her eyes.

It was in 1862 during the American Civil War, when Union Army Captain Robert Ellicombe with his soldiers had taken up their defensive position near Harrison's Landing in Virginia. And facing him was the Confederate Army on the other side of the narrow strip that separated them. During the night, Captain Ellicombe heard the moans of a soldier who lay severely wounded on the battlefield. Not knowing if it was a Union or Confederate soldier, the Captain decided to risk his life and bring the stricken man back to his trench. Crawling on his stomach through gunfire, the Captain reached the stricken soldier and began pulling him toward his encampment. And when the Captain finally reached his own lines, he discovered it was actually a Confederate soldier, but the soldier was dead. The Captain lit a lantern and suddenly went numb with shock when he saw the face of the soldier. It was that of his own son. He had been studying music in the South when the war broke out and the boy without telling his father had enlisted in the Confederate Army. The following morning, the heartbroken father asked permission from his superiors to give his son a full military burial, and despite his enemy status his request was only partially granted.The Captain had asked if he could have a group of Army band members play a funeral dirge for his son at the funeral. But that request was turned down since the soldier was a Confederate. But out of respect for the father, they however gave him a choice to choose only one musician and the Captain chose the bugler. Then he requested the bugler to play a series of musical notes that he had found on a piece of paper in the pocket of his dead son's uniform. This wish was granted. And this is the haunting melody that we just heard and which is now known as 'The Last Post' and which is still played at military funerals. And the words of those musical notes are:—

Day is done—Gone the sun.
From the lakes—From the hills-.-From the sky.
All is well—Safely rest—God is nigh.
Fading light—Dims the sight-.-And a star—Gems the sky.
Gleaming bright.
From afar—Drawing nigh-Falls the night.

Thanks and praise—For our days.
Neath the sun—Neath the stars—Neath the sky
As we go.—This we know.—God is nigh

"Aren't those words really beautiful? And I too wish that when I die there will be atleast one bugler playing it at my funeral also," said Shiraz as he took out a bundle of photographs that he had taken on the cruise from his briefcase to show them to Shups.

"But if they come to know that Imran Hussein, alias Riaz Mohammed Khan is also Major Shiraz Ismail Khan from the Indian Army and a Param Veer Chakra winner at that, then I am afraid that honour will not be bestowed upon you at all. And certainly not by Pakistan and that's for sure,"'said Shupriya in good humour when one particular group photograph caught her eye.

"But tell me who this slim, tall and pretty girl standing next to you. And though she is wearing sunglasses, but to me it looks like your daughter Sherry," said Shupriya with a look of surprise in her face.

"Yes you are right and that is Sherry ofcourse," said Shiraz as he showed her another photograph of his favourite daughter without the sunglasses.

"But tell me does she have a twin sister?" asked Shupriya.

"No of course not. But what made you ask that. Do you also know somebody who resembles her? asked Shiraz.

"Well in a way yes. But that does'nt matter. And I must say that your daughter is strikingly beautiful.'"

"Thank you very much for the complement and now that it is getting late, we will discuss the final composition of the Track 3 channel at our next meeting which will be on Sunday the 9th of September and for which I will select the time and venue and will let you know soon,"'said Shiraz as they got into two separate cabs.

That evening Shupriya on return to her residence took out the photograph of her son standing next to the girl and who Peevee had said was a tourist from Istanbul. And she now wondered as to how two people could have so much of resemblance with each other, unless they were twins. And the possibility that Peevee might have met Sherry by chance somewhere in Moscow when he visited her was also now playing on her mind. That night she was in a real dilemma. She first thought of ringing up Peevee and asking him point blank if the girl was the Pakistan Ambassador's daughter Sherry. But realizing that it could further complicate matters since Sherry and Peevee were children of the same father; Shupriya shelved the idea for the moment.

She now decided to wait and in a roundabout way discreetly find out from Dablo at the next meeting whether his daughter was friendly with the Indian Bollywood actor Deepak Kumar.

And while Dablo and Shups kept working independently about the final composition of their respective members for the Track-3 channel, in the United States a highly motivated, fanatical group of young Muslim fedayeens, suicide bombers from the dreaded Al-Qaida were getting ready to wage a deadly war against the United States of America and that too on America's own sacred soil. Unknown to the world in general and the United States in particular, a group of four youngmen from four different Muslim countries and who were hardcore members of the dreaded Al Qaida had arrived in America a year or more earlier. They had enrolled in various flying schools and had completed their training in flying commercial passenger aircrafts and were now all set to declare war on the world's only super power. Led by their 33 year old Egyptian ring leader Mohammed Atta, a diehard Muslim fanatic from Hamburg, Atta together with 23 year old Marwan Yousef Al-Shehhi the son of a Muslim cleric from the United Arab Emirates had both completed their flying training from The Huffman Aviation School in South Florida and were now confident of piloting big passenger commercial aircrafts. Simultaneously Hani Saleh Hanjour the 29 year old Saudi Arabian together with Ziad Samir Jarrah the 26 year old son of a wealthy Lebanese businessman had completed their flying lessons from Arizona Aviation and from the Florida Flight Training Centre in Venice respectively. And they too were also now ready to hijack and take control of commercial passenger aircrafts of various American airline companies that were flying on the many domestic routes within the country. Besides the four pilots, another group of 15 young fanatical Al Qaida members who were all from Saudi Arabia had also by now entered the United States. They had arrived piecemeal using the many entry points of that vast country. And by the first week of September 2001 most of them had married up up with their respective pilot team captains. The 15 of them in groups of three and four were to be used as musclemen during the various flights that were to be hijacked by the respective team leaders who had been trained as commercial pilots on big Boeing aircrafts.

And while the Al Qaida Fedayeens were getting ready to strike, it was not as if the CIA and the FBI were sleeping. The top bosses in the CIA including George Tenet the Director Central Intelligence in mid July had warned President George Bush and his cabinet members including

Condoleezza Rice who was the National Security Advisor that there were clear indications of a likely massive Al Qaida strike against Americans, but they did not ever think that it will be on American soil. They believed that though it was imminent, it would most likely be somewhere beyond the frontiers of the United States. However, there seemed to be a lack of coordination between Tenet's CIA, and Louis Freeh's and Robert Mueller's FBI. And also among some of the State Police Force who in a few cases had penalized some of the members of this suicide squad for motor traffic offences. Their leader Atta Mohammed had been booked for driving without a license and on 23rd August, 2001 his driving license had been revoked in absentia since he failed to show up in the traffic court to answer the earlier citation for driving without a license. On 1st August another pilot Hani Hanjour was fined 70 dollars by the Virginia police for driving a Toyota Corolla at 55 mph in a 30 mph zone in Arlington Virginia. Khalid-al-Mihdhar with a fellow hijacker Nawaf-al-Hazmi who was his childhood friend had arrived in California in January 2000. Both of them had earlier attended the Al Qaida summit in Kuala Lumpur and though the CIA was aware of the duo's arrival in the United States, they failed to keep the FBI informed of their presence in the country. And what was still more mystifying was the arrest of Habib Zacarias Moussaoui, a French African on 16th August 2001. He was arrested by Harry Samit of the FBI in Minnesota for immigration violation. Zacarias had earlier attended flight training courses at Airman Flight School in Norman, Oklahama, but despite 57 hours of flying lessons had failed the test. On 13th August, Habib Zacarias had also paid 6,800 dollars in 100 dollar bills to receive training in a Boeing 747-400 simulator at the Pan Am International Flight Academy in Eagan, Minniesota. And what was still more surprising was that the man was more interested in learning how to fly the aircraft in the sky and he was least interested in learning on how to take off and land. And though all these facts were brought to the notice of the FBI, there was a complete lack of following up on that vital lead. Hence despite the various positive inputs that the American intelligence agencies had been receiving from its various sources about a likely impending and deadly Al Qaida attack that was on Bin Laden's agenda against the Americans, both the CIA and the FBI it seems were probably still off the view that it would most likely be beyond the land frontiers of the United States. On 23rd August, 2001 even after the Counter Terrorism Centre had given the big boss of the Director Central Intelligence, George Tenet a threat update and which included an item on the briefing chart which had the name of Moussaoui with the caption "Islamic Extremist Learns to Fly', it did not bring home to the American sleuths about the impending terrorist threat from the air and that to in the very heart of the United States of America.

Chapter-39

Deadly Attacks Kamikazi Style

On that Sunday afternoon of the 9th of September, 2001 when Shups and Dablo once again met at the restaurant in Rus Solnichny Hotel on the Warsaw Highway, little did they know that the dreaded Al Qaida would soon redeem with vengeance the deadly 'Fatwa' (Dictat)that their revered leader Osama Bin Laden had promised and declared to all the Muslims of the world on 23rd February 1998. And in which he had said that to kill the Americans and their allies was an individual duty of every Muslim. Both Shups and Dablo also did not know that besides the sleuths from the Russian FSB, the Federal Security Service constantly tailing them, their own respective intelligence agency sleuths from the ISI and the RAW who were posted as diplomats in their respective embassys had also secretly informed their respective heads in Pakistan and India about this very strange meetings that were taking place on the sly between the two heads of mission in Moscow.

That evening while Shiraz was having a quiet dinner at home with his wife and daughter Sherry, there was a call from his son Tojo. He was speaking from New York to give the good news that he was playing in a professional golf tournament at the Dyker Beach Golf Course in Brooklyn and that at the end of day two, having played 144 holes he was number four on the leader board and only three shots behind the leader. And since he was sure of making some good money he had therefore shifted from the four stars Condor Hotel in Brooklyn to the more sophisticated and posh five star Millenium Hilton Hotel near the World Trade Centre in downtown Manhattan.

"Hey Dad this is real luxury hotel and they have given me a room on the 50th floor that faces the huge twin towers of the World Trade Centre on one side and the Statue of Liberty on the other. Tomorrow is a Monday and though my tee off time is around mid-afternoon, but I intend to be on the course after breakfast so that I get some more time to practice my putting on the practice green. And if I can improve upon my present score with atleast a one under par score tomorrow, then hopefully I will pocket a cool one hundred thousand dollars if not more. And if I do get that cheque then I will also take the entire Rehman clan on a seven day grand cruise on the 'Celebrity" from Seattle to Alaska next summer," said an excited Tojo as Saira took the phone from her husband to speak to her darling son.

"But do be very careful because the city of New York is not always safe after sunset and I wish you had not shifted from Brooklyn. I always felt that Downtown Manhattan and especially the area of the business district where this hotel is located is quite a boring place after sunset and somehow after the attack on the World Trade Centre by that Islamic fanatic Ramzi Yousef that took place in February 1993, I have an uncanny feeling that the place is somewhat jinxed,' said Saira.

"But Ammijaan why are you always so cynical? That happened more than eight years ago and Ramzi Yousef is now serving a life sentence and that to without parole. And I believe he is now in some very high security prison in Colorado," said Sherry as she took the phone from her mother and wished her brother all the luck.

"Thank you dear Sis for the good wishes and if I do make a packet then the Steinway grand piano that you always wanted will be yours,'"said Tojo while bidding everybody a very goodnight.

And on that night while Shiraz was enjoying his night cap and listening to the world news on the BBC television news channel, he was shocked to learn about the bizarre assassination of Ahmad Shah Masood, the Lion of Panjshir at a place in the Thakhar Province of north eastern Afghanistan. Claiming to be foreign journalists who had come to interview the young Afghan leader, the two assasins, both fanatical Muslims had triggered off the powerful bomb that was hidden in their video camera. Born on 2nd September, 1953, Masood was a Kabul University engineering student turned military leader who had played a leading role in driving the Soviet army out of Afghanistan. In early 2001, he had addressed the European parliament in Brussels and while asking for humanitarian help to the people of Afghanistan, he had also stated that both the Taliban and the Al Qaida's perception of Islam was also very wrong. While in Europe he had also warned the western world that there was every likelihood of a large scale attack by the Al Qaida on US soil in the near future. A moderate who was known for his daring raids on Soviet convoys, Masood also believed that both men and women were created by the Almighty as equals and therefore both have equal rights. In his area of influence it was therefore not compulsory by law for women and girls to wear the burqa. Much admired by the American CIA, Masood with his goatee beard was like a Che Guevara figure to his people. He was not only well read, he was also a good poet, a fiery orator and above all a decent human being. During the civil war in Afghanistan, when General Zia-ul—Haq was the Pakistan Chief of Army Staff, thousands of regular Pakistani soldiers had been sent to fight alongside the Taliban and Osama Bin Laden's Al Qaida to defeat the Lion of Panjshir, but they had failed. And according to Shiraz the finger of suspicion for the brutal assassination of the progressive Afghan leader pointed towards the Al-Qaida and the Taliban.

On the 10th of September 2001 and having scored a two under par in the third round of the golf tournament that day, Tojo felt very happy and he decided to splurge a bit in anticipation of the expected monetary windfall that would make him richer by atleast 125,000 US dollars the next day. Therefore to celebrate the evening with his faithful caddy, he decided to go to the 230 Restaurant on 5th Avenue. And though it was a Monday, the popular open air Rooftop Garden West Deck was fairly crowded. With a double single malt Glenfiddich on the rocks in his hand as he surveyed the many well lit skyscraper buildings of Manhattan, he really felt proud of what the Americans had achieved since the 4th of July, 1776 when they became an independent country. Though it was basically now a country of immigrants from various parts of the world, but the spirit of the Americans and irrespective of their colour, creed or religion was something that was more than spectacular. Their pride in the stars and the stripes of the national flag and true to the words of their national anthem, the star spangled banner, it was indeed a land of the free and a home of the brave.

With the final round that was scheduled for his tee off at 10.20 AM next morning, Tojo decided to have an early evening and go to bed. Therefore after a sumptuous supper of delicious sea bass that was served with an aromatic coconut broth and short ribs beef rendang, he was back in his hotel room by 10 PM.

The 11th of September, 2001 was a Tuesday. Early that morning at around 6.30 A.M. Tojo as was his routine went for his morning road walk and run towards the Statue of Liberty and around the few blocks that were near his big hotel. As he went past the big sculpture of the 'Big'Bull' on Wall Street and the massive Twin Towers of the World Trade Centre, he kept thinking about what strategy he would adopt on the fourth and final round of the tournament that he was scheduled to play that day. But little did he know that in a few hours time nothing would remain of those two magnificent edifices and that his dream of a getting his first big prize money in golf would also be shattered.

And around that time while he was jogging and working out his plans on how to outwit his opponents, the four Al-Qaida terrorist teams were getting ready to outwit the mighty Americans. Having selected the three main airports of Logan in Boston, Dulles in Washington D.C. and Newark in New Jersey for the start of their murderous missions, the men from Al Qaida in small groups by half past seven that morning had all successfully gone through the security checks at their respective airports and were waiting to board their respective flights. The first and the second group led by their pilots Mohammed Atta and Merwan-al-Sheehi respectively had by now also boarded their respective aircrafts and were waiting for the final take off.

The American Airlines Boeing 767 Flight 11 from Logan under Captain John Ognovski with its 92 passengers including the crew was bound for Los Angeles. The aircraft took off at 7.59 A.M. which was 14 minutes later than the scheduled time of 7.45. Approx after 15 minutes of flying, the five terrorists on board including Atta Mohammed the pilot had taken over the aircraft and its controls. Some 14 minutes later at 8.14 AM the United Airlines Boeing 767 Flight 175 under Captain Victor Saracini and with 65 passengers including the crew also took off from the same Logan airport. The departure of this aircraft which was also bound for Los Angeles was also delayed by 14 minutes. And approx 20 minutes later the five terrorists on board including Marwan-al—Sheehi the pilot had also hijacked the aircraft and Marwan had taken over the controls.

Meanwhile in New York and inside his hotel room on the 50th floor, Tojo was having his light breakfast and was getting ready to leave for the golf course, when all of a sudden he heard the loud noise of an aircraft. He checked his watch it was 8.45. The aircraft It seemed was flying rather low, but by the time Tojo looked out of the widow to check what kind of an aircraft was flying so very low, the big Boeing 767 of the American Airlines Flight 11 at a very high speed of approximately 500 kph had crashed between the 93rd and the 99th floor of the North Tower of the World Trade Centre. Pilot Atta Mohammed and his team of Al-Qaida Fedayeens had sucessfully completed their mission.

Tojo initially thought that it was an accident and that it was probably caused by some technical malfunctioning. But when he saw the thick clouds of black smoke bellowing from the massive building, he was simply horrified. He just stood at the window and kept watching as hundreds of people kept rushing out of that building from every possible exit point. But the building was soon like a burning inferno. And minutes later though the rescue workers from the fire brigade had arrived and others too had joined in the massive rescue operation, the big drone of another big aircraft was heard. And as Tojo and many others like him looked up to see what was happening, the Boeing 767 of the United Airlines Flight 175 piloted by Marwan-al—Sheehi at nearly 600 kph crashed into the 77th and 85th floor of the South Tower.

"Oh my God, these are not accidents but deliberate suicide attacks in the good old Japanese Kamikazi style,"said Tojo as he immediately got in touch with his father in Moscow on the cell phone and told him what he had seen with his very own eyes. And soon thereafter, when Shiraz switched on the CNN channel on his television, he too could not believe what he saw. And when he tried to get through to his counterpart in Washington, DC, he was surprised to learn about the presence of Lt General Mehmood Ahmed, the Pakistani DGISI n the American capital.

"I only hope it is not Bin Laden and his Al-Qaida who is behind all this, and if that be the case then I am afraid we too will be in big trouble. The Americans have been breathing down our necks and they have been time and again asking us to help them in getting hold of Osama and his cohorts who are inside Afghanistan, but we have so far only been paying lip service to it. And now that the Pakistan DGISI is very much on the scene and if the Americans conclusively prove that both the sensational strikes on the World Trade Centre in New York was the handiwork of the Al-Qaida, then I am afraid not only Lt General Mehmood Ahmed will be in the dock, but General Musharraf and Pakistan's present policy to hold the hand of Mullah Omar and his Taliban will all go topsy-turvy,"said Shiraz to his wife as he helped himself to some more black coffee. And while they were all glued to the CNN channel and the news arrived that a third aircraft had struck the Pentagon, the mighty bastion of America's defence planning and war strategy, Shiraz just could not believe it. The American Airlines Boeing 757 Flight 77 under Captain Charles Burlingame with 58 passengers and 6 crew members had taken off from the Dulles International Airport in Virginia at 8.20 AM. Its destination was also Los Angeles. While on its flight it was hijacked by Hami Hanjour and his four Al-Qaida associates. Hami Hanjour sitting on the pilot's seat thereafter had changed course and having headed back towards the national capital, he at 9.37 AM ploughed the aircraft headon into the western section of the Pentagon.

"My God Ammijaan was absolutely right. The World Trade Centre in New York is realy jinxed. And this is the third strike in a little over an hour and I wonder how many more such like suicide missions are still to come," said a visibly shaken Sherry while seeing those horrifying pictures of people stranded on the two towering buildings of the World Trade Centre and despearately calling out and waving to the people for help.

"Well all I can say is that the people who have done these dastardly acts either must be bloody crazy lunatics or they are a bunch of highly motivated anti Americans like McVeigh and Nichols who want to destroy their own country. But if they are Muslims from Al Qaida, and if this sort of mad terrorist strikes on innocent people by radical Muslim fanatics continues, then it will only add to more miseries and sufferings of the impoverished Muslim world and Pakistan is no exception. And if Mr Bin Laden thinks that Americans and the non Muslim world will be cowed down by such cowardly tactics by his henchmen and his fatwas then he is sadly mistaken," said Saira when the news reader announced that a fourth passenger aircraft that had also being hijacked had crashed in a field in Stony Creek, Somerset County, Pennsylvania some 240 miles northwest of Washington DC at 10.03 AM.

The Boeing 757 of the United Airlines Flight 93 had taken off from Newark, New Jersey at 8.42 AM and it was after a good 42 minutes of delay that it finally got airborne. Piloted by Jason Dhall it had only 44 passengers and a crew of 7. The aircraft was on its way to San Francisco, when half and hour after take off and at around 9.10 AM, it was hijacked by four Al Qaida terrorists. But by then Captain Dhall it seems had been alerted about the World Trade Centre disaster and the crew and the passengers were therefore ready to put up a fight. The target this time was the historical and impressive US Capitol Building in Washington DC. And though the young 26 year old Al Qaida pilot Ziad Samir Jarrah from Lebanon had managed to take over the controls, but with the spirited challenge that was put up by the crew and the passengers, the deadly mission to blow up the State Capitol had failed. And it was probably in desperation that Jarrah at high speed was forced to crash the aircraft into the fields at Stony Creek. And like the other three deadly crashes, there were no survivors from this one either.

That evening, when Shupriya too saw on her television screen the manner in which the two massive towers of the World Trade Centre in New York had come crumbling down like a pack of cards and which had resulted in the deaths of so many innocent civilians from so many countries who had made the United States of America their permanent homes, she wondered if Americans would ever remain safe even in their own country. Next morning and after the Americans had confirmed conclusively with hard evidence that it was a cowardly attack on the United States by the Al-Qaida and that America had declared war on Bin Laden, Mulla Omar and his Taliban, she rang up her Dablo on his mobile phone to find out if Pakistan would side with the Americans or with those who were now ruling over Afghanistan.

"Well I guess beggars cannot be choosers and I am afraid General Musharraf has no other choice but to go along with the Americans," said Shiraz while informing Shups that the big boss from the ISI was already in Washington DC when disaster struck.

"And what is he doing there and don't tell me he is there to do a disaster study for Mr Laden," said Shupriya jokingly.

"Well I am not too very sure about that. But one thing is clear and that is he is not going to last on that powerful chair for sure. The ISI General I am afraid was not only reluctant to keep America informed about the whereabouts of Mr Bin Laden and his activities, but on the quiet he was I believe also helping the Al Qaida boss to strengthen his organization. And now that the balloon is up, I will not be surprised if the sleuths in his department help Mr Laden to escape to some safer sanctuary in the high mountains of Afghanistan or even inside some Pakistani tribal area bordering Afghanistan."said Shiraz.

"But whatever has happened is certainly not good for the people of the world in general and definitely not for the Americans and the Muslims of the world in particular,"said Shupriya while requesting Dablo to keep her informed if there were any further developments during the visit of the Pakistan DGISI to the United States.

"Well such things cannot be disclosed over the phone and if I do get any worthwhile inputs, I will definitely get in touch with you and maybe we could meet over a cup of coffee sonewhwere," said Shiraz before switching off his mobile phone.

That evening when he rang up a close friend of his in the Pakistani Embassy in Washington DC, Shiraz was surprised to learn that during a lunch meeting with George Tenet the head of the CIA on 9th September, 2001 when Lt General Mehmood Ahmed the DGISI was categorically told that Mullah Omar and his Taliban were actively supporting and protecting Bin Laden and his Al Qaida, the Pakistani General not only feigned utter ignorance, but he also conveyed to his American counterpart that as far as Afghanistan was concerned, Mullah Omar was only doing whatever he felt was good for his people. And on 9/11, when reports of the World Trade Centre being hit was received in Washington, the DGISI of Pakistan was at that time having a meeting on Capitol Hill with some influential

Congressmen. And when he was told about that disaster there was hardly any worthwhile reaction on the man's face. And after the meeting was over and while his big official limousine with him on the rear seat was on its way back to the Pakistan Embassy and he was told that the Pentagon had also been targeted, he very well now knew that he would have to do a lot of explaning to the Americans. Shiraz also learnt from his friend that at the time of the attack on the World Trade Centre, the U.S President George Bush was visiting the Emma Brooker Elementary School in Sarasota, Florida to promote his education program. He was reading from a book titled 'The Pet Goat' to the second graders in that school. But when he was told by one of his staffers about the attack, it did not immediately get his goat. And though he did not show any anger, but he definitely looked somewhat mystified and puzzled. Thereafter on being told that America was under attack, he boarded the Air Force One. But instead of heading for Washington, the sophisticated aircraft of the American President zig-zagged its way across America's skies and landed at the Offutt Air Force Base in Nebraska. That afternoon at an underground bunker of the U.S. Strategic Command, when he was briefed about all the attacks, it literally got his goat alright. And that evening by the time the angry President returned to Washington DC, White House was like an armed fortress. There was also a fear that it was still not over yet and the possibility of the terrorists having smuggled in a weapon of mass destruction therefore could not be ruled out either. That evening the US President probably for the first time conducted his first ever cabinet meeting in a bunker below the White House. That was also the emergency situation room and later when he spoke to the nation, and to the world, he minced no words. He said that he had directed the full resources of the country's intelligence and law enforcement agencies to find those who were responsible and to bring them to justice. And when he added that America would not make any distinction between the terrorists who committed those heinous acts and those who have been harbouring them, Shiraz who was listening to that broadcast knew that Pakistan was now going to be in deep trouble.

And on 12th September, 2001, while the American intelligence agencies were busy in finding out who was behind those deadly attacks, in the Middle East, Israeli tanks and troops surrounded the West Bank towns of Jericho and Jenin. And while the heavy fighting between the Israelis and the Palestinians continued and the loudspeakers in the mosques called people to defend their towns, it looked that the world was heading for a major disaster, but luckily better sense prevailed when General Colin Powell the American Secretary of State spoke to both the sides and urged them to show restraint.

On 13th September, when the Pakistan Ambassador to the United States, Maleeha Lodhi and the Pakistani DGISI Lt General Mehmood Ahmed were categorically told by the burly and well built Richard Armitage, the Deputy Secretary of State that enough was enough and that the United States would make no distinction whatsoever between terrorists and the nations that protected them, it was clearly a hint to Pakistan that they must stop playing games. And when the giant of a man also added that Pakistan was either with the U.S or against the U.S. both the DGISI and the charming Pakistani lady ambassador realized that it was nothing short of an ultimatum to Pakistan to mend its ways. And it was as a result of this meeting that the Pakistani DGISI agreed to meet Mulla Omar after his return to Pakistan and convince him to hand over the Al Qaida chief and his henchmen to the Americans.

On learning about the latest development in the Pakistan-US relationship and which had a direct bearing on Pakistan's foreign policy on Afghanistan and on the Taliban regime that Pakistan had been strongly supporting, Shiraz rang up Shups from his mobile phone. He wanted to have an urgent meeting with her and apprise her of Pakistan's likely indirect involvement with the Al Qaida in carrying out the recent devastating attacks on America.

"Alright we will meet at the usual Rus Solnechni Hotel on Warshavskaya Highway tomorrow at 7 P.M, sharp,"said Shups as she instructed her private secretary to send a big bouquet of white roses with the personal condolence note from her to the U.S. Ambassador in Moscow.Shiraz and Shups however did not know that unlucky 13th of September, 2001 would be the last meeting for both of them at that place. Not only had that short meeting between the two heads of missions been video taped by the Russian sleuths who had their mole now working as one of the many waiters in that restaurant, but they also decided to discreetly and indirectly inform the Indian and Pakistan foreign office in Islamabad and New Delhi of what the hell was going on in Moscow. Luckily there was no audio recording on that tape or else Shiraz would have been in serious trouble. Because at that meeting, Shiraz had indirectly mentioned to Shups that some of the hijackers who had taken part and had died as martyrs and fedayeens in that daring but bizarre operation of 9/11 had possibly on their way to Afghanistan transited through Paksitan to meet and seek the blessings of the Al Qaida chief. And with the Pakistani ISI chief's presence in Washington on that day there was therefore every possibility of the Pakistan ISI having had an indirect hand in funding the large amount of money that was required to train all the Al Qaida pilots in the many flying schools in America.

And during that terrifying week while the Americans were mourning the deaths of their nearest and dearest ones and there were also strong rumours that all was not over as yet. A series of letters containing the deadly anthrax pores had been mailed to several news media offices and to two US Democratic Senators. And as a result of that a few people had died and a fear phobia had gripped the general public. And when Shupriya was told by her Defence Attaché that Anthrax could be used as a biological weapon, she just could not believe it. The very fact that it could be mailed to people whom you wanted to get rid off was like sending a death warrant by speed post she thought.

"Well may be to make the American public more security conscious they should play the good old Elvis Presley hit song 'Return to Sender-Address not known-No such number No such phone," regularly said the Defence Attache jokingly while recommending that a lecture on the subject so as to educate the embassy staff and make them more security conscious would be useful.

On the 20th of September, 2001 and on being fully convinced that Osama Bin Laden and his Al-Qaida were behind those deadly 11th September attacks, the United States issued a five point ultimatum to the Taliban. In that it clearly stated that the Taliban must not only deliver to the U.S. government all leaders of the AL Qaida including Bin Laden, but the Taliban must also release all imprisoned foreign nationals, immediately close all terrorist camps, handover all terrorists and supporters to the appropriate authorities and also give the United States full access to all the terrorist camps for inspection. And failing which the United States government will take all actions that they deem fit against the Taliban regime in Afghanistan. And on the very next day, when the Taliban rejected the ultimatum by stating that there was no evidence in their possession that could link Bin Laden to the September 11 attacks, the ball was immediate set rolling to oust the Taliban regime from Afghanistan. And it got a further boost when both the United Arab Emirates and Saudi Arabia withdrew their recognition of the Taliban as the legal government of Afghanistan while leaving an isolated and neighbouring Pakistan as the only country in the world with diplomatic ties with that regime.

During that week and with whatever inputs that Shupriya had from time to time gathered from her Dablo, she without mentioning the source wrote a long confidential hand written demi-official letter to her boss in India. Marked confidential and secret It was directly addressed by name to India's Foreign Secretary in New Delhi and was dispatched by the weekly diplomatic courier bag. And on the 30th of September, when the Indian Foreign Secretary personally rang her up and told her that both he and the External Affairs Minister would like to meet her in the Minister's office in South Block at 11 AM on the 3rd of October, it did not at all come as a surprise to her. She was under the impression that it was probably in connection with that confidential letter that she had written to him. But later in the day, when the news arrived that the young Madhavrao Scindia a former cabinet minister from the Congress party had died in an air crash while he was on his way to Kanpur from Delhi to address a party rally, Shupriya indeed felt rather sad. The scion from the princely Scindia family was flying in a chartered 10 seater Cessna that was owned by the Jindal group and accompanying him were some journalists and his private secretary. But what surprised her was that the aircraft had suddenly caught fire while it was flying high over a village in the Mainpuri District of Uttar Pradesh and had crashed. Only a year ago on 11th June, 2000 the Congress party had lost another dynamic and eminent and young politician, when Rajesh Pilot who had also served in the Indian Air Force was killed in a tragic road accident while travelling in his car to Jaipur. Putting two and two together, Shupriya wondered whether these were truly accidents or acts of sabotage. But there was still more bad news to come the next day. On that afternoon of 1st October, 2001 a group of diehard militants had attacked the Jammu and Kashmir State Assembly complex in Srinagar and as a result of which 38 people and 3 Fidayeens were killed. The suicide bombers in a jeep that was packed with high explosives had driven the vehicle to the main entrance of the complex and had detonated it. And later when the terrorist group Jaish-e-Mohammed claimed responsibility for it, and hailed a Pakistani national Wajahat Hussein as the suicide bomber, a livid Faroukh Abdulla the Chief Minister of the state immediately advocated reprisal attacks on the terrorist camps in Pakistan Occupied Kashmir. And though he had said that there is a limit to India's patience, but eventually it only amounted to big talk and nothing more as the Indian foreign ministry only issued a strongly worded statement warning Pakistan not to encourage such manifestations of hate and terror from across its borders. It was no doubt a audacious strike and though some militants had entered the building but no lawmaker was killed and that was because it was around 2 PM in the afternoon and most of the legislators had by that time either left the building or were meeting at a different place since the legislature building had recently been damaged by a fire.

According to one reliable source and eye witness, that afternoon three terrorrists dressed in police uniforms had stopped the official jeep of Ravi Qazi an engineer in the government's telecommunication department somewhere near Habbakadal. Then having thrown him out, they asked his driver Ali Mohammed Machloo to drive to the nearby Fatehkadal area where a fourth terrorist was waiting for them. At Fatehkadal the terrorists loaded four milk containers that were packed with explosives. And at around 2.00 PM after the three armed terrorist in police uniforms had got off and they waited at the entrance to the nearby Jehangir Hotel, the fourth one who was the driver cum suicide bomber drove the vehicle to the entrance of the Assembly complex and blew it up. And it was during that melee that the other three waiting terrorists entered the complex and had started firing. And had they attacked half an earlier they would have succeeded in killing a large number of state politicians too. And surprisingly on that very afternoon and shortly before the Assembly had adjourned at 1.30 p.m. Mr B Srinivas the Senior Superintendent of Police, Srinagar had personally checked the security arrangements around the Assembly building. And as a result of which the police and the Border Security personnel guarding the complex were quite alert and they therefore could kill all the three terrorists.

After a two week lull following the September 11 attacks by the Al Qaida on America, the ISI sponsored terrorist network it seems had been reactivated. On 28th September the LeT had also carried two simultaneous attacks on two Indian army patrols in the area of Kupwara and Handwara and Shiraz was worried that unless the Americans brought pressure on the Musharraf government, there could more such daring attacks not only in the Kashmir valley, but elsewhere in India too.

On the evening of 1st October, while Shupriya got busy doing some last minute shopping for gifts to be given to friends and relatives and was packing her bags to catch the next morning's flight to New Delhi, the news arrived that Hasina Sheikh's Awami Party had received a drubbing in the Parliamentary elections in Bangladesh. At the final count her party had won only a measly 62 seats, whereas the four party alliance led by the good lookng poster lady Khalida Zia of the Bangladesh National Party had secured more than 200 seats and which gave them a clear two thirds majority in Parliament. The eldest of Sheikh Mujib's five children and the wife of a reputed nuclear scientist, Hasina Sheikh it seems had totally miscalculated the voter's mind. And during the last year of her rule whenTransparency International declared Bangladesh as one of the most corrupt countries of the world, and with her pro-India stance, her chances of returning to power was out of question.

Chapter-40

One Surprise too Many

It was on the afternoon of 2nd October, 2001 when Shupriya landed at Palam airport. Being Mahatma Gandhi's birthday it was a national holiday that day and she was pleasantly surprised to see her son Peevee with Monty standing outside the arrival lounge waiting for her. Peevee was in the capital shooting for a new commercial for a men's body deodorant product. That evening at dinner time, when Reeta remarked casually that Peevee would soon be 30 years old next year and that it was time for him to settle down with some nice looking and homely girl, and Shupriya also very cleverly butted in to say that she had found one for him in Moscow but the girl was unfortunately a Muslim from Pakistan and that she was a senior Pakistani diplomat's accomplished daughter, it took Peevee completely by surprise and he simply kept quiet. Thereafter, when Monty also jokingly said that the girl from Istanbul whom Peevee had met in Moscow was also very good looking and even though she too was a Muslim, it would not matter the least if Peevee was keen on getting married her, there was once again a look of bewilderment on Peevee's face. And to add to that, when Mom Number 2 also said that because of the striking resemblance between the two girls, she had once casually asked her Pakistani counterpart if he had twin daughters, and His Excellency thought it was some sort of joke, the look on Peevee's face said it all. Fearing that he will probably soon be cornered by Mom Number 2, Peevee quickly gave an excuse that he was was getting late for the shoot and saying that he would like to talk about it later, he quietly left the table.

Late that night and on his return from the commercial shoot, when Peevee noticed that the reading light was still on in Mom Number 2's bedroom, he knocked softly and walked in. Shupriya was in bed reading the Danielle Steel current best seller that was titled 'The Kiss.' It was ironically also a tragic love story where the couple had to ultimately part ways.That night while sitting close to her on the bed, Peevee held her hand

and confessed to Mom Number 2 about his love for Sherry. And when he also told her how and where they first met and that his trip to Moscow during summer was also to see her again, Shupriya patiently kept listening to her son's love story. But when Peevee told her that he had also proposed to her and was keen to marry her, Shupriya could not hide the tears that were swelling in her eyes. She did not know how to tell or explain to him that Sherry was his half sister and that her father was also his father and that marriage was simply out of question. Therefore in order to hide her emotions from her only son, and change the topic Shupriya put off the reading lamp, switched on the night lamp and having quietly got out of bed from the other side; she made her way to the toilet. Wiping away her tears inside the toilet, she felt sorry for her son and Sherry. She knew that it was not their fault, but somehow and much to her and their sorrow she would now have to somehow convince Peevee and that to without telling him the real truth to break off the relationship for the sake of the family. And had Sherry been any other Pakistani's daughter she and the family would have gladly accepted the match and Shups would have also gladly blessed them as man and wife. Afterall she too had married a Muslim.

Realising that Mom Number 2 was not very happy about the on going affair between him and Sherry and feeling somewhat guilty for hiding the truth from his own family, Peevee asked for forgiveness and excused himself from the room. And on that night neither he nor his Mom Number 2 could sleep. While Shupriya kept thinking on how best and without hurting her son's strong feelings for Sherry she could break that relationship, Peevee kept thinking on how best to convince the family that there was nothing wrong if a shaven off Hindu Sikh from India married a Muslim girl from Pakistan. And next morning Shupriya was in for a still greater shock, when at a closed door meeting with the Indian Foreign Secretary and the Minister for External Affairs she was shown the video film of her sitting with the Pakistani Ambassador at the Hotel Rus Solnechni restaurant that was taken on 13th September and another video clip of both of them having lunch on board the Mama Zoya, which was taken earlier on the 5th of August.

"Perhaps Madam Ambassador would like to explain to us about these private meetings with the Pakistani Ambassador,' said the Minister somewhat firmly and sarcastically as he put the photographs that was on his laptop on the pause mode.

"Well to tell you frankly Sir, these meetings were a fallout of the inconclusive summit levels talks between the two heads of states of both Pakistan and India that took place at Agra in mid July and we both felt that another beginning must be made to revive the talks. On 21st July at the Belgium's National Day reception at the Belgian Embassy where we accidentally met we informally discussed the causes for the failure of the talks at Agra and we were both of the view that a great opportunity for Pakistan and India to live as good peaceful neighbours and as friends and in peace had once again been lost. The Pakistan Ambassador also felt and so did I to be very frank that a third channel or rather a Track-3 channel with some like minded Indians and Pakistanis on both sides of the border and from the diaspora should be set in motion at the earliest so that the agenda for the subsequent summit meeting between the two heads of states and when Mr Vajpayee visits Islamabad could be more broad based and purposeful," said Shupriya very confidently though she knew very well that that was only a part of the real truth. And as far as the real truth was concerned she could not dare to disclose for obvious reasons. Afterall Shiraz was technically and legally now both an Indian and a Pakistani. Moreover he was a highly decorated Indian army officer and also her husband and officially she was a spinster and a Sardarni at that. But with a son from the very man who was now Pakistan's Ambassador to Russia and who was not even aware that they had an issue, she knew very well that it would be suicidal for both of Shiraz and her if the truth ever came to light.

"But regarding this confidential report that you recently sent addressed to the Foreign Secretary and that was written in your hand, could you please tell us from where you got all those classified information. Because I am sure it could not have been delivered to you on a platter by the Pakistani Ambassador," said the Minister somewhat a little sarcastically as he handed back the secret file that was marked with a big cross in red colour to the Foreign Secretary.

"Well Sir, it was definitely not given to me on a platter by His Excellency, but he did give it out indirectly and that too in bits and pieces during our informal meetings. And to be very honest Sir, the meeting on the 13th of September that we just saw on your laptop was the fifth such one on that very subject. I must also admit and add that Mr Riaz Mohammed Khan is genuinely interested in sorting out all matters of dispute and disagreements between the two countries only through bilateral talks and through peaceful means only. And he is also sincerely worried about the future of his own country. He feels that like all military dictators who take over power by pointing the gun barrel towards their own citizens and who don't miss the opportunity of using the services of religious fanatics to remain in power, such men can prove to be not only militarily dangerous, but in the long run their autocratic rule would also be detrimental to the democratic aspirations of its own people. And with more and more money being allotted to defence spending and by producing more nuclear weapons, as also by promoting Islamic fanatical militancy through various religious groups within the country, Pakistan he feels has now put herself on a suicidal mode. Not only are these issues hampering the economic growth of the country, but it is also fostering the Talibanization of Pakistan, and to put it in Mr Riaz Mohammed Khan's own words,' Pakistan is slowly and progressively becoming a Banana Terrorist Republic.' And to tell you the truth Sir, the Pakistani Ambassador has also privately confided in me that he is not only dissillusioned with what is happening in his own country, but he also fears that his outspoken views may one day land him in serious trouble with the military rulers of Pakistan. And he has also hinted to me that for the sake of avoiding another Indo-Pak war which with nuclear weapons on both sides would be disastrous for both the countries, he would also be willing to pass on such like important information that could timely warn India to be on her guard, "said Shupriya as she presented the file that had all the minutes of the various meetings that she had in private with the Pakistan Ambassador and which were written in her own hand on the proposed composition and working of the 'Track-3' channel. Since she had been summoned to India she thought that she would discuss the subject with the Indian Foreign Secretary and take his views, but she never realized that she had been only called to give an explanation for her so called misdemeanors as India's head of mission to Russia.

"I am really sorry if I have violated any rules or if I have inadvertently as India's Ambassador to Russia over stepped my brief. But one thing I can tell you Sir for sure and that is Mr Riaz Mohammed Khan if handled properly by us could be an asset for the future. And he is now also in the race to become Pakistan'snext Foreign Secretary,"said Shupriya with supreme confidence.

"But what makes you so sure and that he is not playing a double game,'said the Minister as he softly whispered into the Foreign Secretary's ear that today's in-house discussion with Miss Yeshwant Kaur Bajwa should till further orders remain strictly within the four walls of his office.

'On that score I am not hundred percent sure Sir, and my gut feeling is that since the man is not a rabid Indian hater and he is genuinely interested in peace and prosperity in the subcontinent, we could count on him if and when the need arises,' said Shupriya.

'Well we will leave it at that today, and in order to ensure what you have just told us and also for the Pakistani gentleman's own safety, I would therefore suggest that you keep this matter entirely to yourself. But henceforth you will not not meet him in such like manner in future, and nor should you talk about your meetings with him to anybody else. Ofcourse meeting him diplomatically in an official capacity and on occasions of national days of various countries must carry on as per the protocol. But there should be nothing beyond that. However, I am afraid that henceforth such formal occasions will only be a few now since we have already selected the new incumbent who will be replacing you in Moscow very soon. Moreover, after all the good work done by you, we want you to be back in Delhi to celebrate both Dusshera and Diwali at home with your family. And on your return you will be taking over as the Secretary East,' said the Minister with a mischievous smile on his face.

'My God that was indeed rather close,' thought Shupriya as she put all the papers back into her briefcase. And before anymore intimate questions could be asked, she thanked the Minister and the Foreign Secretary for giving her an opportunity to explain the circumstances and the reasons why which she had taken the initiative to open the track-3 channel. Thereafter giving the excuse that she was already late for lunch with the family at the Delhi Gymkhana, she wished both of them a very good afternoon and in Indira Gandhi's style briskly walked through the long corridors of South Block to the VIP car park where the driver in the white government of India's Ambassador car with the red beacon light was waiting for her. Getting into his official car at that very moment was Omar Abdullah, the young Minister of State for External Affairs. Realising that the man was a Kashmiri and that too the grandson of Sheikh Abdullah who was once known as the Lion of Kashmir, Shupriya wondered whether the dynastic rule in that perennially troubled state of India that was once a beautiful princely kingdom of pristine lakes and high mountains had come to stay for good. Afterall the young minister's father Dr Faroukh Abdullah was the son of Sheikh Abdullah and he was once again the Chief Minister of the state and young Omar could well be the next one she thought. Shupriya also wondered whether the state of Jammu and Kashmir, which was the root cause of all the trouble between India and Pakistan eversince both the countries became independent will ever be settled amicably and without anymore bloodshed.

'Guess what, the External Affairs Minister has given me a lovely Dussera cum Diwali gift and that too well in advance, and I am going to be back home bag and baggage to celebrate both the festivals with you all very soon,'said a beaming Shupriya as she very affectionately hugged all the members of the family and invited them to celebrate the occasion of her home posting with dinner that evening at her favourite restaurant.

'The Spice Route' restaurant of the Imperial hotel with its southeast cuisine was indeed a gourmet's delight. It was also her late mother and father's favorite hotel. Besides the family, she had also invited the elderly and veteran journalist Unnikrishnan and a few of her senior collegues from the ministry. And for the occasion, she had also booked a table for ten in the farthest corner of the restaurant. That evening after the drinks were ordered for all her guests, the general topic on the table was how would America now react to the deadly attack on their soil, and the general consensus was that like in the case of Saddam Hussein's Iraq, Omar Mullah's Taliban also would not be spared either, and sooner or later the American elite troops would be on Afghan soil and their cruise missiles would once again devastate Afghanistan. In a way everybody's assessment that evening of America's likely direct involvement in sorting out the Taliban and the Al Qaida was generally correct, but that America would be joined by others including Great Britain had not crossed their minds.

By the 14th of September and after a series of high level meetings of the NSC, the National Security Council, the American President as the Commnder-in-Chief of the nation had approved to launch the war on terrorism. Soon thereafter he had also given the green signal to the CIA, and some covert CIA teams were already inside Afghanistan trying to foster the active cooperation of those Afghan warlords who were anti Taliban and who were willing to fight alongside the US troops to get rid of the Taliban and the Al Qaida from their sacred land. In fact the members from the CIA North Alliance Liasion Team had already established themselves in the village of Barak and the CIA team leader had also established contact with Fahim Khan who was one of the Northern Alliance leaders. And also the very fact that President Bush on 22nd September, 2001 in a special memorandum to his Secretary of State General Colin Powell had lifted sanctions against Pakistan and India which were enforced after both the countries tested their nuclear weapons in 1998 was also indicative of the fact that the United States needed the helping hand of India in general and that of Pakistan in particular in getting rid of the Taliban and the Al Qaida and in fighting the war on terror.

On the next topic of whether the recent death of Mr S K Bhatnagar the former Defence Secretary of India who had died a month ago and who was one of the key accused in the never ending Rs 64 crore Bofors payoff scam would effect the on going trial, Unni very candidly said that as far as he was concerned, there was now no question of any more trials because the entire matter together with Bhatnagar had been very conveniently buried by the CBI. And that was amply evident when the CBI once again and very conveniently failed to have the main accused and the mastermind behind this nefarious and shameful deal extradited back to India. He was ofcourse without naming the slimy Italian was referring to none other than Mr Octavio Quattrocchi, the old friend of the Gandhis. And the very fact the Mr Bhatnagar had also very conveniently before his death filed a petition before the Delhi High Court challenging the splitting of the trial was proof enough that the end of the Bofors controversy without punishing any of those accused who who were still living was now very much in sight. Realising that Bofors was still a very sensitive topic, and noticing the forlorn and lost look on Peevee's face, Shupriya very cleverly and diplomatically said.

'Ladies and Gentlemen let us all stop talking shop please and to liven up the evening a bit for everyone, we will therefore now play a lively and interesting party game.' Shupriya also wanted to ensure that nobody that evening even casually opened the touchy subject of finding a partner for her highly eligible Bollywood actor son who was sitting next to her. It was going to be an innovative team game of 'Antakshri' which Shupriya had herself devised, but it was on condition that no loud singing would be allowed. However, whispering the song into the ears of the nominated judge and by writing the correct answers simultaneously on a piece of paper that would be considered good enough to fetch points to the team that responded first. Shupriya had come well prepared with some of the popular songs of yesteryears which were neatly written in Roman Hindi on two sets of coloured papers, one red and one blue. And the lyrics were all from popular Hindi and English songs of the fifties and the sixties. And in order to ensure that both the men and the women had equal representation and participation, Shupriya had not only arranged the seating plan accordingly, but she also ensured that they all sat facing one another and that the husbands and the wives were in the opposite teams. Each team comprised of two ladies and two gentlemen with Shupriya as the compere and with Peevee and Unni as judges. And while the rules of the game were being explained to all the participants, Peevee ordered the starters.

The two teams, Red and Blue were to be given the opening lines of a song and atleast four lines of that song were required to be sung very softly. The old popular song could be in English or in Hindi and the team that sang it first and sang it correctly would be given a point. Simultaneously to earn a bonus point the team had to name the popular singer who was responsible for that particular song's popularity and also give the name of the film wherever it was applicable. With the game commencing with the opening lines of the song Que Sera Sera which was her father's favourite and which was made ever popular by Doris Day in the Alfred Hitchcock film 'The Man Who Knew Too Much,' the game soon became very exciting and interesting. And so much so that it was difficult at times to keep the decibel level down to an acceptable level inside that posh restaurant. And when it ended with the words of the song 'Ye Sham Mastani Madhosh Kiye Jaye' from the film Kati Patang that Kishore Kumar had made very popular, and they all sang it in chorus with Peevee in the lead, there were tears of both joy and sadness in Shupriya's eyes. This was the very song that Shiraz in private had sung to her so lovingly on their wedding day on 15th September 1971 and that was a good thirty long years ago.That night and with only another 12 hours to go before leaving for Moscow again, she kept thinking on how best she could work out a plan that would make her son completely forget his dear Sherry.

Early next morning before leaving for the airport, Shupriya quietly visited the Sai Baba Temple near the big Indira Gandhi stadium which was close to Monty's house in Defence Colony. And there on the steps of that popular temple, with tears in her eyes and compassion in her heart she prayed to the holy man of Shirdi to help her find a sure and safe solution to the problem.

Chapter-41

Caught in the Web

That very evening, Shupriya's prayers to the Sai Baba of Shirdi seemed to have worked and without her doing anything at all, and the problem it seems was in the process of being solved for good. And it was all thanks to the Pakistan ISI. Two days after Shupriya left for Delhi, Riaz Mohammed Khan (Shiraz)the Pakistani Ambassador to Moscow had also received a summons to report to Islamabad for some urgent meeting at the ministry. And the agenda given to him for that meeting was the change of policy that General Musharraf and the Pakistan Foreign Ministry had recently introduced with regard to the Taliban regime in Afghanistan and the activities of the Al Qaida in that country. This was as a fallout from the 9/11 disaster in the United States

In the meantime and a week or so earlier, Shiraz had also been informed by his brother-in-law Salim Rehman Khan who had been posted back to Islamabad from New Delhi that though Lt Gen Mehmood Ahmed, the DGISI on his return to Islamabad from Washington did go and meet Mullah Omar on Taliban turf, but it was an exercise in total futility. Pakistan had asked the Taliban leader to decide once and for all about the fate of the Al Qaida leader Bin Laden who was being sheltered by them and it also wanted the Taliban to demolish all the Al Qaida training camps in that country. But it was not taken very seriously it seems by both the sides. And though the one eyed Mullah was warned that failing which the Americans would make the Taliban pay very heavily for it, the Taliban chief did not seem to be very unduly perturbed or worried. The Mullah however felt that he and his Taliban had been very badly let down both by General Musharaff and by Pakistan who till 9/11 were as thick as theives. And the unexpected and sudden about turn by General Musharraf and his explicit and immediate orders to the DGISI who was once his close friend and colleague to withdraw all the ISI officers and personel from Afghanistan had not only widened the rift within the Pakistan military, but also with the sympathisers of the Taliban in Pakistan. Unknown to Shiraz, and while Lt Gen Mehmood was holding his talks with Mullah Omar, a senior American CIA officer stationed in Pakistan was making friendly overtures to Mullah Osmani, the Taliban Commander of the Kandahar Corps. The meeting took place in a luxury hotel in Baluchistan and the aim was to persuade theTaliban to handover the Al Qaida chief or else allow the Americans to find and extricate him for trial in the United States. But that mission too had failed. However, it was the unconfirmed information that the Pakistan DGISI had allegedly transferred a hundred thousand U.S. dollars in the summer of 2001 to Mohammed Atta who was the ring leader of the 9/11 attacks that had now got Shiraz very worried. And if that was true then God help Pakistan wrote Shiraz in his small secret red diary.

On the 19th of September,2001 General Musharraf the President of Pakistan who because of the 1965 war with India was lucky not to have been court-martialed as a young officer for overstaying his leave had now thanks to American pressure publicly announced a total shift in the country's policy towards Afghanistan. He not only ditched the Taliban for good, but he had also joined the American led coalition in the war against terror. In exchange for debt rescheduling and for more American monetary and economic aid to Pakistan, General Musharraf had offered the U.S. the much needed military bases inside Pakistan that were required for the anti Taliban and anti Al Qaida operations inside Afghanistan. And though he justified it by saying that it was a strategic decision that was aimed at preserving the national interest, but the real fact was that there was also a threat to his remaining in the hot seat. The Americans were breathing down his neck and he had been presented with a fait accompli that had to be met. In other words he was badly caught in a Catch—22 situation. In fact in an address to his people on that day, though General Musharraf had stated that he supported the Taliban, but at the same time and in the same breath he had also said that unless Pakistan reversed its support to the Taliban, it risked the danger of an alliance between the United States and India.

On the 4th of October 2001 it was rumoured that the Taliban had covertly offered to handover Osama Bin Laden to Pakistan for his trial by an international tribunal that operated according to the Islamic Sharia law. And again on 7th October when the Taliban had proposed to try Bin Laden in an Islamic court in Afghanistan, and that too was also rejected by the United States, the green signal to attack Afghanistan was given by the American President. On that very Sunday afternoon of 7th of October 2001, while Shiraz was busy packing his bags and sorting out the official papers that may be required for discussion in Islamabad, the news arrived that the US and the British government had launched "Operation Enduring Freedom.' That evening hordes of American and British military aircrafts with their deadly bombs and missiles including the lethal Tomahawk cruise missiles carried out the massive aerial bombing of theTaliban and Al Qaida bases and training camps inside Afghanistan.

'Though the so called 'War on Terror' as envisaged by the Americans has begun in right earnest, but by bombing the Taliban and the Al Qaida inside Afghanistan that by itself I am afraid will not solve the problem. And the fact that this may result in more Muslim fanatics from Pakistan and elsewhere around the world becoming more anti American simply cannot be ruled out. And what worries me even more is that we have a very large population of tribals in our two provinces of Baluchistan and the Northwest Frontier which borders Afghanistan, and they also have a lot of close ethnic affinity with the Pathan Pashtun tribes across the old Durand Line, and this therefore could be very dangerous for Pakistan in the long run. One must not forget the psyche of the Pathan who simply loves his freedom,' said Shiraz to Saira while asking her and his daughter Sherry if they needed anything from Pakistan.

And on that day of 7th October, 2001 while the Americans and their allies were targeting the Taliban and Al Qaida terrorist camps of the fanatical Muslims in Afghanistan with their deadly smart bombs and missiles, in the Indian state of Gujarat, a dynamic fifty year old fanatical Hindu politician from the BJP, the Bhartiya Janata Party having taken his oath of office as the new Chief Minister of Gujrat was getting ready to teach the Muslims in his state to behave and mend their ways or else be ready to face his music. Born on 17th September, 1950 in a middle class Gujrathi family, Narendra Damodar Modi the fifty one year old politician from Vadnagar with a master's degree in political science had won his political spurs when he was chosen by the Bharatiya Janata Party to direct the party's election campaign in the states of Gujrat and Himachal Pradesh. A fiery orator and an ardent member of the Hindu nationalist right wing Rashtriya Swayamsevak Sangh, the man was a dynamic leader and real livewire. With his frugal lifestyle and no nonsense approach, he was now going to rule Gujrat with an iron hand.

On the afternoon of 8th of October 2001, when Shiraz arrived for the meeting in Islamabad that was scheduled for 1000 hours the next day, he was shocked to learn that on that very morning itself, Lt General Mehmood Ahmed the DGISI had been asked to go home and he had been replaced by Lt General Ehsan ul Haq. The Mardan born air defense gunner officer who was earlier the DGMI of the Pakistan Army and who had recently taken over the Peshawar Corps had been appointed as the new DGISI with immediate effect. And when Shiraz was further told that the changeover was carried out on General Musharraf's specific orders and that all ISI operatives in Afghanistan had been asked to return home, Shiraz knew that it was probably done at the bidding of the Americans. It was now more than evident that the Bush administration had no trust left in the outgoing DGISI because they felt that he was all the time playing a double game and not trying hard enough to get for them the ever elusive Osama Bin Laden and the other top Al Qaida leaders who was hiding in Afghanistan. Indirectly the Americans were also accusing the Pakistanis of not only colluding with the Al Qaida and the Taliban in strengthening their respective cadres, but they were also helping them to promote terrorism across the world.

On 7th October, General Musharraf's tenure as COAS had expired, but since his retirement could have created an imbroglio because the Supreme Court Judgement had mandated him by name to complete the democratic process, before 12th October 2002, he was therefore automatically given a year's extension. To keep the Americans happy and to ensure his continuance as Army Chief, General Musharraf also sent his old friend Lt General Usmani who was the Deputy COAS home and promoted his juniors, Lt General Mohammed Aziz and Lt General Mohammed Yusuf Khan to full generals. They had been appointed as Chairman JCSC and Vice COAS respectively. He also made Lt General Khalid Maqbool the Governor of Punjab and appointed Lt General Jamshed Gulzar, the man who as Force Commander Northern Areas who had helped Musharraf to launch the Kargil operations as the new Adjutant General. And while the new DGISI Lt General Ehsan got busy in tackling the Americans, his two deputy directors, Major General Muhammed Akram and Major General Ehtasham Zamir Jafri were made incharge of looking after the domestic front. Having ordered all ISI officers serving in Afghanistan to get back to base, the orders to the ISI now were to cut off all supplies of oil, arms, ammunition and rations to the Taliban, and instead to provide intelligence and logistic support to the Americans and their allies for the early success of 'Operation Enduring Freedom"

And on that morning of 8th October 2001, when Salim Rehman also told Shiraz that the Foreign Secretary Mr Inam-ul-Haq who was earlier Pakistan's Ambassador to the United Nations was not very happy with the complete turn around of Pakistan's policy vis a vis Talibanised Afghanistan,

Shiraz felt that it was all because of America's arm twisting. But Shiraz was not aware that calling of the head of the mission in Moscow to discuss Pakistan's future foreign policy plans was only a damn excuse. The real aim was to get the truth ot from the man who had been reported by the ISI for hobnobbing with his counterpart from India.Therefore, when Shiraz entered the Foreign Minister's office for the conference and he only found the Pakistani Foreign Secretary present there, he was quite foxed.

'Alright we agree that both the ambassadors from Pakistan and India in Moscow through their proposed track 3 channel were genuinely interested in promoting, or rather should I say in carrying forward the process that got derailed at Agra. But these sets of photographs of the ambassador's pretty daughter Sherry secretly meeting a popular Bollywood filmstar in Moscow and that of you and the Indian ambassador meeting each other in private in some of the restaurants in the Russian capital gives a completely different picture altogether. Does'nt it? And some of the photographs of the young couple kissing in public are not only shocking, but it is totally also against our culture. And it also reflects on the poor upbringing of the two love birds. And don't tell us that you as the father of you favourite and dearest daughter and your wife were completely unaware of what was going on. Or is there a family plot to divulge state secrets to our adversary across the border,' said the Foreign Minister in a rather rough tone as the Foreign Secretary of Pakistan handed over the set of photographs to Shiraz.

'My God and I simply just cannot believe it.' And believe you me Sir I had no idea even till this very moment that my dear daughter is having affair with an Indian Bollywood star,' said Shiraz as he one by one and slowly in utter disbelief went through those photographs.

'So what are you going to do about it? And needless to say that neither you nor Pakistan wants a scandal over this sordid affair,'said the Foreign Secretary rather sternly while hinting to Shiraz that his days in Moscow were now numbered.

'I am sorry for all this, and Allah Kasam there is no question of my family and I being involved in activities that could be detrimental to the sovreignty and security of our beloved Pakistan,' said Shiraz as he wiped the tears that had swelled in his eyes with the spotless silk white handkerchief that was in the top coat pocket of his well tailored blue blazer.

'Alright we believe you and we always appreciated the good work that you have been doing as our country's ambassador to Russia. And therefore we will for the time being also let all that transpired between the three of us on this very subject today remain a complete secret. But take this as a warning and you will have to promise us that there will be no more such clandestine meetings between the two young lovers and the two ambassadors,' said the Foreign Minister firmly as he took back the file with all those photographs for his safe custody.

'But Janab if I have to do something to stop my daughter from continuing with the affair with the Bollywood star, then I do need a few of those photographs as direct proof and evidence to confront her with,' said Shiraz somewhat regretfully.

'In that case you can choose the ones you want,'said the Minister with a sly smile on his face as he handed the file back to Shiraz.Shiraz now knew that the only way he could convince his daughter to breakup the relationship with the Bollywood star was to pose a death threat to the entire family by some fanatical Muslim organization in Pakistan and of which there were now many. The plot was not exactly the same, but it was somewhat similar to what Shupriya's mother had done to breakup his relationship with her daughter, when during the thick of the Indo-Pakistan war in December 1971, she had sent him a false wedding card intimating that Shupriya'smarriage had already been consummated with a well qualified Bengali boy from Gaya.

Being well versed in Urdu, Shiraz wrote all that he wanted to write in that very language but it was in a somewhat crude manner and rustic style. Using an old piece of grimy paper and by adding some of his own bloodstains to it, he quickly made it look quite menacing. Then he wrote the well thought out and clever ultimatum to his family and which he would now on return confidentially show to his daughter together with those photographs of the love birds kissing in public. What he wrote was a strong indictment of his entire family. It was a very strongly worded statement that said in no uncertain terms that his daughter with utter disregard to the tenets of Islam had violated the Sharia law and the Muslim code of conduct which totally prohibited Muslims cohabiting with non Muslims, and therefore a fatwa has been issued to Riaz Mohammed Khan and his family for violating the sacred Muslim law. And incase cognizance of this fatwa was not taken immediately by him and his family members and if the relationship still continued between the two lovers, then as per the punishment required by law it would be meted out to the sinners. And the punishment besides the mandatory lashings to be given to the guilty, would also end up with a death penalty for all members of the family for conspiring in the commitment of this shameful and sinister act.

On that night of 8th of October 2001, while Shiraz was busy writing the fake 'Fatwa' and when he heard that the western coalition forces that was being led by the United States with all their mighty military power had been relelentlessly bombarding the Taliban and Al Qaida bases and camps inside Afghnistan, he felt that possibly the bloody on going war in Afghanistan that had started with the intervention of the Soviets in the winter of 1979 would now finally end and that Mulla Omer and Bin Laden will be dealt with nice and proper. But he was sadly mistaken. And on that very day, when the American President in a worldwide broadcast from the Treaty Room of the White House where all the past Presidents of America always declared that America always worked for peace, Shiraz wondered whether it could be achieved by the use of brute military force alone. Though the President had declared that the United States was not only a friend of the Afghan people, but also friends with all the billion Muslims who practice the Islamic faith, Shiraz wondered whether that statement would cut ice with the Muslim fundamentalists like Bin Laden and Maulana Masood Azhar. And now that he too was under a cloud, Shiraz it seems was now no longer interested in international politics, but about his own future and that of his family. And the only silver lining that day was General Musharraf's personal telephone call to Mr Vajpayee and his promise to investigate the attack on the Kashmir assembly and to which the Indian Prime Minister had reciprocated by offering Indian aid to the Afghan refugees in Pakistan.

The daring attack in broad daylight on the seat of the Jammu and Kashmir government in the state capital which was well guarded had come as a shock to Shiraz and he was now apprehensive that such like attacks could also now take place in the major Indian cities of Delhi and Mumbai which were the national and financial capitals of the country. A day after the attack on 2nd October, the Prime Minister of India had also written to President Bush claiming that India had established that the group that attacked the Kashmir assembly building also had very close links with the Al Qaida and therefore there was need for the US led coalition force to get after them too.

On the 11th of October, and a day prior to his scheduled departure for Moscow, Shiraz with Salim Rehman made a one day trip to Peshawar to visit the two old patriarchs from the Rehman clan and to have lunch with them. Shiraz was glad that none of the family members were yet aware of Sherry's involvement with the Bollywood movie star or about his hobnobbing with the Indian Ambassador in Moscow. During the drive to Peshawar, when Salim Rehman in all seriousness mentioned to him that the joint American-Northern Alliance military operations that was currently in progress to sort out the Taliban and the Al Qaida had literally got off to a flying start, Shiraz jokingly remarked that if the Russian Bear could not sort out the Afghans in a whole damn decade and more, the chances of the American Yankee conquering Afghanistan and subjugating the Pashtun Pathans of that region by only using its massive air power was also a far cry from reality.

'And if the Americans think that by bombing Afghanistan and by defeating the Taliban and the Al Qaida militarily, the war on terror wll completely end, then I feel that they are living in a fool's paradise. And as history shows, the proud Afghans from that inhospitable terrain of high mountains and fast flowing rivers who have never been conquered or subjugated by a foreign power ever will simply keep fighting and they will never accept the fact that they will in future be ruled by an outside power. And no matter how powerful a military power that may be, the people of Afghanistan simply will not accept it. And as far as getting rid of terrorism is concerned from this world, it can only be done if all countries of the world and especially Pakistan agree to join hands with all the others who are also being targeted. Unfortunately Pakistan today has become a haven for terrorists from all over the world and it is we who are to be blamed for it. And unless we sincerely resolve and cooperate whole heartedly with the rest of the world, only then we may probably get rid of this deadly menace,' concluded Shiraz as the car slowly made its way through that historic city which was traditionally also the main gateway to Afghanistan.

And on the next morning of 12th October, while on his way to the airport to catch the PIA flight to Moscow, when Salim Rehman told him that the United States had frozen all the assets of the Jaish-e-Mohammed, the happiest person was Shiraz. But he also knew that by itself it wont solve the problem since the ISI and the Pakistani government were always ready to provide the JeM with all the wherewithal that was required to keep the Indians bleeding and especially so in Kashmir.

On the 3rd of October, when India asked Pakistan to hand over Maulana Masood Azhar the leader of the Jaish-e-Mohammed, Salim Reham thought it was some sort of a joke. And on 10th October, when the United States President released the initial list of the FBI's top 22 most wanted terrorists that included Osama Bin Laden and his deputy Dr Al-Zawahiri, Shiraz too wondered whether Pakistan would now seriously cooperate in helping the Americans to get hold of them. There was no doubt in his mind that both Pakistan and Afghanistan had become a haven for most of those who were on that big wanted list. And he also now wondered whether the cigarette smoking President of Pakistan who also liked listening to gazals and who enjoyed a few tots of Black Label whisky before dinner would be capable of delivering atleast some of those fanatical terrorists to his new found ally and friend George Bush, the American President who had become even more desperate now to bring the culprits to book.

On the evening of 12th October 2001, when Shiraz landed in Moscow, he was surprised to see his wife Saira and daughter Sherry at the airport. It seems that his posting back to Islamabad had been received that very morning by the embassy and the fact that he had been asked to report to Islamabad as an Additional Secretary in the Ministry of Foreign Affairs latest by the end of the month and to hand over charge to the Minister who would officiate till the new incumbent arrived had taken everybody by complete surprise.

'But where is the fire to get back to Islamabad in such a hurry Abbu? And I have yet to complete my dissertation in music from here,' said Sherry as she lovingly hugged her father.

'Well all one can say is that it is a fallout from the new equation that we have established with the United State in fighting terror, and in anycase there is much more to do in Islamabad on this very important subject, than by my sitting here in Moscow,' said Shiraz with a complete poker face. Shiraz too could never imagine that his posting back to Islamabad would come so very soon and so very suddenly. And he was now apprehensive and worried that all his actions and movements henceforth would also come under the constant scanner of the ISI.

The next day 13th of October was a Saturday and Shiraz before confronting his daughter with the carefully worded ultimatum that he had falsely prepared on behalf of the Jaish-e-Mohammed, he also wanted to caution her lover in India with a similar warning. He therefore desperately wanted Deepak Kumar's mobile number and he knew that the only way he could get it was from his daughter's mobile phone. At the same time he also wanted that his wife Saira should not be told about the on going affair between her daughter and the Indian matinee idol and about his meetings with his counterpart from India. Shiraz was also aware that off late Sherry had not just one but two mobile phones. And he had also observed that at times and while at home whenever Sherry received an SMS on the new big Blackbury, she would conveniently excuse herself and go either to the toilet or to her own room. Otherwise that Blackberry phone was hardly being used by her and most of the phone calls that were received and made by her were from the old Nokia phone and for which all the bills were being paid by him.

That evening in celebration for his posting back home, Shiraz held an impromptu drinks and dinner party for all the senior officers in the embassy. And once the party was over and all the guests had finally left, he very cleverly opened a bottle of Dom Perignon champagne. And as the cork from the bottle with a big bang hit the ceiling, he expertly poured the bubbly contents into the three tall flouted crystal champagne glasses and spiked the ones for Sherry and Saira with a sleeping pill each.

'Let us all drink to a better tomorrow and let us hope that the war on terror will soon come to an end,' said Shiraz somewhat matter of factly as they all clinked glasses.

'Maybe we should drink to the early success of 'Operation Enduring Freedom,' because that will be the key to ending the war on terror,' said Saira who genuinely felt happy about the home posting. With her brother Salim Rehman back in Islamabad and with her parents getting older by the day, it would also give all of them the opportunity and time to look after their dear parents.

'And now that President Musharraf has once again extended his hand of friendship to India, maybe we should also drink to a better and more prosperous Indo-Pak friendship in future,' said Sherry, when the blip on her Blackberry indicated that there was a message for her.

'Cheers to that, but that I think is still a far cry from reality' said Shiraz as he poured some more champagne into his wife's glass, while an excited Sherry quickly excused herself and went to the toilet.

At around 11 o'clock every night Moscow time Peevee invariably rang up Sherry and today was no different. And when Sherry conveyed to him that his father had suddenly received a home posting and that she with her parents would be back in Pakistan by the end of the month, Peevee was not only surprised but also confused.

'Well that's news to me, but guess what, my Mom Number 2 has also received her home posting back to India and she will be back in Delhi to celebrate Dushhera with us. And as a result of which I am afraid we will not be able to meet during Diwali in Moscow as planned. In fact I wanted to convey this to you a couple of days ago, but I was not sure about my Mom Number 2 and whether she would be able to make it back to Delhi within the short notice period that has been given to her. And frankly speaking the sudden home posting of my Mom Number 2 to Delhi and that of your father to Islamabad and with both coming in such quick succession has really upset all our plans for the gala Divali date that we had planned to celebrate in Moscow,' said Peevee.

'That is rather strange and sad, but why don't you make it even for a couple of days before Dushhera. Because once we are back in Pakistan, it will be rather difficult for me to get away from my parents and to meet you in some third country. Right now you can always make the excuse to your Mom Numnber 2 that you can be of some help to her in packing her bags, and thus make it to Moscow before Dusshera,' said Sherry in a very depressed and subdued tone as she pleaded with Peevee to atleast give it a try.

'OK, I will not promise but I will definitely give it a good try. Today is already the 13th of October and since Mom Number 2 is expected back in India on the 22nd which is two days prior to Dusshera, I will try and reach Moscow by this coming weekend and fly back with her to Delhi on the 22nd. And Allah Talla—God willing if it works out then we will be with each other atleast for a couple of hours on the 20th and 21st which happens to be a Sunday and Monday. Needless to say I too want to desperately hold you in my arms darling,' said Peevee as he kissed Sherry a very goodnight over the phone.

No sooner she came out of the toilet, Sherry felt somewhat drowsy. The sleeping pill had started having its effect. So giving the excuse that she was very tired and sleepy, she wished her parents a very good night and retired to her room and was soon fast asleep. An hour or so later and having ensured that the effect of the sleeping pill also had its required effect on Saira, Shiraz quietly got into Sherry's room. And having got hold of her Blackberry he noted the telephone number of the last caller and that of the last SMS sender. And since both the numbers were identical and they were from India, Shiraz was a hundred percent sure that it was none other than the matinee idol from Bollywood.

Next morning being a Sunday, Shiraz too got up late. And while Saira got busy making the usual Sunday breakfast of stuffed parathas with curd and homemade pickle, Shiraz on the pretext that he needed some personal help to sort out his personal files, mementoes and letters that were lying in the office, requested Sherry to get ready and accompany him to the office after breakfast. On that very Sunday morning and feeling the heat of 'Operation Enduring Freedom,' the Taliban had once again proposed to handover Bin Laden to a third country for trial, but only if they were given evidence of Bin Laden's involvement in the 9/11attacks. And when that too was rejected by the United States, Shiraz knew that for Mullah Omar and his Taliban it was probably now the end of the road.

And after a sumptous breakfast as the father and daughter duo got into the car and drove away, Shiraz in a rather serious tone told his daughter that he urgently needed to speak to her on something very important and highly confidential. And since he did not want her mother to know about it right now, he had therefore given the excuse to Saira that with time being at a premium for their return to Pakistan, he needed his daughter's help in the office.

'Maybe we could first go to Park Pobedy and over a good cup of coffee work it all out and to everybody's satisfaction too,' said Shiraz as he smiled at Sherry and casually told her how he first met her mother and later proposed to her. Hearing that coming without any relevant context, there was a confused look on Sherry's face, And it was only when they were comfortably seated in the park's only restaurant and Shiraz once again very diplomatically asked Sherry if she was ready to get married, that Sherry realized that probably some marriage proposal had come for her.

'But Abbu, I am only twenty one and I have still to complete my studies in classical music and thereafter submit my thesis on the works of Tchaikovsky to the Russian Academy of Music, and I therefore need atleast another year or two to make up my mind about marriage,'said Sherry somewhat apprehensively as Shiraz took out the envelope with the set of photographs and the ultimatum that was lying inside the dashboard of the car. And having kept them on to one side said.

'Yes and that is exactly what I intended to discuss with you too. And though I personally will have no objections if you want to marry someone whom you really love and care for, but that is not the issue right now. And even if the gentleman of you choice is not a Pakistani that too would not have mattered the least as far as your mother and I are concerned. But I am afraid that under the present circumstances and for your own sake and that of the entire family you will have to call off the affair and relationship that you are now so very seriously into, and you have to do it immediately. And I do not have to tell you about whom I am talking about, because it is all here in the photographs and the ultimatum that is inside the envelope and which I was presented to me by a fundamentalist Islamic group when I was summoned at short notice to Islamabad. And which also unfortunately has led to my posting back to Pakistan and that too so very suddenly. And let me also tell you my love that I personally have nothing against that gentleman, but thanks to our fanatical Mullas and Dons, the man you so deeply love his life I am afraid is now in grave danger too. And let me also add that the both the Pakistani ISI and radical Islamic group are under the impression that you as my daughter have been leaking classified information to someone who they think as a Bollywood actor is actually working as a mole for RAW. And RAW as we all know is the foremost Indian intelligence agency that is always fishing for classified and secret information on Pakistan,'said Shiraz with a sad and pitiful look in his eyes, as he handed over the envelope to his daughter.

As Sherry looked at those revealing photographs, there was a look of complete disbelief on her beautiful face. Then with tears swelling in her eyes, when she broke down and said. 'I am terribly sorry for keeping you and Ammijaan in the dark, but Allah Kasam and I swear by the Holy Koran that I have not passed any classified or secret information to Deepak Kumar. And he is not a mole,' Shiraz knew that his daughter was telling the truth. And when Sherry with tears in her eyes further added and said.

'Yes Abbu I do admit that we are both madly in love with each other and we also want to get married, but why is fate being so cruel to us, and why are the Mullas and the ISI taking it all out on you,' said a heartbroken Sherry while Shiraz felt rather sad for his only daughter. And though he was reminded of the fact that he as a Muslim had married a Hindu and that too secretly, but under the present circumstances he could ill afford to put his daughter and family at risk. He was afraid that in case the Jaish-e-Mohammed, the so called Army of Mohammed became actually aware of this love affair and also about his secret meetings with the Indian Ambassador in Moscow then they would not hesitate to eliminate all of them.

'I know it is rather sad but we just cannot take a chance my dear. The Mullahs and their goons and especially those from the Jaish-e-Mohammed whose leader Maulana Masood Azhar is a rabid and diehard Hindu hater will not spare us, nor will he spare the Bollywood hero. The members of the JeM are absolute fanatics and if we do not bow to their dictates; they will brutally kill all of us. And now that we are going back to Pakistan, not only will they make life hell for all of us, but the ISI too will squarely accuse me of spying for the Indians. And as we all know the penalty for treason is death,' lied Shiraz as he tried to consol his heartbroken daughter.

'Oh my God I just cannot believe all this. I love you so much Dad, but I also love Peevee as much as I love you and Mom. And now I am in a real quandary and I simply do not know how I should convey it to him,' said Sherry as Shiraz wiped away the tears that were trickling down his daughter's pink cheeks.

'Maybe you should tell him a lie and say very firmly that your parents are absolutely against your getting married to a Hindu and that too an actor from Bollywood. However, frankly speaking neither your Mom nor I have anything against such a marriage. But under the present difficult circumstances this is the best excuse that one can think off or else we will be putting Peevee's life in danger too. But do also tell me what does Peevee stand for,' said Shiraz as he smiled at his daughter and thanked her for being so very understanding and cooperative.

'The initials P.V. stands for Paramveer and actually he is a shaven Sikh and not a Hindu. And Deepak Kumar is only his screen name Dad,'said Sherry as she once again looked at those photographs and then handed them back to her father.

'And since I know that it will be very difficult for you to convey this diffricult decision to the man whom you so deeply love over the phone, I suggest you send him a long SMS giving the reasons as to why the relationship has to end. And you can also message to him that besides your own parents, the JeM and the 'D" company Don, Dawood Ibrahim who is now safely ensconced in Karachi too have also somehow come to know about the affair. And therefore not only your life but that off your dear parents and Deepak Kumar's too is now in real danger. And much that you would have loved to carry on with this relationship, but you are now absolutely helpless. And it is even more so now because fearing a reprisal from the diehards in the JeM, your parents have therefore found a suitable match for you in Pakistan. Though I know that this is not true, but nevertheless you have to message this to him also. Maybe this last factor will also reduce the threat that is on us from the JeM and Peevee will also understand that,' said Shiraz very confidently.

That very afternoon, when Sherry like a good devoted daughter while sitting in his father's office and with tears running down her beautiful face sent the required long SMS that her father wanted her to, Shiraz really felt sad for his beautiful and talented daughter. And in the last sentence, when she asked for forgiveness and requested Peevee that for his own sake and for the safety of her own family, he should therefore never ever contact her again, and that the affair was a closed chapter as far as she and her family was concerned, Shiraz knew that the affair thank God was finally over.

Sherry was however not aware that her father too had already sent Peevee a somewhat threatening SMS earlier. Using the name of the Pakistani based Indian Don and mentioning the fact that he was was also an ardent follower of the JeM Mullah Leader, Masood Azhar, Shiraz warned Deepak Kumar not to mess with the life of the Pakistani girl. And in case the warning was not heeded to by him and by the girl in question, and then the 'D' Company goons in Mumbai and the Jaish-e-Mohammed followers in Pakistan will ensure that both the families pay very heavily for it.

When Peevee received the first SMS, he thought that it could be another ruse by a Pakistani based Indian Don to extort some hush money from him through his underworld links in Mumbai. But a couple of hours later, when the second SMS from Sherry was received by him, he began to realize that the matter could be indeed serious. And later when he kept trying to get Sherry on her mobile and Sherry did not respond to either of his messages or calls, he was convinced that things had probably gone out of hand. Nonetheless he kept waiting for a response from her. And it was only well after midnight, when he received a series of threatening calls from some person who claimed to be a devoted follower of Masood Azhar and was warned that the JeM would spare nobody unless Peevee called off the affair immediately', Peevee realized that the matter was indeed very grave and serious, and more so because the caller did not demand any extortion money from him. Peevee was also afraid that these goons may also blackmail him and that would also affect his career very badly. Therefore for the sake of Sherry and her family and that of his own kith and kin, he decided that it was better to call it quits for the time being atleast.

Peevee ofcourse had no idea that those late night threatening calls had been made by none other than Shiraz, his own biological father and about which both of them were totally ignorant. There was now no question of his going to Moscow to help out Mom Number 2 with her packing and to meet Sherry again secretly. Therefore next morning, when he rang up Shupriya and told her that for the sake of the family he had finally decided to end the affair with the Pakistani Ambassador's daughter, the happiest person was his own biological mother. Though he was the one and only issue and son of Shiraz and Shupriya, Peevee however was blissfully unaware that the Pakistani Ambassador to Moscow was his real father and the Lady Indian Ambassador was his real mother.

Though the affair seem to have ended, but there was more bad news for Shiraz when a letter threatening him and his family with dire consequences and death was actually received by him. It was from the Lashkar-e-Toiba's headquarters at Muridke near Lahore. Though the letter was like an ultimatum and it was unsigned, but it could not be taken lightly. It seems that someone from the ISI had intentionally leaked the news of his clandestine meetings with the Indian lady ambassador in Moscow and about his daughter's love affair with the shaven off Sikh Indian cinestar to this deadly fanatical and radical Muslim organization. And with that Shiraz was now more than certain that not only his and his family's every move henceforth would be under the radar of the ISI, but it would also now be under the scanner of the dreaded LeT also.

Chapter-42

Dasvidaniya and Till We Meet Again

On his return to Moscow, when Shiraz learnt that the Indian Ambassador had also received her posting orders to return to India, he too was surprised. And he wondered whether this too was because of their clandestine meetings and that of his daughter's affair with the Bollywood star in Moscow. Therefore in order to find out a little more, he decided to take a chance and have one last meeting with Shups. With only a little over a week left for Shupriya to fly back to India and in order to apprise Shupriya that he too was now on the radar of the ISI and that there was now also a grave danger to his own life and to the lives of his family members from the LeT also, he decided to call her up from a public telephone booth. Aware of the fact that Deepak Kumar while secretly dating his daughter in Moscow had stayed as the guest of the Indian Ambassador, and that both he and his daughter were now being suspected by the ISI of passing classified imformation to the Indian cinestar who according to the ISI was a RAW agent, Shiraz on the evening of 15th Octobert rang up Shupriya on her mobile. It was well after office hours and speaking from a private telephone booth, when he too conveyed to her about his sudden posting back to Islamabad, it also took Shupriya completely by surprise.

'Now listen and listen very carefully and please do not interrupt. My family and I it seems are in very serious danger and before you leave for Delhi, I must meet you. This may well be my last meeting with you and I need to pass on some very important information that may be of value to both the countries in the near future. For our own security and safety we will not meet in any public place, but I will be waiting for you in a local taxi near the main entrance to the Yaroslavsky railway station. Be there sharp at 7p.m. tomorrow,' said Shiraz.

'Alright I will be there as suggested by you,' but you also be very careful because we are both also now on the Russian FSB's radar,' said Shupriya.

Next evening as the two of them while sitting in the cab went on a non stop hour's drive around the city, and Shiraz speaking softly and only in Hindi so that the Russian driver hopefully would not be able to understand told Shupriya about her daughter's involvement with the Bollywood star while he was in Moscow as her personal guest, to that revelation, Shupriya not only showed surprise but she also feighned total ignorance. And thereafter, when Shiraz told her that the ISI and the LeT both were fully aware about their one to one secret meetings in Moscow and that there was now a distinct possibility of the Pakistan government under General Musharraff branding him and his family as spies and traitors,' Shupriya realizing that her husband's life and that of his family were now in real danger therefore agreed to help, provided Shiraz was willing to defect with or without his family and was willing to provide the Indian government with those vital classified information that he had talked about on the phone earlier.

'I have some of it right here with me in this little red diary of mine, but it is all written in my own secret code. I have however also made a decoded copy for you and you may keep both these very safely for the time being. And if ever I have to defect and I need your help, I will send you a gift parcel and that will not only contain a similar small red diary with more classified information in it, but it will also contain a set of microfilms or a compact disk of some top secret classified information regarding Pakistan's military and nuclear arsenal that I intend getting hold off once I get to sit on my chair in Islamabad. It will also contain a letter giving the details of my latest whereabouts and whether I intend to defect alone or with my family. Incase it is going to be a family affair then the unsigned letter will simply have four prominent red dots on top and at the bottom of the page indicating that all the four members of my family will need your help. And incase I decide to make it alone then it will be the usual two zeroes at the end of the letter indicating that it is from 'Dablo' who alone needs your help, said Shiraz as he handed over the little red diary with the decoded copy to her.

'But do be very careful and please do not stretch out your neck too far,'said Shupriya as she put the little red diary and the decoded copy inside her purse.

'Don't worry and if the worst comes to worst and if I have to really ensure that no harm comes to my family, I may even fake my own death and take on another new identity. In the meantime let me warn you that the latest attack by the Lashkar-e-Toiba on the state legislature building at Srinagar is only the beginning, and there may be more such dare devils attacks to come. And the possibility of these being carried out beyond the state boundary of Jammu and Kashmir and on important targets deep inside India is also very much a possibility now. While in Islamabad I also came to know that the Musharraf government is under very heavy pressure at home and his sudden turn around to join the Americans in "Operation Endure Freedom' has greatly angered the fanatical Muslim Mullah leaders of Pakistan and especially those who have a mass following in the volatile Northwest Frontier Region of the country. And with India's support for the Northern Alliance to fight the Taliban in Afghanistan it has only made matters worse. And though the Americans and their allies with their massive air and fire power together with active support from those who are part of the Northern Alliance Forces may succeed in quickly ousting the Taliban from power in Afghanistan, but that alone I am afraid will not eliminate the war on terror. Pakistan I am afraid is now caught in a vicious circle and for General Musharaff and his government these are very testing and trying times. The Americans after the recent visit of General Colin Powell, the American Secretary of State to Pakistan has now made it very clear to the flamboyant General that either Pakistan is with them or not with them and there can be no via media. Therefore 'Dasvidaniya' till we meet again. And if I am in real great trouble then I will certainly from somewhere despatch to you some more highly classified documents and these could be either through micro films or through a compact disc. I will send these together with a letter to you at Monty Bhaiya's address and it will be a gift from Dablo to Shups and to India,'said Shiraz as he smartly saluted and bid a final farewell to his beloved Shups.

With the sudden posting out of both the ambassadors of India and Pakistan from Moscow to their respective capitals, there was a spate of farewell diplomatic send off party for both them. Most of these were hosted by those heads of mission that had close ties with both India and Pakistan and it was at the farewell cocktail party in honour of the Indian Ambassador that was hosted by the Bangladeshi Ambassador to Moscow on the 20th of October that Shiraz and Shupriya again came face to face with one another.

That evening Shupriya was very keen to tell her Dablo that Deepak Kumar the Bollywood film idol who was in love with his pretty daughter was their son, but when she saw Sherry at the party and realised that it would be a shocking revelation that would further endanger both the families, she very wisely kept it to herself. And while she was leaving when she affectionately hugged both Saira and Sherry and told them that she would be looking forward to meeting them again, little did she know that it would never be so.

On the afternoon of 22nd October 2001, with the entire embassy staff at Moscow's Shremetovo International Airport wishing her farewell and a safe journey back to India, Shupriya with tears swelling in her eyes boarded the Air India International flight to Delhi. And as the aircraft took off, seated in her seat in the first class section of the jet liner, Shupriya closed her eyes and said a prayer for the safety of her loving Dablo and his family.

Given the mandatory joining time, Shupriya decided to spend most of it with Monty and Reeta in Delhi. On the fourth day of Durga Puja, she together with Monty and Reeta Bhabi for the first time in many years visited the Durga Puja Pandal at Chittaranjan Park. Considered to be the biggest festival for the Bengali community in the capital, she too dressed up like a typical Bengali that day. Wearing an off white plain silk saree with a big red border Shupriya despite her years looked stunning.The last time she had been there was with her parents and that was way back in October 1971. That was the time when the war clouds over Kashmir had started gathering and the Indian armed forces were getting ready to liberate Bangladesh. Like on that day in 1971, she once again today prayed to the Goddess Durga to keep her Dablo safe and happy. And keeping the safety of her beloved in mind, she never mentioned a word about Dablo's existence in this world to Monty and Reeta. To them he was dead and gone and she was still his widow.

A week later, when she reported for duty at South Block as Secretary East, the entire Ministry of External Affairs was busy preparing the many briefs for the Prime Minister of India's forthcoming visit to Russia and the United States in November. Earlier in February 2001, Ilea Klebanov, the Russian Deputy Prime Minister during his visit to New Delhi had signed the deal for the supply and manufacture in India of the T-90 Main Battle Tank. Consequent to that defence deal, the Defence Minister of India, Jaswant Singh during his visit to Moscow in June 2001 had also signed many more protocols that had elevated the defence ties between both the countries to a new level. The recent visit to India of the US Secretary of State, General Colin Powell, and his assurance that the war on terrorism that America had embarked upon would also include the menace that India had been battling with in Kashmir was also very encouraging. However keeping all these developments in mind, Shupriya was a little skeptical of whether the Russians would be able to honour the various defence deals without raising the prices, and whether the United States will be able to convince the Pakistan President, General Musharraf to stop 'Operation Tupac' in Kashmir. Moreover, the impending high profile visit of the Indian Prime Minister to

Russia and the United States had also got Pakistan worried. There was a fear that the tempo of the proxy war that the ISI had sponsored through militant organizations like the LeT and others in Kashmir and which was gaining added momentum by the use of Fedayeens suicide bombers may have to be curbed since America had indicated that the war on terror cannot be fought in isolation. The U.S. had also warned Pakistan that either Pakistan is with them or not with them.

Operation Tupac was a proxy war that was started by the late General Zia-ul-Haq way back in 1987 and even after the 1999 Kargil war it had shown little or no signs of abating whatsoever. Infact the problem had become worse since then, as Pakistan in close collaboration with the militant organizations like the Hizbul Mujahideen, the Jaish-e-Mohammed and the Lashkar-e-Toiba kept intensifying their ISI sponsored terrorist operations in Jammu and Kashmir. Just before leaving Moscow, Shiraz had told Shupriya very categorically that the humiliation that Pakistan had suffered in 1971 during the Bangladesh War and also during the Kargil misadventure in the summer of 1999 was still very fresh in the minds of the people. And to add to that and thanks to General Zia' policy of Islamization, the fanatical Mullas of that country have therefore been constantly poisoning the minds of the illiterate younger generations with the dictum that the Hindus of India were not only Kafirs, but the Indian leaders were also bent upon destroying Pakistan. Shiraz had therefore warned Shupriya that these militant organizations were hell bent on taking revenge. And the possibility of these militant groups with the help of the ISI and their Indian collaborators further spreading their tentacles into India to create more mischief therefore was now a distinct possibility. He had also mentioned to her that some of these fanatical militant groups that were being armed and trained by the ISI may sooner or later for revenge focus their attention on strategic targets in India.

In mid October, while General Colin Powell was visiting India and Pakistan, the tension on the LOC, the Line of Control had progressively increased as both the Indian army and the Pakistan army traded artillery barrages in the Mendhar and Akhnur Sectors of Jammu and Kashmir. Pakistan had also reverted to pushing in more and better trained militants as suicide bombers into the state to further bleed the Indians.

On the 26th of October 2001 with America's 'Operation Enduring Freedom' in Afghanistan gaining further momentum, President George Bush signed into law the USA Patriot Act. It was an act in response to the terrorist attacks on the USA on 11 September and the acronym 'Patriot; stood for

'Uniting and Strengthening America by Providing Appropriate Tools Required to Intercept and Obstruct Terrorism.' The law now dramatically reduced restrictions on the law enforcement agencies and the immigration authorties in the country to monitor the activities of not only their own citizens, but also those visiting the United States of America. These agencies therefore were now given much wider powers to ensure the safety and security of the nation.

On the 30th of October 2001, and a couple of days before the Indian Prime Minister's sceduled visit to Moscow, Shiraz having handed over charge to the Minister in the Pakistan Embassy, he together with Saira and Sherry boarded the PIA flight to Islamabad. And as the aircraft taxied its way for the take off, Shiraz kissed the lucky locket, closed his eyes and thanked Allah. He had never in his dream ever imagined that after a lapse of thirty years he would be reunited with his beloved Shups in Moscow. But he was also now afraid of being suspected by the ISI and the LeT as an Indian spy.

On the 3rd of November, 2001 while visiting Russia, the Prime Minister of India Mr Atal Bihari Vajpayee signed a declaration with his Russian counterpart condemning all countries that sheltered terrorists and both the leaders had also emphasisied the fact that the United Nations must give a legal basis to the war on terror. Besides the massive defence contracts that were already in the pipeline, and when the Indian Prime Minister also confirmed India's intention to buy the aircraft 'Admiral Groshkov' and an MOU was also signed to implement the Russian designed Kudankulam nuclear power project in the Indian state of Tamil Nadu, all this had got Pakistan very worried. On the 4th and 5th of November, the U.S. Secretary of Defense, Donald Rumsfield during his vist to Pakistan and India had also indicated that the global campaign against terrorism will not exclude Kashmir and this was another set back for Pakistan. And on 9th November, while visiting Washington, when the Indian Prime Minister and President George Bush in a joint statement declared that both countries would now look forward to a new era of peace, friendship and prosperity and that they would wage a joint battle against all forms of terrorism, the happiest person was Shiraz.

On the 7th of November, Carl W. Ford Jr the American Assistant Secretary of State for Intelligence and Research had categorically stated in a memo to Colin Powell that after the attack on America on September 11, the Pakistan public in general had become more sympathetic to the Taliban and knowing that to be a fact, Shiraz was fearful of its future consequences. While on the one hand Pakistan government and the Pakistan military under

General Musharraf were now going hell for leather with the Americans to oust the Taliban from Afghanistan, the people of Pakistan at the same time were giving the fleeing Taliban fighters safe sanctuary in the volatile area of their own North West Frontier and Baluchistan Provinces.

On the 13th of November, 2001 when President George Bush signed an executive order authorizing the creation of military tribunals for the detention, treatment and trial of certain non-citizens in the war against terrorism, it became apparent to Shiraz that the focus of America's war on terror not only included the Al Qaida hardliners but also those who were sheltering them. It was a first such act after the Second World War and it could take appropriate and strict actions against all foreigners who were suspected of having links and connections to terrorist organizations that were engaged in waging a war of terror on the United States. And with Pakistan still very much involved in this tricky cloak and dagger game, the possibility of Pakistanis aided by the ISI being involved in such like anti US activities therefore could not be ruled out. Moreover by helping the Taliban to find safe sanctuary inside Pakistan, the emergence of a strong highly motivated Talibanised Pakistan in the near future was also now a distinct possibility. On the 9th of November, the Northern Alliance had captured Mazar-e-Sharif and by the weekend it had gained control of most of northern Afghanistan. And by the time the ink had dried up on President Bush's latest executive order to create military tribunals, Kabul too had fallen. Surprisingly the Taliban without even giving a fight unexpectedly left the capital city and most of them had fled to Pakistan.

Fearing that Pakistan's policy on Afghanistan was backfiring on him, and that Afghanistan could no longer be used as a buffer, when the President of Pakistan, General Musharraf in a speech on 16th November, 2001 accused India of planning aggression against his country, Shiraz knew that it was only an excuse to divert the attention and minds of the Pakistanis from the mess up that Pakistan had created by recognizing the Taliban regime and by arming them to the hilt. With Pakistan's game plan of having a friendly Afghanistan as its neighbor now in tatters and with the Americans dictating terms to him, the ex SSG Commando was now only looking for excuses to save his own skin.

The massive US air raid on a safe house in Kabul in mid November had also resulted in the death of Mohammed Atef and a few others from the Al Qaida. Atef was the top most military chief of the Al Qaida and was the person who had masterminded the bombing of US embassies in Kenya and Tanzania in 1998. Born in 1944, Atef had served two years in the

Egyptian Armed Forces before becoming a volunteer to fight the Soviets in Afghanistan. As a member of the the Egyptian Islamic Jihad, he was very close to Ayman-al-Zawahiri, the number two man of Al Qaida who was also an Egyptian. Basically a quiet man, Atef's relationship with Bin Laden was further strengthened when he got his daughter married to one of Bin Laden's many sons. That was sometime in January 2001 at Kandahar. On that occassion as the two sat smiling and sipping tea, Bin Laden for the first time claimed responsibility for the suicide attack on the USS Cole and in which 17 US sailors were killed. And though Atef was now dead, there were still 21 such others who were on the United States most wanted list.

Late on that evening of 16th November, Shiraz having got some reliable inputs about the activities of the LeT, the Lashkar-e-Toiba, he made a note of them in his secret red diary. Known as the 'Army of the Pure', the LeT was now undoubtedly one of the largest and most active Islamist militant organizations in the whole of South East Asia. That morning being a Holy Friday, Shiraz who was on an official visit to Lahore had attended a prayer meeting in the LeT's sprawling campus and was surprised to see the large number of young people who had gathered there to listen to the man who was now known as the founder patriarch of the LeT. It was founded by Hafiz Mohammed Saeed, a former professor of engineering from Punjab University, and the well constructed complex with its headquarters, offices, madrassas, hospital and camps was located at Muridke. It was a little outside Lahore and was now something like a national landmark. Popularly and reverendly addressed as the Amir by his ardent followers, Hafiz Mohammed was well known for its extreme hardline views on Islam and he was also a great motivator. Together with his seething hatred for India and zeal to promote and restore Islamic rule in Southeast Asia and elsewhere, he had become a cult like figure in the country. The Markaz-ud-Dawa-wal-Irshad, or the Centre of Preaching at Muridke had become a rallying point for the young and illiterate young men and boys of Pakistan to spread the Jihad as they voluntarily joined the LeT which was the military wing of the organization and was the one that would train them to become fedayeen fighters. The military wing was headed by Zaki-ur-Rehman Lakhvi. He was also a founder member of the LeT and a rabid Indian hater. Popular known as 'Chacha' (Uncle) by the young Jihadi trainees, Zaki had also directed military actions against the Russians in Chechnia and against the Serbs in Bosnia. Till recently, the LeT's focus was on Kashmir and to generate funds for the liberation of the state, the radical fundamentalist organization through their propaganda wing had started a big donation drive. So much so that all shops in the main bazaar of the many cities and towns in Pakistan had become big collection centres to raise funds for their fight for Kashmir. Though it was based in Muridke, it also had a large number of militant training camps in Pakistan administered Kashmir and Shiraz had made a note of all them.

The LeT's presence in Jammu and Kashmir was first noticed in 1993, when 12 Pakistani and Afghan mercenaries infiltrated across the Line of Control in tandem with another Islamic militant organization in the Poonch area of the state. And off late, the LeT had also carried out a large number of suicide bombing attacks inside Jammu and Kashmir including the one on the Kashmir Legislature in Srinagar on 1st October. 2001. But now with the sudden change of policy by the Musharraf government to rally with the Americans and join them in the fight against the Taliban and the Al Qaida, some of the hardliners within the LeT had become disgruntled and there was therefore now every possibility of this breakaway group joining the Taliban and the Al Qaida. Besides receiving large donations from Muslim communities from all over the world, the LeT in the garb of humanitarian aid was also receiving considerable financial, material and other forms of assistance from the Pakistan government. These were being primarily routed through the ISI who were also arming and training their cadres. And according to another reliable source, the Markaz campus at Muridke was also being used to shelter terrorists from other countries. Keeping all these inputs in mind, Shiraz was afraid that given a free hand, this very organization with its very large following inside Pakistan and abroad, may one day well become Pakistan's nemesis. Though it was already on the radar of the United States as a terrorist organization, and General Musharraf was now under great pressure to ban it, but it was easier said than done. He was in a quandary whereby he could neither displease the Americans, nor the many fanatical militant organizations that Pakistan had spawned during the last two and more decades, and certainly not the LeT which now had a mass following. Soon after the Kargil fiasco in 1999, Lakhvi as the Supreme Commander of operations in Kashmir during a three day congregation of the Let's General Council at Muridke had said very categorically and openly that the fidayeen missions in Jammu and Kashmir would not only teach the Indians a lesson in the valley, but his next target would be Delhi. And Shiraz was apprehensive that an attack on Delhi may well provoke a fourth round and one that could be disastrous for both the countries.

And while Shiraz in Islamabad was busy updating his new little secret red diary with more classified information about Pakistan's ever expanding nuclear arsenal and the ISI spawned fanatical militant organizations nexus with the prime intelligence agency in the country, in New Delhi Shupriya was quietly busy trying to collate all the information that was in the old red diary which Dablo had given to her before her departure from Moscow. The contents of the diary besides containing vital information about the storage and deployment of Pakistan's nuclear arsenal in the country's Punjab Province, it also spelt out in no uncertain terms about Pakistan's future plans to produce plutonium based nuclear weapons and spiking them with tritium. And if Pakistan did succeed in doing that, then even a few grams of tritium could result in vastly increasing the explosive yield in a nuclear warhead. And as far as the proxy war in Jammu and Kashmir was concerned, it clearly showed that the Musharraf government and the Pakistan ISI were clearly hand in glove with the LeT and other such like militant groups to keep the issue constantly alive. And not only were they bent in creating more mischief in the valley, but there were also indications that the ISI-Let nexus with Hafiz Mohammed Saeed's full backing were also preparing to spread their tentacles and attack strategic targets in India.

With that constantly at the back of his mind, Shiraz was now very apprehensive of what would happen if terrorist organizations like the LeT and the Al Qaida managed to equip themselves with a nuclear bomb. The very fact that there was a greater possibiliy of a nuclear meltdown in Pakistan and that the country was thinking of commissioning a plutonium reactor which could in future produce smaller and more lethal weapons of mass destruction was itself very frightening. And he felt even if a handful of these fell into the hands of the LeT and the Al—Qaida and they in tandem and in the name of Islam launched a nuclear attack on the United States to avenge the massive attacks that America and her allies had launched to oust the Taliban and the Al Qaida from Afghanistan, then it would probably lead to a global nuclear war and one that would be catastrophic for the whole world. There was no doubt that the Al Qaida had been making persistent efforts in the nuclear and biological blackmarket to acquire such a capability and with the HEU, the highly enriched uranium now being available in many countries, the quantity required to produce a deadly nuclear bomb was therefore not very difficult at all. With just around 25 to 50 Kgs of HEU one could make such a deadly weapon of mass destruction that would be in the size no larger than that of a volleyball or a football, but it could cause massive destruction.Therefore in order to ensure that such an eventuality did not occur, or it was considerably reduced, Shiraz decided to probe a little more about Pakistan's present nuclear capability and the steps taken by the

Pakistan military and the Pakistan Atomic Energy Commission to safeguard them from falling into the hands of terrorist organizations. According to one reliable source, Pakistan by now had around 30 to 40 nuclear warheads and more were now in the process of been added to its nuclear arsenal. The SPD, the Strategic Plans Division of Pakistan under a Lt General as the Director General had been made in charge of all aspects of Pakistan's nuclear weapons except field operations, and together with the Army Strategic Force Command it had a combind strength of nearly 10,000 and more. Presently the weapons were stored unassembled and with the nuclear cores separate from the rest of the weapon. And the weapon storage areas which were highly sensitive were also some distance away from the delivery vehicles. Though they were said to be widely dispersed, but according to one source, most of them were stored in arsenals that were south of Islamabad and at Sargodha. And with the Pakistan Number 9 and Number 11 Squadrons that were equipped with the state of the art sophisticated F-16 fighter aircrafts and were deployed at Sargodha Air Force Base, it had considerably increased Pakistan's first strike capability. Together with the F-16's capability to conduct long range nuclear missions, the assembled nuclear bombs were most likely also kept in the big Sargodha Weapons Storage Complex that was located 10 kilometers south of the city. However, fearing a first strike by India, the possibility of these bombs being stored at operational or satellite bases that were located west of Sargodha and from where the F-16's could easily pick them up was also very much a possibility. But the slipshod manner in which these very sensitive storage areas were being guarded was what was bugging Shiraz now. And with Pakistan now in the process of producing both short range and medium range missiles that were capable of also delivering a nuclear warhead, together with its desire to also develop the cruise missile in the near future, all these developments to Shiraz looked rather sinister and frightening. Though the United States had started providing Pakistan with helicopters, night-vision goggles and nuclear detection equipment that would help in guarding its nuclear material, warheads and laboratories, but the very fact that the region now had more violent extremists than any other country in the world, and with Pakistan's desire to have more nuclear weapons constantly on the rise, the threat from Islamic extremists like the Al Qaida seeking nuclear weapons had only become greater. Moreover, with Pakistan turning down the U.S. offer of providing PAL, the Permissive Action Link technology, a sophisticated nuclear weapon release program which kicks off its use via specific checks and balances, the chances of such weapons being triggered off by those sympathetic to the Taliban and the Al Qaida could not be ruled out either. Therefore having made a note of all these facts in his secret red diary and having managed to microfilm certain highly classified documents about Pakistan's rapid nuclear expansion program, Shiraz now waited for an opportune moment to pass these on to Shups. The very fact that during the Kargil War in 1999, when General Musharraf as the Army Chief on realizing that his clandestine military operation was heading for a complete debacle and that there was every chance of the Indian Army crossing the LOC, he had on his own initiative had activated Pakistan's nuclear might. Hence the chances of his doing so again in the future as the President and Commander-in-Chief of Pakistan was also playing on Shiraz's mind. Shiraz was also aware that the sudden volte face by the flamboyant golf loving military president of Pakistan to help the Americans in getting rid of the Taliban and the Al Qaida from Afghanistan had not been taken well at all by most of his own people. And in order to divert their attention from the ongoing war in Afghanistan, there was therefore also a possibility of Pakistan provoking India and indirectly creating a warlike situation. And with the growing nexus between the ISI and the LeT, such a strike against some strategic target by the ISI trained LeT in India could well be the answer, thought Shiraz as he kissed the lucky locket and slid the small red diary and the microfilms into the secret compartment under his leather briefcase.

On the 23rd of November 2001, when the Taliban Forces surrendered at Kunduz, the capture of John Walker Lindh, a white American fighting for the Taliban also took America by surprise. Lindh was born in Washington DC and though he was baptized, but he was not raised as a Roman Catholic by his parents. Inspired by the film 'Malcolm X' and with a troubled childhood, he had converted to Islam in 1997. In 1998, he travelled to Yemen to learn Arabic and in February 2000, the nineteen year old young American came to Pakistan to study at a madrassa. While in Pakistan he was trained by the Harkat-ul-Mujahideen and soon thereafter in May 2001 he made his way to Afghanistan to join the Al Qaida. He received his training at the Al-Faroukh training camp that was run by the Al Qaida. Located close to the Kandahar airport, it was also known as the airport training camp. Lindh was captured by General Dostum's Northern Alliance Forces on 25th November and on being initially questioned by CIA officers had said that he was Irish. But soon thereafter the makeshift prison known as the Qala-i-Jangi near Mazar-e-Sharif where Lindh and other Taliban prisoners were kept erupted with a massive uprising that resulted in the deaths of many including the CIA officer who had first interrogated Lindh. And during that fighting though Lindh was shot in the right upper thigh, he had managed to find refuge in a basement bunker with many other Taliban fighters, but was eventually captured again.The very fact that a white American citizen who had converted to Islam was captured fighting for the Taliban against the American coalition in faraway Afghanistan was a real eyeopener for Shiraz. And he now wondered whether the present trend of Muslim population explosion in the world, together with the rising militancy in their ranks, and with more and more people being converted to follow the teachings of Prophet Mohammed, the Caliphate of Islam that Bin Laden and Saeed Hafiz had been dreaming off could therefore would one day come true.

Chapter-43

'Chalo—Delhi"

On the 25th of November 2001.the day Lindh was captured, 750 American Marines from the 15th Marine Expeditionary Unit were airlifted in helicopters to create a forward base at a camp that was 100 miles south of Kandahar city. Known as Camp Rhino, it had now become the firm base for the capture of the Taliban's last and foremost stronghold in Afghanistan. With the total support of their superior fire and air power, the eastern alliance under the command of Hamid Karzai and those under Gul Agha Sherzai soon had Mullah Omar and the Taliban on the run. And on 7th December, 2001 with the Kandahar airport in their hands, it signaled the end of organized Taliban control of Afghanistan.

Late on that evening of 7th December, while Shiraz was returning home from his office he realized that all his movements were probably now being shadowed by the ISI and possibly also by the LeT. That morning when he left home and was on his way to the Pakistan Foreign Service Academy in Sector F-5/2 Islamabad to deliver a lecture to the Junior Diplomats Course, on the subject of 'Diplomatic Etiquette and Norms', he had noticed two men in a typical Pathani attire following him on a motor-cycle. And on his return from office he also noticed two more people loitering around his bungalow. Therefore in order to find if both he and the bungalow were under twenty four hours of surveillance, Shiraz decided to take his wife and daughter out for shopping and then for dinner at their favourite restaurant 'Nirvana', which was one of the best eating places in the capital and the crispy beef that they served was simply out of this world.

Before leaving the house, Shiraz also told his old faithful servant Abdul Mian to discreetly keep a vigil on the two men who were seen loitering outside the house and to let him know on his return as to what were they upto. As his silver grey BMW with Sherry at the wheel drove out of the gate and got on to the main road, Shiraz noticed that one of them who was sitting on a nearby culvert and smoking a cigarette was probably noting down the car plate number, and the other while sitting on a motorcycle was talking to somebody on what looked like a police walkie talkie to him. And ten minutes later Shiraz's gut feeling was right. As the car drove past the President's House on Constitution Avenue and got on to the Jinnah Avenue, he noticed through the left side rear view mirror that the same two persons were now following his car on the motorcycle. There was therefore now no doubts in his mind that all his movements were now been closely monitored also, but the crude and unprofessional manner in which it was being done was probably to warn him and his family to refrain from doing anything that would be considered as anti-national. Fearing that talking about it would alarm his family, he therefore kept the matter to himself.

Two days later on 9th December, which happened to be a Sunday, Shiraz after playing his eighteen holes of golf at the Rawalpindi Golf Club was in for another surprise. That afternoon as he got into his car to go home, he was surprised to find a plain white envelope stuck under the windscreen of his car. Since there was no name or address written on it, he through curiosity opened it. It was a four line anonymous letter from some fanatical militant organization that called itself the Kashmir Revolutionary Army. It was written in Urdu and it categorically stated that because of his unbecoming conduct as the country's head of mission in Russia and for his many clandestine meetings with the Indian Ambassador in Moscow, he and his family had therefore been branded as an enemy of the people. It was some kind of a threat no doubt, but he wondered how a militant organization that was relatively unknown had come to know about his activities in Moscow. Maybe it is a ploy by the ISI to uncover his real true identity now that is real name Imran Hussein and that of family tree has been established, thought Shiraz as he discreetly while sitting on the driver's seat readjusted his rear view mirror to check if he was been watched or observed by anybody.

That morning after the first nine holes by his foursome had been played and while they were enjoying their breakfast in the club house, Shiraz was surprised to overhear a somewhat casual remark by a senior Pakistani Brigadier who was now serving in the ISI headquarters at Islamabad. The Brigadier's golf foursome were also having their breakfast at the adjacent table and according to the Brigadier who had recently returned from Afghanistan, it was Lt General Mehmood the ex ISI boss who after the 9/11 disaster in America had categorically warned the Taliban and the Al Qaida to strengthen their defences and to move to safer areas in the mountains that were closer to Pakistan. General Mehmood it seems was also aware that the United States and their allies were planning to come down heavily on the Taliban and the Al Qaida in case the ultimatum that was given to Mulla Omar by the Americans was not honoured. But at the same time Pakistan's ISI boss it seems was also not keen to see the Taliban and the Al Qaida bow down to the dictates from the White House. This aspect had also been spelt out earlier and quite clearly by Brigadier Shaukat Qadir, a Piffer officer who had sought early retirement in 1998. He was a very high caliber officer who had initially wanted to become a pilot in the PAF, but had now become fairly critical in the manner in which Pakistan was being run by the Musharraf coterie and he made no bones about it either.

Retired Lt General Aslam Rehman who that morning was partnering Shiraz was also of the view that the ISI which was always controlled by the military and which had virtually become a state within the state must not be allowed to have a free run anymore, and those sitting at the ISI Headquarters behind those high walls across the Khayaban-e-Suhrawardy Avenue in Islamabad must be made more responsible and accountable. And when most of those golfers at both the breakfast tables generally agreed that the ISI which had created the Taliban and which was also responsible for the mushrooming of the many fanatical militant organizations in the country should stop fraternizing with them and it should not be used to destabalize the subcontinent further, Shiraz was in complete agreement with them. But when the Brigadier from the ISI remarked that in order to keep the militants in good humour, and in order to divert the attention of the people of Pakistan who were generally upset with General Musharraf's sudden complete 'U' turn on the Mulla Omar' Taliban government in Afghanistan, and the ISI therefore may well come up with something even more sensational soon, everybody thought he was joking. But when the Brigadier further added that it could well be 'Chalo Delhi' next, Shiraz was a bit confused. He very well knew that with the senior ISI man coming up that kind of remark like 'Chalo Delhi' it definitely could not be for holding bilateral talks between the two top intelligence agencies of India and Pakistan and he therefore wondered what the man was trying to get at. A year ago on 22nd December 2000, the LeT had carried out an attack on the Red Fort in New Delhi and Shiraz was now apprehensive that the same outfit with the help of the ISI may now carryout another such surprise attack on India's capital as was promised by Lakhvi, the LeT's Supreme Commander soon after the Kargil War.

The next couple of nights were rather sleepless ones for Shiraz as he kept thinking as to what would happen not only to him and his family, but to the good name of the entire Rehman clan of which he was now very much a part of if the exploits of Imran Hussein alias Major Shiraz Ismail Khan, alias Riaz Mohhammed Khan for passing top secret and other such classified information to India ever became known and he was caught for his spying activities. Since he knew he was under surveillance, he also toyed with the idea of whether he should seek help and guidance from the elders in the Rehman clan. But realizing that it may lead to further complications and it could also endanger their lives, he gave up the idea. But something had to be done to ensure that no harm came to his wife and children, and that too without anybody in India or Pakistan coming to know about his real Indian identity and connection. The only person who was aware of his existence and that to as a Pakistani diplomat now was his dear Shups. She knew that Major Shiraz Ismail Khan the very highly decorated Indian Army Officer and her ex husband was still very much alive and she had assured him that she would always keep that a secret. She had also told him that if ever he required any help, he could totally count on her. But the problem now was how to secretly get in touch with her, because any such move at this juncture could well be suicidal for him and his family.

On the morning of 12th December 2001, while Shiraz was seriously thinking of how to contact Shups without arousing any suspicion, massive air strikes by the American led coalition forces were pulverizing the suspected Al Qaida headquarters of Osama Bin Laden in the Tora Bora complex of caves in the mountains near the Pakistan-Afghanistan border. Earlier on 3rd December, suspecting that the Al Qaida leader and his deputy Al-Zawahiri were hidng in a complex of caves near Jalalabad, the Americans had carried out a similar air bombardment of that area, but it proved to be abhortive. And though some reports indicated that a few Al Qaida fighters and members of Al-Zawahiri's family including his wife and three children had been killed in that attack, but the rest of them had managed to escape towards Tora Bora.

Tora Bora that was known as 'Black Dust' in the local Pashtu language was an intricate complex of caves in the White Mountains called 'Safed Koh'. Located close to the border with Pakistan, it was a multi-storeyed cave complex that could besides harnessing hydroelectric power from the nearby mountain streams, it could also with its big interconnecting corriders shelter more than a thousand Al Qaida fighters. The caves that had existed for centuries had been modified earlier with the assistance of the CIA during 'Operation Cyclone', and these were thus extensively used by the Afghan Mujahideens during the Soviet invasion of Afghanistan in the 1980's. The caves also held a large cache of arms, ammunition and missiles that were left over after the Soviet withdrawal from Afghanistan. This was now the last remaining strong formidable bastion of the Al Qaida fighters and America was determined to capture dead or alive the man who had dared to wage a war against the world's most powerful nation.

On the 3rd of December 2001, a group of 20 people from the CIA N.C.S. team codenamed 'Jaw Breaker' together with 70 others from the American Special Forces had been heli-lifted and paradropped into that area. And by 5th December, they together with the Afghan Northern Allince fighters had wrested control of the low ground below Tora Bora. And as the American Air Force bombers kept relentlessly bombarding the area, the Al-Qaida fighters withdrew to higher fortified positions. Backed by air strikes and swift action from the U.S. and British Special Forces, the Northern Alliance also continued their steady advance to flush out the enemy from the many caves that they were hiding in. Fearing defeat and subsequent annihilation, the Al Qaida forces very cleverly negotiated a temporary truce with the Northern Alliance Afghan Leader. It was on the plea that they required time to muster their men and surrender their weapons. And being the Holy month of Ramzan and taking the Taliban commander's word for it, the local Northern Alliance commander fell into the trap. It was a clever ruse by the Al Qaida to gain time and as a result off which there was a lull in the fighting during that crucial period of the battle. Taking full advantage of this stalemate, a large number of them including Osama Bin Laden and other important Al Qaida leaders therefore managed to escape. And on the 12th of December, when the Americans again resumed their deadly bombing of the Tora Bora complex, it was already a bit too late. Fighting a desperate rear guard action, the Al Qaida fighters had ensured that the main force had made good their escape through the White Mountains into the tribal areas of Pakistan near Parchinar. And as a result of which the Americans lost another golden chance to kill or capture the ever elusive Bin Laden and his henchmen. Realising that Afghanistan was now in the hands of the Northern Alliance and that Mullah Omar and his Taliban would no longer be able to host him or offer him safe sanctuary, Osama Bin Laden probably realized that his next best option was to seek refuge in Pakistan. It was the very country from where he had founded his dreaded Al Qaida and Mullah Omar had founded his Taliban.

On that afternoon of 12th Decmber, while Shiraz was watching the battle for Tora Bora live on his television screen, a group of six diehard fanatical Islamic militants from Pakistan were getting ready to deliver their deadliest terrorist act against India on the following day. On the late morning of 13th December, 2001 the 'Chalo Delhi' comment that was made by the Pakistani Brigadier four days earlier at the Rawalpindi Golf Club had literally come true. It was a Thursday and the Indian Parliament was holding its winter session in the historic circular red sandstone building that was created by the architects Sir Edwin Luteyns and Sir Herbert Baker during the British Raj. Inaugurated in1927, it was also the scene of the transfer of power from Britain to India in 1947. But now 54 years later on that wintry 13th of December, 2001 morning it would be witness to a dastardly attack that would make headlines all over the world.

That morning Monty and Reeta at the invitation of their old dear journalist friend Unnikrishnan were both at the parliament house. Reeta had never witnessed a debate in parliament before and Unni with his good contacts had managed to procure two guest passes for them in the visitor's gallery. Sitting in the press gallery, Unni was also very keen to follow the debate on the POTO that was scheduled to be passed as an act on that day. At around 10.00 A.M. and as soon as the Lok Sabha Speaker Mr Balayogi took his chair in the Central Hall of Parliament where a large number of Members of Parliament were present, the pandemonium began as the opposition members kept shouting and demanding for the resignation of George Fernandes the Indian Defence Minister over the infamous coffin scandal and they raised slogans to block the POTO, the Prevention of Terrorism Ordinance from being passed as an act. The Defence Minister in the Vajpayee government had not only paid vastly inflated sums for the 500 aluminium coffins, but the U.S.based supplier had also failed to meet the Indian specifications. The coffins were not only substandard, but they were of poor quality too. George Fernandes the Defence Minister who had resigned in April following the scandalous Tehelka expose had once again returned to head the same ministry in October, and the opposition was livid on his reinduction to the cabinet. And while the blaring shouts of 'Coffin Theives' echoed across the hallowed precincts of the circular hall, and the opposition kept shouting to block the POTO, the Speaker of Lok Sabha disgusted with their unruly behavior at 10.45 hours decided to adjourn the house. Following the adjournment quite a large number of parliamentarians had left the house and had headed home, but around 150 MP's were still present inside that circular complex. And while Monty and Reeta with Unni and a few others while sitting in their respective galleries kept watching the sordid drama that was being played out by the members of the ruling party and the opposition, the six fedayeens from the LeT managed to gatecrash into the complex. And then suddenly as the honourable members of parliament were still trading charges of corruption and nepotism against one another, the rat a rat of rapid gunfire was heard outside. Because of the din in the house most of them including Monty thought that they were probably the noise of firecrackers and that some supporters from the ruling NDA government were probably celebrating for the adjournment of parliament. But the reality was something that they never could have ever thought of or even imagined. The time was 1120 in the morning and the imposing and majestic parliament building which was heavily guarded from all sides was under attack by the six Fedayeens.

Ironically while the ruling party and the opposition were having it out as a free for all inside the well of the house on these two very contentious issues, a suicide squad of six hardcore fanatical Islamic militants dressed in military style fatigues and armed with deadly automatic weapons, grenades and explosives were on their way to storm the historic building and create mayhem. At 1120, when the six armed terrorists in a white ambassador car and like the one that are normally used by ministers and M.P.'s with the red beacon light and with the Home Ministry and Parliament label stickers stuck on it entered at a fairly high speed through one of the many guarded VIP gates of the parliament house, the alarm was sounded. On hearing the alarm, the fedayeen driver of the car it seemed panicked and lost control of his vehicle. And as it came to a screeching halt it rammed into the car of the Indian Vice President Mr Krishna Kant who luckily was still inside the building. Meanwhile the second tier security inside the complex was also alerted and as a result of which all gates and entrances to the building were closed. Then the firefight began. And as the terrorists quickly got out of the vehicle and started firing their weapons and lobbying grenades at random, the security personnel crouching behind anything and everything that could give them some cover and protection started firing back at them. And while the gun battle kept raging for about an hour, the dramatic stand off was being broadcast live on television. It seemed that the six member fidayeen squad had come determined to wreck the historic building and take as many lives as possible, but luck was not on their side. One of the terrorists whose body was strapped with explosives was luckily felled before he could enter the building and the massive explosion simply had ripped apart his entire body. The 13th of December thus proved unlucky for all the six Fidayeens since they were unable to complete the task that they had been assigned to carry out. But nonetheless it was a wake up call for

India and for the Vajpayee government. Like Kargil the brazen surprise attack on the Indian Parliament was a massive intelligence failure and which clearly brought to focus the need for better vigilance and for better coordination between the country's various intelligence agenies. And as Shupriya sitting in her office in South Block watched the stand off live on the television screen that was in her office, she prayed for the safety of those who were still inside the building and the armed Indian police force who had taken up the challenge to eliminate the six terrorists.

That morning the pandemonium in the parliament that was created by the opposition on the coffin scandal and the POTO turned out to be a blessing in disguise. And had the honourable speaker delayed his decision to adjourn the house by even half an hour that day, it may have also led to the deaths of many political leaders, including Mr Vajpayee the Prime Minister of India and Sonia Gandhi the leader of the opposition. It seems that as soon as parliament was adjourned both of them had left the premises, or else they too would have fallen prey to the bullets of the ISI trained terrorists from the Lashkar-e-Toiba and the Jaish-e-Mohammed. Though six Indian policeman and one gardner had lost their lives and all the Fedayeens were shot dead, and a fairly large number were injured in the crossfire, it was an eye opener and a warning to the Indian leaders and to the Indian public that the country's intelligence network was indeed very poor. There was no doubt whatsoever that there was a clear nexus between the fedayeens and their collaborators in India, or else how could they have planned and executed such a daring daylight operation in the very heart of India's capital and that to on a prime strategic target and which the attackers very well knew was very well guarded and protected, thought Monty as he with Reeta and Unni left the premises once the all clear signal was given.

Peevee who had also watched the dramatic face off live on television however was a bit skeptical. He wished that some of those politicians who were basically corrupt and incompetent should have also bought it that day. And moreover since no politician was killed or wounded, he wondered whether the threat given by the Indian Prime Minister in his televised broadcast to the nation that evening of waging a do a die war against terrorism would ever be taken to its logical end. Because that he felt could only be achieved if all the terrorist camps that were inside Pakistan and inside Pakistan Occupied Kashmir were completely demolished and their colloborators in India very severely punished.

That morning as the entire world watched the face off between the Indian security forces and the Fedayeens outside the very portals of the

Indian parliament building, Shiraz was more than convinced that it was only the beginning of another likely confrontation between the two nations. And since both the countries were now armed with deadly nuclear weapons, he knew it would be really disastrous if both the countries went to war again.

Chapter-44

It's Now or Never

That day when the Indian Prime Minister's warning that it was not just an attack on the building, but it was also an attack on India, and that India was ready to take up the challenge was flashed on the television screen, General Musharraf the President of Pakistan immediately put the Pakistan armed forces on high alert. Though Pakistan had condemned the attack on the Indian Parliament, Shiraz knew very well that it was only a diplomatic ploy by Pakistan to please the Americans who were now deeply involved with them in the war against terror in neighbouring Afghanistan.The Indian cabinet immediately after the attack had held an emergency meeting. Besides ordering a complete review of the security arrangements in parliament, the Prime Minister had also sounded the three Indian service chiefs of the Indian army, navy and the airforce to get ready for a likely showdown with Pakistan. Mr Vajpayee had categorically stated that India had accepted the challenge and there was a limit to her patience. And that evening, when the coffins of the Indian martyrs who died fighting the Pakistani terrorists outstde the parliament house draped in the Indian tricolour were given a ceremonial farewell to the heart rendering sound of the bugles playing the taps, there were tears in Shupriya's eyes.

A week later on 20th December, 2001 when the mobilization order to the Indian armed forces was issued and Pakistan too moved its troops to their battle locations in Jammu-Kashmir, Punjab and Sind, it looked as if the fourth round between India and Pakistan was imminent. And as far as the world was concerned, the advent of the new millennium had also signaled the dawn of a new era of unprecedented terror, death and destruction. Thus as the first year of the new millennium came to a close, and both India and Pakistan now armed with deadly nuclear weapons were getting ready to destroy each other, and the Americans and her allies in Afghanistan were desperately trying to get Osama Bin Laden, it was more than evident that the war on terror had only just begun. But to both Shiraz and Shupriya it was imperative that under no circumstances should India and Pakistan be allowed to once again go for each others throat militarily.

Consequent to the warning by the Indian Prime Minister, Pakistan had moved its Hatf-1 and Hatf-2 to their battle locations in the west, while India too it was reported had deployed the Prithvi missiles to the northern Punjab region and which was within range of Islamabad, Rawalpindi and Kahuta. With both the countries now having ordered total mobilization of all its forces and with dark war clouds gathering over the horizon, Shiraz was desperate to find out whether the trigger happy Supremo of Pakistan, General Musharraf would use the nuclear option against India incase Pakistan was attacked. The very fact that the Taliban in Afghanistan was now on the run and the once friendly Afghans in that country could no longer provide Pakistan with the much required strategic depth was also now playing on the Pakistan President's mind. Moreover, with America joining hands with the warlorlds from the Afghan Northern Alliance to oust the Al Qaida and the Taliban from Afghanistan, and a large number of fanatical Pakistani Mulla leaders from the many Islamist militant organizations that the ISI had spawned over the years openly criticizing the General's sudden U-turn on Afghanistan, the possibility of the ambitious General Musharraf using the nuclear option as a last resort therefore could not be altogether ruled out. And while Shiraz debated all these thoughts and options in his mind, there was a telephone call from Fazal Rehman Khan. The Bangladesh Ambassador to Thailand was speaking from Dhaka to convey the good news that their only daughter Samira's wedding had atlast been finalized.

'Well though it is a love marriage, but nonetheless it would be held in the traditional Bangladeshi style in Dhaka. And since all the ceremonies and the traditional 'Nikka' will be held at our house in Dhanmondi on the 15th of January, you with your entire family will have to come and bless the couple. And once the learned Mulla pronounces them as man and wife, all close family members from both the bride's and the bridegrooms side will fly to Bangkok on the next day for the joint reception that will be held at the luxurious Riverside Peninsula Bangkok Hotel on 17th January. And on the 18th of January morning after the couple depart for their honeymoon to New Zealand, the entire Rehman clan wil move to the Karma Samui luxury resort at Koh Samui for a 3 nights and four day delightful seaside holiday,' said an excited Fazal Rehman.

Realising that this could give him an ideal opportunity to contact Shupriya and ask for her help if need be, Shiraz spontaneously accepted the invitation. 'Don't worry we will all be there in full strength to grace the solemn occasion and I will make sure that the entire Rehman clan reaches Dhaka on the 12th of January as proposed by you. And since the bridegroom is serving as the Second Secretary in the Pakistan Embassy in Bangkok and his father who is currently our High Commissioner in Nepal and whom I also personally know fairly well, we must also invite him and his wife to Koh Samui. Both are excellent bridge players and we could make a good foursome,' said Shiraz to Fazal as he also loudly conveyed the good news to his wife Saira.

On the very next day and giving the excuse that their dear neice was soon to get married in Dhaka and that the groom was a career diplomat from the Pakistan Foreign Service, both Shiraz and Salim Rehman requested for a fortnight's leave from the 12th of January. Though initially due to the rising tension between Pakistan and India, there was some hesitation by the Pakistan Foreign Office to grant them leave, but on the personal request and recommendation of Arif Rehman and that of the Pakistani High Commissioner to Nepal, the Pakistani Foreign Minister finally gave the green signal to both of them on Christmas Eve. On that very evening of Christmas Eve, when Shiraz rang up his son Tojo in San Francisco to tell him that he too must also plan and reach Dhaka on the 12th of January for Samira's wedding, he was shocked to learn that Tojo was on the same flight that Richard Reid the shoe bomber had planned to blow up on the 22nd of December over the Atlantic Ocean. Richard Colvin Reid, the 28 year old British citizen of mixed descent who had converted to Islam was a member of the Al Qaida. He had been trained at an Al Qaida camp in Afghanistan and had been motivated to become a suicide bomber. On the 22nd of December, Reid had boarded the American Airlines Flight 63 from Paris to Miami wearing his special high ankle shoes that were packed with plastic explosives in its hollowed bottoms. During the flight and shortly after the meal service was over and on complaints by some passengers that there was smoke smell in the cabin, the cabin crew started looking for the source. When one of the passengers pointed to Reid who was sitting alone near a window, Hermis Moutardier the alert lady flight attendant approached Reid and cautioned him against smoking. Thereafter on noticing that that there was a big shoe on Reid's lap and that Reid was desperately trying to light a fuze that was sticking out from the shoe and which led to the bottom of the shoe, she tried to grab it, but the burly 6 foot four inch man of mixed British and Jamaican blood simply pushed her down to the floor. Hermis then yelled for help. Another flight attendant Christina Jones who tried to subdue Reid was also bitten on the thumb. Thereafter the passengers came to their rescue. They overpowered Reid and bound him up. The aircraft was then immediately diverted to the Logan International Airport in Boston. The passengers and the crew were indeed very lucky because had Reid succeeded in lighting the fuze then nobody would have remained alive to tell the tale. Reid had in fact planned to catch a Miami bound flight a day earlier from the same airport, but his boarding on that flight got delayed when the airport security seeing his disheveled appearance and with no check in luggage tag on his ticket, started questioning him. Not being able to answer some specific questions, Reid was then sent for additional screening by the French National Police. And as a result of that crucial delay, the fuze inside the shoe because of the rainy weather and accumulated foot perspiration had become too damp to get ignited instantaneously. Tojo who had gone to Paris to participate in a golf tournament and who was also one of the many passengers who came to the aid of the crew had now decided that it would be probably much safer to fly by one of the Gulf airways or any other Asian or Middle East airline rather than an Amrican one. Therefore on the advice of his father, he on the very next day booked his flight for the 11th of January from San Francisco to Dhaka by the Cathay Pacific Airways. Surprisingly the 22nd of December was also the day when the Americans appointed Hamid Karzai as the Acting President of Afghanistan.

Karzai was born on 24th December, 1957 in the Karz area of Kandahar City. An ethnic Pashtun he had done his post graduation in political science from the Himachal Pradesh University in Simla which was once the summer capital of the British Raj. In 1983, after his post graduation he went to Pakistan to work as a fund raiser for the Mujahideens who were fighting the Soviets in Afghanistan and he soon became a reliable secret contact for the CIA. And while Karzai remained in Pakistan, his siblings immigrated to the United States. In 1992, when Najibullah's Soviet-backed government collapsed and Afghan political parties as per the Peshawar Acccord established the Islamic State of Afghanistan, Karzai accompanied the Mujahideen leaders into Kabul. Thereafter he also served as the Deputy Foreign Minister in Burhanuddin Rabbani's government. But when he tried to broker peace between Gulbuddin Hekmatyar and Ahmad Shah Massoud, he was jailed and beaten up by the Northern Alliance. He then fled from Kabul to Pakistan in a vehicle that was provided by Hekmatyar. On 14th July, 1999 Karzai's father who was an eminent politician and who supported the return of King Zahir Shah to Afghanistan was allegedly gunned down by the Taliban as he came out of a mosque in the city of Quetta. Thereafter Hamid Karzai travelled to Europe and the United States to gather support for the anti-Taliban movement. Though he was now on the hot seat, Karzai had always considered the late Ahmad Shah Massoud to be a very patriotic Afghan. And he now felt that a man like Masooud should have been there to hold his hand and to guide Afghanistan to a brighter and better future.

And while the appointment of Karzai was being discussed in the corridors of power in Islamabad and Delhi, Fazal Rehman with his wife Samina were busy making all the necessary arrangements for their daughter Samira's wedding. At the same time the armed forces of both India and Pakistan were also getting ready to take each other on. During the next two weeks, while both the Pakistani and the Indian troops came in eyeball to eyeball contact with each other and they geared up for the fourth round, Shiraz kept his fingers crossed. Besides being discreetly shadowed by the ISI he and his famiy were also now being threatened both by the LeT and the JeM. Both these militant organizations thanks to their close contacts with the ISI it seems on been sounded about the peace initiative that Shiraz with his Indian counterpart in Moscow had initiated, and they having been told about his daughter's affair with the Indian matinee idol who was a shaven off Sikh were now also planning to get rid of him and his family. Both these factors had angered the militants and the ISI. And though the so called track 3 channel was a complete non starter, and the affair between his daughter and Deepak Kumar was also over, but nonetheless it had brought Shiraz and his family under the radar of the ISI, the LeT and the JeM. Therefore being fully aware that his own life and that of his family was now in real danger, Shiraz decided that the time had now come for him to take the final plunge. The place and the timing of Samira's wedding had come as a blessing in disguise and he had to now take that crucial decision of whether he should defect alone or with his family to India and if so when. Should it be after the wedding of Samira at Dhaka, or after the reception at Bangkok, or during the holiday at Koh Samui.! For him it was therefore now a question of now or never, and he would now have to decide once and for all about his own and his family's survival. Moreover, time too was also at a premium for him.

Meanwhile with the frenzied and heavy build up troops, weapons, and tanks on the borders and on the LOC by both the sides, together with the deployment of long range heavy artillery and ballistic missiles by both the armies in areas close to the international border, it seemed that the time to start the fourth and final round between Pakistan and India had arrived. But what both Shiraz and Shupriya were really worried about was that the armed conflict should not escalate into nuclear showdown between the two countries. Fearing a severe backlash from India, Pakistani troops who till now with the Americans and other coalition forces were fighting the Taliban and the Al Qaida forces on the Pak-Afghanistan border had now also been moved post haste to the Indo-Pak border. And with India mobilizing its three strong armoured divisions and 500,000 troops on the border and Pakistan responding with its armoured divisions and 300,000 soldiers to take on the Indans, it was now a question of who would pull the trigger first. This was undoubtedly the largest mobilization and build up by both the sides since the 1971 war, and the chances of the conflict escalating into a nuclear holocaust therefore was very much a possibility. Though in retaliation to the attack on the Indian Parliament, an immediate and quick surgical strike against the militant camps inside Pakistan occupied Kashmir by the Indian army and the airforce could have been a valid and justifiable military action, but it was not carried out because the political leaders from the ruling NDA government simply could not make up their minds and give the much needed green signal to the men in military uniform. With the delay in decision making by the NDA government, the strategy of 'Cold Start 'that was being talked about as India's new military doctrine had therefore also lost it relevance in the present context. It should have been executed across the LOC, the line of control in Jammu and Kashmir atleast immediately after the Indian parliament was attacked, thought Shiraz as he made a list of the people who were to be invited to his house for the New Year's Eve party on 31st December. Besides the entire Rehman clan, the party list also included a few of his very close friends and colleagues who had served with him in various missions abroad. And included in that list were also a few senior army, naval and air force officers who had served as senior Defence attaches under him in Paris and Moscow. Amongst them was a Major General and an Air Vice Marshall who were now servng in key appointments in Pakistan's newly created SPD, the Strategic Plan Division. Known previously as the Combat Development Directorate of the Pakistan GHQ, the SPD was established only in February 2000, and Pakistan's nuclear arsenal was put under its control. Besides acting as the secretariat for the NCA, the National Command Authority of Pakistan, it also had an elaborate Security Division which included a counter intelligence network to safe guard the activities of this organization, as also a multi-layered security apparatus to protect its strategic nuclear assets.

Soon after the debacle in Kargil and consistent with the obligations as a nuclear weapons state, Pakistan in February 2000 had formally instituted an elaborate Nuclear Command and Control mechanism that comprised of the NAC, the SPD and the SPC, the Strategic Forces Command.Though in normal peace time the nuclear weapons were kept in a disassembled state, but with the armed forces of both the nations now waiting for the balloon to go up, Shiraz was desperate to find out if Pakistan was geared up and ready to launch a nuclear first or second strike if need be against India. On that New Year's Eve and soon after midnight, when Shiraz opened the champagne bottles and everyone with that bubbly drink in their hands clinked glasses and wished each other a very Happy New Year, Shiraz as the host then very cleverly raised a toast to the armed forces of Pakistan.

'Ladies and Gentlemen, tonight on this New Year's Day let us hope and pray that after the humiliation we faced 30 years ago in Bangladesh, our valiant and gallant armed forces who are bravely standing by to face India's challenge will give them the bloody nose that they so richly deserve. And to quote Winston Churchill's own words, we shall therefore fight on the beaches, we shall fight on the hills, we shall fight on the streets, but we will not give up. Therefore let us drink to the health, happiness and victory to those Pakistani officers and soldiers who as the true sentinels of our great nation are braving it out right now in their trenches posts and picquets,' said Shiraz as he raised his glass and ended his toast with a loud Pakistan Paindabad. And while everybody applauded his thoughtful gesture, Shiraz very diplomatically asked the Major General from the SPD if Pakistan nuclear arsenal was safe from attacks by the Indian Airforce.

'Oh don't you worry Sir because it will be Pakistan who will set the nuclear ball rolling first if India dares to attack us. And to tell you the truth our long and short range ballistic missiles with their nuclear warheads are already in a state of absolute readiness and let not India fool herself that we will not use them. Because this time if the balloon does go up again it will be a fight to the finish,' said the Major General very proudly. And when the Air Vice Marshall from the PAF also echoed the same views, Shiraz was more than convinced that the fourth round would definitely lead to a dreadful holocaust unless both sides saw reason. Though the United States was trying to adjudicate and diffuse the on going crisis, but both India and Pakistan with their arsenal of long range ballistic missiles and big stockpile of nuclear weapons it seemed were hell bent in destroying each other. With the Americans and their allies including the Northern Alliance now also hell bent in ousting the Taliban and the Al Qaida from Afghanistan, a large number of them it seems had now perforce taken refuge in the mountains of Baluchistan and the Northwest Frontier Province of Pakistan, and this had further added to General Musharraf's woes. Some unconfirmed reports also indicated that quite a large number of Al Qaida fighters some days ago were seen boarding a passenger ship at Karachi. Though most of them were from Arab countries, but there were also quite a few from Bangladesh and though the ship had sailed from Karachi, but no one knew its final destination. One source however indicated that the ship was probably bound for Chittagong in Bangladesh. And if that be the case then the possibility of these very people on Bangladesh soil could spell more trouble for India thought Shiraz as he microfilmed a few more top secret letters that the Pakistan GHQ had initiated on this very subject to the Strategic Force Command. And though Shiraz knew that Pakistan was now well on the defensive as far as India was concerned, but the use of the nuclear option that was now in the hands of Pakistan's military President and who had earlier too during the fag end of the Kargil conflict as the army chief had nearly exercised that crucial decision was indeed rather frightening for him. And at the same time Shiraz also knew that he was playing a dangerous game of spying for India and the consequences in case he was caught would be simply dreadful not only for him but for his family also.

Late that night after all the guests had left, the entire Rehman clan got into a huddle. While the women folk kept discussing what items of jewellery would go with their dresses at Samira's wedding, the men folk were busy in debating what would be Pakistan's best military option to once again rake up the Kashmir issue at this moment of time when things were really hotting up.

'Well to my mind the best option would be to launch a limited offensive with the aim to capture a strategic objective across the LOC and one that would if need be give the army subsequent access routes both to the valley and to the passes on the Pir Panjal range in Indian occupied Kashmir. In other words the force level together with plans to have it reinforced subsequently must be allotted dedicated air, artillery and missile support and it must be capable of isolating the valley completely for a limited period of time. Needless to say that the objective chosen to be captured and occupied should not be too deep inside enemy territory either and it should be within the range of Pakistan's long range artillery guns and short range ballistic misslies that are deployed for operations in Jammu and Kashmir. Moreover after capturing the objective our holding formations deployed on the LOC should also be able to provide the necessary logistic support when needed to sustain this attacking force. Simultaneously, the capture of such an objective should also give Pakistan the bargaining power to maintain the pressure on India once the ceasefire is declared,' said Salim Rehman.

'Yes that could be a viable and workable option provided we are able to achieve surprise and sustain the attacking force atleast for a fortnight if not more. But looking at the prevailing severe wintry weather conditions in the valley and on the Pir Panjal Mountain range that I am afraid may not be possible as of now. However, we could once again think of going in for the capture of Akhnur and Rajauri with a major offensive while using armour and infantry in much greater strength than heretofore and with a preponderance of dedicated arillery, air and short range ballistic missile support during the entire opertaion. And if the plan does succeed then we would have achieved in isolating a major part of India's 16 Corps and whose units and formations are tactically deployed in these sectors', said retired Lt General Aslam Rehman.

While retired Lt General Aslam Rehman felt that because of severe winter conditions in the high mountains and in the main Kashmir valley the best option would be to go in for a two pronged sustained attack on Akhnur and Rajauri with armour and infantry, his son Major Samir Rehman felt somewhat differently. Samir Rehman had recently returned after successfully completing the ardous and tough Rangers Course from the US Army Army Ranger School at Fort Benning and was currently posted as a Company Commander in one of the elite SSG Battalions of the Pakistan army that was deployed for operations in the Kashmir valley. Known as the maroon berets and Black Storks, this battalion had been equipped and trained for special operations including operations behind the enemy lines. Having also undergone extensive training in winter warfare in the difficult and ardous Siachen Sector, Major Samir Rehman was of the view that a self contained Brigade Group spearheaded by his SSG Battalion could be the answer to Salim Rehman's suggestion.

'I feel that if we can under today's wintry conditions on a moonlit night take a calculated risk and surprise the enemy by heli-lifting the entire SSG Battalion of which I am now very much a part in the first phase of the operation to the area of Tosha Maidan, the big sprawling meadow on the Pir Panjal and which is only a few kilometers away from Gulmarg as the crow flies, and if we are able to establish a firm base there by midnight D-Day then half the battle will be one. Subsequently and by first light next morning that is D plus 1, the newly raised Special Forces Brigade should be para dropped into that vital area that has already been secured by us. Thereafter by launching a strong attack from the rear with our Special Forces Brigade we should capture Gulmarg by first light D plus 2. And since the entire operation can be easily supported by our own troops and artillery that are deployed on our side of the the LOC, it will be all the easier and we would have achieved our aim of capturing a strategic objective. Thereafter with additional build up of troops from the Divisional and Corps reserves from across the LOC and into the Gulmarg sector, we could also pose a direct threat to the valley. Needless to say that such an operation cannot be done in total isolation and our holding formations that are deployed all along the LOC in Jammu and Kashmir must also therefore carry out limited offensive and diversionary operations against our adversaries all along the LOC and more so in the Poonch, Uri, Leepa, Tangdhar and the Kupwara sectors. The first 48 hours therefore will be very crucial and our aim should be to not only to keep the enemy guessing about where our main thrust will be finally delivered, but it should also ensure that the enemy's Divisional and Corps reserves do not react to our limited offensive operations in the Gulmarg sector during those crucial 48 hours,' added Major Samir Rehman very confidently as his father the retired Lt General Aslam Rehman looked at him with awe and congratulated him for his well thought out plan.

'I must say that it is definitely a well thought out and workable plan and needless to say that we today also have the necessary wherewithal to execute it. However, we have to also be careful because the enemy too in retaliation and as a tit for tat may also carry out such an operation against us in the Tithwal, Gurez and Kargil sectors to cut off our lines of communication that runs perilously close to the LOC and along the picturesque Neelum Valley to Gilgit via Chilas,'said Lt General Aslam Rehman while narrating to them as to how because of bad planning, inadequate intelligence and false bravado, the SSG operations against Indian airforce bases during the 1965 war became an unmitigated disaster.

That night after the grand party finally ended during the wee hours of the morning, Shiraz too kept thinking about Major Samir Rehman's daring plan. It was no doubt an ambitious one, but one that was worth considering no doubt. Later on that New Year's Day, which happened to be a Tuesday and a working day at that, Shiraz while driving to his office made a very serious New Year resolution to himself. He had decided that come what may, he for the sake of his family would defect to India, but that would be only after Samira's wedding at Dhaka and the reception at Bangkok. And it would be executed in a novel manner while holidaying with the rest of the Rehman family at Koh Samui. There at the seaside resort he would fake his own death by drowning. And thereafter with help from Shups, he would secretly resurface in New Delhi to give whatever classified information he had gathered on Pakistan's nuclear deployment and intentions. Since both the nations were now armed with deadly nuclear weapons, his only aim it seems was to somehow ensure that under no circumstances should both the countries go to war. He was however fully convinced that driven to a tight corner there was every possibility of General Musharraf unleashing Pakistan's nuclear arsenal on India. And according to one reliable source Pakistan was now in possession of atleast 40 to 50 nuclear bombs or warheads and if not more.

Soon after the September 11 attack on the United States and fearing that the US may conduct military strikes against Pakistan's nuclear assets if Islamabad did not tow the American line to get rid of the Taliban and the Al Qaida, General Musharraf had at that time redeployed Pakistan's nuclear arsenal to various different secret locations. But thereafter, when the Pakistani President did a complete U-turn on the Taliban and decided to join the Americans in "Operation Enduring Freedom', the nuclear warheads and bombs were back to where they were suppose to be. But after the recent attack on the Indian Parliament and with India threatening to teach Pakistan a bloody lesson, General Musharraf it seems was left with no other solution but to sound the alarm and adopt the first strike option if need be. Though both India and Pakistan on that New Year's day had exchanged lists of their respective nuclear facilities which was in accordance with the agreement that no side would attack each other's nuclear installations and facilities, but that was all on paper and there was no guarantee. On the 29th of December it was reported by the Hindu newspaper that the Indian army was preparing to launch a large scale military exercise to test it's readiness against a nuclear attack by Pakistan. And a day earlier prior to that, India had banned all overflight facilities to Pakistan and the strength of their respective High Commissions in New Dlehi and Islamabad had also been reduced by fifty percent. On New Year's Eve, the United States intelligence is reported to have also predicted that the war may well begin in the next few days. These were all not only ominous signs, but clear battle indications that another round was in the offing and which would have disastrous effects on both the countries.

Shiraz had however also decided that his defection to India would also have certain conditions attached to it. Like the spy who came in from the cold, his first condition would be that as a high profile defector and on completion of his debefriefing and interrogation by the Indian authorites, he should be given a brand new identity together with a passport and he should be allowed to leave the country. His second condition to Shups would be that under no circumstances whatsoever should India come to know about his true and real identity. To him Major Shiraz Ismail Khan, P.V.C. Riaz Mohammed Khan from the P.F.S. and Imran Hussein were all dead and gone. And his third condition would be that his wife Saira and family should be protected and well compensated if need be.

With only three more weeks available to put all his plans into action and to make his death by drowning look like an accident or a freak mishap, Shiraz now desperately needed Shups help. And with the limited time available at his disposal he had not only to gather more authentic classified information about Pakistan's nuclear deployment, but also on Pakistan's final game plan incase India went on the offensive. Realising that putting it all in his little red diary and then carrying it with the micro films in the secret compartment of his brief case to Dhaka would be rather dangerous, he therefore during the next few days got busy transferring all the classified information and data from his little red secret diary and from the micro films into a compact disk. But before doing that he first recorded into the CD a few popular songs and Qwalis that were sung by his favourite Pakistani singer the late Nusrat Fateh Ali Khan, and it included the one that had the words 'Saya Bhi Saath Jub Chod Jaye'-Aaisi Hai Tanhai-Rohna Bhi Chahun Toh Ansoo Bhi Na aye' (When even your shadow leaves you-such great is the suffering that even if you want to cry, tears won't come to you). That song was sung by the great Pakistani singer in the 1998 Sunny Deol-Urmila Matondkar film 'Dillagi' and it was one of his favourites.The lyrics of that song was no doubt very apt and Shiraz wondered how his wife and children would take the shock of his sudden disappearance from this world. There was no doubt that he loved them very much. His only aim to record those few songs right at the beginning of that very unobtrusive looking compact disc that contained those highly classified and explosive information about Pakistan was primarily to ensure that it would pass scrutiny at the immigration and custom posts that he would have to go through at various airports.

Thinking about how best his disappearance act could be done and without arousing any suspicion whatsoever, Shiraz was reminded about 'Operation Mincemeat.' It was a top secret military operation and a very clever master deception plan that was executed by the British intelligence sleuths from MI-5 to fool Hitler and his Nazi Generals during the Second World War. And as a result of which the German High Command was convinced that the planned allied landings in Southern Europe in 1944 would take place in Greece and Sardinia instead of the intented island of Sicily. Made into a classic war movie in the mid fifties with the title 'The

Man Who Never Was 'it was a true story of how one dead body of a fictitous British officer by the name of Major Martin that was secretly transported in a submarine from England to the Spanish coast at Huelva and which subsequently altered the course of war in Europe.

The holiday at the Karma resort at Koh Samui was scheduled to begin on the 18th of January 2002 afternoon and it was scheduled to end on the 21st morning. Thereafter they were to fly back from there via Bangkok to Islamabad. Therefore based on that, Shiraz decided that he would perhaps have to do his disappearing act late on the evening of the 20th by going for a swim in the sea. However in order to ensure that his wife would be eligible for pension he had to also make sure that his death by drowning was purely accidental. But that could only be done if there was an eye witness to it. He was no doubt a good swimmer who could swim for hours together and he therefore needed help from Shups to have him picked up from the high seas and later have him secretly whisked away to some unknown destination for a quick facial surgery including a face lift and rhinioplasty before finally touching down at Delhi with his new identity. Therefore the immediate need of the hour for him was to somehow get in touch with Shups as quickly as possible and to discreetly inform her about the plan and also to get a feedback from her at the earliest on its feasability.

With PIA flights over India once again banned, the only way to get to Dhaka from Islamabad was now through Colombo and the possibility of his getting in direct touch with Shups was therefore either during the few hours stopover at Colombo airport or soon after reaching Dhaka. But with so many family members flying together and congregating in Dhaka it would not be safe either reckoned Shiraz. Therefore the one and only choice for him was to get in touch with Shups on the telephone from Colombo airport and immediately follow it up with a detailed letter to her from there He would write the letter with his plan during the long flight and together with the CD post it from Colombo's International airport by registered post addressed to Miss Simran Bajwa care off Monty's Defence Colony address. For easy and immediate identification he would highlight the figure 00 on the reverse of the envelope and sign the letter as Dablo. And as far as that particular CD was concerned it would be be part of his CD music library which he always carried with his laptop.

In order to ensure that no other Rehman family member except his wife and daughter would be on the same flight to Dhaka via Colombo, Shiraz therefore decided to leave twenty four hours earlier than the rest of the clan. On the excuse that since all PIA flights to Dhaka will have to perforce now be via Colombo, and since he and his family had never been to that emerald island, he with his family would therefore take a twenty four stop over and go on a sight seeing tour of the Sri Lankan capital. And on the next day they would join the rest of the Rehman family at Colombo airport and be with them on the same flight to Dhaka.

On the 11th of January morning, Shiraz with his family boarded the PIA flight to Colombo via Karachi and by lunch time arrived at the Sri Lankan capital. Giving the excuse that he urgently needed to go to the toilet and have the hotel booking confirmed and also order a cab to take them to the hotel, he told Saira and Sherry to collect the checked in luggage from the conveyor belt and to wait for him outside the arrival lounge. No sooner they were out of sight, Shiraz quickly made his way to the airport post office. And having sent the letter and the CD by registered post to Shups, Shiraz from an airport public booth immediately called her up on her mobile. And as soon as she came on the line he simply said.

'Dablo needs your help immediately. I am speaking from Colombo airport and I with my family are on our way to Dhaka and Bangkok for a family wedding. The details for the kind of help required by me are given in the letter that I have just posted to you from here. Enclosed with the letter is a CD that may prove to be useful to diffuse the present volatile situation on our borders. I will contact you again once you have gone through the letter and the CD. Needless to say that it is time for me to be reborn again and that too with a brand new identity and only you can help me out. I won't say anything more right now but do wait for my call which I will make to you after reaching Bangkok. And hopefully by that time you will also be ready with your action plan. From 12th to the 16th I will be in Dhaka and from 17th to 21st January in Thailand. The D-Day selected by me is the 20th of January. The place for your people to launch 'Operation Dablo' will be the Lamai Beach on the island of Koh Samui. The beach is on the east coast of a popular tourist resort in the Gulf of Thailand and the time to pick me up by your men in a fast speed boat from the high seas will be approximately ten minutes after sunset Thailand Standard Time on the 20th January. And my approx location would be a kilometer from the centre of that beach. For easy and quick identification and recognition I will flash a scuba diver's light three times at regular short intervals. All this at the moment is however still tentative and I will get back to you with more details later. Saira, my daughter Sherry and I are presently in Colombo for a day and I will try and contact you again soon. Tomorrow afternoon we will be leaving for Dhaka. While in Dhaka I will buy another new mobile phone and again try and get in touch with you. In the meantime please SMS to me your land line numbers both of your office and residence. Right now I am speaking to you from a public booth at the airport. My mobile number is 0305377080 but don't ever call me up on this number. Goodbye for now.'

Hearing his voice, Shups was indeed very thrilled and all that she could say to her Dablo in reply was 'Thank you for the call and do take good care of yourself.'

That afternoon after they had checked in at the luxurious Hilton Colombo Hotel, Shiraz felt that a big load was finally off his chest. He had at last managed to send all those highly classified information to Shups and with the hope that India would not escalate the present crisis by going to war with Pakistan. Later that evening Shiraz took his wife and daughter out sightseeing. Having been a colony first under the Portuguese, then the Dutch and finally the British, the port city of Colombo was proud of its many well maintained beautiful old churches and colonial architecture. Besides the many colonial type structures like the historical Cargill and Millars building, they also visited the Jami ul Alfar Mosque, and the neoclassical style Colombo Musuem. Later in the evening they had an early dinner of real good delicious authentic Chinese food at the 'Emperor's Wok', the Chinese restaurant of the hotel. After the hearty meal and giving the excuse that he needed to go for a little walk, Shiraz took the walkway that linked the hotel to the World Trade Centre. Shups had already messaged to her the required landline numbers and he needed to talk to her again from a public booth. The idea was to apprise Shups in a little more detail about 'Operation Dablo' so that she could get a little more lead time to plan and set the ball rolling. Luckily he found a public booth near the World Trade Centre and got her on her residence land line number. And speaking to her only in Hindi and Urdu so that the people around may not understand, Shiraz explaned to her in a little more detail about his bizarre plan to fake his own death by drowning.

The next day afternoon Shiraz with his wife and daughter and the entire Rehman clan were on board the PIA flight to Dhaka from Islamabad via Colombo. The only one missing from the group was Major Samir Rehman Khan. Because of the warlike situation on the border he had not been granted any leave and since his wife was eight months pregnant she on her doctor's advice could not make the trip either.

On that very morning of 12th January, the President of Pakistan, General Pervez Musharraf in a hard hitting speech to his people that was televised live by all international media channels had given them a long sermon. And while a day earlier on 11th January 2002, General Padmanabhan, the Indian Army Chief who was popularly known to his friends as Paddy had also officially certified to the Indian government that mobilization of his troops on the Pakistan border had been completed and he was now waiting for the green signal to be given to him by the government.

In his speech, Musharraf not only admitted that fanning terrorisn was against Pakistan's interest, but he also slammed the Mullas hard and proper as he vowed to finish religiously the kind of extremism that had engulfed the country. He also condemned the attack on America and on the Indian Parliament and he even announced the ban on the LeT and the JeM, the two terrorist outfits that was responsible for the attack on the Indian Parliament. But he refused to hand over the 20 hardcore Indian terrorists that were wanted by India.Musharraf also admitted that the use of force would not resolve the Kashmir problem, and he also invited the Indian Prime Minister for talks. But at the same time and in the same breath, he also said that moral and diplomatic support to the freedom struggle in Kashmir would continue. He also emphasized that Jihad should be directed against the widespread poverty and illiteracy in the country and not against non Muslims and neighbouring countries. He also asked all Pakistanis not to burst their arteries for other Muslims around the world. Having admitted that Pakistan's image had been badly tarnished because of the rise in militancy and fundamentalism in the country, he directed and passed a decree that said very categorically that all madrassas in Pakistan must be registered by end March 2002, and all foreign students seeking admission in madrassas in Pakistan would have to compulsorily first seek permission from the government. Delivered in Urdu with a generous leavening of English, the General's hour long address to the nation was no doubt impressive. According to the General the lawlessness that had spread under the garb of righteous religiosity in Pakistan had to end, and the writ of the state had to be respected at all cost.

To emphasize that he really meant business, the Pakistani police even before the President began his address had already rounded up a few hundred Islamic militants from places across the country, and the majority of them were from Pakistani held Kashmir. That day the police also raided the offices of some of the more extreme religious organizations and had them sealed. This speech too was reminiscent of the two key words "Trust me' and "Pakistan First". Those were the very words that general Musharraf had used in his speech to the nation in September 2001, when he formally annulled Pakistan's military unholy alliance with the Taliban.

Shiraz who had heard the President's speech live that morning while sitting at the VIP lounge inside the Bandarnaike International Airport in Colombo and while waiting for the PIA flight from Islamabad to arrive was no doubt very impressed in the forthright manner in which the flamboyant General had castigated the fundamentalist religious leaders of the country. But at the same time Shiraz also felt that it would be difficult at this stage for the General to turn the clock around full circle. According to Shiraz, not only the politicians, but the Pakistan armed forces and the ISI were all equally responsible for the growth of this fundamentalist monster and he sincerely hoped that the President will be true to his words in eradicating this ever growing menace.

That evening during the flight to Dhaka the only subject under discussion was General Mushharraf's magnificent speech. While most of them felt that this would act as a good catalyst to diffuse the tension on the border, but whether the General would go the whole hog to rein in all the fundamentalists organizations in the country still remained the 64 million dollar question. His speech in September had not been well received by the fundamentalist hardliners and looking at the manner in which the Taliban and the Al Qaida militants were being given safe sanctuaries inside Pakistan, it was definitely not going to be easy even if he tried his level best.

'I think General Musharraf gave a good speech no doubt, but saying is one thing and implementing it is a different cup of tea altogether. Therefore to keep everybody happy including the Americans and the Indians on one side and and the many hardcore fundamentalist groups in Pakistan on the other side, he will have to I am afraid do some very fine balancing acts and tight rope walking. With the Americans and it allies breathing down our backs in the west while they keep chasing the Taliban and the Al Qaida from Afghanistan into Pakistan, and with India continuing to mass her tanks, troops and missiles in the east, the next few days I am afraid will be very crucial for him and the country. And though the expected visit of General Colin Powell, the American Secretary of State to Pakistan and India that is scheduled for the 15th and 16th of January may act as a softener, but there is no guarantee that the balloon won't go up. And one foolish and belligerent act by either side could lead to a veritable nuclear holocaust, and that is what has to be avoided at all costs. But by using the phrase that Kashmir runs in the blood of every Pakistani and that Pakistan is the fort of Islam, the General I am afraid has only managed to confuse the issue further,' said Shiraz as the voice of the pilot over the intercom announced all passengers to fasten their seat belts. It was not for landing, but because of some expected bad weather over the Bay of Bengal.

'I hope we are in safe hands young lady,'said Salim Rehman jokingly to the pretty air hostess as she went around checking that everyone was following the Captain's orders.

'We are great people to fly with Sir and with that being our motto you can be rest assured that you will reach your destination not only on time, but also safe and sound too,' said the smart air hostess very confidently. Thereafter though the big Boeing 747-300 did go through some rough turbulent weather that had quite a few of the passengers including Ruksana Begum, and Farzana counting their prayer beads, it nevertheless landed dot on time at Dhaka's General Zia International airport.

That evening the exclusive special Rehman family get together dinner that was organized by Fazal Rehman at the Bengal Art Lounge of the Dhaka Club was indeed a gala affair. Founded in 1911, and modelled on the lines of the Bengal Club in Calcutta, it was one of the oldest Clubs of undivided Bengal before partition and which now catered for the top most elite and the high and the mighty of the city. Located near the Shabagh intersection and close to the historic Ramna Park and Suhrawardy Udyan, the main club house with its wood—panelling reminded Arif Rehman of the British era, when membership to the club was only given to the British officers from the heaven born ICS, and to those officers serving in the police department, the judiciary and the military. Except for Arif Rehman and Ruksana Begum who were staying with their nephew Fazal Rehman and Samina in their house in the up market area of Dhanmondi, the rest of them had been accommodated in 15 of the 19 guest houses of the Dhaka Club. And with Karim Malik being the eldest among the son's-in-law, he and his wife Mehmuda were therefore given the privilege and honour of occupying the Presidential suite, while the rest were all accommodated in the deluxe suites.

The day happened to be a Saturday and it looked as if all the high and the mighty of the city with their wives and girlfiends had congregated at the club that evening. But what surprised Shiraz was the large number of nattily dressed young and middle aged women at the bar, some of whom were not only enjoying their skotch and soda, but quite a few were also puffing away at their imported Dunhill cigarettes. Too him therefore like Pakistan, Bangladesh too had become a country of either the very rich or the very poor, and the very previledged and the least previledged Bangladeshi.

'Though the tenets of Islam prohibits the drinking of alcohol and smoking of cigarettes, but that I guess only applicable to those who either cannot afford that luxury or to those who have become addicted to it and it has nothing to do with religion I guess,' said Shiraz to his brother-in-law Salim Rehman while ordering two large Black Label whisky with soda and ice.

'But what ever you may say, some of these Bangladeshi ladies with their natural tanned skin, hour glass figures and sharp features are really very beautiful, and therefore one cannot blame Mr Zulifiqar Ali Bhutto in creating this new country. After all he was very much in love with Husna Sheikh who was from this part of the world too and whom he had met way back in 1961 and therefore it can be rightly said that Bangladesh was probably given as a dowry to her. Afterall she still claims that the crown prince of Larkhana did marry her and the dowry was probably on the one condition that she would have to remain with him in Pakistan for good. But after Mr Bhutto was hanged, in 1977, Husna Sheikh I believe fled to London and their long 16 year relationship soon became the talk of the town,'said Salim Rehman jokingly as Fazal Rehman also joined them in the light hearted discussion on the great Husna-Bhutto love affair.

'Well though the two love birds first met in1961 in Dhaka, when the ever dapper Mr Bhutto was a dashing 34 year old cabinet minister in Field Marshall Ayub Khan's government, and later the lady virtually ran a kitchen cabinet after Mr Bhutto came to power in December 1971, the fact is that she has always been a damn thorn as far as the Bhutto family is concerned. And though she still claims that she is Bhutto's third wife, but there is no legal proof to sustain it,' said Fazal while reminding them that the rest of the family were waiting for them at the reserved Bengal Art Lounge to begin the party game that Samira had so thoughfully devised.

The party game by the soon to be bride Samira was indeed a very novel and a well thought out one. It was meant to remind all the members of the Rehman clan about their rich lineage and heritage. It not only conveyed to the younger lot their rich family tree but also who was who and who is who in the big Afridi family. She aptly named it 'Humbola" and it was a mini version of the popular game called tambola. Whereas in the game of tambola one was required to cut the fifteen numbers on his or her ticket, when it was called out by the compere, in this case one had to only cut the fifteen names of the individual that was on his or her ticket and which Samira as the compere was required to announce at random.

Samira with the help of his father and grandfather had also very conveniently displayed on a giant chart the big family tree of the five generations of the Rehman clan with their photographs. On top of the tree was the name and photo of the late Haji Abdul Rehman and his wife who were Samira's paternal great great grandparents. And to make the game even more interesting for the younger generation so that they would come to know a little more about the person concerned, Samira was also required to say a few words about the individual once the name was called. And in case the person was no longer living, then together with the short biodata a big framed photograph of the person concerned would also to be shown to all the young participants on the big screen. Besides that Samira also very wisely kept some attractive prizes for the winners of the jaldi five, each line and the full house.

'Ladies and gentlemen, dear cousins, brothers, sisters and children, eyes down for the first name please' said the beautiful beaming Samira as she gave her grandmother Ruksana Begum the privilege and honour to take out the first name from her maternal grandfather's old solar pith hat. And lo and behold it was that of Colonel Attiqur Rehman who was Samira great grandfather and Ruksana Begum's father-in-law. He was an army doctor who had fought against the Germans in both the world wars. For the next name to be taken out from the hat it was now the turn of her paternal grandfather, the 82 year old and the senior most patriarch of the proud Afridi Rehman clan. And when Arif Rehman pulled out the name it happened to be that of his late younger sister Shenaz Hussein, but about whom poor Samira knew very little it seems. Samira had only heard about this grand aunt of hers who had died very young. Therefore to help Samira out, Arif Rehman gave out the story of how Shenaz and her husband Nawaz Hussein were killed by the Pathan raiders at a place called Rampur-Buniyar in Kashmir in late October 1947, while they were returning from a holiday in Srinagar in their new Studebaker car with their only son Imran Hussein.Then pointing towards Shiraz when he further added and said. 'And it is only thanks to the lucky talisman that had Allah's name written on it in Urdu and which is even today around my dear nephew's neck that had saved him from the marauding Pathans,' there was hushed silence. Very few among the fourth and fifth generation Rehman family knew the full story and Shiraz that evening after that fabulous party was in two minds of whether to go ahead with his plan and disappear from Koh Samui or scuttle the plan for good. During the game when a black and white photograph of his mother Shenaz and father Nawaz Hussein and with their nine month old Imran Hussein sitting on his mother's lap was flashed on the big screen, that had got Shiraz thinking. That night as he kept thinking about them, he just could'nt go to sleep and neither could he firmly make up his mind.

But on the next day during the sit down lunch that was hosted by the Pakistan High Commissioner in Dhaka at his residence and which was in honour of the bridegroom's father, the Pakistan High Commissioner to Nepal and his wife and to which Shiraz and Salim Rehman with their wives had also been invited, when the topic of whether General Musharraf would be able to tighten the screws on the fanatical Mullas and their militant organizations, and whether Bangladesh as a Muslim country would back Pakistan in case there was a fourth round with India, Shiraz was shocked to learn about the manner in which Bangladesh too was being radically Islamized, and that the ISI and the Al Qaida too had a big hand in that bizarre game. The focus was not only to try and Talibanize the younger lot of Bangladeshis, but also to create and generate a hate and terror campaign against India. The generation that were born soon after the sordid 1971 Bangladesh massacres and genocide that were so inhumanly carried out by the Pakistanis from West Pakistan on them and vice versa were now 30 years of age and for them all that it seems was now forgotten history and a completely closed chapter.

Soon after that sumptuous Baluchi lunch, and while they were all enjoing their cup of good coffee, there was an urgent call from the Pakistani Foreign Ministry. It was from the Foreign Secretary and he wanted to speak to Riaz Mohammed Khan (Shiraz) urgently and in private only on the land line. That sudden unexpected call from non other than his immediate boss wanting to speak to him in private did unnerve Shiraz, but being a seasoned diplomat he simply smiled and said in good humour.

'Lagta hai ke muj ko us hot seat pur jaldi hi baitna padega-ye foreign office wale aur khas karke mera ye boss chutti pur bhi mera picha nahin chodenge—pata nahin ub kiya aafat aa gayeee. Magar unhe pata kaise laga ke mein yahan pur hun is waqt ?' (It looks that they do want me to sit on that hot seat because these foreign office chaps and particularly this boss of mine even while I am on leave will not leave me alone. And I wonder where the fire is this time. But how the hell did he come to know that I am at our High Commissioner's house right now?}Then as he was escorted to his host's study room to take the call, Shiraz kissed the lucky talisman and silently said a prayer. He had a hunch that probably he had been exposed and he also feared that he may be recalled immediately, arrested and charged with treason. His guilty conscience was playing on his mind and he feared the worst. But it came as a big surprise and a welcome relief to him, when his boss congratulated him and told him over the phone very confidentially that he had also put his name on the panel for the selection of the next Foreign

Secretary of Pakistan. The Foreign Secretary who was two batches senior to him was also a good friend of his and they had also served together both in erstwhile USSR and in the US. They were also on the save wave length when it came to extending the hand of friendship to India was concerned, and for the need for both Pakistan and India to settle the Kashmir dispute peacefully. But Shiraz knew that he stood no chance at all because his efforts to promote the track 3 channel from Moscow had gone against him and he was already under the ISI scanner. Moreover, he had unofficially heard before leaving Islamabad that Riaz Hussein Khokar who was Pakistan's Ambassador to China and who was senior to him had already been tipped for that coveted post. Nevertheless he felt a lot more reassured and happy that his name had at least been recommended by his immediate boss and there was therefore no need to scuttle his escape plan. And since he had been categorically told not to share this confidential information with anybody else till such time it was officially announced by the government, Shiraz decided to pull another fast one on everyone. He therefore came back to the drawing room with a sullen face and when he was asked by the host and the other fellow diplomats if all was well, Shiraz in all seriousness said.

'Khak thik hai yaar. Ab toh lagta hai ke ub mera number Foreign Secretary banne ka kabhi nahin ayega. Kyun ke mera ye kambakt boss mero ko Timbaktu bhej raha hai—aur wahan aissi jor ki aag lagi hai ke hokum diya gaya ke mujhe kal tak wahan zaroor paunchna padega. Ab sawal ye paida hota hai ke mein kiya karoon—Jaoon ya na jaoon Aur Kaal thak wahan pahunchne ka sawal hi nahin paida hota hai.'Mali koi padosi desh toh nahin (Damn it all-nothing is well—because now it seems I will never ever become the Foreign Secretary,because my damn boss has now posted me to Timbaktu—because there is a big fire on there and I have been ordered to report there latest by tomorrow to put it off-And now the question is what the hell should I do-should I go or not go but my reaching there by tomorrow simply is next to impossible because Mali is not in the immediate neighbourhood)'

Salim Rehman realizing that his brother-in-law as usual was pulling a fast one, he at once took his side and added. 'In that case dear brother-in-law, please take all of us all along with you, because today the fire in Pakistan is much bigger than anywhere else in this world. And it will get even bigger, bloodier and beyond anybody's control if the present on going crisis leads to an all out nuclear war with India. And the only consolation will be that Dr A Q Khan, who claims to be the father of the Islamic bomb and who has built a lavish hotel there and named it after his wife Hendrina he will also probably be there to welcome us. And if we decide to keep quiet and not to open our big mouths about Dr Khan's other nefarious activities of making slush money by selling nuclear secrets to others, he I am sure will even provide all of us and our families with free accommodation and messing for the rest of our lives.'

With the party ending on that jovial but sarcastic note about Dr AQ Khan, Shiraz on the pretext that he was keen to visit the old Nawab of Dhaka's palace that was in the heart of the old city quietly peeled off from the rest of the group. On the way he first stopped at a cellular phone store to buy a mobile phone with a new number, but when he was told that the Grameen mobile phone could not be used for overseas calls, he gave up the idea. Since it was already well over forty eight hours since he had dispatched that very confidential letter with the highly explosive CD to Shups from Colombo's Internatinal airport, he was very keen to find out if it had reached her safely. And he was also apprehensive that if by chance it fell into the wrong hands then he could possibly be in very big and serious trouble, since it was sent by registered post and it had the name of the sender as Dablo and a fictitious Colombo address on it. He initially thought of calling Shups on her office land line from a public booth, but finally reckoned that probably it was still a bit too early. And knowing the efficiency of the postal services in India, he therefore postponed it till the day of the wedding when everybody he knew would be very busy and he would be able to quietly slip away for a while and call her up on her office land line from some public booth in Dhaka. Not only would that be a safer bet, but it would have also give more time to Shups to give him a preliminary feedback on his proposed Houdini style vanishing act.

Whereas, Harry Houdini the Hungarian born American master magician had to impress the world with his famous 'Overboard Box Escape,'and 'Buried Alive Stunt' acts, Shiraz would have to impress the top sleuths from the Indian RAW and the military intelligence authorities in India not only with the factual data about Pakistan's nuclear might, but also about its future proxy war strategy against India. He knew very well that General Musharraf's much touted plans to totally ban the LeT, the JeM and such like other militant organizations was all bunkum and he was certain that these militant groups would at a later stage surface again. But the manner in which both the countries were now flexing their military muscles and deploying their respective and deadly, short, medium and long range ballistic missiles close to the international border and which were also capable of carrying nuclear warheads, Shiraz was indeed very worried.

Moreover, having come under the long shadow of both the Pakistan ISI and the JeM, time was also now now running out for him. There was no question of his going back to Pakistan anymore. The time for now or never had finally arrived for him.

Chapter-45

Home Sweet Home Again

On the morning of the 15th of January, 2002 after the formal Nikka ceremony by the learned Kazi had been conducted and Yusuf Khan the bridegroom and Samira Rehman the bride were declared as man and wife, Shiraz looked at his watch. It was nearing mid afternoon and he was getting a bit impatient. He desperately wanted to get in touch with Shups. With only five days more to go for his vanishing act, he needed a firm confirmation and a guarantee that the Indian government would help him to disappear from Koh Samui for good and accept him as a defector. And that they would be also willing to escort him back safely and secretly to resurface in India. He initially thought of skipping the traditional 'Walima,' the big feast that is hosted immediately after the wedding, but decided not to because his absence on that festive occasion would not only be in bad taste, but it could also raise a few eyebrows. After all there were quite a few representatives from the Pakistan High Commission in Dhaka at the wedding too and some of them could well be from the ISI. Moreover, it was a Tuesday and calling Shups on the office landline he knew would serve no purpose either because she may not be able to speak to him so very freely and openly. He therefore decided that the best time for him to make that important call would be around 9 PM in the evening,when Shups hopefully would be alone at home in Delhi and everybody in Dhaka would be enjoying the gala reception at the Dhaka Sheraton Hotel.

That evening just before leaving for the reception, Shiraz complained of a mild stomach ache to his wife and attributed it to his eating a bit too many of those delicious king size lobsters at the wedding. But like a good sport he did go along with the family to attend the reception. It was of course a plain white lie. He only needed an excuse to get away early from there and make that all important phone call to Shups.

At around 8.30 PM, and while everybody was enjoying their drinks and snacks, Shiraz on the excuse that he was not feeling very bright simply kept sipping plain soda water and did not even touch the snacks and that had got Saira worried.

'I think you should go back to the club and take complete rest. The indigestion tablet that I gave you before leaving for the reception I think has not worked. And if you do feel hungry you can always order for some plain curd and rice and which I am sure the Dhaka Club will be able to provide,' said Saira as she asked the young lady at the hotel's front desk to quickly arrange for a cab for her husband.

On the way back to the Dhaka Club which was not very far from the hotel, Shiraz first went looking for a fully enclosed public telephone booth. And then with the help of the hired cab driver having found one near the Dhaka University Campus, he made that all important phone call to Shups. Luckily she was at home and she by then had also received his long confidential letter and the highly classified CD that Shiraz had dispatched to her from the Colombo International Airport. Getting her immediately on the line Shiraz felt a lot relieved, but before he could say anything Shupu's simply shut him up and said.

'Now please do not interrupt and just keep listening to me very carefully till I finish. It has all been worked out and 'Operation Dablo' will commence at the place selected by you at 6.55 PM, Thailand time and which is 10 minutes after sunset on 20th January. Our representative will contact you personally on the 17th with all the details and it will be during the wedding reception at the Peninsula Bangkok Hotel. At around 7.45 PM that evening you should conveniently position yourself near the bar and wait for our man to approach you. For easy identification you should wear your white silk Pathani suit. Our man will come up to you at the bar and in a matter of fact way will simply say to you. 'They do make a charming couple, don't they!! And you have to only answer by saying.' Undoubtedly so but marriages are only made in heaven.' Thereafter you will ask him if he can help change a 1000 Baht note for you and which he will do so by giving you ten notes of hundred Bahts each. So do remember to keep a 1000 Baht note in your purse. The ten notes of hundred denomination will be serially numbered and details of your new identity, profession and other details of how the operation will be carried out will be written on them serially and in very fine print. Therefore do equip yourself also with a powerful magnifying glass. Thereafter you will have to memorize the entire data and then destroy all the currency notes. Have you understood?

'Yes I have and thank you very much. Hope to see you soon,' said Shiraz as he quickly put the phone back on the receiver, paid for the short one and a half minute call and got back into the car for his drive back to the Dhaka Club. And in order to carry on feigning his illness, he stopped by first at a chemist shop and picked up a box of Alka-Seltzer Effervescent tablets and then went to a stationery and book store to buy the magnifying glass. That day also happened to be the Army Day in India and Shiraz remembered very vividly how after the parade on that 15th January 1971, he had picked Shups up from outside the Kotah House Officers Mess and while having lunch at Karim' s restaurant proposed to her.

On the next day morning and in order to get more time to himself and to convince the others that he was still feeling unwell, Shiraz did not stir out of his room. And while all of them went sightseeing and shopping, he helped himself to a chilled beer and read the book 'Operation Cicero" that he had borrowed from the Dhaka Club library. It was a true story of how the valet of the British Ambassador to Turkey during the Second World War secretly photographed a large number of highly classified secret and top secret documents and sold it to the Germans. Later on that very evening of 16th January, when the entire marriage party from both the families boarded the Bangladesh Biman flight to Bangkok from Dhaka, Shiraz kept wondering whether he would be able to do his disappearing act without arousing any suspicion.

On the 17th evening for the reception at the Peninsular Bangkok Hotel, Shiraz for the sake of easy recognition and as directed by Shups wore a traditional off white raw silk Pathani suit and sharp at 7.40 with a large peg of Black Label whisky and soda in his hand he stood with his back against the bar and kept surveying the crowd. Five minutes later and as per the given time, a middle aged gentlemen who looked every inch a Thai and who was dressed in a well cut three piece suit with a big bouquet of flowers in his hands came up to the bar, stood close to him and ordered his drink. Shiraz who was looking out for some Indian face was however very pleasantly surprised when the man even before his screw driver cocktail could arrive said the words that he was waiting to here. Soon thereafter having helped Shiraz to change his 1000 Baht note, the gentleman with the drink in hand stood in line and waited for his turn to present the bouquet of flowers to the bride. The entire act was so very professional and natural that nobody could ever think that the person concerned who had probably gate crashed was a spy or a courier and who was working for the Indian RAW. And Shiraz also was mighty impressed with the supreme confidence and the suave manner in which the man had conducted himself for those 25 to 30 minutes before disappearing from the scene.

With three nights and four days to go before doing his disappearing act, Shiraz was now required to memorize and act on what was written on those ten currency notes and it had to be done without his showing any anxiety or nervousness and in complete secrecy. The flight to Koh Samui from Bangkok was scheduled for the next day afternoon and time was running out for him. So as not to arouse any suspicion he therefore decided to get up very early next morning and spend more time in the loo with those monetary notes and the magnifying glass.

It was five o'clock on that morning of 18th of January 2002 and giving the excuse to Saira, that his stomach problem had not recovered fully, Shiraz with those precious Thai bank notes in his purse and the magnifying glass inside his night gown and with the latest copy of the Time magazine in his hand he quietly went and sat inside the loo. And by the time he memorized the contents from the fine prints of half of those currency notes that were each worth only a hundred Thai bahts, he knew that he had been reborn again and that to with a completely new identity. His life was about to once again come full circle. He had been given his new cover story.

After his disappearance from Koh Samui, he would be known as Shiraz Rehmatullah Khan, the only son of Dr Ismail Rehmatullah Khan and Mumtaz Rehmatullah Khan. He was born in Calcutta on 15th August 1945 and after his parents were killed in the great Calcutta Hindu Muslim riots of 1946, he was adopted and brought up by Dr Riaz Rehmatullah Khan and his wife Shabnam Rehmatullah Khan. The Doctor was his own paternal Uncle and his wife was from a very well to do Muslim family of Lucknow. They had been married for five years years but were issueless. And since Shabnam's father too was a doctor, Dr Riaz Rehmatullah Khan the son-in-law also settled down in Lucknow to run the family clinic. They were very well off financially and since Lucknow had a large population of Muslims, they did not migrate to Pakistan during partition. In 1950, and after his father Dr Riaz Rehmatullah Khan successfully completed his F.R.C.S from England, the family settled down there. After 10 years of stay in England they were all given British citizenship. In 1960, because of growing racial tensions in England, the family moved to Georgetown in what was then known as British Guyana and where there were a very large number of immigrant Indians. After Guyana attained its independence from Britain in 1966, the family now became citizens of that country. In 1962, Shiraz completed his high school in Georgetown from the prestigious 'Queens College'. It was the same college where the former President Cheddi Jagan had also studied and like Jagan he too was in Percival House.

Thereafter on getting his Bachelors degree in Business Manaagement from Georgetown University in 1966, Shiraz Rehmatullah Khan joined Unilever as a management trainee. In 1970 and having worked with Unilever for four years in England in the food department, he returned to Guyana soon after the country became a republic in February 1970. At Georgetown he then started his own business of selling spices and food products and which mainly catered to the taste buds of the large number of people of Indian origin who had migrated and settled in the capital city. Though most of them were Hindus, but there was a sizeable population of Indian Muslims also. As a young and eligible bachelor, Shiraz had fallen in love with a Hindu girl from Georgetown, but he could'nt marry her because there were serious objections from her parents of his being from the Muslim community. He therefore remained a bachelor all his life. After his parents died in the early eighties and being the only issue, he therefore had inherited a lot of money and property. In 1990, he sold off his business in Guyana and returned to his roots in India and was now an Indian citizen. Because of his love for nature, solitude, books and wild life, he had built himself a nice bungalow at Naukuchiya Tal in the Kumaon Hills of Uttar Pradesh and had settled there. With his passion for photography, history and travelling, and being a bachelor he therefore now spends most of the winter season visiting various places of historical and archeological interests both within India and around the world.'

There was no doubt that Shups was the brain behind that well thought out fictional character and cover story thought Shiraz as he sat inside the loo memorizing all the details. And like the Bofors case where the recipients of those kickbacks on the murky gun deal were always one step ahead of the CBI sleuths in ensuring that the money received by them would never be traced and they would all getaway scotfree, in this case too Shiraz Rehmatullah Khan would now have to remain a step ahead of the Pakistani sleuths from the ISI and convince them that Riaz Mohammed Khan while holidaying in Koh Samui had accidently died by drowning there and then get away scotfree. However that cover story would only begin after his defection and interrogation by the Indian intelligencies authorities and only thereafter would he be given a new passort with that new name and a new identity to vanish once again from India to any place of his own choosing. Therefore with that convincing story about his new life that was soon to begin, Shiraz soon memorized all the given details and then tore up the first five currency notes and flushed them down the toilet. Soon after midday that day and after seeing the happy newly wedded couple off for their honeymoon to New Zealand, Shiraz with the rest of the Rehman clan and the bridegroom's parents as their guests boarded the Bangkok Airways flight to Koh Samui, With that new identity of his, Shiraz was more than convinced that 'Operation Dablo' would only be successful if he did not unnecessary worry and remained cool all the time. At around 2 'oclock that afternoon and after a comfortable one hour flight, when they arrived at the island's luxurious and most sought after beach resort in Koh Samui, Shiraz silently prayed to the Sai Baba of Shirdi to give him the courage to successfully carryout his mission.

The Karma Samui Resort on the Cheong Mon beach with its exclusive pool villas on a steep cove that led to a pristine beach was the ultimate in luxury that one could have asked for on that beautiful island. The three nights and four day stay at Koh Samui had also been very meticulously planned. The first day would be utilized to go around the entire island and its many beaches. The second day they would go snorkeling and have a grand picnic on the Koh Tao island that was famous for its crystal clear waters and abundance of marine life. And on the third day they would all visit the famous Ang Thong National Marine Park. Thereafter on the 4th day morning after breakfast they would catch the flight back to Bangkok. And after an overnight stay at Bangkok everyone would depart for their respective destinations.

That evening after a good swim in the sea and a bottle of Blue Label whisky to go with the delicious fish and prawn snacks that Samina and Saira kept preparing in the well equipped kitchen of their big three bedroom villa, Fazal Rehman with Shiraz as his bridge partner took on the challenge from the Pakistani High Commissioner to Nepal and his wife. The had decided to play the best of five rubbers and the losers were required to foot the bill for the entire group for the next day's planned day trip by a chartered speedboat to the Ang Thong National Marine Park,and which was inclusive of the on board Thai lunch, the beer, soft drinks and snacks.

Late that evening before going to bed and with only 48 hours left for him to plan and do his own disappearing act, Shiraz finally got the time to read the fine print on the other five Thai bank notes. In those currency notes were the details of his entire escape plan together with his cover story. Sitting in that luxurious bathroom he had to also make a quick mental note of all those details and thereafter destroy all the bank notes and flush them down the toilet. As per those instructions, Shiraz was required not to swim, but to hire a sea kayak and go kayaking from the Lamai beach for at least a mile and a half in the easterly direction towards the South China Sea and it was to be on a compass bearing of approximately 90 degrees east.But before setting out from that beach, he was also required to ensure that there would be atleast a couple of eye witnesses including one or two from his own group, who should have seen him go kayaking from there. He was also required to leave behind his wallet with all his credit cards, driving licence and some other personal items with a member from his own group for safe custody. That was required to be done in order to establish the fact that he did go kayaking from that beach and had all the intentions of coming back. He had however been told to keep the lucky talisman that was around his neck because that was required to be shown to the Indian sleuths directing the operation for recognition and identification. At around 6.50 P.M. and soon after sunset and whilst kayaking, he was also required to establish contact with the fishing trawler on a prearranged torchlight signal. The trawler too in reponse would also flash a green light thrice.Thereafter he must abandon the kayak and swim towards the trawler. But before abandoning the kayak, he would also be required to ensure that traces of his own blood was left on the life jacket and that the life jacket was made unusable. Before boarding the trawler and for correct identification he would first have to show his lucky talisman and thereafter hand it over to the man in charge of the entire operation. And once he was safely inside the fishing trawler, his kayak would be hit by the trawler and badly damaged. That would make it look like an accident. On board the trawler, his beard and moustache would be shaved off and he would be given a crew cut. He would also be also required to dorn the wig that woul be given to him. Some blood stained bandages would also be put on his right leg and around his right shoulder and arm and his left arm would be placed in a sling. Thereafter the trawler would head for the high seas and at a predetermined time and place the rendez vous with an Indian naval ship would take place. On the excuse that the trawler had picked up an injured individual and two others who proclaimed to be an Indian tourists after their sailing boat had met with an accident with the trawler, they would all be handed over to the Captain of the Indian naval ship and the ship would then head back to the Indian Naval Base at the Andaman and Car Nicobar Islands. At the naval hospital at Port Blair a team of plastic surgeons would carry out a series of quick surgeries on his face including rhinoplasty. And a few days later with a relatively changed face, a much younger looking Shiraz Rehmatullah Khan with his new Indian passport and escorted by a senior officer from the RAW would be flown to New Delhi in a special aircraft. On arrival at Palam airport he would be taken to a safe house. His expected date of arrival at the safe house in New Delhi would be on the late evening of 25rd January and thereafter for the next few days or so he would be in the hands of India's top sleuths from the RAW, the IB and the Military Intelligence Directorate who will then interrogate and debrief him. During his interrogation and debriefing by the JIC, the Joint Intelligence Committee, Shiraz would be required to elaborate in a lot more detail the veracity of all the classified information that he had made in his little red diary and on the CD and which he had sent to Shupriya from Colombo airport. The JIC on being satisfied with the genuineness of the information would then through the Secretary RAW apprise and brief the Prime Minister of India personally. And once that formality was completed, and the Prime Minister was fully satisfied that the defector was indeed the high ranking Pakistani career diplomat, Shiraz Rehmatullah would be given his freedom. However, he would not be allowed to settle in India and nor would he be allowed to go back to Pakistan or Bangladesh. He would no doubt be paid very handsomely and which would enable him to settle down comfortably in his new life. He would also be given every assistance and help to go to any other country of his choice, but once he was out of India he must not under any circunstances get in touch with any individual who had helped him to defect.

That whole night Shiraz did not get any sleep at all. He was in a big dilemma. On the 20th of January, the entire Rehman clan togther with the Pakistani High Commissioner to Nepal and his wife were required to go on the day long excursion to the Ang Thong National Marine Park and there was hardly any time for him to to cook up a reasonably good excuse to stay back. Moreover, he was also required to have atleast one reliable eye witness from the group on the Lamai beach on that evening to see him go kayaking. After a very restless night, Shiraz next morning was still in a quandary. Time was running out on him and he had to think of a plausible and good excuse to skip the excursion. At the bridge table with Fazal Rehman as his partner, they had also lost the best of five rubbers and they were therefore required to play host for the day long excursion to the marine park the next day. He also could not again give the same old excuse that he was suffering from indigestion and an upset stomach. He had therefore to think of a legitimate excuse and think fast.

And the idea struck him, on the 19th morning, when they were on the ferry boat to the Koh Tao Island and where they were to do snorkelling. He remembered that during his cadet days at the National Defence Academy in Kharakwasla, Poona he at times in order to skip the out door rigorous drill and physical training periods would conveniently report sick by complaining of a badly sprained ankle. And though it was a self inflicted and painful exercise, it did serve the purpose alright. And all he did was to severely beat his left ankle with the wooden side of his boot brush till it got a nice pinkish colour and a reasonably good swelling. So while snorkeling with the others, Shiraz quietly picked up a nice big stone that had a smooth surface from the bottom of the sea. Soon thereafter giving the excuse that he would like to explore the island a bit, he left the group and having found a secluded cove and got on with the job. And after an hour or so when he came back limping and gave the excuse that he had badly sprained his left ankle while trying to jump across some stones that led to that secluded cove, everybody got a bit worried.

'I think the swelling is quite bad and you need to show it to a good doctor when we get back to Koh Samui,' said Arif Rehman as he examined his son-in-law's badly swollen ankle.

'Maybe we could find a chemist shop on this island and put a crepe bandage over it temporarily. Or maybe we could get hold off some turmeric and salt and make a paste and apply it gently on the ankle since it is a proven household remedy and it works,' said Ruksana Begum.

'Maybe we could find a doctor among the many tourists and have the injury examined here itself. And I only hope it is not a fracture' said a worried Saira.

With everybody feeling pity for him, Shiraz was more than convinced that he now had the right excuse to shy away from the next day's planned trip to the National Maritime Park. Therefore now all that was needed was to get some people from the group who would keep him company while the others were out exploring the beauty of the underwater world.

On their return journey to Koh Samui and while enjoying their tea and snacks on board the ferry boat, Shiraz very cleverly decided to find out whether the rumours that some Al Qaida and Taliban fighters from Afghanistan had found refuge in Bangladesh was true or not, and he therefore opened the topic by saying very casually.

'You know though the Americans and their allies are still pounding the Taliban and the Al Qaida training camps and hideouts in Aghanistan, but a large number of them including their leaders Mulla Omar and Bin Laden I believe have escaped from there and have found refuge in other countries. And what is even more surprising is the fact that a small number of them from the Al Qaida and the Taliban who were lucky to escape from Tora Bora were Bangladeshis.'

'Yes and undoubtedly so and it is now a big problem for us too. And a month or so after the Americans launched 'Operation Endure Freedom,' a large number of them were seen disembarking from the ship M.V. Mecca' at Chittagong, our major port on the Bay of Bengal. That was sometime in the third week of December, 2001 and according to one reliable eye witness who happened to be a port worker, the ship had anchored near a sand bank which was quite some distance away from the main port and from there five or six big water launches were used to ferry them to the shore. And the men who landed on that early winter moring of 21st December were not only tall and well built, but they also had big beards and black turbans on their heads and were dressed in the traditional Islamic dress of salwar-kameez. And according to one rough estimate they were around 150 of them who had arrived in that first batch to Bangladesh from Karachi and most of them were speaking in Arabic. However there were alao a few Bangladeshis and Rohingyas, the stocky Muslim refugee tribe from western Myanmar. All these men were also seen unloading crates of ammunition and each one of them had an AK-47 rifle slung around his big shoulder,' said Fazal Rehman as Shiraz kept massaging his swollen ankle with oil and listening patiently.

'But where did they go and why did they have to come all all the way to Bangladesh from Afghanistan? Asked Shiraz.

'I have a gut feeling they have come to Bangladesh because of Bin Laden's growing desire to stage an Islamic revolution in this vastly populated but poor Muslim country,' said the Pakistani Ambassador to Nepal.

'Yes you may be right because there are now a very large number of Bangladeshi Jihadists and more are being indoctrinated through the many madrassas that have mushroomed in this country in the recent past. However one report indicates that the group that had landed at Chittagong soon after their arrival had disappeared from that city. And while some of their leaders later surfaced in Dhaka, but most of them went to a place near the village of Ukhia. It is a village which is south of Cox Bazaar on the southern most tip of Bangladesh. There are also now reports that they are trying to establish some kind of a training camp in the jungles around Ukhia. I have also heard that the ship M.V.Mecca had sailed from Karachi and if that is true then the Pakistan's ISI must have had a hand in it too or else how could they managed to just get away so very easily, and especially so after General Musharraf had become an ally of George Bush,'added FazalRehman.

'Ofcourse without the help from the ISI and also without the connivance of the D.G.F.I and the present Bangladesh government of

Khalidia Zia, they could have never reached this far. And I must also add that our ISI sleuths in Nepal are doing a good job too. They are not only very active in that country, but they have also established very good contacts with the HUJI of Bangladesh, and the Bodos of Assam to stir up trouble in India,' said the Pakistan High Commissioner to Nepal very proudly.

'Well in that case, that calls for a drink tonight and maybe we could play a rubber or two of bridge once we get back to our villas,' said Shiraz while complaining of acute pain in his left ankle.

'But you must get an x-ray done and see a doctor first,'said Ruksana Begum while sounding a little worried about her son-in-law's swollen ankle.

That evening after the x-ray showed no fracture, and the doctor advised him to apply some iodex ointment and to take complete rest atleast for the next twenty-four hours, Shiraz knew that his good old NDA trick had worked. The National Defence Academy, the cradle of the Indian army besides teaching the cadets how to become physically strong, it also taught some of them how to at times sham also. His only problem now was how to lure a few others from the group to keep him company the next day. And he got the answer on that very evening at the bridge table itself when he asked for volunteers who would like to keep him company.

'In anycase I will be with you,' said Saira.

'And so will we, since both my wife and I have visited the marine park on Sentosa Island in Singapore a number of times when I was posted there as Consul General, And maybe we could as a foursome go sight seeing around the island and have a picnic of our own,'said Mohammed Hayat, Pakistan's High Commissioner to Nepal.

'Oh that is indeed very thoughtful and sporting of you, and with my wife as my partner maybe we could play some bridge too,' said Shiraz as he handed over fifteen thousand Bahts to Fazal Rehman as his share for the marine park trip the next day.

On the 20th of January, Shiraz got up early in the morning to see off those who were leaving for the Ang Thong National Park and which included his in-laws and most importantly his son Tojo and daughter Sherry. He knew that this would be the last time he would see them. And though he was filled with emotion but he simply could not show it. Standing at the door of his villa he simply waved his hand and told them to enjoy the trip. At the breakfast table later that morning, when Shiraz suggested that since his ankle after applying the iodex ointment and the hot water fermentation was now much better and that he could now also walk a bit without limping, and that an outing to the Namuang waterfalls and the Secret Buddha

Gardens on the island would be a good idea, all of them immediately agreed. And when Shiraz further suggested that after visiting the Secret Buddha Gardens they could also spend some time at the Lamai Beach which is far less crowded and have lunch at Rocky's Beach restaurant which he had heard specializes in exotic Thai food, all of them once again unanimously agreed.

'Not a bad idea at all and after lunch we could also play a couple of rubbers of bridge and have our evening tea sitting by the poolside of Rocky's Boutique Resort,' added Mohammed Hayat.

'I think that will be simply great and after tea while the ladies go for a nice and refreshing Thai massage which I believe the resort specializes in, you and I will go kayaking. And the resort I believe also provides good ocean kayaks and therefore there will be no problem in hiring them. Thereafter we could all have a couple of drinks at the pool bar and return back to our villas for the camp fire night on the beach that the children have so thoughtfully planned for the elders and what say you Hayat,' said Shiraz.

'Well since I am not the adventurous type you can do your kayaking my friend and I will rather join the ladies and go for a massage,' said the Pakistani High Commissioner to Nepal with an impish smile on his face.

'Well whatever suits you my friend', said Shiraz while feeling very happy that Mohammed Hayat had declined his invitation to go kayaking with him.

'But with that ankle of yours, how will you manage,' asked Saira

'Oh by evening and with some more of that iodex massage, I am sure it will be alright. Why even now there is hardly any swelling left,'said Shiraz as he lifted his trousers for Saira to inspect.

For that day's outing, Shiraz got into his favourite grey flannel pants, a spotless white shirt, wore the red silk scarf that Sherry had presented him with on his last birthday and over it the ferrari style windcheater that his son had brought for him from America. Thereafter having checked the powerful hand held special torch light that Scuba divers normally use and the prismatic compass that he had bought in Bangkok, he called for a Hertz rental car. Before leaving the villa, he also put a sharp fruit cutting knife and his Charles-Hubert pocket watch that his father-in-law had presented him with on his fiftieth birthday inside the lower right hand pocket of his windcheater.

That morning after the sightseeing trip and a sumptuous lunch at Rocky's restaurant, they all sat down near the beachside swimming pool of the resort and played a couple of rubbers of bridge. At five o'clock in the evening having ordered tea and some snacks, Shiraz asked the concierge to have the ocean going kayak that he had selected earlier together with the life jacket and paddle to be placed near the pool and close to the beach. Since Shiraz had done a good deal of ocean kayaking when he was posted in Washington D.C. Shiraz had selected a Cape Ann Storm kayak that had a span of 160 to 230 lbs and which was ideal for his weight and height. He also new that to cover the required distance he would have to kayak for at least an hour if not more depending upon the tidal conditions. Therefore to be at the designated rendez-vous at 6.50 PM Thailand time he had to start kayaking latest by 5.30 P.M and it was now already a little past 5.00.

'Unless I start soon I will not be able to get back before sunset and I believe the sunset here is out of this world,' said Shiraz as he called out once again to the concierge to quickly arrange for the kayak. Ten minutes later, when the tea arrived and the kayak was also placed on the beach, Shiraz felt a lot relieved. While telling everyone to enjoy themselves and to have their massage at the spa and that he would be back before sunset, he calmly had his tea. Then having handed over his Rolex Oyster wrist watch that Saira had presented to him on his 50th birthday and his wallet to his wife, he gently squeezed her hand and ran towards the beach where the kayak had already been placed. Thereafter having donned his life jacket, he got into the light blue coloured sit on top ocean kayak and carried out a quick check that all the required articles were there inside his windcheater pockets. And before he was ready to paddle away he again waved out to his wife for the last and final time.

Shiraz no doubt felt very sorry for her, but he had made up his mind. He had to do it not only for the safety of his family whom some of the radical Mullas had threatened to kill because of his daughter's involvement with an Indian shaven of Sikh and for his secret liaison with the Indian ambassador in Mioscow. He was also aware about the shame that he would bring to the family in case he was arrested, unmasked and tried for treason. Moreover he had to prevent at all cost the nuclear disaster and the fourth round that both Pakistan and India were getting ready to unleash.

Though the visit of General Colin Powell, the American Secretary of State to India and Pakistan in mid January to de-escalate the rising military tension on the borders was welcomed by both the sides, but it was more of an act of friendly persuasion and mediation. But that had not stopped the sabre rattling by both the countries. With Pakistan refusing to pull back its troops from the borders unless India did likewise first, and India insisting that it will not pull back unless the cross-border terrorism in Kashmir is stopped completely, there was now a serious logjam and Shiraz was worried that the more Islamic hawks in the Pakistan army may well force

General Musharraf to go for a first strike nuclear kill. And though President Musharraf in his presidential address on the 12th of January had met some of India's demands by ordering the disbandment of the LeT, the JeM, and a few other such like fanatical militant terrorist groups, but it had in no way stopped these militant organizations from functioning under different names. They were still shouting from the rooftops and some of them even more vociderously that there will be no scaling down of the Jihad against the Indian rule in Kashmir. And one senior JeM spokesman from Muzaffarabad had even reiterated that they were not afraid of war. Though even Beena Sarwar, the noted and charming Pakistani journalist from Pakistan in her recent article that was titled 'Time to Provoke Peace' had categorically stated that Pakistan had no other choice but to take action against these groups that had caused as much or more havoc within the country, these militant groups it seems were bent upon destroying both India and Pakistan. Shiraz also dreaded the day when one of these fundamentalist militant groups in the name of saving Islam may arm themselves with weapons of mass destruction. And while Shiraz kept debating whether good sense will prevail on the rulers of boh the countries, he checked the time on his pocket watch.

Luckily at that time of the evening most of those who had gone kayaking and sailing or were indulging in other kinds of watersports were returning back to base and so were the fishing boats and trawlers. With the sunset time scheduled at 6.47, the dusk time Shiraz calculated would be around 7P.M.00 and it would be at around that time that he must establish contact with the concerned fishing trawler. It was nearing 6.30 when he again checked his compass bearing and according to his calculation and as per the navigational map, he had covered fairly good distance and was heading in the right direction also.

As the giant sun on the horizon began to turn into a golden fireball and started to slowly disappear from the scene, Shiraz became a little nervous. He was now way out into the Gulf of Thailand and there was still no trace of the fishing trawler. And while he was trying to recheck his bearings on the compass there appeared in view about a hundred yards away a typical Thai fishing trawler. Shiraz immediately and in all excitement took out the torch and as was required flashed it thrice at five second intervals, but there was no corresponding response of the three green light sgnals that he was expecting from it. Shiraz was disappointed no doubt, but he did not lose heart. He looked up towards the crimson sky and prayed to the Sai Baba of Shirdi. Ten minutes later he heard the sound of another trawler and as it came closer he once again signaled with his torchlight. It was already dusk, but luckily the trawler had spotted him. And when the trawler responded thrice in quick succession with the green light, there was a smile on Shiraz's face as he with the sharp fruit cutting knife made a fairly big slit first on his left shoulder and then on his left thigh. With the blood oozing out from his shoulder and thigh, he took off his life jacket and from the inside soaked it with his own blood. He then made a few incisions on the life jacket with the knife and together with the torch and the pocket watch threw the jacket into the water. Thereafter he abandoned the kayak and in Tarzan style while holding the knife between his teeth, he quickly swam towards the waiting trawler. This was not a typical fishing trawler that the Thais normally use, but it was one of those ocean going big Alexandra trawlers that had an extended range and was quite luxurious from the inside too.

With its engine switched off, there was an eerie silence as Shiraz doing the fast crawl approached the waiting trawler. And when he was only a couple of yards from it, a long rope was thrown to him. He clutched it firmly and while he was being pulled by a tall gentleman who was dressed in somewhat Sherlock Holmes style, Shiraz as was required for correct identification indicated to him the talisman that was around his neck.

'I hope we did'nt keep you waiting for too long,' said the tall gentleman in good Urdu as he extended his hand to Shiraz and told him to speak to him only in that language.

'Not really! Though the ten minute delay did make me a little nervous, but I was confident that I would be rescued. But under such circumstances what I was really scared off was being spotted and questioned by some Thai marine police patrol boat. Because one such boat from the marine police did pass by me a little while ago,' said Shiraz in his fluent Urdu as his host escorted him to the wood panelled bedroom that had a small bathroom also attached to it.

'Suggest you wrap this big towel around you before my colleague attends to your wounds, and please don't ask any questions and do not talk to any of the three member crew' said the man again in good Urdu as he handed over the plain navy blue coloured towel to Shiraz, while the big trawler with its revved up engine banged into the kayak with speed and sent it flying into the air. As the broken pieces came falling down into the sea, the trawler headed back towards the high seas. Soon thereafter from the adjacent sitting lounge appeared another gentleman with a first aid kit and who also spoke fairly good Urdu.

'Though your wounds are only superficial but there is a need to apply some iodine and put bandages on them. And I will also put a splint on your right arm to make you look like a wounded sailor,' said the nursing assistant as the senior gentlemen in charge handed over a set of naval uniforms that were normally worn by the sailors of the Indian Navy, together with a pair of black shoes and white socks.The two men from the contact team were no doubt both Indian sleuths from the RAW, but definitely not the other three crew members of the trawler. With their typical broken English accent and features, they seem to be locals from the area. There was therefore now a doubt in Shiraz's mind whether the sophisticated trawler belonged to the RAW or had been chartered by the Indian intelligence agency for this very purpose. And with sea piracy and drug smuggling on the rise in this region, the possibility of the trawler belonging to some drug lord could not be ruled out either.

'We have another four hours or so to go before we marry up with the Indian Naval Ship in international waters and I therefore suggest that you have a tot of brandy and some food and take some rest,' said the senior sleuth who had introduced himself as Dev Kumar from Lucknow.

And while Shiraz rested on the bed with his tot of brandy and kept thinking about Saira and his children and what they must be going through right now, the two Indian sleuths sitting in the adjoining lounge were busy preparing for their next phase of operation.

Meanwhile at the Lamai Beach at Koh Samui there was panic. It was nearing 8'oclock and there was still no sign of her husband's kayak. Fearing the worst, Saira contacted her brother Salim Rehman who had by then returned with the others from the Marine Park. Not wishing to alarm them and not wishing to upset the final day's camp fire that was being organized by the younger crowd for the elders, Salim Rehman together with Fazal Rehman quietly drove down to Rocky's Resort on the Lemai Beach to get more details.

'Maybe because of his ankle sprain, he may have got severe cramps while Kayaking and that may have slowed him down,' said Salim Rehman, while Fazal Rehman using his diplomatic rank and status contacted the main Koh Samui Police Station, the Lamai Police Service Unit and the Marine Poice on the island for help. Half an hour later they were all on a fast marine police patrol boat searching the area in and around the Lamai Beach. And though they kept searching for nearly two hours, there was no sign of Riaz Mohammed Khan (Shiraz) and his kayak. By the time they got back to the resort it was well past 10 P.M. and a pall of gloom had descended on the entire Rehman family. And with only 12 hours left for all of them to board the flight back to Bangkok, for the elderly Ruksana Begum it was indeed very nerve racking and sad. With the prayer beads in her hands she kept praying the whole night for the safe return of her loving son-in-law.

And that night, while the entire Rehman family kept praying for his safe return, Shiraz in an Indian naval ratings uniform was safely on board the Indian naval frigate. At around 11 P.M. that night and having established contact with the Captain of the Indian Naval Ship over the satellite phone, the two Indian sleuths had also donned their naval uniforms. While Dev Kumar became a Senior Petty Officer, his junior colleague became a Leading Seaman. It was a part of a cover plan to show that the ship was conducting a sea rescue exercise and drill by night. On being taken aboard, all three of them were whisked away to a special and secluded cabin. Though this was a top secret operation that only the Naval Captain of the Indian Frigate had been made aware off, he however had no idea about the true identity of the injured person who had been rescued and why.

On the next morning while a clean shaven Shiraz with a crew cut and a wig over his head was enjoying his breakfast inside that secluded special cabin of the Indian frigate, at Koh Samui the Marine Patrol had sighted the wreckage of the kayak, but there was no sign at all of the person who was in it. They therefore sought the help of some scuba divers and all they found was the torch light, the pocket watch and the life jacket with blood stains on it and nothing else.

'I think it was an accident, but we have yet to find the body. With the blood stains on the life jacket, it seems to me that the person had been hit on his left shoulder and had possibly drowned, but as off now it is only a conjecture. Preliminary reports indicate that the kayak had either been hit by a fishing trawler or by some other bigger sea going vessel. Nonetheless the search for the body is still on,' said the Marine Patrol Boat Master.

'Maybe after the accident he became a victim of Bull Sharks. They are found at times in the waters in this region and though they are supposed to be typically solitary hunters, but at times they also hunt in pairs,' said one of the marine police personnel.

After a full forty eight hours of search and when there was still no trace of the body, Salim Rehman first informed the Pakistani Embassy in Bangkok and he also called up the Pakistan Foreign Office at Islamabad to inform them about the tragedy. He also had his leave extended and stayed back with his sister Saira and her family at Koh Samui with the hope that his brother-in-law may still be alive or atleast his body would be found.

On the fourth day and early in the morning a half eaten left limb of a human being together with the talisman wound around the wrist was found by some locals on a beach at the Koh Phangan island which was 20 miles north of Koh Samui. And later that morning when on being showed the talisman, Saira confirmed to the local police and to the Pakistani Ambassador to Thailand who had arrived a day earlier for investigation, that the talisman indeed belonged to her husband, the death by accidental drowning of Riaz Mohammed Khan was recorded by the local police and on the same very evening it was also officially announced by Radio Pakistan. Unknown to Shiraz 'Operation Dablo' like "Operation Mincemeat' had also been very meticulously planned by the Indian intelligency agency. The broken limb of a man of roughly Shiraz's age, colour and size and with the same blood group had been procured from a government mortuary in Kolkata and had been carried by the Indian sleuths in a sealed icebox on the 19th of January first to Bankok by an international flight from Kolkata and and then from Bankok to Surat Thani by a domestic flight. Surat Thani was a commercial port in the south of Thailand and it was also close to Koh Samui. That same evening at Surat Thani the two sleuths with the ice box had boarded the chartered trawler that belonged to a private company. The ice box was then put inside the trawler's freezer. On the next day and at around 4.30 in the evening they left Surat Thani for their secret rendezvous. That late evening before all of them boarded the Indian Naval Ship on the high seas, the talisman and the broken limb was handed over by the Indian sleuths to the man in charge of the trawler and who as instructed had it placed on that particular beach. Ofcourse he had been paid quite handsomely for it too. Surprisingly that day happened to be the 23rd of January and the 105th birth anniversary of Netaji Subhash Chander Bose, the great Indian patriot whose death and disappearance during the Second World War had always remained a mystery. On that day very early in the morning the Indian Naval Frigate had also dropped anchor at Port Blair and well before sunrise, and injured Shiraz was taken inside the operation theatre of the INHS Dhanwantari, the multi speciality well equipped naval hospital on the main island. Coincidentally the islands of Andaman and Nicobar had been renamed as 'Shaheed' (Martyr) and 'Swaraj' (Freedom) by Subhas Bose when it was handed over to him by the Japanese in 1943 and where the first provisional government of free India was set up by him. And today unknown to the whole world except for his beloved Shups, Major Shiraz Ismail Khan of the Indian army who had been awarded the Param Veer Chakra posthumously and who had died as a martyr in December 1971 while fighting the Pakitanis had been once again reborn and had found his freedom too.

However, on that late evening and while recouping in the hospital bed when Shiraz read the day's newspaper, he was shocked to learn about the terrorist attack on the American Center in Kolkata. In the early hours on the morning of 22nd Jamuary at about 6.30 a.m. four gunmen on two motorcycles had opened automatic gun fire on the security personnel who were guarding the premises. The action it seemed was well planned and well timed. It was fairly foggy that morning and the security guards were in the process of being changed at that time. There were some three dozen policemen outside the American Center and and they were taken completely by surprise. So shocked were the policemen that they did not even return the fire. As a result of that dastardly act five policemen had been killed and seventeen others wounded and some of them very seriously too. The U.S Consulate in Kolkata is located about half a kilometer away from the Center on the Jawaharlal Nehru Road and a police contingent at the nearby Maidan were rehearsing for the Republic day parade at that time, but the terrorists had made good their escape.

'I only hope the terrorist groups in Pakistan don't have a hand in this, because if they do then it will only precipitate matters. As it is there is so much tension on the Indo-Pak border and we don't want another war,' said Dev Kumar

'I hope not too and the possibility of the group belonging to the HUJI of Bangladesh should not be ruled out either,'said Shiraz.

For the next three days the three specialist plastic surgeons from the Indian armed forces who had been especially flown in from the Command Hospital in Pune diligently worked on Shiraz's face. They had been told not to ask any questions and to get on with the task of transforming his face to the best of their ability and to give him a much younger look, While the first doctor did a rhinoplasty on his nose to shorten and widen it a bit, the other two plastic surgeons carried out a complete face lift. With expert cosmetic surgery and face restructuring they not only removed the big battle scar that was on his cheek, but they also removed the extra flab and wrinkles that was around his face, on his neck, under the eyes, and on his forehead. And by the time they finished the entire surgery which took a full day, Shiraz by late evening had a completely new look.

Very early on the morning of 26th of January which happened to be India's 52nd Republic Day and Shups 52nd birthday also, while a heart broken Saira with her son Tojo and daughter Sherry, and accompanied by her brother Salim Rehman and his family boarded the PIA flight from Bangkok to Islamabad, Shiraz with the two Indian sleuths boarded a private

Cessna executive jet at Port Blair. The sleek aircraft either belonged to RAW or it may have been been chartered by the agency thought Shiraz as he took the first window seat. It was a special flight that would take him to New Delhi on that cold Saturday morning. A while later after the aircraft was airborne and the seat belt sign was switched off, Shiraz was handed over his new Indian passport. Though it looked rather funny when he saw his latest photograph on it, but he felt no doubt a bit flattered. He was not only looking young but he could not even recognize himself. He was now officially Shiraz Rehmatullah Khan son of the late Dr Riaz Rehmatullah Khan, a 44 year old Indian citizen with his permanent home address as 'The Tiger's Den" Naukuchiatal, Distict Nainital, Uttaranchal, India.

'Well looking at the manner in which our plastic surgeons have worked on you, I don't think even the top Pakistan ISI sleuths from the ISI will ever be able to nab you ever,' whispered Dev Kumar the senior Indian police officer from RAW very confidently. Dev Kumar had also earlier served as a Counsellor in the Indian Embassy in Thailand and had therefore been specially chosen for this top secret assignment.

Chapter-46

Farewell My Love

It was at around 0800 hours on that wintry Saturday morning of 26th January 2002, when the sleek eight seater Cessna jet with its very valuable passenger landed at Palam airport and it was immediately taken to one of the hangers of the Indian Air Force Air Headquarters Communication Squadron. This was the squadron that primarily catered for the flight of the VVIP's, such as the President and the Prime Minister of India and the foreign heads of states who visit the country in an official capacity. Once the aircraft was fully inside the hangar, the aircraft door was opened and as soon as, Shiraz together with Dev Kumar and his buddy stepped out of the aircraft, they were greeted by two other very senior officers from the RAW.

'Hope you had a comfortable flight and we are sorry we could not serve you any tea or coffee on board, but there is breakfast waiting for all of us in the guest house where you will be staying for the next couple of days,' said the short statured bald gentleman who introduced himself as Kailash Chandra. And in the bossy but friendly manner in which he was conducting himself, Shiraz could make out that the gentleman probably was either an Additional Secretary (RAW) from the Cabinet Secretariat or the prinicipal controlling officer for 'Operation Dablo'. Minutes later while they were on their way to the safe house near Mehrauli in the two black Ambassador cars with tinted glasses, Shiraz who was sitting in the rear seat with the bald gentlemen by his side made a small request to them.

'If you don't mind Mr Chandra can I make a little request I would very much like to send a big bouquet of flowers to someone special today and it is only to thank the person concerned for all the help and assistance,' said Shiraz as the two cars made their way to a secluded big farm house on the Mehrauli Road.

'Sure, and it can be done over the telephone through Inter Flora or through a good reliable florist once we get to the guest house,' said Dev Kumar who was at the wheels.

By the time they reached the guest house which was one of RAW's important safe houses around New Delhi, Dev Kumar ordered for some tea and coffee and also asked for breakfast to be laid quickly. Then he switched on the television for all of them to watch the Republic Day Parade that was being telecast live from Rajpath that day. Because of the tension on the borders, this was one of the most unusual and lackluster republic day parade that morning.There were no contingents from the army, navy or the airforce, and the public galleries too were largely empty. There was no display of India's military power and might, and the colourful pageant that normally befits the occasion were not too many and they were not very colourful and impressive either. There was no doubt that the parade was being held under very tight security conditions and the sky too had been effectively sanitized.

Unknown to Shiraz, Shups too that morning while sitting in the VIP section that was meant for senior government officials and their families was witnessing the parade and where President Hugo Chavez of Venezuela was to be the chief guest. But because of the India-Pakistan standoff, the President of Venezuela had pulled out at the last minute and he was replaced by Cassam Uteem, the President of Mauritius. When the winners of the Ashok Chakra, the highest gallantry awards that are given in peace time were being presented by President K R Narayanan to the winners there were tears in Shupriya's eyes. All the four Ashok Chakras that were awarded that morning were all given posthumously to the next of kin and. while only one of them was from the Indian army, the other three were from the police and the watch and ward staff at Parliament House who had shown exemplary courage and bravery during the terrorist attack on the Indian Parliament. When the next of kin of Naik Ranbeer Singh Tomar of the 26th Rastriya Rifles who had in a dare devil operation single handedly killed four armed terrorists in the valley before being gunned down was presented with the gallantry medal, there was pin drop silence. Monty who had accompanied Shupriya to the parade was also reminded of the day thirty years ago when he also stood in front of the President of India to receive the Param Veer Chakra on behalf of his foster brother Major Shiraz Ismail Khan, but he had no idea about his arrival and presence in the Indian capital that day.

That morning seeing the poor turnout of the participants at the 52nd Repuplic Day Parade in Delhi and the very poor attendance of the public in general, together with the unprecedented security at Raj Path all this gave a clear indication to Shiraz that both India and Pakistan were bent upon destroying each other militarily. Both sides had more or less completed the mobilization of their armed forces and it was now only a question of time as to who would fire the gun first.With 'Operation Endure Freedom' by the United States and its allies gaining momentum in the west, and with the plans to launch 'Operation Anaconda' in the offing to oust the Taliban and the Al Qaida from Afghanistan, General Musharraf and his government had been caught in a very tricky and dicey situation. Where as in the west he had assured the Americans that he would help them in the war against terror, in the east the Indian armed forces were threatening to unleash their superior forces against him. Moreover, his sudden 360 degree about turn in Afghanistan and the tough sermon that he gave to the Mullahs and to the people of Pakistan on the 12th of January asking them to direct their Jihad against poverty and illiteracy in the country, and not against the kafirs and non Muslims had not gone down well with the fundamentalist and radical militant groups in Pakistan. With the war clouds getting darker and more ominous, and fearing that more delay would only precipitate matters, Shiraz soon after breakfast told his handlers that he was ready to talk. Soon thereafter and after his handlers had arranged to send the beautiful bouquet of 52 red roses through a local florist to the address in New Delhi that was given by him, he said somewhat abruptly.

'Gentlemen, I think the time has come for me to bare it all. Though most of it is already there inside the secret red diary and the CD that I had sent to Miss Simran Kaur Bajwa earlier, but the need of the hour is to prevent an all out nuclear war between India and Pakistan and which would be disastrous for both the countries.Therefore if you all have any questions or doubts, or you need any further elaboration or clarifications, I will be only too glad to answer them."

'In that case we shall start the debriefing soon after our big boss arrives and he is expected to be here any minute since the parade is over now,' said the short statured bald man as another ambassador car with a beacon light entered through the gate and stopped at the portico.

'Welcome to India and with time being at a premium, we shall therefore start the proceedings right now,' said the tall gentleman with the salt and pepper hair who was dressed impeccably in churidar pyjamas and an embroidered sherwani. He with two other officers from RAW it seems had come directly from the parade

'And needless to say we will not carry out any polygraph test on you and nor shall we term this as an interrogation, but you have to tell us the truth, the whole truth and nothing but the truth," said Kailash Chander.

'But before you start with your story which will be recorded by us, you must first tell us a bit more about yourself, about your family, your career and what was the main reason or compulsion for you to defect,"said the tall gentlemen who appeared to Shiraz to be the one who was heading the JIC, the Joint Intelligence Committee, while the other two who accompanied him were probably Joint Secretaries from Area 'A' which dealt with Pakistan and the other from Area 'B' which dealt with China and South East Asia. And though the Secretary 'R' the big boss of RAW was notably absent that morning, but that was understandable since he would be kept in full picture soon after the initial debreifing of the high profile defector from Pakistan was over.

Giving the reason that he was both an Indian and a Pakistani because he was born in Kolkata to a Muslim family before the country was partioned and that the family migrated to Pakistan soon after it was divided and which was not his fault, his decision to defect was therefore of his own free will and volition. Therefter hiding the fact that he was actually a highly decorated officer of the Indian Army, he very confidently gave out his life history as Riaz Mohammed Khan. And the main reason for him to defect by planning his own death by drowning was because of the threat to his own life and the threat to the lives of his near and dear ones in Pakistan. For it was not only him, but also his wife and children too whose lives were now in danger. The JeM and the LeT had threatened to kill all of them and with he and his family now also on the radar of the Pakistan ISI, he therefore had no other choice. And all this was simply because he as the Pakistani Ambassador to Russia, had got in touch with his Indian counterpart in Moscow and both of them together had decided to work towards a lasting peace in the subcontinent. But this had angered both the men in uniform who were now ruling the country and the radical Mullas and their militant organizations and I was being labeled as an Indian spy.It all started soon after the failure of the Indo-Pak talks at Agra, when Miss Bajwa and I at my own initiative decided to open a Track-3 channel consisting of like minded Indians and Pakistanis and with the sincere aim to settle the ever burning Kashmir problem peacefully once and for all. And the only other reason for my crossing over was to ensure that both the countries should not go for a fourth round. And it is with that very purpose in mind that I had sent those vital topsecret in puts about Pakistan's nuclear stockpile, capability and likely intentions. There is now also every possibility of some of those falling into the hands of the highly fanatical Al-Qaida, the LeT and such like other fanatical and militant organization, and looking at the manner and the direction in which Pakistan is heading today, these radical outfits may well will also soon start dictating terms to General Musharraf. With the increase in instability in the country and the growing fundamentalism in Pakistan, it has made the country's nuclear weapons and stockpiles highly vulnerable to theft and proliferation by such like militant groups. A reliable source has also indicated that Dr AQ Khan, who is one of Pakistan's top nuclear scientists has also opened a smuggling ring which besides selling bomb related parts to Libya, Iran and North Korea, it has also provided Colonel Gadaffi with design information of a nuclear bomb. Moreover, with some of Pakistan's top serving and retired military brass who are stil smarting over the 1971 debacle and the loss of East Pakistan, they it seems are still determind to take their revenge and therefore the chances of some rogue element from within the present Pakistan military hierarchy going for a first nuclear strike could not be ruled out. The war on terrorism is going to be a long drawn battle and in the near future this factor too will subject Pakistan to more instability,' added Shiraz as he on the giant blow up map of the subcontinent pointed out the deployment of Pakistan's nuclear weapons, there effective ranges, there storage locations, the security and access control arrangements at those sites and other operational details. His focal points were Chaklala, the old British Cantonment area of Rawalpindi and where the Headquarters of the Strategic Plans Division was also located and Sargodha where the squadron of F-16 fighter aircrafts were based. Shiraz also pointed out that despite General Musharraf's sermon to the nation on 12th January, the Pakistan military and the ISI are still maintain very strong ties with the Tali ban, the LeT, the JeM and the Al Qaida. And like most Pakistanis there are many among the rank and file in the military and also in the officer corps who are also very sympathetic to these fundamentalist militant organizations. And as a result of which their hostility towards the United States, India and even towards General Musharaff would only keep growing, and especially so now that Pakistan too has joined America and its western allies in 'Operation Enduring Freedom'. Today there are two distinct factions in the armed forces of Pakistan. One is the Kemalist faction or the moderate faction that is being led by General Musharraf and the other is the Jehadi faction that is led by a group of second rung serving generals and which is also being actively supported by fundamentalist generals like retired Lt General Usmani, Lt General (retired) Hamid Gul and others including Lt General Aziz who is a serving Corps Commander and the man who also helped Musharraf to come to power. Even some of the top Pakistani nuclear scientists and those from the ISI are also still maintaining close clandestine links with the Al-Qaida and the LeT. There is no doubt that the Pakistan Jihadi faction share an unbilical cord with the Taliban and after all theTaliban is Pakistan's child and therefore it cannot exist without that lifeline. And I am afraid if this ISI-Pakistan Military-Al Qaida-LeT nexus is allowed to continue then it could lead to a civil war in Pakistan and a more destabilized and Talibanised Pakistan would be even a greater threat to India and the world. And what is even more ironic is the fact that the Taliban was also actively being supported by the daughter of the east, Benazir Bhutto and her government during its second term of ofiice from 1993 to 1996, and allegedly a large number of her husband's business friends including her husband Asif Ali Zardari had made quite a killing by exporting fuel to that country. And as the Taliban army expanded further and became more mechnized, the permits to export fuel supplies from Pakistan also became a major earner for some of the other Pakistani politicians also. And even under Benazir's regime the policy of exploiting Islamic fundamentalist terrorism had become a state sponsored tool. So much so that Pakistan was flooded with thousands of Islamist militants from nearly 20 diferent countries. They were not only given free visas to enter Pakistan, but they were also equipped and trained by the ISI to fight against the Indian rule in Kashmir and elsewhere too including Bosnia and Chechniya, and they are still doing so as far as Kashmir is concerned. And I must also tell you that the drug trade continues unabated even today and the money that is laundered in this hawala fashion is also a significant source for funding not only terrorist activities in the country, but it also provides illicit funds for international terrorism. Heroin the lucrative contraband is also very much tied into Pakistani politics and the militarization of the Pakistani armed forces. Prior to the launching of 'Operation Endure Freedom' the opium production under the Taliban eradication program had declined by nearly 90 percent, but once again now on the orders of President Bush not to destroy the opium harvest since it might lead to destabilizing of the Musharraf government, it has once again become a thriving business. The laundering of drug money has again begun in right earnest and this multibillion dollar trading activity is being protected both by the CIA and the ISI. And with Pakistanis still protecting the likes of Khalid Sheikh Mohammed and others who had masterminded the 9/11 attacks on Washington and New York, the situation is indeed very grave today,' added Shiraz.

That whole day and for the next forty eight hours, while Shiraz with his vital inputs on Pakistan kept the JIC spellbound, Shups who was not included in the loop started getting a bit worried. She had promised Dablo his complete freedom and was keen to find out a little more about his whereabouts. Though she had received the fifty two red roses on her birthday, but after that there was no other communication from him at all. On the evening of 29th January 2002, after watching the beating of the retreat at Vijay Chowk, Shupriya called on the Cabinet Secretary who was working still in his office. She had been promised by none other than the Prime Minister and the Foreign Minister of India that no mental and physical harm would come to the defecting Pakistani diplomat and she wanted to know if that promise was being kept.

'Well Madam, I think you have arrived right on time because the gentleman concerned and the Secretary 'R' together with the Foreign Minister are right now in the Prime Minister's office and I must say that the suave Pakistani diplomat has given us some very vital and highly classified information. And if you desire to meet him then you may wait here in my office. After all this whole game of cloak and dagger was started by you Miss Bajwa and it should end with you too I guess,' said the Cabinet Secretary, who was the senior most bureaucrat of the country but who had no idea at all that the Pakistani gentleman was none other than Major Shiraz Ismail Khan, PVC and an officer from the Jammu and Kashmir Rifles of the Indian army and the lady Miss Simran Kaur Bajwa from the Indian Foreign service was actually Shupriya Sen the defector's legally wedded wife

It was around 8 o'clock on that cold wintry Tuesday evening, when Shiraz immaculately dressed in a three piece warm pin striped black and grey suit and accompanied by the Secretary RAW walked into the Cabinet Secretary's ofiice. And had Shupriya not been told, even she would never have recognized her Dablo.The only heartening news that day was Pakistan's offer for talks on a phased plan to withdraw troops to their peacetime locations, but India had rejected the offer stating that tensions could only be reduced if Pakistan took effective steps to reduce infiltration in Kashmir.

'Let me introduce you to Mr Shiraz Rehmatullah Khan, said the Secretary RAW as Shups gazed in amazement at Dablo. And while she kept looking at him, the top boss from RAW extended an invitation to Shiraz for cocktails at Henri's bar. Located on the top most floor of the Le Meridien Hotel in New Delhi it not only offered a panoramic view of the capital but it also served very good delicious snacks too. There was no doubt at all that India's top sleuth and his intelligent agency had very meticulously planned and executed 'Operation Dablo' and he therefore wanted to celebrate it with the very person who was not only a very high ranking Pakistani Foreign Service Officer but also a distinguished career diplomat. This was probably India's biggest catch ever since RAW came into existence in 1968. Also invited to the cocktails were the two RAW officers who were instrumental in catching the big fish from the waters of the Gulf of Thaland and an Indian Brigadier who had only recently been posted on deputation to RAW and he was now a part of the Cabinet Secretariat.

That evening, when Shiraz was introduced to the Brigadier, he got a shock of his life. He was not only from his own N.D.A batch and seniority, but also from the same 'India Squadron'. Though he had passed out from the Indian Military Academy Dehradun with the coveted sword of honour, but now it seems he had missed the boat for futher promotions. And according to the grapewine his appointment on deputation was mainly thanks to his political connections.That evening, when the topic of whether there were Indian army officers who had been declared missing after the 1971 Indo-Pak war and who had been taken as prisoners by Pakistan were still in Pakistani jails was put to Shiraz by the Brigadier, and Shiraz very cleverly answered it by saying that though everyone in Karachi knows that Dawood Ibrahim the Mumbai Don who was responsible for the 1993 Bombay serial blasts was very much in Pakistan, but the government of Pakistan will never admit, the Brigadier had got the answer.

That evening before being taken back to a government guest house that was in a posh locality of Lodhi Road in South Delhi, Shiraz was handed over a first class air ticket from New Delhi to Port of Spain (Guyana) via New York and a large envelope containing a big wad of U.S. hundred dollars. Though he was now a free man, the men from RAW were not taking any chances. Since Shiraz was scheduled to catch the Air India flight to New York from Delhi late next evening of 30th January, he therefore requested if he could have breakfast with Miss Simran Kaur Bajwa(Shupriya) next morning.

'Most certainly, but no more Track-3 solutions please,' said the RAW Chief in good humour, as he shook hands with Shiraz and bid him a final goodbye.

It was dot at 9 a.m.next morning, when Shupriya with a biggish handbag arrived at the guest house. Not wishing to have anybody else around the breakfast table, she very cleverly requested the guest house incharge if they could have their breakfast sitting in one far corner of the lawn and while enjoying the winter sun.

'Most certainly Madam and we will have it served in the food trolley,'said the housekeeper as he asked the bearer to quickly put two garden chairs with peg tables out in the lawn.

'Wearing her sunglasses to hide away the tears that were swelling in her eyes, Shuprya took out the big packet from her hand bag and while handing it over to Dablo said.

'Inside the bag there are the things that rightly belong to you and it includes the gold Victorian guinea that was presented by Lord Curzon to Curzon Sikandar Khan and the Victoria Cross that was awarded to him by King George the Fifth of England, the Mahavir Chakra medal that was awarded to Colonel Shiraz Ismail Khan who adopted you, and your own Param Veer Chakra and Veer Chakra medals.'

'But what will I do with them and in anycase I do not have anybody to hand them over to when I die,' said Shiraz feeling rather emotional about it.

'Well then let me confess and tell you that you do have a somebody and he is very much your own flesh and blood too, He also happens to be our one and only son and he is very much alive. I never told you this because even the son who is now nearly 30 years old does not know the real truth. Right from his birth Monty has been his father and Reeta his mother. And thanks to both of them, he therefore knows that he is their son and he calls me Mom Number 2,'said Shupriya as she wiped away the tears from her eyes.

'But where the hell is he and why did you not tell me about all this earlier and what is his name. And now let me atleast see and meet him in flesh and blood before I finally leave the country for good, 'said Shiraz as he pleadingly and with folded hands kept looking at Shups.

'You can see him alright but I cannot let you meet him and there are many reasons as to why you should not meet him also. He is presently working in Mumbai and though the notice is very short, but I will give some excuse and request him to come immediately. Because that I think is the least that I can do as his mother and your wife and for you as the father. And if that suits you then you will have to come to the India Gate a few minutes before sunset this evening. Because every year on the 30th of January we all pay homage to the Unknown Soldier and we will also do the same today. And while we will be paying our homage while facing the 'Amar Jawan Jyoti' from the direction of Rashtrapati Bhawan, you will be required to do the same, but from the opposite direction. And for that you will have to therefore enter the complex from the National stadium side. And hopefully not only will you see your handsome son, but also the others from the remarkable and great Bajwa family. This is a ritual with candles that Monty Bhiaya, Reeta Bhabhi and I religiously carry out every year on the 30th of January. It is Martyr's Day today and we will be there not only to pay our respects to all those brave soldiers who sacrificed their lives for the nation, but we will also pray for the departed souls of Lt Colonel Daler Singh Bajwa, Colonel Ismail Sikandar Khan, and Major Shiraz Ismail Khan, my husband and India's war hero. This will also give you an opportunity after thirty one long years to see your near and dear ones from fairly close quartes in flesh and blood for the last and final time probably', said Shupriya as she tried to control her emotions and kept wiping away the tears from her eyes.

'Well now that you have told me, I will definitely be there at the appointed time. But in order to get rid of my anxiety you could atleast show me his photograph. And all these medals and memorabilia therefore should remain a part of my son's inherited legacy' said Shiraz softly as he handed back the big packet containing those medals to Shups.

'For reasons best known to the family and me I never carry his photograph on my person and I also cannot afford to present one to you either. And as far as the medals are concerned I think I will be more apt if these are presented by Monty Bhaiya in your memory to the Jammu and Kashmir Rifles Regimental Centre Musuem at Jabalpur during the coming regimental reunion that the regiment will be celebrating later this year,' said Shups rather softly while putting the packet back into her handbag. Thereafter as they quietly kept having their breakfast, Shupriya said.

'You know it is really a strange world where people it seems only live to part with their near and dear ones, but one simply cannot forget the past I guess. And I am sure you too would like to one day reunite with Saira and your children And if you ever desire my help and assistance in finding out how your family in Pakistan is doing, and you need my help and assistance, you can always count on me at whatever distance,'said Shups as she called out to her driver to get ready for the journey back home. Strangely enough Shupriya was occupying the same official bungalow on Pandara Road that her father and mother had stayed in earlier while she was secretly dating her Dablo.

'Yes I would love to get back to them, but certainly not in Pakistan and definitely not as Riaz Mohammed Khan. But may be I will hopefully someday Inshallah return to them as Shiraz Rahimtullah Khan. My death by accident may have in some way reduced the death threat to them from those fanatical Mullas, but I think it would be much better and safer too, if Saira and Sherry shift house permanently to the United States where my son Tojo who is now a green card holder and he can look after them in a much better manner. And if that does become a reality someday, then rest assured that I as Shiraz Rehmatullah Khan will once again reappear on the scene and maybe get reunited with them for good. Afterall I have still to get my Sherry and Tojo married. And you have to do me a favour too. You have to get our son married to a nice girl who should be as beautiful, as considerate and as gentle as you. But by the way you have not told be my son's name and what does he do for a living?' said Shiraz softly as he gently squeezed Shups hand.

'We call him Param Veer in honour of the medal that was won by you for gallantry and valour and he works for an event management company in Mumbai and let me also tell you that he is as tall and handsome as you and maybe even more,' said Shupriya very proudly as she got into the car.' She did not want to tell him that he was a popular Bollywood filmstar who was once in love with his pretty daughter.

'Well that is indeed a very nice name and I am eagerly looking forward to seeing him in flesh and blood this evening,' said Shiraz as he bid Shups goodbye. The name Param Veer was quite a common name among the Sikhs and to Shiraz it did not ring a bell because it also stood for Peevee in short. And as soon as the car went out from the big gate, Shups called up Peevee on his mobile and in a very sad and emotional tone said.

"I am sorry for the short notice but if you really love your Mom Number 2 then please take the first flight out of Mumbai and reach Delhi positively by sundown this evening. Just leave everything and come fast and if need be even charter a flight if you have to, but I need you very urgently.Suddenly something very important has cropped up and I need you here to sign some important legal papers and documents. Off late I have not been keeping well at all and I do not know for how long more I will live. I have made my will and since I have no children, I want all my wordly possession should go to you and to you alone before God decides to give me his last and final call. And I do not think I have much time left either.'

Hearing those words coming from his Mom Number 2 and whom he dearly loved, Peevee who was shooting in Film City, immediately left the studio and took the first flight to Delhi. And while he was on his way, Shups called up her lawyer and told him to get the will ready. And in order to make it look even more dramtic and authentic she also visited the All India Medical Sciences hospital and complained of chest pain. There she got an ECG and a cardiogram also done and with those medical papers in her hand she went straight to Monty's house in Defence Colony.

'Since I am not feeling too bright I think I will skip going to office today. I developed some chest pain this morning and I also got myself checked up by the cardiologist at the AIMS. The ECG that was taken was not very good and though the doctor said that it could be due to gas, but

I decided not to take any chances. So I called up Peevee and told him to come positively by this evening. And I also told my lawyer to make a will bequeathing all that I have and posses in the name of Param Veer Singh Bajwa and to bring it along with him to your house at the earliest so that both of you can sign as witnesses. And my only other request is that all these gallantry medals that I have in this packet should be handed over for prosperity to the JAKRIF Regimental Centre Musuem at Jabalpur,' said Shupriya in all seriousness as Reeta made her lie down on the bed, while Monty fetched her a glass of water to have the medicines that the docter at the A.I.M.S. had prescribed for her.

And at around 3.15 p.m. when Peevee arrived from Mumbai, Shups knew that her good acting had done the trick. But Peevee seeing her lying in bed insisted on getting a second opinion from another reputed cardiologist who was also an ex Sanawarian and a good family friend. And when that doctor too after examining the cardiogram and the patient said that there was nothing to really worry about and that it could be because of gas, there was a sense of relief on everybody's face. And a little while later when her lawyer arrived with the will and Shupriya quickly got the needful done, she felt very happy indeed.

The sunset time on that 30th of January 2002 was at 17.59 hrs and calculating that Dablo would definitely be there atleast 5 to10 minutes earlier, Shupriya suggested that like every year on 'Martyrs Day' today also all of them must go and pay homage to late Colonel Ismail Sikandar Khan, Lt Colonel Bajwa, Major Shiraz Ismail Khan and also to the Unknown Soldier, and therefore they should all be at the 'Amar Jawan Jyoti' well before sunset.

'But you need to rest and maybe we could skip it this year, or postpone it till you are better', said Reeta.

'But right now I am feeling absolutely fine, and since both the doctors have said that it could be because of gas and that there was no real cause to worry, we could just go for a few minutes may be. After all today is 'Martyr's Day isn't it 'said Shupriya

'Yes and maybe a bit of fresh air and an evening walk in this lovely winter weather will also be good for Mom Number Two. It would also help her to get rid of the gas and that's what the good doctor had also suggested and advised. So therefore let us all go for a quick cup of tea to Mom Number Two's bungalow. That will also give her time to change and freshen up a bit and from there India Gate is only a stone's throw away and we could all walk it to that place if need be' said Peevee.

At around five o'clock that evening, while Monty and family were all enjoying their tea with sizzling hot pakoras at Mom Number Two's bungalow on Pandara Road, Shiraz was getting ready to go to the India Gate. He had very cleverly given the excuse to his handlers that before leaving India he wanted to to visit that historic place and it was primarily because he wanted to pay homage to his late grandfather Naik Curzon Sikandar who had been posthumously awarded the Victoria Cross in the First World War and whose name was etched in gold on that historic monument. The beautiful designed edifice in the shape of a huge gate was designed by Sir Edwin Lutyens and it was constructed as a war memorial to honour all those who died for the British Empire in the First World War and in the Third Afghan War. However, though the construction began in 1921, it was only unveiled in 1931 by the British government and the beautiful red and pale sandstone and granite structure had now become a very popular tourist landmark. After the 1971 war a cenotaph was added to it and that became the tomb of the Indian Army's Unknown Soldier and which was depicted by the traditional helmet on top of a reversed rifle and where an eternal fire was always kept burning. The cenotaph that was named as the 'Amar Jawan Jyoti' or the flame of the immortal solldier had also now become a place of pilgrimage for the next of kin of those soldiers who had sacrificed their lives for the honour and the territorial integrity of the country after India had gained her freedom. The black marble structure that was guarded round the clock by four Indian army soldiers with four fires perpetually burning in the four corners of the cenotaph was inaugurated by Mrs Indira Gandhi the Prime Minister of India soon after the 1971 Indo-Pak war. It was in tribute to those gallant Indian armed forces servicemen who had died fighting during that short war. And since Shiraz had heard that the name of his grandfather Naik Curzon Sikandar Khan who died at Flanders in 1915 during the Battle of Loos was also engraved in golden letters on that monument, he only wanted to check it out if his name was still there.

It was nearing 5.45 in the evening, when the Government of India's black Ambassador Car wth Dev Kumar at the wheels and with Shiraz and another officer from RAW as co-passengers arrived near the India Gate. Seeing the big crowd near the monument and with no parking allowed in the general area of Raj Path and the India Gate, Dev Kumar therefore decided to park the car inside the Union Public Service Commisssion office at Dholpur House on the nearby Shah Jehan Road and from there walk to the monument which was only a short distance away. Surprisinly though it was a Wednesday and a working day at that, but being the 'Martyr's Day,' in India there were bus loads of men, women and children who had congregated inside the historic monument and at the "Amar Jawan Jyoti'. Though quite a few of them were foreigners, but the majority of them were Indians and they were mostly from Punjab, Haryana and Uttar Pradesh. Tradtionally the 'Martyr's Day' is linked to India's Father of the Nation Mahatma Gandhi because it was on that day of 30th January 1948, that he died from an assassin's bullet, and a solemn function in the presence of the Prime Minister and the President of India and the three service chiefs is always held in the morning at Raj Ghat. And during the day a large number of families of India's freedom fighters and from those of the Indian armed forces who had sacrificed their lives for the nation also gather there at the India Gate on that auspicious day to pay their respects to the 'Unknown Indian Soldier'.

As part of the Republic Day celebrations in the capital, the India Gate had been lit up very aesthetically that evening and as all three of them approached the magnficent edifice, Shiraz noticed that a large number of people who were mostly young boys and girls were shouting and jostling to get as close to the cenotaph as possible.

'I wonder why all this commotion and chaos at this time of the evening and I hope it is not another security concern. So therefore let me first check it out,' said Dev Kumar as he went ahead alone to first verify with the police van that was on duty in that area and find out what the commotion was all about.

'Kuch Nahin Saheb, suna hai ke ek koi Bollywood ka mashur actor aya hua hai aur log unke saath hath milana aur photo lehna chahaten' said the Head Constable very matter of factly. (There is nothing to worry about Sahib. I believe some famous Bollywood actor has come and the people want to shake hands and have a photograph taken with him.)

'Ye toh bahut hi sharam ki baat hai. Aur Khas karke aaj ka din, jab log aate hai yahan shardhanjali dene hamere shahid huye jawanon ko, aur hamare naujawan ko ek filmy hero ke se hath milane ka aur uske saat photo khichne ki naubat padi hui ha—Kiys hoga is desh ka !,' ('This is really shameful and especially so on this particular day when people come here to pay their respects to our martyred soldiers who sacrificed their lives for the nation and it seems that the young people are more interested in shaking hands and getting themselves photograph with some popular Bollywood hero. And I wonder what will happen to this damn country,' said a visibly upset Dev Kumar as he beckoned his comrade and Shiraz to come forward.

It was already nearing sunset and Shiraz was now worried that the presence of the Bollywood star at this critical moment of time and with the crowd milling around him could well prevent him from seeing his long lost son.

'I think we should hurry up and get in from the other side, before the crowd becomes unmanageable,' said Shiraz as they with the help of a police constable managed to enter the precincts of the hallowed monument from the National Stadium side. There was now a huge crowd both inside and ouside the India Gate as Shiraz with his big frame made a desperate attempt to get as close to the 'Amar Jawan Jyoti' as possible. And thanks to his tall height he somehow finally did manage to spot Shups. But as a result of his desperation to see her with his son, Shiraz had lost physical contact with Dev Kumar and his partner in that big crowd. Though he finally managed to spot Shups standing with Monty and Reeta on the other side of the cenotaph, but he found it difficult to get closer to them.Because standing a little ahead of them was a tall handsome young gentleman who it seems was literally being mobbed by the big crowd. He could not see him very clearly and did not know even know the name of the Bollywood star who was literally being mobbed by the crowd till a young teenage boy who was standing not very far from him with his camera held high above his head kept shouting loudly to some of his friends to get a little closer to Deepak Kumar so that he could take a group photograph of all of them with the actor.

'Oh so that's the Bollywood star who had swept my daughter of her feet,' but where is my son thought Shiraz as he took the big red handkerchief out from his top coat pocket and kept waving it at Shups. He was frantically trying to catch her attention, and when he finally did manage to do that, he not only shouted at the top of his voice,'where is my son', but he also tried to gesture the same with his hand and palm. But when he saw Shups repeatedly putting her right hand on Deepak Kumar's head as if she was blessing him and with her left hand kept pointing at the Bollywood star. Shiraz just could not believe that his son was Deepak Kumar, the Bollywood actor. Unable to control his emotions and with tears of joy in his eyes he now tried to edge as forward as possible. He wanted not only to get a closer look at his son, but he also wanted to physically touch him and shake his hand. And while Shiraz in that big crowd kept waving his hand in happiness and tried to push his way through the big crowd, suddenly there were a couple of loud deafening explosions. There was already a red alert in Delhi and the huge crowd fearing that it could be a terrorist bomb attack started running helter skelter and which resulted in a massive stampede. There was complete chaos both inside and outside the India Gate, as the small police force with Deepak Kumar's bodyguard tried to whisk him and his family away. In his desperate endeavour to atleast be able to touch his son, Shiraz tried to lunge forward and in that melee lost his balance and fell down. At that very moment the team of four army sentries who were positioned in the four corners of the cenotaph in their ceremonial uniforms and fearing that the sacred resting place of India's Unknown Soldier that they were suppose to protect at all costs may be targeted by the terrorists, they too in order to keep the big crowd at bay cocked their rifles and fired a few rounds in the air. But the sound of the rifle fire only added to the chaos and confusion as more people in that crowd while trying to quickly get away from the scene fell on top of one another. Most of them were old men and women who had come with their war widows and grandchildren to pay homage at the 'Amar Jawan Jyoti.' They were the next of kin of those Indian soldiers who had so gallantly sacrificed their lives during the 1971 Indo-Pak war. Thanks to Peevee alert bodyguard and the small posse of police force that was trying to pevent the Bollywood star from being mobbed, Peevee and his family had been quickly whisked away from the scene no sooner those explosions were heard. And by the time the Rapid Action Force with the sniffer dogs could arrive, there were eight dead including Shiraz and twenty one others injured and some of them fairly seriously too. That evening by the time the situation was brought totally under control at India Gate, Shups with Monty, Reeta and Peevee were safely back at her residence on Pandara Road. But Shupriya did not know that her loving Dablo was no more. And it was only on the next day morning, when she read the headlines in the newspapers that the stampede at the India Gate was not a terror attack at all there was a big sigh of relief on her face. Because she very well knew that if there had been another terrorist attack, then the guns on the borders definitely would have also opened up by now. The Indian Prime Minister had already warned Pakistan after the attack on the Indian Pariament on 13th December that India's patience was running out, and with both the countries armed with nuclear weapons that were ready to srike at each other,it would have been simply catastrophic

According to the headlines in the newspaper, the stampede was caused by some young enthusiast who with his friends was celebrating his eighteenth birthday at the India Gate. They were bursting fire crackers nearby and which unfortunately resulted in the death of eight people and had injured twenty one others. But when Shupriya turned to page seven to read in a little more detail about the tragic incident and then read the names of those who had died, she was shocked beyond belief and realized that she actually now was a widow. The only consolation was that on the same page was the photograph of her son Deepak Kumar paying homage at the memorial to the Unknown Indian Soldier. For her that 30th of January 2002 was truly a martyr's day. Though there were no obituaries and no gun salutes for the fallen and forgotten Indian war hero, she was atleast happy that Major Shiraz Ismail Khan, P.V.C had died at the feet of India's Unknown Soldier. But her only regret and complaint was that even after 55 years of India being a free democratic country, the Government of India was yet to design and construct a befitting War Memorial in the nation's capital with the names of all those soldiers from India's gallant armed forces who had with valour, courage and devotion to duty sacrificed their lives for the nation. And included in the list of martyrs and written in golden letters would have also been for sure the name of her dear husband Major Shiraz Ismail Khan, PVC. Though Shiraz with many other such young officers of the Indian army had sacrificed their young lives for India's tomorrow in the many wars that India and Pakistan had fought over Kashmir ever since India gained her freedom, but they unfortunately were always forgotten by the politicians soon after the wars were over.

On that night of 31st January, 2002 Shupriya took out the photograph of his beloved Dablo. It was a photograph of the young and handsome Second Lieutenant Shiraz Ismail Khan dressed in his winter Green Patrols receiving the Veer Chakra from the President of India at Rastrapati Bhawan. It was presented to her by Dablo the day after they became man and wife and before he left for the battle front. Written behind the photograph were the words.

'To My Beloved Shups,

'Sare Jahan Se Acchha—ye Hundustan Hamara—Hum Bulbule hain iski ye gulistan hamara. Jaraha hun ek bar phir jung ke maidan mein dushman ke upar vijay pane ke liye-lekin roh math meri jaan—rahunga mein hamesha tumhare hi daman mein—Zaroor aunga mein wapas tumhare hi pass-intezar karna meri jaan kyon tum hi toh ho mere humnawaz.

Off all the places in this world Hindustan (India) is the best-and we are the nightingales of this beautiful garden on earth-Once again I am on my way to the battlefield to defeat the enemy—but you must not cry my love because I will always ever remain by your side and I will definitely comeback my darling-so you just wait because you are my only sweetheart. Below those touching words were Dablo's traditional OO and it was dated 16th September 1971.And that night as she silently cried and read those beautiful words and kissed her husband's photograph, she prayed to God to give eternal peace to her unforgettable Dablo and reunite them again in their next life. She had no doubt that it was because of Dablo's timely revelation of the desperate situation that Pakistan was in that had made Indian leaders think twice before deciding to finally give the green signal to the armed forces of the country to attack Pakistan. On the 25th of January 2002, India had successfully tested the short range version of the deadly Agni ballistic missile and both the countries it seemed were now poised to destroy each other. Pakistan had been pushed into a very tight corner not only by the Americans and their allies who were fighting the war against terror in Afghanistan, but also by some of their own radical islamists within the country who were bent upon Talibanizing Pakistan.' Operation Sangram', the biggest ever troop mobilization of the Indian armed forces to take on Pakistan had been fully completed, but if pushed to the wall Pakistan was also ready to carry out a nuclear first strike. It was therefore a question of touch and go as General S.Padmanabhan, Admiral Madvendra Singh and Air Chief Marshall S Krishnaswamy the three Indian service chiefs waited with baited breath the NDA government's decision to launch or not to launch Operation Parakram. The United States too it seems had conducted its own secret analysis and they also feared that an attack on Pakistan by India could very well trigger of a nuclear war between the two nations.

Early on the morning of 1st February 2002, when the Secretary RAW rang up Shupriya and told her that Shiraz Rahimtullah Khan on the previous evening had been given a proper Muslim burial and offered his heartfelt condolences to her, she imediately visited the same Bangla Sahib Gurudwara where they both as Sikhs had got married thirty two years ago. Quite fittingly the kirtan that was being sung by the Raagis at that moment of time when she entered the gurudwara was 'Deh Shiva Bar Mohe-ii-Hai"Grant me this boon O God-May I never refrain from the righteous acts-May I fight without fear all foes in life's battles-With confident courage claiming the victory-May thy glory be ingrained in my mind and my highest ambition be singing thy praises—when this mortal life comes to end-May I die fighting with limitless courage.'And as the holy proccedings in the Gurudwara ended with the long Sikh cry of victory 'Bole Sonihal'(Who ever utters the phrase will be happy) and the huge congregation responded full throatedly with 'Saat Sri Akaal, (Eternal is the Holy Lord) and which was followed with 'Wahe Guruji Ka Khalsa-Wahe Guruji Ki Fateh'(The Pure Ones Belong to God and Victory to belongs to God and his followers.) Shupriya knew that this too was the greatest victory for her dear Dablo because as the days passed by, the war clouds too started slowly disappearing over the horizon. From her it was truly 'Farewell My Love'

The very next day and inspite of knowing that she had been approved to become the first women Foreign Secretary of India, Shupriya put in her papers. The tragic loss of her dear Dablo was too much for her to bear. She wanted the secret of Major Shiraz Ismail Khan, alias Riaz Mohammed Khan, alias Shiraz Rehmatullah Khan to go with her to her grave. That day she also wrote a small note to Saira in Pakistan and which read.

'I was indeed very shocked and sad to learn about your beloved husband Riaz Mohammed Khan accidental death while you all were holidaying in Koh Samui. This was conveyed to me by our High Commissioner in Islamabad officially over the telephone only this morning. Your dear husband was not only a wonderful man and a thorough gentleman, but also a true well wisher of goodwill and peace in the Indian subcontinent. In his untimely death not only has Pakistan lost a suave diplomat, but India too has also lost a good friend and I a good rival. May the almighty therefore give you and your family the courage to bear this great and irreparable loss?And when she ended the letter with Mirza Ghalib's famous Urdu couplet 'Har ek makan ko hai makeen se sharaf azad-majnu jo mar gaya hai-toh jungle udaas hai.-(It is the inmates of the house who enhance its beauty and glow, but with Majnu now dead and gone, only desolate lie in the wilderness). And then with tears running down from her beautiful face when she lovingly kissed Dablo's photograph and prayed for his soul to rest in eternal peace, she knew that once again her Shiraz Ismai Khan had truly become immortal.

Synopsis

"NOTHING BUT!" is a saga of the 20th Century history of India and the Indian Subcontinent in particular and the world in general covering the period 1890-2002 It is a story of eight Indian families and one British family and their five generations. Though they were from different religions they were all once very close friends and comrades and how circumstances beyond their control separated them and some even became each other's sworn enemy

The complete book is in 6 parts and its main focus is on the disputed Indian Territory of Jammu and Kashmir—a volatile region that has been in the eye of the storm ever since the Great Game began in the late 19th century and remains the main bone of contention between India and Pakistan ever since the two countries became independent in 1947.

Book One—'—The Awakening' covers the period 1890-1919 and tells the story of the advent and rise of Indian nationalism through the eyes of these fictional characters and how the Great Game was played and how and the Great War (1914-1918) effected the lives of these people.

Book-2—"The Long Road to Freedom' covers the period 1920-1947 and tells the story about the sacrifices made to attain freedom and how partition came about.

Book-3—"What Price Freedom' covers the period 1947-1971 and tells the story of the horrors of partition and the 3 major wars that took place between India and Pakistan and which also gave birth to a new nation called Bangladesh.

Book-4—'—Love has no Religion' covers the period 1971-1984. It is a tragic love story of two couples from the fourth generation with different religious and cultural backgrounds and how it affected their lives and those of their countrymen.

Book-5 'All is Fair In Love and War' covers the period 1984-1994 and tells us about the rise of communal, religious and regional politics in the subcontinent and corruption in politics together with the rise of fanatical religious organizations throughout the world in general and the subcontinent in particular.

Book-6 "Farewell My Love" covers the period 1994-2002 tells the story of the people from the 4th and 5th generation of these families and how the rise of militancy, terrorism and selfish coalition politics affected their lives and those of the people on the streets.